KEEPING TRACK OF AGATHA CHRISTIE'S
76 NOVELS,
158 SHORT STORIES, AND
15 PLAYS
DOESN'T HAVE TO BE MURDER!

Whether you're a die-hard Christie aficionado, or a case-by-case crime fiction fan, you'll find everything you want to know about the doyenne of modern mystery in
THE COMPLETE CHRISTIE

Painstakingly researched and unmatched in its depth of coverage, this marvelous illustrated reference captures the spirited imagination of Dame Agatha—and the intriguing atmosphere of her tales—on every page. From her most confounding plot puzzles to her most memorable characters, from her fictional murder weapons of choice to the writer's own real-life mysteries, here is the essential companion to the life and works of one of the most beloved authors of all time.

THE COMPLETE CHRISTIE

By the same author

Prophecies: 2000

Encyclopedia of the Roman Empire

The Vampire Encyclopedia

Encyclopedia Sherlockiana

The Angelic Doctor:
The Life and World of St. Thomas Aquinas

Our Sunday Visitor's Encyclopedia
of Catholic History

The Pope Encyclopedia

Encyclopedia of the Middle Ages

Papal Wisdom:
Words of Hope and Inspiration
from Pope John Paul II

The Wisdom Teachings of
the Dalai Lama

The Complete Christie

An Agatha Christie Encyclopedia

Matthew Bunson

POCKET BOOKS

NEW YORK LONDON TORONTO SYDNEY SINGAPORE

This book is dedicated to Agatha Christie, without whose genius the vast realm of detective fiction would be a plain one indeed. This book is also dedicated to Mathew Prichard, who has done so much to perpetuate the legacy of his grandmother.

An *Original* Publication of POCKET BOOKS

 POCKET BOOKS, a division of Simon & Schuster, Inc.
1230 Avenue of the Americas, New York, NY 10020

Library of Congress Cataloging-in-Publication Data

Bunson, Matthew.
    The complete Christie : an Agatha Christie encyclopedia / Matthew Bunson.
      p.   cm.
    Includes bibliographical references.
    ISBN: 0-7434-0785-7
    ISBN: 0-671-02831-6 (trade paperback)
    1. Christie, Agatha, 1890–1976—Encyclopedias. 2. Women and literature—England—History—20th century—Encyclopedias. 3. Authors, English—20th century—Biography—Encyclopedias. 4. Detective and mystery stories, English—Encyclopedias. I. Title.
    PR6005.H66 Z459 2000
    823'.912—dc21
    [B]   00-042793

First Pocket Books hardcover printing September 2000
First Pocket Books trade paperback printing September 2000

10 9 8 7 6 5 4 3 2 1
10 9 8 7 6 5 4 3 2 1 (trade paperback)

Designed by Joseph Rutt
Cover design and illustration by William Sloan/Three

Printed in the U.S.A.

Contents

Acknowledgments

There are a number of individuals to whom special thanks are owed for their kind assistance during the preparation of this book. Among them are: the staffs of several libraries, including the Sahara West Library; Jerry Ohlinger; the Mandelbaum brothers; Kim Clanton-Green; Marie Cuglietta; and Lisa Grote.

Particular thanks are owed to Martha Casselman, my exceedingly patient agent; Jane Cavolina and Paul Schnee, the initial project editors; and Kim Kanner, my equally patient editor, who has made the completion of this project a genuine pleasure.

Introduction

Even by the standards of modern global communications, it is still difficult to comprehend fully the success of Dame Agatha Christie. It has been estimated that her books have sold in excess of one-half billion copies in over 100 languages. This achievement makes Christie the most successful author of all time, eclipsing even the Bard, William Shakespeare. Her characters, especially the eccentric Belgian Hercule Poirot and the venerable spinster Miss Marple, are virtual cultural icons, known even to the most casual reader or fan of mystery stories.

There is no secret to the success of Dame Agatha. She was possessed of a truly brilliant mind, an astonishing attention to detail, and a nearly infallible sense for plotting and pacing. Such gifts have been possessed in abundance by many writers, but she combined them with a staggering capacity for work, even under the most grim or peculiar circumstances. As her marriage to Archie Christie deteriorated in the 1920s, Dame Agatha kept writing, finding solace in her labors. When she found herself happily traveling the globe and working on archaeological digs with her second husband, Max Mallowan, she was still writing books, stories, and plays. Even as she entered the twilight of her life, when she could physically write nothing more, she still delighted her fans with a final adventure for Miss Marple in *Sleeping Murder* and a sad farewell for Hercule Poirot in *Curtain.* Both had been written decades before and had been stashed away in a bank vault for just such a time.

Agatha Christie's legendary labors commenced in 1920 with the publication of *The Mysterious Affair at Styles* and ended only with her death in 1976. In between, there were years of stupendous productivity. In 1934, for example, Christie published three novels—*Murder on the Orient Express, Why Didn't They Ask Evans?,* and *Unfinished Portrait*—and two collections of short stories—*The Listerdale Mystery* and *Parker Pyne Investigates.* In all, that one year saw the release of twenty-eight literary creations. Christie kept up such a pace, off and on, for half a century. By the time of her death, she had written nearly 300 works, including mystery novels, nonfiction books, poetry, radio plays, short stories, stage plays, and an autobiography. It is little wonder that she earned, and can still claim, the title of Grand Dame of Mystery. It is her genius, endurance, and place of honor that this book celebrates.

The Complete Christie is intended to provide both the general reader and the devoted fan of Dame Agatha Christie with an easy-to-use, comprehensive guide to the vast world of Christie. This reference book contains virtually every aspect of Christie's works and their adaptations in film, television, or stage. Devotees of the subject hopefully will find *The Complete Christie* an enjoyable resource for consultation and quick reference to particular characters and short stories, or for answering some arcane question of who played who in the many Christie movies and television programs.

There are, of course, many readers who will come to this book with only a passing familiarity with Christie's writings. Indeed, it is true that there are many Christie fans who have read only a few of her books but are intimately connected with Poirot and Miss Marple through the film and television adaptations over the last decades. To assist them, this book has been organized with reader ease in mind. There are three main sections: The

Writings, the Characters, and the Adaptations. The first section brings together all of her books and short stories. It is recommended that the novice Christie reader begin with the short biography on Dame Agatha, to establish some context to her life and writings. From there, readers should move on to the titles that are most familiar to them (e.g., *Murder on the Orient Express, Evil under the Sun,* or *The Body in the Library*). After reading some of the articles on the novels and short stories, it might be helpful to read the longer entries on the detectives and major characters. The two obvious places to start are the long entries detailing the lives, methods, habits, and appearances of Miss Marple and Hercule Poirot. Logically, from here one can go on to the third section to read the assorted cinematic and television versions of favorite novels and stories, completing a circle of reading. The reader, of course, need never fear that the solution to a case that he or she has not read will be revealed. Plots, clues, suspects, and a few subtle hints are included in the entries, but at no time is the actual solution ever given.

The Complete Christie offers several other valuable elements to Christie fans. First, it is the most up-to-date reference currently available. This book includes the happy release of several new Christie works in the last years, including the collection *The Harlequin Tea Set and Other Stories* (1997) and the two novels by Charles Osborne, *Black Coffee* (1998) and *The Unexpected Guest* (1999), adaptations to novel form of two Christie plays. *The Complete Christie* also provides details on the latest television adaptations, including the triumphant return of David Suchet as Hercule Poirot in *The Murder of Roger Ackroyd* (1999).

Second, this book also includes rarely seen book covers and photographs from the past. Thanks to the efforts of the staff of Pocket Books, the first section offers covers of Christie books from over the decades, including many that are now virtually unobtainable. There are also rare photographs from old films and plays, such as the movie *Alibi* (1931) and the stage plays *Love from a Stranger* (1936) and *Witness for the Prosecution* (1953). It is hoped that these enhance the enjoyment of the book and give further testimony that Christie's genius extended well beyond the printed page.

The
Complete
Christie

Agatha Christie in the 1940s. *(Photofest)*

Agatha Christie
1890–1976

Agatha May Clarissa Miller was born at Ashfield, the family home of Frederick Alvah Miller and Clara "Clarissa" Miller (née Boehmer), in Torquay, England, on September 15, 1890. Her father was an American who had business connections to both America and England, and her mother was the niece of Frederick's stepmother. The family established firmer ties to the United States with their decision to move to New England from Torquay in 1879 shortly after the birth of their first child, Madge. While in America in 1880, Clara gave birth to their second child, Monty. Soon after, the family set off for England again, but Frederick was forced by business to return across the Atlantic, and suggested that the family continue on to Torquay and rent a house. Upon his return, however, Frederick learned that Clara had actually purchased a house, Ashfield, and, despite initial plans to sell it after a time and return to America, the Millers decided to remain at the home and become permanent residents in England.

The third child of the family, Agatha grew up essentially an only child. Madge and Monty were much older than she was and were away at school most of the time. Her early education was at home, and her parents initially were worried that she might be developmentally challenged because of her severe shyness. This concern was proven groundless as Agatha soon displayed much of the curiosity and love of learning that characterized her later years. The happiness of her youth was shattered, however, in 1901, when Frederick died. It was a severe a blow to the family, both from a personal and a financial standpoint. It became necessary, for example, for Agatha's mother to rent out Ashfield from time to time to make ends meet, meaning that she and Agatha would travel under

very austere circumstances during the times when Ashfield was occupied.

Her mother made certain that Agatha received a suitable education, and, in 1906, she was sent to Paris to attend a finishing school. While there, she earned a reputation as a gifted singer and showed a talent for music. There was, in fact, some discussion about the possibility of Agatha's becoming a professional singer, but the notion did not long endure. Throughout her long life, she retained a love of music and an ability to play the piano.

An attractive and intelligent young woman, Agatha became the recipient of a number of marriage proposals. She declined all of them until 1912, when she accepted the offer of a major in the Gunners (Artillery). The very next year, she met the dashing Captain Archibald Christie, who swept her off her feet at a party. He was a guest at Ashfield a few days later, making a grand entrance on a motorcycle. Within a short time, she accepted his offer of marriage and sat down to write the painful letter to her first fiancé announcing the cancellation of their planned wedding. On Christmas Eve, 1914, Agatha and Archibald were wed. Two days later, Archie was sent off to fight in World War I.

While Archie was away, Agatha volunteered in a local hospital as a nurse and was eventually moved to the hospital pharmacy and dispensary. There, she encountered many of the poisons that were to be featured in her later writings and even gained firsthand knowledge of at least one possible plot for a murder (see *The Pale Horse,* page 115, for details). By 1916, she had decided to try her hand at writing and had been working on a mystery novel. Partly to alleviate the boredom of being a war wife and also because she seemed to have a natural gift for plotting out the details of a novel, Christe stayed at her book. The result was *The Mysterious Affair at Styles*. After submitting it unsuccessfully to several publishers, her first novel found a home at John Lane and was published in 1920. Owing to the terms of her contract, she made virtually no money from the book, and she remained initially uncertain whether a writing career was feasible.

After Archie's return and the end of the war, the Christies settled in London, where Archie took a position in a bank. In 1919, Rosalind Christie, Agatha's only child, was born. Christie continued writing, and in 1922 her second novel, *The Secret Adversary,* was published. It was written mainly to assist with the upkeep of Ashfield, although Archie encouraged her in her writing. She soon signed with the literary agents Hughes Massie, Ltd., and, before long, her unprofitable and draconian contract with John Lane was terminated. After that, she was signed with the ambitious publisher William Collins Sons and Co., Ltd. Her first book with them was *The Murder of Roger Ackroyd* (1926), one of the most breathtaking, innovative, and popular mysteries of the twentieth century. Her relationship with Collins endured to the end of her life.

Agatha dedicated her third novel, *Murder on the Links* (1923), "To my husband," and noted in her autobiography that she was "happy" during this period. Strains began to appear as early as 1924, however, stemming at least in part from Archie's obsession with golf. By 1926, there was considerable distance between Archie and Agatha, so much so that Agatha took a holiday to Corsica without him in the early part of the year. It proved a portentous beginning to a very dramatic year.

Upon returning home, Agatha learned that her mother was seriously ill with bronchitis. Clara Miller died only days later, and Agatha faced the disaster alone, as Archie was away in Spain. He returned to England, learned of the death of his mother-in-law, and promptly set out again. Even after he came back, he still stayed away from Agatha, preferring to remain in London or at the recently acquired family home in Berkshire, Styles House.

In the midst of this tragedy, Christie earned national acclaim with the June release of *The Murder of Roger Ackroyd*. She was still recovering from her mother's death when Archie made the announcement that he wanted a divorce. He had fallen in love with another woman, Nancy Neele. Out of consideration for Rosalind, Archie moved back to Styles House for an attempted reconciliation. As Christie wrote in her autobiography, it was "a period of sorrow, misery, heartbreak." By early December, the reunion was over. Archie announced that he was leaving again, this time for good, to be with Nancy. The episode that followed still remains a mystery.

One day, Agatha Christie returned home to Styles House and discovered Archie gone. She then packed a bag and drove away. Her car was found the following morning over an embankment at Newlands Corner, Berkshire. The hood was up and the lights were on; inside the car was a fur coat and a suitcase, as well as Agatha's expired driver's license. The police subsequently issued a missing person report, a news flash that gripped the imagination of the country, especially as *Roger Ackroyd* was still one of the best-selling books of the year. *The Daily Mail* offered a reward of one hundred pounds for Agatha's discovery and police everywhere were on the lookout for her.

The uproar ended unceremoniously when the reward was claimed by Bob Tappin, a musician at the Hydro Hotel in Harrogate. He recognized Christie as a guest (she was registered under the name Teresa Neele) and claimed the money. Police and Archie Christie raced to the hotel. After meeting with Agatha in private, Archie made a public statement that his wife "has suffered the most complete loss of memory and does not know who she is." This was the position reiterated in public statements by the author. The matter is still a "mystery, with no complete answer given to the disappearance's many nagging questions. Christie herself did not touch upon the matter in her autobiography, and the closest thing to an official statement made by her about it in later years was published in Janet Morgan's authorized biography. Morgan, who had access to many papers unavailable to other writers, supported Christie's original claims of amnesia.

The disappearance of Agatha Christie remains one of the most intriguing episodes in the eventful life of the author. As she never addressed the issue publicly, Christie's precise activities during her several missing days served as fodder for rumor and theory, and the amount of gossip and speculation, combined with the vicious treatment she received from the press left Christie understandably reluctant for the rest of her life to deal with the media and to have her private life once more the subject of ridicule and scandalmongering.

There was, however, a continuing interest in the disappearance, with researchers and writers attempting to piece together the author's activities. A fictional account of the disappearance was penned in 1978 by Kathy Tynan (with an adaptation to film in 1979, starring Vanessa Redgrave and Dustin Hoffman). Another theory was recently offered by Jared Cade in his *Agatha Christie and the Eleven Missing Days* (1998). He postulated that the disappearance was a calculated effort by Agatha to humiliate her husband, Archie. The theory was rejected forcefully by Mathew Prichard, the dedicated defender of his grandmother's memory.

During the period of recovery from the trauma, Agatha lived at Styles with Archie, but their marriage was at an end. She finally granted him, albeit reluctantly, a divorce. By the end of 1927, after a long period of writer's block, she was back at work. Her divorce was finalized in 1928, and Christie was able to make a joke about the entire ghastly affair in the dedication of *The Mystery of the Blue Train* by giving praise to members of the "O.F.D." (Order of the Faithful Dogs). She considered the divorce to have been an "acid test" for her friends. Those who remained devoted were members of the O.F.D., while those who had abandoned her were made members of the Order of the Rats, third class. The two most conspicuous members of the Faithful Dogs, as noted in her dedication, were Carlo (her secretary, Charlotte) and Peter, her wire-haired terrier.

In 1928, Christie also went to the Middle East and visited the archaeological dig at Ur. She became friendly with the dig director, Leonard Woolley, and his wife, Katharine. While on a second visit, she met Max Mallowan, the twenty-six-year-old archaeological assistant to Woolley. The two were married on September 11, 1930, in Scotland. Their marriage proved a genuinely happy one, lasting for forty-six years and ending only with Agatha's death. At the time of their union, Agatha was thirty-nine and Max was twenty-six. For purposes of her books, Agatha retained the name Agatha Christie, but, in private life, she always referred to herself as Mrs. Mallowan, and her nonfiction account of life on an archaeological dig, *Come Tell Me How You Live,* was published under the name Agatha Christie Mallowan.

Max was a brilliant archaeologist, and Agatha happily devoted much of her time to working with him on his many digs in the Middle East. She became a bona fide member of the archaeological team, and recorded the details of her daily activities in *Come Tell Me How You Live.* Max's most important dig was at Nimrud, which began around 1949. As always, Agatha was at his side, assisting him for the next ten years. It was while at the dig at Nimrud that she first started work on her autobiography, at which laboring sporadically for fifteen years. In 1960, Max was honored with the rank of Commander of the British Empire, not for being the husband of Agatha Christie but for his many contributions to archaeology and to the advancement of our knowledge about the ancient world. He published a documentary history of the dig at Nimrud, *Nimrud and Its Remains,* in 1966. Two years later, Queen Elizabeth II knighted him for his work.

Even as she assisted her husband—and adored

work on the digs—Christie continued her staggeringly prolific writing career. She produced about one book a year and enjoyed an especially productive period during World War II, when she wrote such works as *Sad Cypress* (1940), *One, Two, Buckle My Shoe* (1940), *Evil under the Sun* (1941), *N or M?* (1941), *The Body in the Library* (1942), *Five Little Pigs* (1943), *The Moving Finger* (1943), *Towards Zero* (1944), *Death Comes As the End* (1945), *Sparkling Cyanide* (1945), and *Sleeping Murder* and *Curtain,* the two long final cases for Miss Marple and Hercule Poirot, respectively.

Aside from its period of great productivity, the war brought to Christie the terrible uncertainty of the London Blitz and bombings by the Luftwaffe as well as a personal tragedy. Her daughter, Rosalind Christie, had married Hubert Prichard early in the war, and, in 1944, the young man was killed in the fighting. The grief of his death was relieved in many ways by the presence of Mathew Prichard, Christie's grandson, who had been born on September 21, 1943. Agatha loved her grandson, regularly sending him advance copies of her books while he was away at school and even giving him the copyright to *The Mousetrap* as a present for his tenth birthday. In 1949, Rosalind was married again, this time to Anthony Hicks, of whom Agatha approved most enthusiastically.

In addition to her work on archaeological digs and her gargantuan literary efforts, Christie also enjoyed a career as a playwright. Her first play, *Black Coffee,* was staged in 1930 and starred the great actor Francis Sullivan. Christie never saw it, however, as she was in Mesopotamia at the time. It was the success of *Ten Little Indians* (1940) that convinced her to continue on as a playwright and sparked a period of much stage writing, which included *Appointment with Death* (1945), *Murder on the Nile* (1946), *The Murder at the Vicarage* (1949),

and *The Hollow* (1951). These were, in many ways, mere preludes to her most successful play—and one of the most successful and enduring plays of all time—*The Mousetrap*. Her triumph was followed the next year by the immensely popular *Witness for the Prosecution* (1953).

In 1956, Christie was given formal recognition for her place in literature and the arts. She was named a Commander of the British Empire. In 1971, she was declared a Dame of the British Empire by Queen Elizabeth II. That same year, she suffered a leg injury. It marked the beginning of a sharp decline in her health and her productivity. It is commonly agreed that her last two novels, *Elephants Can Remember* (1972) and *Postern of Fate* (1973), were not of the same quality as her previous works, and *Postern of Fate* proved to be her last original work. Later, however, Christie published her final Poirot and Marple novels, *Curtain* (1975) and *Sleeping Murder* (1976), which had been sitting in vaults since World War II. They were a fitting cap to an unprecedented literary career.

Dame Agatha made her final public appearances at the 1974 gala premiere of the film *Murder on the Orient Express,* screened at the ABC cinema on Shaftesbury Avenue, London, with Queen Elizabeth in attendance, and at the banquet held at Claridge's afterward. She died on January 12, 1976, at her home at Wallingford, Berkshire. Max Mallowan survived his beloved Agatha by two years, dying on August 19, 1978. As per her request, Christie was buried in a private ceremony at Saint Mary's churchyard, Cholsey, Berkshire. Her simple tombstone was inscribed with two lines from Edmund Spenser's *The Faerie Queene*:

Sleepe after toyle, port after stormie seas,
Ease after warre, death after life, does greatly
please.

Agatha Christie's Writings

At the time of her death, Dame Agatha Christie's writings had sold a total of some four hundred million copies worldwide. She has been read in more languages than Shakespeare, and her famed and beloved sleuths Miss Marple and Hercule Poirot are perhaps better known than any literary figures in history. The following is a list of all Agatha Christie's writings, including her plays; alternate titles for many of her novels, which may differ between American and English editions, are also included but are not designated as such.

Novels and Story Collections

The A.B.C. Murders (1936)

Absent in the Spring (as Mary Westmacott, 1944)

The Adventure of the Christmas Pudding and a Selection of Entrées (1960)

After the Funeral (1953); also *Funerals Are Fatal*

And Then There Were None (1939); also *Ten Little Niggers* and *Ten Little Indians;* also *The Nursery Rhyme Murders*

Appointment with Death (1938)

At Bertram's Hotel (1965)

The Big Four (1927)

Black Coffee (1998 adapted by Charles Osborne from the 1930 play)

The Body in the Library (1942)

The Burden (as Mary Westmacott, 1956)

By the Pricking of My Thumbs (1968)

Cards on the Table (1936)

A Caribbean Mystery (1964)

Cat among the Pigeons (1959)

The Clocks (1963)

The Crooked House (1949)

Curtain (1975)

A Daughter's a Daughter (as Mary Westmacott, 1952)

Dead Man's Folly (1956)

Death Comes As the End (1945)

Death in the Clouds (1935); also *Death in the Air*

Death on the Nile (1937)

Destination Unknown (1954); also *So Many Steps to Death*

Double Sin and Other Stories (1961)

Dumb Witness (1937); also *Poirot Loses a Client*

Elephants Can Remember (1972)

Endless Night (1967)

Evil under the Sun (1941)

Five Little Pigs (1943); also *Murder in Retrospect*

The Floating Admiral (1931); Christie contributed one chapter

4.50 from Paddington (1957); also *What Mrs. McGillicuddy Saw!*

Funerals Are Fatal (1953); also *After the Funeral*

Giant's Bread (as Mary Westmacott, 1930)

The Golden Ball and Other Stories (1971)

Hallowe'en Party (1969)

The Harlequin Tea Set and Other Stories (1997)

Hercule Poirot's Christmas (1938); also *A Holiday for Murder* and *Murder for Christmas*

Hickory Dickory Dock (1955); also *Hickory Dickory Death*

The Hollow (1946); also *Murder after Hours*

The Hound of Death and Other Stories (1933)

The Labours of Hercules (1947)

The Listerdale Mystery (1934)

Lord Edgware Dies (1933); also *Thirteen at Dinner*

The Man in the Brown Suit (1924)

The Mirror Crack'd from Side to Side (1962); also *The Mirror Crack'd*

Miss Marple's Final Cases and Two Other Stories (1979)

The Moving Finger (1943)

Mrs. McGinty's Dead (1952)

The Murder at the Vicarage (1930)

Murder in Mesopotamia (1936)

Murder in the Mews and Other Stories (1937); also *Dead Man's Mirror and Other Stories*

A Murder Is Announced (1950)

Murder Is Easy (1939); also *Easy to Kill*

The Murder of Roger Ackroyd (1926)

Murder on the Links (1923)

Murder on the Orient Express (1934); also *Murder in the Calais Coach*

The Mysterious Affair at Styles (1920)

The Mysterious Mr. Quin (1930)

The Mystery of the Blue Train (1928)

Nemesis (1971)

N or M? (1941)

One, Two, Buckle My Shoe (1940) ; also *An Overdose of Death;* also *The Patriotic Murders*

Ordeal by Innocence (1958)

The Pale Horse (1961)

Parker Pyne Investigates (1934); also *Mr. Parker Pyne, Detective*

Partners in Crime (1929)

Passenger to Frankfurt: An Extravaganza (1970)

Peril at End House (1932)

A Pocket Full of Rye (1953)

Poirot Investigates (1924)

Poirot's Early Cases (1974); also *Hercule Poirot's Early Cases*

Postern of Fate (1973)

The Regatta Mystery and Other Stories (1939)

The Rose and the Yew Tree (as Mary Westmacott, 1947)

Sad Cypress (1940)

The Secret Adversary (1922)

The Secret of Chimneys (1925)

The Seven Dials Mystery (1929)

The Sittaford Mystery (1931); also *Murder at Hazelmoor*

Sleeping Murder (1976)

Sparkling Cyanide (1945); also *Remembered Death*

Star over Bethlehem and Other Stories (1965)

Taken at the Flood (1948); also *There Is a Tide*

They Came to Baghdad (1951)

They Do It with Mirrors (1952); also *Murder with Mirrors*

Third Girl (1966)

Thirteen Clues for Miss Marple (1966)

Thirteen for Luck (1961)

The Thirteen Problems (1932); also *The Tuesday Club Murders*

Three-Act Tragedy (1935); also *Murder in Three Acts*

Three Blind Mice and Other Stories (1950); also *The Mousetrap and Other Stories*

Towards Zero (1944)

The Under Dog and Other Stories (1951)

The Unexpected Guest (1999, adapted by Charles Osborne from the 1958 play)

Unfinished Portrait (as Mary Westmacott, 1934)

Why Didn't They Ask Evans? (1934); also *The Boomerang Clue*

Witness for the Prosecution and Other Stories (1948)

Short Stories

"Accident"

"The Actress"

"The Adventure of the Cheap Flat"

"The Adventure of the Clapham Cook"

"The Adventure of the Egyptian Tomb"

"The Adventure of the Italian Nobleman"

"The Adventure of the Sinister Stranger"

"The Adventure of 'The Western Star'"

"The Affair at the Bungalow"
"The Affair at the Victory Ball"
"The Affair of the Pink Pearl"
"The Ambassador's Boots"
"The Apples of the Hesperides"
"The Arcadian Deer"
"At the 'Bells and Motley'"
"The Augean Stables"
"The Bird with the Broken Wing"
"Blindman's Bluff"
"The Bloodstained Pavement"
"The Blue Geranium"
"The Call of Wings"
"The Capture of Cerberus"
"The Case of the Caretaker"
"The Case of the City Clerk"
"The Case of the Discontented Husband"
"The Case of the Discontented Soldier"
"The Case of the Distressed Lady"
"The Case of the Middle-Aged Wife"
"The Case of the Missing Lady"
"The Case of the Missing Will"
"The Case of the Perfect Maid"
"The Case of the Retired Jeweller"
"The Case of the Rich Woman"
"The Chess Problem"
"The Chocolate Box"
"A Christmas Tragedy"
"The Clergyman's Daughter"
"The Coming of Mr. Quin"
"The Companion"
"The Cornish Mystery"
"The Crackler"
"The Cretan Bull"
"The Dead Harlequin"
"Dead Man's Mirror"
"Death by Drowning"
"Death on the Nile"
"The Disappearance of Mr. Davenheim"
"The Double Clue"
"Double Sin"
"The Dream"
"The Dressmaker's Doll"
"The Edge"

"The Erymanthian Boar"
"The Face of Helen"
"A Fairy in the Flat"
"Finessing the King"
"The Flock of Geryon"
"Four and Twenty Blackbirds"
"The Four Suspects"
"The Fourth Man"
"A Fruitful Sunday"
"The Gate of Baghdad"
"The Gentleman Dressed in Newspaper"
"The Gipsy"
"The Girdle of Hyppolita"
"The Girl in the Train"
"The Golden Ball"
"Greenshaw's Folly"
"Harlequin's Lane"
"The Harlequin Tea Set"
"Have You Got Everything You Want?"
"The Herb of Death"
"The Horses of Diomedes"
"The Hound of Death"
"The House at Shiraz"
"The House of Dreams"
"The House of Lurking Death"
"How Does Your Garden Grow?"
"The Idol House of Astarte"
"In a Glass Darkly"
"The Incredible Theft"
"Ingots of Gold"
"Jane in Search of a Job"
"The Jewel Robbery at the Grand Metropolitan"
"The Kidnapped Prime Minister"
"The Kidnapping of Johnnie Waverly"; also "The Adventure of Johnnie Waverly
"The King of Clubs"
"The Lamp"
"The Last Séance"
"The Lemesurier Inheritance"
"The Lernean Hydra"
"The Listerdale Mystery"
"The Lonely God"
"The Lost Mine"
"The Love Detectives"

"Magnolia Blossom"
"The Man from the Sea"
"The Manhood of Edward Robinson"
"The Man in the Mist"
"The Man Who Was No. 16"
"Manx Gold"
"The Market Basing Mystery"
"The Million-Dollar Bond Robbery"
"Miss Marple Tells a Story"
"Mr. Eastwood's Adventure"
"Motive vs. Opportunity"
"Murder in the Mews"
"The Mystery of Hunter's Lodge"
"The Mystery of the Baghdad Chest"
"The Mystery of the Blue Jar"
"The Mystery of the Crime in Cabin 66"
"The Mystery of the Spanish Chest"
"The Mystery of the Spanish Shawl"
"The Nemean Lion"
"Next to a Dog"
"The Oracle at Delphi"
"The Pearl of Price"
"Philomel Cottage"
"The Plymouth Express"
"A Pot of Tea"
"Problem at Pollensa Bay"
"Problem at Sea"
"The Rajah's Emerald"
"The Red House"
"The Red Signal"
"The Regatta Mystery"
"Sanctuary"
"The Second Gong"
"The Shadow on the Glass"
"The Sign in the Sky"
"Sing a Song of Sixpence"
"SOS"
"The Soul of the Croupier"
"The Strange Case of Sir Arthur Carmichael"
"Strange Jest"
"The Stymphalean Birds"
"The Submarine Plans"
"The Sunningdale Mystery"
"Swan Song"

"The Tape-Measure Murder"; also "A Village Murder"
"The Theft of the Royal Ruby"; also "The Adventure of the Christmas Pudding"
"The Third Floor Flat"
"Three Blind Mice"
"The Thumb Mark of Saint Peter"
"The Tragedy of Marsdon Manor"
"Triangle at Rhodes"
"The Tuesday Night Club"
"The Unbreakable Alibi"
"The Under Dog"
"The Veiled Lady"
"A Village Murder"
"The Voice in the Dark"
"Wasps' Nest"
"While the Light Lasts"
"Wireless"; also "Where There's a Will"
"Within a Wall"
"The Witness for the Prosecution"
"The World's End"
"Yellow Iris"

Nonfiction and Other Works and Poetry
An Autobiography (1977)
Come, Tell Me How You Live (1946)
The Road of Dreams (1924)
Poems (1973)

Plays
Akhnaton (never staged but published in 1973)
Appointment with Death (dramatized by Christie from her novel, 1945)
Black Coffee (1930)
Fiddlers Three (1971)
Go Back for Murder (dramatized by Christie from her novel *Five Little Pigs,* 1960)
The Hollow (dramatized by Christie from her novel, 1951)
The Mousetrap (dramatized by Christie from her story "Three Blind Mice," 1952)
Murder on the Nile (dramatized by Christie from her novel *Death on the Nile,* 1946)

Rule of Three: Afternoon at the Seaside, The Patient, The Rats (1962)

Spider's Web (1954)

Ten Little Niggers (dramatized by Christie from her novel, 1943)

Towards Zero (dramatized by Christie and Gerald Verner from her novel, 1956)

The Unexpected Guest (1958)

Verdict (1958)

Witness for the Prosecution (dramatized by Christie from her novel, 1953)

PART ONE

The Writings

It was while I was working in the dispensary that I first conceived the idea of writing a detective story.

—Agatha Christie, An Autobiography

A 1960s edition of The A.B.C. Murders.
(Pocket Books)

The A.B.C. Murders

PUBLISHING HISTORY: First published by William Collins Sons and Co., Ltd., London, 1936. First published in the United States by Dodd, Mead and Co., New York, 1936.

CHARACTERS: Hercule Poirot; Captain Arthur Hastings; Chief Inspector James Japp; Colonel Anderson, Alice Ascher, Franz Ascher, Mr. Barnard, Mrs. Barnard, Elizabeth Barnard, Megan Barnard, Nurse Capstick, Sir Carmichael Clarke, Lady Charlotte Clarke, Franklin Clarke, Inspector Crome, Alexander Bonaparte Cust, Deveril, Roger Downes, Mary Drower, George Earlsfield, Donald Fraser, Thora Grey, Tom Hartigan, Milly Higley, Commissionaire Jameson, Dr. Kerr, Sir Lionel, Dr. Thompson.

Captain Arthur Hastings returns to England from his ranch in Argentina for a six-month visit and wastes little time in paying a call on Hercule Poirot. He finds the sleuth years older, but as vain as he had remembered, obviously using a bottle of dye to maintain the jet-black appearance of his hair. The Belgian is not so old, however, that he needs to retire permanently. In fact, he may very well be on the verge of a new case.

A letter arrives addressed to Poirot that contains a most disturbing message:

> MR. HERCULE POIROT — *You fancy yourself, don't you, at solving mysteries that are too difficult for our poor thick-headed British police? Let us see, Mr. Clever Poirot, just how clever you can be. Perhaps you'll find this nut too hard to crack. Look out for Andover on the 21st of the month. Yours, etc., A.B.C.*

Inspector Japp has seen the note, but the Scotland Yard policeman thinks little of it beyond that it is the work of a crackpot. Poirot, of course, has other ideas and waits with some anticipation for the twenty-first. His fears are confirmed when word arrives on the morning of the twenty-second. Alice Ascher, in Andover, has been found brutally murdered, with an open copy of the *A.B.C Rail Guide* placed on a counter next to her corpse. The book is open to the page listing trains from Andover.

A month later, Poirot receives a second taunting letter, warning of the impending murder of someone in Bexton-on-Sea. True to its fiendish prediction, Elizabeth "Betty" Barnard is found strangled in Bexton-on-Sea. Once again, the *A.B.C. Guide* is found next to the body. More killings follow, and Poirot sets out to find the crafty and arrogant murderer, forming a special legion to assist him—a group of relatives of the murder victims who likewise cry out for justice.

• • •

One of the most ingenious and successful of Christie's novels and a genuine puzzle for the Belgian detective, *The A.B.C. Murders* offers up a rare serial killer, one with a nasty disposition. As the novel makes clear early on, the title is derived from the *A.B.C. Rail Guide,* the popular British railway guide that presents its listing of station stops in alphabetical order. The murders in the novel correspond to the guide, with the first victim, A.A., found at a station in the *A* section; the *A.B.C Guide* is placed near the body to make the connection obvious. Fortunately for the book's general population, the killer reaches only to the letter *D* before Poirot closes in and captures his prey.

The narrative is presented in two different styles. The first is an account from the pen of Captain Hastings and the second is a set of eight chapters, "Not from Captain Hastings' Personal Narrative," which contains material to which Hastings was not exposed or of which he had no knowledge.

The novel was adapted for film as *The Alphabet Murders* (1966), starring Tony Randall as Hercule Poirot. The novel was also adapted for television by London Weekend Television in 1992 for the series *Agatha Christie's Poirot* starring David Suchet.

Absent in the Spring

PUBLISHING HISTORY: First published by William Collins Sons and Co., Ltd., London, 1944. First published in the United States by Farrar & Rinehart, New York, 1994.

CHARACTERS: Michael Callaway, Rupert Cargill, Miss Gilbey, Blanche Haggard, Myrna Randolph, Major Reid, Princess Sasha Hohenbach Salm, Joan Scudamore, Rodney Scudamore, Tony Scudamore, Captain Charles Sherston, Leslie Sherston, Barbara Wray, William Wray.

Absent in the Spring is an often intense psychological study of Joan Scudamore, a lonely woman who has become isolated from both friends and family. When, while traveling in Iraq, her train becomes stranded at Tell Abu Hamid, she is forced to take the time to ponder intently her life and her many mistakes over the years. Chief among her concerns is her relationship with her daughter. Gradually, with much pain, she receives a revelation about herself. The question next becomes what she plans to do about it.

• • •

Absent in the Spring was the third non-mystery novel penned by Agatha Christie under the pseudonym Mary Westmacott. According to Christie, she commenced work on the book almost immediately after the completion of *Death Comes As the End* (1945). She claimed to have written the book in a marathon session of creativity that lasted for three days; she finished the first and last chapters before the rest. She was working at the time as a volunteer in a dispensary, and called in sick on the third day of her furious writing session. When Christie returned to work on the next day, she looked so drained and exhausted that her coworkers had little trouble accepting the idea that she had been grievously ill.

The title for this book comes from William Shakespeare's Sonnet 98: "From you I have been absent in the spring."

"Accident"

PUBLISHING HISTORY: First published by William Collins Sons and Co., Ltd., London, 1934, in the short story collection *The Listerdale Mystery.* First published in the United States by Dodd, Mead and Co., New York, 1948, in the short story collection *Witness for the Prosecution and Other Stories.*

CHARACTERS: Mrs. Anthony, Inspector Evans, Captain Haydock, George Merrowdene, Margaret Merrowdene.

While visiting his old friend Captain Haydock, Inspector Evans, a one-time member of the police's Central Intelligence Division, has a chance encounter with Haydock's neighbors. He immediately notes that there is something very familiar about Mrs. Merrowdene, and his memory is jolted upon hearing that she has taken out a very large insurance policy on her husband. Several years before, she had been acquitted of murdering her husband by poison; only the shortage of evidence prevented her conviction. Convinced that she is now planning another murder, Evans takes the bold step of entering Mrs. Merrowdene's lair to try and save her husband from what he is sure is his impending murder.

• • •

"Accident" presents one of the most calm and calculating murderers in the body of Christie writings. It also makes use of one of the perennial detective types in her works, a stolid, determined, and relatively unimaginative policeman whose primary errors are missing the obvious threat and underestimating severely the intelligence and cunning of his opponent.

"The Actress"

PUBLISHING HISTORY: First published in *Novel Magazine*, London, 1923. First published in the United States by G. P. Putnam's Sons, New York, 1997, in the short story collection *The Harlequin Tea Set and Other Stories*.

CHARACTERS: Cora, Syd Danahan, Miss Jones, Jake Levitt, Olga Stormer.

Jake Levitt sits in the fourth row of the theater and stares in amazement at the actress on the stage. He recognizes the performer as Nancy Taylor and then laughs cynically when he notes in the program that she is now going by the name of Olga Stormer. A petty and shabby blackmailer, Jake smiles to himself and declares: "Olga Stormer! So that's what she calls herself . . . Quite forgotten your name was ever Nancy Taylor, I dare say . . . I wonder now what you'd say if Jake Levitt should remind you of the fact."

Jake proceeds with his blackmail scheme, sending a letter to Olga Stormer that hints at dire consequences for her should she not be agreeable to paying a generous amount of money. For Olga, the risks are truly grim, especially as revelations from her past will cost her not just her reputation but the career of the man she loves. Two choices

remain to her: pay up or disappear and start over again. Olga, however, decides on a third route, one involving trapping a blackmailer with his own methods.

• • •

"The Actress" had never been published in the United States before 1997, nor had it been collected in any other compilation before *The Harlequin Tea Set and Other Stories*.

"The Adventure of"

Stories beginning with this phrase are listed under the next word in each individual title. For example, for "The Adventure of the 'Western Star,' " see " 'Western Star,' The Adventure of the."

The Adventure of the Christmas Pudding and a Selection of Entrées

See Christmas Pudding, The Adventure of the, and a Selection of Entrées

"The Affair at the Bungalow"

PUBLISHING HISTORY: First published by William Collins Sons and Co., Ltd., London, 1932, in the short story collection *The Thirteen Problems*. First published in the United States by Dodd, Mead and Co., New York, 1933, in the short story collection *The Tuesday Club Murders*.

CHARACTERS: Miss Jane Marple; Jane Helier; Colonel Bantry, Mrs. Bantry, Sir Henry Clithering, Sir Herman Cohen, Leslie Faulkener, Netta Green, Mary Kerr, Dr. Lloyd.

One of the mysteries presented during the gathering of the Tuesday Night Club, "The Affair at the Bungalow" is told by the actress Jane Helier, who, despite her clumsy efforts at concealment, soon admits that the events described actually happened to her. A riverside bungalow in which she had been staying is burglarized, and the police arrest a young man. The suspect, a playwright named Leslie Faulkener, claimed that he had met Jane Helier at the bungalow—after sending a play for her to read—had been invited for cocktails, and had then apparently been drugged as he awakened some time later out in the road by a bridge. The same bungalow was later robbed, and Faulkener is the only suspect, as the police are unable to find any witness to corroborate his story. The solution to this mystery is offered by the different members of the club, but only Miss Marple provides the real meaning to the particular course of events. Jane Helier, who knows the truth, is suitably impressed.

"The Affair at the Victory Ball"

PUBLISHING HISTORY: First published by Dodd, Mead and Co., New York, 1951, in the short story collection *The Under Dog and Other Stories.*

CHARACTERS: Hercule Poirot; Captain Arthur Hastings; Inspector James Japp; the Honorable Eustace Beltrane, Coco Courtenay, Lord Cronshaw, Mrs. Davidson, Mr. Chris Davidson, Mrs. Mallaby.

This case is recounted by its redoubtable "author," Captain Arthur Hastings, to demonstrate the particular talents of his friend Hercule Poirot: "I have long felt that it is only fitting that Poirot's connection with the solution be given to the world." Hastings refers to the "strange tangle" that surrounded the murder of the young aristocrat Lord Cronshaw and the mysterious death of his fiancée, Coco Courtenay, from an overdose of cocaine.

Even as Poirot and Hastings are discussing the affair at the Victory Ball, they are consulted by Inspector Japp, who tells Poirot that it is "a case that strikes me as being very much in your line, and I came along to know whether you care to have a finger in the pie." While attending a previous Victory Ball with his friends, Lord Cronshaw was moody, and it was clear that he and Coco Courtenay were not even speaking. Courtenay was unable to maintain her demeanor and went home early in hysterics in the care of the young actor Chris Davidson. Davidson was unable to return to the ball and went home to his flat in Chelsea, where his young wife told him of the disaster at

the gathering. Lord Cronshaw remained moody and was aloof with his friends. Finally, after searching for him, the other members of the party found him sprawled across the floor in an empty room with a table knife stuck in his heart.

Poirot unravels the seemingly obtuse mystery by concentrating on the two most important clues: a small enamel box containing a stash of cocaine and having the name Coco written across it in diamonds; and a small pom-pom of emerald green silk with ragged threads hanging from it. Of vital importance to Poirot are the costumes worn by Lord Cronshaw and his friends, the characters from the commedia dell'arte. With the costumes of Harlequin, Punchinello and Pulcinella, Pierrot and Pierrette, and Columbine, the detective traps both the killer and a drug dealer.

• • •

This was the first appearance in the Christie writings of the *commedia dell'arte* and the harlequinade. They would reappear in a significant way in the cases featuring the mysterious Mr. Harley Quin. "The Affair at the Victory Ball" also features a rare intermission, offering the reader the chance to work out the solution to the crime before finishing the story.

"The Affair of the Pink Pearl"

PUBLISHING HISTORY: First published by William Collins Sons and Co., Ltd., London, 1929, in the short story collection *Partners in Crime.* First published in the United States by Dodd, Mead and Co., New York, 1929, in the short story collection, *Partners in Crime.*

CHARACTERS: Tommy Beresford; Tuppence Beresford; Lady Laura Barton, Mrs. Hamilton Betts, Gladys Hill, Colonel Kingston-Bruce, Beatrice Kingston-Bruce, Mr. Rennie.

The Beresfords are visited at their offices in Blunt's International Detective Agency by Beatrice Kingston-Bruce and her mother after a disaster has befallen the Kingston-Bruces. A house guest of theirs has had a precious pink pearl stolen, and someone mentioned to them that the

Beresfords were quite good at solving this sort of problem.

The case takes on a special interest for the Beresfords as they adopt—for the first time in the series of investigations recorded in *Partners in Crime*—the personae of fictional detectives while at work. In this case, Tommy adopts the character and mannerisms of Dr. John Evelyn Thorndyke, a brilliant detective, physician, and forensic expert created by R. Austin Freeman (d. 1943).

After the Funeral

PUBLISHING HISTORY: First published by William Collins Sons and Co., Ltd., London, 1953. First published in the United States by Dodd, Mead and Co., New York, 1953, under the title *Funerals Are Fatal*.

CHARACTERS: Hercule Poirot; Inspector Morton; Helen Abernethie, Maude Banks, George Crossfield, Mr. Entwhistle, Miss Gilchrist, Mr. Gobey, Alexander Guthrie, Lancombe, Cora Lansquenet, Dr. Larraby, Michael Shane, Rosamund Shane.

The Abernethie family of Enderby Hall has gathered to attend the funeral of its most prominent member, Richard Abernethie, the heir of the old and long-dead patriarch of the family, Cornelius Abernethie. The times are rather grim for the Abernethies, as members of the family seem to be dying with appalling regularity, and Richard's passing was both sudden and unexpected.

All seems quite normal, however, when the family gathers for the reading of the will by the Abernethie lawyer, Mr. Entwhistle. The will is clear and simple. The estate is to be divided evenly among the heirs, so all have benefited from Richard's passing. Things, however, take a rather ominous turn when the eccentric and loud-mouthed Cora Abernethie Lansquenet, Richard's younger sister, openly states what all of her relatives seem to be thinking, namely that "It's been hushed up very nicely, hasn't it? . . . But he was murdered, wasn't he?"

Stunned by her question, Mr. Entwhistle decides to visit Cora at Lytchett-St. Mary to ask her directly what she meant. Before he can reach her, word arrives. Cora has been found hacked to death. Now convinced that she was telling the truth, Entwhistle turns to someone who will discover the perpetrator of at least two murders (and perhaps several more): Hercule Poirot.

• • •

Christie dedicated the novel thus: "For James—In memory of happy days at Abney." The James was James Watts, Jr. (III), her nephew, with whom she spent many happy hours at the Watts family home of Abney Hall. The estate also served as the model for the fictional Enderby Hall.

After the Funeral was loosely (very loosely) adapted for the film *Murder at the Gallop* (1963), starring Margaret Rutherford as Miss Marple (who replaced Hercule Poirot for the film).

"The Ambassador's Boots"

PUBLISHING HISTORY: First published by William Collins Sons and Co., Ltd., London, 1929, in the short story collection *Partners in Crime*. First published in the United States by Dodd, Mead and Co., New York, 1929.

CHARACTERS: Tommy Beresford; Tuppence Beresford; Albert Batt, Cicely March, Richards, Ralph Westerham, Randolph Wilmott.

Tommy and Tuppence Beresford receive a curious request from a prospective client. The United States ambassador to the Court of St. James, Randolph Wilmott, asks them to help him retrieve a piece of his luggage that was accidentally switched with the bag of an American senator, Ralph Westerman. The situation becomes even more bizarre when the senator's "valet" shows up at the embassy to exchange the bags. It soon turns out that the senator has never heard of the valet; nor has he heard of any trouble with the bags.

• • •

As is the case with other stories in *Partners in Crime,* the sleuths adopt the personae of various fictional detectives to assist in the solution of the crime. In this outing, Tuppence declares herself to

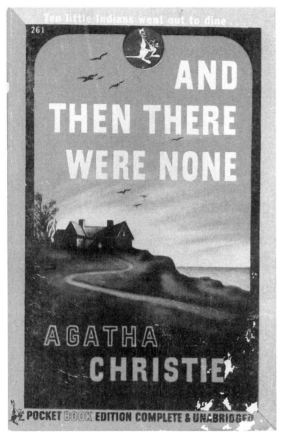

A 1944 edition of And Then There Were None. *(Pocket Books)*

be Reggie Fortune, a detective created by H. C. Bailey (d. 1961), an elegant surgeon and snob.

And Then There Were None

PUBLISHING HISTORY: First published by William Collins Sons and Co., Ltd., London, 1939, under the title *Ten Little Niggers*. First published in the United States by Dodd, Mead and Co., New York, 1940, under the title *And Then There Were None*.

CHARACTERS: Dr. Edward George Armstrong, William Henry Blore, Caroline Brent, Vera Elizabeth Claythorne, Sir Thomas Legge, Captain Philip Lombard, General John MacArthur, Inspector Maine, Anthony James Marston, Fred Narracott, Ethel Rogers, Thomas Rogers, Mr. Justice Laurence Wargrave.

In a series of short chapters, the reader is introduced to eight different people, all of whom have as their ultimate destination an isolated island to which they have been invited by a mysterious host, Mr. U. N. Owen. After arriving on the island, each of the guests is shown to a room where a nursery rhyme is framed above the mantel, a disturbing poem by Septimus Winner (1868) about a group of doomed Indians (see below).

Ten Little Indians
Septimus Winner
1868

Ten little Indian boys went out to dine;
One choked his little self and then there nine.

Nine little Indian boys sat up very late;
One overslept himself and then there were eight.

Seven little Indian boys chopping up sticks;
One chopped himself in halves and then there were six.

Six little Indian boys playing with a hive;
A bumblebee stung one and then there were five.

Five little Indian boys going in for law;
One got in Chancery and then there were four.

Four little Indian boys going out to sea;
A red herring swallowed one and then there were three.

Three little Indian boys walking in the zoo;
A big bear hugged one and then there were two.

Two little Indian boys sitting in the sun;
One got frizzled up and then there was one.

One little Indian boy left all alone;
He went and hanged himself and then there were none.

The guests gather for dinner and, gradually, the reason for their invitation is revealed by a loud voice booming out across the dining hall: Everyone in attendance, even the butler and cook, has been brought to the island so that they might at last face justice. All of them have caused the deaths of other human beings and all of them will face the ultimate penalty for their crimes. A short time later, the fate of the guests is first revealed when Anthony Marston takes a sip of his drink and drops dead in agony.

What follows is a masterpiece of terror, mutual suspicion, and death as each guest is stalked and murdered in inventive and brutal ways, their deaths marked in a grisly fashion by little statues of ten Indians that disappear one by one after each murder. The "executions" continue until only one guest remains, faced with the prospect of forced suicide or being hanged by the police, for there is no way to escape what has become an absolute trap of justice. The final solution to the crime is revealed to the police months later, when a fisherman sends them a letter he discovered in a bottle. Only then does Sir Thomas Legge, assistant commissioner at Scotland Yard, fully understand the incredible events on the island.

• • •

Christie was justifiably proud of *And Then There Were None,* noting in her autobiography: "I had written the book . . . because it was so difficult to do that the idea had fascinated me. Ten people had to die without it becoming ridiculous or the murderer being obvious. I wrote the book after a tremendous amount of planning, and I was pleased with what I had made of it. It was clear, straightforward, baffling, and yet had a perfectly reasonable explanation; in fact, it had to have an epilogue to explain it."

As Christie also observed in her autobiography, the book was ideally suited for adaptation to the stage. The resulting play, *Ten Little Indians,* debuted in 1940 with a deliberately chosen happier ending than the grim climax of the novel. The basis for the ending was a second version of the last stanza of the Septimus Winner rhyme by Frank Green:

One little Indian boy left all alone;
He got married and then there were none.

This ending was also used in the 1945 film adaptation, directed by René Clair, and provided a more satisfying, less downbeat, and even romantic denouement. It was thus even more appealing as a project for performers. (For details of the stage and film adaptations, see under Film and Stage.)

Not surprisingly, Dodd, Mead, Christie's primary publisher in the United States, found the appalling original title, *Ten Little Niggers,* to be wholly unacceptable, despite the fact that it was taken faithfully from the original rhyme. The publisher chose the title *And Then There Were None,* although other editions appeared with other titles: *Ten Little Indians* (which many, understandably, consider as offensive as *Ten Little Niggers*) and *The Nursery Rhyme Murders.* The changes in title necessitated as well the adaptation of certain locations in the text. Thus, Nigger Island becomes Indian Island.

"The Apples of the Hesperides"

PUBLISHING HISTORY: First published by William Collins Sons and Co., Ltd., London, 1947, in the short story collection *The Labours of Hercules.* First published in the United States by Dodd, Mead and Co., New York, 1947, in the short story collection *The Labors of Hercules.*

CHARACTERS: Hercule Poirot; Inspector Wagstaff; Atlas, Patrick Casey, George, Emery Power, Ricovetti, Reuben Rosenthal, Marchese di San Veratrino.

The eleventh labor of Hercule Poirot in honor of the twelve labors of the mythological hero, this case sets the sleuth on the trail of an expensive goblet with an evil past. The wealthy art connoisseur Emery Power enlists Poirot's help in recovering a gold chased goblet that had been used by the infamous Borgia pope, Alexander VI: "He sometimes presented it to a favored guest to drink from. That guest, M. Poirot, usually died . . . Its career has always been associated with violence." Not the history but the design attracts Poirot—"a tree round which a bejeweled serpent is coiled, and the apples on the tree are formed of very beautiful emeralds." Power had purchased the goblet ten years before, but it had been stolen by a gang of international thieves. Two of the gang were caught, but a third, Patrick Casey, was never brought to justice. However, he fell to his death from the fifth floor of a building while about to rob the house of a millionaire. As a result, the goblet, which had been in his keeping, was never recovered, as it was never offered for sale.

Poirot embarks upon his search by consulting Inspector Wagstaff, who had been involved in the affair, and then, like the mythological Hercules, he consults the modern day version of Prometheus or Nereus, he consults detectives from across the globe—New York, Sydney, Rome, Istanbul, Paris—inquiries that climax with Poirot's arrival in Inishgowlan, on the Irish coast, and a rendezvous with history in a convent.

• • •

In classical mythology, Hercules was forced to retrieve golden apples—given as a wedding gift to the goddess Hera—that were guarded by Ladon, a dragon with a hundred heads, and the Hesperides, the vile daughters of Atlas.

This case includes an appearance by Poirot's unflappable manservant, George (or Georges), who was also mentioned or took part in *Murder on the Links, Curtain,* "The Nemean Lion," and "The Lernean Hydra."

Appointment with Death

PUBLISHING HISTORY: First published by William Collins Sons and Co., Ltd., London, 1938. First published in the United States by Dodd, Mead and Co., New York, 1938.

CHARACTERS: Hercule Poirot; Abdul, Mrs. Boynton, Carol Boynton, Ginerva Boynton, Lennox Boynton, Nadine Boynton, Raymond Boynton, Colonel Carbury, Jefferson Cope, Dr. Theodore Gerard, Sarah King, Mahmoud, Miss Amabel Pierce, Lady Westholme.

Hercule Poirot arrives in Jerusalem for a vacation and takes up residence in the Hotel Solomon. On his very first night, he is initially amused to hear a voice from an adjacent window. In a hushed, furtive whisper, the voice declares: "You do see, don't you, that she's got to be killed?" At first the detective dismisses the sentence as part of a collaboration on a play or a book, but he notes "a curious intensity in the voice . . ."

Also in the hotel are Dr. Theodore Gerard, a famous French psychologist; Sarah King, an English medical student vacationing in the Holy Land; and, above all, the Boynton clan, headed by the odious and imperious matriarch Mrs. Boynton, described by Dr. Gerard as "a horror of a woman! Old, swollen, bloated, sitting there immovable—a distorted old Buddha—a gross spider in the center of a web!" Entangled in her web are her entire family and in-laws, trapped by her evil and dominating cruelty. Her malign influence is seen keenly in the behavior of her children, all of whom harbor open or secret hatred for their mother.

The family departs Jerusalem and heads for the ancient city of Petra. There, to everyone's surprise, Madame Boynton permits her enslaved children to go exploring without her. When they all return, however, they make an appalling discovery— Madame Boynton has been murdered, in plain view of the entire camp, with an injection of digitoxin.

Poirot, meanwhile, pays a visit to Amman, Jordan, where he introduces himself to Colonel Carbury, the local police commander. Carbury warms to Poirot, especially after reading the letter of introduction from their mutual friend, Colonel Race. Taking Poirot immediately into his confidence, Carbury details the Boynton death. Although listed officially as death from natural causes, her passing was, he suspects, most unnatural. Poirot must agree, lamenting that he will take the case, even though her death was a blessing to all.

• • •

The backdrop for murder in *Appointment with Death* is the famed ancient city of Petra; the site was also used in the Parker Pyne story "The Pearl of Price" (1934), although neither work gives extensive detail on the great city of the Nabataeans. Christie visited Petra for the first time in 1933 with her husband, the archaeologist Max Mallowan.

There are two especially memorable characters in *Appointment with Death:* the tyrannical matriarch and former prison warden Mrs. Boynton and the American-born member of Parliament and social climber Lady Westholme. The novel also contains several references to other Poirot cases: Colonel Carbury knows Poirot through Colonel Johnny Race and the detective's success in the Shaitana murder (recounted in *Cards on the Table*); Nadine Boynton makes reference to Poirot's moral and conscience-challenging solution to the murder that took place on the Orient Express; and Miss Pierce knows Poirot as the man who solved the A.B.C. murders.

Appointment with Death was adapted for the stage by Christie in 1945 in London. It was also adapted for film in 1988, with Peter Ustinov as Hercule Poirot.

"The Arcadian Deer"

PUBLISHING HISTORY: First published by William Collins Sons and Co., Ltd., London, 1947, in the short story collection *The Labours of Hercules*. First published in the United States by Dodd, Mead and Co., New York, 1947, in the short story collection *The Labors of Hercules*.

CHARACTERS: Hercule Poirot; Marie Hellin, Nita, Katrina Samoushenka, Ted Williamson.

In the third of the twelve labors performed by Hercule in emulation of the classical hero Hercules, the detective is not challenged with a dire murder or theft but with a romantic mystery of lost love. The labor follows its mythological counterpart rather aptly: Hercules captured the golden-horned hind in Arcadia near the Cerymean River. Poirot's method is far less brutal than Hercules's. The mythological hero

caught the hind by shooting through her forelegs, earning the displeasure of the goddess Artemis.

When Poirot's car does not behave "with that mechanical perfection which he expected of a car," he finds himself in the riverside village of Hartly Dene and at the small hotel of the Black Swan. There, he meets the local garage mechanic, Ted Williamson, "a simple, young man with the outward appearance of a Greek god." Williamson beseeches his help in finding a mysterious young woman, Nita, who told him that she was a lady's maid to one of the guests in a local house. Nita added that he should return in several weeks, when the lady would once more be a guest. Going back to the house, Ted was informed that Nita was no longer in the employ of the lady; adding to his frustration was his inability to contact her— the letters he sent to her new house were returned unanswered.

Poirot's involvement takes him from England to the Continent, including Pisa and Vagray les Alpes, Switzerland. He hunts down the elusive maid and succeeds in convincing a dying woman that she truly has much to live for.

Poirot performs in this case in a manner quite similar to Mr. Satterthwaite, the chief investigator for the enigmatic Mr. Harley Quin.

While this is the third labor of Hercule Poirot in this collection, Hercules's labor of hunting the Arcadian deer is traditionally his fourth.

At Bertram's Hotel

PUBLISHING HISTORY: First published by William Collins Sons and Co., Ltd., London, 1965. First published in the United States by Dodd, Mead and Co., New York, 1966.

CHARACTERS: Miss Jane Marple; The Honourable Elvira Blake, Mrs. Carpenter, Chief Inspector Fred Davy, Michael Gorman, Miss Gorringe, Sir Ronald Graves, Lady Selina Hazy, Robert Hoffman, Mr. Humfries, Colonel Derek Luscombe, Ladislas Malinowski, Contessa Martinelli, Mildred Melford, Canon Pennyfeather, Mr.

Robinson, Lady Bess Sedgwick, Rose Sheldon, Emma Wheeling, Raymond West.

Miss Marple has benefited over the years from the kindness of her favorite nephew, Raymond West. A year before, Raymond and his painter wife, Joan, had sent the old spinster to the West Indies, where "she had to get mixed up in a murder case" (recounted in *A Caribbean Mystery*). This year, Raymond is happy to report that his latest novel is "doing very well indeed" and that he and Joan would like to send Jane on another holiday. They offer her Torquay, Bournemouth, or Eastbourne, but she would rather have a more special trip. London beckons, as Miss Marple longs to see once more the venerable institution of Bertram's Hotel, with its refinement, elegance, service, comfortable chairs, and tea and muffins.

Settling into the grand hotel, Miss Marple notes keenly that somehow all is not as it should be in Bertram's. Small but not insignificant changes have wormed their way into the once sacrosanct refinery of the place: There is a distinct American presence (heating in the rooms, a television room, and, most horrible of all, jelly doughnuts served at breakfast); and there is also a tingling sense of danger and crime beneath the still beautiful veneer. Yes, Miss Marple notes, things are definitely amiss.

She is not alone in her concerns. Scotland Yard has its eye on Bertram's, and when the hotel's name surfaces in several seemingly unrelated investigations, one of its best men, Inspector Davy, is launched onto the case. Events take an even more serious note when the doorman of the hotel, Mickey Gorman, is shot to death, dying from a bullet apparently intended for the young heiress Elvira Blake. Her mother, the adventuress and wealthy romantic Lady Bess Sedgwick, is also staying at the hotel, as is Blake's current love interest, the race car driver Ladislaus Malinowski. Interestingly, the key to the investigation is an absent-minded cleric, Canon Pennyfeather, who disappears from the hotel and is found in the countryside, the victim of kidnapping.

• • •

The traditional assumption among Christie aficionados is that Bertram's Hotel was based on the venerable London hotel Brown's. At least one biographer, Janet Morgan (in *Agatha Christie: A Biography,* 1985), stands opposed to this hypothesis. She contends instead that the model for Bertram's Hotel was Fleming's.

As with the other later Christie novels—in particular, *Third Girl*—At Bertram's Hotel paints a sharp contrast between the traditional culture in England (staid, urbane, and lingeringly Victorian) and the wild, rebellious, and, to Christie, horrible youth movement of the 1960s. This tension and social struggle is played out in the hotel, and the embodiment of traditional English values does not survive the invasion of new culture.

Christie dedicated the book thus: "For Harry Smith because I appreciate the scientific way he reads my books." The novel was adapted for television in 1987 by the BBC.

"At the 'Bells and Motley' "

PUBLISHING HISTORY: First published by William Collins Sons and Co., Ltd., London, 1930, in the short story collection *The Mysterious Mr. Quin.* First published in the United States by Dodd, Mead and Co., New York, 1930, in the short story collection *The Mysterious Mr. Quin.*

CHARACTERS: Mr. Satterthwaite; Mr. Harley Quin; Mr. Cyrus Bradburn, Stephen Grant, Captain Harwell, William Jones, Eleanor Le Couteau, John Mathias, Mrs. St. Clair.

Mr. Satterthwaite finds himself stranded with an inoperative car in the "godforsaken hole" of Kirtlington Mallet, near the Salisbury Plain and far from his original destination of Marswick Manor. Settling in at the only local inn, Bells and Motley, he is astonished to discover that a fellow guest at the inn is the mysterious Mr. Quin. As always occurs when Mr. Quin makes an appearance, a mystery soon follows. This is presented by the landlord, who tells of the peculiar disappearance three months before of Captain Harwell. Adding to the puzzle is the decision of Mrs. Harwell, the former Miss Eleanor Le Couteau, to sell their house, Ashley Grange, for sixty thousand pounds to the American millionaire Cyrus Bradburn. The only suspect in the disappearance and possible murder of Captain Harwell is the former master of horses at Ashley Grange, Stephen Grant, the fiancé of the daughter of Bells and Motley's landlord. As there was lack of evidence of foul play, Grant was released, leaving the police baffled. Their confusion only deepens when they can find nothing remotely substantial in the background of Captain Harwell.

"The Augean Stables"

PUBLISHING HISTORY: First published by William Collins Sons and Co., Ltd., London, 1947, in the short story collection *The Labours of Hercules.* First published in the United States by Dodd, Mead and Co., New York, 1947, in the short story collection *The Labors of Hercules.*

CHARACTERS: Hercule Poirot; Miss Thelma Anderson, Sir George Conway, Dagmar Ferrier, Edward Ferrier, John Hammett, Dr. Henderson, Percy Perry.

Whereas the Hercules of legend was responsible for cleaning out the unpleasant stables of King Augeas of Elis, the detective Hercule Poirot completes his version by washing away the stench and grime surrounding a political scandal involving a former British prime minister, John Hammett. The "manure" in this case was piled high by one particular muckraking journal, *X-Ray News,* published by the ambitious Percy Perry.

Poirot is consulted by Edward Ferrier, prime minister, and Sir George Conway, home secretary, in the hope that he might prevent Ferrier's reputation from being destroyed by the *X-Ray News.* In taking up his task, Poirot enters into combat on a large scale with Percy Perry. Throughout the struggle, it seems that Perry has the upper hand, especially when Dagmar Ferrier, wife of Edward Ferrier and daughter of John Hammett, is suddenly embroiled in a sex scandal. This moment of apparent victory offers Poirot his chance, and he

seizes it, securing a crushing blow and triumph over the muckraker.

• • •

This case places Poirot once again in contact with the highest levels of the British government. His value to the state was demonstrated in several investigations, including his rescue of Prime Minister David MacAdam in "The Kidnapped Prime Minister."

In classical mythology, the powerful and clever Hercules accomplished the seemingly impossible task of cleaning out the Augean stables in one day (in return for one-tenth of King Augeas's prized cattle) by diverting the courses of the Peneus and Alpheus Rivers. It was ranked number six of the twelve labors; for Poirot, the feat of the Augean stables is his fifth labor.

An Autobiography

PUBLISHING HISTORY: First published by William Collins Sons and Co., Ltd., London, 1977. First published in the United States by Dodd, Mead and Co., New York, 1977.

An Autobiography offers Agatha Christie's often charming account of her own life, covering the years from her birth until 1965. She began the work in April of 1950 and ended it fifteen years later, when, at the age of seventy-five, she could write, "I am satisfied. I have done what I wanted to do." The book was subsequently edited by her daughter, Rosalind, and finally released in 1977, a year after Christie's death.

Because the book ends in 1965, it does not cover the last ten years of Christie's life, a period that boasted the publication of her last novels featuring Poirot and Marple, *Curtain* and *Sleeping Murder* respectively, the 1974 release of the Oscar-winning film *Murder on the Orient Express,* and the continued success of her works around the world. Also during this time, Christie was named a Dame of the British Empire (1971) and her husband, Max Mallowan, was knighted (1968).

Christie chose a basic chronological structure for her autobiography. This did not prevent her, however, from moving around in her coverage of events and stories. There are rich details about her early life and her relationships, especially her marriage to Max Mallowan. She devotes much time to travel stories and to the archaeological digs with her husband in the Middle East. Of particular interest is her account of how she embarked upon her writing career, with splendid details on the creation of Hercule Poirot and Miss Marple and assorted insights into some of her most memorable works.

The autobiography does not include any information on Christie's much-heralded 1926 disappearance. This is in keeping with Christie's long-standing policy of never addressing the mystery, although she does make potentially critical observations about amnesia and says, "I have remembered, I suppose, what I wanted to remember." In her epilogue, she wrote:

> *I live now on borrowed time, waiting in the anteroom for the summons that will inevitably come. And then—I go to the next thing, whatever it is. One doesn't luckily have to bother about that.*
>
> *I am ready now to accept death. I have been singularly fortunate. I have with me my husband, my daughter, my grandson, my kind son-in-law—the people who make up my world.*

The Big Four

PUBLISHING HISTORY: First published by William Collins Sons and Co., Ltd., London, 1927. First published in the United States by Dodd, Mead and Co., New York, 1927. (See also below for the history of "The Chess Problem.")

CHARACTERS: Hercule Poirot; Captain Arthur Hastings; Achille Poirot; Countess Vera Rossakoff; Chief Inspector James Japp; Joseph Aarons, Betsy Andrews, Colonel Appleby, Sydney Crowther, Claud Darrell, Monsieur Desjardeaux, Robert Grant, Mr. and Mrs. Halliday, John Ingles, Captain Kent, Li Chang Yen, Miss Martin, Mr. Mayerling, Mr. McNeil, Inspector Meadows, Flossie Monro, Madame Olivier, Mabel Palmer, Mr. Paynter, Mrs. Pearson, Dr. Ridgeway, Abe Ryland, Mr. and Mrs. Templeton, Dr. Treves, Jonathan Whalley, Gilmour Wilson.

Captain Arthur Hastings returns to England after a decade away on his ranch in Argentina. Journeying to see his old friend, Hercule Poirot, he is shocked to discover that the detective is planning on going to South America himself, to Rio, on a case for the American soap magnate Abe Ryland. Just as Poirot is ready to depart, however, they are surprised by an unexpected guest. A stranger, "coated from head to foot with dust and mud" and emaciated as though from some long imprisonment, collapses on Poirot's floor. He is only able to speak Poirot's name and to scribble the number four repeatedly on a piece of paper. After helping the man come to his senses, the detective hears a wild tale of a sinister international crime cartel called the Big Four, headed by a mysterious Chinese mastermind named Li Chang Yen, known as Number One. Number Two is an American, Number Three is French, and Number Four is utterly unknown.

Poirot leaves the stranger in the care of his housekeeper and sets off for the train with Hastings. At last, Poirot surmises that he has been sent on a false mission to South America to get him out of the way. They hurriedly return to Poirot's flat only to discover the stranger dead; the clock on Poirot's mantelpiece has stopped at four o'clock, announcing that the stranger has been murdered by Number Four, the "Destroyer."

Poirot consults with Inspector Japp and is told that the dead man was a British agent with the code name of Mayerling, who had disappeared five years before and who had been murdered by being gagged and forced to inhale prussic acid. With great determination, Poirot sets out not merely to defeat the Big Four but to tear apart the entire organization. His investigation takes him to the Italian Tyrol and throws a host of challenges before him: secret laboratories, assassins, secret weapons, and even death. Above all, the case signals the appearance of Achille Poirot, Hercule's able but lethargic brother. Achille and Hastings prove of great importance in the resolution of the case and the defeat of the Big Four.

• • •

The Big Four was published only a year after the brilliant and groundbreaking mystery *The Murder of Roger Ackroyd* (1926) and was never able to escape the latter's very large shadow. The initial publication of the book, however, was aided by an all-too-real event in Christie's life. Just before the release of *The Big Four,* on December 3, 1926, Christie disappeared, the greatest personal mystery surrounding the author. (For details, see page 2.)

As a result of her famous disappearance, the new book, released only a few weeks after her sudden reappearance, was a financial hit and actually sold more than twice the number of copies that *Roger Ackroyd* did (what seems today the paltry quantity of 8,500 copies in its first printing). Its success is even more surprising because of the absence of the traditional murder mystery format that had by then become the hallmark of the Poirot cases. Here, rather than making inquiries into the death of some country squire, Poirot and Hastings are caught up in international intrigue and espionage. It set a precedent for the future and opened up the possibilities for the character.

The Big Four was also notable for the appearance of two most interesting characters: Achille Poirot and Countess Vera Rossakoff. Achille is to Poirot what Mycroft Holmes was to Sherlock Holmes, the equally brilliant but sadly indolent older brother. There is, of course, less to Achille than meets the eye, but Hastings, ever gullible, fails to note the obvious. As for Vera Rossakoff, Poirot had met her previously in the case of "The Double Clue," and had clearly fallen for the charming Russian émigré. Whereas Achille was Mycroft to Poirot's Sherlock, Countess Vera is the perfect equivalent of Irene Adler (the only woman ever to catch the eye of Holmes). He will meet her for the last time years later in "The Capture of Cerberus." The case has one final distinguishing feature: Chief Inspector Japp, one of the favorite mainstays of the Poirot cases, makes his second Christie appearance after his involvement in *The Mysterious Affair at Styles.*

In an interesting side note to the publishing history of *The Big Four,* Chapter Eleven from the novel has been published separately at times as a stand-alone short story under the title "The Chess Problem."

"The Bird with the Broken Wing"

PUBLISHING HISTORY: First published by William Collins Sons and Co., Ltd., London, 1930, in the short story collection *The Mysterious Mr. Quin.* First published in the United States by Dodd, Mead and Co., New York, 1930, in the short story collection *The Mysterious Mr. Quin.*

CHARACTERS: Mr. Satterthwaite; Mr. Harley Quin; Gerard Annesley, Mabelle Annesley, Doris Coles, Roger Graham, Mrs. Graham, David Keeley, Madge Keeley.

Mr. Satterthwaite finds himself at a party in London, having declined an invitation to visit Laidell. While he is at the party, however, a group of young people attempt a round of table-turning—contacting the spirits—and receive a message from QUIN for Mr. Satterthwaite. It says simply: LAIDELL. Comprehending fully, Satterthwaite rushes to Laidell, complying with the obvious summons from the enigmatic Mr. Quin.

Arriving at Laidell, Satterthwaite makes the acquaintance of the household and becomes fascinated by the ravishing Mabelle Annesley, a member of the ill-fated Clydesley family—a brother had killed himself, one sister had drowned, and another had died in an earthquake. Mabelle joins them in death, for she is found hanged by a rope from a hook high up on a door. The police soon discover that Mabelle did not die by her own hand but was murdered by an unknown assailant while she entered a room to fetch a ukelele. Satterthwaite solves the murder, but he cannot help feeling guilty for having failed Mr. Quin and having failed to prevent the death. Quin reminds him, however, that "death is not the greatest evil."

Black Coffee

PUBLISHING HISTORY: First published by St. Martin's Press, New York, 1997, as an adaptation of the 1930 play of the same name.

CHARACTERS: Hercule Poirot; Captain Arthur Hastings; Chief Inspector James Japp; Barbara Amory, Miss Caroline Amory, Sir Claud Amory, Lucia Amory, Richard Amory, Dr. Carelli, Dr. Graham, Johnson, Edward Raynor, Tredwell.

The novel *Black Coffee* is an adaptation of the original Christie stage play, first penned in 1930. The adaptation was undertaken by Charles Osborne, a veteran actor and writer who also played the role of Dr. Carelli in a 1956 summer production of *Black Coffee* at Tunbridge Wells.

The novel follows the basic events of the original stage play and features the murder of Sir Claud Amory and the theft of a secret formula. Hercule Poirot must solve both the murder and the theft while avoiding a clever effort to have him join Sir Claud in death. (For more details, see under Film and Stage.)

"Blindman's Bluff"

PUBLISHING HISTORY: First published by William Collins Sons and Co., Ltd., London, 1929, in the short story collection *Partners in Crime*. First published in the United States by Dodd, Mead and Co., New York, 1929.

CHARACTERS: Tommy Beresford; Tuppence Beresford; Duke of Blairgowrie, Captain Harper.

While dining at the Gold Room, a very posh eatery, Tommy and Tuppence are approached by the powerful and elegant Duke of Blairgowrie, who asks their help in locating his missing daughter. The two detectives agree immediately and solve the crime while Tommy adopts the persona and methods of the fictional detective Thornley Colton, a blind sleuth created Clinton Holland Stagg (d. 1916). Tuppence acts as Thornley's assistant. (Throughout the collection *Partners in Crime,* the Beresfords impersonate assorted fictional detectives while solving their cases.)

"The Bloodstained Pavement"

PUBLISHING HISTORY: First published by William Collins Sons and Co., Ltd., London, 1932, in the short story collection *The Thirteen Problems*. First published in the United States by Dodd, Mead and Co., New York, 1932, in the short story collection *The Tuesday Club Murders.*

CHARACTERS: Miss Jane Marple; Joyce Lemprière; Captain Denis Dacre, Mrs. Margery Dacre, Miss Carol Harding, Raymond West.

One of the seemingly enigmatic stories of murder recounted by members of the Tuesday Night Club, of which Miss Marple is a member, this dark case is told by Joyce Lemprière, "an artist, with her close-cropped black head and queer hazel-green eyes" (as she is described in "The Tuesday Night Club"). While visiting Rathole, "a queer little Cornish fishing village," Joyce observes the chance meeting of Captain Denis Dacre and his wife with Miss Carol Harding. While painting the quaint inn, Joyce notices that she has included in the painting not only wet bathing suits hanging from a line and drying in the sun but a disturbing bloodstain on the pavement. By the time she reaches the stain, however, there is to be found only water that had dripped from suits dangling above. Soon after, Joyce learns of Mrs. Dacre's accidental death by drowning. From only a few details, Miss Marple solves the crime, perceiving immediately the significance of the bathing suits.

• • •

The *modus operandi* in this particular case bears striking similarity to the Poirot case *Evil under the Sun* (1941).

"The Blue Geranium"

PUBLISHING HISTORY: First published by William Collins Sons and Co., Ltd., London, 1932, in the short story collection *The Thirteen Problems*. First published in the United States by Dodd, Mead and Co., New York, 1932, in the short story collection *The Tuesday Club Murders.*

CHARACTERS: Miss Jane Marple; Colonel Arthur Bantry, Dolly Bantry, Sir Henry Clithering, Nurse Copling, Jane Helier, Dr. Lloyd, George Pritchard, Mary Pritchard, Zarida.

The Tuesday Night Club reunites after a year's separation, and the members—Miss Marple included—hear a tale of mysterious death from Colonel Arthur Bantry and his wife, Dolly. Mrs. Mary Pritchard, the semi-invalid who "really had something wrong with her, but whatever it was, she played it for all it was worth," becomes obsessed with impending danger. This idea is both planted and exaggerated by a fortune-teller, Zarida, "Psychic Reader of the Future," who pays Mrs. Pritchard a visit. Her long-suffering husband, George, attempts to calm his wife down, but she insists that evil is present and presents him with a heavily scented paper with large black writing from Zarida:

I have seen the Future. Be warned before it is too late. Beware of the full moon. The Blue Primrose means warning, the Blue Hollyhock means Danger; the Blue Geranium means Death . . .

Soon, the primrose flowers in the flower decorated wallpaper in Mrs. Pritchard's house turn inexplicably blue, followed soon after by the hollyhock flower that was just above her head. The day finally comes, of course, when Mrs. Pritchard is found dead in her room. There, on the wall, one of the once pinky-red geraniums on the wallpaper had turned bright, deep blue.

An autopsy follows, but the cause of death is uncertain, focusing local gossip on George Pritchard. Adding to the mystery is the absolute disappearance of Zarida, for the address where she was supposedly to be found proves a dead end. As a result, partly because of her musings about the sad destruction of wasps on a beautiful summer's day, Miss Marple deduces how a murder was committed and who the true murderer was.

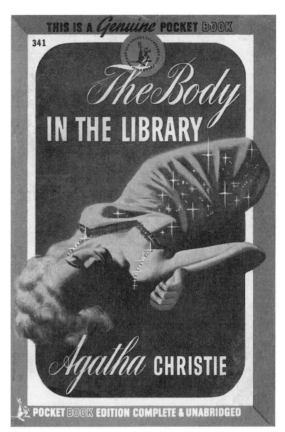

A *1946 edition of* The Body in the Library. *(Pocket Books)*

The Body in the Library

PUBLISHING HISTORY: First published by William Collins Sons and Co., Ltd., London, 1942. First published in the United States by Dodd, Mead and Co., New York, 1942.

CHARACTERS: Miss Jane Marple; Colonel Arthur Bantry, Dolly Bantry, Mrs. Bartlett, George Bartlett, Basil Blake, Peter Carmody, Griselda Clement, Leonard Clement, Sir Henry Clithering, Mark Gaskell, Superintendent Harper, Miss Hartnell, Dr. Haydock, Adelaide Jefferson, Conway Jefferson, Ruby Keene, Dinah Lee, Hugh Maclean, Colonel Melchett, Dr. Metcalf, Constable Palk, Martha Price Ridley, Pamela Reeves, Inspector Slack, Raymond Starr, Josephine Turner, Caroline Wetherby.

The early morning serenity of Gossington Hall, St. Mary Mead, home of the Colonel and Dolly Bantry, is shattered when the housemaid, Mary, runs into the couple's bedroom and shouts hysterically, "Oh, ma'am, there's a body in the library!" At first doubting her ears, Dolly finally decides that yes, she has heard correctly that there is a body in the library. Of course, she has a rather difficult time convincing her husband of this, but he eventually staggers downstairs and, sure enough, there, sprawled on the hearth rug in the library, is the corpse of a young blond woman in an evening dress. Her "face was heavily made up, the powder standing out grotesquely on its blue, swollen surface, the mascara of the lashes lying thickly on the distorted cheeks."

Dolly wastes little time in contacting the most competent person she knows concerning murder: Miss Marple. As the old spinster is "so good at bodies," she is brought to Gossington Hall and is soon at work in her own quiet but relentless style. Leading the police investigation is an old nemesis of Miss Marple's, Inspector Slack, "an energetic man who belied his name and who accompanied his bustling manner with a good deal of disregard for the feelings of anyone he did not consider important." The body is identified as Ruby Keene, a dancer and hostess at the nearby Majestic Hotel. The investigation soon turns up a connection with Conway Jefferson, a wealthy invalid who had taken such a shine to Ruby that he planned to adopt her as his heir.

Matters seem to deepen when another corpse is discovered, this time in a burned-out car near the quarry. The new body is identified as a Girl Guide named Pamela Reeves; she had been strangled before the car was set on fire. In a seemingly incriminating admission, George Bartlett, a guest at the Majestic, admits that his car had been stolen but he had not reported it until the following morning. As the investigation turns up a number of likely suspects, Miss Marple closes in on the killer and brings about the person's capture.

• • •

The Body in the Library marks the return of Miss Marple to novel form after an absence of twelve years, following the publication of *The Murder at the Vicarage* (1930). While Christie commented that there were far too many characters in *The Murder at the Vicarage,* she wisely brought back to life a number of the inhabitants of St. Mary Mead. The characters became virtual mainstays of the Miss Marple universe, including Marple's physician, Dr. Haydock, as well as Colonel Melchett, the Bantrys, Sir Henry Clithering, and Leonard and Griselda Clement (the vicar and his wife). According to Christie's autobiography, she wrote *The Body in the Library* during the early part of World War II, when London was being bombed by the Luftwaffe in what the Germans hoped was a prelude to their invasion of Britain. The writer also confessed (in a *Life* magazine interview in 1956) that the opening segment of the novel was the best she ever wrote. It is hard to disagree with her, given the description of the body on the hearth rug in the library of the Bantrys' house, and the tortured efforts of Dolly Bantry to convince her husband that their domicile has truly been invaded by a corpse. The novel was adapted for television in 1984 by the BBC, with Joan Hickson as Miss Marple.

The Boomerang Clue

See *Why Didn't They Ask Evans?*

The Burden

PUBLISHING HISTORY: First published by William Heinemann, London, 1956. First published in the United States by Dell Publishing Co., New York, 1963.

CHARACTERS: Mr. Baldock, Ethel, Lady Muriel Fairborough, Angela Franklin, Arthur Franklin, Charles Franklin, Laura Franklin, Shirley Franklin, Henry Glyn-Edwards, Dr. Graves, Reverend Eustace Henson, Mr. Horder, Llewellyn Knox, Susan Lonsdale, Mrs. Rouse, Miss Weekes, Sir Richard Wilding.

Much concerned with family love, relationships, and the price of personal sacrifice, *The Burden* follows the life of Laura Franklin. A young woman who has grown up in the shadow of her dead brother, Charles, Laura once harbored hopes of winning her parents' love after her brother's death, but her prayers were left unanswered when her parents arrived home from a cruise and announced that they were expecting another child. That child, Shirley, enjoys the full attention of Laura's parents, causing Laura to hate Shirley until a house fire almost results in Shirley's death in the flames.

Subsequent to the fire, Laura becomes devoted completely to her sister, especially after the death of their parents in a plane crash. This sacrifice comes at a severe price, for Laura now obsessively controls her sister's life at the expense of her own happiness. Ultimately, even her smothering concern cannot keep Shirley from tragedy or protect Laura from facing her own crisis of self-worth.

• • •

The Burden was the last book written by Agatha Christie under the pseudonym Mary Westmacott. The American edition of the novel was not published until 1963, and it was released only as a paperback. The American hardcover edition was published in 1973 by Arbor House. Readers of this book will note the close similarity of its plot to the plot of *A Daughter's a Daughter.*

By the Pricking of My Thumbs

PUBLISHING HISTORY: First published by William Collins Sons and Co., Ltd., London, 1968. First published in the United States by Dodd, Mead and Co., New York, 1968.

CHARACTERS: Tommy Beresford; Tuppence Beresford; Albert Batt; Gertrude Bligh, Emily Boscowan, Mr. Copleigh, Mrs. Copleigh, Mr. Eccles, Ada Fanshawe, Mrs. Lancaster, Dr. Murray, Nurse O'Keefe, Miss Packard, Sir Josiah Penn, Alice Perry, Amos Perry, Robert, Ivor Smith, Sir Philip Starke, the Vicar.

The aging Tommy and Tuppence Beresford pay a call on Tommy's very elderly Aunt Ada at the Sunny Ridge rest home and discover that while she may be getting up there in years and displaying tendencies toward senility, she is still a fearsome old gal. Upon seeing Tuppence, she chides Tommy that he "shouldn't bring that type of woman in here. No good her pretending she's your wife."

Taking the hint, Tuppence makes a tactical retreat and takes a walk through the halls of Sunny Ridge. She meets a variety of peculiar patients, including one who swallows her thimble to attract attention and another who is willing to drink her milk because it is not poisoned today. The milk lady then asks a curious question: "I see you're looking at the fireplace—was it your poor child? That's where it is, you know. Behind the fireplace." Before she can continue with other details, Tommy arrives and the Beresfords depart the rest home.

Three weeks later, Aunt Ada dies, and Tommy and Tuppence return to the home to collect the old girl's possessions. Among her effects is a painting of a pale pink house by a canal and a small bridge that had not been there at their last visit. It turns out that it was a gift from Mrs. Lancaster, the little old lady with the glass of milk. The painting stirs vague memories in Tuppence, and she tries to find Mrs. Lancaster to ask her about the painting and to inquire if she would like it back. Mrs. Lancaster is gone from the home, removed by her family. Attempts to locate Mrs. Lancaster prove fruitless, and all letters forwarded to her are not answered.

The painting continues to bother Tuppence, and she is convinced that she has passed the house by train. With her usual perseverance, she sets out to locate the house. With the help of the ever-faithful servant Albert Batt, Tuppence finds the house and learns that it was once called Waterside. The house proves to be a dangerous place, and the words of Mrs. Lancaster are horribly prophetic.

• • •

The title of the novel is taken from William Shakespeare's *Macbeth* (act 4, scene 1); the line is recited by the three witches as they wait for the arrival of Macbeth.

The character of Mrs. Lancaster was used a total of three times in Christie's writings. She first appeared in *Sleeping Murder* (published in 1976 but written during World War II) as a "charming old lady with white hair" carrying a glass of milk in a rest home, who tells Gwenda Reed that there is a child buried behind a fireplace. She appears again in *Pale Horse* (1961) in a home for the mentally ill, again speaking of a child buried behind the fireplace. In the case of *By the Pricking of My Thumbs,* the little old lady actually plays a vital role in the plot.

"The Call of Wings"

PUBLISHING HISTORY: First published by William Collins Sons and Co., Ltd., London, 1933, in the short story collection *The Hound of Death and Other Stories.* First published in the United States by Dodd, Mead and Co., New York, 1971, in the short story collection *The Golden Ball and Other Stories.*

CHARACTERS: Silas Hamer; Dick Borrow, Bernard Seldon.

A tale of the supernatural and profound spiritual transformation, "The Call of Wings" follows the final days of the wealthy Silas Hamer and the mysterious flute music that beckons him into the next world. His experience begins with a conversation between him and his friend Dick Borrow. The latter observes that Hamer is the only contented millionaire he has ever known. Hamer freely declares himself contented because "he is out and out a materialist," who does not believe in anything he cannot hear or see.

While walking home that night, Hamer has a brush with death and turns a street corner, where the only sound to be heard is that of a flute. The sound is unlike anything he has ever heard, and is played by an unknown but clearly gifted musician. The musician has no legs, but his skill is beyond dispute. When he stops playing, Hamer has deep trouble retaining his composure and senses that he is leaving his body.

Unable to shake the powerful sensations he experienced, Hamer consults his friend Sheldon. His friend suggests that Hamer endure a struggle between the flesh and the spirit and see what happens. The experience transforms Hamer, and he meets his "flute" in the autumn air on a London street.

"The Capture of Cerberus"

PUBLISHING HISTORY: First published by William Collins Sons and Co., Ltd., London, 1947, in the short story collection *The Labours of Hercules.* First published in the United States by Dodd, Mead and Co., New York, 1947, in the short story collection *The Labors of Hercules.*

CHARACTERS: Hercule Poirot; Countess Vera Rossakoff; Chief Inspector James Japp; Detective Inspector Charles Stevens; Dr. Alice Cunningham, Miss Lemon, Paul Varesco.

In the final of Hercule Poirot's twelve labors recreating the heroic endeavors of the mythological Hercules, the detective brings an enormous dog, the equivalent of the legendary Cerberus, out of the underworld, destroys a cocaine ring, and encounters for the first time in twenty years the woman for whom he possessed a "fatal fascination." This remarkable woman is Countess Vera Rossakoff, and Poirot meets her again in the London Underground, while ascending the escalator to the cool air of the evening. The countess is descending, and when the detective asks her how they might meet again, she gives him a cryptic two-word answer: "In Hell." With her usual skill and knowledge of the seemingly most obscure details, Miss Lemon responds to Poirot's inquiry about "Hell" by booking a table there, dialing Temple Bar 14578 and reserving a spot for 11:00 P.M.

Poirot arrives in Hell, a stylish nightclub, replete with the largest and ugliest dog Poirot has even seen! The dog is Cerberus, who guards the entrance and is kept pacified by an offering of dog biscuits from a small basket. Penetrating the deeper confines of the club, the detective at last meets Countess Vera, the apparent owner, and encounters several of her friends, including Alice Cunningham, the fiancée of the countess's son;

Professor Linkeard, an archaeologist; and the sinister Paul Varesco. A psychologist, Dr. Cunningham arouses Poirot's interest because of her dowdy attire and the fact that she is so thoroughly unimpressed with the great Hercule.

Poirot soon learns that Scotland Yard suspects that Hell is the nerve center of a ring of criminals dealing in gems and narcotics. Poirot, however, must learn if his friend the countess is involved, especially given her colorful past. Poirot solves the matter, relying on several clues, such as the massive jaws of Cerberus, Miss Cunningham's big pockets, the countess's tendency toward crime, and a tiny piece of checked tweed.

• • •

In the labors undertaken by Hercules in mythology, he was forced to descend into the underworld and find Cerberus, the giant dog, at the gate of Tartarus. The beast possessed three heads, and Hercules had to subdue its spirit without any weapons and bring it back to earth. The enchanting Countess Vera first met Poirot in "The Double Clue," and then again in *The Big Four.*

Cards on the Table

PUBLISHING HISTORY: First published by William Collins Sons and Co., Ltd., London, 1936. First published in the United States by Dodd, Mead and Co., New York, 1937.

CHARACTERS: Hercule Poirot; Colonel Johnny Race; Mrs. Ariadne Oliver; Superintendent Battle; Mrs. Benson, Mrs. Craddock, Charles Craddock, Rhoda Dawes, Major John Despard, Gerald Hemmingway, Mrs. Lorrimer, Mrs. Luxmore, Anne Meredith, Sergeant O'Connor, Dr. Roberts, Mr. Shaitana.

Hercule Poirot attends an exhibit of snuffboxes at Wessex House and meets the mysterious and rather sinister Mr. Shaitana, a man of whom virtually everyone is afraid but whose parties, "lavish" and "macabre," are an absolute must socially, despite the pervasive unease of the guests. It is precisely to one of these parties that Shaitana invites Hercule Poirot, offering the detective an irresistible invitation: In attendance at the dinner will be four murderers, four individuals who have successfully committed murder and who got away with it.

The four guests at the dinner party seem innocent enough. There is Major Despard, the explorer; Anne Meredith, a charming ingenue; Dr. Roberts, a physician of some note; and Mrs. Lorrimer, a widow. Adding even further interest to the assemblage are the three other guests: Colonel Race, Superintendent Battle, and Mrs. Ariadne Oliver. It is obvious to the detective that none of the latter three is a murderer, and he settles in to observe the accused.

After the meal, Shaitana suggests bridge, leading his guests to two tables. There, while he sits by the fire, the eight guests play bridge, four murderers at one table and four champions of justice at the other. At the end of the evening, Race bids his host farewell and discovers the seemingly impossible. While all sat playing bridge, someone had walked over to Shaitana—in plain view of the other guests—and stabbed him to death with a thin blade. The hunt is then on to find the deft and composed murderer. Without question, the killer was at the table of accused murderers. But which bridge player could it have been?

• • •

Cards on the Table is a novel of great significance in the Christie works, as it brings together four expert criminologists and provides them with a suitable puzzle for their talents: Poirot, Oliver, Race, and Battle. This is also Mrs. Oliver's first appearance in a novel, subsequent to her two appearances in the short story collection *Parker Pyne Investigates* (1934). The germ of the fascinating method and setting for the murder in *Cards on the Table* was first set out in chapter three of *The A.B.C. Murders:*

"Supposing," murmured Poirot, "that four people sit down to play bridge and one, the odd man out, sits in the chair by the fire. Then into the evening the man by the fire is found dead. One of the four, while he is dummy, has gone over and killed him,

and, intent on the play of the hand, the other three have not noticed. Ah, there would be a crime for you! Which of the four was it?"

While there are only four suspects—one of the members of the group of four bridge players—Christie uses the subtle and superbly crafted plot to provide the reader with enough questions to keep them guessing right to the end. Of particular interest is the interplay among the four detectives who make up the second foursome of bridge players in the home of the mysterious Mr. Shaitana. This case was mentioned in *Appointment with Death* as a notable success for Poirot.

Similarly, *Cards on the Table* includes a mention of *Murder on the Orient Express,* but also includes a clear indication of that solution; this is a point of some importance to those readers who have not read *Orient Express* and accidentally read *Cards on the Table* before picking out the other Christie masterpiece.

Another less positive aspect of the novel is the repeated presence of then-acceptable racial and cultural epithets, such as a description of a solicitor who is "rather alert and Jewish" and that "damned dago, Shaitana." Such references appear in Christie's early works and have been, at times inconsistently and incompletely, edited out of later editions. *Cards on the Table* was adapted for the stage by Leslie Darbon and opened in London in 1981.

"Caretaker, The Case of the"

PUBLISHING HISTORY: First published by Dodd, Mead and Co., New York, 1950, in the short story collection *Three Blind Mice and Other Stories.* Reprinted by William Collins Sons and Co., Ltd., London, 1979, in the short story collection *Miss Marple's Final Cases.*

CHARACTERS: Miss Jane Marple; Dr. Haydock, Harry Laxton, Louise Laxton, Mr. Murgatroyd, Mrs. Murgatroyd.

This story concerns a rather grim tale of murder given by Dr. Haydock to Miss Marple in the form of an unpublished manuscript. The doctor's purpose is twofold: first, he wishes to see if she can solve the puzzle, and second, he is attempting to revive her spirits after a bout with the flu. The murder in question involves a young couple, Harry Laxton and his French-English bride, Louise, who return home to their little village after making their fortune. To create a suitable domicile for his family, Laxton tore down the derelict old Kingsdean House and replaced it with a new mansion, "white and gleaming among the trees."

This destruction and rebirth has come at the expense not only of Kingsdean House but of the decades-old job of the caretakers, Old Murgatroyd and her husband. Angry at losing her position—despite her generous pension—Murgatroyd curses the Laxtons, and begins haunting the couple. Tragedy ensues when Louise's horse is frightened while the young bride is riding. Thrown from the horse, Louise is killed, to the great sorrow of her husband. Miss Marple perceives the truth, and the doctor is pleased to announce that "You're looking almost yourself again."

A Caribbean Mystery

PUBLISHING HISTORY: First published by William Collins Sons and Co., Ltd., London, 1964. First published in the United States by Dodd, Mead and Co., New York, 1965.

CHARACTERS: Miss Jane Marple; Señora de Caspearo, Gregory Dyson, Lucky Dyson, Big Jim Ellis, Dr. Graham, Colonel Edward Hillingdon, Arthur Jackson, Victoria Johnson, Molly Kendal, Tim Kendal, Major Palgrave, Canon Jeremy Prescott, Joan Prescott, Jason Rafiel, Esther Walters, Raymond West.

In a remarkable change of scenery for the venerable sleuth of St. Mary Mead, Miss Marple finds herself in the Caribbean, on the island of St. Honoré in the West Indies. Her generous nephew, the novelist Raymond West, has made the trip possible by providing the funds to his aunt after her recent bout with pneumonia. He has been doing quite well with his novels, and he insists that she get away and recuperate properly. She seems quite taken with the holiday and is soon observing the other guests with her customarily keen eye. There are the Kendals, the young couple who run the hotel; the Dysons and Hillingdons, two couples who are also apparently very good friends; Jason Rafiel, a crusty old invalid who is immediately impressed with Miss Marple's mental faculties; and the talkative Major Palgrave, "purple of face, with a glass eye," who insists on regaling Miss Marple with long-winded tales of his days in Kenya.

Listening patiently, Miss Marple suddenly has her attention riveted when the Major asks her, "Like to see the picture of a murderer?" Just as he is about to show it to her, he glances over her shoulder and sees something (or someone) so alarming that he puts the photo away into his wallet and hurriedly changes the subject. Miss Marple is anxious to speak with the Major again, but she learns the next morning that Palgrave died during the night, supposedly from his high blood pressure. Deepening the mystery is the revelation that the photo has disappeared. Not only does Miss Marple have to find out how and why the Major was killed, but who committed the crime.

• • •

A *Caribbean Mystery* presents the only known published case solved by Miss Marple that was undertaken outside of England. Not only does her setting change, she is also uncharacteristically vigorous in her investigation. Normally, Miss Marple would sit and ponder a problem while knitting. Here, seemingly rejuvenated by the sun, she is quite active, even going so far as to spy on several suspects by hiding in a flower bed. One of the characters, Jason Rafiel, is so impressed by the abilities of the sleuth that he later posthumously commissions her to solve another murder and prove the innocence of his son, in *Nemesis* (1971).

The book is dedicated "To my old friend (J. C. R.) with happy memories of my visit to the West Indies." J. C. R. was John Cruikshank Rose, an architect who hosted Christie and her husband, Max

Mallowan, on several occasions in the West Indies. The novel was adapted twice for television: in 1983 by CBS television, with Helen Hayes as Miss Marple, and in 1989 by the BBC, with Joan Hickson as Miss Marple.

"The Case of the . . ."

Stories beginning with this phrase are listed under the next word in each individual title. For example, for "The Case of the Discontented Soldier," see "Discontented Soldier, The Case of the."

Cat among the Pigeons

PUBLISHING HISTORY: First published by William Collins Sons and Co., Ltd., London, 1959. First published in the United States by Dodd, Mead and Co., New York, 1960.

CHARACTERS: Hercule Poirot; Prince Ali Yusef, Miss Blake, Angele Blanche, Sergeant Percy Bond, Miss Bulstrode, Alice Calder, Miss Chadwick, John Edmundson, Georges, Adam Goodman, Miss Johnson, Detective Inspector Kelsey, Derek O'Connor, Colonel Pikeaway, Denis Rathbone, Bob Rawlinson, Eileen Rich, Mr. Robinson, Miss Rowan, Princess Shaista, Ann Shapland, Miss Grace Springer, Jennifer Sutcliffe, Joan Sutcliffe, Mrs. Upjohn, Julia Upjohn, Miss Vansittart.

Summer session has arrived for the exclusive Meadowbank School, and the imperious headmistress of the academy, Miss Bulstrode, welcomes back her prized students—invariably, the daughters of the wealthy and powerful from Europe and beyond. In sharp contrast to the serene atmosphere of Meadowbank is the scene two months before in the Middle Eastern country of Ramat. There, a revolt has toppled its ruler, Prince Ali. The elegant and still determined prince must leave his country, but not before entrusting to his private pilot, Bob Rawlinson, a cache of precious stones to be smuggled out of the country.

Rawlinson barely has time to send a mysterious message to an undersecretary at the British embassy and to write a hasty note to his sister, Joan Sutcliffe, who is visiting Ramat with her daughter, Jennifer. They are ordered out of Ramat by the British embassy, as the country is not safe, and depart without ever seeing Bob.

Upon returning home, Jennifer Sutcliffe enrolls for the current semester at Meadowbank just in time to hear the terrible news from the Middle East. The principality of Ramat has fallen, and the prince and his pilot, Bob Rawlinson, were killed in a plane crash while fleeing the strife.

More bad news follows. Miss Springer, the very unpopular games mistress, is shot to death in the sports pavilion. The only fingerprints found by the police are Miss Springer's, on a flashlight. Not long after this, Princess Shaista, cousin of the dead Prince Ali of Ramat and a student at Meadowbank, is kidnapped, Miss Chadwick, another teacher, is murdered, and several lockers are broken into and searched by some unknown criminal. As things are now utterly out of hand, Julia Upjohn, the daughter of a one-time British agent and a clever student at Meadowbank, turns to an outside detective: Hercule Poirot.

• • •

Cat among the Pigeons introduces the mysterious (and rather malevolent) character Mr. Robinson, described as "not definitely Jewish, nor definitely Greek nor Portuguese nor Spanish, nor South American." Nor is he English. Robinson appears in three other novels: *At Bertram's Hotel* (1965), *Postern of Fate* (1973), and *Passenger to Frankfurt* (1970). As he has dealings with Poirot, Miss Marple, and the Beresfords, he holds the distinction of appearing with four of the major detectives in the Christie pantheon. Another associate of Mr. Robinson, Colonel Ephraim Pikeaway, appears with Robinson in *Postern of Fate, Passenger to Frankfurt,* and *Cat among the Pigeons.* There is also a reference to *Mrs. McGinty's Dead,* as the character of Mrs. Upjohn knows Maureen Summerhaye, who appeared in that novel.

"Cheap Flat, The Adventure of the"

PUBLISHING HISTORY: First published in *Sketch* magazine, London, 1923–24; reprinted by John

Lane Publishers, London, 1924, in the short story collection *Poirot Investigates.* First published in the United States by Dodd, Mead and Co., New York, 1925, in the short story collection *Poirot Investigates.*

CHARACTERS: Hercule Poirot; Captain Arthur Hastings; Chief Inspector James Japp; Mr. Burt, Elsa Hardt, Gerald Parker, Stella Robinson.

In a case narrated by Captain Arthur Hastings, Poirot investigates an affair that begins with the establishment of a seemingly mysterious and heaven-sent low rent for an apartment (or flat) and climaxes in international secrets and murder. The matter is brought to the attention of Captain Hastings, who tells Poirot that Mrs. Robinson was the recipient of extraordinary good luck when she and her husband found an affordable flat in the most fashionable Montagu Mansions complex, near Knightsbridge, for only eighty pounds a year, and no premiums. Poirot commences immediately to investigate the curious matter, going so far as to rent a flat for himself in Montagu Mansions only two floors above the fortunate Robinsons and to actually break into their domicile.

Hastings is next astonished to learn that the flat is only part of a complicated scheme involving stolen American naval plans, the murder of a young navy department employee named Luigi Valdarno, and the sudden disappearance of his girlfriend, Miss Elsa Hardt, a concert singer. Poirot ties both events together, captures a dangerous assassin, and returns to the Americans a valuable set of secret plans. A vital set of clues points to the resolution of the matter, Poirot's skills as a thief, and to the fact that the detective does not care for his friends to carry loaded pistols, all contribute to the resolution.

• • •

This case was adapted for television in 1990 by London Weekend Television as part of the series *Agatha Christie's Poirot* starring David Suchet.

"The Chocolate Box"

PUBLISHING HISTORY: First published in *Sketch* magazine, London, 1923–24; reprinted by John

Lane Publishers, London, 1924, in the short story collection *Poirot Investigates*. First published in the United States by Dodd, Mead and Co., New York, 1925, in the short story collection, *Poirot Investigates*.

CHARACTERS: Hercule Poirot; Captain Arthur Hastings; Virginie Mesnard; Madame Déroulard, Paul Déroulard, Felicie, M. de Saint Alard, Mr. John Wilson.

"The Chocolate Box" is unique among the recorded cases of Hercule Poirot, for, as Poirot declares to Captain Hastings, "See here, my friend, you have, I know, kept a record of my little successes. You shall add one more story to the collection, the story of my failure." Against the backdrop of a rainstorm with howling winds, Poirot tells of a time some years before, when the detective was still serving with distinction as a member of the Belgian police, although the events he describes took place under the technical auspices of his leave, meaning that Poirot conducted the investigation in his capacity as a private sleuth.

While on vacation, Poirot is consulted by Virginie Mesnard, a cousin of Madame Déroulard, the late wife of the French minister, Paul Déroulard. Madame Déroulard had died from a fall down a flight of stairs, and she was eventually followed by her husband; he had died quite suddenly. It was this death that Virginie had asked Poirot to investigate, for, despite a complete absence of proof, she was convinced that Paul Déroulard had been murdered. There were certainly many people who might have contemplated Déroulard's murder, for he was a leading enemy of the Catholic church in France, and even Poirot, *bon Catholique,* greeted his death as fortunate. There were, however, several very likely suspects, who seemed more likely once the detective determined that Déroulard had died from poison. He closed in on his suspect, only to have his theory dashed by the willing confession of the real murderer. Poirot's failure was brought about because he neglected to note the most important and simple clue of the case: a pink box of chocolates with a blue lid.

• • •

A version of this case was adapted by London Weekend Television in 1993 for the series *Agatha Christie's Poirot* starring David Suchet. This case provides a rare glimpse of Poirot's early life, including the fact that the scientific and coldly rational sleuth was a good Catholic. He also uses the occasion to note his other failures: *"La bonne chance,* it cannot always be on your side. I have been called in too late. Very often another, working toward the same goal, has arrived there first. Twice have I been stricken down with illness just as I was on the point of success. One must take the downs with the ups, my friend."

"Christmas Pudding, The Adventure of the"

PUBLISHING HISTORY: First published by William Collins Sons and Co., Ltd., London, 1960, in the short story collection *The Adventure of the Christmas Pudding and a Selection of Entrées.*

CHARACTERS: Hercule Poirot; Prince Ali Yusef, Annie Bates, Mr. Jesmond, Colin Lacey, Em Lacey, Colonel Horace Lacey, Sarah Lacey, Mr. Desmond Lee-Wortley.

Hercule Poirot is consulted by an official of the British government, a Mr. Jesmond, in the hopes that he will be willing to assist the Crown. It seems that the son of a powerful ruler in the Middle East has been visiting London and has been separated from a priceless royal ruby by a clever gang of thieves, including a pretty woman who had caught his eye. As the theft has potentially severe repercussions for relations between England and the kingdom of the prince, the detective's skills are badly needed to recover the gem. It turns out that the woman in question will be spending the holidays with the Lacey family at their country estate, King's Lacey, meaning that Poirot will likewise have to surrender his plans for the holiday.

Once ensconced in the Lacey estate, Poirot shrewdly puts a fright into the young woman and causes her to make a severe mistake in hiding the gem. The family is given quite a surprise when the ruby turns up in the Christmas pudding. Events do not end there, however, for Poirot must also bring the case to a close without incident while performing a bit of reverse matchmaking, as the beloved granddaughter of the Laceys, Sarah Lacey, seems to have fallen for the wholly unsuitable Desmond Lee-Wortley.

• • •

This short story is also known as "The Theft of the Royal Ruby." It was adapted for television in 1991 by London Weekend Television for the series *Agatha Christie's Poirot* starring David Suchet.

Christmas Pudding, The Adventure of the, and a Selection of Entrées

PUBLISHING HISTORY: First published by William Collins Sons and Co., Ltd., London, 1960. There was no American edition, although all the stories appeared in other collections published in the United States.

CONTENTS:

"The Adventure of the Christmas Pudding"
"The Mystery of the Spanish Chest"
"The Under Dog"
"Four and Twenty Blackbirds"
"The Dream"
"Greenshaw's Folly"

"Greenshaw's Folly" was published here for the first time in a book, having appeared previously only in a magazine, in 1957. "The Mystery of the Spanish Chest" and "The Dream" were subsequently published in *The Regatta Mystery and Other Stories*. "The Under Dog" was published in *The Under Dog and Other Stories*. "Four and Twenty Blackbirds" was published in *Three Blind Mice and Other Stories*.

"The Adventure of the Christmas Pudding," "The Under Dog," "Four and Twenty Blackbirds," and "The Dream" were adapted for television by London Weekend Television as part of the series *Agatha Christie's Poirot* starring David Suchet.

"A Christmas Tragedy"

PUBLISHING HISTORY: First published by William Collins Sons and Co., Ltd., London, 1932, in the short story collection *The Thirteen Problems*. First published in the United States by Dodd, Mead and Co., New York, 1933, in the short story collection *The Tuesday Club Murders*.

CHARACTERS: Miss Jane Marple; Colonel Bantry, Dolly Bantry, Sir Henry Clithering, Dr. Coles, Gladys Sanders, Jack Sanders.

During a gathering of the Tuesday Night Club, Sir Henry Clithering complains that thus far that night all the stories had been told by men. He thus insists that the ladies do "their fair share," suggesting that Miss Marple relate a story, perhaps "the 'Curious Coincidence of the Charwoman,' or the 'Mystery of the Mother's Meeting.'" Not one to disappoint, Miss Marple does remember a dark tale of murder.

Some years prior, during Christmas, Miss Marple visited a spa, and there met a married couple, Jack and Gladys Sanders. Within a short time, she became convinced that Gladys was the target of murder at the hands of her husband. Planning on setting a trap for him, Miss Marple was surprised by Sanders's swift execution of both his plan and his wife: "He knew I would suspect an accident. So he made it murder." Mrs. Sanders was found bludgeoned to death in a sand bog, and her husband had a seemingly airtight alibi. Miss Marple, however, seizes upon a few apparently insignificant details—especially a hat—and unravels the carefully woven alibi for murder.

"City Clerk, The Case of the"

PUBLISHING HISTORY: First published by William Collins Sons and Co., Ltd., London, 1934, in the short story collection *Parker Pyne Investigates*. First published in the United States by Dodd, Mead and Co., New York, 1934, in the short story collection *Mr. Parker Pyne, Detective*.

CHARACTERS: Mr. Parker Pyne; Mr. Bonnington, Grand Duchess Olga, Mr. Roberts, Mrs. Roberts, Madeleine de Sara.

Mr. Roberts answers Parker Pyne's newspaper advertisement in the hopes of relieving the boredom in his life; Pyne promises to solve people's dilemmas. A "small sturdily built man of forty-five with wistful, puzzled, timid eyes," Roberts has spent years in safe employment, raising his family, and now he longs for some excitement. Parker Pyne agrees to hire him for five pounds, sending him off to Geneva as the secret courier of an important cryptogram. Roberts soon finds himself rescuing a gorgeous Russian countess and helping to bring the Russian crown jewels into England. For his gallantry, Roberts is awarded by the grateful countess the "Order of St. Stanislaus—tenth class with laurels."

"Clapham Cook, The Adventure of the"

PUBLISHING HISTORY: First published by William Collins Sons and Co., Ltd., London, 1951, in the short story collection *The Under Dog and Other Stories;* reprinted by William Collins Sons and Co., Ltd., London, 1974, in the short story collection *Poirot's Early Cases.*

CHARACTERS: Hercule Poirot; Captain Arthur Hastings; Annie, Eliza Dunn, Mr. Simpson, Mr. Todd, Mrs. Todd.

Just as Poirot is expressing little interest in cases that are not of national importance, the solitude of his rooms is shattered by the panting and truculent Mrs. Todd, who is eager for the detective to devote himself to finding a missing cook: "A good cook's a good cook—and when you lose her, it's as much to you as are pearls to a fine lady." Poirot takes the case as a novelty, as never yet had he pursued a missing domestic. The fabulous cook, Eliza Dunn, had gone out on Wednesday and had not returned.

Visiting Clapham, 88 Prince Albert Road, the detective and Hastings question Mrs. Todd's household, and Poirot makes note of the fact that Miss Dunn's trunks had been packed and corded well before they were picked up by a company and sent away. After further inquiries, the sleuth is stunned to receive a letter from Mrs. Todd termi-

nating his employment and giving him the appalling sum of one guinea as a consultation fee. Angered by such an affront to his dignity, Poirot vows to carry on, advertising in the paper for the elusive cook. His efforts are rewarded when Miss Dunn arrives and tells her tale of why she left the employ of the Todds. Her explanation confirms to Poirot that there is much more at stake than a missing domestic. He is, in fact, on the trail of a gifted embezzler and a murderer. Poirot is satisfied with the resolution of the case: "A disappearing domestic at one end—and a cold-blooded murderer on the other. To me, one of the most interesting cases." As a reminder, Poirot does not cash the check for a guinea; instead, he frames it and hangs it on the wall of his sitting room.

• • •

This case was adapted by London Weekend Television for the series *Agatha Christie's Poirot* starring David Suchet. A small piece of the domestic arrangement between Poirot and Hastings (they shared an apartment in London) is revealed in this case, namely the fact that it was customary for Hastings to read the morning headlines in the newspaper, *The Daily Blare.*

"The Clergyman's Daughter"

PUBLISHING HISTORY: First published by William Collins Sons and Co., Ltd., London, 1929, in the short story collection *Partners in Crime.* First published in the United States by Dodd, Mead and Co., New York, 1929, in the short story collection *Partners in Crime.*

CHARACTERS: Tommy Beresford; Tuppence Beresford; Albert; Theodore Blunt, Monica Deane.

Tommy and Tuppence Beresford are consulted by Monica Deane in the hopes that they might clear up not necessarily a corporeal mystery but a haunting. Monica's aunt has died and left her and her mother a house. Unfortunately, there was no money available for its upkeep, so they have taken in lodgers to support themselves. Keeping tenants is proving rather difficult, however, for the house seems infested with poltergeists. Adding to their discomfort is the persistence of a self-proclaimed psychic investigator who is determined at any price to own this particular haunted house. As occurs with their other cases in *Partners in Crime,* Tommy and Tuppence solve the mystery while impersonating fictional detectives; in this case, they go about their business in the person of Roger Sheringham, a detective created by Anthony Berkley Cox (d. 1970); Cox was a member of the Detection Club, which also claimed Agatha Christie as a member.

The Clocks

PUBLISHING HISTORY: First published by William Collins Sons and Co., Ltd., London, 1963. First published in the United States by Dodd, Mead and Co., New York, 1964.

CHARACTERS: Hercule Poirot; Colonel Beck, Josiah Bland, Valerie Bland, Edna Brent, Mr. R. H. Curry, Detective Inspector Dick Hardcastle, Mrs. Hemmings, Colin Lamb, Mrs. Lawton, Miss Martindale, Mrs. McNaughton, Angus McNaughton, Millicent Pebmarsh, Professor Purdy, Mrs. Ramsey, Ted Ramsey, Dr. Rigg, Merlina Rival, Edith Waterhouse, James Waterhouse, Sheila Webb.

Sheila Webb, a member of the Cavendish Secretarial Bureau, is informed that her next assignment will be at the home of Miss Millicent Pebmarsh of 19 Wilbraham Crescent. She arrives and receives no answer at the door. As she had been given instructions to let herself in, Sheila enters the Pebmarsh house and is struck immediately by the large number of clocks. There is a Dresden china clock, a French gilt ormolu clock, a travel clock, and a silver clock. They have all stopped at 4:13.

There are still more surprises in store for Sheila. On the floor, behind the sofa, is sprawled a dead man. Just as Sheila finds the corpse, Miss Pebmarsh walks into the house, and Sheila sees that she is blind. What's more, when interviewed by the police, Miss Pebmarsh denies ever telephoning the agency and requesting a secretary. She also states categorically that the only clock that should be in the sitting room is a grandfather clock.

• • •

The Clocks is dedicated "To my old friend Mario (Galotti) with happy memories of delicious food at the Caprice."

It is a matter of speculation as to the father of the British intelligence operative, Colin Lamb, one of the characters in the novel. Based on certain clues—including Lamb's revelation that his father was a friend and colleague of Poirot—it is likely that Lamb is the son of the popular Christie sleuth Superintendent Battle. *The Clocks* also affords Poirot the opportunity to express his many opinions of contemporary writers and detective fiction; he has high regard for *The Leavenworth Case* (1878) by Anna Katharine Green (a favorite of Agatha Christie), *The Mystery of the Yellow Room* (1908) by Gaston le Roux, and, of course, *The Adventures of Sherlock Holmes* by Sir Arthur Conan Doyle. As for the writings of Ariadne Oliver (Christie's literary alter ego), Poirot notes that she "makes an occasional crude deduction."

Come, Tell Me How You Live

PUBLISHING HISTORY: First published by William Collins Sons and Co., Ltd., London, 1946. First published in the United States by Dodd, Mead and Co., New York, 1946.

In a sharp departure from her detective novels and her romances (written under the pseudonym Mary Westmacott), Agatha Christie decided to write an account of her travels in the Middle East during the 1930s, focusing on the archaeological digs she attended with her husband, Max Mallowan, from 1935 to 1938. While on the digs in Iraq and Syria, Christie kept detailed journals of events, paying close attention to the daily happenings in the camps and to her dealings with the many colorful people of the region. Written in chronological order, the account is both charming and informative. The genuine love Christie felt for the Middle East is explained and easily understood, and the reader learns a great deal about the field of archaeology as practiced during the 1930s. Of even greater interest, of course, is that Christie reveals many intimate aspects of herself and the events that shaped her life—happily—with Max Mallowan, even in the midst of the hardships of the desert.

• • •

Christie dedicated the book thus: "To my husband, Max Mallowan; to the Colonel, Bumps, Mac and Guilford, this meandering chronicle is affectionately dedicated." The "Colonel" was A. H. Burn, a retired colonel of the Indian army, an amateur archaeologist; "Bumps" was Louis Osman, a young architect and assistant to Max; "Mac" was Robin Macartney, another young architect, who was described by Christie as "a man endowed with a cast iron stomach and a few words"; Guilford was yet another architect and assistant, whose primary ability, in Christie's view, was in "trimming horses' toe-nails."

As it was with her Mary Westmacott books, Christie's publisher was opposed to the notion of publishing these memoirs, especially as the firm disliked "anything, in fact, that enticed me away from mysterious stories." To make clear to readers that this book was not a mystery, it was released under the proximate pseudonym Agatha Christie Mallowan. The book proved a success and laid the groundwork for her autobiography (1977).

"The Coming of Mr. Quin"

PUBLISHING HISTORY: First published by William Collins Sons and Co., Ltd., London, 1930, in the short story collection *The Mysterious Mr. Quin*. First published in the United States by Dodd, Mead and Co., New York, 1930, in the short story collection *The Mysterious Mr. Quin*.

CHARACTERS: Mr. Satterthwaite; Mr. Harley Quin; Derek Capel, Laura Conway, Sir Richard Conway, Alec Portal, Eleanor Portal.

The first story to introduce the characters Mr. Satterthwaite and Mr. Harley Quin, "The Coming of Mr. Quin" establishes the general patterns of the Quin stories, in which the enigmatic Mr.

Quin makes unexpected appearances in the lives of people, usually leaving them changed forever. The upheavals take place as part of the solution to a mystery, a romantic misunderstanding or entanglement, or as part of even darker events, such as a murder; but, unlike Poirot, Quin is most concerned with human emotion and resolving the personal crises and needs of those with whom he has had contact. His methods, as seen in "The Coming of Mr. Quin," are quite subtle, however, and he utilizes the skills and the sensibility of Mr. Satterthwaite to implement his plans and the practical aspects of the resolution. Thus, Satterthwaite fulfills the vital role of the detective and arbiter, using his intelligence and diligence to examine clues, interrogate suspects, and bring criminals to justice. Quin acts as a quiet catalyst for Satterthwaite's efforts, but the abilities and success of Satterthwaite do nothing to detract from Quin's seemingly supernatural tendencies or his apparent omniscience.

In this case, Mr. Quin makes his peculiar appearance at Royston Hall in need of assistance, as his car has broken down. He arrives just as the guests at the hall are discussing the suicide some ten years before of Derek Capel. Quin seems to have greater knowledge of the affair than one would imagine and carefully steers the conversation: "It was he who was staging the play—was giving the actors their cues. He was at the heart of the mystery pulling the strings, making the puppets work." Adding to the drama is the discovery by Mr. Satterthwaite that Eleanor Portal, a widow and long a suspect in the death of her husband, crouches against the balustrade of the gallery above, listening to the conversation with great intensity. As a result of Quin's carefully placed proddings and clues, the discussion climaxes with the discovery of true reason for Derek Capel's suicide and the reason behind the murder of Eleanor's first husband.

• • •

This story was the basis for the first film adaptation of a Christie work ever produced in English, *The Passing of Mr. Quinn* (sic), released in 1928. (For details, see page 390.)

"The Companion"

PUBLISHING HISTORY: First published by William Collins Sons and Co., Ltd., London, 1932, in the short story collection *The Thirteen Problems*. First published in the United States by Dodd, Mead and Co., New York, 1933, in the short story collection *The Tuesday Club Murders*.

CHARACTERS: Miss Jane Marple; Dr. Lloyd; Colonel Arthur Bantry, Dolly Bantry, Miss Mary Barton, Sir Henry Clithering, Miss Amy Durrant.

One of the unsolved cases of murder told by a member of the Tuesday Night Club, Dr. Lloyd, "The Companion" concerns the peculiar events surrounding the wealthy Miss Mary Barton and her companion, Miss Amy Durrant, and their trip to the Canary Islands. The pair go swimming one afternoon, and the unfortunate Miss Durrant drowned. What is inexplicable, however, is the eyewitness account by someone who had been on the shore that Mary Barton had not tried to save Amy Durrant but had actually held her head under the water. Evidence, of course, was insufficient, but Dr. Lloyd was chronically nagged by doubts and by his inability to learn anything significant about the poor drowned woman. As for Miss Barton, a few months later, she left a note to the coroner and apparently walked into the ocean, driven by guilt. Only the clothes were found on the beach; no body was ever discovered. Reminded of the criminal Mrs. Trout in her own little village, Miss Marple deduces—correctly—the true events of the crime and why Miss Barton should commit a crime devoid of any motive.

"The Cornish Mystery"

PUBLISHING HISTORY: First published by Dodd, Mead and Co., New York, 1951, in the short story collection *The Under Dog and Other Stories*.

CHARACTERS: Hercule Poirot; Captain Arthur Hastings; Dr. Abrams, Miss Marks, Mrs. Pengelly, Edward Pengelly, Jacob Radnor.

Hercule Poirot is paid a visit by the distraught Mrs. Pengelly, who has come all the way from Polgarwith, in Cornwall, to beg the detective's assistance. She is convinced that someone is poisoning her, despite the assurances of the doctor that her discomfort is caused by a case of gastritis. After asking a few questions, Poirot readily takes the case and sets out for Polgarwith. Upon arrival, however, he is given the stunning news that his client has died most unexpectedly.

It takes only hours for the detective to hear the rumors that Mrs. Pengelly was murdered, a notion dismissed out of hand by the dead woman's pompous physician, Dr. Abrams. Poirot next meets Mrs. Pengelly's relations, especially her niece, Freda, and Freda's fiancé, Jacob Radnor, for whom it seems, the late Mrs. Pengelly had developed a passion. This apparent desire was the source of much embarrassment and consternation to Freda. Jacob Radnor, meanwhile, encourages Poirot to let "sleeping dogs lie. I don't want my wife's uncle tried and hanged for murder." On the way home by train with Hastings, the sleuth announces calmly and prophetically, "I give just three months. Then I shall have him in the dock."

Poirot's words came true in exactly the manner he predicted. Gossip spread like wildfire in Cornwall, climaxing with the exhumation and autopsy of Mrs. Pengelly. When large amounts of arsenic were discovered, Mr. Pengelly was charged with her murder. Poirot returns to Cornwall and catches the murderer—using his skills and personality to secure a signed confession without a shred of proof.

• • •

This story was adapted by London Weekend Television in 1990 for the series *Agatha Christie's Poirot* starring David Suchet.

"The Crackler"

PUBLISHING HISTORY: First published by William Collins Sons and Co., Ltd., London, 1929, in the short story collection *Partners in Crime*. First published in the United States by

Dodd, Mead and Co., New York, 1929, in the short story collection *Partners in Crime*.

CHARACTERS: Tommy Beresford; Tuppence Beresford; Jimmy Faulkener, M. Heroulde, Inspector Marriot, Hank Ryder, Lawrence St. Vincent.

The Beresfords are visited by Inspector Marriot, who enlists their help in catching a clever counterfeiter who has been virtually mass-producing counterfeit notes and using them on both sides of the Channel. As much of the money is being passed in nightclubs, the Beresfords seem the ideal choice for investigating. They set about their task impersonating the Busies, detectives created by Edgar Wallace (d. 1932). Tommy catches the counterfeiter by using catnip.

"The Cretan Bull"

PUBLISHING HISTORY: First published by William Collins Sons and Co., Ltd., London, 1947, in the short story collection *The Labours of Hercules*. First published in the United States by Dodd, Mead and Co., New York, 1947, in the short story collection *The Labors of Hercules*.

CHARACTERS: Hercule Poirot; Admiral Sir Charles Chandler, Hugh Chandler, George Frobisher, Diana Maberley.

A modern-day Hercules—embodied by Hercule Poirot—must accomplish another major task, the seventh of his twelve labors. Whereas the original Hercules had brought back to the goddess Pasiphae her beloved Cretan bull, Hercule Poirot accomplishes a similar feat. He proves the sanity of young Hugh Chandler and permits his return to the loving embrace of his adoring Diana Maberley.

It is Diana Maberley who comes to Poirot with a plea for his help. Her ex-fiancé, Hugh Chandler, has broken off their engagement in response to his fear—and that of his family—that young Hugh is going insane. He has apparently suffered blackouts and, upon waking, once found himself with bloodstained weapons. Adding to his sense of fear is the spreading tale of animals being slaughtered in the surrounding district. Poirot takes the case

and journeys to Lyde Mann to meet with Hugh. A friend of Sir Charles, Colonel George Frobisher, informs Poirot that insanity runs in the Chandler family and tends to skip generations.

The solution to this case involves terrible and overwhelming jealousy and rage. The key to the resolution is the revealing of a dark family secret, a revelation that ends in sudden and unexpected tragedy.

• • •

The Hercules of myth brought back the Cretan bull to Pasiphae by riding the bull as it swam from Crete to Greece. The returned bull was then freed from all captivity to wander through the Greek countryside. Similarly, Hercule Poirot frees Hugh Chandler to live a happy and healthy life.

"Crime in Cabin 66"

See "Problem at Sea"

The Crooked House

PUBLISHING HISTORY: First published by William Collins Sons and Co., Ltd., London, 1949. First published in the United States by Dodd, Mead and Co., New York, 1949.

CHARACTERS: Mr. Agrodopolous, Lawrence Brown, Miss Edith de Haviland, Mr. Gaitskill, Dr. Gray, Assistant Commissioner Sir Arthur Hayward, Charles Hayward, Mr. Johnson, Detective Sergeant Lamb, Aristide Leonides, Brenda Leonides, Clemency Leonides, Eustace Leonides, Josephine Leonides, Magda Leonides, Philip Leonides, Roger Leonides, Sophia Leonides, Janet Rowe, Chief Inspector Tavener, Magda West, Janet Woolmar.

Aristide Leonides, a one-time Greek immigrant who earned a fortune through hard work and intelligence in the restaurant and catering business, has been found dead in his massive gabled half-timbered mansion in suburban London, Swinley Dean. His obituary is printed in a newspaper in Egypt at the end of World War II and is read by Charles Hayward, who reports the news to the woman he loves, Aristide's granddaughter, Sophia Leonides. Both Charles and Sophia have been stationed in Egypt and both vow to get together once more back home in England. As it turns out, the chief investigating officer into Leonides's mysterious death is Charles's father, Sir Arthur Hayward, an assistant commissioner at Scotland Yard.

Sir Arthur has determined that Aristide was, in fact, murdered by having his insulin—needed daily for his diabetes—replaced with a barbiturate, eserine. Most of the family members had a motive to commit the crime, but chief among the suspects is Brenda Leonides, Aristide's second wife, who happens to be fifty years younger than her now-dead husband. In order to investigate thoroughly, not to mention to ensure that no suspicion falls on Sophia, Charles agrees to insinuate himself into the Leonides household and investigate from the inside. The solution to the murder of Aristide proves a most surprising one.

• • •

Agatha Christie gave an interview in the *Daily Mail* in September of 1970, and was asked if *Three Blind Mice* was her favorite work. No, she answered, her favorite was *Crooked House*. Subsequently, in her autobiography, she confirmed her opinion, listing *Crooked House* alongside *Ordeal by Innocence* (1958) as her favorites. (There are also different lists of Christie's favorites from other sources, which mention *Sleeping Murder, The Murder of Roger Ackroyd,* and *Ordeal by Innocence.*)

According to Christie, *The Crooked House* was also memorable because of the effort by the publisher to change the ending. The editors were unhappy with her choice of murderer, but Christie, as was her policy, refused to budge. Thus, *Death Comes As the End* (1945) remains the only Christie murder mystery to have its ending changed under external pressure. The ending for *The Crooked House* remained untouched, and the novel continues to shock new readers, much like *The Murder of Roger Ackroyd.*

The title for this book is derived from the nursery rhyme that begins "There was a crooked man" and ends with the line "and all lived together in a crooked house." The image is applied to the withered, little, crooked, and wealthy patriarch, Leonides, whose family resides in a half-timbered estate. As was often the case in her writings, Christie created a very memorable detective for the occasion, Charles Hayward, but then never used him again. A similar situation occurred in *4.50 from Paddington* (1957; Lucy Eyelesbarrow) and *Ordeal by Innocence* (1958; Dr. Calgary).

Curtain

PUBLISHING HISTORY: First published by William Collins Sons and Co., Ltd., London, 1975. First published in the United States by Dodd, Mead and Co., New York, 1975.

CHARACTERS: Hercule Poirot; Captain Arthur Hastings; George; Major Allerton, Sir William Boyd–Carrington, Elizabeth Cole, Nurse Craven, Curtiss, Barbara Franklin, Dr. John Franklin, Judith Hastings, Colonel George Luttrell, Daisy Luttrell, Stephen Norton.

Captain Arthur Hastings, now a widower and growing older, has been summoned away from Argentina and returns to England at the urging of Hercule Poirot. He journeys to Styles Court—site of his first great success and adventure with the Belgian detective—where a reunion of sorts has been arranged. Not only will Hastings meet once more and for the last time his longtime friend, he will also meet his daughter, Judith, which has been arranged by Poirot as a further inducement.

Just as Hastings's own journey is a melancholy one, given the recent death of his wife, so too is his arrival at Styles Court. Styles is no longer a grand estate. It is now a guest house, and both he and Poirot must pay to stay there. Even worse, Poirot is dying and is pathetically confined to a wheelchair.

Hastings soon discovers, of course, that Poirot has lost none of his "little grey cells," and he has brought Hastings to England so that he might work with him one last time to catch a murderer. One of the guests at Styles is, in Poirot's view, a clever murderer of five people, although none of the other guests seems a likely prospect, in Hastings's mind, as a serial killer. Poirot, of course, is most certain, further assuring Hastings that his suspect, "X," has come to Styles Court to commit yet another murder.

Complicating matters for Hastings is the apparent relationship between his daughter and the highly dubious Major Allerton. Hastings dreads that his daughter will be humiliated by the Major and will commit suicide in shame, the fate of another woman who had become involved with the Major. Indeed, so concerned does Hastings become that he actually plans to poison Allerton. His plan is never fulfilled and is all but forgotten when another guest dies from poisoning and when Poirot takes a serious turn for the worse.

• • •

This last case of Hercule Poirot—in which he dies at the end—was written by Agatha Christie, along with *Sleeping Murder,* during the early 1940s and the terrible London Blitz, when German bombing raids were devastating the city. Concerned that she would be killed during the attacks, Christie finished two manuscripts, insured them, and then put them into vaults in banks for safe-keeping. The two works were also final safety valves should her inspiration fail her. While *Sleeping Murder* was Miss Marple's last case and was dedicated to Max Mallowan, *Curtain* was dedicated to her daughter, Rosalind. Christie had long tired of the meticulous and (to her) annoying Belgian detective and was delighted to finish him off, especially as it ensured that no writer would be tempted to keep him alive after she passed away herself (this has been a regular event in the world of Sherlock Holmes).

The reader is little prepared for the shocking condition of the beloved detective. He is crippled and clearly dying, and Christie adds a few—some would argue deliberately cruel—additional touches to the characterization, including reducing Poirot's legendary vanity to a pathetic effort to dye his hair and mustache. At the end of the book, Poirot bids farewell to Arthur Hastings (who seems remarkably hale despite the passage of time) in a touching letter. His old friend has returned to Styles, the scene of their first triumph together. Poirot writes:

Goodbye, cher ami, I have moved the amyl nitrate ampules away from beside my bed. I prefer to leave myself in the hands of the bon Dieu. May his punishment, or his mercy, be swift!
We shall not hunt together again, my friend. Our first hunt was here—and our last.
They were good days.
Yes, they have been good days.

(For other details on Poirot, please see Poirot, Hercule.)

A Daughter's a Daughter

PUBLISHING HISTORY: First published by William Heinemann, London, 1952. First published in the United States by Dell Publishing Co., New York, 1963 (see also below).

CHARACTERS: Richard Cauldfield, Edith, Geoffrey Fane, Jennifer Graham, James Grant, Gerald Lloyd, Mrs. Massingham, Ann Prentice, Sarah Prentice, Lawrence Steen, Dame Laura Whitstable.

Ann Prentice, an attractive forty-one-year-old widow and mother of a nineteen-year-old daughter, Sarah, has finally met someone with whom she believes she will be able to find happiness, Richard Cauldfield. She is now faced with the difficult decision about whether to pursue her own happiness or continue to devote her full attentions to her daughter. Sarah tries to decide the matter for her by selfishly doing everything in her power to sabotage her mother's happiness, and Ann finally chooses to give up her love for Richard.

Having wrecked her mother's life, Sarah decides to marry the dissipated playboy Lawrence Steen, who leads her on a swift road to personal chaos and agony. Her mother, meanwhile, learns that Richard Cauldfield has married, but she knows that he is still in love with her.

The relationship between Ann and Sarah finally undergoes a crisis when both suffer terrible personal struggles. Ann has sunk into severe depression and Sarah has become such a cocaine addict that she finds herself in a nursing home. In the end, Sarah has one last chance for happiness, an opportunity that has eluded her mother.

• • •

A Daughter's a Daughter was originally published in 1952. The American edition, however, was not published until 1963, and then only in paperback format. The American hardcover edition was not published until 1972, by Arbor House. Readers will note the similarity between this novel and *The Burden* (1956).

"The Dead Harlequin"

PUBLISHING HISTORY: First published by William Collins Sons and Co., Ltd., London, 1930, in the short story collection *The Mysterious Mr. Quin.* First published in the United States by Dodd, Mead, and Co., New York, 1930, in the short story collection *The Mysterious Mr. Quin.*

CHARACTERS: Mr. Satterthwaite; Mr. Harley Quin; Frank Bristow, Alix Charnley, Hugo Charnley, Lord Reggie Charnley, Monica Ford, Aspasia Glen, Colonel Monckton.

Mr. Satterthwaite purchases from the Harchester Galleries a painting that catches his breath: *The Dead Harlequin.* The picture catches his eye for two reasons. First, the face of the dead harlequin bears a striking resemblance to his enigmatic acquaintance Mr. Harley Quin. Second, the scene of the painting reminds Satterthwaite of the terrace room at Charnley.

Satterthwaite arranges to meet the artist, Frank Bristow, an encounter that leads him to the estate of Charnley and a retelling of the mysterious suicide fourteen years before of old Lord Charnley. Lord Charnley had apparently shot himself through the heart in the oak parlor room. It must have been suicide because all of the doors to the room were locked—and the keys were in the locks—and the window was shut, with its shutters fastened. Satterthwaite believes otherwise and slowly unravels the true events of Lord Charnley's murder. Central to Satterthwaite's solution are the multiple bullet holes in the oak parlor room and the odd disappearance of a Bokhara rug from the terrace room.

Dead Man's Folly

PUBLISHING HISTORY: First published by William Collins Sons and Co., Ltd., London, 1956. First published in the United States by Dodd, Mead and Co., New York, 1956.

CHARACTERS: Hercule Poirot; Mrs. Ariadne Oliver; Superintendent Baldwin, Dectective Inspector Bland, Miss Amanda Brewis, Elsa, Amy Folliat, Marilyn Gale, Robert Hoskins, Alec Legge, Peggy Legge, Felicity Lemon, Mrs. Connie Masterton, Major Merall, Merdell, Etienne de Sousa, Sir George Stubbs, Lady Hattie Stubbs, Marilyn Tucker, Marlene Tucker, Captain Jim Warburton, Michael Weyman.

Hercule Poirot is interrupted while dictating his memoirs to the efficient Miss Lemon by a telephone call from Mrs. Ariadne Oliver. The flamboyant mystery writer and sometime investigating associate delivers a brief but urgent plea for the Belgian detective to come at once to Nasse House, Nassecombe, Devon, where she is staying as a houseguest. Convinced that Mrs. Oliver has become embroiled in a murder mystery, Poirot sets out for Nasse House. To his surprise, she is not involved in a murder mystery but a murder hunt. A charity murder game has been organized as part of a larger charity event, including food stalls, other games, fortune-telling, and assorted appearances by celebrities. Mrs. Oliver has placed assorted clues around the estate, leading to the "discovery" of the "victim" in the boathouse at Nasse House. The "victim" in the game is a teenage girl named Marlene Tucker, whose task for the day is to remain in the boathouse reading comic books until someone finally turns up.

Poirot finds all of the goings-on quite charming, but Mrs. Oliver confesses that her summons to him was only in part out of fun. She has a sense that something is vaguely wrong at Nasse House.

Her fears are confirmed when Marlene Tucker becomes a real victim and is discovered murdered by Hercule Poirot and Mrs. Oliver.

• • •

Dead Man's Folly offers readers a combination of Hercule Poirot and Mrs. Ariadne Oliver, a collaboration that was a regular event in Poirot novels in later years. The case is notable in that it has a young murder victim, the fourteen-year-old Marlene Tucker. The setting of the story, Nasse House, is based on Greenway House, the home that Christie and her husband purchased in 1939 and that was Christie's favorite residence; this view was advanced by Max Mallowan in his memoirs. The similarities between Nasse House and Greenway House include the placement of the first murder in a boathouse on the river at Nasse House (modeled on the Greenway House boathouse) and the quotation by Mrs. Folliat of a verse from Edmund Spenser's *The Faerie Queene*:

Sleepe after toyle,
Port after stormie seas,
Ease after warre,
Death after life
Does greatly please.

The verse has particular significance because it was included on Dame Agatha's tombstone, along with the inscription "Agatha Christie the writer." *Dead Man's Folly* was adapted by CBS television in 1986, starring Peter Ustinov as Hercule Poirot and Jean Stapleton as Ariadne Oliver.

"Dead Man's Mirror"

PUBLISHING HISTORY: First published by William Collins Sons and Co., Ltd., London, 1937, in the short story collection *Murder in the Mews*. First published in the United States by Dodd, Mead and Co., New York, 1937, in the short story collection *Dead Man's Mirror and Other Stories*.

CHARACTERS: Hercule Poirot; Mr. Satterthwaite; Godfrey Burrows, Colonel Ned Bury, Susan Caldwell, Gervase Chevenix-Gore, Ruth Chevenix-Gore, Lady Vanda Elizabeth Chevenix-Gore, Ogilvie Forbes, Captain Lake, Miss Lingard, Chief Constable Major Riddle, Snell, Hugo Trent.

Hercule Poirot receives a curious letter from Sir Gervase Chevenix-Gore requesting the assistance of the detective. Chevenix-Gore tells Poirot, "[I have] heard good account of you and have decided to entrust the matter to you." He goes on to say, however, that, although he is the victim of fraud, the detective should be prepared to come to Hamborough Close only when summoned, nor should he reply to the letter. Poirot's eyebrows are raised by the note, and his interest is piqued, so he investigates his would-be client, with the assistance of Mr. Satterthwaite. He then awaits—and receives—the note of summons from Chevenix-Gore.

Poirot arrives in Hamborough Close in time for the call to dinner, when a gong is sounded and the butler announces that "dinner is served." The long-held ritual is ruined by the realization that the host, Lord Chevenix-Gore, is not present. The friends and family go immediately to the study and find it barred. The door is broken down, and the grisly scene within is revealed: Lord Chevenix-Gore is slouched down in his chair, dead, and "on the floor was a small gleaming pistol," the instrument of his apparent suicide.

What seems an obvious suicide gradually falls under doubt for Poirot, as details of Chevenix-Gore's life come under closer scrutiny and the crime scene is examined. Adding further weight to the growing certainty of murder are the terms of Chevenix-Gore's will. Vital clues include a broken mirror, a small piece of glass embedded in a heavy bronze statuette, the placement of the gong, and a torn paper bag in the dead man's wastebasket.

• • •

This case was adapted in 1993 by London Weekend Television for the series *Agatha Christie's Poirot* starring David Suchet. The plot of this case is virtually identical to that of another Poirot case, "The Second Gong."

"Death by Drowning"

PUBLISHING HISTORY: First published by William Collins Sons and Co., Ltd., London, 1932, in the short story collection *The Thirteen Problems*. First published in the United States by Dodd, Mead and Co., New York, 1933, in the short story collection *The Tuesday Club Murders*.

CHARACTERS: Miss Jane Marple; Sir Henry Clithering; Mrs. Bartlett, Inspector Drewitt, Joe Ellis, Rose Emmott, Tom Emmott, Colonel Melchett, Rex Sandford.

While visiting his friends at St. Mary Mead, Sir Henry Clithering, ex-commissioner for Scotland Yard, is visited by Miss Marple. She asks his assistance in solving the unfortunate drowning death of young Rose Emmott; Miss Marple contends that not only did "she not drown herself she was *murdered . . .* and I know who murdered her." Clithering believes her because of their past association and interjects himself in the investigation, conducted by the chief constable of the county, Colonel Melchett, and the local inspector, Drewitt. The obvious suspect, the aspiring architect Rex Sandford, was admittedly in the woods near the river in which Rose drowned; he confessed that he was the father of the child she was carrying, and had a girl in London to whom he was engaged, thereby giving him a clear motive for murder. The case seems firm against Sandford, but Clithering is interested in two other witnesses, Joe Ellis and his landlady, Mrs. Bartlett. After further investigation, Clithering uncovers the murderer, with the help of Miss Marple. The perpetrator is, of course, the same person named initially by the old sleuth and whose name and address were scribbled by Miss Marple on a piece of paper.

Death Comes As the End

PUBLISHING HISTORY: First published by Dodd, Mead and Co., New York, 1944. First published in England by William Collins Sons and Co., Ltd., London, 1945. (As occurred several times in the publishing history of Christie's works, the American edition of *Death Comes As the End* was published before the British edition.)

CHARACTERS: Esa, Henet, Hori, Imhotep, Ipy, Kait, Kameni, Khay, Divine Father, Mersu, Montu, Nofret, Renisenb, Satipy, Sobek, Teti, Yahmose.

A wealthy farmer and priest in ancient Thebes, in Egypt. Imhotep is also the patriarch of a family whose members regard him with both trepidation and resentment upon his return home. The primary cause for their hostility is the installation of Imhotep's new concubine, Nofret, who is beautiful but quite arrogant. The young woman does little to change the atmosphere in the household, and, while Imhotep is away, she is discovered dead at the base of a cliff. Her death is reported to Imhotep, who naturally assumes that Nofret was murdered, thanks mostly to his dead concubine's own letters, which detail numerous threats and unpleasantness from his own family.

The tragedy of Nofret's death does not long remain an isolated incident. Satipy, Imhotep's daughter-in-law, falls to her death, shouting "Nofret!" as she plunges downward. Even more deaths follow, as terror stalks the family of Imhotep.

• • •

Death Comes As the End is unique among Christie's many imaginative writings. Not only is it the sole book to offer a historical setting (save for the murder mysteries solved by reminiscences, such as "The Chocolate Box"), it also was the only one of her published books to have its ending changed after displeasure was expressed by a rather prominent reader.

The key figure in both events was a famous Egyptologist, Stephen R. K. Glanville, a friend of Max Mallowan and fellow archaeologist. He suggested to Christie that she set a murder mystery in ancient Egypt, subsequently providing so much help that she dedicated the book to him. In the dedication, she declared that, without Glanville's aid, "this book would never have been written."

As a kindness to her invaluable consultant, Christie permitted Glanville to read the finished manuscript. The Egyptologist was quite candid in admitting that he did not much care for the ending. What exactly he disliked is unclear, but he did suggest an alternate ending. Surprisingly, Christie accepted his idea, the first and only time that she changed an ending at someone else's urging. It was a decision she regretted, declaring in her autobiography: "I still think now, when I re-read the book, that I would like to rewrite the end of it—which shows that you should stick to your guns in the first place."

Death in the Air

See *Death in the Clouds*

Death in the Clouds

PUBLISHING HISTORY: First published by William Collins Sons and Co., Ltd., London, 1935. First published in the United States by Dodd, Mead and Co., New York, 1935, under the title *Death in the Air.*

CHARACTERS: Hercule Poirot; Chief Inspector James Japp; Raymond Barraclough, Dr. James Bryant, Daniel Clancy, Lord Dawlish, Armand Dupont, Jean Dupont, Monsieur Fournier, Norman Gale, Madame Giselle, Elise Grandier, Jane Grey, Lady Cicely Horbury, Lord Stephen Horbury, the Honorable Venetia Anne Kerr, Andrew Leech, Henry Charles Mitchell, Ruth Mitchell, Anne Morisot, Jules Perrot, Miss Ross, James Bell Ryder, Maitre Alexandre Thibault, Dr. James Whistler, Detective Sergeant Wilson, Henry Winterspoon, Monsieur Zeropoulos.

Hercule Poirot needs to go to London from Paris and has decided to fly. With his ten fellow passengers, he boards the airplane, the *Prometheus,* and settles into the rear compartment. With his usual knack for detail, he notes immediately that there is eye contact between two of the passengers and actually takes little notice of the assorted other fliers. The flight is subsequently routine, with a meal and coffee served by the two stewards and with the passengers seemingly engrossed in their own affairs. Indeed, the only event out of the ordinary is the irritating presence of a wasp, which is finally killed by a passenger. Following the meal, a steward makes the rounds to collect money for the food and attempts to wake the passenger in seat number two. An ugly old lady "dressed in heavy black," the passenger has traveled several times on the flight from Paris to London, but it becomes obvious that her travel days are over. The passenger—identified as Madame Giselle—is dead.

It is assumed at first that she was stung by the wasp and somehow had died from an allergic reaction. This is supported by a small puncture on her neck, but this cause of death is dismissed by Poirot, who discovers a small black-and-orange object on the floor. It is not another wasp. Madame Giselle was murdered by a blowgun dart. Incredibly, she was killed in a locked cabin by one of the passengers who shot her with a dart while in full view of the other passengers.

Aside from being an interesting case from the standpoint of criminal detection, the murder of Madame Giselle proves of great personal importance to the Belgian detective. When searching the plane, police discovered the murder weapon hidden beneath a cabin seat. The occupant of the seat, it is learned, was none other than Hercule Poirot. Based on this evidence, a court of inquest determines a verdict of willful murder by the Belgian. The coroner, of course, refuses to accept such a ludicrous notion, but it is up to Poirot to clear his name and bring a murderer to justice. As he investigates Madame Giselle and her varied life, it becomes clear that quite a few people had a motive to see her dead.

• • •

Death in the Clouds presents a rather challenging murder for Hercule Poirot—Madame Giselle is killed in the locked cabin of an airborne plane. The murder method, a blow gun, is also unique in the Christie annals. The book was dedicated: "To my old friend Sybil Healey, with affection." This case was adapted for television in 1992 by London Weekend Television for the *Agatha Christie's Poirot* series starring David Suchet.

Death on the Nile

PUBLISHING HISTORY: First published by William Collins Sons and Co., Ltd., London, 1937. First published in the United States by Dodd, Mead and Co., New York, 1938.

CHARACTERS: Hercule Poirot; Colonel Johnny Race; Mrs. Allerton, Tim Allerton, Dr. Carl Bessner, Gaston Blondin, Louise Bourget, Miss Bowers, Mr. Burnaby, Jacqueline de Bellefort, Linnet Ridgeway Doyle, Simon Doyle, James Fanthorp, Mr. Ferguson, Mr. Fleetwood, Jules, Marie, Rosalie Otterbourne, Salome Otterbourne, Andrew Pennington, Signor Guido Richetti, Cornelia Ruth Robson, Sterndale Rockford, The Honourable Joanna Southwood, Mrs. Marie van Schuyler, Charles Windlesham.

The glamorous heiress Linnet Ridgeway, worth millions of dollars, arrives at the village of Malton-under-Wode to settle into her newly bought estate, Wode Hall. The villagers are unsure about the new mistress of Wode Hall, especially as she has already extravagantly spent sixty thousand pounds for the estate's refurbishment. She soon demonstrates that she is headstrong, arrogant, and proud. She is also, however, a faithful friend, welcoming her oldest friend, Jacqueline de Bellefort, who has been wiped out financially by the stock market crash. Jackie arrives with the far happier news that she is engaged to be married to the charming, adorable, but thoroughly broke Simon Doyle. She asks Linnet if she will consider hiring him on as an estate manager, and Linnet agrees. Within a short time, Simon Doyle has married and is seemingly quite happy. Linnet is also quite pleased, because she has married as well—her best friend's fiancé, Simon. The happy couple will honeymoon in Egypt.

While staying at the Cataract Hotel in Aswan, Egypt, Hercule Poirot meets the Doyles and is approached by Linnet, who asks his help in a matter of increasing annoyance to them. Jackie de Bellefort did not take being jilted well at all and has pursued the couple relentlessly throughout their honeymoon. Linnet hopes that Poirot might rea-

son with the young woman and discourage her in her absurd vendetta. The detective does speak to Jackie, urging her not to open her "heart to evil." She admits that she could kill Linnet, as the heiress has robbed her of everything she loved in the world.

Poirot next joins a group of assorted American and British travelers, including the Doyles, on a journey on the Nile on board the steamer *Karnak*. Interaction with the passengers soon reveals that almost everyone on board has some connection to Linnet Doyle, and the heiress has also managed to offend virtually all of them. Tensions mount on board with Jackie's presence and because of a supposed accident that nearly kills Linnet and Simon. Finally, hostilities erupt when Jackie becomes drunk, has an argument with Simon, and accidentally shoots him in the leg. The situation soon deteriorates even further when, in the morning, Linnet Doyle is found murdered, shot through the head with the same pistol used by Jackie to shoot Simon. A further clue points to Jackie: A "J" is scrawled in blood on the wall next to Linnet's corpse, although Dr. Bessner, who examined Linnet, proclaims it impossible for Linnet to have written it, as she was killed instantly.

Poirot now faces a murder investigation with a ship full of likely suspects. His inquiry becomes even bloodier with the murders of two more passengers.

• • •

One of the most popular of all Christie writings, *Death on the Nile* was also a personal favorite of Agatha herself, especially among those mysteries set in exotic locales. Her preference for the novel is understandable, as the case involving the murder of Linnet Doyle, the maid Marie, and the awful Mrs. Otterbourne is a challenge for Poirot.

Christie had considerable knowledge of Egypt prior to writing *Death on the Nile*. She first visited the country when she was around eighteen years old and returned in the 1930s with her archaeologist husband, Max Mallowan; the couple sailed up the Nile on a steamer, probably identical to the

Karnak, the vessel in the novel. Her personal experiences find their way into the narrative (to a greater degree than her knowledge of Petra, which was barely touched upon in *Appointment with Death*), with such interesting observations as a description of the ship's passage through the "Assuan" (Aswan) dam—built by the British between 1899 and 1902 and not to be confused with the colossal achievement of the high Aswan Dam, which was constructed between 1950 and 1979—and a description of Abu Simbel, which is visited twice by the characters, including once at night, by torchlight. The novel also boasts extensive details concerning ancient Egyptian architecture and history, no doubt supplied with the help of Max Mallowan. The novel was dedicated "To Sybil Burnett, who also loves wandering about the world." Sybil Burnett was the wife of Sir Charles Burnett, an air vice-marshal stationed in Algiers and a fellow passenger of Christie's on a boat trip from Trieste to Beirut. The two did not get along at first, but they eventually became friends.

Death on the Nile was adapted for film in 1978, with Peter Ustinov as Hercule Poirot (the first of his outings as Poirot in film and television) and David Niven as Colonel Race; supporting roles were played by Angela Lansbury (who played Miss Marple in *The Mirror Crack'd*); Bette Davis, Maggie Smith (who also appeared in *Evil under the Sun*), George Kennedy, and Olivia Hussey. The novel was also adapted for the stage by Christie under the title *Murder on the Nile,* opening in London in 1946; the American production, with the title *Hidden Horizon,* opened in 1946.

"Death on the Nile"

PUBLISHING HISTORY: First published by William Collins Sons and Co., Ltd., London, 1934, in the short story collection *Parker Pyne Investigates.* First published in the United States by Dodd, Mead and Co., New York, 1934, in the short story collection *Mr. Parker Pyne, Detective.*

CHARACTERS: Mr. Parker Pyne; Lady Ariadne Grayle, Sir George Grayle, Pamela Grayle, Elsie Macnaughton, Basil West.

Foreshadowing the murderous events that would take place in Christie's famed novel *Death on the Nile* (1937), this short story offers up a murder on a cruise ship steaming up the Nile River; instead of the redoubtable Hercule Poirot, however, the detective in this case is Mr. Parker Pyne, who displays Poirot's attention to detail and his ability to bluff the perpetrator into a confession. There is little similarity in the plot between the two deaths on the Nile. Indeed, the case is closer to the Poirot case "Problem at Sea," which features an equally unpleasant murder victim.

While traveling through Egypt, Parker Pyne boards a cruise ship for a journey on the Nile, much to the chagrin of one of the passengers, the spoiled and very wealthy Lady Ariadne Grayle, who "had suffered since she was sixteen from the complaint of having too much money." Parker Pyne, of course, is unmoved by her protestations, and before long he is consulted by Lady Grayle, who is aware of Parker Pyne's work in London. She asks him to look into the possibility that her husband, George, might be trying to poison her, especially as her health tends to improve when he is away. Within a short time, Lady Grayle is dead from strychnine poisoning. The only clue is the tiny fragment of a burned letter, which contains the barely legible words: ". . . chet of dreams. Burn this!"

Parker Pyne's investigation uncovers the murderer, but only by clever maneuvering does he elicit a confession.

• • •

Egypt was the setting for several of Christie's works, including the novel *Death on the Nile* (1937), her play *Akhnaton* (1937), "The Adventure of the Egyptian Tomb" (1924), and "Problem at Sea" (1939).

Destination Unknown

PUBLISHING HISTORY: First published by William Collins Sons and Co., Ltd., London,

1954. First published in the United States by Dodd, Mead and Co., New York, 1955, under the title *So Many Steps to Death.*

CHARACTERS: Alcadi, Mr. Aristides, Mrs. Calvin Baker, Dr. Louis Barron, Olive Betterton, Thomas Betterton, Hilary Craven, Herr Director, Torquil Ericsson, R. Evans, Major Boris Gloyr, Walter Griffiths, Janet Hetherington, Miss Jennson, Mr. Jessop, Mademoiselle la Roche, Henri Laurier, Monsieur Leblanc, Dr. Mark Lucas, Professor Mannheim, Mohammed, Bianca Murchison, Dr. Simon Murchison, Helga Needheim, Andrew Peters, Dr. Rubec, Carol Speeder, Paul van Heidem, Colonel Wharton.

A young American scientist, Thomas Betterton, has disappeared from a conference in Paris. He is a researcher of increasing importance because of his recent discovery of ZE fission. His sudden disappearance has also set off alarms across the world because he joins an growing number of scientists who have vanished off the face of the planet.

Participating in the investigation to locate the missing scientists is a British agent, Mr. Jessop. Unfortunately, there are few clues to follow. Olive Betterton, the American's wife, has gone to Morocco, supposedly for a rest after the tension and stress of her husband's disappearance. Jessop follows her, but his trail seems to end as her plane crashes while bound for Casablanca.

Jessop, however, refuses to be daunted, convincing a young, suicidally depressed woman, Hilary Craven, that she looks exactly like Olive Betterton and that, if she is looking for death, there is no better way to go than on a dangerous mission. Hilary agrees and sets off to impersonate Mrs. Betterton. Her mission takes her into the heart of a vast organization engaged in espionage, dangerous research, and world domination.

• • •

Destination Unknown is one of Christie's espionage novels. Other novels featuring similar themes include *They Came to Baghdad* (1951), *Cat among the Pigeons* (1959), *Passenger to Frankfurt* (1970), and *Postern of Fate* (1973). Written after World War II and often connected with the grim days of the Cold War, the novels were nevertheless intended to be frothy and light espionage thrillers—especially this novel, *Passenger to Frankfurt,* and *Postern of Fate.* They thus are not to be compared with John le Carré but with the contemporaneous books featuring James Bond written by Ian Fleming (the first novel featuring James Bond, *Casino Royale,* was published in 1953). In comparison with the often brooding, misanthropic, sexually preoccupied, and brutal environment of the Bond novels, Christie's efforts seem rather dated, even though they are set in the same period.

Christie dedicated the book "To Anthony—who likes foreign travel as much as I do." Anthony is Christie's son-in-law, Anthony Hicks, who wed Rosalind Christie Prichard in 1949.

"The Disappearance of Mr. Davenheim"

PUBLISHING HISTORY: First published by *Sketch* magazine, London, 1924; reprinted by John Lane, London, 1924, in the short story collection *Poirot Investigates.* First published in the United States by Dodd, Mead and Co., New York, 1925, in the short story collection *Poirot Investigates.*

CHARACTERS: Hercule Poirot; Captain Arthur Hastings; Chief Inspector James Japp; Mr. Davenheim, Mrs. Davenheim, Billy Kellett, Mr. Lowen.

In a case similar to that recounted in "The Mystery of the Hunter's Lodge," Hercule Poirot solves the disappearance of a wealthy financier; whereas in "Hunter's Lodge" the detective was recovering from influenza and could not venture outdoors, in this mystery he proposes to Japp that he can solve the matter without leaving his chair in his fashionable flat. As always, Hastings serves as Poirot's earnest eyes and ears, and as a source of useless and incomplete theories. Hastings proves especially off the mark in this case, enumerating four points that supposedly demonstrate why the leading suspect must be guilty. Poirot then courteously shreds each of them in succession.

Mr. Davenheim, senior partner of Davenheim and Salmon—bankers and financiers—departed from his estate, The Cedars, after tea, to stroll down to the village to post some letters. He left by the front door, passed leisurely down the drive and out the gate, and was never seen again. From that hour, he vanished completely. After hearing the particulars, Poirot assists Japp (by giving advice from his flat, of course) in finding the clothes of the missing man. The detective then solves the mystery by finding the perpetrator in a place virtually no one would think to look. His clues for solving the mystery include Davenheim's passion for buying jewelry, his trip to Buenos Aires, his beard, and his sudden decision to sleep in separate quarters from his wife.

• • •

This case bears a striking similarity to the Sherlock Holmes case "The Man with the Crooked Lip."

"Discontented Husband, The Case of the"

PUBLISHING HISTORY: First published by William Collins Sons and Co., Ltd., London,1934, in the short story collection, *Parker Pyne Investigates*. First published in the United States by Dodd, Mead and Co., New York, 1934, in the short story collection *Mr. Parker Pyne, Detective*.

CHARACTERS: Mr. Parker Pyne; Sinclair Jordan, Mrs. Massington, Madeleine de Sara, Mrs. Iris Wade, Mr. Reginald Wade.

In a case similar to that presented in "The Case of the Middle-Aged Wife," Mr. Parker Pyne is consulted by Mr. Reginald Wade, whose wife has asked him for a divorce so that she can marry another man. A taciturn and inexpressive husband—he sums up his feelings for his wife by saying "I'm fond of her . . .You see—well, I'm fond of her"—Mr. Wade is willing to do anything to restore his marriage. Fortunately for him, his wife has agreed to give him six months. If, at the end of that time, her feelings are unchanged, Mr. Wade will stand aside. For his scheme, Parker Pyne enlists the assistance of the ravishing Madeleine de Sara, whom Parker Pyne describes as

the "Queen of Vamps." While it is executed perfectly, Pyne's solution proves to have unforeseen results, and Parker Pyne suffers one of the few setbacks in his career.

"Discontented Soldier, The Case of the"

PUBLISHING HISTORY: First published by William Collins Sons and Co., Ltd., London, 1934, in the short story collection *Parker Pyne Investigates*. First published in the United States by Dodd, Mead and Co., New York, 1934, in the short story collection *Mr. Parker Pyne, Detective*.

CHARACTERS: Mr. Parker Pyne; Miss Freda Clegg, Ariadne Oliver, Madeleine de Sara, Major Wilbraham.

Mr. Parker Pyne is consulted by Major Wilbraham, a soldier recently returned from East Africa, in the hopes of relieving his excruciating boredom: "It's the boredom I object to. The boredom and the endless tittle-tattle about petty village matters . . . My neighbors are all pleasant folk, but they've no ideas beyond this island." Parker Pyne assures the Major that he can provide him with sufficient excitement in London in return for fifty pounds, payable in advance, and guarantees him that if, within a month, the Major is still in a state of boredom, he will refund his money. With the help of the stunning Madeleine de Sara and the ingenious Ariadne Oliver, the Major embarks on an adventure with Miss Freda Clegg concerning a hidden African treasure.

• • •

This story was adapted by Thames Television in 1982 as part of *The Agatha Christie Hour*.

"Distressed Lady, The Case of the"

PUBLISHING HISTORY: First published by William Collins Sons and Co., Ltd, London, 1934, in the short story collection *Parker Pyne Investigates*. First published in the United States by Dodd, Mead and Co., New York, 1934, in the short story collection *Mr. Parker Pyne, Detective*.

CHARACTERS: Mr. Parker Pyne; Lady Dortheimer, Claude Luttrell, Mrs. Daphne St. John, Madeleine de Sara.

Mr. Parker Pyne is consulted by Mrs. Daphne St. John, who is desperate for his help. It seems she has amassed severe gambling debts and, to pay them off, stole a diamond ring from Lady Dortheimer and replaced it with a paste replica. Having retrieved the ring from the pawn shop and being deeply ashamed of her deed, she hopes Parker Pyne will find a way of restoring the ring to the hand of Lady Dortheimer without the owner discovering the truth. With the assistance of Madeleine de Sara and Claude Luttrell, Parker Pyne uncovers the whole truth of the affair. The case is notable for the fact that Parker Pyne refuses to accept his customary fee.

"The Double Clue"

PUBLISHING HISTORY: First published by Dodd, Mead and Co., New York, 1961, in the short story collection *Double Sin and Other Stories.*

CHARACTERS: Hercule Poirot; Captain Arthur Hastings; Vera Rossakoff; Marcus Hardman, Mr. Johnston, Bernard Parker, Lady Runcorn.

This mystery is most remarkable for introducing Hercule Poirot to the formidable character of Vera Rossakoff. The case that brings them together is launched by Marcus Hardman, a wealthy collector, who has lost an emerald necklace said to have belonged to Catherine de' Medici. The necklace was stolen during a tea party at which he had shown his guests his collection of medieval jewels and entertained them with chamber music. After the guests had departed, Hardman discovered that his safe had been rifled. Aside from his desperation to recover the jewel, Hardman is equally concerned with the risk of publicity: "My own guests, my personal friends! It would be a horrible scandal!"

Hardman describes four likely suspects: Mr. Bernard Parker, Lady Runcorn, the Countess Vera Rossakoff, and Mr. Johnston. Each had the means to steal the necklace, although Hardman has his eye on one suspect in particular. Matters are deepened by the discovery in the safe of a man's glove and a cigarette case with the initials *B* and *P,* causing everyone to draw the obvious conclusion that it belongs to Bernard Parker. Poirot, however, has his doubts—bolstered by Parker's energetic denials and his interviews with the remaining suspects, including the dramatic Vera Rossakoff.

In keeping with Hardman's request, Poirot solves the case with total discretion, even permitting the thief to escape justice and leave the country. As for the countess, Poirot has very high praise for her (making her unique in the accounts of Poirot's cases): "A remarkable woman, I have a feeling, my friend—a very decided feeling—I shall meet her again. Where, I wonder?"

• • •

Poirot's premonition is twice proven correct, as he meets the countess again in "The Capture of Cerberus" and *The Big Four.* This case was adapted by London Weekend Television in 1990 for the series *Agatha Christie's Poirot* starring David Suchet.

"Double Sin"

PUBLISHING HISTORY: First published by Dodd, Mead and Co., New York, 1961, in the short story collection *Double Sin and Other Stories.*

CHARACTERS: Hercule Poirot; Captain Arthur Hastings; Joseph Aarons, Mary Durrant, Norton Kane, Miss Elizabeth Penn, Mr. J. Baker Wood.

Captain Arthur Hastings takes pity upon his seriously overworked friend, Hercule Poirot, and persuades him to take a week's holiday in the well-known resort Ebermouth. While there, however, the detective is contacted by a friend, the theatrical agent Joseph Aarons, who is staying at Charlock Bay, near Ebermouth. The agent requires Poirot's assistance. While on their way to Charlock, Poirot and Hastings encounter an attractive young woman, Mary Durrant, who is engaged on a business trip for her aunt, who owns "a most interesting antique shop in Ebermouth." Her aunt's clients are located all over England, and one, an American, is interested in a set of miniatures. Mary has been sent to represent the firm in the matter. Poirot warns her to be on guard against malefactors, especially as she will be traveling with five hundred pounds. Sure enough, once she arrives at Charlock Bay, the young woman discovers that the case is absent its valuable contents. A brief investigation reveals that the American had been visited by a lady who claimed to be representing Mary's aunt. This fraudulent person had used the miniatures as a lure and made off with the money.

The obvious suspect in the case, Mr. J. Baker Wood, was first drawn to the attention of Poirot sometime before the crime, and Hastings takes an instant dislike to the young man upon their interview with him. The second suspect is Mr. Norton Kane, a traveler in a brown suit. Poirot, of course, proceeds methodically, using a brown piece of luggage, evidence of the odd forcing of the luggage, and the adage that "a criminal is either clean-shaven or he has a proper mustache" to solve the case.

• • •

Poirot observes Hastings's propensity for noticing pretty women, especially his tendency toward "Auburn hair—always the auburn hair!" As is made clear in this story, whatever matter was troubling Joseph Aarons is remedied by Poirot—quickly—so that the sleuth can turn to the more intriguing history at hand. This case was adapted by London Weekend Television in 1990 for the series *Agatha Christie's Poirot* starring David Suchet.

Double Sin and Other Stories

PUBLISHING HISTORY: First published by Dodd, Mead and Co., New York, 1961. (For further details, see below.)

CONTENTS:
"Double Sin"
"Wasps' Nest"
"The Theft of the Royal Ruby"
"The Dressmaker's Doll"
"Greenshaw's Folly"
"The Double Clue"
"The Last Séance"
"Sanctuary"

This collection of stories was published for an American audience, and includes four cases featuring Hercule Poirot, two with Miss Marple, and two stories of a supernatural nature. "The Theft of the Royal Ruby" had been published originally in the collection *The Adventure of the Christmas Pudding* (1960); "Greenshaw's Folly" was also originally collected in the same book. "The Last Séance" was originally published in the collection *The Hound of Death* (1933).

"The Dream"

PUBLISHING HISTORY: First published by Dodd, Mead and Co., New York, 1939, in the short story collection, *The Regatta and Other Stories.*

CHARACTERS: Hercule Poirot; Inspector Barnett, Hugo Cornworthy, Benedict Farley, Louise Farley, Joanna Farley, Holmes, Dr. Stillingfleet.

Comfortable with being consulted by the powerful and wealthy, Hercule Poirot arrives at Northway House, "relic of an earlier age," in reply to a letter of invitation by the reclusive and eccentric millionaire Benedict Farley. The peculiar Farley first questions the detective in an attempt to ascertain that he is the genuine article and then tells a strange tale indeed. The millionaire is plagued night after night by the same dream. He is in his room, sitting at his desk, and at twenty-eight minutes past three he opens his desk drawer, takes out a revolver, loads it, and walks over to the window. Farley then dreams that he shoots himself, and wakes up. He has consulted three doctors, without satisfaction, and now consults Poirot because he wants his experience. The detective assures him he has never encountered such a peculiar circumstance, a statement that seems to satisfy the millionaire, for he cuts short their interview and demands from Poirot the letter he had sent to the detective. Poirot hands over a document, and then apologizes: he has mistakenly given Farley not the letter but his correspondence with his laundress. Quite baffled, the detective gives Farley the right letter and departs the presence of the millionaire.

The following week, Poirot receives a call from Dr. John Stillingfleet, who is at Northway House—Benedict Farley has shot himself. The police see Poirot's visit noted in Farley's appointment book, and the physician hopes that Poirot will be able to shed light on the matter. The detective goes to Northway House and encounters Inspector Barnett, along with Dr. Stillingfleet; Mrs. Farley, his widow; Joanna Farley, his daughter; and Hugo Cornworthy, his private secretary. The circumstances of Farley's death seem to match perfectly the events of his dream, but Poirot suspects murder. Clues in finding the murderer include Mr. Farley's excellent vision with his glasses on, a pair of lazy tongs, Farley's hatred of cats, and a small, stuffed black cat.

• • •

This case was adapted in 1989 by London Weekend Television for the series *Agatha Christie's Poirot* starring David Suchet.

"The Dressmaker's Doll"

PUBLISHING HISTORY: Published by Dodd, Mead and Co., New York, 1961, in the short story collection *Double Sin and Other Stories.*

CHARACTERS: Alicia Coombes, Mrs. Fellow-Brown, Sybil Fox, Mrs. Grove.

The owner of a shop that makes dresses, Alicia Coombes, becomes fascinated by a doll that seems to have been in the store for as long as anyone can remember, but no one knows when it arrived or who might have first brought it into the establishment. If this were not odd enough, the doll is apparently moving around a room, appearing in a different spot every day. As all of her employees swear they did not move it, the doll has a life of its own. Hoping to put an end to the mystery, Alicia locks the door to the room, only to discover some time later that the doll has escaped its confinement and has taken up a place in a different room. Now genuinely disturbed, Alicia tries to be rid of the doll entirely by hurling it out the window. A little girl, however, finds it and reveals the true secret of the haunted doll.

• • •

"The Dressmaker's Doll" is one of the several stories written by Christie with a supernatural theme. Also included in the collection, *Double Sin and Other Stories,* was another of Christie's tales that dabble in the occult and horror, "The Last Séance." Other notable stories of the supernatural by Christie included "The Hound of Death," "The Red Signal," "The Lamp," "The Call of Wings," "SOS," and "The Strange Case of Arthur Carmichael." (For more on these stories, see *The Hound of Death and Other Stories.*)

Dumb Witness

PUBLISHING HISTORY: First published by William Collins Sons and Co., Ltd., London, 1937. First published in the United States by Dodd, Mead and Co., New York, 1937, under the title *Poirot Loses a Client.*

CHARACTERS: Hercule Poirot; Captain Arthur Hastings; Angus, Charles Arundell, Emily Arundell, Theresa Arundell, Bob, Nurse Carruthers, Dr. Rex Donaldson, Dr. Grainger, Wilhelmina Lawson, Caroline Peabody, William Purvis, Bella Tanios, Dr. Jacob Tanios, Isabel Tripp, Julia Tripp.

The Arundell family gathers for Easter at Little Green House, the Market Basing home of Emily Arundell, daughter of the late General Arundell and keeper of the family fortune. It is obvious to her that all her relatives desire her money, and thus the dinner is both tense and unpleasant. Not long after, Emily tumbles down the stairs of her house during the night, and the incident is blamed on the little rubber ball that is a favorite toy of her dog, Bob. Emily, however, suspects that there is more to her accident, especially as Bob was out of the house and his ball had been put away in a drawer. The very next day, Emily writes two letters. The first is to her attorneys and the second is to Hercule Poirot.

Two months later, Poirot is reading his mail and opens the letter from Emily. He notes immediately that there was a two-month delay in its arrival. With his interest aroused, he sets off with

Captain Hastings (who is visiting from Argentina) for Little Green House. Upon their arrival, they learn that Little Green House is up for sale and that Emily has been dead for some time.

It does not take long for Poirot to learn the details of her death. Emily had died from a sudden attack of jaundice. Her relatives, however, were soon given the stunning news that she had changed her will just before her death. Instead of dividing her estate among her family, she left everything to her companion, Miss Minnie Lawson. Without delay, Poirot launches his investigation into what he knows was the murder of Emily Arundell.

• • •

Dumb Witness features perhaps the most unusual witness to a murder in the vast Christie library: Bob, a loyal wire-haired terrier who provides Poirot with the vital clues necessary for the solution of the case. Bob was based almost certainly on Christie's own beloved terrier, Peter. Mentioned in the dedication of *The Mystery of the Blue Train* (1928)—"Dedicated to Two Distinguished Members of the O.F.D., Carlotta and Peter")—the terrier was the sole recipient of the dedication in *Dumb Witness*: "To Dear Peter—most faithful of friends and dearest of companions, a dog in a thousand."

Dumb Witness was the last appearance of the dim but redoubtable Captain Hastings until his involvement in the very sad events recounted in *Curtain* (1975). Hastings goes off to Argentina, but he takes with him the intelligent Bob. While the dog was given to Poirot at the end of the novel, Hastings insists that the little fellow will be staying with him, and not the Belgian detective. Hastings observes to his friend, "You're not really any good with a dog, Poirot. You don't understand dog psychology!" As for Christie, she noted in her autobiography that she was "getting a little tired" of Hastings. She was willing, albeit reluctantly, to carry on with Poirot, but her days of writing about Hastings were over.

The germ for this story was originally planted in the short story "How Does Your Garden Grow?" although that case was not published in book form until 1939 (in *The Regatta Mystery*). The basic premise involved a woman who suspects she is being poisoned and so consults Poirot. The detective, however, does not arrive in time and finds his client dead. As was often the case, the seed of a plot planted in a short story finds superb and captivating fulfillment in a fuller, novel-length treatment.

"The Edge"

PUBLISHING HISTORY: First published in *Sovereign Magazine,* London, 1926. First published in the United States by G. P. Putnam's Sons, New York, 1997, in the short story collection *The Harlequin Tea Set and Other Stories.*

CHARACTERS: Clare Halliwell, Sir Gerald Lee, Vivien Lee.

Clare Halliwell has long harbored a passion for the wealthy Sir Gerald Lee. They had played together as children and had remained very close friends. She considered it inevitable that they should wed; it was only a matter of time. It thus came as a bitter blow when Gerald announced his marriage to the beautiful, elfin, red-haired Vivien, a young woman who displayed little interest in the usual amusements to be found in the area around Gerald's estate, Medenham Grange. Clare took an instant dislike toward Vivien, an aversion that wormed its way into her very soul.

Her hatred for Vivien finds wicked expression one day when Clare learns that Vivien has been lying to Gerald and is in an adulterous affair with a married man. Clare carefully builds a scheme not just to wreck Vivien's marriage but to destroy the woman completely. Blackmailing Vivien—who lives in terror of her lover being ruined—Clare proposes a simple solution. Vivien should take a run along some perilous cliffs and simply keep running, right over the edge.

• • •

"The Edge" had never been published in the United States prior to appearing in *The Harlequin*

Tea Set and Other Stories, nor had it been collected in any other compilation.

"Egyptian Tomb, The Adventure of the"

PUBLISHING HISTORY: First published by *Sketch* magazine, London, 1924; reprinted by John Lane Publishers, London, 1924, in the short story collection *Poirot Investigates.* First published in the United States by Dodd, Mead and Co., New York, 1925, in the short story collection *Poirot Investigates.*

CHARACTERS: Hercule Poirot; Captain Arthur Hastings; Dr. Ames, Mr. Bleibner, Rupert Bleibner, Mr. Schneider, Dr. Tosswill, Lady Willard, Sir Guy Willard, Sir John Willard.

In another case that brings Hercule Poirot to Egypt, the detective solves a cunning triple murder disguised as an ancient curse. Within weeks of discovering the tomb of King Men-her-Ra, "a shadowy king of the Eighth Dynasty," the two chief excavators, Sir John Willard and Mr. Bleibner, both died. Willard died suddenly of heart failure, and Bleibner was killed by acute poisoning. Compounding the tragedy was the suicide by self-inflicted gunshot wound of Bleibner's nephew, Rupert. The deaths were attributed immediately to the curse of opening the tomb of King Men-her-Ra, causing a huge public uproar.

Poirot is brought into the dark affair by Sir John Willard's wife, Lady Willard, who now fears for her son's safety, as he intends to carry on the excavations. The detective agrees to do all in his power to save young Willard from death. He suspects, of course, that there is a human cause for the deaths. This is confirmed when an attempt is made to murder Poirot, a gambit that allows him to trap the killer.

• • •

This case was adapted in 1993 by London Weekend Television for the series *Agatha Christie's Poirot* starring David Suchet. It is notable that Poirot's fear of and susceptibility to seasickness, the *mal de mer,* are displayed in the detective's journey to Egypt. Poirot also investigated murder in Egypt in *Death on the Nile* and "Problem at Sea." The cases permitted Agatha Christie to provide details of her extensive archaeological excavations and travels to Egypt.

Elephants Can Remember

PUBLISHING HISTORY: First published by William Collins Sons and Co., Ltd., London, 1972. First published in the United States by Dodd, Mead and Co., New York, 1972.

CHARACTERS: Hercule Poirot; Mrs. Ariadne Oliver; Mrs. Buckle, Mrs. Burton-Cox, Desmond Burton-Cox, Julia Carstairs, Kathleen Fenn, Chief Inspector Garroway, Mr. Goby, Dorothea Jarrow, Felicity Lemon, General Alistair Ravenscroft, Celia Ravenscroft, Lady Margaret Ravenscroft, Madame Rostenelle, Superintendent Bert Spence, Dr. Willoughby.

The mystery writer Mrs. Ariadne Oliver finds herself at a much-dreaded literary luncheon—she dislikes all such gatherings, where fans rush up to gush about her books—but she soon is hemmed in not by a fan but by the imperious Mrs. Burton-Cox. Instead of speaking about her books, Mrs. Burton-Cox raises an unexpected issue concerning one of Mrs. Oliver's goddaughters, Celia Ravenscroft. Mrs. Oliver can barely remember the young woman, beyond the fact that she gave Celia a Queen Anne silver strainer as a christening gift. The initial inquiry is followed by an even more stunning question: Which one was the murderer, Celia's mother or father? She does not know "whether the wife shot the husband and then shot herself, or whether the husband shot the wife and then shot himself."

The matter is of great importance to Mrs. Burton-Cox, as Celia plans to marry her son, Desmond. It becomes of interest to Mrs. Oliver as well, given her intense curiosity and given that the tragedy had taken the lives of one-time friends of hers and also involved her goddaughter. Mrs. Oliver goes straight to the one person she knows will solve the mystery, even though it is now decades old. The old detective sits her down and encourages her to find the right people who have all the little bits of ancient information that will lead to a solution. After all, the detective assures her, some people have the memories of elephants, and elephants never forget.

• • •

Elephants Can Remember was Christie's second to last book (not counting *Curtain* and *Sleeping Murder,* which were written during World War II) and offers up the eighth and last appearance of Mrs. Ariadne Oliver, who, once again, teamed up with Hercule Poirot to solve murders. The novel is considered one of Christie's weakest, in terms of its lack of the fabled details that were once a hallmark of the Christie genius. The characters have consistently hazy memories, and there are assorted misstatements to which nitpickers point in discussing inconsistencies or continuity errors. The primary cause of the small, but hardly unforgivable, lapses was Dame Agatha's advancing years and deteriorating health.

A murder solved mainly through retrospective analysis, in the style of Mr. Harley Quin, this novel is especially notable for Mrs. Oliver's final involvement with the Belgian detective. Ever the alter ego of Agatha, Mrs. Oliver is even more so in *Elephants Can Remember,* echoing in the early chapters Agatha's own dislike for public events, social gatherings, and gala luncheons thrown in her honor. Dame Agatha was always shy, as she noted in her autobiography, dreading "parties, and especially cocktail parties."

Endless Night

PUBLISHING HISTORY: First published by William Collins Sons and Co., Ltd., London, 1967. First published in the United States by Dodd, Mead and Co., New York, 1960.

CHARACTERS: Greta Anderson, Dimitri Constantine, Claudia Hardcastle, Sergeant Keene, Mrs. Esther Lee, Andrew P. Lippincott, Stanford Lloyd, Major Phillpot, Gervase Phillpot, Mrs. Rogers, Ellie Rogers, Michael Rogers, Rudolf Santonix, Dr. Shaw, Cora van Stuyvesant.

A chauffeur in the area of Kingston Bishop, Michael Rogers, visits an old Victorian mansion up for auction, The Towers, and becomes entranced not with the house itself but with the land around it. Called Gipsy's Acre, the land is reputedly cursed, and Michael is even warned away from the property by old Mrs. Lee, who is herself a local gypsy. Undeterred, Michael dreams of someday owning the land, and eventually meets a beautiful heiress, Ellie Goodman, who shares his passion for the property.

Within a short time, Michael and Ellie have fallen in love and have married. Not long after that, they acquire Gipsy's Acre and hire the noted architect Rudolf Santonix to build them their dream home. This idyllic beginning is marred by growing jealousy and the pernicious work of what feels like a dread curse upon the house.

• • •

According to Max Mallowan, *Endless Night* was ranked with *The Murder of Roger Ackroyd* (1926), *The Pale Horse* (1961), and *Moving Finger* (1943) as one of Christie's favorite works, although Mallowan admitted that "her opinions change from time to time." Mallowan believed that Agatha liked *Endless Night* because it gave the reader a "penetrating understanding of the twisted character who had a chance of turning to the good and chose the course of evil." *Endless Night* is also notable because the murders or deaths take place quite late in the narrative. The book was dedicated "To Nora Prichard from whom I first heard the legend of Gipsy's Acre." Nora Prichard was the paternal grandmother of Christie's only grandson, Mathew Prichard. The novel was adapted for film in 1972, starring Hayley Mills and Hywel Benett.

"The Erymanthian Boar"

PUBLISHING HISTORY: First published by William Collins Sons and Co., Ltd., London, 1947, in the short story collection *The Labours of Hercules.* First published in the United States by Dodd, Mead and Co., New York, 1947, in the short story collection, *The Labors of Hercules.*

CHARACTERS: Hercule Poirot; Inspector Drouet, Madame Grandier, Inspector Gustave, Commissionaire Lementeuil, Dr. Karl Lutz, Marrascaud, Mr. Schwartz.

Having successfully accomplished his third labor—"The Arcadian Deer"—Hercule Poirot finds himself in Switzerland and decides to spend several days seeing the sights. His journey climaxes at Rochers Neiges, ten thousand feet above sea level. While ascending in a funicular, the detective receives a note from Commissionaire Lementeuil that the very dangerous murderer Marrascaud, the equivalent of the mythological Erymanthian boar, has journeyed to Rochers Neiges with his gang. The Commissionaire suggests that Poirot get in touch with the policeman on the scene—Inspector Drouet.

The detective arrives at the Hotel Rochers Neiges and is contacted by Drouet, in disguise as a waiter. Knowing that a desperate and cunning murderer is loose in the hotel with his gang, Poirot must unravel the potential lies of his fellow guests: the American tourist Mr. Schwartz, the German doctor Lutz, and the tall, dark, and mysterious Madame Grandier. Complicating matters is the sudden isolation of the hotel when an avalanche cuts it and its guests off from the rest of the world. Poirot uses the isolation to lay a trap for Marrascaud and survives an attempt on his life. The trap is sprung with the aid of Commissionaire Lementeuil, who arrives once the funicular is repaired.

• • •

"The Erymanthian Boar" relies on isolation as an essential element in the setting and the plot for the mystery. Similar circumstances were used in other stories, including *And Then Were None* and *Murder on the Orient Express*. In mythology, Hercules captured the famed boar in a snowdrift.

Evil under the Sun

PUBLISHING HISTORY: First published by William Collins Sons and Co., Ltd., London,

A 1945 edition of Evil under the Sun. *(Pocket Books)*

1941. First published in the United States by Dodd, Mead and Co., New York, 1941.

CHARACTERS: Hercule Poirot; Major Barry, Horace Blatt, Emily Brewster, Mrs. Castle, Inspector Colgate, Alice Corrigan, Edward Corrigan, Rosamund Darnley, Carrie Gardener, Odell Gardener, Reverend Stephen Lane, Arlena Marshall, Captain Kenneth Marshall, Linda Marshall, Gladys Narracott, Dr. Neasdon, Sergeant Phillips, Christine Redfern, Patrick Redfern, Colonel Weston.

Hercule Poirot has come to the Jolly Roger Hotel on Smuggler's Island, Leathercombe Bay, to enjoy the sea air and the sun (in his own fashion). Rather than the sun, however, he takes the most interest in his fellow guests: Rosamund Darnley, a fashion designer; Reverend Stephen Lane, a cleric with an eye for the ladies; an American couple, Mr. and Mrs. Odell Gardener; the obnoxious millionaire Horace Blatt; Major Barry, a retired soldier; and the Redferns, Patrick and Christine, who are quite a contrast—she is shy and retiring and hides her white skin from the sun, while he is robust, active, and quite obviously attractive to women. Into this assembly is thrown the trio of the Marshalls. Captain Kenneth is joined by his teenage daughter, Linda, and, above all, by his wife, Arlena Marshall, a glamorous and domineering beauty who takes an instant interest in Patrick Redfern.

With Poirot ever observing the interplay, it becomes increasingly obvious that most of the guests have some connection to Arlena Marshall and a very good reason for hating her. It thus comes as no great shock to Poirot that Arlena is found strangled to death on a deserted beach. As he is present at the hotel, Poirot becomes embroiled in the investigation into her death, proving vitally useful to the two police officials in charge, Inspector Colgate and Colonel Weston. In this case, Poirot pays the greatest attention to time and the way that people do exactly what they should because of it.

• • •

Evil under the Sun is ranked by many readers among their favorite Christie works, and features Poirot at his fussy best, obsessed with maintaining his elegant appearance in the heat and the sea air. The plot seems similar to several other Christie cases, most notably *Death on the Nile* (1937) and the short stories "The Bloodstained Pavement" (1932) and "Triangle at Rhodes" (1937). The novel was adapted for film—with a number of location changes—in 1982's *Evil under the Sun*. Peter Ustinov reprised his work as Hercule Poirot; the stellar support cast included Diana Rigg, Maggie Smith and Jane Birkin (who were also in *Death on the Nile*), James Mason, Roddy McDowall, and Colin Blakely.

"The Face of Helen"

PUBLISHING HISTORY: First published by William Collins Sons and Co., Ltd., London, 1930, in the short story collection *The Mysterious Mr. Quin*. First published in the United States by Dodd, Mead and Co., New York, 1930, in the short story collection *The Mysterious Mr. Quin*.

CHARACTERS: Mr. Satterthwaite; Mr. Harley Quin; Charles Burns, Philip Eastney, Gillian West.

With the enigmatic Mr. Quin's chimerical assistance, Satterthwaite prevents a murder but is unable—or unwilling—to stop a suicide. The case begins at the opera, where the cultured Satterthwaite hears *Pagliacci* performed by the tenor Yoaschbim. To his surprise and delight, Satterthwaite encounters Harley Quin, who maneuvers him subtly into following a stunning beauty in the audience. Once outside, Satterthwaite rescues the woman—Gillian West—from a fight between two suitors. The two men vying for her attentions are Charles Burns, a shipping clerk, and Philip Eastney, a musical genius and expert in glassmaking. It is soon learned that West's troubles with the young men are not her first; there have been others, often ending in tragedy. Her present attachments also threaten disaster, but Satterthwaite is able to anticipate and save West from murder. The method chosen, relying upon "The Shepherd's Song" and a rare, deadly poison, is one of the most unique in Christie's writings.

"A Fairy in the Flat"

PUBLISHING HISTORY: First published by William Collins Sons and Co., Ltd., London, 1929, in the short story collection *Partners in Crime*. First published in the United States by Dodd, Mead and Co., New York, 1929, in the short story collection, *Partners in Crime*.

CHARACTERS: Tommy Beresford; Tuppence Beresford; Theodore Blunt, Mr. Carter.

The first story in the collection *Partners in Crime*, "The Fairy in the Flat" also serves as an introduction to the rest of the cases in the book, which are investigated by the Beresfords in their own inimitable and elegant style. Tuppence expresses the wish that there were a fairy in their flat who might help in relieving her boredom. Tommy replies by showing her a photograph with a flash of light that could be mistaken easily for a fairy. Even more exciting, however, is the arrival of Chief Carter, a high-ranking member of British intelligence. He brings with him a special assignment for the Beresfords. A double agent, Theodore Blunt, has been placed in prison and Carter needs two clever operatives to run his detective service, Blunt's International Detective Agency. Most important, Carter wants Tommy to be on the watch for a letter bearing the significant number sixteen and to await someone who might arrive and use the code phrase "sixteen" in his or her opening sentence. The number is a significant identifying phrase in a spy ring operating in England.

"Finessing the King" and "The Gentleman Dressed in Newspaper"

PUBLISHING HISTORY: First published by William Collins Sons and Co., Ltd., London, 1929, in the short story collection *Partners in Crime*. First published in the United States by Dodd, Mead and Co., New York, 1929, in the short story collection, *Partners in Crime*.

CHARACTERS: Tommy Beresford; Tuppence Beresford; Captain Bingo Hale, Inspector Marriot, Sir Arthur Merivale, Lady Vere Merivale.

In a period of relative quiet for the Beresfords at Blunt's International Detective Agency, Tommy and Tuppence peruse the personals columns in the local papers. They take note of one especially unusual message: "Three hearts . . .12 tricks . . .Ace of Spades . . .finesse the king." Tuppence ponders the message and deciphers what proves to be a relatively simple code. Three hearts refers to the Three Arts Ball; twelve tricks signifies midnight; and Ace of Spades is a popular club. "Finesse the king" proves more inscrutable, and the pair decides to attend the ball to see if they

can find out what it means. "Finesse the king" becomes clear at the ball. It means murder.

● ● ●

This case begins in "Finessing the King" and concludes in "The Gentleman Dressed in Newspaper." As they do throughout this collection of stories, the Beresfords in this case impersonate fictional detectives. Here, they adopt the style and manner of the detectives McCarty and Riordan, created by Isabel Ostrander (d. 1924). Both cases were adapted in 1984 for the series *Partners in Crime* by London Weekend Television.

Five Little Pigs

PUBLISHING HISTORY: First published by William Collins Sons and Co., Ltd., London, 1943. First published in the United States by Dodd, Mead and Co., New York, 1943, under the title *Murder in Retrospect*.

CHARACTERS: Hercule Poirot; Meredith Blake, Philip Blake, Caroline Crale, Sir Montague Depleach, Lord Dittisham, Alfred Edmunds, Quentin Fogg, Elsa Greer, Inspector Hale, Caleb Jonathan, Carla Lemarchant, George Mayhew, John Rattery, Angela Warren, Cecelia Williams.

Hercule Poirot receives a visit from Miss Carla Lemarchant, as she desires the detective to investigate a murder. What makes the crime especially intriguing to Poirot is that it occurred sixteen years ago, and the murderer in the case was apparently brought to justice. Caroline Crale, Carla's mother, was arrested for the murder of the artist Amyas Crale, Carla's father. Caroline was convicted of the crime and sentenced to life in prison; she died after only a year as a prisoner.

Raised in ignorance of her family past, Carla was given the shocking news about her parents when she turned twenty-one. A letter, written by her mother, was handed to her. In its pages, Caroline assures her daughter that she was innocent of the crime. Carla believes her and seeks now to prove her mother guiltless. Her desire has an added poignancy, for Carla plans to marry and is concerned that her husband will never be entirely certain about his own wife's tendencies.

Overcome with excitement at the challenge of solving a case so seemingly obvious and so bereft of surviving evidence, Poirot readily agrees to help. He goes immediately to see Quentin Fogg, the Crown Attorney, and receives from him particulars of the case against Caroline Crale. He then interrogates the family's old lawyers and the chief investigating officer, Inspector Hale. Based upon his inquiries, Poirot settles on five chief suspects, "five little pigs": Elsa Greer, Amyas's old mistress; Angela Warren, Caroline's younger sister; Philip Blake, Amyas's best friend; Meredith Blake, a country squire; and Cecelia Wiiliams, Angela's old governess.

• • •

Five Little Pigs was the first of the five novels written by Christie that present a murder case solved in retrospect. The other four are: *Sleeping Murder* (1976, but written during World War II), *Sparkling Cyanide* (1945), *Ordeal by Innocence* (1958), and *Elephants Can Remember* (1972). Of the five books penned in this style, *Five Little Pigs* is considered the best, although it is one of Christie's lesser-known works.

The novel is notable for two other reasons. First, the book uses—entirely with success—the most complicated of narrative styles. Hercule Poirot must interrogate witnesses who provide their own personal views of distant events. Thus, the murder of Amyas Crale and the trial of his wife, Caroline Crale, are recounted several times, albeit from the differing perspectives of the individual witnesses. The novel consequently has a *Rashomon* quality to it.

Second, the story details the complex psychological and emotional components of a marriage that disintegrates, mirroring in many ways the unfortunate events in Christie's own life during her failed marriage to Archie Christie. A triangular (and deadly) relationship was used in several Christie stories and novels, including *Evil under the Sun* (1941), *Death on the Nile* (1937), "The Bloodstained Pavement" (1932), and "Triangle at Rhodes" (1937).

Christie dedicated the novel to Stephen Glanville, a friend of the family and a noted Egyptologist. He was given the rare honor of having two books dedicated to him (the other one is *Death Comes As the End*) despite not being a member of the immediate Christie family. *Five Little Pigs* was adapted for the stage by Christie and debuted under the title *Go Back for Murder* in 1960.

The Floating Admiral

PUBLISHING HISTORY: First published by Doubleday, Doran and Co., Inc., Garden City, New York, 1932.

The Floating Admiral is an unusual collaborative effort, bringing together some of the more famous detective writers of the early 1930s. All the contributors were members of the Detection Club, a prestigious organization of mystery writers.

The novel was organized into twelve chapters and an introduction, each written by a different writer. Dorothy L. Sayers penned the introductory chapter, which also established the parameters for the chapters to follow. Each contributor wrote a chapter that had "a definite solution in view—that is, [the writer] must not introduce new complications merely 'to make it more difficult.' " The murder in question is that of Admiral Penistone, who is found dead in the vicar's boat floating down the Whyn River. The case is investigated by Inspector Rudge of the Whynmouth police.

Agatha Christie was asked to write the fourth chapter, titled "Mainly Conversations." The other contributors were G. K. Chesterton, Canon Victor L. Whitechurch, G. D. H. and M. Cole, Henry Wade, John Rhode, Milward Kennedy, Ronald Knox, Freeman Wills Crofts, Edgar Jepson, Clemence Dane, and Anthony Berkeley.

"The Flock of Geryon"

PUBLISHING HISTORY: First published by William Collins Sons and Co., Ltd., London,

1947, in the short story collection *The Labours of Hercules*. First published in the United States by Dodd, Mead and Co., New York, 1947, in the short story collection *The Labors of Hercules*.

CHARACTERS: Hercule Poirot; Chief Inspector James Japp; Dr. Andersen, Amy Carnaby, Emmeline Clegg, Mr. Cole.

Hercule Poirot is visited by Miss Amy Carnaby, the lady's companion who so impressed the detective with her intelligence and ingenuity in "The Nemean Lion." The industrious Miss Carnaby consults the detective in the hope that he might assist her in enlivening her rather humdrum life. She already has a suggestion in mind, and Poirot gives his approval.

A very dear friend of Miss Carnaby's, the widow Emmeline Clegg, has fallen under the influence of a cult leader, a Dr. Andersen, and his society, the Great Flock. The members of the Great Flock are mostly women, and, in the last year, no less than three wealthy female members have died. In each case, they left their sizable fortunes to the society. While the deaths were seemingly from natural causes, Miss Carnaby is suspicious, a view clearly shared by Hercule Poirot.

While the detective begins his own investigation of Dr. Andersen, it is agreed that Miss Carnaby will allow herself to be recruited into the Great Flock, providing Poirot with an agent inside the cult. This proves a very dangerous assignment, as Miss Carnaby is exposed to the powerfully influential rites of the Great Flock and the Great Shepherd, Dr. Andersen. She is especially concerned about one member, Mr. Cole, who seems mad with his obsession for "reflecting on the Fullness of Life, on the Supreme Joy of Oneness." With Carnaby's help and several surprise developments, Poirot unravels the Great Flock and the schemes of its "Shepherd."

• • •

This case, the tenth labor of Hercule Poirot in honor of the twelve labors of the mythical Hercules, concerns Poirot's effort to free women from the slavery of the Great Flock. The mythological

Hercules labored at setting free the cattle owned by Geryon and kept on the island of Erythea. Hercules slew Orthus, the hound guarding the flock, followed by Eurytion, the herdsman, and, finally, the villain Geryon. Christie's knowledge of narcotics, hallucinogens, and lethal bacilli is displayed in this story. This story also contains a reference to Adolf Hitler, unusual in her writings despite the presence of the dictator on the world stage during much of the period in which Christie wrote.

"Four and Twenty Blackbirds"

PUBLISHING HISTORY: First published by Dodd, Mead and Co., New York, 1950, in the short story collection *Three Blind Mice and Other Stories*.

CHARACTERS: Hercule Poirot; Henry Bonnington, Anthony Gascoigne, Henry Gascoigne, Dr. George Lorrimer, Molly.

In a superb demonstration of Hercule Poirot's obsession with order and method, the detective becomes convinced that something is seriously amiss solely because a long-time customer in a restaurant orders a different meal from his usual fare. While dining at the Gallant Endeavour, Kings Road, Chelsea, with his friend Henry Bonnington, Poirot hears the story of a customer—an old fellow nicknamed Old Father Time by the staff—who has been coming to the restaurant on Tuesdays and Thursdays for ten years and never orders suet pudding or blackberries or thick soup. Suddenly, the old man turns up on a Monday night and orders thick tomato soup, beefsteak and kidney pudding, and blackberry tart. Poirot observes, "I find that extraordinarily interesting."

Three weeks later, the detective learns of the death of Henry Gascoigne, an aged eccentric who died from an accident and whose body had been discovered after several days, owing to the accumulation of milk bottles outside his door. Curiously, on the very day that Henry Gascoigne died, his brother, the one-time artist Anthony Gascoigne, passed away also. The brothers were survived by only one relative, Anthony's son, George Lorrimer.

Poirot, of course, is convinced that a murder has taken place precisely because of the routine that was disrupted and also because everything "is beautifully in order . . ." The absolutely vital clue in the case is the meal of Henry Gascoigne at the Gallant Endeavour.

• • •

In this case, there is reference to the rhyme "Sing a song of sixpence." This is only one of the many children's rhymes quoted in Christie's writings. This case was adapted by London Weekend Television in 1989 for the series *Agatha Christie's Poirot* starring David Suchet.

4.50 from Paddington

PUBLISHING HISTORY: First published by William Collins Sons and Co., Ltd., London, 1957. First published in the United States by Dodd, Mead and Co., New York, 1957, under the title *What Mrs. McGillicuddy Saw!*

CHARACTERS: Miss Jane Marple; Inspector Bacon, Alfred Crackenthorpe, Lady Alice Crackenthorpe, Cedric Crackenthorpe, Emma Crackenthorpe, Harold Crackenthorpe, Luther Crackenthorpe, Chief Inspector Dermot Craddock, Armand Dessin, Alexander Eastley, Bryan Eastley, Miss Ellis, Lucy Eylesbarrow, Florence Hill, Madame Joliet, Mrs. Kidder, Elspeth McGillicuddy, Dr. Morris, Dr. Quimper, Lady Stoddard-West, James Stoddard-West, Anna Stravinska, David West, Mr. Wimbourne.

Elspeth McGillicuddy, "short and stout," has journeyed down from Scotland for a holiday and awaits the whistle to board the 4:50 train that will take her to Brackhampton and her connecting rides to the village of St. Mary Mead and her dear friend Miss Marple. She has puffed her way through Paddington Station toward the train, as she is much burdened by Christmas packages. Finally, she finds an empty compartment, slumps into a cushioned seat, and begins reading a magazine. The train sets out slowly from the station and runs parallel for a moment with another train on the next track. What happens next is burned into her memory:

At the moment when the two trains gave the illusion of being stationary, a blind in one of the carriages flew up with a snap. Mrs. McGillicuddy looked into the lighted first-class carriage that was only a few feet away.

Then she drew her breath in with a gasp and half rose to her feet.

Standing with his back to the window and to her was a man. His hands were round the throat of a woman who faced him, and he was slowly, remorselessly, strangling her. Her eyes were starting from their sockets, her face was purple and congested. As Mrs. McGillicuddy watched, fascinated, the end came, the body went limp and crumpled in the man's hands.

The trains then separated and the image was gone. The train authorities on hand, of course, greet her story with considerable incredulity, and she is still upset when she at last reaches St. Mary Mead and tells Jane Marple of her shocking experience. The old sleuth replies soothingly, "Most distressing for you, Elspeth, and surely most unusual. I think you had better tell me about it at once."

Marple believes Elspeth from the first and suggests that they wait to see if the papers report the crime. No word is ever published, and even Inspector Cornish can find nothing about an incident on a train. With virtually everyone doubting Elspeth's story, Miss Marple sends her friend off to Ceylon to enjoy the holidays with her son. She then takes matters into her own hands and plots out the likely places for a corpse to be hidden. Her quiet inquiries lead her to the Crackenthorpe family of Rutherford Hall. To spearhead her investigation into the Crackenthorpes, she enlists the assistance of a clever young woman, Lucy Eylesbarrow. The amateur detective soon uncovers a corpse and proves the value of confiding in Miss Marple.

• • •

Lucy Eylesbarrow became one of the author's most popular and memorable characters. As Miss Marple was getting up there in age, she needed a youthful and mobile assistant to conduct the more laborious aspects of her investigations. Lucy proves both talented and resourceful, earning Miss Marple's confidence and praise. Inexplicably, Christie chose to leave Lucy behind in other Marple cases, preferring to concentrate on Inspector Craddock, who also appeared in *A Murder Is Announced, The Mirror Crack'd from Side to Side,* and "Sanctuary." There is a curious discrepancy between the English and American editions of *4.50 from Paddington* that concerns time. In the American edition, the train taken by Mrs. McGillicuddy departs from Paddington Station for Brackhampton, Milchester, etc., at 4:54; in the British edition, the departure time is 4:50. The cause of the difference has to do with the original manuscript, which was to be published with the title *4.54 from Paddington.* The publisher, Collins, decided to change the title to *4.50 from Paddington.* By the time Collins informed the American publisher, Dodd, Mead and Co., of the change, the book had already gone to press (with, of course, the different title), and the departure time remained 4:54.

The novel was adapted twice: for the feature film *Murder, She Said* (1962) starring Margaret Rutherford, and for a television film, produced by the BBC in 1987, starring Joan Hickson.

"The Four Suspects"

PUBLISHING HISTORY: First published by William Collins Sons and Co., Ltd., London, 1932, in the short story collection *The Thirteen Problems.* First published in the United States by Dodd, Mead and Co., New York, 1933, in the short story collection *The Tuesday Club Murders.*

CHARACTERS: Miss Jane Marple; Colonel Bantry, Dolly Bantry, Sir Henry Clithering; Mr. Dobbs, Dr. Rosen, Mrs. Gertrud Schwartz.

The question of guilt or innocence and the terrible ordeal of living under the suspicion of a crime one did not commit serve as the backdrop to Sir Henry Clithering's account of murder with four suspects; one of them is a murderer, while the other three live under a cloud of suspicion. Related as part of the Tuesday Night Club gathering, "The Four Suspects" is concerned with the assassination of the German counterspy Dr. Rosen, whose work in Germany helped to break up the terrorist ring of the *Schwarze Hand.* Forced to flee his homeland for England, Rosen is hunted down and murdered in a small, remote English village. Rosen had lived there in deliberate obscurity with his niece, Greta, a personal secretary—actually a German-speaking member of Scotland Yard—an old German servant who had served Rosen for forty years, and a gardener and handyman, who was a native of a village in Somerset, King's Gnaton. When Rosen dies from a broken neck after falling down a flight of stairs, it is certain that a member of the household is guilty of murder. The most vital clue in solving the crime is a peculiar letter sent to Dr. Rosen, a missive that is of special import to Miss Marple, who deciphers a clever code because of her knowledge of the language of flowers.

"The Fourth Man"

PUBLISHING HISTORY: First published by William Collins Sons and Co., Ltd., London, 1933, in the short story collection *The Hound of Death and Other Stories.* There was no American edition of the collection.

CHARACTERS: Felicie Bault, Dr. Campbell Clark, Sir George Durand, Raoul Letardean, Canon Parfitt, Annette Ravel.

Three men on a train—Sir George Durand, a lawyer, Canon Parfitt, a cleric, and Dr. Campbell Clark, a psychologist—enter into an intense conversation about the peculiar case of Felicie Bault. That unfortunate young woman, a peasant girl from Brittany, developed multiple personalities at the age of twenty-two, including a lazy personality, an intelligent personality, an immoral personality, and an unearthly personality. Their speculation is interrupted by a long-silent passenger named Raoul Letardean, who provides stunning firsthand information about Felicie.

"A Fruitful Sunday"

PUBLISHING HISTORY: First published by William Collins Sons and Co., Ltd., London, 1934, in the short story collection *The Listerdale Mystery*. First published in the United States by Dodd, Mead and Co., New York, 1971, in the short story collection *The Golden Ball and Other Stories*.

CHARACTERS: Edward Palgrove, Dorothy Pratt.

Miss Dorothy Pratt and her beau, Edward Palgrove, set out for a Sunday picnic and pick up along the way a small wicker basket full of fruit at a corner stall. After discussing the newspaper headlines, including the amazing theft of a ruby necklace worth fifty thousand pounds, the couple enjoys the fruit. Suddenly, at the bottom of the basket, Dorothy finds a ruby necklace. It matches exactly the description of the stolen necklace, and the pair of picnickers figure that somehow, through a bizarre twist of fate, they have come into possession of the precious gems. The question now becomes what they should do about it.

After discussions, Dorothy and Edward decide that the police will not believe them and that they would do well to try and sell the necklace to what Edward excitedly calls a "fence." The plan is short-circuited by the newspaper, which contains two stories of great interest.

Funerals Are Fatal

See *After the Funeral*

"The Gate of Baghdad"

PUBLISHING HISTORY: First published by William Collins Sons and Co., Ltd., London, 1934, in the short story collection *Parker Pyne Investigates*. First published in the United States by Dodd, Mead and Co., New York, 1934, in the short story collection *Mr. Parker Pyne, Detective*.

CHARACTERS: Mr. Parker Pyne; Mr. Hensley, Flight Lieutenant Loftus, Mrs. Pentemian, General Poli, Netta Pryce, Captain Smethurst, Flight Lieutenant Williamson.

Unlike most of his other published cases (save for "Death on the Nile"), "The Gate of Baghdad" offers Parker Pyne a murder case; his other cases regularly concern matters of the heart, or, at worst, theft or kidnapping. The setting is also far more rugged than those of his other cases—it takes place while the sleuth is traveling from Damascus to Baghdad. The cast of characters is also wonderfully typical for Christie at her best, with redoubtable soldiers, a buoyant young woman, and a murderer in disguise anxious to conceal a terrible secret.

While journeying through the Middle East, Parker Pyne joins a group of travelers crossing the desert. During the trip, one of the RAF officers is murdered, and Parker Pyne oversees the brief investigation. He soon uncovers the murderer.

There is much in this story that is quite reminiscent of Hercule Poirot investigating a crime. Parker Pyne displays the same meticulous attention to detail so routinely displayed by the Belgian detective. It is also likely that many of the aspects of the story were based on Christie's own journey to the region around 1933 with her second husband, the archaeologist Max Mallowan.

"The Gentleman Dressed in Newspaper"

See "Finessing the King"

Giant's Bread

PUBLISHING HISTORY: First published by William Collins Sons and Co., Ltd., London, 1930. First published in the United States by Doubleday and Co., New York, 1930.

CHARACTERS: George Chetwynd, Phillis Deacon, Myra Deyre, Vernon Deyre, Walter Deyre, Mr. Fleming, Nurse Frances, Mr. Green, Jane Harding, Katie, Mr. and Mrs. Levinne, Sebastian Levinne, Aunt Nina, Mrs. Pascal, Miss Robbins, Susan, Uncle Sydney, Nell Vereker, Josephine Waite, Winnie.

Giant's Bread follows the life and progress of Vernon Deyre, a potentially brilliant composer. Born and raised on the family estate of Abbots Puissants, he loves the family land and lives in dread of losing it. He is also a genuinely gifted composer and decides to invest his entire family fortune and prospects on an opera. Larger events intervene, however, and Vernon marches off to the trenches of World War I.

Vernon's wife subsequently receives a telegram informing her that her husband has been killed in combat. In fact, he was captured and managed to escape from a German prison camp. In the aftermath of his experience, Vernon succumbs to amnesia and becomes a lowly chauffeur, while his wife, still believing him dead, remarries. What follows is a series of crises that threaten both their marriage and their lives.

• • •

Giant's Bread was the first novel written by Christie under the pseudonym Mary Westmacott. The book came about after she had established herself as a full-time writer of mysteries. As time wore on, however, she developed a desire to write other types of books, as noted in her autobiography. Her work on the manuscript was coupled "with a rather guilty feeling," but upon completion of the book, Collins agreed to publish it. The decision was made, however, to release the book under a pseudonym—given its content, there was an understandable desire to maintain Christie's name in association only with mysteries. Christie noted the reluctance of her publishers to support the Westmacott books, as there was a sense that somehow they would detract from the mysteries. The sentiment was most manifest with the manuscript of *Come, Tell Me How You Live* (1946). Christie persisted, and the first Westmacott book was well received by critics. She dedicated the book to her mother, Clara Miller.

"The Gipsy"

PUBLISHING HISTORY: First published by William Collins Sons and Co., Ltd., London, 1933, in the short story collection *The Hound of Death and Other Stories*. First published in the United States by Dodd, Mead and Co., New York,

1971, in the short story collection *The Golden Ball and Other Stories*.

CHARACTERS: Dickie Carpenter, Mrs. Alistair Haworth, Esther Lawes, Mr. Macfarlane.

Another work by Christie featuring a supernatural rather than a mystery theme, "The Gipsy" is concerned with a man's seemingly irrational fear of gypsies. This aversion on the part of Dickie Carpenter is noticed by Mr. Macfarlane, but he has never asked Carpenter for the reason. When a mutually distressing event in their private lives momentarily punctures the air of formality between them, Carpenter reveals that his terror began with a dream that came to him during his childhood. He subsequently had an encounter with a gypsy that sealed his fear as a hidden but palpable secret until his meeting with Mrs. Haworth. She warns him about his future and a proposed leg operation. Carpenter goes ahead anyway and dies.

This odd and tragic event compels Macfarlane to journey to see Mrs. Haworth. Like his friend, he finds her beguiling and haunting, but even more disturbing is her certain declaration that they will not meet again.

"The Girdle of Hippolita"

PUBLISHING HISTORY: First published by William Collins Sons and Co., Ltd., London, 1947, in the short story collection *The Labours of Hercules*. First published in the United States by Dodd, Mead and Co., New York, 1947, in the short story collection *The Labors of Hercules*.

CHARACTERS: Hercule Poirot; Chief Inspector James Japp; Miss Bourshaw, Inspector Hearn, Winifred King, Miss Lavinia Pope, Alexander Simpson.

Confirming one of Hercule Poirot's favorite sayings, "One thing leads to another," this ninth of the twelve labors of Hercule Poirot—in emulation of the great hero Hercules of Greek mythology—takes the detective on two seemingly unrelated investigations that become intertwined. Poirot is initially consulted by Alexander Simpson, owner of Simpson's Gallery, in the hopes that the Belgian might recover a stolen Rubens. The small but virtually priceless painting was taken right out of the gallery. The crime, according to Simpson, had been orchestrated by a certain unscrupulous millionaire. Poirot takes the case with little enthusiasm, but finds that it permits him to undertake a very different matter, a case brought to him by Inspector Japp that he finds far more intriguing. A schoolgirl, young Winnie King, had disappeared somewhere along the Calais-Paris line, sometime after lunch, for when the train arrived in Paris, eighteen girls were counted, not the nineteen who had been at Amiens, even though the other girls were sure that Winnie King had been present.

As Poirot sets out for France, he is informed by Japp that Winnie King has turned up alive, near Amiens, dazed and incoherent. The detective presses on, consulting with Inspector Hearn over the kidnapping and the persons in charge at Winnie King's school, a posh institution run by Miss Lavinia Pope. By using his "little grey cells," Poirot not only explains the meaning behind the kidnapping but recovers the missing Rubens; a magnificent painting called *The Girdle of Hyppolita*.

"The Girl in the Train"

PUBLISHING HISTORY: First published by William Collins Sons and Co., Ltd., London, 1934, in the short story collection *The Listerdale Mystery*. First published in the United States by Dodd, Mead and Co., New York, 1971, in the short story collection *The Golden Ball and Other Stories*.

CHARACTERS: Grand Duchess Anastasia, Lady Elizabeth Gaigh, Detective Inspector Jarrold, Prince Karl, Prince Osric, George Rowland.

In an adventure more reminiscent of a caper orchestrated by Mr. Parker Pyne than a true-life event, "The Girl in the Train" offers the amazing tale of George Rowland. Having just been fired by his uncle for showing up late at work after a long evening of fun the night before, George decides to flee his humdrum existence and seek the colonies. As Australia is too far away, he decides to head for

the aptly named Rowland's Castle. At Waterloo Station, George is suddenly confronted by a stunning young woman who begs to hide in his compartment. He secrets her away beneath the seat in the compartment just in time to face a repellent little man demanding to know what George has done with his niece. George adroitly deflects the man's accusation and escapes on the train. The young woman is immensely grateful and sends George on a further mission to follow a sinister black-bearded traveler.

George is soon caught up in international espionage, an imbroglio involving the grand duchy of Catonia and a curious letter hidden in a bathroom. Dogged himself for a time by would-be duelers and Scotland Yard, George foils a spy plot, recovers a valuable ring, and wins the hand of a beautiful woman.

• • •

This story was adapted by Thames Television in 1982 for *The Agatha Christie Hour*.

"The Golden Ball"

PUBLISHING HISTORY: First published by William Collins Sons and Co., Ltd., London, 1934, in the short story collection *The Listerdale Mystery*. First published in the United States by Dodd, Mead and Co., New York, 1971, in the short story collection *The Golden Ball and Other Stories*.

CHARACTERS: George Dundas, Ephraim Leadbetter, Mary Montresor, Bella Wallace, Rube Wallace.

George Dundas finds himself standing on a street in the City of London, having just been disowned by his serious uncle Ephraim Leadbetter for failing to grasp "the golden ball of opportunity." While meditating on his misfortune, he is confronted by a scarlet touring car driven by the gorgeous but precocious Mary Montresor. She invites him for a drive and asks him, with utter casualness, if he would like to marry her. He accepts immediately, and she answers, rather ominously, "Perhaps you may someday."

On a whim, Mary takes George into the country to look for a prospective house. She chooses one, seemingly at random, for its charm, and the pair begin peeking into the windows when they are invited inside by the butler. The situation soon becomes dangerous when a revolver is drawn on them by a sinister occupant, and they are ordered upstairs. It is at that moment that George seizes the opportunity so colorfully described by his uncle.

The Golden Ball and Other Stories

PUBLISHING HISTORY: First published by Dodd, Mead and Co., New York, 1971. Two stories were previously unpublished; five were reprinted from *The Hound of Death and Other Stories;* and three were reprinted from *The Listerdale Mystery.*

CONTENTS:
"The Listerdale Mystery"
"The Girl in the Train"
"The Manhood of Edward Robinson"
"A Fruitful Sunday"
"The Golden Ball"
"The Rajah's Emerald"
"Swan Song"
"The Hound of Death"
"The Gipsy"
"The Lamp"
"The Strange Case of Sir Arthur Carmichael"
"The Call of Wings"
"Jane in Search of a Job"
"Magnolia Blossom"
"Next to a Dog"

"Magnolia Blossom" and "Next to a Dog" had not been published previously in earlier collections; "The Listerdale Mystery," "The Girl in the Train," "The Manhood of Edward Robinson," "A Fruitful Sunday," "The Golden Ball," "The Rajah's Emerald," "Swan Song," and "Jane in Search of a Job" were published previously in *The Listerdale Mystery* (1934); "The Hound of Death," "The Gipsy," "The Lamp," "The Strange Case of Sir Arthur Carmichael," and "The Call of Wings" were published previously in *The Hound of Death* (1933).

This collection is a mix of lighter stories (from *The Listerdale Mystery*) and tales of the supernatural (from *The Hound of Death*). There is, consequently, a sharp change in mood and atmosphere as the stories move from one to the next, with "Magnolia Blossom" standing out as a romantic tragedy and "Next to a Dog" being notable as a very personal and exceedingly touching story of the love of an owner for her pet.

Perhaps the most remarkable tidbit in the collection is the confusing typographical error in the contents page and on the title page of the story "The Strange Case of Sir Arthur Carmichael." In the original version of the story as it appeared in *The Hound of Death,* the title was correct; in *The Golden Ball and Other Stories,* however, the title was printed as "The Strange Case of Sir Andrew Carmichael," even though in the text it remained "Arthur Carmichael." Incredibly, the error was not corrected in subsequent paperback editions.

"Greenshaw's Folly"

PUBLISHING HISTORY: First published by William Collins Sons and Co., Ltd., London, 1960, in the short story collection *The Adventure of the Christmas Pudding and a Selection of Entrées.*

CHARACTERS: Miss Jane Marple; Raymond West; Horace Bindler, Mrs. Creswell, Nat Fletcher, Miss Katherine Greenshaw, Louise Oxley, Alfred Pollock, Inspector Welch, Joan West.

Miss Marple's nephew, Raymond West, visits with his friend Horace Bindler, a literary critic, at the eccentric mansion and "outrageous pile" called Greenshaw's Folly, built by a wealthy success story who virtually bankrupted himself in its construction. They meet Katherine Greenshaw, the aged owner of the estate, and become witnesses to her will, in which she leaves her entire estate to her housekeeper, Mrs. Creswell. Miss

Greenshaw is subsequently murdered—shot in the chest by an arrow—and all three suspects have seemingly airtight alibis. Mrs. Creswell was locked in a room at the time of the murder; the gardener Alfred Pollock was at the local pub, Dog and Duck, consuming his usual bread and cheese and beer; and Nat Fletcher, Greenshaw's supposed nephew, was filling up his car at a nearby garage and asking for directions. Evidence certainly points to Pollock, as he is a member of the local bow and arrow club and had been feuding with Mrs. Creswell. Miss Marple is able to solve the murder by noting that Miss Greenshaw twice wore a peculiar old-fashioned print dress, hid her will in a copy of the book *Lady Audley's Secret,* and that Alfred is prone toward laziness.

Hallowe'en Party

PUBLISHING HISTORY: First published by William Collins Sons and Co., Ltd., London, 1969. First published in the United States by Dodd, Mead and Co., New York, 1969.

CHARACTERS: Hercule Poirot; Mrs. Ariadne Oliver; Beatrice Ardley, Judith Butler, Miranda Butler, Hugo Drake, Rowena Arabella Drake, Miss Emlyn, Dr. Ferguson, Lesley Ferrier, Jeremy Fullerton, Michael Garfield, Mrs. Goodbody, Mrs. Hargreaves, Desmond Holland, Harriet Leaman, Mrs. Llewellyn-Smythe, Elspeth McKay, Inspector Henry Timothy Raglan, Nicholas Ransome, Mrs. Reynolds, Ann Reynolds, Joyce Reynolds, Leopold Reynolds, Olga Seminoff, Superintendent Bert Spence, Janet White, Elizabeth Whittaker.

The popular and best-selling mystery author Mrs. Ariadne Oliver travels to the town of Woodleigh Common, near Medchester, to visit her friend Judith Butler and to assist in organizing a Halloween party for the children at the Elm School in town. Assorted games and entertainments are planned for the occasion, and Mrs. Oliver notes with some pleasure that there will be the game of bobbing for apples—she, of course, has a passion for apples.

During the preparations, the author is peppered with questions from the children about murder and mysteries and also encounters a loquacious thirteen year-old girl named Joyce Reynolds, who complains that Mrs. Oliver's books don't have "enough blood" in them. The girl then adds that she saw a murder herself a while ago but had not told anyone because she did not realize until recently that it really was a murder.

No one seems to pay Joyce any attention, and the party begins with a game of "snap-dragon" in the drawing room. Not long afterward, Joyce is found in the library. She has been drowned in the tub of water that was to be used for the apples. It is immediately assumed that the girl was murdered by some unknown lunatic, her claims of having seen a murder herself being roundly dismissed. Bolstering the assumption is Joyce's habit of telling lies and embellishing stories. Mrs. Oliver, however, is convinced that Joyce had said something of importance and a murderer had overheard her. She takes her belief to a fellow expert in crime, Hercule Poirot. The Belgian agrees with her, placing much significance on Joyce, for "the victim, you see, is so often the cause of the crime." Before Poirot and Mrs. Oliver can bring a murderer to justice, another victim is claimed, bringing the total number of deaths to six in this bloody case.

• • •

Hallowe'en Party presents Hercule Poirot in his thirty-first full-length novel and his fortieth book overall (including short story collections). It also constitutes his fifth mystery with Mrs. Ariadne Oliver (following *Cards on the Table,* 1936; *Mrs. McGinty's Dead,* 1952; *Dead Man's Folly,* 1956; and *Third Girl,* 1966).

The novel is unique in two other ways. First, it is only the second Christie mystery in which one of the victims is a juvenile, besides *Dead Man's Folly* (1956). Second, the novel contains the only instance of the word "lesbian" in the entire body of Christie's writings. Christie dedicated the book "To P. G. Wodehouse—whose books and stories have brightened my life for many years. Also, to show my pleasure in his having been kind enough to tell me he enjoyed my books."

"Harlequin's Lane"

PUBLISHING HISTORY: First published by William Collins Sons and Co., Ltd., London, 1930, in the short story collection *The Mysterious Mr. Quin.* First published in the United States by Dodd, Mead and Co., New York, 1930, in the short story collection *The Mysterious Mr. Quin.*

CHARACTERS: Mr. Satterthwaite; Mr. Harley Quin; Anna Denman, John Denman, Prince Oranoff, Lady Roscheimer, Molly Stanwell, Claude Wickham.

As does the Harley Quin story "The Man from the Sea," "Harlequin's Lane" presents a romantic and often bittersweet tale of lost love and fate. Mr. Satterthwaite journeys for a visit to the Denmans, Anna and John, despite considering them "dull Philistines" and despite being incapable of grasping why exactly he goes to their home repeatedly. This time he finds that the Denmans have also invited none other than Mr. Harley Quin. Whereas Quin's presence has often been accompanied by some kind of mystery or murder, this time Harley Quin brings with him forgotten love and abandoned lovers.

The planned festivities for the weekend include a ballet performance of the harlequinade. This is put in jeopardy when a minor car accident injures several performers. The disaster, however, makes possible the return to ballet of Kharsanova, the great Russian ballerina, after years of exile from her native Russia. The performance, in which she plays Columbine to Mr. Quin's Harlequin, proves her last.

• • •

"Harlequin's Lane" is one of several Christie works that include Russian émigrés. Outside the Harley Quin stories, Harlequin and Columbine, with other figures from the *commedia dell'arte,* also appeared in "The Affair at the Victory Ball."

"The Harlequin Tea Set"

PUBLISHING HISTORY: First published by Macmillan London, Ltd., 1971, in *Winter Crimes 3;* Published in the United States in *Ellery Queen's Magazine,* 1973, and collected in *The Harlequin Tea Set and Other Stories,* by G. P. Putnam's Sons, New York, 1997.

CHARACTERS: Mr. Satterthwaite; Mr. Harley Quin; Tom Addison, Beryl Gilliat, Roland Gilliat, Simon Gilliat, Timothy Gilliat, Dr. Horton, Inez Horton, Mary Horton.

Mr. Satterthwaite has another unexpected encounter with the enigmatic Mr. Harley Quin in a most fitting place, the Harlequin Café. Satterthwaite is on his way to visit a friend who now shares an estate with his son-in-law, daughter-in-law, and two grandchildren. Mr. Quin, in his usually mysterious fashion, departs Satterthwaite's company with a single word, "Daltonism."

Quin's reference—to a tendency toward being color-blind—becomes clear when Satterthwaite meets his old friend and notices that he is wearing two different colored slippers. Indeed, Daltonism lies at the heart of the mystery into which Satterthwiate becomes embroiled and constitutes a vital clue in the prevention of a murder.

The Harlequin Tea Set and Other Stories

PUBLISHING HISTORY: First published by G. P. Putnam's Sons, New York, 1997.

CONTENTS:
"The Edge"
"The Actress"
"While the Light Lasts"
"The House of Dreams"
"The Lonely God"
"Manx Gold"
"Within a Wall"
"The Mystery of the Spanish Chest"
"The Harlequin Tea Set"

All the stories in this collection were previously unpublished in the United States except "The Mystery of the Spanish Chest," which was published in *The Regatta Mystery and Other Stories* in 1939. (For details on the publishing history of other stories, please see under individual titles.)

"Have You Got Everything You Want?"

PUBLISHING HISTORY: First published by William Collins Sons and Co., Ltd., London, 1934, in the short story collection *Parker Pyne Investigates.* First published in the United States by Dodd, Mead and Co., New York, 1934, in the short story collection *Mr. Parker Pyne, Detective.*

CHARACTERS: Mr. Parker Pyne; Elsie Jeffries, Edward Jeffries, Madame Subayska.

The collection *Parker Pyne Investigates,* marks a sharp change in both setting and substance when compared to the types of cases usually undertaken by Parker Pyne. The remaining stories (see *Parker Pyne Investigates* for details) have as their backdrops exotic locales, including this particular case, which is set on board the Simplon Express and climaxes in Trieste. Subsequent stories are set in Baghdad, Damascus, and on the Nile.

"Have You Got Everything You Want?" opens with Mr. Parker Pyne traveling on the Simplon Express to Trieste. On the train, he meets a young American woman, Elsie Jeffries, who recognizes his name and his remarkable powers to solve personal problems. Her particular dilemma stems from the accidental discovery of a message preserved on an ink blotter and written by her husband: "Wife . . . Simplon Express . . . just before Venice would be the best time." Parker Pyne takes command of the situation and remains with Elsie on the train near Venice. Surprising events follow, and, to Elsie's disappointment, her jewels are stolen. The only suspect, Madame Subayska, does not have the jewels on her person or in her possession. Parker Pyne, of course, solves the case, returning the jewels and offering some peculiar advice to Edward Jeffries, Elsie's husband.

"The Herb of Death"

PUBLISHING HISTORY: First published by William Collins Sons and Co., Ltd., London, 1932, in the short story collection *The Thirteen Problems.* First published in the United States by Dodd, Mead and Co., New York, 1933, in the short story collection *The Tuesday Club Murders.*

CHARACTERS: Miss Jane Marple; Colonel Bantry, Dolly Bantry, Sir Ambrose Bercy, Mrs. Adelaide Carpenter, Sylvia Keene, Jerry Lorimer, Maude Wye.

During a gathering of the Tuesday Night Club, Dolly Bantry relates the case of a tragic death that initially seems to be sad but hardly overly sinister: "One day, by mistake (though very stupidly, I've always thought), a lot of foxglove leaves were picked with the sage. The ducks for dinner that night were stuffed with it and everyone was very ill, and one poor girl—Sir Ambrose's ward—died of it."

From this simple exposition, a more complex case of deliberate murder is extracted through the probing questions of the other club members, including Miss Marple. It is discovered that Sylvia Keene had not died by accident but had been murdered with digitalin. One obvious suspect was her fiancé, Jerry Lorimer, who had married a different woman, Maude Wye. Some months after Sylvia's death, Wye stood to inherit a fortune. One other seemingly insurmountable problem in proving murder was the fact that Sylvia had picked the foxglove herself, thus making impossible some preconceived notion of murder. Murder, it was, however, and Miss Marple uncovers a bitter story of unrequited love and jealousy.

• • •

This case is one of many examples of Agatha Christie's extensive knowledge of poisons and chemicals.

Hercule Poirot's Christmas

PUBLISHING HISTORY: First published by William Collins Sons and Co., Ltd., London, 1938. First published in the United States by Dodd, Mead and Co., New York, 1939, under the title *Murder for Christmas;* reprinted in paperback under the title *A Holiday for Murder.*

CHARACTERS: Hercule Poirot; Gladys Best, Mr. Charlton, Stephen Grant, Sydney Horbury, Colonel Johnson, Queenie Jones, Joan Kench, Adelaide Lee, Alfred Lee, David Lee, George Lee, Harry Lee, Hilda Lee, Lydia Lee, Magdalene Lee, Simeon Lee, Conchita Lopez, Beatrice Moscomb, Emily Reeves, Gladys Spent, Superintendent Sugden, Edward Tressilian.

Simeon Lee, the "thin, shrivelled figure of an old man" and the master of Gossington Hall, has very cruel plans for his grasping relatives when they gather at the Hall to celebrate Christmas. Even though his body is withered, his fiery eyes reveal his determination and hark back to his past, when he earned millions in South Africa by striking it rich in the gold mines. As though drawing assurance from the uncut gems and pondering the delicious oppression they will inflict, Simeon Lee withdraws from his safe a cache of uncut diamonds and strokes and talks to them.

On Christmas, the family assembles: Alfred, one of Simeon's sons, who acquiesces to his every whim; Lydia, Alfred's wife, who openly despises the controlling Simeon; Harry, another son, who has been away for years; David, Simeon's youngest son, who hates his father for destroying the happiness and the life of his mother; Simeon's son George and his wife, Magdalene, both dependent upon Simeon, especially now, as their debts have piled up; Stephen Farr, whose father had known Simeon in Africa; and Conchita Lopez, a mysterious woman who has some connection to Simeon's past.

Simeon wastes little time in tearing into his relatives about their greed and stupidity, making certain that they overhear his conversation with his attorney in which he changes his will, leaving all of them out of an inheritance. He then orders all of them out of his study to ponder their impending doom.

Dinner is served, but Simeon fails to respond. Suddenly, from upstairs, there comes the horrendous sound of murder, as furniture is hurled around in Simeon's study and Simeon lets out a hair-raising scream for his life. Rushing upstairs, the family finds Simeon sprawled on the floor, his blood spewed about the room (see below) and his diamonds missing.

The police arrive to investigate and are posed with the obvious challenge of solving a locked-room murder with no apparent suspects. It turns out, however, that the local chief constable, Colonel Johnson, is hosting a houseguest for Christmas: Hercule Poirot.

• • •

Hercule Poirot's Christmas came about as a result of a complaint. James Watts, husband of Madge, Agatha Christie's sister, expressed his personal sentiment that he wished Agatha's murders had a little more blood in them. Watts' sister-in-law replied with one of her best novels, a locked-room murder that contains one of the more brutal assassinations in her writings, although, compared to other writers, Christie's effort remains rather refined:

Heavy furniture was overturned. China vases lay splintered on the floor. In the middle of the hearthrug in front of the blazing fire lay Simeon Lee in a great pool of blood . . . Blood was splashed all-around . . .

The theme of blood is first introduced in the preface, in a line from Shakespeare's *Macbeth*: "Yet who would have thought the old man to have had so much blood in him?"

The dedication takes up directly James Watts' challenge:

My Dear James
    You have always been one of the most faithful and kindly of my readers, and I was therefore seriously perturbed when I received from you a word of criticism.
    You complained that my murders were getting too refined—anaemic, in fact. You yearned for a "good violent murder with lots of blood." A murder where there was no doubt it's being murder!
    So this is your special story—written for you. I hope it may please.
                    Your affectionate sister in law,
                    Agatha

This novel was adapted by London Weekend Television in 1995 for the series *Agatha Christie's Poirot* starring David Suchet.

Hercule Poirot's Early Cases
See *Poirot's Early Cases*

Hickory Dickory Death
See *Hickory Dickory Dock*

Hickory Dickory Dock

PUBLISHING HISTORY: First published by William Collins Sons and Co., Ltd., London, 1955. First published in United States by Dodd, Mead and Co., New York, 1955, under the title *Hickory Dickory Death*.

CHARACTERS: Hercule Poirot; Miss Felicity Lemon; Mr. Akibombo, Achmed Ali, Celia Austin, Leonard Bateson, Sergeant Bell, Nigel Chapman, Mr. Endicott, Sally Finch, Geronimo, Valerie Hobhouse, Mrs. Hubbard, Elizabeth Johnston, Chandra Lal, Patricia Lane, Colin McNabb, Mrs. Nicoletis, Inspector Sharpe, Jean Tomlinson.

Things are amiss in the normally well-oiled machine of Hercule Poirot's office. Miss Lemon, the detective's usually perfect secretary, has made three mistakes in typing one letter, a virtually impossible event. Poirot questions her and learns that she is deeply troubled by her sister, Mrs. Hubbard. A widow, Mrs. Hubbard has returned to England after many years in Singapore and has taken up a post as matron in a youth hostel in Hickory Road. Unfortunately, crimes have been taking place at the hostel; items are being stolen, but the crime spree is taking on a more sinister tinge because of the "unnatural" aspects of the thefts.

Mrs. Hubbard is invited to tea by the detective and provides him with a list of the stolen items, including a stethoscope, a rucksack, a cookbook, and a diamond ring. Upon returning to the hostel, Mrs. Hubbard is informed that one student plans to leave because of the thefts, while another one is upset at having green ink poured all over her study sheets.

Poirot arrives on the scene and makes the stunning suggestion that they call the police. This threatening development prompts one of the students, Celia Austin, to admit to some of the thefts, prompting the psychiatry student, Colin McNabb, to ask her hand in marriage so that he might observe her at close range. He never has the chance, however, as Celia is soon discovered dead from an overdose of morphine. It is clearly not suicide, as the putative suicide note is not even in her own handwriting. What began as petty thefts in a student hostel has now escalated to murder, and by the time Poirot solves the crime two more people will be dead.

• • •

Hickory Dickory Dock is one of the novels that displays Agatha Christie's vast knowledge of poisons. Two murders are committed using morphine tartrate. This is also the sixth novel to utilize a nursery rhyme in its title.

A Holiday for Murder
See *Hercule Poirot's Christmas*

The Hollow

PUBLISHING HISTORY: First published by William Collins Sons and Co., Ltd., London, 1946. First published in the United States by Dodd, Mead and Co., New York, 1946, under the title *Murder after Hours*.

CHARACTERS: Hercule Poirot; Albert, Madame Alfredge, David Angkatell, Edward Angkatell, Sir Henry Angkatell, Lady Lucy Angkatell, Gerda Christow, Dr. John Christow, Zena Christow, Beryl Collins, Mrs. Crabtree, Veronica Cray, Inspector Grange, Mr. Gudgeon, Midge Hardcastle, Elsie Patterson, Doris Saunders, Henrietta Savernake.

The beautiful estate called the Hollow will be the scene of a planned weekend gathering of friends. The lady of the estate, Lady Lucy Angkatell, has assembled an odd group of guests, realizing too late that her choices may not be ideal, given past associations, and may result in "discordant personalities boxed up indoors." Her fears are confirmed as her weekend guests arrive: Dr. John

Christow and his vulnerable and unhappy wife, Gerta; Henrietta Savernake, a fiery and capricious sculptress, who also happens to be Dr. Christow's mistress; Edward Angkatell, Sir Henry Angkatell's nephew; Edward's relative David Angkatell, a loudmouthed and sullen brute who will inherit Edward's estate should he die childless; and Midge Hardcastle, a cousin of Lady Angkatell.

Only adding to the tension is Veronica Cray, a glamorous film star and neighbor of the Angkatells. She, too, had a relationship with Dr. Christow and insists that he accompany her home after a short visit to borrow matches. Christow returns to the Angkatells—and his wife—three hours later and then receives a note the following morning summoning him to Cray's nearby cottage.

Hours later, a final guest arrives at the Hollow. Hercule Poirot has been invited for Sunday luncheon and makes his way down to the pool. There he sees a memorable vision. It looks at first as though a *tableau vivant* (or living tableau) has been staged in his honor. Dr. Christow lolls next to the pool with blood pouring out of him while his wife stands over him, a gun in her hand. Around the couple stand unmoving the other houseguests, staring in horror and disbelief at the scene before them. The detective realizes quickly that this is not some staged scene. Hurrying to Dr. Christow's side, the Belgian knows it is too late to save him, but he hears the doctor's dying word: "Henrietta."

• • •

The Hollow was the first Christie novel published after the end of World War II (a struggle that cost the life of her son-in-law, Hubert Prichard). The setting for this story, the country house of the Angkatells, was based on the real-life house of the famous British stage actor Francis L. Sullivan and his wife at Hazlemere, Surrey. Sullivan portrayed Poirot in the plays *Black Coffee* (1930) and *Peril at End House* (1940), and Christie acknowledged her use of his home in the novel by writing in her dedication: "For Larry and Danae, with apologies for using their swimming pool as the scene of a murder."

As was typical of Christie's fatigue with Hercule Poirot, she regretted including the detective in the book. She wrote in *An Autobiography* that *The Hollow* was "ruined by the introduction of Poirot. I had got used to having Poirot in my books and so naturally he had come into this one, but he was all wrong there." Christie also noted in her autobiography that the anecdote recounted in chapter six was based on actual events from Christie's childhood.

"The Horses of Diomedes"

PUBLISHING HISTORY: First published by William Collins Sons and Co., Ltd., London, 1947, in the short story collection *The Labours of Hercules*. First published in the United States by Dodd, Mead and Co., New York, 1947, in the short story collection *The Labors of Hercules*.

CHARACTERS: Hercule Poirot; Lady Carmichael, Patience Grace, General Grant, Pam Grant, Sheila Grant, Anthony Hawker, Mrs. Beryl Larkin, Dr. Michael Stoddart.

In his eighth of twelve labors in emulation of Hercules, Hercule Poirot sets out to tame the horses of Diomedes. In mythology, the horses were mares, owned by Diomedes of Thrace, who raised them to be man-eaters by feeding them human flesh. In Poirot's case, the "mares" are the daughters of General Grant, of Mertonshire.

Poirot is introduced to the case by young Dr. Michael Stoddart, who brings him to see a patient, Mrs. Patience Grace. She has fallen prey to a cocaine addiction, "stuff that starts off making you feel just grand and with everything in the garden lively, it peps you up and you feel you can do twice as much as you usually do. Take too much of it and you get violent mental excitement, delusions, and delirium."

Making his way to Ashley Lodge, the residence of General Grant and his four daughters, Poirot puts an end to a gang of clever cocaine dealers. He also uncovers the ringleader, a master conspirator who has long escaped any suspicion.

• • •

In classical mythology, Hercules tamed the horses of Diomedes by feeding them the flesh of Diomedes. Similarly, Poirot ends the activities of the mares in this case by forcing them to acknowledge the presence of Diomedes in their own lives.

"The Hound of Death"

PUBLISHING HISTORY: First published by William Collins Sons and Co., Ltd., London, 1933, in the short story collection *The Hound of Death and Other Stories*. First published in the United States by Dodd, Mead and Co., New York, 1971, in the short story collection *The Golden Ball and Other Stories*.

CHARACTERS: Sister Marie Angelique, Mr. Anstruther, Dr. Rose, William P. Ryan.

"The Hound of Death" continues the supernatural theme of the other works in *The Hound of Death and Other Stories*. In this story, more reminiscent of H. P. Lovecraft and August Derleth than Hercule Poirot, a young Englishman named Anstruther visits his sister in Cornwall and learns of a unique Belgian nun. Sister Marie Angelique supposedly destroyed an entire convent in Belgium when it was occupied by invading Germans during World War I. The symbol of the power that she unleashed was a shadow burned onto one of the surviving walls of the convent in the shape of a dog or hound.

It turns out that Sister Angelique is living in Cornwall, in a house in Trearne, Foldbridge. The nun is a source of great interest to the young doctor in the town, Dr. Rose, especially as he becomes convinced that she has been able to tap into some arcane power from an ancient time.

The Hound of Death and Other Stories

PUBLISHING HISTORY: First published by William Collins Sons and Co., Ltd., London, 1933.

CONTENTS:
"The Hound of Death"
"The Red Signal"

"The Fourth Man"
"The Gipsy"
"The Lamp"
"Wireless"
"The Witness for the Prosecution"
"The Mystery of the Blue Jar"
"The Strange Case of Sir Arthur Carmichael"
"The Call of Wings"
"The Last Séance"
"SOS"

The Hound of Death and Other Stories is notable in ways. First, it offers a collection of stories that are taken up mostly by the supernatural in some form or another. Also, one of tales that does not involve the supernatural is the most famous of the collection and one of Christie's most popular works, "The Witness for the Prosecution." Interestingly, "The Witness for the Prosecution" in its original incarnation as a short story has largely been forgotten in favor of its two successive lives—as a stage play and a film (produced in 1953 and 1957 respectively; the film version starred Charles Laughton, Tyrone Power, and Marlene Dietrich; another film version was released in 1982).

Although this collection was not published in the United States, all the stories in it were available there in later collections (see under individual titles for details). "The Red Signal," "The Mystery of the Blue Jar," and "The Fourth Man" were adapted by Thames Television and aired from 1983 to 1985.

"The House at Shiraz"

PUBLISHING HISTORY: First published by William Collins Sons and Co., Ltd., London, 1934, in the short story collection *Parker Pyne Investigates*. First published in the United States by Dodd, Mead and Co., New York, 1934, in the short story collection *Mr. Parker Pyne, Detective*.

CHARACTERS: Mr. Parker Pyne; Lady Esther Carr, Muriel King, Herr Schlagel.

While traveling through the Middle East,

Parker Pyne visits the Persian city of Shiraz. There, he becomes intrigued with a magnificent house, "all tiled in blue and rose and yellow, set in a green garden with water and orange trees and roses." Even more interesting to Parker Pyne is the house's occupant, Lady Esther Carr, a wealthy British eccentric who will have nothing "to do with anything or anyone British." The house was darkened some three years before by the tragic death of Muriel King, Lady Esther's maid, who fell to her death while carrying a breakfast tray to her mistress. Mr. Parker Pyne pays the English-woman a visit and unravels a tale of deception, death, and unrequited love.

• • •

The house at Shiraz was based on a real, albeit empty, house in that Persian city that Christie visited in 1933 with her archaeologist husband, Max Mallowan, according to his memoirs.

"The House of Dreams"

PUBLISHING HISTORY: First published in *Sovereign Magazine,* London, 1926. First published in the United States by G. P. Putnam's Sons, New York, 1997, in the short story collection *The Harlequin Tea Set and Other Stories.*

CHARACTERS: Allegra Kerr, John Segrave, Maisie Wetterman.

As the first line announces, "This is the story of John Segrave—of his life, which was unsatisfactory; of his love, which was unsatisfied; of his dreams, and of his death . . ." Segrave fails to find the kind of happiness in life that he seeks, but his thoughts and his hopes are ultimately shaped and directed by a dream. He is blessed with a dream of a house, a perfect white house on high ground. He longs to see more of it, for all that is visible is the outside, with the promise of beholding more in the days to come. Setting off for adventures in Africa, he falls ill with fever and, at last, has the chance to enter the house of his dreams—but at what price?

• • •

"The House of Dreams" is one of the short stories in the 1997 collection *The Harlequin Tea Set*

and Other Stories. The story had never before been published in the United States, nor had it been collected in any other compilation.

"The House of Lurking Death"

PUBLISHING HISTORY: First published by William Collins Sons and Co., Ltd., London, 1929, in the short story collection *Partners in Crime.* First published in the United States by Dodd, Mead and Co., New York, 1929, in the short story collection *Partners in Crime.*

CHARACTERS: Tommy Beresford; Tuppence Beresford; Dr. Burton, Mary Chilcott, Hannah, Lois Hargreaves, Miss Logan, Esther Quant, Dennis Radclyffe.

Lois Hargreaves comes to the International Detective Agency terrified for her life. Recently made wealthy, thanks to an inheritance from an aunt, Lois received a box of chocolates that contain arsenic. Several members of the household are already ill, and by the time the Beresfords arrive on the scene two people are dead and a third is perilously close to death.

• • •

As is their custom in the collection *Partners in Crime,* Tommy and Tuppence solve this case while adopting the personae of detectives from fiction. For this particular investigation, Tommy adopts the character and methods of Inspector Gabriel Hanaud, the brilliant French detective created by Alfred Edward Woodley Mason (d. 1948), while Tuppence becomes Mr. Ricardo, Hanaud's faithful assistant.

"How Does Your Garden Grow?"

PUBLISHING HISTORY: First published by Dodd, Mead and Co., New York, 1939, in the short story collection *The Regatta Mystery and Other Stories.*

CHARACTERS: Hercule Poirot; Felicity Lemon; Amelia Barrowby, Henry Delafontaine, Mary Delafontaine, Katrina Rieger, Inspector Sims.

The Belgian detective receives a letter, marked "Private and Confidential," from Amelia Barrowby, requesting a meeting with him to discuss certain concerns and to determine if her suspicions are correct. Intrigued, Poirot replies that he will see her at any time. No reply is forthcoming, however, and Poirot learns that his prospective client is dead. Determined to find out the significance of Miss Barrowby's letter, he sets out for Rosebank, Charman's Green. Arriving at the deceased's house, Poirot is reminded instantly of a peculiar English children's rhyme, a little song that has great importance in the solution of the case.

Meeting Miss Barrowby's aunt, Mary Delafontaine, and her weak-willed husband, the detective learns from Inspector Sims the exact details of Miss Barrowby's death. She had eaten dinner on Tuesday night and had become convulsively ill. By the time a doctor arrived, the elderly woman had died. As the matter was rather odd, the doctor refused to sign a death certificate and an autopsy subsequently found her death to have been caused by a large dose of strychnine.

The matter is complicated by the fact that it seems impossible for her to have ingested such a large dose of poison, given its bitter taste. The police suspect the Delafontaines, but the evidence points instead to Miss Barrowby's helper and nurse-companion, Katrina Rieger. Poirot unmasks a murderer, using the children's rhyme and the essential symmetry of a charming garden.

• • •

This story was adapted by London Weekend Television in 1991 for the series *Agatha Christie's Poirot* starring David Suchet. The plot of "How Does Your Garden Grow?" served as the basis for the expanded and much more developed plot in *Dumb Witness* (1937). The story also marked the first appearance of Miss Felicity Lemon as Poirot's extremely competent secretary.

"The Idol House of Astarte"

PUBLISHING HISTORY: First published by William Collins Sons and Co., Ltd., London, 1932, in the short story collection, *The Thirteen Problems.* First published in the United States by Dodd, Mead and Co., New York, 1933, in the short story collection *The Tuesday Club Murders.*

CHARACTERS: Miss Jane Marple; Dr. Pender; Diana Ashley, Elliot Haydon, Richard Haydon, Lady Mannering, Dr. Symonds.

One of the seemingly insoluble murder mysteries presented by members of the Tuesday Night Club, this particular story is presented by the old clergyman Dr. Pender. Set in the very atmospheric region of Dartmoor, the case involves the peculiar goings-on in the large estate Silent Grove, which had recently been purchased by Sir Richard Haydon. There, in the center of a grove steeped in the atmosphere of ancient trees, where sacred rites had been performed, stands the Idol House of Astarte, a summerhouse made of stone. The guests at the house take part in a fancy dress party and one, Diana Ashley, is seemingly overwhelmed by the spiritual power of the Idol House, proclaiming herself the Priestess of Astarte and promising death to any who might approach. Ignoring her warnings, Richard Haydon comes too near and, inexplicably, falls to the ground and is found dead. He has been stabbed in the chest, although no one was close enough to have committed the deed. Miss Marple immediately knows the truth, and Dr. Pender admits she is correct, for he had learned the truth five years after the tragedy took place.

"In a Glass Darkly"

PUBLISHING HISTORY: First published by William Collins Sons and Co., Ltd., London, 1929, in the short story collection *Partners in Crime.* First published in the United States by Dodd, Mead and Co., New York, 1929, in the short story collection *Partners in Crime.*

CHARACTERS: Alan Carslake, Sylvia Carslake, Charles Crawley, Derek Wainwright.

The narrator of the story, a houseguest at Badgeworthy, the country home of the Carswells, beholds a frightening reflection in the mirror of his bedroom. A man with a vicious scar is strangling a beautiful young woman. Shaken by the vision, the guest is given an even greater shock at dinner that evening when he is introduced to the very couple he had seen in the mirror.

• • •

This story was adapted in 1982 by Thames Television.

"The Incredible Theft"

PUBLISHING HISTORY: First published by William Collins Sons and Co., Ltd., London, 1937, in the short story collection *Murder in the Mews.* First published in the United States by Dodd, Mead and Co., New York, 1937, in the short story collection *Dead Man's Mirror and Other Stories.*

CHARACTERS: Hercule Poirot; Carlisle Charlie, Air Marshal Sir George Carrington, Lady Julia Carrington, Reggie Carrington, Leonie, Mrs. Macatta, Lord Charles McLaughlin Mayfield, Mrs. Vanderlyn.

Lord Mayfield, the minister of defence, known as the most excellent of hosts, invites to his home for a weekend conference a variety of influential and powerful figures in political society, including Air Marshal Sir George Carrington, Mrs. Macatta, M.P., and the rather enigmatic Mrs. Vanderlyn, an American who has had three husbands—an Italian, a Russian, and a German. It seems that Lord Mayfield has fallen for "the siren," Mrs. Vanderlyn, but he gives assurance instead to Carrington that he is merely baiting the dangerous woman. Mrs. Vanderlyn is considered a possible agent for a European power, and Mayfield hopes to trap her. This scheme apparently goes horribly awry when the plans for a top-secret bomber mysteriously disappear from Mayfield's office.

At the urging of Carrington, Mayfield summons Hercule Poirot to his estate and impresses upon him the need for discretion and the likelihood that Mrs. Vanderlyn has somehow orchestrated the theft. Mayfield swears that he saw a man in the shadows during the moment that the maid screamed and his secretary ran out to investigate. From the first, Poirot has problems with this chain of events and sets out methodically to investigate. Slowly, the sleuth reveals the complete picture of events in the house during the weekend. He succeeds brilliantly, but the plans are never recovered.

• • •

This case was adapted by London Weekend Television in 1989 for the series *Agatha Christie's Poirot* starring David Suchet. "The Incredible Theft" has a plot very similar to that of the much shorter "The Submarine Plans."

"Ingots of Gold"

PUBLISHING HISTORY: First published by William Collins Sons and Co., Ltd., London, 1932, in the short story collection *The Thirteen Problems.* First published in the United States by Dodd, Mead, and Co., New York, 1933, in the short story collection *The Tuesday Club Murders.*

CHARACTERS: Miss Jane Marple; Raymond West; Inspector Badgworth, Sir Henry Clithering, Bill Higgins, Mr. Kelvin, John Newman.

One of the mysteries recounted by the Tuesday Night Club, of which Miss Jane Marple is a member, "Ingots of Gold" is told by Raymond West, Miss Marple's nephew, who is also a talented novelist and poet. West's artistic tendencies and naiveté are on display in the story. Invited to visit the Cornish village of Polperran by his friend John Newman, West is hopeful of taking part in the quest for the sunken Spanish treasure ship *Juan Fernandez,* which sank centuries before off the rocky coast. Another ship, the recently sunk *Otranto,* is also gaining much attention from authorities because of its precious cargo. It does not take long, of course, for West to become embroiled in a scheme to steal the sunken treasure of the *Otranto,* a plot that leaves Newman bound and gagged and the evidence pointing toward the landlord of the local pub, the Three Anchors.

"Italian Nobleman, The Adventure of the"

PUBLISHING HISTORY: First published in *Sketch* magazine, London, 1923; reprinted by John Lane, London, 1924, in the short story collection *Poirot Investigates*. First published in the United States by Dodd, Mead and Co., New York, 1925, in the short story collection *Poirot Investigates*.

CHARACTERS: Hercule Poirot; Captain Arthur Hastings; Signor Paolo Ascanio, Count Foscatini, Mr. Graves, Dr. Hawker., Miss Rider.

While enjoying a visit with their friend Dr. Hawker, Poirot and Hastings are interrupted by Miss Rider, the good doctor's housekeeper. She informs the physician that a terrible call has come from someone who has cried out for help: "They've killed me!" Hawker recognizes the name as a patient, Count Foscatini. Poirot and Hastings accompany him to Foscatini's flat in Regent's Court and find him seated at a large writing table, battered to death. He was still grasping the telephone base with his right hand, and the weapon, a statuette of marble covered in blood, stood in a spot clearly denoting its hasty placement. Adding to the grisly scene was a round table in the center of the room from which three chairs had been pushed back and upon which a meal had been consumed.

Poirot is soon impressed with the murderer, observing, "We have decidedly to do with a man of method." He also has severe doubts about the suspect arrested for Foscatini's murder, Signor Paolo Ascanio, an Italian who had visited Foscatini on the very night of his murder. Important clues in fingering the real murderer are a fastened window, a smashed clock stuck at 8:47 P.M., and an uneaten rice soufflé. Hastings is forced to write at the end of his account, "Poirot was right. He always is, confound him!"

• • •

This case was adapted by London Weekend Television for the series *Agatha Christie's Poirot* starring David Suchet.

"Jane in Search of a Job"

PUBLISHING HISTORY: First published by William Collins Sons and Co., Ltd., London, 1934, in the short story collection *The Listerdale Mystery*. First published in the United States by Dodd, Mead and Co., New York, 1971, in the short story collection *The Golden Ball and Other Stories*.

CHARACTERS: Jane Cleveland, Detective Inspector Farrell, Colonel Kranin, Grand Duchess Pauline, Princess Poporensky, Count Stylptitch.

A young woman in need of work, the lovely Jane Cleveland, reads the pages of the *Daily Leader* for a likely position. The paper yields rather depressing results, until she reads a curious advertisement:

> *If a young lady of twenty-five to thirty years of age, eyes dark blue, very fair hair, black lashes and brows, straight nose, slim figure, height five feet seven inches, good mimic and able to speak French, will call at 7 Endersleigh Street between 5 and 6 P.M., she will hear of something to her advantage.*

Going to the appointed location, Jane takes part in a massive competition with other young women and is then sent to Harridge's Hotel for the final decision by her mysterious would-be employer. Once there, she is surveyed by a group of Russians, including Count Stylptitch and Princess Poporensky, and is finally approved for some mysterious task by the Grand Duchess Pauline of Ostrova, who bears a very striking resemblance to Jane. Her job soon becomes clear: She is to impersonate the grand duchess during her visit to London in order to foil a possible threat to the noblewoman's life. The role proves to be full of surprises, and Jane faces a grim future only to be saved by a hero with an eye for shoe heels.

• • •

This story was adapted by Thames Television in 1983 for the series *The Agatha Christie Hour.*

"The Jewel Robbery at the Grand Metropolitan"

PUBLISHING HISTORY: First published in *Sketch* magazine, London, 1923–1924; reprinted by John Lane, London, 1924, in the short story collection *Poirot Investigates*. First published in the United States by Dodd, Mead and Co., New York, 1925, in the short story collection *Poirot Investigates.*

CHARACTERS: Hercule Poirot; Captain Arthur Hastings; Célestine, Mrs. Opalsen, Ed Opalsen.

Hercule Poirot and Captain Hastings investigate the seemingly inexplicable theft of a piece of jewelry. Their involvement stems from Poirot's determination to find "a change of air," as he and Hastings journey to Brighton for a restful weekend in the Grand Metropolitan Hotel. The plush surroundings, in particular the marvelous dresses and jewels being worn by the guests, cause Poirot to wish that he had turned his "brains to crime instead of detection." The interest in jewels continues after Poirot meets some acquaintances of Hastings, the Opalsens; Ed Opalsen, a rich stockholder who made a fortune in the recent oil boom, had given his wife a string of pearls. As Poirot has seen some of the finest gems and jewels of the time, Mrs. Opalsen is eager to display her prized possession. She disappears to retrieve her pearls, but soon Poirot is summoned upstairs, where he is told of the incredible theft of the jewels. Instantly, Poirot agrees to undertake the investigation.

The devious suspect in this crime is the maid, Célestine, especially as she is always present with the jewels, even when the chambermaid enters the room to perform her daily functions. A search of Célestine and her belongings turns up nothing, and a similar search of the chambermaid is equally fruitless. Suddenly, however, a pair of jewels is discovered in a most unlikely place—the bed of the maid, Célestine. Poirot has his doubts and solves the case by deciphering a set of clues that includes a set of fake pearls, a strange white card, and French chalk. Settling the matter to his own satisfaction, Poirot suggests to Hastings that they re-turn for another weekend in Brighton, this time at the expense of Ed Opalsen, who gave the detective a generous reward.

• • •

This case was adapted by London Weekend Television in 1993 for the series *Agatha Christie's Poirot* starring David Suchet.

The title of this short story was initially considered for the title of the collection *Poirot Investigates* after the first proposed title, *The Curious Disappearance of the Opalsen Pearls,* was rejected.

"Johnnie Waverly, The Adventure of"

PUBLISHING HISTORY: First published by Dodd, Mead and Co., New York, 1950, in the short story collection *Three Blind Mice and Other Stories.*

CHARACTERS: Hercule Poirot; Captain Arthur Hastings; Miss Collins, Tredwell, Ada Waverly, Johnnie Waverly, Marcus Waverly, Miss Jessie Withers.

Hercule Poirot is consulted by an exceedingly distraught Mr. and Mrs. Waverly. Their son, young Johnnie Waverly, has been kidnapped, despite the best efforts of the police to prevent it, and they have turned to Poirot as their last hope. Ten days prior, the Waverlys had received a note demanding 25,000 pounds or their son would be taken. Mr. Waverly had dismissed this as nonsense, but the note was followed by a second demand five days later. As his wife was disturbed by the matter, Mr. Waverly contacted Scotland Yard. They, too, were of the view that the affair was not a serious one, at least until the day when the next note arrived: "You have not paid. Your son will be taken from you at twelve o'clock noon tomorrow, the twenty-ninth. It will cost fifty thousand pounds to recover him." Apparently calmed by Scotland Yard's assurances, Waverly returned home only to discover a final note pinned to a pillow in his own room: "At twelve o'clock." Sure enough, the next day Johnnie disappeared, despite every effort by the Yard to keep him safe. The boy was taken at exactly noon, as had been threatened.

Poirot considers the case a "pleasing little

problem, obscure and charming." With his customary skill at cutting to the heart of the matter, Poirot focuses on three main points: the curious poisoning of Mrs. Waverly, the pinning of the note to the pillow, and the setting of a clock ten minutes fast. The detective secures the return of the boy, but in a generous decision, he permits the culprit to escape justice.

• • •

The name of the butler to the Waverly family, Tredwell, was used in two other cases: *The Secret of Chimneys* and *The Secret Adversary.* This case was adapted by London Weekend Television in 1989 for the series *Agatha Christie's Poirot* starring David Suchet.

"The Kidnapped Prime Minister"

PUBLISHING HISTORY: First published in *Sketch* magazine, London, 1923–1924; reprinted by John Lane, London, 1924, in the short story collection *Poirot Investigates.* First published in the United States by Dodd, Mead and Co., New York, 1925, in the short story collection *Poirot Investigates.*

CHARACTERS: Hercule Poirot; Captain Arthur Hastings; Chief Inspector James Japp; Captain Daniels, Bernard Dodge, Bertha Ebenthal, Lord Estair, David MacAdam, O'Murphy.

In one of his most important cases, Hercule Poirot is commissioned by the British government to find Prime Minister David MacAdam. The P.M. disappeared on the very eve of an important conference regarding what Captain Hastings describes vaguely as the end of World War I. While it is publicly revealed that an attempt was made to assassinate MacAdam, it is not generally known that the P.M. disappeared somewhere between Boulogne and Paris. His presence is desperately needed at the conference, especially as the personality of "Fighting Mac" will be decisive in overcoming a growing pacifist sentiment.

Traveling to Boulogne, Poirot there ceases his frantic energies and checks into a hotel. To his astonished companions, he makes a startling statement that reveals much of his method: "It is not so that a good detective should act, eh? . . . He must be full of energy. He must rush to and fro. He should prostrate himself on the dusty road and seek the marks of tires through a little glass. He must gather up the cigarette-end, the fallen match?" Instead, Poirot sits for five hours, "motionless, blinking his eyelids like a cat, his green eyes flickering and becoming steadily greener and greener."

Poirot and his companions set off for England. Having used the clues at hand and his many "little grey cells," Poirot stuns Hastings and other officials by retrieving the P.M. The following morning, the detective receives from the P.M. one of the most memorable telegrams of his life: "In time."

• • •

This case was adapted by London Weekend Television in 1990 for the series *Agatha Christie's Poirot* starring David Suchet. Poirot had another case involving a prime minister in "The Augean Stables," in *The Labours of Hercules.*

"The Kidnapping of Johnnie Waverly"

See "Johnnie Waverly, The Adventure of"

"The King of Clubs"

PUBLISHING HISTORY: First published by Dodd, Mead and Co., New York, 1951, in the short story collection *The Under Dog and Other Stories.*

CHARACTERS: Hercule Poirot; Captain Arthur Hastings; Mr. Oglander, Mrs. Oglander, Miss Oglander, Prince Paul of Maurania, Henry Reedburn, Valerie Saintclair, Madame Zara.

Hercule Poirot is consulted by Prince Paul of Maurania in the hopes that the detective can assist his fiancée, the famous dancer Valerie Saintclair, who has become embroiled in the murder of Henry Reedburn, the powerful and most unpopular impresario. As reported in the paper, a middle-class English family, the Oglanders, was at home and enjoying an evening of bridge when, suddenly, Valerie Saintclair burst through their French windows. Her dress was stained with blood, and she uttered one word, "Murder!" before sinking into unconsciousness. The murder of which she spoke was that of Reedburn, whose skull had been crushed. Seemingly anticipating the grisly event was the warning given to Valerie by Zara, a clairvoyant who warned her of "a man who holds you in his power . . . Beware of the king of clubs." As Reedburn was this man and as he was in love with Valerie—an unrequited love—the prince is deeply concerned that Valerie might somehow have been responsible for the crime.

Poirot and Hastings set out for Streatham and the scene of the murder, Reedburn's spacious and modern house, Mon Désir. After investigating the well-worn crime site, the sleuth wanders over to Daisymead, the neighboring house, belonging to the Oglanders. At first denied access to Valerie by the curiously protective Oglanders, the detective finally meets the dancer and hears her account of the crime. Her description of the tramp who struck Reedburn elicits from Poirot the simple declaration that "Hercule Poirot does not hunt down tramps." The true solution to the crime hinges for Poirot on the back window of Mon Désir and the absence of the telltale king of clubs from a pack of cards.

• • •

This case was adapted by London Weekend Television in 1989 for the series *Agatha Christie's Poirot* starring David Suchet. "The King of Clubs" presents one of the rare cases in which Poirot permits the real killer to escape justice.

The Labours of Hercules

PUBLISHING HISTORY: First published by William Collins Sons and Co., Ltd., London, 1947. First published in the United States by Dodd, Mead and Co., New York, 1947, under the title *The Labors of Hercules.*

CONTENTS:
The Labours of Hercules features an introductory chapter and twelve stories:
"The Nemean Lion"
"The Lernean Hydra"
"The Arcadian Deer"
"The Erymanthean Boar"
"The Augean Stables"
"The Stymphalean Birds"
"The Cretan Bull"
"The Horses of Diomedes"
"The Girdle of Hyppolita"
"The Flock of Geryon"
"The Apples of Hesperides"
"The Capture of Cerberus"

Perhaps the best collection of Christie's short stories, *The Labours of Hercules* uses a unifying theme to pull together twelve examples that show off the formidable "little grey cells" of Hercule Poirot. The Belgian ponders retirement after a brilliant career so that he can settle down and cultivate vegetable marrows. The thought occurs to him, however, that before his retirement he will undertake twelve labors, in emulation of the mythological hero Hercules. The detective thinks very little of the ancient Hercules: "Hero indeed . . . What was he but a large muscular creature of low intelligence and criminal tendencies." The result is twelve adventures to match the feats of his famed namesake. While the stories seem at times rather a stretch (the "Nemean lion," for example, is a Pekingese), several offer up some genuinely dangerous enemies for Poirot to defeat. The most memorable of the stories is generally considered "The Capture of Cerberus," for it reunites Poirot with Countess Vera Rossakoff in the unlikely location of hell.

"The Lamp"

PUBLISHING HISTORY: First published by William Collins Sons and Co., Ltd., London, 1933, in the short story collection *The Hound of Death and Other Stories.* First published in the United States by Dodd, Mead and Co., New York, 1971, in the short story collection *The Golden Ball and Other Stories.*

CHARACTERS: Mrs. Lancaster, Geoffrey Lancaster, Mr. Raddish, Mr. Winburn.

A moving tale of the supernatural, "The Lamp"

features a haunted house and the love of one child for another; an innocent love that sets a captive spirit free. The events take place in an old house, No. 19, in Weyminster, a town that "was averse from ghosts and considered them hardly respectable except as the appanage of a 'county family.' " No. 19 is thus not advertised as haunted, but it has remained unoccupied for years. Mrs. Lancaster approves of the house and takes it, ghosts and all. She moves in with her father, Mr. Winburn, and her son, Geoffrey Lancaster, and soon seems to hear evidence of the ghost—the spiritual remnant of a poor little boy who died under tragic circumstances.

Young Geoffrey loves the house, but he shocks his mother by asking her why he cannot be permitted to play with the "other" little boy who sits in the attic floor crying. Mrs. Lancaster's father understands fully the import of the encounter, quoting some poetry to drive home his point:

"What Lamp has Destiny to guide
Her little Children stumbling in the Dark?"
"A Blind Understanding," Heaven replied.

Soon after, Geoffrey falls ill with a long-present lung problem. In his suffering, the child makes possible the freedom of eternal happiness for a dead spirit.

"The Last Séance"

PUBLISHING HISTORY: First published by William Collins Sons and Co., London, 1933, in the short story collection *The Hound of Death and Other Stories*.

CHARACTERS: Raoul Daubreuil, Elise, Madame Exe, Madame Simone.

"The Last Séance" is one of Christie's tales that showcases the supernatural, especially the supernatural power that can be cruelly misused by someone without scruples. It presents the final, disastrous séance of the brilliant medium Madame Simone. Planning to retire from her work as a medium, Simone agrees to perform one last séance, at the behest of her fiancé, Raoul, for a grieving mother, Madame Exe. Madame Exe hopes to contact her deceased daughter, a spirit who has displayed the unusual ability to manifest herself in physical form during previous séances. Once under way, Madame Exe reveals her true plans for the session, and the séance sinks into horror.

"The Lemesurier Inheritance"

PUBLISHING HISTORY: First published by Dodd, Mead and Co., New York, 1951, in the short story collection *The Under Dog and Other Stories*.

CHARACTERS: Hercule Poirot; Captain Arthur Hastings; John Gardiner, Hugo Lemesurier, Major Roger Lemesurier, Ronald Lemesurier, Sadie Lemesurier, Captain Vincent Lemesurier.

Hercule Poirot confronts a deadly curse that, over the centuries, has claimed the firstborn sons of the Lemesurier family. He is introduced to the grim affair during World War I, when he meets Captain Vincent Lemesurier and his uncle, Hugo, and cousin, Roger. The latter relates how the family fell prey during the Middle Ages to a curse by which no firstborn son ever succeeds to the estate. In what seems a peculiar twist, Vincent—the firstborn—has remained untouched, while his two younger brothers have been killed. A short time later, however, Poirot is informed of Captain Vincent's death under odd circumstances, followed by other Lemesuriers in swift and gruesome succession.

The detective is consulted by the wife of Hugo Lemesurier—now the heir—who is desperately worried about the safety of her older son, Ronald. In the previous six months, the boy has had three narrow escapes from death, and Mrs. Lemesurier is convinced that a real-life assailant, and not the family curse, is at work. Poirot accepts the commission to keep the boy safe, journeying northward to the Lemesurier estate.

The detective observes to Hastings that the recent deaths in the Lemesurier household could easily have been planned. Hugo, meanwhile, seems resigned to the possibility that Ronald will soon be taken by the curse. His words prove prophetic, as Ronald's life is definitely placed in danger.

• • •

This case is yet another in which Agatha Christie's extensive knowledge of poison and chemicals—including atropine and formic acid—is displayed.

"The Lernean Hydra"

PUBLISHING HISTORY: First published by William Collins Sons and Co., Ltd., London, 1947, in the short story collection *The Labours of Hercules*. First published in the United States by Dodd, Mead and Co., New York, 1947, in the short story collection *The Labors of Hercules*.

CHARACTERS: Hercule Poirot; George(s), Gladys, Nurse Harrison, Beatrice King, Miss Leatheran, Jean Moncrieffe, Dr. Charles Oldfield.

In the second of his cases emulating the labors of Hercules, Poirot is consulted by Dr. Oldfield, who is desperate to clear himself of suspicion in the death of his wife and to put an end to the vicious gossip that swirls around in his little village, Market, Loughborough, Berkshire. His wife had been an invalid for some years and then, a year before the doctor consults Poirot, she died. Foul play was soon suspected, especially when gossip spread that Oldfield was in love with his dispenser, Jean Moncrieffe. Poirot replies appropriately, "Rumor is indeed the nine-headed Hydra of Lernea, which cannot be exterminated because as fast as one head is cut off two more grow in its place."

Journeying to the country with his valet, Georges, Poirot interviews Jean Moncrieffe, a frank woman who admits to wanting to wed Dr. Oldfield. That she is the obvious suspect seems certain when a pink enamel compact is discovered among her belongings; in the compact is arsenic, the same poison that was used to murder Dr. Oldfield's wife. Poirot has other ideas, however, and proves her innocence with help of his valet.

• • •

Poirot's unflappable valet, Georges, makes an appearance in this story, one of his twenty-one participations in Poirot cases.

The Listerdale Mystery

PUBLISHING HISTORY: First published by William Collins Sons and Co., Ltd., London, 1934. This collection was not published in United States.

CONTENTS:
"The Listerdale Mystery"
"Philomel Cottage"
"The Girl in the Train"
"Sing a Song of Sixpence"
"The Manhood of Edward Robinson"
"Accident"
"Jane in Search of a Job"
"A Fruitful Sunday"
"Mr. Eastwood's Adventure"
"The Golden Ball"
"The Rajah's Emerald"
"Swan Song"

The Listerdale Mystery collection was published in the same year as *Murder on the Orient Express* and is, not surprisingly, far less known. The collection is also quite different in atmosphere and theme, for the assembled stories are generally light and frothy. There are no brutal murders solved by Poirot or Miss Marple. Rather, there are some minor mysteries, romantic misunderstandings, and the devotion of an owner for her beloved pet.

While this collection was not published in the United States, all the stories were subsequently included in other American collections. "Philomel Cottage" was adapted for the stage in 1936 and for film in 1937 and 1947. "The Girl in the Train," "Jane in Search of a Job," and "The Manhood of Edward Robinson" were adapted for television between 1983 and 1985 by Thames Television.

"The Listerdale Mystery"

PUBLISHING HISTORY: First published by William Collins Sons and Co., Ltd., London,

1934, in the short story collection *The Listerdale Mystery*. First published in the United States by Dodd, Mead and Co., New York, 1971, in the short story collection *The Golden Ball and Other Stories*.

CHARACTERS: Colonel Maurice Carfax, Lord Listerdale, Quentin, Mrs. St. Vincent, Barbara St. Vincent, Rupert St. Vincent.

Owing to the untimely death of her husband (who "was never, in any sense of the word, a businessman"), Mrs. St. Vincent and her children, Barbara and Rupert, find themselves living in grim but genteel poverty in a London flat. Their financial predicament is matched by Barbara's embarrassment about showing their home to her prospective husband, a wealthy young man. There thus is great surprise in the household when Mrs. St. Vincent picks up the *Morning Post* and reads an advertisement for a small house in Westminster: "exquisitely furnished, offered to those who would really care for it. Rent purely nominal."

Happily ensconced in their new home, the St. Vincents still ponder the mystery of why their rental is so inexpensive. Rupert then adds to their questions by remembering that 7 Cheviot Place was the home of Lord Listerdale, who walked out of the place one evening and has never been seen since. He supposedly went to East Africa and communicates with his cousin and representative, Colonel Carfax, but Rupert is convinced that foul play has taken place.

• • •

While offering an interesting mystery involving mistaken identities, "The Listerdale Mystery," like the other stories in *The Golden Ball and Other Stories,* is not a conventional murder mystery in the Christie tradition.

"The Lonely God"

PUBLISHING HISTORY: First published in *Royal Magazine,* London, 1926. First published in the United States by G. P. Putnam's Sons, New York, 1997, in the short story collection *The Harlequin Tea Set and Other Stories.*

CHARACTERS: Lonely Lady, Frank Oliver.

Frank Oliver finds himself back in London after a time in Burma and begins to note the deep sense of loneliness in his life. He has his sister and a few friends, but there is no one to claim his heart, and he seems incapable of solving the dilemma of his personal life. Aimlessly, he wanders into the British Museum and there encounters a statue of a little god from Mexico. He declares the small, all-but-forgotten deity to be the Lonely God and returns day after day to ponder the pathetic block of stone.

One day, Oliver discovers there is another "worshipper" of the Lonely God, a woman around twenty years old, "a little bit of a thing . . . in a shabby black coat and skirt that had seen their best days . . . with fair hair and blue eyes, and a wistful droop to her mouth." Gradually, hesitantly, Oliver strikes up a conversation with this "Lonely Lady." Beneath the gaze of the Lonely God, a relationship forms between two equally lonely souls, but fate must decide the ultimate path of their love.

• • •

"The Lonely God" had never been published in the United States, nor had it been collected in any compilation, prior to being included in *The Harlequin Tea Set and Other Stories.*

Lord Edgware Dies

PUBLISHING HISTORY: First published by William Collins Sons and Co., Ltd., London, 1933. First published in the United States by Dodd, Mead and Co., New York, 1933, under the title *Thirteen at Dinner.*

CHARACTERS: Hercule Poirot; Captain Arthur Hastings; Chief Inspector James Japp; Carlotta Adams, Alton, Alice Bennet, Miss Carroll, Sir Montague Corner, Jenny Driver, Ellis, Dr. Heath, George Alfred St. Vincent Marsh, Geraldine Marsh, Captain Ronald Marsh, Brian Martin, Dowager Duchess of Merton, Duke of Merton, Donald Ross, Mrs. Wilburn, Jane Wilkinson.

Hercule Poirot and Captain Hastings attend a

performance in London given by the suddenly famous actress Carlotta Adams in her one-woman show. Adams stuns the audience with her many talents, including an uncanny ability to impersonate the even-more-famous American actress Jane Wilkinson. As luck would seemingly have it, after the performance, Poirot and Hastings dine at the Savoy and see both Miss Adams and Miss Wilkinson, at separate tables. Poirot, however, does not remain long outside of Miss Wilkinson's sphere of personal interest. Her husband, Lord Edgware, arrives at the table and invites the detective and Hastings up to his wife's suite.

Poirot is greeted by Lady Edgware, who wastes little time in explaining her dilemma to the Belgian: "M. Poirot, somehow or other I've just *got* to get rid of my husband!" She has high hopes of ending her loveless marriage and marrying the exceedingly wealthy and most eligible duke of Merton, but Lord Edgware has thus far refused steadfastly to grant her a divorce. To Hastings's considerable surprise, Poirot accepts her request and sets off to secure her divorce.

Events take an unexpected turn right from the start. Lord Edgware confides to Poirot that he regrets bitterly his marriage to Jane Wilkinson and has already written his wife with his acceptance of her request for a divorce. This news comes as a surprise to Jane, as she claims never to have received the letter.

Once again, however, a shocking development takes place. Lord Edgware is found stabbed to death in his library, and, as the butler attests, the last person to see him alive was Lady Edgware. Jane is thus arrested by Scotland Yard, but she has an unimpeachable alibi: At the time of the murder, she was at dinner with a room full of friends at the home of Sir Montague Corner.

• • •

Lord Edgware Dies was written by Agatha Christie between 1931 and 1932, while her husband, the archaeologist Max Mallowan, was on a dig in Nineveh, in northern Iraq. As ever, she accompanied him, but part of the book was completed while she was on vacation in Rhodes. Her husband worked on the dig as an assistant to Reginald Campbell Thompson (d. 1941), a noted archaeologist, to whom she dedicated the book, along with Thompson's wife, Barbara. The novel has been adapted twice for film and television. The first adaptation was the 1934 film starring August Trevor as Hercule Poirot. The second adaptation, this time for television, was made in 1985 by Warner Brothers Television and released under the title *Thirteen at Dinner.* It starred Peter Ustinov as Hercule Poirot; David Suchet, who went on to fame as Hercule Poirot on television, played Inspector Japp.

"The Lost Mine"

PUBLISHING HISTORY: First published in *Sketch* magazine, London, 1923–1924; reprinted by John Lane, London, 1924, in the short story collection *Poirot Investigates.* First published in the United States by Dodd, Mead and Co., New York, 1925, in the short story collection *Poirot Investigates.*

CHARACTERS: Hercule Poirot; Captain Arthur Hastings; Mr. Dyer, Charles Lester, Mr. Wu Ling, Inspector Miller, Mr. Pearson.

In a case that begins with an insightful exchange between Poirot and Hastings on the subject of personal finance, the detective relates the story of his investigation into the murder of a wealthy Chinese mine owner, Wu Ling, who had journeyed to England with the records of a fabulously rich mine. He failed to attend an important meeting of the board of a major company, however, and was soon known to have disappeared. One of the directors, Mr. Pearson, initially left the matter in the hands of the police, but as no trace of Wu Ling or his luggage was found, the director turned to Poirot.

Poirot turned his attention to two main areas of search: those members of the company who knew of Wu Ling's plans and the passengers of the S.S. *Assunta,* on which the man sailed. He shared his pursuit of the latter group with Inspector Miller, a line of inquiry that proved to be fruitful, yielding two definite suspects, Charles Lester (who was heavily in debt, thanks to his gambling activities) and a Mr. Dyer (who had known connections to Chinese criminals). The pursuit of the murderer of Wu Ling took Poirot to the dark and seedy underworld of London and the infamous Limehouse. There, in the middle of an opium den, the detective concluded his investigation. For his genius, Poirot was awarded 14,000 shares of the Burma Mines, Ltd. Given his experience of fraud and murder, Poirot is understandably hesitant to purchase shares—as suggested by Hastings—in the Porcupine oil fields.

• • •

This case was adapted by London Weekend Television in 1990 for the series *Agatha Christie's Poirot* starring David Suchet. Poirot's methodical nature is not confined to his detective work or his attire, as this case demonstrates. According to the Belgian sleuth, he has a perpetual bank balance of "four hundred and forty-four pounds, four and four-pence."

"The Love Detectives"

PUBLISHING HISTORY: First published by Dodd, Mead and Co., New York, 1950, in the short story collection *Three Blind Mice and Other Stories.*

CHARACTERS: Mr. Satterthwaite; Mr. Harley Quin; Inspector Curtis, Paul Delangua, Sir James Dwighton, Lady Laura Dwighton, Janet, Jennings, Colonel Melrose, Miles.

Mr. Satterthwaite pays a visit to his old friend Colonel Melrose and is told of the recent murder of Sir James Dwighton, one of Melrose's neighbors. The obvious suspects in the crime are Mrs. Dwighton, the widow, and Paul Delangua, a family friend thrown out of the house by Sir James. A vital clue to solving the murder is two broken timepieces.

"Magnolia Blossom"

PUBLISHING HISTORY: First published by Dodd, Mead and Co., New York, 1971, in the short story collection *The Golden Ball and Other Stories.*

CHARACTERS: Richard Darrell, Theodora Darrell, Vincent Easton.

Theodora Darrell resolves to leave her husband for Vincent Easton, a young man who awaits her anxiously under a clock at Victoria Station. His nagging doubts that she will come are put to rest when he sees her walking toward him down the platform, with "a faint smile on her face." Once on the train, Vincent still cannot relax completely as he tries to decipher the thoughts of the woman he loves. Finally, he asks of her enduring silence and learns of her fear—of happiness. Arriving at Dover, they settle into a hotel to await the morning, when they will cross over to the Continent. Vincent purchases several evening papers and soon finds Theodora riveted to a headline: FAILURE OF HOBSON, JEKYLL AND LUCAS; it is the firm of her husband, Richard Darrell.

Theodora announces to Vincent calmly that she must return to her husband. Once home, she learns that her husband's firm is ruined financially and he will have to make a fresh start of things. She agrees to stay with him, especially as creditors will not be able to touch the house and marriage settlement, for they are in her name. She knows, however, that he has not told her all. At last he confesses the truth. He has been involved in dealings that, while in his mind were right and honest, authorities might consider illegal. What is more, the very papers that might destroy him can be retrieved; they are the possession of one man, Vincent Easton.

• • •

This story was adapted in 1982 by Thames Television.

"The Man from the Sea"

PUBLISHING HISTORY: First published by William Collins Sons and Co., Ltd., London, 1930, in the short story collection *The Mysterious Mr. Quin.* First published in the United States by Dodd, Mead and Co., New York, 1930, under the title *The Mysterious Mr. Quin.*

CHARACTERS: Mr. Satterthwaite; Mr. Harley Quin; Anthony Cosden, the Signora.

Mr. Satterthwaite has come to a Mediterranean island from his favorite haunts on the Riviera. Taking a walk along the edge of the cliffs near a shuttered villa called La Paz, he meets Anthony Cosden, a young man who is preparing to leap to his death. Satterthwaite talks to Cosden for a time and learns that he had actually planned to commit suicide the night before but had been prevented by the intervention of a mysterious figure. Satterthwaite realizes quickly that Cosden had received a visit from the great enigma, Mr. Harley Quin. Cosden is convinced to forego death for one more evening.

Satterthwaite next meets a tortured woman who lives in the villa. Soon, he is able to discern that her dark fate is connected in some way to that of Cosden. Their futures and their happiness are dependent upon his actions, guided as ever by the hand of Mr. Quin. Harley Quin appears again only after the storm has passed.

• • •

Mr. Satterthwaite displays his knowledge of opera in this story.

"The Manhood of Edward Robinson"

PUBLISHING HISTORY: First published by William Collins Sons and Co., Ltd., London, 1934, in the short story collection *The Listerdale Mystery*. First published in the United States by Dodd, Mead and Co., New York, 1971, in the short story collection *The Golden Ball and Other Stories*.

CHARACTERS: Lady Noreen Elliot, Maud, Edward Robinson.

Edward Robinson puts down a romantic novel and ruminates about the adventurous life led by its hero compared to his own rather dull existence. He ponders his job, his excellent health, and his commonsense fiancée, Maud. All these considerations leave him quite depressed, especially as he thinks about ways to spend the five hundred pounds that he has just won in a contest. He

knows what he wants to do with it, at least four hundred and sixty-five pounds of it—buy an elegant, fast, two-seater car.

To Edward's surprise, he walks into the auto dealership and buys the car. To his further surprise and delight, he drives out of London to enjoy his new possession. He stops for lunch and to see the sights, discovering in the pocket of the car (the glove compartment) not the muffler (or scarf) that had been put in there that morning but a diamond necklace. He realizes then that there had been an identical car parked nearby during one of his stops; he was driving the wrong car. Searching the car, Edward finds what proves to be a vital clue, a note that reads simply, "Meet me, Greane, corner of Salter's Lane, ten o'clock." Edward has a rendezvous with courage and his romantic destiny.

• • •

This story was adapted by Thames Television for the series *The Agatha Christie Hour* in 1983. The idea for the story came to Christie from a suggestion made by her husband, Archie, that they should buy a new car. She wrote in her autobiography: "Why not indeed? It was possible . . . I will confess here and now that of the two things that have excited me most in my life the first was my car; my grey bottlenosed Morris Cowley."

The Man in the Brown Suit

PUBLISHING HISTORY: First published by John Lane, London, 1924. First published in the United States by Dodd, Mead and Co., New York, 1924.

CHARACTERS: Batani, Anne Beddingfield, Suzanne Blair, L. B. Carton, Mr. and Mrs. Flemming, Anita Grünberg, Caroline James, Harry Lucas, Arthur Minks, Lord Nasby, Guy Pagett, Sir Eustace Pedler, Colonel Johnny Race, Henry Rayburn.

A popular dancer, Madame Nadina, is met in her dressing room in Paris by Count Sergius Paulovitch, and the two are soon deep in conversation about international intrigue, stolen diamonds, and the mysterious mastermind known simply as the Colonel. Nadina plans to blackmail the Colonel by using against him his superstitious fear that he will be destroyed by a beautiful woman.

Meanwhile, the young and clever Anne Beddingfield finds herself in a difficult situation. Her father, a noted anthropologist with whom she worked, has died suddenly from pneumonia, leaving her in financial straits. She has received a kind offer of housing from her father's former solicitor, but she cannot bring herself to accept. Instead, she has decided to "have adventures and see the world," although she is not entirely certain where to start. Fate takes care of this when Anne walks to the tube station and watches as a small, thin man falls backward onto the track and is electrocuted by the third rail. A man dressed in a brown suit pushes his way to the body, claims to be a doctor, and pronounces the accident victim dead. He then hurries away and leaves behind a scrap of paper containing the words "17–122 Kilmorden Castle."

Scotland Yard investigates and pronounces the death an accident, but Anne is certain that something else is involved. As the Yard refuses to accept her opinions, she decides to take matters into her own hands. She barges her way into the offices of Lord Nasby, the wealthy owner of the *Daily Budget,* and convinces him that she can get to the bottom of the mystery, especially as she has an obviously vital clue. Nasby admits that "I rather like cheek—from a pretty girl" and agrees to her proposal. Anne sets out to find Kilmorden Castle and the man in the brown suit. Her search takes her to South Africa and encounters with such colorful characters as Sir Eustace Pedler, Colonel Race, Harry Rayburn, and the dangerous criminal the Colonel.

• • •

The Man in the Brown Suit owes much of its inspiration to a friend of Agatha Christie, Major Ernest R. Belcher. The director of the British Empire Mission, Belcher traveled extensively across the globe to promote comity among the nations of the Empire. A good and a longtime friend of Archie Christie, Belcher convinced Archie to become his traveling business manager on the world tour. Archie took Agatha with him, and she devoted an entire chapter of her autobiography to the memory of the journey. She described Belcher as "a man with terrific powers of bluff . . ." The major was full of stories and even had the gall to suggest that Agatha write a book called *The Mystery of Middle House* (taken from Belcher's home, Middle House, in Dorney) and that she should include him in the story. Agatha agreed that the title might work, but she refused to budge on including him in the story. As it turned out, while the major made it into the novel, the title did not. In this very rare instance, Christie surrendered to outside pressure (see also *Death Comes As the End*); she actually included Belcher in the novel, albeit in the person of Sir Eustace Pedler. As she wrote in her autobiography, Pedler was not technically Major Belcher, "but he used Belcher's phrases and told some of Belcher's stories. He too was a master of the art of bluff, and behind the bluff could easily be sensed an unscrupulous and interesting character." As for the house, however, it didn't make it into the book: Christie changed the title to *The Man in the Brown Suit,* as *Murder at Mill House* was too close to *Murder on the Links.*

In her dedication, Christie wrote: "To E.A.B.— in memory of the journey, some lion stories, and a request that I should someday write the history of the Mill House!" The novel was adapted loosely for CBS Television in 1989, starring Stephanie Zimbalist and Edward Woodward as Sir Eustace Pedler. The novel is also remarkable for the introduction of one of Christie's recurring characters, Colonel Johnny Race. He appeared subsequently in *Cards on the Table* (1936), *Death on the Nile* (1937), and *Sparkling Cyanide* (1945).

"The Man in the Mist"

PUBLISHING HISTORY: First published by William Collins Sons and Co., Ltd., London, 1929, in the short story collection *Partners in*

Crime. First published in the United States by Dodd, Mead and Co., New York, 1929, in the short story collection *Partners in Crime.*

CHARACTERS: Tommy Beresford; Tuppence Beresford; Ellen, Mervyn Estcourt, Gilda Glen, Mrs. Honeycutt, Mr. Marvell, James Reilly.

Over cocktails at the Grand Aldington Hotel, Tommy and Tuppence drown their misery over a failed case. Their depressed spirits are soon lifted by a meeting with the actress Gilda Glen; it seems that she is being followed by someone, and the Beresfords set out to keep an eye on her, agreeing to meet with her at the White House on Morgan's Avenue. The path to Morgan's Avenue, however, is shrouded in mist, and the detectives encounter assorted characters before coming across the grisly sight of Gilda Glen. She has been battered to death by one of the people in the fog on Morgan's Avenue.

• • •

As was the case in the other stories recounted in *Partners in Crime,* Tommy and Tuppence adopt the character and manners of detectives from fiction. In this investigation, Tommy becomes the inimitable Father Brown, the priest-detective created by G. K. Chesterton (d. 1936).

"The Man Who Was No. 16"

PUBLISHING HISTORY: First published by William Collins Sons and Co., Ltd., London, 1929, in the short story collection *Partners in Crime.* First published in the United States by Dodd, Mead and Co., New York, 1929, in the short story collection *Partners in Crime.*

CHARACTERS: Tommy Beresford; Tuppence Beresford; Albert, Mr. A. Carter, Mrs. Cortlandt van Snyder, Paul de Varez, Prince Vladiroffsky.

This case, the last recounted in the collection *Partners in Crime,* brings to a conclusion the recurring thread of mystery that had been sewn in the first case, "A Fairy in the Flat." In that investigation, the Beresfords were first installed in the International Detective Agency by British Intelligence with the warning to be on the watch for a foreign agent identified by the number sixteen.

At last, the agent arrives at the establishment, announces the code number, and proclaims his name to be Prince Vladiroffsky. The prince displays great generosity to the couple, but he then disappears suddenly with Tuppence, even as British Intelligence has him under close observation. Tommy is able to find his beloved wife and helps bring the case to a close. At its end, he suggests to Tuppence that they should retire from the detective business. She agrees enthusiastically and gives Tommy one final surprise.

• • •

As was the case throughout the collection *Partners in Crime,* Tommy and Tuppence solve this case by adopting the mannerisms and personae of detectives from fiction. In this final case, Tommy becomes a very special literary detective: Hercule Poirot. Tuppence becomes Poirot's faithful sidekick, Captain Arthur Hastings.

"Manx Gold"

PUBLISHING HISTORY: First published in *The Daily Dispatch,* Manchester, 1930. First published in the United States by G. P. Putnam's Sons, New York, 1997, in the short story collection *The Harlequin Tea Set and Other Stories.*

CHARACTERS: Ewan Corjeag, Juan Faraker, Dr. Fayell, Fenella Mylecharane, Mrs. Skillicorn.

"Manx Gold" is one of the most unusual mysteries ever written by Agatha Christie. The genesis of the story goes back to 1929 and an idea proposed by Arthur B. Crookall, an alderman and chairperson of the June Effort, a committee devoted to promoting tourism on the Isle of Man, the small island situated off the northwest coast of England. Crookall thought that if a treasure hunt could be organized, tourists might be induced to visit. To make the hunt even more interesting, Crookall proposed to have the island filled with clues that the participants would have to find and decipher. To present all the clues in one tidy format, it was decided that a short story should be written. The author who came to mind immediately was Agatha Christie.

For the fee of sixty pounds, Agatha Christie accepted the commission. She visited the Isle of Man, toured varied sites for the story, and then wrote her tale. It was published in five installments toward the end of May, 1930, in the *Daily Dispatch,* a newspaper in Manchester. Additionally, a quarter of a million copies were sent out to all the hotels, guest houses, and likely tourist spots on the island, and the five clues were published separately to give added help to the amateur detectives who were preparing to descend on the island. Naturally, the residents of the island were not permitted to take part, a decision that did little to encourage enthusiasm by the locals. It is still a matter of debate as to whether the hunt was successful in generating a large increase in tourism. For each of four lucky souls who solved the very challenging puzzles, there was a treasure of a snuffbox containing an eighteenth-century Manx halfpenny with a hole in it; through the hole was tied a ribbon connected to a declaration signed by Alderman Crookall that instructed the hunter to go at once to the town hall in the island's capital of Douglas. There, he could redeem the prize of one hundred pounds.

The story itself is one of the more convoluted efforts by the great mystery writer. Juan Faraker and Fenella Mylecharane are given the task of locating four chests of treasure that have been buried in different locations across the island by their late eccentric uncle Myles. Adding a bit of spice to the hunt is the fact that Uncle Myles made two other possible heirs participants in the chase. He provides clues to Juan and Fenella a mere twenty-four hours before two other relatives, Myles's unscrupulous nephew Ewan Corjeag and the otherwise unknown cousin, Dr. Richard Fayell, arrive on the scene.

• • •

Christie clearly enjoyed the plot idea of a treasure hunt, as she used it several times over the years. The two most obvious examples are "The Case of the Missing Will" (1924) and "Strange Jest" (1941), which had the original title "A Case of Buried Treasure." There is also the murder hunt game that is staged by Ariadne Oliver in *Dead Man's Folly* (1956), which is used as the setting for a real murder.

"The Market Basing Mystery"

PUBLISHING HISTORY: First published by Dodd, Mead and Co., New York, 1951, in the short story collection *The Under Dog and Other Stories.*

CHARACTERS: Hercule Poirot; Captain Arthur Hastings; Chief Inspector James Japp; Miss Clegg, Dr. Giles, Mr. and Mrs. Parker, Constable Pollard, Walter Protheroe.

Chief Inspector Japp convinces Hercule Poirot and Captain Arthur Hastings to spend a restful weekend with him in the countryside town of Market Basing, especially as "nobody knows us, and we know nobody . . . That's the idea." Poirot enjoys the diverting trip, observing that when he retires he shall have "a little place in the country. Far from crime, like this." Unfortunately, Market Basing is not far enough away, for the local constable, Pollard, recruits Japp and the detective in an investigation into a death at Leigh House. Walter Protheroe was found shot in the head, but the matter is exceedingly curious, for he was found in a room, a pistol clasped in his right hand, with the door locked and the window bolted. The local doctor is firmly convinced, however, that Protheroe could not have shot himself, on the basis of some fine points, including the peculiar entry wound.

Poirot and Japp examine the room with much interest, noting the pile of cigarette butts in an ashtray and a broken cufflink on the floor near the dead man. They then interrogate the household, starting with the thin and calm Miss Clegg, who subtly points a finger toward Protheroe's guests.

It is soon learned that a guest, Mr. Parker, had come to Leigh House to blackmail Protheroe. He is arrested for murder. Poirot is not satisfied with the solution, pressing ahead with the real investigation. He reveals all with a handkerchief, a pile of cigarettes, and the fresh air in the murder room.

• • •

This case includes an intriguing thought from Inspector Japp that echoes the sentiments of many readers over the years concerning Poirot: "You'd have been a holy terror if you had taken to crime."

"Middle-Aged Wife, The Case of the"

PUBLISHING HISTORY: First published by William Collins Sons and Co., Ltd., London, 1934, in the short story collection *Parker Pyne Investigates.* First published in the United States by Dodd, Mead and Co., New York, 1934, in the short story collection *Mr. Parker Pyne, Detective.*

CHARACTERS: Mr. Parker Pyne; Claude Luttrell, George Packington, Maria Packington.

The first case recounted in the collection *Parker Pyne Investigates,* "The Case of the Middle-Aged Wife" brings to Mr. Parker Pyne's offices a Mrs. Maria Packington. She is most unhappy at the recent behavior of her husband. He has been spending far too much time with and has certainly been paying too much attention to his office secretary. Answering Parker Pyne's advertisement, she has come to the detective with the demand that he restore her marriage.

Parker Pyne adopts a very practical strategy for Mrs. Packington. Hiring the services of the talented and very charming Claude Luttrell, Parker Pyne instructs Mrs. Packington to be seen with Claude in very public circumstances and to make certain that her husband finds out. The reaction of Mr. Packington is quite predictable.

"The Million-Dollar Bond Robbery"

PUBLISHING HISTORY: First published in *Sketch* magazine, London, 1923–1924; reprinted by John Lane, Publishers, London, 1924, in the short story collection *Poirot Investigates.* First published in the United States by Dodd, Mead and Co., New York, 1925, in the short story collection *Poirot Investigates.*

CHARACTERS: Hercule Poirot; Captain Arthur Hastings; Esmée Farquhar, Philip Ridgeway, Mr. Shaw, Mr. Vavasour.

While Hercule Poirot and Captain Arthur Hastings are discussing the theft of a million dollars' worth of Liberty bonds that were being sent by the London and Scottish Bank on board the ocean liner *Olympiá,* they receive a visitor. Miss Esmée Farquhar, fiancée to Philip Ridgeway (the bank employee in charge of the bonds on their crossing), implores Poirot to assist in clearing him of any possible complicity. The bonds had sailed from Liverpool on the *Olympiá* and had been handed to Ridgeway that morning by the two joint general managers of the bank, Mr. Vavasour and Mr. Shaw. The bonds had been enclosed, packed, and sealed in his presence and then locked in Ridgeway's portmanteau. The portmanteau had a special lock and had been stored at the bottom of Ridgeway's trunk. Incredibly, the bonds disappeared only a few hours before reaching New York harbor as though into thin air, reappearing inexplicably a mere half hour after the docking of the *Olympiá,* when they were sold in small parcels. One broker swore that he had purchased some of the bonds even before the *Olympiá* had arrived. Ridgeway was the obvious suspect.

After several interviews, Poirot is confident that he knows who stole the bonds, prompting Hastings to exclaim, "Do you know, I'd give a considerable sum of money to see you make a thorough ass of yourself—just for once." As always, of course, Hastings is disappointed. Vital clues to the solution of this crime include the apparent arrival of the bonds in New York ahead of the *Olympiá,* the presence of an aged gentleman wearing glasses, Mr. Ventner, in the cabin next to Ridgeway, and the existence of several master keys.

• • •

This case was adapted by London Weekend Television for the series *Agatha Christie's Poirot* starring David Suchet. Poirot's traditional suffering from seasickness is mentioned in this case.

The Mirror Crack'd from Side to Side

PUBLISHING HISTORY: First published by William Collins Sons and Co., Ltd., London,

1962. First published in the United States by Dodd, Mead and Co., New York, 1962, under the title *The Mirror Crack'd*.

CHARACTERS: Miss Jane Marple; Arthur Badcock, Heather Badcock, Mary Bain, Cherry Baker, Jim Baker, Mrs. Dolly Bantry, Margaret Bence, Lola Brewster, Chief Inspector Craddock, Gladys Dixon, Ardwyck Fenn, Dr. Gilchrist, Giuseppe, Marina Gregg, Dr. Haydock, Mrs. Jameson, Miss Knight, Hailey Preston, Jason Rudd, Dr. Sanford, Detective Sergeant William Tiddler, Ella Zielinsky.

Miss Jane Marple may be too old to be as active as she once was, but she is not so infirm that she can be content to sit and endure the endless ministrations of Miss Knight. Already depressed over the increasing suburban sprawl that has found its way into St. Mary Mead in the shape of a new housing development, she finds her live-in companion, hired by her doting nephew Raymond West, to be so efficient and overly kind and attentive that Miss Marple is desperate to get out of the house. Sending Miss Knight on an errand, Miss Marple makes a dash for temporary freedom by heading outdoors and taking a stroll through the development.

While walking, Miss Marple slips and falls and is given assistance by Heather Badcock. Taken in for tea, Miss Marple hears a great deal of gossip from Miss Badcock, with talk centering on Gossington Hall and its new residents (the longtime inhabitant, Miss Marple's old friend the widowed Dolly Bantry, has vacated the mansion)—the movie star Marina Gregg and her latest husband, the director Jason Rudd. Gregg is making her comeback film and finds Gossington Hall a convenient center for going to and from the studio. After returning home, Miss Marple calls Dr. Haydock, who checks her out and finds her doing just fine; he notes, of course, that what she really needs "is a nice juicy murder."

A short time later, Marina Gregg and her husband host a charity benefit at Gossington Hall to raise money for the St. John's Ambulance Brigade

and to win the good will of St. Mary Mead's inhabitants. The residents eagerly attend the charity, not only to see the famous movie star but also to see what she has done with the renovated estate. Among those in attendance is Heather Badcock, who hangs on Marina Gregg and then falls ill. Stricken with a seizure, Heather collapses and dies.

Miss Marple hears of the death the following morning, along with word that a postmortem will be held. The word is soon out: Heather Badcock died from a massive overdose of a sedative that had been apparently intended for someone else at the party. Inspector Craddock wastes little time in arriving at Miss Marple's house to fill her in on the crime and to begin benefiting from her remarkable insights.

• • •

The Mirror Crack'd from Side to Side was the first Miss Marple novel to have appeared since *4.50 from Paddington* in 1957. It was also the last Miss Marple story (and, indeed, the final Christie work) that was set exclusively within the confines of an English village—specifically, St. Mary Mead. The subsequent books, including the other Miss Marple books, are set elsewhere, and St. Mary Mead is seen only briefly. The title of the book is taken from "The Lady of Shallott," a poem by Alfred, Lord Tennyson:

Out flew the web and floated wide;
The mirror crack'd from side to side;
"The curse is come upon me," cried
The Lady of Shallott.

Christie dedicated the book "To Margaret Rutherford, in admiration." She had great respect for the famed actress (who died in 1972), although she disliked passionately Rutherford's outings as Miss Marple. The novel was adapted twice, once for film and once for television. Released as *The Mirror Crack'd* in 1980, the film starred Angela Lansbury as Miss Marple, and featured Elizabeth Taylor, Tony Curtis, Edward Fox,

Kim Novak, and Rock Hudson. The television version, produced by the BBC in 1992, starred Joan Hickson as Miss Marple.

Miss Marple's Final Cases and Two Other Stories

PUBLISHING HISTORY: First published by William Collins Sons and Co., Ltd., London, 1979. This collection was not published in United States (see below for details).

CONTENTS:

This collection contains six stories featuring Miss Marple and two stories that do not feature Marple or Poirot.

"Miss Marple Tells a Story" (Marple)

"In a Glass Darkly"

"Strange Jest" (Marple)

"The Tape-Measure Murder" (Marple)

"The Case of the Caretaker" (Marple)

"The Case of the Perfect Maid" (Marple)

"Sanctuary" (Marple)

"The Dressmaker's Doll"

"Miss Marple Tells a Story" and "In a Glass Darkly" were published originally in *The Regatta Mystery and Other Stories* (1939); "Strange Jest," "The Tape-Measure Murder," "The Case of the Caretaker," and "The Case of the Perfect Maid" were published in *Three Blind Mice and Other Stories* (1950); "Sanctuary" and "The Dressmaker's Doll" were published originally in *Double Sin and Other Stories* (1961).

Prior to the publication of this collection, the stories had been published in Britain only in magazines. All the stories, however, had been published in collections in the United States.

"Miss Marple Tells a Story"

PUBLISHING HISTORY: First published by Dodd, Mead and Co., New York, 1939, in the short story collection *The Regatta Mystery and Other Stories*.

CHARACTERS: Miss Jane Marple; Raymond West; Miss Carruthers, Mrs. Granby, Mary Hill, Mr. Petherick, Mr. Rhodes, Joan West.

A charmingly written tale of murder told from the perspective of Miss Marple, this narrative is addressed to Marple's dear nephew Raymond West and his wife, Joan. The old sleuth writes of her efforts to free the unfortunate Mr. Rhodes from the suspicion of murdering his wife. The case is brought to her by her longtime solicitor, Mr. Petherick, on behalf of Rhodes, his client, who had expectations of being arrested shortly afterward and being accused of stabbing his wife to death. He was the logical suspect because of the circumstances of the room in which the couple had been staying in the Crown Hotel in Barnchester:

He {Mr. Rhodes} discovered the electric light on and his wife laying on the bed stabbed through the heart. She had been dead at least an hour—probably longer . . . There was another door in Mr. Rhodes's room leading to the corridor. The door was locked and bolted on the inside. The only window in the room was closed and latched. According to Mr. Rhodes nobody had passed through the room in which he was sitting but a chambermaid bringing hot water bottles. The weapon found in the wound was a stiletto dagger which had been lying on Mrs. Rhodes's dressing table. She was in the habit of using it as a paper knife. There were no finger prints on it.

Miss Marple cuts to the heart of the problem, elucidating four ways that Mrs. Rhodes may have died. She then very calmly reveals who the murderer is, concluding the narrative by asking: "Now I do hope you don't think I've been running on too long . . ."

• • •

This story includes a most interesting description of herself by Miss Marple: "I am hopelessly Victorian. I admire Mr. Alma-Tadema and Mr. Frederick Leighton and I suppose to you they are hopelessly *vieux jeu.*"

"Missing Lady, The Case of the"

PUBLISHING HISTORY: First published by William Collins Sons and Co., Ltd., London, 1929, in the short story collection *Partners in Crime*. First published in the United States by Dodd, Mead and Co., New York, 1929, in the short story collection *Partners in Crime.*

CHARACTERS: Tommy Beresford; Tuppence Beresford; Lady Susan Clonray, the Honourable Hermione Crane, Dr. Horriston, Mr. Gabriel Stavansson.

Tommy and Tuppence Beresford are visited by the explorer Gabriel Stavansson. After two years in the Arctic, Stavansson has returned to England and is anxious to be with his fiancée, the Honourable Hermione Crane. She has disappeared, and her own family is unable, or unwilling, to tell investigators exactly what has become of her. The Beresfords use assorted clues to arrive at a nursing home in the country. There, they uncover Miss Crane's shocking and weighty secret.

• • •

As is the custom in the cases recounted in *Partners in Crime,* the Beresfords solve their investigation while impersonating the characteristics of detectives from fiction. For their hunt for Hermione Crane, Tommy and Tuppence impersonate Sherlock Holmes and Dr. Watson. Tommy's rendition of Holmes is finely detailed, even down to his violin playing.

"Missing Will, The Case of the"

PUBLISHING HISTORY: First published in *Sketch* magazine, London, 1923–1924; reprinted by John Lane, London, 1924, in the short story collection *Poirot Investigates*. First published in the United States by Dodd, Mead and Co., New York, 1925, in the short story collection *Poirot Investigates.*

CHARACTERS: Hercule Poirot; Captain Arthur Hastings; Mr. Baker, Mrs. Baker, Andrew Marsh, Miss Violet Marsh.

In what is described by Hastings as "rather a pleasant change from our usual routine work,"

Poirot is asked by Miss Violet Marsh to accomplish an unusual task: He must, within a year, find a will that has been deliberately hidden by her uncle or she stands to lose her entire inheritance. An orphan, Violet had been raised by her uncle, Andrew Marsh, an old-fashioned farmer who had a mistrust of "book knowledge." He was thus strenuously opposed to Violet's receiving a college education, and the young woman was forced to use her own money, left by her mother, to educate herself. Uncle Andrew, however, was determined to have the last say, and his last words to her were, "I've no book learning, but for all that, I'll pit mine against yours any day: We'll see what we shall see." The old man died a month before Violet's meeting with Poirot, and his will was subsequently read. By its terms, Crabtree Manor— Uncle Andrew's estate—and its contents are to be at Violet's disposal for one year from his death, "during which time my clever niece may prove her wits." If, at the end of the year, the puzzle still defies her, the house and its rather large fortune go to assorted charities.

As Poirot is intrigued by the challenge of matching wits with Violet's deceased uncle, he readily accepts her request for aid. An essential clue to the solution is a key attached to a simple envelope. Poirot, however, openly admits that throughout much of the case he has been "not a triple imbecile, but thirty-six times one."

• • •

A very loosely adapted version of this case was produced in 1993 by London Weekend Television for the series *Agatha Christie's Poirot* starring David Suchet. "The Case of the Missing Will" is quite similar to the case investigated by Miss Marple in "Strange Jest"; it, too, involves an uncle with a most eccentric sense of humor.

"Motive vs. Opportunity"

PUBLISHING HISTORY: First published by William Collins Sons and Co., Ltd., London, 1932, in the short story collection *The Thirteen Problems*. First published in the United States by

Dodd, Mead and Co., New York, 1933, in the short story collection *The Tuesday Club Murders.*

CHARACTERS: Miss Jane Marple; Mr. Petherick; Cristobel Clode, George Clode, Simon Clode, Lucy David, Emma Gaunt, Eurydice Spragg.

At a gathering of the Tuesday Night Club, the attorney Mr. Petherick relates a tale of a will and the influence of a spiritualist. A man of considerable wealth, Simon Clode becomes obsessed with contacting his recently deceased and much beloved granddaughter. He meets an American medium, Eurydice Spragg, who gains "an immense ascendancy over Simon Clode." She conducts séances and supposedly summons the spirit of the granddaughter, Cristobel. Completely enthralled with the spiritualist, Simon changes his will in favor of Eurydice Spragg at the expense of the original heirs. The will is signed and witnessed and placed in a blue envelope. Two months later, Simon dies, and the will is opened and read. To everyone's astonishment, the sealed envelope contains only a sheet of blank paper. How this act of apparent substitution might have happened proves a mystery soluble only by Miss Marple, who recalls "little Tommy Symonds, a naughty little boy, I am afraid, but sometimes very amusing."

"The Mousetrap"

See under Plays; see also "Three Blind Mice"

The Mousetrap and Other Stories

See *Three Blind Mice and Other Stories*

The Moving Finger

PUBLISHING HISTORY: First published by Dodd, Mead and Co., New York, 1942. First published in England by William Collins Sons and Co., Ltd., London, 1943.

CHARACTERS: Miss Jane Marple; Colonel Appleby, Emily Barton, Jerry Burton, Joanna Burton, Mrs. Cleat, Reverend Dane Calthorp, Mrs. Maud Dane Calthorp, Florence, Miss Ginch, Inspector Graves, Mary Grey, Aimee Griffith, Dr. Owen Griffith, Elsie Holland, Megan Hunter, Dr. Marcus Kent, Superintendent Nash, Mr. Pye, Mona Symmington, Richard Symmington, Agnes Woddell.

A young pilot who had survived a crash and then endured five months of anxious waiting to see if he would ever walk again, Jerry Burton is delighted to learn that he will not be a helpless cripple. Nevertheless, he faces a lengthy period of rehabilitation and recuperation: "Good air, quiet life, nothing to do—that's the prescription for you. That sister of yours will look after you. Eat, sleep, and imitate the vegetable kingdom as far as possible." "That sister" is Joanna, and the site Jerry chooses for his recovery is Little Furze, on the outskirts of Lymstock.

Not long after settling into their house, the Burtons receive a letter with a local postmark and typed address. The missive is a vicious poison-pen letter that accuses Jerry and Joanna of an incestuous relationship. When Jerry is visited by the local doctor, Griffith, he is informed that several people have received similar letters, including Griffith and the local solicitor, Symmington.

The letters continue to be delivered over the next several days, making increasingly disgusting accusations, some of which, it is rumored, are especially accurate. Finally, one of the letters goes so far that a recipient actually commits suicide.

With things now out of hand, Mrs. Dane Calthorp, wife of the local vicar, decides to bring in someone who can deal with the problem. Jerry and Joanna are invited to tea at the vicarage and are introduced to a dear friend of the Dane Calthorps, a visitor from St. Mary Mead named Miss Marple.

• • •

The Moving Finger ranks with *The Murder of Roger Ackroyd* (1926), *The Pale Horse* (1961), and *Endless Night* (1967) as one of Christie's favorite works. She noted her pleasure with the novel in her autobiography, observing as well that she wrote it during the difficult period of the war, when London was being bombed by the Luftwaffe. The Tommy and Tuppence Beresford novel *N or M?* (1941) was written around the same time. In a way, many parts of the novel are more reminiscent of Christie's romances (penned under the pseudonym of Mary Westmacott) than the Marple murder mysteries. *The Moving Finger* contains several subplots involving the romantic aspirations of Jerry Burton for the young Megan Hunter. As was often the case with Christie's novels, the American edition of this book is shorter than its British counterpart. The novel was adapted for television in 1996 by the BBC and starred Joan Hickson as Miss Marple.

"Mr. Eastwood's Adventure"

PUBLISHING HISTORY: First published by William Collins Sons and Co., Ltd., London, 1934, in the short story collection *The Listerdale Mystery*.

CHARACTERS: Carmen, Detective Sergeant Carter, Anthony Eastwood, Verrall.

A successful writer of newspaper mysteries, Mr. Eastwood struggles to complete a short story with the dubious title of "The Mystery of the Second Cucumber." His labors are interrupted by a strange call, and he is soon embroiled in a mystery that becomes more peculiar with every passing episode. Eastwood is mistaken for a murderer named Conrad Fleckman and falls into the hands of two odd policemen who insist on inspecting his home.

Mr. Parker Pyne, Detective

See *Parker Pyne Investigates*

Mrs. McGinty's Dead

PUBLISHING HISTORY: First published by William Collins Sons and Co., Ltd., London, 1952. First published in the United States by Dodd, Mead and Co., New York, 1952.

CHARACTERS: Hercule Poirot; Mrs. Ariadne Oliver; James Bentley, Bessie Burch, Joe Burch, Eve Carpenter, Guy Carpenter, Edna, Mrs. Eliot, Deirdre Henderson, Evelyn Hope, Pamela Horsefall, Mrs. Kiddell, Mrs. McGinty, Michael, Dr. Rendell, Shelagh Rendell, Superintendent Bert Spence, Major Johnnie Summerhayes, Maureen Summerhayes, Mrs. Sweetimen, Mrs. Laura Upward, Robin Upward, Mr. Wetherby, Mrs. Wetherby, Maude Williams.

Hercule Poirot is paid a visit by Superintendent Bert Spence of the Kilchester police in the hopes that the Belgian detective will assist the policeman in a special investigation. James Bentley, a boarder in the home of Mrs. McGinty, has just been convicted of his landlady's death, a case that was of little interest to Poirot but one that had bothered Spence considerably. The evidence seems clear, but Bentley did not look like a murderer, and, in terms of the jury, the policeman declares, "I know a lot more about murderers than they do."

The facts are certainly against Bentley. The widow Mrs. McGinty was found beaten to death in her cottage parlor. Her property was pillaged and overturned and even the floorboards had been pulled up. While there are assorted other possible suspects—she had worked, after all, as a domestic in various other houses—the police immediately targeted Bentley. He was "sometimes cringing and sometimes truculent," but, above all, he was discovered with Mrs. McGinty's blood and hair on his coat sleeve. A short time later, he was convicted by a jury.

Accepting the opinion of Spence, Poirot departs for the less urbane surroundings of Broadhinny, taking up residence in an overwhelmingly dreadful boardinghouse run by the Summerhayeses. The detective suffers much throughout his inquiries because of Mrs. Summerhayes's cooking and total inability to run an efficient house.

Following his usual method, Poirot rolls ahead with the assistance of Mrs. Ariadne Oliver, interrogating the assorted witnesses and suspects, an inquiry that frightens the murderer into committing more crimes and even threatening Poirot's safety. As with many other cases, Poirot assembles the suspects and reveals the name and motive of the murderer at the end.

• • •

Mrs. McGinty's Dead marked the second partnership between Hercule Poirot and Mrs. Ariadne Oliver, Christie's alter ego and a crime writer in her own right. Poirot had not been included in a novel since *Taken at the Flood* (1948), and Mrs. Oliver had not been seen since 1936, in *Cards on the Table.* Two characters of note in the novel are Mrs. Maureen Summerhayes and Superintendent Spence. Maureen, wife of Major John Summerhayes and co-manager of a guest house in which Poirot stays, is the source of deep frustration for the detective because of her utter lack of organization. Poirot can only lament, "Yes, I suffer," but, in a charming moment, he teaches Maureen, using his superbly organized methods, how to prepare an omelet. (See also *Cat among the Pigeons.*) The second character, Superintendent Spence, is introduced for the first time. He reappears in *Hallowe'en Party* (1969) and *Elephants Can Remember* (1972).

The novel is dedicated to the producer Peter Saunders (who produced a host of Christie plays, including *The Mousetrap*). Having performed this kindness, Christie used Mrs. Oliver to vent some frustrations about the adaptation of her works for the stage: "You've no idea of the agony of having your characters taken and made to say things they never would have said, and do things that they never would have done. And if you protest, all they say is that it's 'good theatre.'"

The novel was used loosely as the basis for the 1964 film *Murder Most Foul,* starring Margaret Rutherford as Miss Marple.

Murder after Hours

See *The Hollow*

Murder at Hazelmoor

See *The Sittaford Mystery*

The Murder at the Vicarage

PUBLISHING HISTORY: First published by William Collins Sons and Co., Ltd., London, 1930. First published in the United States by Dodd, Mead and Co., New York, 1930.

CHARACTERS: Miss Jane Marple; Dennis Clement, Griselda Clement, Reverend Leonard Clement, Miss Cram, Gladys, Miss Hartnell, Mr. Hawes, Dr. Haydock, Mrs. Lestrange, Colonel Melchett, Mrs. Price Ridley, Anne Protheroe, Lettice Protheroe, Lawrence Redding, Inspector Slack, Dr. Stone, Caroline Wetherby.

Reverend Leonard Clement serves as the narrator of the brutal events that trouble St. Mary Mead and that claim the life of the much hated Colonel Protheroe. In the village, the colonel is one of the most disliked personages, and even the religious Reverend Clement confesses that "any one who murdered Colonel Protheroe would be doing the world at large a service." As the local magistrate and churchwarden, Protheroe demands a stern financial policy, "militant Christianity," and nearly Victorian personal habits. Everyone thus has some kind of complaint about him, especially his daughter, Lettice, who objects to his controlling her life. The colonel is especially upset that Lettice has been posing in a bathing suit for the painter Lawrence Redding, who rents a small studio on the vicarage grounds.

Redding, Lettice, and the gossip of the village are the chief topic of conversation at an afternoon tea in the vicarage drawing room. Miss Marple is a guest, and she makes the observation that it is unlikely that Lettice and Redding are having an affair—at least not with each other. Not long afterward, Reverend Clement discovers Redding with a woman, not Lettice but her mother, Anne Protheroe. Redding erupts with emotion, admitting that he wished Colonel Protheroe were dead.

Colonel Protheroe remains an important topic in Clement's affairs, as he must meet with him to discuss vicarage business. Running late, Clement finally arrives at the vicarage and discovers Protheroe sprawled over Clement's own writing table. He has been shot in the head.

The investigation into the murder is headed by Inspector Slack and Colonel Melchett, and it takes little time for Slack to encounter Miss Marple. The case, of course, seems fairly cut and dried, as

Redding is a likely suspect. Things soon become complicated when Anne Protheroe confesses to the crime and the evidence seems to exonerate Redding. Miss Marple, of course, only adds to the mystery by observing that there are numerous possible suspects in the crime.

• • •

The Murder at the Vicarage marks the debut of Miss Jane Marple and the first incarnation of the beloved village of St. Mary Mead in novel form.

Christie wrote in her autobiography: *"Murder at the Vicarage was published in 1930, but I cannot remember where, when or how I wrote it, why I came to write it, or even what suggested to me that I should select a new character—Miss Marple—to act as a sleuth in the story."* Christie noted that she did not create Miss Marple as a rival for Poirot, nor did she plan on offering many more Marple novels; this fact was borne out by the absence of a new Marple novel until 1942's *The Body in the Library.* Miss Marple, however, did appear in the short story collection *The Thirteen Problems* (1932).

The novel introduces the residents of St. Mary Mead, who became definite favorites with readers, including Dr. Haydock (Miss Marple's physician), Reverend Leonard Clement and his wife, Griselda Clement, Colonel Melchett, and Raymond West; also present is Inspector Slack, who takes part in *The Body in the Library,* "The Tape-Measure Murder," and "The Case of the Perfect Maid."

Christie dedicated the book "To Rosalind." The object of the dedication was Rosalind Christie Prichard Hicks, Agatha Christie's only child. The novel was adapted for the stage in 1949 and adapted for television in 1986, starring Joan Hickson as Miss Marple.

Murder for Christmas

See *Hercule Poirot's Christmas*

Murder in Mesopotamia

PUBLISHING HISTORY: First published by William Collins Sons and Co., Ltd., London,

1936. First published in the United States by Dodd, Mead, and Co., New York, 1936.

CHARACTERS: Hercule Poirot; Ali Yusef, Frederick Bosner, Richard Carey, Bill Coleman, David Emmott, Anne Johnson, Major Kelsey, Mary Kelsey, Father Lavigny, Amy Leatheran, Dr. Eric Leidner, Mrs. Louise Leidner, Captain Maitland, Raoul Menier, Joseph Mercado, Marie Mercado, Major Pennyman, Dr. Giles Reilly, Sheila Reilly, Carl Reiter, Monsieur Verrier.

A young nurse, Amy Leatheran, is hired to accompany Major and Mrs. Kelsey to Baghdad and to take care of Mrs. Kelsey's expected baby. Plans change, however, and Miss Leatheran faces the prospect of having to return home to London. Instead, she is hired unexpectedly by Dr. Leidner, a Swedish-American archaeologist who needs a nurse to care for his wife, a nervous woman who suffers from bouts of terror. Her position requires Amy to travel to the remote archaeological dig of Tell Yarimjah, on the Tigris River.

Although she is a nervous wreck, Mrs. Leidner comes to trust Amy and confide in her, revealing assorted details about her earlier life—especially her first marriage, to a German spy. Amy also notes the strange happenings in the camp, but most odd occurrences are blamed on Mrs. Leidner's nervous problems. It is soon obvious that Mrs. Leidner was right about her own suspicions: Louise Leidner is murdered. The murderer must be a member of the archaeological expedition.

As luck would have it, Hercule Poirot is traveling through Mesopotamia. Dr. Reilly, in charge of the dig, consults with the detective and convinces him to take the case. Poirot finds a number of suspects and unravels a host of secrets and motives. He is helped throughout the investigation by Amy Leatheran.

• • •

Christie wrote *Murder in Mesopotamia* using the extensive knowledge she had acquired about the Near East and archaeology from traveling to various digs with her archaeologist husband, Max Mallowan. In recognition of her debt to the archaeologists in Iraq—who supplied both technical details and models for characters—Christie dedicated the book thus: "To my many archaeological friends in Iraq and Syria."

Murder in the Calais Coach

See *Murder on the Orient Express*

"Murder in the Mews"

PUBLISHING HISTORY: First published by William Collins Sons and Co., Ltd., London, 1937, in the short story collection *Murder in the Mews*. First published in the United States by Dodd, Mead and Co., New York, 1937, in the short story collection *Dead Man's Mirror and Other Stories*.

CHARACTERS: Hercule Poirot; Captain Arthur Hastings; Chief Inspector James Japp; Barbara Allen, Major Eustace, Charles Laverton-West, M.P., Mrs. Pierce, Jane Plenderleith.

After spending the evening of Guy Fawkes Day with Chief Inspector Japp and discussing the subject of murder, Poirot is summoned the following morning by the policeman to number 14 Bardsley Gardens Mews. There, the body of Mrs. Barbara Allen has been discovered, dead from an apparent suicide: The poor woman had seemingly shot herself in the head with a Webley .25. Subsequent investigation casts this preliminary conclusion into doubt. The pistol is in the wrong position and the door to the room was locked and the window bolted. Presumably, the murderer locked the door and hoped no one would notice that the key was missing.

Poirot and Japp undertake a thorough scrutiny of Mrs. Allen's death site, and the detective pays particular attention to the deceased's wristwatch and writing bureau, noting additionally the absence of a suicide note.

The roommate of Mrs. Allen, Jane Plenderleith, proves a valuable source of information to the investigators, pointing them to the men in Mrs. Allen's life, Charles Laverton-West, M.P., and the distinctly unpleasant Major Eustace. The latter

proves the likely suspect and is confronted with what seems damning evidence, including a cufflink. Poirot, of course, sees the clues in a very different light. He uses the clues—including cigarette remains, a set of golf clubs, and a briefcase—to unravel the true events in the death of Mrs. Allen.

• • •

This case was adapted in 1989 by London Weekend Television for *Agatha Christie's Poirot* starring David Suchet. The structure of the plot in "Murder in the Mews" follows that of "The Market Basing Mystery," with both having as their central element an inexplicable death in a locked room. Poirot boasts to Japp of his potential powers as a murderer: "My dear Japp, if I committed a murder you would not have the least chance of seeing—how I set about it! You would not even be aware, probably, that a murder has been committed."

Murder in the Mews and Other Stories

PUBLISHING HISTORY: First published by William Collins Sons and Co., Ltd., London, 1937. First published in the United States by Dodd, Mead and Co., New York, 1937, under the title *Dead Man's Mirror and Other Stories*.

CONTENTS:
"Murder in the Mews"
"The Incredible Theft"
"Triangle at Rhodes"
"Dead Man's Mirror"

Murder in the Mews is of particular interest because of the way each of the stories bears a very striking similarity to other cases. "Murder in the Mews" is a locked-room murder quite close to "The Market Basing Mystery." "The Incredible Theft" is a revised and lengthened version of "The Submarine Plans." "Triangle at Rhodes" is strikingly similar to *Evil under the Sun*. "Dead Man's Mirror" is a longer and more complicated version of "The Second Gong." "The Incredible Theft" was, for no specific reason, omitted in the American edition. "Murder in the Mews," "The Incredible Theft," and "Triangle at Rhodes" were adapted in 1989 by London Weekend Television for the series *Agatha Christie's Poirot* starring David Suchet.

Murder in Retrospect

See *Five Little Pigs*

Murder in Three Acts

See *Three-Act Tragedy*

A Murder Is Announced

PUBLISHING HISTORY: First published by William Collins Sons and Co., Ltd., London, 1950. First published in the United States by Dodd, Mead and Co., New York, 1950.

CHARACTERS: Miss Jane Marple; Old Ashe, Charlotte Blacklock, Letitia Blacklock, Dora Bunner, Johnny Butt, Sir Henry Clithering, Detective Inspector Craddock, Colonel Archie Easterbrook, Laura Easterbrook, Sergeant Fletcher, Belle Goedler, Randall Goedler, Sonia Goedler, Dian "Bunch" Harmon, Reverend Julian Harmon, Myrna Harris, Phillipa Haymes, Miss Hinchcliffe, Jim Huggins, Mitzi, Amy Murgatroyd, Mr. Rowlandson, Chief George Rydesdall, Rudi Scherz, Patrick Simmons, Emma Stamfordis, Mrs. Swettenham, Edmund Swettenham, Tiglath-Pileser.

The inhabitants of the quaint town of Chipping Cleghorn receive their usual delivery of the Chipping Cleghorn *Gazette* on October 29. In the personals column, one ad catches the attention of nearly everyone:

A murder is announced and will take place on Friday, October 29, at Little Paddocks, at 6:30 P.M. Friends please accept this, the only intimation.

The arrival of the news about the impending murder comes as a surprise to the residents of Little Paddocks: Leitita Blacklock, the mistress of the house; Dora Bunner, Letitia's old school friend and guest; Patrick and Julia Simmons, distant cousins of Letitia; Phillipa Haymes, the gardener at Little Paddocks; and Mitzi, the Eastern European maid and cook, who is perpetually uptight. As guests will no doubt be arriving in reply to the ad, Letitia decides to make the best of the situation and to prepare for a gathering.

As the appointed hour approaches, guests do begin to show up: Colonel Easterbrook and his much younger wife; Reverend Julian Harmon—the vicar of Chipping Cleghorn—and his wife, Bunch; the spinsters Hinchcliffe and Murgatroyd; and Mrs. Swettenham and her son, Edmund.

Letitia gives them a grand welcome, and all await the moment with much anticipation. At 6:30 P.M., the lights go out suddenly and the darkness is broken only by a flashlight beam that sweeps searchingly across the room. A voice calls out, "Stick 'em up," and two bullets are fired, accompanied by screaming. When the lights finally return, the dazed guests see an even more amazing sight: Letitia has been shot in the ear, and an unknown man, clearly the intruder, is dead, slumped on the floor.

• • •

A Murder Is Announced marked the first time in seven years that Miss Marple solved a published case (she last appeared in *The Moving Finger,* 1943). Henceforth, Miss Marple made more regular appearances, especially as the spinster sleuth came to match Poirot in popularity among readers.

The number fifty assumed considerable importance in the publication of the novel. It was released in 1950, the first printing was 50,000 copies, and it was touted as Christie's fiftieth novel. The last claim was not entirely accurate, as this was not her fiftieth novel; rather, it was her fiftieth book (there were several short story collections included in the account). The book is dedicated: "To Ralph and Anne Newman, at whose house I first tasted . . . Delicious Death." The lethal-sounding dessert was served at a dinner party hosted by the Newmans and found its way into the story. *A Murder Is Announced* was the first

Marple novel to be shown on television. It was broadcast live on December 30, 1956, on NBC Television's *Goodyear Playhouse.* The second adaptation was made by the BBC in 1986, and starred Joan Hickson as Miss Marple. The novel was also adapted for the stage in 1977.

Murder Is Easy

PUBLISHING HISTORY: First published by William Collins Sons and Co., Ltd., London, 1939. First published in the United States by Dodd, Mead and Co., New York, 1939, under the title *Easy to Kill.*

CHARACTERS: Mr. Abbott, Mrs. Anstroth, Superintendent Battle, Harry Carter, Lucy Carter, Miss Church, Bridget Conway, Lord Easterfield, Mr. Ellsworthy, Luke Fitzwilliam, Lavinia Fullerton, Amy Gibbs, Major Horton, Jessie Rose Humbleby, Dr. John Humbleby, Jimmy Lorrimer, Sir William Ossington, Mrs. Pierce, Tommy Pierce, Dr. Geoffrey Thomas, Alfred Wake, Honoria Waynflete.

After years spent away in the colonial police, Luke Fitzwilliam has returned to England and now finds himself on the connecting train from Dover to London. He shares his compartment with a little old lady named Miss Lavinia Fullerton. Once she learns of Luke's police background, she tells him straight away the cause of her journey to London. She is, in fact, on her way to Scotland Yard to report a series of bizarre deaths that have been terrorizing her village of Wychwood. Luke listens attentively, but he has a difficult time accepting her story, especially as Scotland Yard no doubt must deal quite often with old ladies reporting murders. Miss Fullerton is quite sincere, however, and even predicts the next death, the local doctor named Humbleby.

The very next day, Luke reads in the *Times* that a Miss Fullerton had been killed by a hit-and-run driver while crossing Whitehall. If this is not enough of a coincidence, one week later, Luke reads a death notice concerning a Dr. Humbleby of Wychwood. Convinced that Lavinia Fullerton was right all along, Luke sets out for Wychwood and pretends to be researching a book on folklore

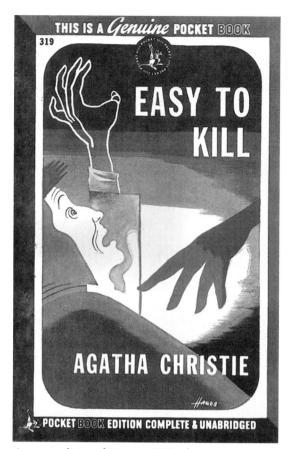

A 1945 edition of Easy to Kill, *the American title for* Murder Is Easy. *(Pocket Books)*

and superstitions. It does not take him long to uncover the terrible truth that a prolific murderer is loose in the village.

• • •

Murder Is Easy is a deceptive novel, for even though it boasts none of Christie's famous sleuths (save for Superintendent Battle), it offers perhaps the most diabolical and prodigious murderer in the many pages of Christie's works. Even before the novel opens, the murderer has massacred five people: with arsenic, by pushing one off a cliff, by pushing another off a building, by poison again (oxalic acid), and by inducing septicemia (a scratch from a rusty nail proves fatal). During the events of the novel, two more people die; one is run over by a car and another is crushed in the skull by part of a lamppost.

Assisting Superintendent Battle in his investigation is Luke Fitzwilliam. Luke proves an able and interesting assistant, similar to Lucy Eylesbarrow in *4.50 from Paddington;* like the redoubtable Lucy, Luke's appearance is a one-time occurrence.

A loose adaptation of the novel was made for CBS Television in 1982, starring Bill Bixby, Olivia de Havilland, and Lesley-Anne Down.

The Murder of Roger Ackroyd

PUBLISHING HISTORY: First published by William Collins Sons and Co., Ltd., London, 1926. First published in the United States by Dodd, Mead and Co., New York, 1926.

CHARACTERS: Hercule Poirot; Mrs. Cecil Ackroyd, Flora Ackroyd, Roger Ackroyd, Major Hector Blunt, Ursula Bourne, Colonel Carter, Mrs. Ferrars, Mrs. Richard Folliott, Miss Garnett, Mr. Hammond, Charles Kent, Parker, Captain Ralph Paton, Inspector Denis Raglan, Geoffrey Raymond, Miss Russell, Caroline Sheppard, Dr. James Sheppard.

The residents of the little village of King's Abbot are preoccupied with the death of one of Dr. James Sheppard's patients, Mrs. Ferrars. She was found dead from an apparent overdose of veronal, and everyone, including James' inquisitive sister, Caroline, believes that she committed suicide out of remorse for murdering her husband with arsenic. The death is a particular subject of conversation between Dr. Sheppard and his sister, and Caroline is very well informed about the gossip circulating around the village. Mrs. Ferrars was expected to wed the very eligible Roger Ackroyd at the end of a suitable time of mourning for her husband. Sheppard next speaks with his neighbor, a retired Belgian detective named Hercule Poirot, who has left his profession for the quiet life in the country, and spends his time growing vegetable marrows. Their topic of interest is again the Ackroyd household, namely Roger

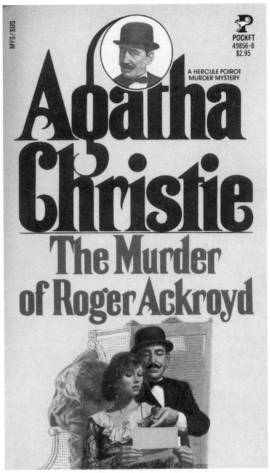

A 1970s edition of The Murder of Roger Ackroyd. *(Pocket Books)*

Ackroyd's niece, Flora, and stepson, Ralph Paton. The two young people hope to marry, but Ackroyd has poor relations with his stepson, and Paton has even been heard to exclaim that he wishes Roger were dead.

Dr. Sheppard is invited the next evening for dinner at the home of Roger Ackroyd, Fernly Glen. Ackroyd tells Sheppard that he is anxious to speak with him about something important, and after dinner the two men speak in seclusion. Ackroyd admits that he feels terrible guilt about Mrs. Ferrars's death, as she had admitted to him on the very night before their engagement was to be announced that she had in fact poisoned her husband and was now being blackmailed by someone in the village. While he subsequently canceled their engagement, Ackroyd certainly did not anticipate that she would commit suicide.

Sheppard leaves Ackroyd and returns home for the night. A mere hour later, he is summoned back to the Ackroyds'. Roger Ackroyd has been found stabbed to death.

It is learned that Roger Ackroyd had been heard speaking with someone for about half an hour after Dr. Sheppard left, so the time of death can be placed between 9:30 and 10:00 P.M. There are also several obvious suspects, including Ralph Paton; Major Blunt, a big-game hunter; Flora, Ackroyd's niece, and her impoverished mother; Miss Russell, the housekeeper of Fernly Glen, who was in love with Ackroyd and was distraught at the sudden appearance of Mrs. Ferrars; and Ursula Bourne, the parlor maid.

It takes little time for Hercule Poirot to abandon his vegetable marrows and to begin working with the Sheppards to solve the crime. Caroline Sheppard proves an invaluable assistant and a fine complement to Poirot's "little grey cells."

• • •

Had Agatha Christie not written any other works before or after *The Murder of Roger Ackroyd,* she would still be given an honored place in the history of detective fiction. *Roger Ackroyd* shatters some of the most conventional and hallowed rules of mysteries and has thus long been a source of great controversy among readers and experts. Christie acknowledged the controversy in her autobiography: "A lot of people say that *The Murder of Roger Ackroyd* is cheating; but if they read it carefully they will see that they are wrong. Such little lapses of time as there have to be are nicely concealed in an ambiguous sentence."

Credit was given by Christie for the original idea to two people: James Watts, her brother-in-law, and Lord Louis Mountbatten, who went on to serve as a World War II hero and the last viceroy of India and who was murdered in 1979 by IRA terrorists. Mountbatten also had a role in bringing *Murder on the Orient Express* to the screen in 1974 (see under Film for details).

Ackroyd is also notable for the presence of Hercule Poirot and Caroline Sheppard, sister of the narrator, Dr. James Sheppard. Miss Sheppard is curious, smart, and imaginative, possessing many attributes that characterized another spinster detective, one from St. Mary Mead.

Murder on the Links

PUBLISHING HISTORY: First published by John Lane, London, 1923. First published in the United States by Dodd, Mead and Co., New York, 1923.

CHARACTERS: Hercule Poirot; Captain Arthur Hastings; Joseph Aarons, Francoise Arrichet, Lucien Bex, Madame Daubreuil, Marthe Daubreuil, Bella Duveen, Dulcie Duveen, Monsieur Giraud, Monsieur Hautet, Mrs. Renauld, Jack Renauld, Paul Renauld, Gabriel Stonor.

Captain Arthur Hastings journeys by train from Paris to London and meets a memorable young woman who is thoroughly modern; she is heavily made up, smokes, and has little reticence about swearing. She terms herself Cinderella, and even though he does not much approve of her habits, Hastings is quite charmed. Cinderella admits to Hastings that she is an actress and acrobat and is also much worried for her sister, likewise an actress, who has disappeared. Hastings tells her that, as luck would have it, he knows a detective.

That particular detective, Hercule Poirot, wastes little time upon Hastings's return telling him that a letter has arrived from a potential client, Paul Renauld, requesting the detective's help in an unspecified matter. Hastings recognizes the name at once as that of a millionaire from South America.

The two set off across the Channel and arrive at Renauld's estate, between Boulogne and Calais, only to discover that Renauld has been murdered. Poirot is given entry to the estate by the much-impressed

French police. The Belgian learns the details of the crime. Renauld had been abducted from his house, stabbed in the back, and placed in a freshly dug grave on the golf course adjoining his property. Madame Renauld had been gagged and tied and left in the house by the murderous intruders.

Poirot finds the case to be an intriguing one, especially after looking into the background of the victims. Of special interest is the past of Madame Renauld. As for Hastings, he does not long go without meeting Cinderella again, and the case proves quite memorable for him—he meets the woman who will become his wife.

• • •

Murder on the Links marked the second appearance of Hercule Poirot and Captain Arthur Hastings after *The Mysterious Affair at Styles* (1920). It holds a special place of importance for fans of Captain Hastings, for it is during this case that he meets his future wife, Miss Dulcie Duveen—the happy couple, much later, have two daughters and two sons and move to Argentina. The topic of the title, *Murder on the Links,* is a demonstration that golf is a major part of the story. It is also a reflection of Christie's delight in the game during that time, when her marriage with Archie Christie was still a happy one. Golf was a favorite pastime of the couple.

Murder on the Orient Express

PUBLISHING HISTORY: First published by William Collins Sons and Co., Ltd., London, 1934. First published in the United States by Dodd, Mead and Co., New York, 1934, under the title *Murder in the Calais Coach.*

CHARACTERS: Hercule Poirot; Countess Helena Maria Andrenyi, Count Rudolph Andrenyi, Colonel Arbuthnot, Monsieur Bouc, Dr. Constantine, Mary Debenham, Princess Dragomiroff, Lieutenant Dubosc, Antonio Foscarelli, Cyrus Hardman, Mrs. Hubbard, Hector MacQueen, Edward Henry Masterman, Pierre Michel, Greta Ohlsson, Mr. Ratchett, Hildegarde Schmidt.

Hercule Poirot has just completed a successful "little affair in Syria" and arrives in Istanbul (called Stamboul in the novel) for a bit of personal enjoyment and sightseeing. His hopes of being a tourist are cut short by a telegram summoning him back to London. He makes a booking on the Orient Express for the journey and runs into M. Bouc, director of the train line. The two are old friends and are delighted to know that they will be traveling together. There is thus an unpleasant surprise awaiting them at the station. Incredibly, the sleeping car is booked completely, a virtually unprecedented event in the winter. Fortunately for Poirot, one passenger fails to arrive and the detective is able to secure accommodations by sharing a com-

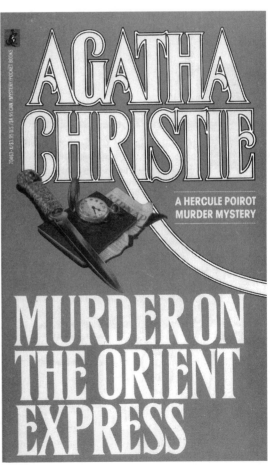

A *1970s edition of* Murder on the Orient Express. *(Pocket Books)*

partment with Hector MacQueen, the American secretary to a wealthy American businessman and philanthropist, Samuel Ratchett.

The detective observes his fellow passengers and is struck immediately by the remarkably cosmopolitan gathering in the Calais Coach. There are representatives of every social class, but the one passenger who most strikes him is Ratchett, whose eyes belie his outwardly "benevolent personality." Ratchett himself approaches Poirot and expresses his desire to employ the detective as a bodyguard, promising him *"big* money." Poirot declines on the simple basis that he does not like Ratchett's face.

After a night full of noises and disturbances, Poirot awakens to the startling news from M. Bouc that Ratchett has been brutally stabbed to death in his compartment. There will be no immediate investigation by the police because the train has been stopped in its tracks by a snowdrift and will be stranded for an unknown period of time. Not surprisingly, Bouc insists that Poirot take the case. It proves a very complicated matter, even though there are clues littering Ratchett's compartment, and it is deceptively obvious that the murderer has to be one of the other passengers in the sleeping car. Even more stunning is the identification of Ratchett as someone who deserved death for one of the most infamous crimes of the century.

• • •

Whereas *The Mousetrap* is Christie's most famous play, *Murder on the Orient Express* is Christie's most widely read work overall, with the exception of *The Murder of Roger Ackroyd* (1926). Ironically, the book is perhaps best known today because of the 1974 film adaptation of the same name. Indeed, there are many fans who know the plot in general terms and can even name some of the characters, even though they have never read the original novel. This is unfortunate, for *Orient Express* remains one of Christie's genuine masterpieces.

Trains figured prominently in many of Christie's works, including *The Mystery of the Blue Train,* "The Plymouth Express," and "The Girl in the Train." Christie noted in her autobiography her love of trains, adding her special admiration for one train: "All my life I had wanted to go on the Orient Express. When I had travelled to France or Spain or Italy, the Orient Express had often been standing at Calais, and I had longed to climb up into it. *Simplon-Orient Express-Milan, Belgrade, Stamboul."* She thus took great care in framing the world-famous train in just the right setting and providing a truly intriguing puzzle for Hercule Poirot.

The inspiration for the story is not difficult to fathom for anyone familiar with the tragedy that befell the Lindberghs in 1932. On March 21, the infant son of Charles and Anne Lindbergh was kidnapped from their home in Hopewell, New Jersey. Despite the payment of the ransom of $50,000, the child was found dead near Hopewell. The following year, Bruno Richard Hauptmann was arrested after being discovered with some of the ransom money. After a trial that has only grown in controversy over the years, Hauptmann was convicted for complicity in the kidnapping and electrocuted.

Christie was well informed of the details of the Lindbergh case and adapted it neatly to the mystery format. Rather than present the actual kidnapping, she instead focused on the kidnapper and his final encounter with justice. In terms of the novelization, Christie created a stricken couple that was based only loosely on the Lindberghs—Colonel Armstrong, a half-British, half-American soldier, and his wife, the daughter of a renowned American actress. Again swerving from history while pointing the finger of guilt at the kidnapper, Christie had the child's mother die from the shock and grief over her child's death and then had Colonel Armstrong shoot himself in despair. As for the kidnapper, he escaped from America and subsequently roamed the world under the new name of Ratchett. Revenge finally catches up with him on board the Calais Coach.

The book was dedicated "To M.E.L.M, Arpachiyah, 1933." M.E.L.M. was Max Edgar

Lucien Mallowan, Agatha's husband; Arpachiyah was an archaeological dig in Iraq where Mallowan worked.

Murder with Mirrors

See *They Do It with Mirrors*

The Mysterious Affair at Styles

PUBLISHING HISTORY: First published by the Bodley Head, London, 1921.

CHARACTERS: Hercule Poirot; Captain Arthur Hastings; Dr. Bauerstein, John Cavendish, Lawrence Cavendish, Mary Cavendish, Mr. Denby, Sir Ernest Heavyweather, Evelyn Howard, Alfred Inglethorpe, Emily Agnes Inglethorpe, Chief Inspector James Japp, Manning, Cynthia Murdoch, Mrs. Raikes, Superintendent Summerhayes.

Captain Arthur Hastings, still recovering from his war injuries and on sick leave, receives a kind invitation from a friend, John Cavendish, to recuperate at Styles Court, an estate near the village of Styles St. Mary in Essex. After arriving at Styles, Hastings discovers that the tension level is very high among the members of the Cavendish family. The mistress of the estate, Emily Cavendish, stepmother to John and Lawrence Cavendish, has total control of the family fortune since their father's death a year before, and both John and Lawrence are completely dependent upon her for their financial survival. They are thus quite disturbed when Emily gets married to Alfred Inglethorpe, a man twenty years younger and of very questionable background. Hastings also meets the other members of the household, including Mary, John's wife; Dr. Bauerstein, a friend of Mary Cavendish and an expert in poisons; Evelyn Howard, Mrs. Inglethorpe's secretary; and Cynthia Murdoch, an orphan given a home by Emily.

Emily also has assorted philanthropic projects. One of them is giving assistance to refugees of the war, including a group of Belgians. One of the Belgian refugees is actually known to Hastings, and the two have a joyous reunion in Styles St. Mary. Hastings's old friend is the famous detective Hercule Poirot.

The fears of Hastings that something terrible might happen at Styles come to pass when Emily falls ill and "seems to be having some kind of a fit." She is grievously stricken with convulsions and dies after muttering Alfred's name. The examining doctor diagnoses a heart complication, but Dr. Bauerstein recognizes at once the symptoms of poisoning.

The possibility of poison compels Hastings to consult his friend Poirot. Within a short time, the detective is at work on the case, bringing him into contact with the two police officers assigned to the case, Inspector Japp and Superintendent Summerhayes. The evidence points to Alfred Inglethorpe, but Poirot is not as eager as the police for his arrest.

• • •

The Mysterious Affair at Styles is most memorable for introducing to the world the great Belgian detective Hercule Poirot and for being the first book by Agatha Christie ever published. Christie began work on the book in 1916, during World War I, while working at a hospital dispensary, and used all of her spare time to bring the complicated case and the eccentric detective to life. Once it was finished and then revised extensively, she sent it off to the publisher Hodder and Stoughton, which wasted no time in rejecting it. Five more publishers declined the book, and then Christie received an invitation to go to London and meet with John Lane, head of the publisher Bodley Head. The publisher held the book for more than a year and a half before replying. The terms to which Agatha agreed were not generous (she learned much about contracts and rights from this early experience). There was no advance, nor were any royalties to be paid until 2,500 copies were sold.

The Mysterious Affair at Styles was finally published in February of 1921 (the copyright was technically registered in 1920) and sold 2,000 copies. This meant, unfortunately, that Christie saw no money for her efforts, save for twenty-five pounds for the serial rights, which were sold to a magazine.

The Mysterious Mr. Quin

PUBLISHING HISTORY: First published by William Collins Sons and Co., Ltd., London, 1930. First published in the United States by Dodd, Mead and Co., New York, 1930.

CONTENTS:

"The Coming of Mr. Quin"
"The Shadow on the Glass"
"At the 'Bells and Motley' "
"The Sign in the Sky"
"The Soul of the Croupier"
"The World's End"
"The Voice in the Dark"
"The Face of Helen"
"The Dead Harlequin"
"The Bird with the Broken Wing"
"The Man from the Sea"
"Harlequin's Lane"

The collection of stories featuring the cryptic Mr. Harley Quin was one of Agatha Christie's favorite works, and both Harley Quin and the urbane Mr. Satterthwaite were also two of her favorite characters. (For details on the birth of the character of Mr. Quin, please see page 324.) Such was her love of the harlequin that Christie dedicated the collection "To Harlequin, the Invisible." This marked the only time that she actually dedicated a book to one of her characters.

"The Mystery of Hunter's Lodge"

PUBLISHING HISTORY: First published in *Sketch* magazine, London, 1923–1924; reprinted by John Lane, London, 1924, in the short story collection *Poirot Investigates*. First published in the United States by Dodd, Mead and Co., 1925, in the short story collection *Poirot Investigates*.

CHARACTERS: Hercule Poirot; Captain Arthur Hastings; Chief Inspector James Japp; Roger Havering, Zoe Havering, Harrington Pace.

In a case similar to that of "The Disappearance of Mr. Davenheim," Poirot solves a murder entirely by long distance, relying upon the earnest Captain Hastings to keep him informed of all the particulars. Recovering from severe influenza, Poirot is unable to travel to Derbyshire with Roger Havering to look into the murder of Havering's uncle, Harrington Pace, at Hunter's Lodge. Commanded to send repeated telegrams to the detective, Hastings sets out with Havering and arrives in Derbyshire to find Inspector Japp already there on the case.

The chief suspect in the murder is a mysterious man with a black beard and a light overcoat who called on Harrington Pace just before his death and who disappeared. The murder weapon—later found at Ealing station in a parcel—is one of two identical revolvers owned by Pace, a fact of some importance to Poirot. A second vital clue for the detective is the indisputable fact that Roger Havering was at his club at the time of Pace's murder and thus could not possibly have pulled the trigger. Unlike virtually every other case, however, this case leaves the detective unable to provide enough evidence to capture and convict the killers. Japp, too, knows the full truth of Poirot's theory, but the guilty escape justice—albeit for a short time.

• • •

This case was adapted in 1991 by London Weekend Television for the series *Agatha Christie's Poirot* starring David Suchet.

"The Mystery of the Baghdad Chest"

PUBLISHING HISTORY: First published by Dodd, Mead and Co., New York, 1939, in the short story collection *The Regatta Mystery and Other Stories*.

CHARACTERS: Hercule Poirot; Captain Arthur Hastings; Burgoyne, Lady Chatterton, Edward Clayton, Marguerita Clayton, Major Curtiss, Major Jack Rich.

Poirot and Hastings are caught up in a discussion about the sensational murder case involving Major Rich. As described in blaring headlines and lurid news stories, the Major was arrested for murdering a friend, Edward Clayton, and stuffing the corpse into a Baghdad chest in his flat; he was further accused of hosting a party half an hour later and dancing in the same room with the victim's ravishing wife. The detective is drawn directly into the case by a friend, Lady Chatterton, who makes it possible for Poirot to receive a plea for help from Marguerita Clayton. She is certain that Major Rich did not murder her husband, even though she knew that he loved her and thus had ample motive for murder.

The subsequent investigation by Poirot certainly seems to point to Rich as a murderer. He had been the last to see Clayton alive, and his valet, Burgoyne, testifies that he did not hear Clayton depart, thereby confirming how the body may have ended up in the chest. Several vital clues offer Poirot the solution to the case. These include the movement of a screen that had customarily blocked the Baghdad chest; curious holes cut into the chest; and the cumbersome wooded tool found in Clayton's pocket. As was thought all along, jealousy and desire are at the heart of the case.

• • •

While this particular short story has not been adapted for television, "The Mystery of the Spanish Chest"—an expanded version of this case—was adapted in 1991 (see page 110). Poirot is brought into the matter of Clayton's murder by Lady Chatterton, one of Poirot's most ardent admirers. The detective had solved the case of a burglar and housebreaker by examining the mysterious conduct of a Pekingese.

"The Mystery of the Blue Jar"

PUBLISHING HISTORY: First published by William Collins Sons and Co., Ltd., London, 1933, in the short story collection *The Hound of Death and Other Stories*.

CHARACTERS: Uncle George, Jack Hartington, Dr. Ambrose Lavington, Felice Marchaud, Mrs. Turner.

A fanatical golfer, Jack Hartington enjoys playing every morning at the same time and on the same course. His recent game has been disturbed, however, by the same incident every morning: A scream emanates from a nearby cottage, a plaintive cry from a woman. In speaking with the resident of the cottage, Jack discovers that the poor man has been plagued by dreams of a woman and a blue vase. Convinced that somehow a psychic link has been established with a dead woman, Jack enlists a psychic investigator with dramatic consequences.

The Mystery of the Blue Train

PUBLISHING HISTORY: First published by William Collins Sons and Co., Ltd., London, 1928. First published in the United States by Dodd, Mead and Co., New York, 1928.

CHARACTERS: Hercule Poirot; Joseph Aarons, Alice, Monsieur Carrege, Monsieur Caux, Comte Armand de la Roche, Olga Demiroff, Ellen, Charles Evans, Mr. Goby, Katherine Grey, Boris Ivanovitch, Derek Kettering, Ruth Kettering, Major Richard Knighton, Ada Beatrice Mason, Pierre Michel, Mirelle, Demetrius Papopolous, Zia Papopolous, Lenox Tamplin, Rosalie Tamplin, Rufus van Aldin, Amelia Viner.

The wealthy American Rufus van Aldin is concerned about his daughter, Ruth Kettering. Her marriage to the penniless English aristocrat Derek Kettering is drawing to an end, and Rufus has long encouraged her to be rid of the faithless husband. Rufus sent his secretary, Major Knighton, to try and buy off Derek, especially as Derek has been involved of late with his mistress, the dancer Mirelle. To improve his daughter's outlook, Rufus gives her the priceless and famous Heart of Fire rubies, gems that have about them "a trail of tragedy and violence." He warns her, however, not to take the jewels out of the country.

Disregarding her father's advice, Ruth sets off from England on board the famous Blue Train from London to Nice to meet her former lover, the Comte Armand de la Roche. While on board, she strikes up a conversation with Katherine Grey, who has recently come into some money after the death of her former employer. Grey is soon shocked to be interviewed by the police at the station in Nice. Ruth Kettering has been murdered while on board and her jewels have been stolen.

• • •

While Agatha Christie had several favorite novels (*The Murder of Roger Ackroyd, The Pale Horse, Moving Finger,* and *Endless Night*), she seemed to have one definite choice as to the worst of her books: *The Mystery of the Blue Train,* which she described as "the worst book I ever wrote." It is perhaps natural for Christie to have little affection for the book, as it was the first book she authored after the dreadful year of 1926—a year that included the death of her mother, her disastrous divorce, and her still unexplained disappearance in December. The book is "Dedicated to two Distinguished Members of the O.F.D., Carlotta and Peter." O.F.D. stood for Order of the Faithful Dogs, which was created by Christie to honor the friends who stood by her during the darkest hours of the year. The friends to prove faithless were inaugurated into the Order of the Rats, third class.

"The Mystery of the Crime in Cabin 66"

See "Problem at Sea"

"The Mystery of the Spanish Chest"

PUBLISHING HISTORY: First published by William Collins Sons and Co., Ltd., London, 1960, in the short story collection *The Adventure of the Christmas Pudding and a Selection of Entrées.* A shorter version, entitled "The Mystery of the Baghdad Chest," was published by Dodd, Mead and Co., New York, 1939, in the short story collection *The Regatta Mystery and Other Stories.*

CHARACTERS: Hercule Poirot; William Burgess, Lady Abbie Chatterton, Arnold Clayton, Margharita Clayton, Miss Felicity Lemon, Inspector Miller, Major Charles Rich, Jeremy Spence, Linda Spence.

"The Mystery of the Spanish Chest" is an expanded and heavily revised version of the "The Mystery of the Baghdad Chest," and features an identical plot. The primary changes are the altered names used for the characters (e.g., Margharita

Clayton in "Spanish Chest" is Marguerita Clayton in "Baghdad Chest") and the fleshing out of Hercule Poirot's investigation. The murder victim is the same, as is the clever but gruesome murder method: A man is lured into a secret chest, where he is stabbed to death by a jealous murderer.

• • •

This case was adapted by London Weekend Television for the series *Agatha Christie's Poirot* starring David Suchet. Miss Felicity Lemon makes one of her memorable appearances in this story.

"Mystery of the Spanish Shawl"

See "Mr. Eastwood's Adventure"

"The Nemean Lion"

PUBLISHING HISTORY: First published by William Collins Sons and Co., Ltd., London, 1947, in the short story collection *The Labours of Hercules.* First published in the United States by Dodd, Mead and Co., New York, 1947, in the short story collection *The Labors of Hercules.*

CHARACTERS: Hercule Poirot; Miss Amy Carnaby, Emily Carnaby, Georges, Mrs. Harte, Sir Joseph Hoggin, Lady Milly Hoggin, Miss Ellen Keble, Mrs. Samuelson.

The first of Hercule Poirot's labors in emulation of the famed mythological figure Hercules, "The Nemean Lion" presents the detective with one of the more seemingly inconsequential and even inane cases of his illustrious career: He must solve the disappearance of a Pekingese dog named Shan Tung. For Poirot, such a case should not command his attention, but as he is duplicating the labors of the great hero, the disappearance of a diminutive lion/dog is ideal for what he has in mind. The case is also not without its merits.

Consulted by Sir Joseph Hoggin, Poirot is asked to investigate the "dognapping" of Shan Tung, who was held for ransom and subsequently released when Lady Milly Hoggin paid the demanded sum. Matters become even more intriguing when Poirot learns that Shan Tung's kidnapping was merely one of a series of disappearances.

Further investigation uncovers one of the most ingenious criminal organizations that Poirot has ever faced: "Your organization must have been indeed excellent . . . your psychology is excellent . . . Your organization is first class . . ." He brings the gang to an end, but he is remarkably magnanimous in victory. As a tangential matter, Poirot also prevents any possibility of murder from taking place, much to the surprise of the would-be killer.

• • •

"The Nemean Lion" includes the brief appearance of Poirot's unflappable "valet and general factotum," Georges, who is present in twenty-one stories in all.

Nemesis

PUBLISHING HISTORY: First published by William Collins Sons and Co., Ltd., London, 1971. First published in the United States by Dodd, Mead and Co., New York, 1971.

CHARACTERS: Miss Jane Marple; Cherry Baker, Miss Barrow, Archdeacon Brabazon, Anthea Bradbury-Scott, Clotilde Bradbury-Scott, Nora Broad, James Broadribb, Mr. Caspar, Miss Cooke, James Crawford, Lavinia Bradbury-Scott Glynne, Verity Hunt, Richard Jameson, Sir Andrew McNeil, Miss Merrypit, Emlyn Price, Jason Rafiel, Michael Rafiel, Mrs. Sandbourne, Mr. Schuster, Elizabeth Temple, Mrs. Vinegar, Esther Walters, Professor Wanstead.

As is her habit, Miss Marple reads two newspapers, one in the morning and the other, the *Times,* in the afternoon with her tea. Of particular interest to her are the assorted notices—the births, the marriages, and, above all, the deaths. On this particular afternoon, one name in the deaths column catches her eye: Jason Rafiel. After searching her memory, she finally recalls; he was the wealthy guest on the island of St. Honoré at which she had stayed during the events of that murder in the Caribbean.

Days later, Miss Marple receives a letter with a London postmark that arrives in a long, good-quality envelope. The letter is from Messrs. Broadribb and Schuster, solicitors and notaries public, with offices in Bloomsbury. It requests that she visit their offices within the next week to hear the details of a proposition that will be to her advantage. After suggesting a specific date, the senders add that they represent the estate of the late Jason Rafiel.

Greeted with the utmost courtesy by the attorneys upon her arrival at their offices, Miss Marple is presented with an astonishing proposal. They give her a letter from Rafiel that declares his intention to reward her with a legacy of twenty thousand pounds in return for her acceptance of a commission:

You my dear, if I may call you that, have a natural flair for justice and that has led to your having a natural flair for crime. I want you to investigate a certain crime . . . I have set aside a year for you to engage on this mission. You are not young, but you are, if I may say so, tough. I think I can trust a reasonable fate to keep you alive for a year at least.

After reading the letter three times, Miss Marple accepts the challenge from beyond the grave. She is next given a note providing details of a tour that had been ordered for her by Rafiel before his death, "Tour No. 37 of the Famous Houses and Gardens of Great Britain." Within a short time, she is on a bus and heading through the English countryside. Her tour brings her into the investigation of the past and a crime that involved Jason Rafiel's son. It is a hunt for justice that must be undertaken by someone who embodies precisely what Rafiel called Miss Marple: Nemesis.

• • •

Nemesis holds the distinction of being the last Marple novel that Christie wrote. While *Sleeping Murder* and *Miss Marple's Final Cases* were published posthumously (in 1976 and 1979, respectively), they had been written prior to her authorship of *Nemesis*. As with Poirot's emulation of the legendary hero Hercules in *The Labours of Hercules* (1947), *Nemesis* features Miss Marple in the role of Nemesis, the dreaded Greek goddess of divine retribution. She was cast in this role by Jason Rafiel, who had seen her talents for detective work in *A Caribbean Mystery* (1964).

The novel was dedicated to Daphne Honeybone, Christie's longtime private secretary. She continued in the capacity of private secretary to Sir Max Mallowan after Christie's death in 1976.

Nemesis was adapted for television in 1987 by the BBC, and starred Joan Hickson as Miss Marple.

"Next to a Dog"

PUBLISHING HISTORY: First published by Dodd, Mead and Co., New York, 1971, in the short story collection *The Golden Ball and Other Stories.*

CHARACTERS: Mr. Allaby, Mrs. Barnes, Arthur Holliday, Joyce Lambert.

The young widow Joyce Lambert finds herself in a desperate financial predicament. In need of a job, she must turn down an offered position as a governess because it means that she must leave the country and journey to Italy. That she cannot do, for she is unable to take along the creature most dear to her in the world: her aged and half-blind terrier named Terry. The beloved dog—her companion and virtually only friend—had been a gift from her husband as he went off to fight and die in France.

With the last reservoir of hope gone in her life, she agrees to marry the odious Arthur Holliday. She does not love him, nor does she even like him, but he is eager to marry her and has money. She regrets her decision, but there is nothing left to do. Nothing, at least, until Terry is grievously injured in an accident and later dies. She is suddenly free to take the job out of the country and has a meeting with destiny.

N or M?

PUBLISHING HISTORY: First published by William Collins Sons and Co., Ltd., London, 1941. First published in the United States by Dodd, Mead and Co., New York, 1941.

CHARACTERS: Tommy Beresford; Tuppence Beresford; Appledore, Albert Batt, Deborah Beresford, Dr. Binion, Major Bletchley, Alfred Cayley, Elisabeth Cayley, Mr. Grant, Commander Haydock, Anthony Marsdon, Sophia Minton, Mrs. O'Rourke, Mrs. Eileen Perenna, Sheila Perenna, Vanda Polonska, Betty Sprot, Mrs. Millicent Sprot, Carl von Deinim.

World War II has begun and England is in its bitter life-and-death struggle with the Axis powers. For the aging Tommy and Tuppence Beresford, the days of the war are made even more gloomy by their remembrance of better days. Both are feeling "middle-aged and past doing things" even as both are eager to help their country in its hour of greatest need. The gloom of the Beresfords is lifted unexpectedly by the arrival of Mr. Grant, a member of British intelligence. He has been sent by their old boss, Mr. Carter, to request that Tommy resume his old duties in hunting down foreign agents in England. Tommy Beresford agrees instantly, and sets off for the seaside resort of Leahampton. Tuppence is left deliberately uninformed of the mission, at the request of Tommy's bosses. It is believed by intelligence that a group of agents is operating out of the resort hotel there, the Sans Souci. The basis for the assumption by intelligence is the recent death of a British agent, whose dying words were: "N or M Song Susie."

Tommy arrives at the resort and finds, to his surprise, another guest there by the name of Mrs. Blenkensop. She claims to have three sons in the war, but Tommy has his doubts about her, especially as he recognizes her immediately as Tuppence Beresford. She had heard Tommy's conversation with Grant and had set out on her own to lend a hand with the investigation. It does not take long for the Beresfords to meet up with adventure and danger, especially after Tuppence's room is searched and Tommy disappears.

• • •

Published in 1941, *N or M?* offered readers in Britain a chance to follow the exploits of two of their favorite characters in a setting very close to home. Britain was in the middle of World War II, and the fun of the book was a welcome relief for fans from the all-too-real daily dangers being posed by the Luftwaffe and the reports of the war overseas. Christie wrote the book in the middle of the frequent bombings during the Blitz.

One, Two, Buckle My Shoe

PUBLISHING HISTORY: First published by William Collins Sons and Co., Ltd., London, 1940. First published in the United States by Dodd, Mead and Co., New York, 1941, under the title *The Patriotic Murders.* Subsequent editions were published under the title *An Overdose of Death.*

CHARACTERS: Hercule Poirot; Chief Inspector James Japp; Colonel Abercrombie, Mr. Amberiotis, Reginald Barnes, Alistair Blunt, Frank Carter, Agnes Fletcher, Gerda Grant, Mr. Harrison, Ram Lal, Mrs. Merton, Georgina Morley, Henry Morley, Gladys Neville, Jane Olivera, Julia Olivera, Howard Raikes, Mr. Reilly, Mabelle Sainsbury Seale.

Not even Hercule Poirot can avoid those "certain humiliating moments in the lives of the greatest of men." Journeying by taxi to 58 Queen Charlotte Street, Poirot enters the offices of Dr. Henry Morley and willingly subjects himself to the "ordeal of the drill." In chatting with the dentist, Poirot learns of Morley's pride that later that day he will be caring for a very important patient, Mr. Alistair Blunt, the immensely wealthy and powerful financier.

Hours later that same day, Poirot receives a call from Inspector Japp. Dr. Morley has been found dead, shot through the head from an apparent suicide. He certainly was not a candidate to take his own life, given the absence of personal and financial troubles; nor did it make sense for him to do himself in during the middle of a busy day of seeing patients.

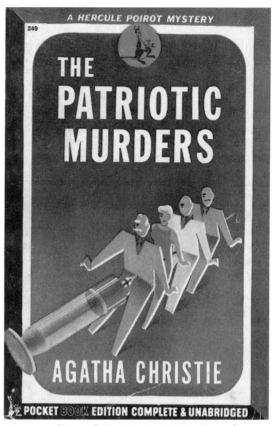

A 1944 edition of The Patriotic Murders, *the American title for* One, Two, Buckle My Shoe. *(Pocket Books)*

Further developments point not to suicide but to murder. Morley's assistant, Gladys, had been called away from the office under false pretenses. Even more peculiar, one of Morley's other patients, seen on the same day, was a mysterious Greek visitor who had phoned from the Savoy for an appointment. He had seen Morley and then gone back to the hotel, where he died. Not long after, an assassination attempt is made on the prime minister of England while he walks with Alistair Blunt. The clues point to the possibility that there is someone after Blunt, but Poirot has other ideas.

• • •

Even though it was published during World War II, *One, Two, Buckle My Shoe* contains only a few, albeit passing, references to Hitler and Mussolini and can be dated to the period just before the Nazi invasion of Poland in September of 1939. The time period is established by the absence of the backdrop of war, the presence of the quasi-military fascist group the Imperial Shirts (modeled after such groups as the very real British Union of Fascists, who disbanded at the commencement of the war), and the generally nice things Poirot's dentist, Dr. Morley, has to say about King Leopold of Belgium. The king earned the bitter hostility of his people and the Allies for his unconditional surrender to the Germans in 1940; he spent the war in Germany and was refused entry into Belgium by its parliament after the fighting, dying as an exile.

This novel is one of Christie's works that uses a nursery rhyme in its title. The novel was adapted in 1992 by London Weekend Television for the series *Agatha Christie's Poirot* starring David Suchet.

"The Oracle at Delphi"

PUBLISHING HISTORY: First published by William Collins Sons and Co., Ltd., London, 1934, in the short story collection *Parker Pyne Investigates*. First published in the United States by Dodd, Mead and Co., New York, 1934, in the short story collection *Mr. Parker Pyne, Detective*.

CHARACTERS: Mr. Parker Pyne; Aristopoulos, Willard J. Peters, Mrs. Willard J. Peters, Mr. Thompson.

While on a visit to Greece, Mr. Parker Pyne pays a call at Delphi and becomes embroiled in the kidnapping case of young Willard J. Peters. Informed by note that her son has been kidnapped by Greek bandits, the adoring Mrs. Peters must produce a ransom of ten thousand pounds or her son's ears will be cut off and then he will be murdered. To her seeming rescue comes Parker Pyne, who arranges for Mrs. Peters to pay the ransom with a diamond necklace worth a hundred thousand dollars. The case is solved and young Willard

is returned safely, but only after a surprising twist in the story.

Ordeal by Innocence

PUBLISHING HISTORY: First published by William Collins Sons and Co., Ltd., London, 1958. First published in the United States by Dodd, Mead and Co., New York, 1959.

CHARACTERS: Christina Argyle, Hester Argyle, Jacko Argyle, Leo Argyle, Michael Argyle, Rachel Argyle, Dr. Arthur Calgary, Joe Clegg, Maureen Clegg, Dr. Donal Craig, Mary Durrant, Philip Durrant, Major Finney, Superintendent Huish, Kirsten Lindstrom, Dr. MacMaster, Andrew Marshall, Gwenda Vaughan.

Dr. Arthur Calgary has returned to England after taking part in an Antarctic expedition that has kept him away from home for many months. His return delivers him a shocking piece of news. Jacko Argyle has died in prison from pneumonia! He realizes that he might have been able to save the man from prison and death had he been in England and, more important, had he been able to remember what happened on a certain night months before.

Rachel and Leo Argyle were a childless couple who used her considerable wealth to convert their home at Sunny Point to a refuge for children evacuated from London. Eventually, they adopted five of the children and raised them as their own. The children were all emotionally disturbed in different ways, and Rachel, with her smothering matriarchal manner, did not help the situation.

One child most of all was a problem—Jacko Argyle, who displayed tendencies toward theft and delinquency. He also argued and fought with his mother over money, with one argument seared into the memories of those who heard it because of what followed. Rachel Argyle was beaten to death with a poker, and the police immediately looked to Jacko as their only suspect. He claimed to have been hitchhiking from Sunny Point to Drymouth at the time of the murder, and said that he had been picked up by a passing motorist. Unfortu-

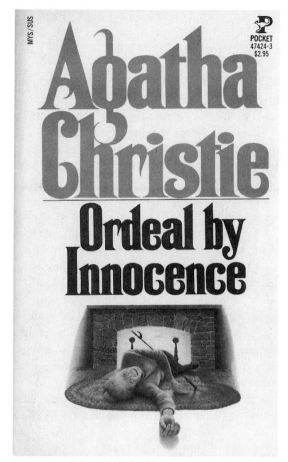

A *1970s edition of* Ordeal by Innocence. *(Pocket Books)*

nately for him, no driver could ever be found, nor did anyone come forward to identify him. Jacko was brought to trial, convicted, and sentenced to life. Within months, he was dead from pneumonia.

To his horror, Dr. Calgary realizes that he was the driver who might have proven Jacko innocent. The very night that he picked up Jacko, Calgary was in a collision and suffered a bout of amnesia. Even as he recovered physically from the trauma, Calgary could remember nothing of the night in question and thus set off for Antarctica to work as a geophysicist. Once discovering what had hap-

pened, Calgary goes straight to the police, who confirm his story, and then visits the Argyles to give them the good news about Jacko's innocence. There is, of course, the dark reality that if Jacko was blameless in Rachel's death, someone else in the Argyle household is a murderer.

• • •

Ordeal by Innocence is ranked among the novels Christie declared to be her favorites—with *The Murder of Roger Ackroyd* (1926), *The Pale Horse* (1961), *Moving Finger* (1943), and *Endless Night* (1967), among others. The novel is notable for the absence of any recurring Christie detective. Instead, the sleuth for this novel is Dr. Arthur Calgary. Similar to Charles Hayward in *Crooked House* (1949), Calgary is a likable and competent lay investigator who, nevertheless, never appears again in any Christie work.

Christie dedicated book "To Billy Collins with Affection and Gratitude." Billy Collins was William Collins, Jr., head of William Collins Sons and Co., Ltd.; he was responsible for convincing Christie to jump from John Lane to Collins in 1926.

The novel was adapted for film in 1985, starring Donald Sutherland and Faye Dunaway.

An Overdose of Death

See *One, Two, Buckle My Shoe*

The Pale Horse

PUBLISHING HISTORY: First published by William Collins Sons and Co., Ltd., London, 1962. First published in the United States by Dodd, Mead and Co., New York, 1962.

CHARACTERS: Mrs. Ariadne Oliver; David Ardingly, C. R. Bradley, Eileen Brandon, Dr. Jim Corrigan, Katherine Corrigan, Reverend Caleb Dane Calthorp, Maud Dane Calthorp, Mrs. Jesse Davis, Colonel Hugh Despard, Rhoda Despard, Mark Easterbrook, Lou Ellis, Father Gorman, Thyrza Grey, Detective Inspector Lejeune, Milly, Hermia Redcliffe, Sybil Stamfordis, Pamela Stirling, Thomasina Tuckerton, Mr. Venables, Bella Webb.

The writer Mark Easterbrook takes a break

from his writing efforts on Mogul architecture to clear his head and departs his Chelsea flat for something to eat. He wanders into Luigi's, a very bohemian hangout, and sees the local wildlife on display. Two young female patrons enter into a brawl, which includes vicious hair-pulling. The violence is finally brought to an end, but one of the participants has managed to yank out handfuls of her opponent's hair. He learns that the red-haired girl who had lost the patches of hair is Thomasina Tuckerton, the daughter of wealthy parents, who had abandoned her family's money privilege for a more unconventional lifestyle. A week later, Easterbrook is surprised to read in the newspaper that Thomasina Tuckerton is dead after a brief stay in a nursing home.

In another part of London, the Presbyterian minister Father Gorman is summoned to a dying woman's bedside in a rooming house. As she dies, she cries out, "Wickedness . . . it must be stopped," and then relates to the minister a fantastic tale of murder. The minister finds her story beyond belief, but there was something about her that he cannot discount. He decides to stop at a café and write down her ramblings. Most important, he has a list of nine names that were of absolute urgency to the dying woman. He puts the list in his shoe and then sets out for home. A short time later, he is killed by someone who, according to a witness, was following him.

The two police officials assigned to the Gorman case, Detective Inspector Lejeune and police surgeon Corrigan, are unable to find a motive for the murder, but they are surprised to learn that most of the names on the list are of people who have died, including Thomasina Tuckerton. As luck would have it, Corrigan meets an old friend of his, Mark Easterbrook, at a party thrown by a friend of Ariadne Oliver. Easterbrook is shown the list of names and recognizes most of them. He also relates a story he had heard while with friends that it is possible to hire a group of murderers who apply witchcraft and the occult in the practice of eliminating one's enemies. They can be contacted

at a place called The Pale Horse Inn, the home of a psychic, Thyrza Grey, a medium, Sybil Stamfordis, and a witch, Bella Webb.

• • •

The Pale Horse features the only published case in which Mrs. Ariadne Oliver appears without Hercule Poirot. Not to disappoint those fans who appreciated Christie's bringing characters from one novel into another, Christie included two people, Colonel Despard and his wife, Rhoda, who had last appeared in *Cards on the Table* (1936). She also reused Reverend Caleb Calthorp, from *The Moving Finger* (1943).

According to Christie's autobiography, the idea for the novel came to her nearly half a century before she wrote it in book form. While studying pharmacology during World War I, Christie caught a mistake made by a well-known pharmacist, a "Mr. P.," but she never revealed his error. It was then that she realized the potentially endless criminal possibilities: "He struck me, in spite of his cherubic appearance, as possibly rather a dangerous man. His memory remained with me so long it was still there waiting when I first conceived the idea of writing my book, *The Pale Horse*."

Christie dedicated the book "To John and Helen Mildmay White—with many thanks for the opportunity given me to see justice done." *The Pale Horse* was adapted for television by the BBC in 1997, and starred Colin Buchanan.

Parker Pyne Investigates

PUBLISHING HISTORY: First published by William Collins Sons and Co., Ltd., London, 1934. First published in the United States by Dodd, Mead and Co., New York, 1934, under the title *Mr. Parker Pyne, Detective*.

CONTENTS:
"The Case of the Middle-Aged Wife"
"The Case of the Discontented Soldier"
"The Case of the Distressed Lady"
"The Case of the Discontented Husband"

"The Case of the City Clerk"
"The Case of the Rich Woman"
"Have You Got Everything You Want?"
"The Gate of Baghdad"
"The House at Shiraz"
"The Pearl of Price"
"Death on the Nile"
"The Oracle at Delphi"

The stories in this collection can be divided into two distinct groups. The first six, set apart by their title ("The Case of . . ."), present Parker Pyne fulfilling his primary role in relieving people of their unhappiness. The cases follow the general pattern of clients responding to his advertisement in the newspaper. There is among the cases one conspicuous failure and one that reveals the elaborate lengths to which Parker Pyne goes to satisfy his clients' demands.

The second set of stories contains cases set in climes far removed from England. Instead of romantic entanglements, Parker Pyne must deal with murder, theft, and deception. The settings make use of some of the more exotic locales used by Christie in other, more famous works (e.g., the Orient Express, Baghdad, Egypt, and Petra) and put to use as well Christie's extensive travel experience in the Middle East with her second husband, the archaeologist Max Mallowan.

The collection makes use of two minor and two significant characters. Parker Pyne relies upon the services of the beautiful Madeleine de Sara and the handsome Claude Luttrell for those cases requiring the presence of irresistible or enchanting objects of affection. The significant characters, Miss Felicity Lemon and Ariadne Oliver, appear elsewhere in Christie's writings: Miss Lemon becomes Hercule Poirot's invaluable secretary and Miss Oliver, beloved as Christie's literary alter ego, serves as an interesting foil to Poirot. Miss Lemon appears in six Christie short stories and four novels, while Mrs. Oliver appears in eight novels and two short stories (both in this collection).

Of these short stories "The Case of the Discon-

tented Soldier" and "The Case of the Middle-Aged Wife" have been adapted for television—both in 1982, by Thames Television, for *The Agatha Christie Hour.*

Partners in Crime

PUBLISHING HISTORY: First published by William Collins Sons and Co., Ltd., London, 1929. First published in the United States by Dodd, Mead and Co., New York, 1929.

CONTENTS:
"A Fairy in the Flat"
"A Pot of Tea"
"The Affair of the Pink Pearl"
"The Adventure of the Sinister Stranger"
"Finessing the King"
"The Gentleman Dressed in Newspaper"
"The Case of the Missing Lady"
"Blindman's Bluff"
"The Man in the Mist"
"The Crackler"
"The Sunningdale Mystery"
"The House of Lurking Death"
"The Unbreakable Alibi"
"The Clergyman's Daughter"
"The Red House"
"The Ambassador's Boots"
"The Man Who Was No. 16"

Partners in Crime offers a series of loosely connected short stories starring the spirited and fun-loving couple Tommy and Tuppence Beresford. Having been married and deliriously happy in each other's company at the end of *The Secret Adversary* (1922), the Beresfords are still bitten with the adventure bug. Their hopes are fulfilled when Mr. Carter, Tommy's superior in the British secret service, enlists them to assist their country by taking an assignment guaranteed to keep them busy. They are to assume control of Blunt's International Detective Agency and await the arrival of foreign agents. In the meantime, they are free to solve any various cases that may come their way.

What elevates the collection is the habit adopted by the Beresfords of conducting their investigations in the personae of different detectives of fiction. Thus, Tommy becomes Father Brown, Hercule Poirot, and several other lesser-known detectives, while Tuppence also takes part as various characters, including Captain Hastings.

The collection was adapted by London Weekend Television in 1983.

Passenger to Frankfurt

PUBLISHING HISTORY: First published by William Collins Sons and Co., Ltd., in London, 1970. First published in the United States by Dodd, Mead and Co., New York, 1970.

CHARACTERS: Lord Edward Altamount, Squadron Leader Andrews, Karl Arguileros, Clifford Bent, Admiral Philip Blunt, Jim Brewster, Lady Matilda Check-Heaton, Gordon Chetwynd, Mildred Jean Cortman, Sam Cortman, Dr. Donaldson, Professor Eckstein, Professor Gottlieb, Monsieur le President Grosjean, Henry Horsham, Sir James Kleek, Cedric Lazenby, Amy Leatheran, Lisa Neumann, Sir Stafford Nye, Colonel Ephraim Pikeaway, Eric Pugh, Dr. Reichardt, Mr. Robinson, Robert Shoreham, Herr Heinrich Spiess, Signor Vitelli, the Grafin Charlotte von Waldhausen, Countess Renata Zerkowski.

While waiting at the Frankfurt airport for his connecting flight to London, British diplomat Sir Stafford Nye is approached by a young woman with "a very faint foreign accent." She makes to him a most unusual proposal. Desperate to reach London—indeed, her very life depends upon it—the young woman begs Sir Stafford to imbibe some of a drugged drink and allow her to make off with his cloak and passport. These she will use to enter England. Always a most unconventional personality (one of the reasons for his inconspicuous career in the foreign service), Sir Stafford agrees and takes the potion. When he awakens, he discovers that his cloak and his passport are gone. He reports them stolen and heads home to London.

Upon returning, Sir Stafford is congratulated for his ingenuity in assisting the young woman to reach England, the first inkling that she is a person of some importance. As though in response to his deed, Sir Stafford is twice nearly killed by automobiles and then receives his passport in the mail. Hoping to meet the young woman again, Stafford places an advertisement in the personals column. He receives a reply and meets a contact on the Hungerford Bridge, who gives him a ticket for the Wagnerian opera *Siegfried* the next night. At last, he meets the woman again, but once more their encounter is fleeting, and, for the first time, Sir Stafford sees the ominous name "young Siegfried." Not long afterward, he meets the woman yet again, this time at the American embassy. It is there that he learns her real name, Countess Renata Zerkowski.

Having proven himself trustworthy, Sir Stafford is assigned by his superiors to a special mission. With the countess, he must go to Germany and begin working against a secret organization struggling to achieve world domination. Sir Stafford and the countess must deal with dangerous youth gangs, assassins, a monstrously obese intriguer nicknamed Big Charlotte, and the illegitimate son of Adolf Hitler.

• • •

Passenger to Frankfurt was a deviation from Christie's usual mystery fare. As one of her espionage novels, it is not one of the most popular among readers and seemed from the first rather pale in comparison to the spy thrillers of the period, especially the intense novels by Ian Fleming featuring James Bond.

Patriotic Murders

See *One, Two, Buckle My Shoe*

"The Pearl of Price"

PUBLISHING HISTORY: First published by William Collins Sons and Co., Ltd., London, 1934, in the short story collection *Parker Pyne Investigates.* First published in the United States by Dodd, Mead and Co., New York, 1934, in the short story collection *Mr. Parker Pyne, Detective.*

CHARACTERS: Mr. Parker Pyne; Caleb Blundell, Carol Blundell, Dr. Carver, Colonel Dubosc, Abbas Effendi, Jim Hurst, Sir Donald Marvel.

While journeying across Jordan, Parker Pyne becomes involved in solving the disappearance of an expensive earring, supposedly worth $140,000. The earring, the pearl of price, had apparently slipped off the ear of a young American woman, Carol Blundell, the daughter of the American magnate Caleb Blundell. With the stark Jordanian desert as the backdrop, Parker Pyne must achieve a most difficult set of tasks: recover Carol Blundell's pearl earring and prove the innocence of the young man she loves, despite her would-be fiancé's criminal past. Fortunately, the rich heritage of the desert provides Parker Pyne with his solution and a successful resolution to the case.

• • •

Christie's familiarity with archaeology, derived from her marriage to the archaeologist Max Mallowan, is nicely displayed in this story (as it is in other stories and novels).

"Perfect Maid, The Case of the"

PUBLISHING HISTORY: First published by Dodd, Mead and Co., New York, 1950, in the short story collection *Three Blind Mice and Other Stories.*

CHARACTERS: Miss Jane Marple; Edna, Gladys Holmes, Emily Skinner, Lavinia Skinner, Inspector Slack.

In this story, featuring an example of a person who seems too good to be true, Miss Marple uses her deductive powers to solve the case of a maid who is an apparent model of perfection and who all the while plots to rob jewels from her unsuspecting employers.

Two sisters, Emily and Lavinia Skinner, claim that a piece of jewelry is missing. They suspect their maid, Gladys, and dismiss her, even though the item in question turns up in a drawer. The maid they hire to replace Gladys, Mary Higgins, proves so capable and ideal that Miss Lavinia exclaims, "I really feel Mary has been sent here

through prayer." Miss Marple warns her to be "a little careful," and, sure enough, only a few days later, Mary has disappeared, along with diamonds, jewels, and cash from other residents of prosperous St. Mary Mead. The police are baffled, especially Inspector Slack, but Miss Marple finds the missing maid with the help of a striped piece of peppermint candy and a small mirror from her handbag.

Peril at End House

PUBLISHING HISTORY: First published by William Collins Sons and Co., Ltd., London, 1932. First published in the United States by Dodd, Mead and Co., New York, 1932.

CHARACTERS: Hercule Poirot; Captain Arthur Hastings; Chief Inspector James Japp; Reverend Giles Buckley, Jean Buckley, Maggie Buckley, Nick Buckley, Commander George Challenger, Bert Croft, Milly Croft, Dr. Graham, Jim Lazarus, Dr. MacAllister, Mr. Rice, Frederica Rice, Charles Vyse, Dr. Whitfield, Ellen Wilson.

While taking a well-deserved vacation in St. Loo, Hercule Poirot and Captain Arthur Hastings meet a charming young woman named Nick Buckley. She is the last of the Buckleys, a family that has long inhabited the isolated mansion of End House on a nearby promontory. It turns out that Miss Buckley has narrowly escaped harm three times from "accidents," and the Belgian detective finds it unlikely that these events are pure coincidence. Even as they sit and chat, a wasp buzzes around Nick's ear. Poirot, however, investigates the ground around them, as well as Nick's hat, which she has left behind by accident. On the ground, he finds a spent bullet, and in her hat is a bullet hole. The detective wastes no time in visiting Nick at her home and announcing that her "accidents" were not so accidental and that her life is in genuine danger. Poirot's conviction is soon validated when Nick's cousin, Maggie Buckley, is murdered while wearing Nick's red shawl.

• • •

Peril at End House was produced during one of Christie's most fruitful periods (between 1929 and 1932), during which she wrote four novels (*The Seven Dials Mystery,* 1929; *The Murder at the Vicarage,* 1930; *The Sittaford Mystery,* 1931; and *Peril at End House,* 1932) and three short story collections (*Partners in Crime,* 1929; *The Mysterious Mr. Quin,* 1930; and *The Thirteen Problems,* 1932).

Christie acknowledged in her autobiography the cost that such productivity entailed: *"Peril at End House* was another of my books which left so little impression on my mine that I cannot even remember writing it. Possibly I had already thought out the plot sometime previously, since this has always been the habit of mine, and often confuses me as to when a book was written or published."

The dedication of the book read: "To Eden Phillpotts, to whom I shall always be grateful for his friendship and the encouragement he gave me many years ago." Phillpotts was a novelist and poet and the first professional writer to read Christie's writings. He gave her advice and encouragement and started her out on her titanic career.

Peril at End House was adapted for the stage by Arnold Ridley; it opened in 1940 in London. In 1990, the book was adapted by London Weekend Television for the series *Agatha Christie's Poirot* starring David Suchet.

"Philomel Cottage"

PUBLISHING HISTORY: First published by William Collins Sons and Co., Ltd., London, 1934, in the short story collection *The Listerdale Mystery.*

CHARACTERS: Mr. Ames, George, Alix Martin, Gerald Martin, Dicky Windyford.

Beautiful Alix has been the object of love by Dicky Windyford for quite some time, but he has never formally asked for her hand in marriage because he is determined to make something of himself before getting married. His reluctance only increases after Alix inherits two thousand pounds, as he is more determined to make a fortune on his own.

This delay proves critical, for Alix meets Gerald Martin and, quite uncharacteristically, she marries him after the briefest of courtships. Alix is at first quite happy, but tiny details about her new husband begin to trouble her, especially her total ignorance about his earlier life. Her apprehension grows when she discovers old newspapers from America and a diary that reveals terrifying details about Gerald's previous career. Facing what she fears is her imminent murder, Alix contacts Dicky for help, but she must confront the danger on her own.

• • •

This story was adapted for the stage in 1936 with the title *Love from a Stranger.* The film, also called *Love from a Stranger,* was made in 1937, and starred Basil Rathbone and Ann Harding; a remake of the film appeared in 1947.

"The Plymouth Express"

PUBLISHING HISTORY: First published by Dodd, Mead and Co., New York, 1951, in the short story collection *The Under Dog and Other Stories.*

CHARACTERS: Hercule Poirot; Captain Arthur Hastings; Chief Inspector James Japp; The Honourable Flossie Carrington, Rupert Carrington, Ebenezer Halliday, Jane Mason, Count Armand de la Rochefour, Lieutenant Alec Simpson.

Hercule Poirot receives a note from the extremely wealthy American industrialist Ebenezer Halliday asking him to call at the earliest convenience. Poirot answers Hastings's questions as to what the American might want by directing him to the newspaper. There, the captain reads the gruesome tale of the murder of Mrs. Rupert Carrington, whose body—stabbed through the heart—was found stuffed under a seat in a train compartment. Prior to her marriage, the victim was called Flossie Halliday, daughter of the steel king of America.

Ebenezer Halliday comes to the point swiftly—he will spend his last dollar, if necessary, to catch the murderer of his daughter; the recovery of the expensive jewels that were stolen is of minor importance to him. He believes that Flossie's husband, Carrington, is "an unprincipled scoundrel," and urged his daughter to take proceedings against him for his appalling and potentially scandalous behavior. There is a second likely suspect in the crime—an adventurer, the Count de la Rochefour, who had apparently been involved in a relationship with the victim.

Inspector Japp pursues the case from his own direction, but, as ever, he finds the sleuth ahead of him, even anticipating the discovery of the knife used in the murder and its precise location on the line of the Plymouth Express where the crime was committed. Poirot's solution surprises his client and results in Halliday's sending Poirot a massive check to show his gratitude.

• • •

This case was adapted in 1991 by London Weekend Television for the series *Agatha Christie's Poirot* starring David Suchet. "The Plymouth Express" was subsequently used as the basis for the novel *The Mystery of the Blue Train.*

A Pocket Full of Rye

PUBLISHING HISTORY: First published by William Collins Sons and Co., Ltd., London, 1953. First published in the United States by Dodd, Mead and Co., New York, 1954.

CHARACTERS: Miss Jane Marple; Mr. Ansell, Mr. Billingsley, Mr. Crump, Mrs. Crump, Mary Dove, Vivian Dubois, Ellen, Albert Evans, Adele Fortescue, Elaine Fortescue, Jennifer Fortescue, Lancelot Fortescue, Patricia Fortescue, Percival Fortescue, Rex Fortescue, Miss Griffith, Miss Grosvenor, Sergeant Hay, Helen MacKenzie, Ruby MacKenzie, Gladys Martin, Inspector Neele, Miss Effie Ramsbottom, Gerald Wright.

Rex Fortescue, "a large flabby man with a gleaming bald head," always expects his tea to be brought to him in his office at the Consolidated Investments Trust. Fortescue drinks "different tea" and has "different china and special biscuits." It is also carried into him by his wildly glamorous sec-

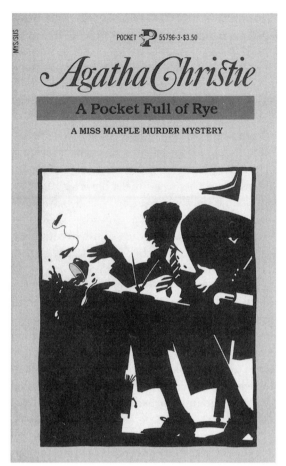

A 1970s edition of A Pocket Full of Rye. *(Pocket Books)*

retary, Miss Grosvenor, and placed with a sense of ritual before him. He replies merely with a grunt, and Miss Grosvenor returns to her other duties.

One day, Miss Grosvenor hears sounds penetrating out of Fortescue's office, "a strangled, agonized cry." Rushing into her employer's office, she finds Fortescue "contorted with agony. His convulsive movements were alarming to watch." Fortescue gasps out one question: "Tea—what the hell—you put in the tea—get help—quick, get a doctor"—it is too late. Rex Fortescue is dead after further moments of agony.

Inspector Neele, assigned to the murder by

Scotland Yard, decides very quickly that he is engaged on an odd case indeed. Fortescue was murdered by taxine, a poison that can take several hours to reach its full effect, so Fortescue was not poisoned by something in his tea. Even more strange was what they found in Fortescue's coat pocket: a handful of rye grain.

Journeying to the family estate at Yewtree Lodge, Neele informs Fortescue's wife, Adele, of her husband's murder and is shocked to detect a slight smile on her face. Adele, however, also dies a short time later, while eating "bread and honey" with her tea. Yet another murder strikes at Yewtree Lodge when the dim-witted maid, Gladys Martin, is found in the garden, with a clothespin cruelly clipped to her nose.

Gladys's former employer, a spinster in the village of St. Mary Mead, impresses Inspector Neele from the start with her keen intelligence, but he is even more interested in her strong sense of justice. Miss Marple will solve the crime for a simple reason: "This is a wicked murderer, Inspector Neele, and the wicked should not go unpunished."

• • •

A Pocket Full of Rye uses a nursery rhyme as the basis for the series of murders in the case. As was often the case with Christie stories, the nursery rhyme serves largely as a clever narrative device, with only a passing connection to the actual crimes committed (see, for example, *Hickory, Dickory, Dock*). In this particular case, however, it serves as a deliciously biting echo of the brutal murders. The rhyme used is "Sing a Song of Sixpence" (see below).

Aside from having the victims of murder perish in ways fitting the rhyme, Christie has Miss Marple make the most significant observation: "But what I mean to say is: have you gone into the question of black birds?" This, of course, is the decisive clue to the resolution of the crime. The novel was dedicated to Bruce Ingram, the editor of *Sketch* Magazine, who first published Christie's short stories. The BBC adapted the novel for television in 1985, with Joan Hickson starring as Miss Marple.

> *Sing a song of sixpence, a pocketful of rye,*
> *Four and twenty blackbirds baked in a pie.*
> *When the pie was opened the birds began to sing.*
> *Wasn't that a dainty dish to set before the king?*
>
> *The king was in his counting house, counting out*
>   *his money,*
> *The queen was in the parlour, eating bread and*
>   *honey,*
> *The maid was in the garden, hanging out the*
>   *clothes,*
> *When there came a little dickey bird and nipped*
>   *off her nose.*

Poems

PUBLISHING HISTORY: First published by William Collins Sons and Co., Ltd., London, 1973. First published in the United States by Dodd, Mead and Co., New York, 1973.

Poems contains two volumes of poetry. The first volume was a republishing of an earlier (1924) volume of poems originally released under the title *The Road of Dreams,* and was divided into four parts: "A Masque from Italy," "Ballads," "Dreams and Fantasies," and "Other Poems." "A Masque from Italy" contains ten poems written around the central theme of the *commedia dell'arte* and the figure of the harlequin. This makes them a foreshadowing of the mysterious Mr. Harley Quin, who became a character in later Christie short stories (see page 324). "Ballads" contains seven stories of romance, including tales of knights and ladies. "Dreams and Fantasies" also has seven poems, but with a different theme: nightmares and dreams. Finally, "Other Poems" offers eleven poems on assorted themes.

Volume two contains twenty-seven poems divided into four sections: "Things," "Places," "Love Poems and Others," and "Verses of Nowadays." "Things" contains four poems, one each on the topics of beauty, water, sculptors, and wandering tunes. "Places" offers five poems about various locations, including Dartmoor, Baghdad, the Nile, and Calvary. "Love Poems and Others" contains eleven poems about love. "Verses of Nowadays" features four poems on such nostalgic topics as a dead love, a picnic, and childhood innocence.

The dating for the poems in Volume two is somewhat difficult, save for the obvious "Picnic 1960." It is likely, however, that at least some of them were completed during Christie's visits to the Middle East.

Poirot Investigates

PUBLISHING HISTORY: First published by John Lane, London, 1924. First published in the United States by Dodd, Mead and Co., New York, 1925.

CONTENTS:
"The Adventure of 'The Western Star' "
"The Tragedy of Marsdon Manor"
"The Adventure of the Cheap Flat"
"The Mystery of Hunter's Lodge"
"The Million-Dollar Bond Robbery"
"The Adventure of Egyptian Tomb"
"The Jewel Robbery at the Grand Metropolitan"
"The Kidnapped Prime Minister"
"The Disappearance of Mr. Davenheim"
"The Adventure of the Italian Nobleman"
"The Case of the Missing Will"
"The Veiled Lady"
"The Lost Mine"
"The Chocolate Box"

Poirot Investigates is a collection of Poirot short stories that had been published originally in *Sketch* magazine by Bruce Ingram, the magazine's editor. The first story, published on March 7, 1923, inaugurated a new era for Christie that resulted in the publication of more than one hundred short stories. The first story was also accompanied by the first illustration of Hercule Poirot, drawn by W. Smithson Broadhead. The stories were subsequently collected and published by John Lane.

Christie gave the collection the title *The Curious Disappearance of the Opalsen Pearls.* This was changed to *The Jewel Robbery at the Grand Metropolitan,* then the publishers suggested *The Grey Cells of Monsieur Poirot.* In the end, Christie decided on *Poirot Investigates* and used her powers of persuasion to compel the publisher to accept.

All the cases in the collection were adapted by London Weekend Television for the series *Agatha Christie's Poirot* starring David Suchet.

Poirot Loses a Client
See *Dumb Witness*

Poirot's Early Cases

PUBLISHING HISTORY: First published by William Collins Sons and Co., Ltd., London, 1974. First published in the United States by Dodd, Mead and Co., New York, 1974, under the title *Hercule Poirot's Early Cases.*

CONTENTS:
"The Lost Mine"
"The Chocolate Box"
"The Veiled Lady"
"Problem at Sea"
"How Does Your Garden Grow?"
"The Adventure of Johnnie Waverly"
"The Third Floor Flat"
"The Affair at the Victory Ball"
"The Adventure of the Clapham Cook"
"The Cornish Mystery"
"The King of Clubs"
"The Lemesurier Inheritance"
"The Plymouth Express"
"The Submarine Plans"
"The Market Basing Mystery"
"The Double Clue"
"Double Sin"
"Wasps' Nest"

All the stories in this collection appeared in earlier volumes: *Poirot Investigates* ("The Lost Mine," "The Chocolate Box," "The Veiled Lady,"

1924); *The Regatta Mystery and Other Stories* ("Problem at Sea," "How Does Your Garden Grow?" 1939); *Three Blind Mice and Other Stories* ("The Adventure of Johnnie Waverly," "The Third Floor Flat," 1950); *The Under Dog and Other Stories* ("The Affair at the Victory Ball," The Adventure of the Clapham Cook," "The Cornish Mystery," "The King of Clubs," "The Lemesurier Inheritance," "The Plymouth Express," "The Submarine Plans," "The Market Basing Mystery," 1951); and *Double Sin and Other Stories* ("The Double Clue," "Double Sin," "Wasps' Nest," 1961). For details on the adaptations of the short stories, please see under individual titles.

Postern of Fate

PUBLISHING HISTORY: First published by William Collins Sons and Co., Ltd., London, 1973. First published in the United States by Dodd, Mead and Co., New York, 1973.

CHARACTERS: Tommy Beresford; Tuppence Beresford; Albert Batt; Andrew, Colonel Atkinson, Deborah Beresford, Henry Bodlicott, Isaac Bodlicott, Miss Collodon, Angus Crispin, Mr. Durrance, Miss Griffin, Gwenda, Janet, Mary Jordan, Miss Iris Mullins, Inspector Norris, Alexander Parkinson, Colonel Ephraim Pikeaway, Mr. Robinson, Rosalie.

Tommy and Tuppence Beresford have at last decided to retire. Their choice for relaxation is a new home, the Laurels, in the resort town of Hollowquay. While unpacking, Tuppence sorts through a collection of children's books that were left behind by previous occupants. There are many titles that she read in her youth, including *The Black Arrow* by Robert Louis Stevenson. She notices one peculiarity about the old book. Certain letters have been underlined throughout the text, and when all the letters are arranged together a message is revealed:

Mary Jordan did not die naturally. It was one of us. I think I know which one.

Tuppence searches for the grave of Mary Jordan and can only find at first the grave of the book's original owner, Alexander Parkinson, who had died at the age of fourteen. Her curiosity now in firm control, Tuppence continues searching and ultimately learns that an au pair in the Parkinson household, Mary Jordan, had died sixty years before, after eating lethal foxglove leaves that had been mixed accidentally into a salad. Soon, Tommy is involved, and the pair learns other details of the long-ago events, thanks to the enduring memories of the villagers. Mary Jordan was supposedly somehow involved in secret government affairs, including the development of a new submarine. Tommy confirms this with his friends in British intelligence.

Having learned that Mary Jordan was a British agent who was probably murdered six decades ago over some secret matter of espionage, the Beresfords are brought suddenly back into the present when their gardener, Isaac Bodlicott, is murdered and found on their doorstep. Someone from the past is determined that Tommy and Tuppence should not discover a long-buried secret.

• • •

Postern of Fate is one of the most significant books in the Christie writings for only one reason. It was the last book that Christie wrote; her last two published novels, *Curtain* (1975) and *Sleeping Murder* (1976), were both published after *Postern of Fate* but had been written decades before and withheld from publication until the very end. That *Postern of Fate* should be Christie's last book is unfortunate because it is considered by many fans to be the worst of all of her works.

Aside from certain lapses in details and logic, *Postern of Fate* was also troubled by an overly ambitious plot. Tommy and Tuppence, who had been around as characters since 1922 (and *The Secret Adversary*), not only had to contend with another espionage case, they also had to solve a murder that took place sixty years before. *Postern* thus relies in one volume on two of the more frequently used plot devices in Christie's late works, espionage (e.g., *Destination Unknown,* 1954, and *Passenger to Frankfurt,* 1970) and murder in retrospect (*Elephants Can Remember,* 1972, and *Ordeal by Innocence,* 1958).

Christie dedicated the book thus: "For Hannibal and his master." Hannibal was the beloved dog of the Beresfords and was based on Christie's own dog, Treacle. Both were Manchester terriers, and Treacle was the last dog owned by Dame Agatha. Treacle's master, of course, was Max Mallowan.

"A Pot of Tea"

PUBLISHING HISTORY: First published by William Collins Sons and Co., Ltd., London, 1929, in the short story collection *Partners in Crime.* First published in the United States by Dodd, Mead and Co., New York, 1929, in the short story collection *Partners in Crime.*

CHARACTERS: Tommy Beresford; Tuppence Beresford; Albert Batt; Janet Smith, Lawrence St. Vincent.

Having been established as the proprietors of Blunt's International Detective Agency (in "Fairy in the Flat"), Tommy and Tuppence Beresford greet their first client, Lawrence St. Vincent. He wishes the detectives to locate a young woman whom he secretly loves, Janet Smith. She is a shop girl in Madame Violette's hat shop and has disappeared.

Tuppence shocks Tommy by making an incredible proposition to their first client. She guarantees that for twice the usual fee they will find Smith in twenty-four hours. Tommy searches through the hospitals for the young woman while Tuppence, oddly calm and in no hurry, decides it is best for her to remain at the agency offices.

• • •

In the stories in the collection *Partners in Crime,* the Beresfords adopt the personae of detectives of fiction while solving their cases. In this first story after "Fairy in the Flat," the Beresfords have not yet begun to imitate other sleuths. Tuppence,

however, does confess that she has some ideas for the future.

"Problem at Pollensa Bay"

PUBLISHING HISTORY: First published by Dodd, Mead and Co., New York, 1939, in the short story collection *The Regatta Mystery and Other Stories.*

CHARACTERS: Mr. Parker Pyne; Mrs. Adela Chester, Basil Chester, Betty Gregg, Madeleine de Sara, Mina Wycherley.

Mr. Parker Pyne takes a holiday away from England on the picturesque island of Mallorca. His work does not permit any rest, though, for a domineering mother, Mrs. Chester, enlists his talents to convince her son, Basil, that he must not marry an unsuitable young woman from the nearby colony of bohemian artists.

"Problem at Sea"

PUBLISHING HISTORY: First published by Dodd, Mead and Co., New York, 1939, in the short story collection *The Regatta Mystery and Other Stories.* (See also below for other details on the publishing history of this story.)

CHARACTERS: Hercule Poirot; Adeline Clapperton, Colonel John Clapperton, General Forbes, Pam Gregan, Miss Ellie Henderson, Kitty Mooney.

Hercule Poirot finds himself at sea—much to his chagrin, owing to his chronic struggles with seasickness—on a trip to Egypt and soon finds the voyage darkened by murder. Mrs. Adeline Clapperton, the imperious and unpleasant wife of Colonel John Clapperton, apparently declines to go ashore with her husband and is later found murdered, with a native dagger plunged in her heart and a string of amber beads found on the floor of her cabin.

A cursory investigation includes the questioning all of the local bead sellers in the port of Alexandria, but the case becomes more mysterious when Poirot learns that no jewelry had been taken, only a small amount of cash. Two other clues are the fact that the door to Mrs. Clapperton's cabin was locked and that the window—not the porthole—was opened onto the deck. Poirot solves the crime and catches the murderer with the help of a wooden doll dressed in a velvet suit and lace collar.

"Problem at Sea" was also published as a separate sixteen-page pamphlet by Vallency Press, Ltd., London, in 1944 under the title "The Mystery of the Crime in Cabin 66."

This case was adapted by London Weekend Television in 1989 for the series *Agatha Christie's Poirot* starring David Suchet. Poirot solved several cases in Egypt, including *Death on the Nile* and "The Adventure of the Egyptian Tomb."

"The Rajah's Emerald"

PUBLISHING HISTORY: First published by William Collins Sons and Co., Ltd., London, 1934, in the short story collection *The Listerdale Mystery.* First published in the United States by Dodd, Mead and Co., New York, 1929, in the short story collection *The Golden Ball and Other Stories.*

CHARACTERS: James Bond, Lord Edward Campion, Grace Jones, Claude Sopworth.

An underpaid clerk, James Bond, is exceedingly self-conscious about his meager pay as he journeys to an expensive resort in Kimpton-on-Sea with his fiancée, Grace. She is ambitious and now earns more than he does in the millinery salons of Messrs. Bartles in the High Street. Bond's aggravation only increases when he learns that Grace is staying at the swanky Esplanade Hotel, while he must room in a much less costly guest house. Even worse, she is paying attention to the wealthy Claude Sopworth. Among the other guests in the resort are Lord Campion and his very special guest, the Rajah of Maraputna.

Miserable with his misfortune, Bond goes for a swim and then accidentally changes into the wrong pair of gray flannel trousers. He discovers his mistake only when he finds in a pocket an enormous emerald. A short time later, his shock turns to terror when he sees the local newspaper's headline: THE RAJAH'S EMERALD STOLEN.

● ● ●

Written before Ian Fleming's works introducing the superspy James Bond, "The Rajah's Emerald" features a hero who bears little resemblance to the urbane and romantic agent 007.

"The Red House"

PUBLISHING HISTORY: First published by William Collins Sons and Co., Ltd., London, 1929, in the short story collection *Partners in Crime.* First published in the United States by Dodd, Mead and Co., New York, 1929, in the short story collection *Partners in Crime.*

CHARACTERS: Tommy Beresford; Tuppence Beresford; Crockett, Monica Deane, Dr. O'Neill.

A continuation of the case first recounted in "The Clergyman's Daughter," "The Red House" brings Tommy and Tuppence to the home of Monica Deane, which is being tormented by some kind of ghost. It is believed that, somehow, the nasty maid, Crockett, or her nephew is behind the supposedly supernatural events in the house, but the question is how to prove it. The vital clues to the resolution of the case are a rhyme and a Bible verse.

● ● ●

This story was combined with "The Clergyman's Daughter" and adapted by London Weekend Television in 1982.

"The Red Signal"

PUBLISHING HISTORY: First published by William Collins Sons and Co., Ltd., London, 1933, in the short story collection *The Hound of Death and Other Stories.*

CHARACTERS: Mrs. Violet Eversleigh, Johnson, Mrs. Thompson, Claire Trent, Alington West, Dermot West.

"The Red Signal" offers the supernatural experience of Dermot West. He experiences a "red signal" that warns him of impending danger, a feeling that is at its keenest one night while Dermot is attending a dinner party that has been organized by the psychiatrist Sir Alington West. The psychiatrist wants to observe one of the guests, a person who, he believes, is mentally ill. The red signal proves accurate when Dermot receives a dire warning during a séance. Later that night, Alington is murdered, and Dermot becomes the prime suspect.

• • •

This story was adapted in 1982 by Thames Television.

"The Regatta Mystery"

PUBLISHING HISTORY: First published by Dodd, Mead and Co., New York, 1939, in the short story collection *The Regatta Mystery and Other Stories.*

CHARACTERS: Mr. Parker Pyne; Eve Leathern, Samuel Leathern, Evan Llewellyn, Sir George and Lady Pamela Marroway, Mr. Isaac Pointz, Mrs. Jane Rustington, Mr. Leo Stein.

Isaac Pointz, a wealthy diamond merchant, has brought a yacht full of guests to the Dartmouth shore to have fun at the fair after the group has been taking part in yacht races. That night, over dinner at the Royal George, Pointz accepts a challenge from young Eve Leathern: She can make a diamond worth thirty thousand pounds disappear right before their eyes. In full view of the table, Eve succeeds in making the diamond disappear, but when she tries to bring it back, she realizes that the stone truly is missing. Despite a desperate search of the restaurant, no gem can be found, and suspicion falls on one young man. Hoping to clear his name, the young man turns for help to Mr. Parker Pyne.

The Regatta Mystery and Other Stories

PUBLISHING HISTORY: First published by Dodd, Mead and Co., New York, 1939.

CONTENTS:

"The Regatta Mystery" (Parker Pyne)
"The Mystery of the Baghdad Chest" (Poirot)
"How Does Your Garden Grow?" (Poirot)
"Problem at Pollensa Bay" (Parker Pyne)
"Yellow Iris" (Poirot)
"Miss Marple Tells a Story" (Marple)
"The Dream" (Poirot)
"In a Glass Darkly" (a tale of the supernatural)
"Problem at Sea" (Poirot)

The Regatta Mystery and Other Stories was the first short story collection (there would be others) that was published for an American audience exclusively. It marked the first appearance of the stories in book form, and details of each had been published only in magazines and had not been previously included in any British short story collection. "How Does Your Garden Grow?" is of special interest because it features the first appearance of Miss Felicity Lemon as Hercule Poirot's secretary. She had first come to literary life as Parker Pyne's secretary in *Parker Pyne Investigates,* 1934.

Four of the stories were subsequently published in British short story collections. "In a Glass Darkly," "How Does Your Garden Grow?" and "Problem at Sea" were adapted for television. "Problem at Sea" was published as a separate sixteen-page pamphlet by Vallency Press, Ltd., London, in 1944 under the title "The Mystery of the Crime in Cabin 66."

Remembered Death

See *Sparkling Cyanide*

"Rich Woman, The Case of the"

PUBLISHING HISTORY: First published by William Collins Sons and Co., Ltd., London, 1934, in the short story collection *Parker Pyne Investigates.* First published in the United States by Dodd, Mead and Co., New York, 1934, in the short story collection *Mr. Parker Pyne, Detective.*

CHARACTERS: Mr. Parker Pyne; Doctor Constantine, Claude Luttrell, Hannah Moorhouse, Ariadne Oliver, Mrs. Amelia Rymer, Madeleine de Sara, Joe Welsh.

One of Parker Pyne's more ambitious and expensive projects, this case deals with a very wealthy widow who is miserable despite her fortune. Mrs. Amelia Rymer grew up as a farm worker, married Abner Rymer, and watched him slowly amass a pile of money in business. Her husband, however, died at the young age of forty-three, leaving her with a vast estate but no family and no friends. She finally consults Parker Pyne in an effort to restore her happiness. He assures her of his ability to solve her dilemma, but it will cost her a thousand pounds. A visit to Dr. Constantine, a sip of tea, and a cure for weariness of the soul convince Mrs. Rymer that her thousand pounds were well spent.

The Road of Dreams

See *Poems*

The Rose and the Yew Tree

PUBLISHING HISTORY: First published by William Heinemann, Ltd., London, 1948. First published in the United States by Holt, Rinehart and Winston, New York, 1948.

CHARACTERS: Doctor Burt, Milly Burt, Captain Carslake, Mrs. Bigham Charteris, Isabella Charteris, Father Clement, John Gabriel, Anne Mordaunt, Hugh Norreys, Lady Adelaide St. Loo, Rupert St. Loo, Lady Tressilian, Catherine Yougoubian.

A romance and a study of human nature, *The Rose and the Yew Tree* follows the travails of Hugh Norreys, a young man who suffers a severe injury in an accident and becomes suicidally despondent. He moves to the seaside resort of St. Loo and becomes embroiled in the political ambitions of John Gabriel, a Conservative candidate for Parliament and a seemingly perfect choice for the local party. Also involved with Gabriel is Isabella Charteris, Hugh's sister-in-law. Their relationship ends in tragedy and brings about a powerful transformation in Gabriel.

• • •

The Rose and the Yew Tree was the fourth novel written by Christie under the pseudonym Mary Westmacott. The title was derived from the final section of T. S. Eliot's *Four Quartets*, "Little Gidding": "The moment of the rose and the moment of the yew tree are of equal duration."

Sad Cypress

PUBLISHING HISTORY: First published by William Collins Sons and Co., Ltd., London, 1940. First published in the United States by Dodd, Mead and Co., New York, 1940.

CHARACTERS: Hercule Poirot; Mr. Abbot, Inspector Brill, Sir Edwin Bulmer, Elinor Carlisle, Mary Draper, Ehpraim Gerrard, Mary Gerrard, Jessie Hopkins, Horlick, James Arthur Littledale, Dr. Peter Lord, Chief Inspector Marsden, Nurse O'Brien, Alfred James Wargrave, Laura Welman, Roderick Welman.

Elinor Carlisle stands in a courtroom and answers resolutely that she is not guilty of the murder of Mary Gerrard back on July 27 at Hunterbury, Maidensford. The trial commences nevertheless, and Elinor ponders the curious events that have brought her to this precarious position.

Some time ago, Elinor received an anonymous letter saying that someone was insinuating her way into the good graces of the aunt of Elinor's boyfriend, Laura Welman, with the aim of being added to the will. Worried about this development, Elinor set off to Hunterbury with her boyfriend, Roddy, "to protect our interests *and* because we're fond of the old dear!"

Once at Hunterbury, Elinor spots immediately the apparent threat to her fortune. Young Mary Gerrard, daughter of the groundskeeper, has made herself indispensable to Aunt Laura, and Elinor grows even more alarmed when Roddy displays a definite fondness for her.

Aunt Laura has already suffered a stroke, and dies during the night after a second occurrence. As Aunt Laura has made no will, Elinor inherits the entire estate and decides to be generous. She even fulfills Aunt Laura's last wishes that she give Mary two thousand pounds, prompting one of Aunt Laura's nurses, Nurse Hopkins, to offer the suggestion that Mary herself should make a will. Elinor's generosity comes at a price, however, as she is tormented by the vision of Roddy madly in love with Mary.

Elinor breaks off her engagement with Roddy because of his feelings for Mary but again treats Mary with courtesy by inviting her and Nurse Hopkins over for sandwiches. Not long after eating, Mary dies from poisoning. As Elinor had made the sandwiches and had a very good motive for murdering Mary, suspicion falls immediately on her. Police pursue an apparently airtight case, and Elinor is arrested. Dr. Peter Lord, who is in love with Elinor, refuses to believe her capable of murder and engages the help of Hercule Poirot.

• • •

Christie dedicated the book to Peter and Peggy MacLeod. During the 1930s, the MacLeods were in charge of a hospital in Mosul, Syria, where Christie and her husband, Max Mallowan, worked on archaeological digs.

As she did with a number of her Poirot novels, Christie candidly observed that *Sad Cypress* should not have included the Belgian detective. Christie also displays her impressive knowledge of poisons by having two victims murdered by morphine hydrochloride.

"Sanctuary"

PUBLISHING HISTORY: First published by Dodd, Mead and Co., New York, 1961, in the short story collection *Double Sin and Other Stories*.

CHARACTERS: Miss Jane Marple; Mrs. Diana "Bunch" Harmon; Rev. Julian Harmon; Police Constable Abel, Inspector Craddock, Mr. Eccles, Pam Eccles, Dr. Griffin, Sergeant Hayes, Edwin Moss, Jewel St. John, Walter St. John, Zobeida.

While preparing flowers to decorate the parish church in Chipping Cleghorn, Diana "Bunch" Harmon discovers a dying man sprawled upon the chancel steps. He clasps a handkerchief and mutters the word "sanctuary" and something else she could not quite catch. The local physician, Dr. Griffiths, determines that the victim has been shot at close range, and has used the handkerchief to staunch the bleeding. Finally, with the words "Please—please," he dies.

It is subsequently learned that the victim was named Sandbourne, and soon his sister, a Mrs. Eccles, arrives with her husband and asks for all his personal effects. Perplexed by these events, Bunch pays a visit to Miss Marple. With the sleuth's help, she deciphers the vital clue, a cloakroom ticket, and helps to catch the murderer of Mr. Sandbourne and a clever group of thieves.

"The Second Gong"

PUBLISHING HISTORY: First published by Dodd, Mead and Co., New York, 1948, in the short story collection *Witness for the Prosecution and Other Stories*.

CHARACTERS: Hercule Poirot; Joan Ashby, Gregory Barling, Diana Cleves, Harry Dalehouse, Mr. Digby, Geoffrey Keene, Captain John Marshall, Hubert Lytcham Roche.

Poirot is called upon to investigate the murder of Hubert Lytcham Roche, an eccentric aristocrat who has a peculiar dinner ritual. A gong is sounded twice in his home to announce that dinner is served, and any guests or family who fail to reach the table before the second gong sounds are ostracized ever after by Lytcham Roche. There is thus considerable shock when the imperious host is himself in violation of the regulation. A brief investigation reveals Roche dead in a locked room, the victim of an apparent suicide.

Poirot, naturally, has his doubts, and overcomes the seemingly impossible problem that the dead man was found in a locked room. The plot and precise method of murder in this case are nearly identical to that of the much more complicated (and longer) story "Dead Man's Mirror."

The Secret Adversary

PUBLISHING HISTORY: First published by John Lane, London, 1922. First published in the United States by Dodd, Mead and Co., New York, 1922.

CHARACTERS: Tommy Beresford; Tuppence Beresford; Albert Batt; Annette, Mr. Brown, A. Carter, Sir James Peel Edgerton, Jane Finn, Dr. Hall, Julius P. Hersheimmer, Boris Ivanovitch, Kramenin, Marguerite Vandemeyer, Edward Whittington.

Shortly after the end of World War I, two childhood friends, Tommy Beresford and Prudence "Tuppence" Cowley, have a chance encounter on Dover Street in London. Thrilled to see each other again, they go for tea at Lyons' and catch up on recent years. At the moment, Tommy is convalescing from war wounds and Tuppence is working on a hospital ward. They lament the poor prospects for employment after the war, especially as both of them are broke. They decide to go into business together by hiring themselves out as adventurers. Their ad in the *Times* will read: "Two young adventurers for hire. Willing to do anything, go anywhere. Pay must be good. No unreasonable offers refused."

After Tommy and Tuppence part, Tuppence is approached in the street by a well-dressed man who identifies himself as Mr. Whittington. He had overheard their conversation in Lyons' and would like to hire her as an adventurer. At his office the next day, Mr. Whittington offers Tuppence one hundred pounds if she will go to Paris and impersonate an American girl for three months. When Mr. Whittington asks Tuppence what her name is, Tuppence decides on an alias, and she plucks from her memory a name used by Tommy the day before. It was Jane Finn, a name he had overheard in a conversation between two men on the street. Whittington responds in a bizarre manner, demanding to know what she has learned. He even tries to bribe her to keep quiet. By the very next day, Whittington and his offices have disappeared, replaced by a locked and empty set of rooms.

After this odd event, Tommy and Tuppence receive two inquiries. The first is from British intelligence, which wishes to hire them to find a missing agent, a young woman who had been handed secret documents on board the doomed ship the *Lusitania,* and had then disappeared. Her name was Jane Finn. The second prospective employer is Mr. Julius Hersheimmer. He wants the pair to find his missing cousin, a young woman named Jane Finn.

• • •

After the moderate success of *The Mysterious Affair at Styles* (1920), for which she earned the grand total of twenty-five pounds in royalties, Agatha Christie still doubted that she could actually have a career as a writer. It was her first husband, Archie Christie, who encouraged her to make a go of writing for money. The question of what to write was answered when she conceived the plot for what became *The Secret Adversary.* Aside from being her first spy thriller, the novel introduced the longtime Christie favorites Tommy and Tuppence Beresford, an incredibly romantic and fun-loving couple who find their way into assorted mysteries, espionage capers, and international intrigues.

Christie dedicated her second novel "to all those who lead monotonous lives, in the hope that they may experience at second hand the delight and dangers of adventure."

The Secret Adversary was adapted for the screen in 1928 under the title *Die Abenteuer G.m.b.H.,* making it the first adaptation of a Christie work for film. The novel was also adapted in 1983 by London Weekend Television.

The Secret of Chimneys

PUBLISHING HISTORY: First published by John Lane, London, 1925. First published in the United States by Dodd, Mead and Co., New York, 1925.

CHARACTERS: Boris Anchoukoff, Chief Inspector Badgworthy, Inspector Battle, Clement Edward Brent, Daisy Brent, Dulcie Brent, Lady Eileen "Bundle" Brent, Anthony Cade, Dr. Cartwright, Dutch Pedro, Bill Eversleigh, Hiram Fish, Herman Isaacstein, Constable Johnson, Monsieur Lemoine, Baron Lolopretjzyl, the Honourable George Lomax, Giuseppe Manelli, Jimmy McGrath, Colonel Melrose, Angele Mory, Prince

Michael Obolovitch, Virginia Revel, Count Stylptitch, Tredwell, King Victor, Professor Wynwood.

Young Anthony Cade, a friendly adventurer, has secured employment with Castle's Select Tours and finds himself leading an expedition through Bulawayo, Africa, that is comprised of "seven depressed-looking females and three perspiring males." Good fortune strikes, however, when he meets his old friend Jimmy McGrath. A fellow adventurer, Jimmy offers Anthony the opportunity to share in a bit of fun and profit. Some time before, Jimmy had saved an older man from muggers and had thus met Count Stylptitch of Herzoslovakia. The count died recently, but it turns out that, just before his death, he mailed to Jimmy the manuscript of his memoirs. If Jimmy will bring the manuscript safely to the count's London publisher, there will be a reward of one thousand pounds. The memoirs are reputedly scandalous, and there are certain parties who will stop at nothing to prevent them from being published. As Jimmy now has the chance to travel to a gold field, he offers the reward to Anthony. Cade wastes little time dumping his party and accepting Jimmy's proposal. Jimmy also gives Anthony a second assignment. A now-dead friend of his was using a cache of letters to blackmail an Englishwoman, Virginia Revel. As he objects to the whole notion of blackmail, Jimmy wants the letters returned to their owner, a poor woman who has suffered severe financial losses, thanks to the extortion.

Anthony is not long back in England before he receives a visit from Baron Lolopretjzyl, a representative of the Loyalist Party of Herzoslovakia. He offers Cade fifteen hundred pounds for the manuscript, but Anthony refuses. This relatively polite offer is followed by several violent attempts at taking the manuscript by force, and, in one of the struggles, Anthony loses the letters. It is clear by now that Cade is embroiled in a mystery far bigger than that generated by a mere scandalous memoir.

• • •

In the history of Christie's writings, *The Secret of Chimneys* is overshadowed by her very next novel, *The Murder of Roger Ackroyd*. It is nevertheless memorable for two points. First, it has a direct sequel, written several years later—*The Seven Dials Mystery* (1929). Second, it introduces the memorable and recurring character Superintendent Battle.

Christie dedicated the book thus: "To my nephew in memory of an inscription at Compton Castle and a day at the zoo." Her nephew was James Watts, Jr., son of Christie's older sister, Madge Miller.

The Seven Dials Mystery

PUBLISHING HISTORY: First published by William Collins Sons and Co., Ltd., London, 1929. First published in the United States by Dodd, Mead and Co., New York, 1929.

CHARACTERS: Alfred, Count Andras, Rupert "Pongo" Bateman, Superintendent Battle, John Bauer, Clement Edward Brent, Lady Eileen "Bundle" Brent, Marcia Brent, Dr. Cartwright, Lady Maria Coote, Sir Oswald Coote, Vera "Socks" Daventry, Ronny Devereaux, Sir Stanley Digby, Herr Eberhard, Bill Eversleigh, the Honourable George Lomax, Colonel Melrose, Mr. Mosgorovsky, Terence O'Rourke, Hayward Phelps, Countess Anna Radzky, Babe St. Maur, Jimmy Thesiger, Tredwell, Gerald Wade, Loraine Wade.

A wealthy businessman, Sir Oswald Coote, and his wife have leased the beautiful house called the Chimneys for two years from the Marquis of Caterham. Because they enjoy parties, especially those attended by young people, the Cootes decide to throw a final bash before their lease is up. They invite a batch of young adults to the Chimneys, but Mrs. Coote confesses to having some difficulty fathoming the habits of the youngsters. For example, there is Gerry Wade, who is a perpetual late riser, much to the annoyance of his friends. A group of them decide that the time has come to play an appropriate joke on the late sleeper. They go into the nearby town of Market Basing and purchase eight alarm clocks. These are set in Gerry's room to go off in deafening sequence starting at 6:30 A.M.

The next morning, they await the thunderous chiming of the clocks. Amazingly, when they go off, they seem to have no effect on Gerry. He fails to come down, and when his friends investigate his room, they find Gerry dead in his bed. He has been poisoned, and one of the clocks has been stolen, leaving seven in the room. The mystery of the death is taken up by Lady Eileen Brent, Jimmy Thesiger (a friend of Gerry's), and Loraine Wade, Gerry's sister.

• • •

The Seven Dials Mystery marks the first time that Christie wrote a deliberate sequel to an earlier novel. Unlike other novels, in which a detective and certain police officers reappear, *The Seven Dials Mystery* continued certain elements from the plot of its predecessor, *The Secret of Chimneys* (1925). The reader who had enjoyed *Chimneys* thus had the fun of spending time again with Superintendent Battle, Colonel Melrose, Eileen Brent, and Clement Brent. The novel was also adapted in 1981 by London Weekend Television.

"The Shadow on the Glass"

PUBLISHING HISTORY: First published by William Collins Sons and Co., Ltd., London, 1930, in the short story collection *The Mysterious Mr. Quin.* First published in the United States by Dodd, Mead and Co., New York, 1930, in the short story collection *The Mysterious Mr. Quin.*

CHARACTERS: Mr. Satterthwaite; Mr. Harley Quin; Captain Jimmy Allenson, Lady Cynthia Drage, Major Porter, Moira Scott, Richard Scott, Mrs. Iris Staverton, Mr. Unkerton, Mrs. Unkerton.

While Mr. Quin often makes his presence felt in stories involving romance, lost love, or the questions of life, in "The Shadow on the Glass" the mysterious man assists Mr. Satterthwaite in solving the murders of two people under peculiar circumstances. The events take place at Greenways House during a gathering hosted by the Unkertons.

"The Sign in the Sky"

PUBLISHING HISTORY: First published by William Collins Sons and Co., Ltd., London, 1930, in the short story collection *The Mysterious Mr. Quin.* First published in the United States by Dodd, Mead and Co., New York, 1930, in the short story collection *The Mysterious Mr. Quin.*

CHARACTERS: Mr. Satterthwaite; Mr. Harley Quin; Sir George Barnaby, Lady Vivien Barnaby, Louisa Bullard, Sylvia Dale, Martin Wylde.

Mr. Satterthwaite sits in a courtroom and hears the verdict against Martin Wylde in the murder of Lady Vivien Barnaby—guilty. The jury had deliberated for a mere half hour, but their decision leaves Satterthwaite dissatisfied. Going for a meal at his favorite restaurant, Arlecchino, Satterthwaite discovers his enigmatic friend, Mr. Harley Quin. Together, they go over the details of the murder case, an examination that leaves Satterthwaite with enough doubts that he begins a fresh inquiry into Lady Vivien's death. Especially curious is the sudden departure of a housemaid, Louisa Bullard, for Canada. Satterthwaite sets off for British Columbia and tracks Bullard down in Banff. She provides much useful information, including the ominous and seemingly spiritual clue that, on the night of Lady Vivien's murder, she saw a great white plume of smoke rising from a train, which "formed itself into the sign of a gigantic hand. A great white hand against the crimson of the sky."

• • •

Mr. Satterthwaite dines at Arlecchino, where he also dines in "The Face of Helen." The restaurant is also, apparently, frequented by Mr. Harley Quin.

"Sing a Song of Sixpence"

PUBLISHING HISTORY: First published by William Collins Sons and Co., Ltd., London, 1934, in the short story collection *The Listerdale Mystery.* First published in the United States by Dodd, Mead and Co., New York, 1934, in the short story collection *Witness for the Prosecution and Other Stories.*

CHARACTERS: Ben, Emily Crabtree, Miss Lily Crabtree, William Crabtree, Martha, Sir Edward Palliser, Magdalen Vaughan, Matthew Vaughan.

Miss Lily Crabtree has been murdered and has left an estate of eighty thousand pounds. Both the size of the estate and the circumstances of her murder make all four of her heirs obvious suspects, but there is a lack of evidence, making the task of finding the murderer virtually impossible. Upset at the murder and at the way mutual suspicions are tearing apart the family, Magdalen Vaughan, niece of Emily, turns to a retired barrister, Sir Edward Palliser, for help.

"Sinister Stranger, The Adventure of the"

PUBLISHING HISTORY: First published by William Collins Sons and Co., Ltd., London, 1929, in the short story collection *Partners in Crime.* First published in the United States by Dodd, Mead and Co., New York, 1929, in the short story collection *Partners in Crime.*

CHARACTERS: Tommy Beresford; Tuppence Beresford; Albert Batt, Dr. Charles Bower, Coggins, Detective Inspector Dymchurch, Inspector Marriot.

As detailed in the earlier stories recounted in *Partners in Crime,* Tommy and Tuppence Beresford have been awaiting the arrival of a letter from Russia that might contain an important clue about espionage and the number sixteen hidden beneath its postage stamp. The letter finally arrives at Blunt's International Detective Agency, but before they can pry the stamp off the Beresfords are interrupted by an obviously foreign stranger. He introduces himself as Dr. Bower and has come to ask their help in preventing someone from stealing his research on alkaloids. Tommy sets off with Dr. Bower, and Tuppence remains behind to guard the letter. It is soon clear that the letter is a magnet for the attentions of sinister agents.

• • •

As was the case throughout *Partners in Crime,* the Beresfords here adopt the characters and methods of detectives of fiction. For this investigation, the Beresfords become Francis and Desmond Okewood, brothers and sleuths first created by Valentine Williams (d. 1946) under the name Douglas Valentine. Normally, Desmond manages to get himself in perilous situations only to be saved at the last moment by Francis. In this case, the role of Francis is definitely played by Tuppence.

The Sittaford Mystery

PUBLISHING HISTORY: First published by William Collins Sons and Co., Ltd., London, 1931. First published in the United States by Dodd, Mead and Co., New York, 1931, under the title *Murder at Hazelmoor.*

CHARACTERS: Mrs. Belling, Major John Edward Burnaby, Mr. Curtis, Amelia Curtis, Mr. Dacres, Martin Dering, Sylvia Dering, Mr. Duke, Charles Enderby, Rebecca Evans, Robert Henry Evans, Jennifer Gardner, Captain Robert Gardner, Ronald Garfield, Constable Graves, Inspector Narracott, Brian Pearson, James Pearson, Caroline Percehouse, Sergeant Pollock, Mr. Rycroft, Emily Trefusis, Captain Joseph Trevelyan, Dr. Warren, Mrs. Willett, Violet Willett, Captain Wyatt.

The small village of Sittaford, in Dartmoor, England, has been stricken by a rare blizzard, and the community finds itself effectively cut off from the rest of the country, especially its nearest neighbor, the town of Exhampton. At Sittaford House, meanwhile, the temporary renters, the Willetts, are hosting a party, despite the weather. The Willetts, Mrs. Willett and her daughter, Violet, have rented Sittaford House for the winter from Captain Joseph Trevelyan, a retired navy officer and athlete, and the Captain has moved for the season to a smaller cottage in Exhampton. This is bad news for Trevelyan's best friend, Major Burnaby, who misses Trevelyan and has little fondness for the current occupants of Sittaford House. Nevertheless, as there is little else to do on a winter's evening without Trevelyan around, Burnaby accepts the Willetts's invitation to dinner.

Later in the party, the gathered guests decide to have a séance. The adventure into the paranormal seems to be a success when rapping sounds are heard, but guests soon discern that the rapping spells out a frightening message: TREVELYAN DEAD—MURDER. Horrified, the members of the séance call an abrupt end to the proceedings, and Burnaby refuses to accept such a ludicrous assertion from beyond. Nevertheless, he is worried about his friend.

Unable to telephone Trevelyan, Burnaby makes his way to Trevelyan's cottage, Hazelmoor, enduring a grueling two-hour trip in the snow. He finally reaches the cottage and receives no answer to his bell. Burnaby fetches the police, and, with Constable Graves, he enters the cottage and finds his friend. Trevelyan has been murdered, beaten to death at what is determined to have been exactly the same time as the séance warned of his impending doom.

• • •

The Sittaford Mystery presents a clever murder mystery, but it is especially notable as the first Christie work to utilize at least the trappings of the supernatural in its structure. The supernatural theme was subsequently adopted in numerous short stories by Christie, especially those collected in *The Hound of Death and Other Stories* (1933).

Sleeping Murder

PUBLISHING HISTORY: First published by William Collins Sons and Co., Ltd., London, 1976. First published in the United States by Dodd, Mead and Co., New York, 1976.

CHARACTERS: Miss Jane Marple; Dorothy Afflick, Jackie Afflick, Colonel Arthur Bantry, Dolly Bantry, Mrs. Cocker, Major Erskine, Eleanor Fane, Walter Fane, Mr. Galbraith, Helen Spenlove Kennedy Halliday, Dr. Haydock, Mrs. Hengrave, Dr. James Kennedy, Lady Abbot Kimble, Manning, Edith Pagett, Dr. Penrose, Detective Inspector Primer, Giles Reed, Gwenda Reed, Mr. Sims, Joan West, Raymond West.

Gwenda Reed and her husband of three months, Giles Reed, have decided to move to England from New Zealand. While Giles finishes up some of his business in New Zealand, he sends Gwenda ahead to find them a suitable house. She journeys through the coastal region of the resort of Dillmouth and happens upon a small Victorian villa called Hillside that is up for sale. While touring the house, Gwenda heads down some stairs and suddenly suffers a bout of absolute terror. The moment passes, and Gwenda purchases the house.

Settling into the house in anticipation of Giles's arrival, Gwenda begins experiencing odd events. She seems to remember a garden path that leads to the sea, and, sure enough, there it is; she keeps walking into a wall as though there was once a door there, and it turns out that there once really *was* a door in the exact spot. Most disturbing of all, Gwenda discovers that beneath the yellow wallpaper in the nursery is paper decorated with cornflowers and poppies, the very wallpaper that she wanted to have installed.

Increasingly rattled and nervous, Gwenda decides to take a break and accepts an invitation to visit London from the novelist Raymond West and his wife, Joan, who are friends of Giles. One of the planned activities is an outing to the theater with their aunt, a formidable old woman named Jane Marple. The play is *The Duchess of Malfi,* and as the final line is delivered—"Cover her face; mine eyes dazzle: she died young"—Gwenda emits a high-pitched shriek and runs from the theater.

The following day, she meets with Miss Marple, and the old sleuth begins unraveling Gwenda's past and the horrifying event of her memories. At that dreadful moment in the play, Gwenda remembered herself as a child looking through the banister on the stairway at Hillside. Below, a golden-haired woman, her face contorted and blue from strangulation, lies upon the foot of the stair. Her murderer stands above her, reciting the same lines from the *Duchess of Malfi.* Gwenda had witnessed a murder and has somehow returned to the same house.

• • •

Sleeping Murder was the last novel featuring Miss Marple to be published. It was not, however, the last Marple novel to be written (that was *Nemesis, 1971*). In fact, *Sleeping Murder* was penned around the same time that Christie wrote *Curtain,* during World War II, when the author was genuinely concerned about dying in one of the German raids on England. The manuscript—like its Poirot counterpart, *Curtain*—was placed into a vault for safekeeping and left untouched for three decades. Unlike *Curtain,* however, *Sleeping Murder* does not include the death of Miss Marple, so its being released so many years after its creation still remains somewhat of a mystery in its own right. In any event, the publication of a brand-new Marple novel was greeted with considerable enthusiasm on both sides of the Atlantic.

The case uses a recurring narrative device similar to one in other novels, namely, a murder in retrospect, and is solved by looking back on distant events and then piecing together the clues. Similar cases include *Five Little Pigs* (1943) and *Sparkling Cyanide* (1945). *Sleeping Murder* was adapted for television in 1987 by the BBC, starring Joan Hickson as Miss Marple.

So Many Steps to Death
See *Destination Unknown*

"SOS"
PUBLISHING HISTORY: First published by William Collins Sons and Co., Ltd., London, 1933, in the short story collection *The Hound of Death and Other Stories.*

CHARACTERS: Mortimer Cleveland, Mr. Dinsmead, Charlotte Dinsmead, Johnnie Dinsmead, Magdalen Dinsmead, Maggie Dinsmead.

A psychic researcher, Mortimer Cleveland, is stranded on the Wiltshire Downs when his car breaks down. He finds shelter in the house of the Dinsmead family. He is startled to discover the S.O.S. written in the dust of his bedroom nightstand, and believes that it was put there by one of the Dinsmead daughters, Charlotte. Cleveland, however, is possessed of certain mediumistic talents, and he reaches the conclusion that Charlotte may have written the note without even being aware of it. The circumstances deepen, however, when Mortimer learns of a large family inheritance and the motive for a murder attempt in a pot of tea.

"The Soul of the Croupier"
PUBLISHING HISTORY: First published by William Collins Sons and Co., Ltd., London, 1930, in the short story collection *The Mysterious Mr. Quin.* First published in the United States by Dodd, Mead and Co., New York, 1930, in the short story collection *The Mysterious Mr. Quin.*

CHARACTERS: Mr. Satterthwaite; Mr. Harley Quin; Countess Czarnova, Elizabeth Martin, Pierre Vaucher.

While on vacation in Monte Carlo, Mr. Satterthwaite becomes involved in the private affairs of several couples, including several young Americans. Miss Elizabeth Martin is growing increasingly jealous over the lavish attentions being paid by Franklin Rudge, a fellow American, toward the beautiful and superbly cosmopolitan Countess Czarnova. Rudge is the countess's latest romantic attachment, the most recent in a long line that has included the king of Bosnia. The fact that the countess is no longer the king's *chère amie* and is in distinct competition with the Parisian stage favorite Mirabelle reveals to Mr. Satterthwaite that the financial and social standings of the countess are not what they once were.

Sparkling Cyanide
PUBLISHING HISTORY: First published by William Collins Sons and Co., Ltd., London, 1945. First published in the United States by Dodd, Mead and Co., New York, 1945, under the title *Remembered Death.*

CHARACTERS: Betty Archdale, Giuseppe Balsano, George Barton, Rosemary Barton, Patricia Brice-Woodworth, Anthony Browne, Charles, Lucilla Drake, Victor Drake, Lady Alexandra Farraday, Stephen Farraday, Chief Inspector Kemp, Lady Victoria Kidderminster, Lord William, Earl of Kidderminster, Ruth Lessing, Iris Marle, Colonel Johnny Race, Mary Rees-Talbot, Chloe Elizabeth West, General Lord Woodworth.

Almost a year has passed since the death of Rosemary Barton, and the feeling that her unexpected and horrible death was not a suicide has only grown in certainty in the mind of her husband, George Barton. Rosemary had died while sitting at a birthday party held in her honor at the Luxembourg restaurant, slumping forward and dying in horrible convulsions. As arsenic had been found in her purse and it was established that she had been very depressed on the day before her death, an inquest determined that she had almost certainly committed suicide.

The succeeding months have done nothing to confirm that finding. Indeed, her husband is even more convinced that she was actually murdered, after receiving two anonymous poison-pen letters that state outright that she was killed. Taking his concerns to a friend, Colonel Johnny Race, Barton ponders the death, and realizes that there are certainly plenty of suspects for a murder investigation.

Barton plans to commemorate Rosemary's death on its one-year anniversary in a very special way. He throws a party at the Luxembourg that is a direct re-creation of the original birthday party, invites all the same guests, and announces that "something important" will happen at 9:30 P.M. At the appointed hour, the lights go out, the guests rise to toast the memory of Rosemary, and George Barton drops dead from cyanide poisoning.

• • •

Sparkling Cyanide is a longer version of the short story "Yellow Iris" (1939), and offers the recurring structural format of a murder in retrospect. The device worked quite well in *Five Little Pigs* (1941), and was also very successful in this mystery. Readers certainly seemed to think so, as *Sparkling Cyanide* sold more than 30,000 copies in its first year.

An adaptation was made by CBS Television in 1983.

A 1947 edition of Remembered Death, *the American title for* Sparkling Cyanide. *(Pocket Books)*

Star over Bethlehem and Other Stories

PUBLISHING HISTORY: First published by William Collins Sons and Co., Ltd., London, 1965. First published in the United States by Dodd, Mead and Co., New York, 1965.

CONTENTS:
"A Greeting"
"Star over Bethlehem"

"A Wreath for Christmas"
"The Naughty Donkey"
"Gold, Frankincense and Myrrh"
"The Water Bus"
"In the Cool of the Evening"
"Jenny by the Sky"
"Promotion in the Highest"
"The Saints of God"
"The Island"

Agatha Christie's only foray into the world of children's literature, this seventy-nine-page book contains five poems and six short stories, all of them on a religious theme.

This collection was published under the author name of Agatha Christie Mallowan.

"The Strange Case of Sir Arthur Carmichael"

PUBLISHING HISTORY: First published by William Collins Sons and Co., Ltd., London, 1933, in the short story collection *The Hound of Death and Other Stories.* First published in the United States by Dodd, Mead and Co., New York, 1971, in the short story collection *The Golden Ball and Other Stories.*

CHARACTERS: Sir Arthur Carmichael, Lady Carmichael, Dr. Edward Carstairs, Miss Phyllis Patterson, Dr. Settle.

A tale of the supernatural, the case is supposedly taken from the notes of the late Dr. Edward Carstairs, M.D., "the eminent psychologist." He recounts the peculiar events that befell the young Sir Arthur Carmichael, a case into which he is brought by a friend, Dr. Settle. Carmichael, a pleasant but not brilliant upper-class young Englishman, goes to bed one evening and wakes up the next morning wandering about the local village in a semi-idiotic state. Adding to the odd nature of the affair is the belief by Dr. Settle, an occultist, that there is something in the Carstairs house, something terrible, that caused the event.

• • •

For the curious publishing history of this short story, please see *The Golden Ball and Other Stories.* (page 68)

"Strange Jest"

PUBLISHING HISTORY: First published by Dodd, Mead and Co., New York, 1950, in the short story collection *Three Blind Mice and Other Stories.*

CHARACTERS: Miss Jane Marple; Jane Helier, Edward Rossiter, Charmian Stroud, Matthew Stroud.

An unusual mystery for Miss Marple to solve, "Strange Jest" is brought to the old sleuth by her actress friend Jane Helier, who has assured two friends, Charmian Stroud and Edward Rossiter, that only Miss Marple is qualified to get to the bottom of things. She tells Miss Marple, "[You will] fix it for them, I know. It will be easy for you." The problem confronting the young couple has to do with a treasure buried somewhere in the estate of their deceased Uncle Matthew. As he grew older, he became more suspicious of people and worried that he would be swindled out of his money. So he took steps before he died to seal his securities and withdrew large sums of money, which he converted into assets that could be hidden or buried. Unfortunately, he left no clues as to their whereabouts save a "faint, weak little chuckle. He said, 'You'll be all right, my pretty pair of doves!' And then he tapped his eye—his right eye—and winked at us. And then—he died . . .'"

Miss Marple assures the couple that the solution must be simple, and they invite her to the estate. There, she is given a tour of the entire grounds, including the well-searched garden, the woods, and once-smooth lawn—now all heavily trenched—as well as the attic, cellar, and rooms. Miss Marple's attention is finally drawn to Uncle Matthew's desk and a packet of love letters, within which is the vital clue for finding the old man's wealth.

"The Stymphalean Birds"

PUBLISHING HISTORY: First published by William Collins Sons and Co., Ltd., London,

1947, in the short story collection *The Labours of Hercules*. First published in the United States by Dodd, Mead and Co., New York, 1947, in the short story collection *The Labors of Hercules,*.

CHARACTERS: Hercule Poirot; Elsie Clayton, Philip Clayton, Mrs. Rice, Harold Waring.

In classical mythology, Hercules slew the dread birds that inhabited the Stymphalean marshes and terrorized the surrounding regions with their bronze beaks and destructive feathers. Poirot takes on a similar labor, ridding the world of a pair of con artists who have grown fat on the suffering and misfortune of their victims.

The chief target of the "Stymphalean birds" is a young British politician, Harold Waring. While on vacation in a hotel at Lake Stempka, in Herzoslovakia, he became involved in the calamitous relationship between Mrs. Elsie Clayton and her apparently abusive husband, Philip Clayton. A violent outburst between husband and wife ends in Philip's death, with only Harold a witness to the real and accidental events that transpired. To ensure that none of them falls prey to the local justice system, it is proposed to bribe everyone who might have knowledge of the event. All seems to go well, until Mrs. Rice informs Harold that two old ladies—"devilish blood-sucking harpies"—are blackmailing the three of them. To their rescue comes Hercule Poirot. With the simple use of a telegram, the detective defeats the plans of the Stymphalean birds "with iron beaks, who feast on human flesh."

• • •

In mythology, Hercules used a pair of castanets, or bronze rattles, to scare the Stymphalean birds from their marshy abode. Once in the air, the birds were slaughtered by Hercules with a bow and arrow. Hercule Poirot's chosen weapon of destruction is the telegraph, a device that makes a similar rattling sound as messages are sent and received.

"The Submarine Plans"

PUBLISHING HISTORY: First published by Dodd,

Mead and Co., New York, 1951, in the short story collection *The Under Dog and Other Stories*.

CHARACTERS: Hercule Poirot; Captain Arthur Hastings; Lord Alloway, Sir Henry Alloway, Mrs. Conrad, Mr. Fitzroy, Leonie, Lady Juliet Weardale, Leonard Weardale.

Hercule Poirot is summoned to the estate of Lord Alloway and implored to undertake—discreetly—an investigation into the shocking and unexpected theft of secret submarine plans. He is unable to refuse the future prime minister and understands the importance of the plans to the safety of England. The chief suspect in the theft is a guest in the house, one of the socially high-placed acquaintances of Lord and Lady Alloway, who had invited her for the weekend. Mrs. Conrad, a wealthy socialite who is thought to have associations with blackmailers, is considered the likely thief, and the plans to trap her went horribly awry.

Poirot finds the precise series of events as described by Lord Alloway to be rather absurd, preferring his own more imaginative—and, of course, correct—solution. Mrs. Conrad, meanwhile, charms the easily charmed Captain Hastings. Despite Hastings's most earnest efforts and Poirot's entirely perfect solution, the plans are not recovered. Nevertheless, Lord Alloway is entirely satisfied.

• • •

This case is virtually identical with that solved by Hercule Poirot in "The Incredible Theft," in which secret bomber plans, rather than submarine plans, are stolen.

"The Sunningdale Mystery"

PUBLISHING HISTORY: First published by William Collins Sons and Co., Ltd., London, 1929, in the short story collection *Partners in Crime*. First published in the United States by Dodd, Mead and Co., New York, 1929, in the short story collection *Partners in Crime*.

CHARACTERS: Tommy Beresford; Tuppence Beresford; Albert Batt; Major Barnard, Doris Evans, Mr. Hollaby, Mr. Lecky, Inspector Marriot, Captain Sessle.

Tommy and Tuppence Beresford are having lunch at a restaurant when they read about the murder of Captain Sessle. The victim had been murdered on a golf course by being stabbed through the heart with a hatpin while playing golf. The chief suspect, a young woman, was seen at the crime scene, thanks to her bright red wool coat. Significantly, Captain Sessle was found with a bit of red wool clasped in his hand; other golfers report seeing the young woman at the scene. As for the suspect, she claims to have been lured to the golf course by the promise of romance. The Beresfords have problems with the police's handling of the case and set out to solve the murder by relying only on the newspaper account, without ever leaving their table. Their solution comes as a surprise to a diner at a nearby table, Inspector Marriot.

•   •   •

As with other investigations recounted in *Partners in Crime,* the Beresfords resolve this case by adopting the habits and personae of detectives in fiction. For this murder, Tommy becomes the Old Man in the Corner, an armchair detective created by Baroness Emma Orczy (d. 1947), who solves assorted puzzles while sitting in the comfortable corner seat of a tea shop. He is assisted by Polly Burton, a role undertaken by Tuppence.

"Swan Song"

PUBLISHING HISTORY: First published by William Collins Sons and Co., Ltd., London, 1934, in the short story collection *The Listerdale Mystery.* First published in the United States by Dodd, Mead and Co., New York, 1971, in the short story collection *The Golden Ball and Other Stories.*

CHARACTERS: Blanche Amery, Edouard Bréon, Mr. Cowan, Elise, Madame Paula Nazorkoff, Miss Vera Read, Signor Roscari, Lady Rustonbury.

A short tale, "Swan Song" presents a neat, complete, and emotional case of revenge and murder set within the world of opera. The magnificent operatic star Paula Nazorkoff—situated in utter opulence in the Ritz—is given by her principal business manager, Mr. Cowan, an invitation to sing in a private concert. The offer comes from the well-known socialite Lady Rustonbury of Rustonbury Castle. She desires Madame Nazorkoff to sing the role of Madame Butterfly, but Nazorkoff will accept only if she sings the role of *Tosca;* the star is exceedingly proud of her *Tosca.*

On the night of the gala event at the castle's private theater, the performance of *Tosca* is imperiled by the sudden illness of the singer Signor Roscari. Taken sick from food poisoning, Roscari cannot sing. Lady Rustonbury comes up with the solution. The retired opera star Edouard Bréon, who lives nearby, is summoned and kindly agrees to undertake the part vacated by Signor Roscari. In a fateful performance, the sinister events of the opera *Tosca* are played out, including the vengeful murder of the villain Scarpia.

•   •   •

This case displays Christie's extensive knowledge of opera and her ability to interweave the plots of notable operas into her stories.

Taken at the Flood

PUBLISHING HISTORY: First published by William Collins Sons and Co., Ltd., London, 1948. First published in the United States by Dodd, Mead and Co., New York, 1948, under the title *There Is a Tide.*

CHARACTERS: Hercule Poirot; Frances Cloade, Gordon Cloade, Jeremy Cloade, Katherine Cloade, Dr. Lionel Cloade, Rosaleen Cloade, Rowland Cloade, Eileen Corrigan, David Hunter, Mrs. Leadbetter, Beatrice Lippincott, Adela Marchmont, Lynn Marchmont, Major George Douglas Porter, Superintendent Spence, Charles Trenton, Captain Robert Underhay.

Hercule Poirot is visiting his club when he overhears a most interesting conversation involving Major Porter, another member. Gordon Cloade, the sixty-two-year-old head of the Cloade family of Warmsley Vale, returned to

England from a visit to America on government affairs with a major surprise for his family. While crossing the Atlantic, he met a young, beautiful widow named Rosaleen Underhay and immediately married her. They arrived in England and were on their way to Furrowbank, the Cloade estate, to introduce her to her new family when an air raid was called. During the bombing, Gordon was killed, leaving Rosaleen in full possession of the estate and Gordon's relatives absolutely stunned at this disastrous turn of events.

While seemingly successful in their own rights as a lawyer, a doctor, and a farmer, Gordon's brothers nevertheless relied heavily upon Gordon's generosity for loans to keep them going. They thus find themselves in the horribly awkward position of having to go Rosaleen, a complete stranger, to ask for money that they had long expected to inherit. Tensions mount at Furrowbank, and Rosaleen's brother, David Hunter, warns her to be careful that one of the Cloades does not try to put strychnine in her food.

Only deepening the strain is a letter that arrives for the Cloades announcing that Rosaleen may not actually be a widow. Her first husband, Robert Underhay, was presumed to have died in Africa, but a mysterious figure named Enoch Arden may know details that threaten Rosaleen's inheritance. Blackmail and intrigue follow, climaxing with the discovery of Arden murdered in the local village inn. One of the Cloades, Rowley, finally goes to Hercule Poirot for help and the Belgian arrives to find a murderer and to unmask the false identities of several scheming people.

• • •

The title of the novel is taken from Shakespeare's *Julius Caesar* (Act 4, scene 3):

There is a tide in the affairs of men,
Which taken at the flood, leads on to fortune . . .

As she did in *One, Two, Buckle My Shoe* (with its veiled references to Hitler and Mussolini),

Christie took the unusual step of using World War II as a backdrop for *Taken at the Flood*. At the start the novel, London is suffering through the Blitz.

"The Tape-Measure Murder"

PUBLISHING HISTORY: First published by Dodd, Mead and Co., New York, 1950, in the short story collection *Three Blind Mice and Other Stories.* Also published under the title "A Village Murder."

CHARACTERS: Miss Jane Marple; Gladys Brent, Ted Gerard, Miss Amanda Hartnell, Colonel Melchett, Miss Politt, Inspector Slack, Mrs. Spenlow, Arthur Spenlow.

Mrs. Spenlow is discovered dead—strangled on a hearth rug—by Miss Amanda Hartnell. The victim was supposed to have been fitted by the dressmaker, Miss Politt, at three-thirty at her house, Laburnam Cottage, and her failure to answer was the first sign that something was amiss. The immediate and obvious suspect is Mr. Spenlow, who does nothing to improve the situation by his peculiar detachment and his feeble alibi. Despite the murder of his wife, Spenlow displays no emotion, but he claims that such is in keeping with the finest elements of the Chinese philosophy he has been studying. Miss Marple, of course, observes that "the people of St. Mary Mead react rather differently. Chinese philosophy does not appeal to them." Further, Spenlow asserts that Miss Marple had telephoned on the afternoon of his wife's murder and had asked that he visit her. Miss Marple swears she made no such call. While things look bleak for Mr. Spenlow, Miss Marple solves the crime with the help of a pin, a tape measure, and the fact that at two-thirty the Much Benham bus draws up outside the post office door in St. Mary Mead.

Tell Me How You Live

See *Come, Tell Me How You Live*

Ten Little Indians

See *And Then There Were None*

"The Theft of the Royal Ruby"

See "Christmas Pudding, The Adventure of the"

There Is a Tide

See *Taken at the Flood*

They Came to Baghdad

PUBLISHING HISTORY: First published by William Collins Sons and Co., Ltd., London, 1951. First published in the United States by Dodd, Mead and Co., New York, 1951.

CHARACTERS: Andre, Richard Baker, Mr. Bolford, Dr. Alan Breck, Mrs. Cardew Trench, Henry Carmichael, Sir Rupert Crofton Lee, Captain Crosbie, Mr. Dakin, Edward Goring, Mrs. Hamilton Clipp, George Hamilton Clipp, Victoria Jones, Otto Morgenthal, Dr. John Pauncefoot, Dr. Rathbone, Anna Scheele, Catherine Serakis, Lionel Shrivenham, Marcus Tio, Sheik Hussein el Ziyara.

Captain Crosbie and Mr. Dakin sit in a nondescript office in the Middle East and discuss with remarkable detail the events of the region. They are most concerned about an upcoming secret meeting in Baghdad that is designed to bring an end to the Cold War. Their concerns are over the emergence of a secret terrorist organization that will seek to assassinate some of the participants, sabotage the meeting, and start another world war.

Meanwhile, in New York, Anna Scheele, private secretary to the international banker Otto Morgenthal, unexpectedly requests a three-week leave of absence so that she can visit her sister in London. What strikes Morgenthal as peculiar is the absence during all the years of her employment of any mention by Anna that she even has a sister.

Meanwhile, young Victoria Jones sits in Fitz-James Gardens in London and ponders the fact that she has just been fired from her latest job for doing an impersonation of her boss's wife that struck a little too close to home. Brightening her day considerably is her chance encounter with a handsome young man named Edward Goring. There is an instant attraction, but Edward is leaving for Baghdad to work with Dr. Rathbone, a philanthropist. Utterly smitten, Victoria does not think it strange that Edward takes several photos of her, including profile shots; rather, she devotes her thoughts to finding a way to follow Edward to Baghdad.

Victoria finds a way to Baghdad by hiring herself out as a companion to Mrs. Hamilton Clipp, a wealthy American woman heading for the Middle East. She wastes little time in tracking down Dr. Rathbone, and finds him at The Olive Branch, a bookstore devoted to promoting world peace. Victoria soon learns more about The Olive Branch, Dr. Rathbone, and Edward than she ever dreamed, plunging herself into a world of intrigue, assassins, and Cold War politics.

• • •

For her first novel featuring espionage since *N or M?* (1941), Christie returned to one of her strongest devices, the setting of stories in exotic locales. In this case, she chose Baghdad, a city she had first visited in 1928 and that she knew quite well, thanks to the archaeological work of her husband, Max Mallowan, in the Middle East. Her connections to the city were clear in her dedication: "To all my friends in Baghdad." Three years later, Christie returned to the espionage theme with *Destination Unknown* (1954).

They Do It with Mirrors

PUBLISHING HISTORY: First published by William Collins Sons and Co., Ltd., London, 1952. First published in the United States by Dodd, Mead and Co., New York, 1952, under the title *Murder with Mirrors*.

CHARACTERS: Miss Jane Marple; Juliet Bellever, Inspector Curry, Ernie Gregg, Christian Gulbrandsen, Gina Hudd, Wally Hudd, Edgar Lawson, Dr. Maverick, Alex Restarick, Carrie Louise Serrocold, Lewis Serrocold, Mildred Strete, Ruth van Rydock.

Miss Jane Marple visits her longtime friend Ruth van Rydock during one of Ruth's annual trips to London. The two have known each other since the days of their youth, when Miss Marple first met Ruth and her sister, Carrie Louise, during a visit to Florence. Ruth and Carrie Louise eventually married (several times), with Ruth settling back home in America and Carrie Louise residing in England.

Carrie Louise and Miss Marple have not met for twenty years, so there is need for some catching up with Ruth. Carrie Louise's first husband was a millionaire philanthropist, Eric Gulbrandsen; her second husband was a wastrel, Johnny Restarick, who left her and died in an auto accident; her third husband, Lewis Serrocold, is another philanthropist, but he has grand plans to reform the world using his wife's money. His present project is to reform juvenile delinquents, adapting their estate, Stonygates, into a home for boys. Ruth, however, is worried that things are not quite right.

Miss Marple arrives at Stonygates and does find things strangely amiss. There is more than enough money, but cost-cutting is evident everywhere, including in the chipped dishes and dire need for repairs throughout the house. This all strikes the insitute trustee, Christian Gulbrandsen, as odd, especially after he pays a surprise visit to the home and questions Miss Marple carefully about Carrie Louise's health, especially her heart. Not long after, Gulbrandsen is shot to death in his room, and the letter he was typing at the time has mysteriously disappeared.

• • •

They Do It with Mirrors reveals a number of personality traits and background details concerning Miss Marple. It is learned, for example, that in her youth, Miss Marple lived for a time in Italy. She resided in a "pensionnat in Florence." While there, she met two characters from this novel, the American sisters Carrie Louise and Ruth Martin. Alas, nothing else is known about her Italian adventures. Miss Marple has very clear views about reform schools, Stonygates, and the "modern" education movement. The old sleuth wonders why so much effort and money is being spent on juve-

nile delinquents, seemingly at the expense of perfectly normal and properly raised children: "The young people with a good heredity, and brought up wisely in a good home and with grit and pluck and the ability to get on in life—well, they are really, when one comes down to it, the sort of people a country needs."

As is, unfortunately, true of several Christie works, *They Do It with Mirrors* contains derogatory statements about Italians and Roman Catholics: "She's half Italian, you know, and the Italians have that unconscious vein of cruelty. They've no compassion for anyone who's old or ugly, or peculiar in anyway. They point with their fingers and jeer . . . The Italians are never truthful. And she's a Roman Catholic of course." The Italian-language editions do not include such remarks. American editions continue to include them, although the prewar anti-Semitic remarks have been omitted. There have been two television adaptations of the novel. The first was made in 1985 by CBS Television, starring Helen Hayes as Miss Marple; the second was produced in 1992 by the BBC, and starred Joan Hickson as Miss Marple. The 1992 version had the original title *Murder with Mirrors* in England; the title was changed in the United States to *They Do It with Mirrors*.

"The Third Floor Flat"

PUBLISHING HISTORY: First published by Dodd, Mead and Co., New York, 1950, in the short story collection, *Three Blind Mice and Other Stories*.

CHARACTERS: Hercule Poirot; Captain Arthur Hastings; Donovan Bailey, Jimmy Faulkener, Patricia Garnett, Mrs. Ernestine Grant, Mildred Hope, Inspector Rice.

Two young couples return from an evening out and discover that the key to one of their apartments—the one belonging to Patricia Garnett—is missing. They are all stranded on her doorstep. After several suggestions for entering the apartment are dismissed as impractical, they hit on the idea of getting in through the coal lift, which they are certain will not be locked or bolted because

"Pat never locks and bolts things." Donovan Bailey and Jimmy Faulkener lift themselves up the coal shaft to what they think is the fourth floor and enter through the kitchen into what they believe is Pat's apartment. They soon discover, however, that they have entered the wrong flat; hastily, they depart and reach the correct floor. Donovan, it seems, has cut his hand in the wrong apartment, but, upon washing his hand, he discovers that the blood is not his own. Jimmy and Donovan return to the wrong apartment and there find a corpse, whom they presume to be Mrs. Ernestine Grant, the occupant.

As the foursome struggles to cope with the horrifying discovery, they are encouraged to contact the police by the tenant in the flat above—Hercule Poirot. The detective is on the case, taking note of the letter found in the pocket of the dead woman's dress:

I WILL COME TO SEE YOU THIS EVENING AT HALF-PAST SEVEN—J. F.

The detective also uses several clues to solve the case: the missing key, an electric light switch, and the fact that things in a room are always in the same place under the same set of given circumstances.

• • •

This case was adapted by London Weekend Television in 1989 for the series *Agatha Christie's Poirot* starring David Suchet. The arrival of Poirot on the scene in this case reveals the curious detail that the detective rents his flat in the building under the unlikely name of Mr. O' Connor. It is also revealed that Poirot has a passion for omelets. This is confirmed two years later when Poirot teaches Maureen Summerhayes how to cook in *Mrs. McGinty's Dead* (1952).

Third Girl

PUBLISHING HISTORY: First published by William Collins Sons and Co., Ltd., London, 1966. First published in the United States by Dodd, Mead and Co., New York, 1967.

CHARACTERS: Hercule Poirot; Mrs. Ariadne Oliver; David Baker, Mr. Bascomb, Miss Battersby, Louise Birell, Peter Cardiff, Frances Cary, Mrs. Louise Charpentier, George, Mr. Goby, Sir Roderick Horsefield, Miss Jacobs, Miss Felicity Lemon, Inspector Neele, Robert Orwell, Claudia Reece-Holland, Andrew Restarick, Mary Restarick, Norma Restarick, Sonia, Dr. John Stillingfleet.

Hercule Poirot is bored. Having just completed "his *magnum opus,* an analysis of great writers of detective fiction," he is already restive without a new case to divert his "little grey cells." His thoughts are disturbed by his valet, George, who announces that a young woman wishes to see him. He starts to refuse until George adds that she wishes to consult him "about a murder she might have committed." This piques his interest, especially the "might have." The young girl is ushered in and is met by Poirot's immediate disapproval of her choice of dress, her dirty, straggly hair, and her "vacant expression." Before he can get very far in his questioning, however, the still nameless girl complains, "You're too old. Nobody told me you were so old . . . I'm really very sorry," and bolts out of his flat.

Still perplexed, Poirot receives a call from his old friend Ariadne Oliver. He learns that Mrs. Oliver had sent the young woman, Norma Restarick, to Poirot after meeting her at a party. Subsequently, Ariadne heads for Norma's flat and meets with the other two residents (Norma is the "third girl"). She has disappeared, and it comes as a shock to Ariadne and Poirot that no one cares that she is missing. They finally track her down in a café and learn that there are periods of time for which she cannot account. It was during one of these periods that she may have murdered someone. The question is, who might be dead and why?

• • •

Third Girl marked the fourth collaboration between Hercule Poirot and Mrs. Ariadne Oliver, and the novel makes the most of their advanced ages (Poirot's especially) as they find themselves in the midst of the then modern youth movement. The story thus contains young people dressed poorly and taking drugs: "swallowing L.S.D." and "sniffing snow." The contrast is quite sharp, especially as Christie expresses genuine dislike of both the young people and Poirot. She clearly disapproved of the unkempt counterculture, and of the appearance of the young people, using the young, grungy, and unwashed Norma Restarick as her exemplar. The woman goes to Hercule Poirot for aid and announces swiftly that the detective is "too old," echoing the same sentiments as Christie herself. Similarly, Ariadne Oliver—constantly an alter ego for Christie in print—laments about her detective: "They say how much they love my awful detective Sven Hjerson. If they knew how I hated him! But my publisher always says I'm not to say so." The dedication for *Third Girl* was to Nora Blacknorow.

Thirteen at Dinner

See *Lord Edgware Dies*

Thirteen Clues for Miss Marple

PUBLISHING HISTORY: First published by Dodd, Mead and Co., New York, 1966. This collection was not published in England.

CONTENTS:
"The Bloodstained Pavement"
"Motive vs. Opportunity"
"The Thumb Mark of Saint Peter"
"The Blue Geranium"
"The Companion"
"The Four Suspects"
"The Herb of Death"
"Strange Jest"
"The Tape-Measure Murder"
"The Case of the Perfect Maid"
"The Case of the Caretaker"
"Greenshaw's Folly"
"Sanctuary"

All the stories in this collection were published previously.

Thirteen for Luck

PUBLISHING HISTORY: First published by Dodd, Mead and Co., New York, 1961. This collection was not published in England.

CONTENTS:
"The Nemean Lion"
"The Girdle of Hyppolita"
"The Blue Geranium"
"The Four Suspects"
"The Bird with the Broken Wing"
"The Face of Helen"
"The Regatta Mystery"
"Problem at Pollensa Bay"
"The Veiled Lady"
"The Market Basing Mystery"
"The Tape-Measure Murder"
"The Unbreakable Alibi"
"Accident"

All the stories in this collection were published previously.

The Thirteen Problems

PUBLISHING HISTORY: First published by William Collins Sons and Co., Ltd., London, 1932. First published in the United States by Dodd, Mead and Co., New York, 1932, under the title *The Tuesday Club Murders*.

CONTENTS:
The Thirteen Problems contains thirteen short stories, all featuring Miss Marple:
"The Tuesday Night Club"
"The Idol House of Astarte"
"Ingots of Gold"
"The Bloodstained Pavement"
"Motive vs. Opportunity"
"The Thumb Mark of Saint Peter"
"The Blue Geranium"
"The Companion"

"The Four Suspects"
"A Christmas Tragedy"
"The Herb of Death"
"The Affair at the Bungalow"
"Death by Drowning"

The Thirteen Problems offers what is technically the first appearance of Miss Jane Marple. While it is true that *The Murder at the Vicarage* (1930) marked the first incarnation of the old sleuth in novel form, she had first appeared in print back in 1928, when six stories were published in magazines featuring the beloved resident of St. Mary Mead. The six mysteries were subsequently collected, added to seven more short stories, and published in 1932 as *The Thirteen Problems.*

The premise for the collection was given by Christie herself in her autobiography: "I wrote a series of six stories for magazines and showed six people whom I thought might meet once a week in a small village and describe some unsolved crime. I started with Miss Jane Marple . . ." The six stories were all originally published in *Sketch* magazine. As stated in "The Tuesday Night Club," the sleuth is the host—in her cottage in St. Mary Mead—of several friends and acquaintances who dine together each Tuesday night and solve a mystery narrated by one of the members. Originally (in the first six stories), there are six members of the club: Jane Marple; her nephew, the novelist Raymond West; the painter Joyce Lemprière (who became Joan Lemprière West); the solicitor Mr. Petherick; the cleric Dr. Pender; and the retired commissioner of Scotland Yard Sir Henry Clithering. The last seven stories introduce a change of location and several new characters. The club meets at the home of the previously unknown couple Colonel and Dolly Bantry. The Bantrys became favorite participants in Marple novels and are perhaps best remembered for waking up one morning to find a corpse sprawled on a hearth rug in their house (in *The Body in the Library,* 1942). Two other new characters are the actress Jane Helier and the physician Dr. Lloyd.

The collection is dedicated to Leonard Woolley and his wife, Katharine. An archaeologist, Woolley, with his wife, introduced Christie to her future husband, Max Mallowan.

Three-Act Tragedy

PUBLISHING HISTORY: First published by Dodd, Mead and Co., New York, 1935, under the title *Murder in Three Acts.* First published in England by William Collins Sons and Co., Ltd., London, 1935.

CHARACTERS: Hercule Poirot; Mr. Satterthwaite; Anthony Astor, Reverend Stephen Babbington, Sir Charles Cartwright, Doris Cocker, Superintendent Crossfield, Cynthia Dacres, Freddie Dacres, Margaret de Rushbridger, Aristide Duval, John Ellis, Colonel Johnson, Hermione "Egg" Lytton Gore, Lady Mary Lytton Gore, Oliver Manders, Mrs. Milray, Violet Milray, Sir Bartholomew Strange, Angela Sutcliffe, Miss Temple, Muriel Wills.

Sir Charles Cartwright, late of the stage, hosts a dinner party at his estate on the sea near Loomouth. Thirteen guests have been invited, including Hercule Poirot and the urbane Mr. Satterthwaite, but given that the crowd for dinner is a superstitious lot, Sir Charles's secretary, Miss Violet Milray, agrees to serve as the fourteenth guest. Dinner is served, and a maid brings a round of cocktails. One of the recipients is Reverend Stephen Babbington, rector of Loomouth. He takes one sip, chokes, collapses on a nearby couch, and dies in agony.

The horrified Sir Charles believes the obvious—that Babbington was poisoned by something in the cocktail, but Poirot disagrees. Sure enough, an analysis reveals a perfectly normal martini. Not long after, another party is held at which a guest from Sir Charles's party, Egg Lytton Gore, is present. This time, a physician, Bartholomew Strange, drops dead after sipping a glass of port. Mr. Satterthwaite contacts Poirot, and the Belgian sets out to trap a murderer with a flair for using nicotine in a fiendish way.

• • •

Agatha Christie, who had already written the play *Black Coffee* (1930) and had a genuine love of the theater, chose to adopt a theatrical format for this Poirot mystery. The original hardcover editions had their title pages designed to look like a theater program, and contained the whimsical line: "Illumination by Hercule Poirot."

As with other Christie works, *Three-Act Tragedy* displays her brilliant knowledge of poisons. Three victims are murdered by the ruthless and cunning use of nicotine. So talented is the murderer that Poirot acknowledges that he might have been poisoned himself. Christie dedicated the novel to Geoffrey and Violet Shepiston—"My Friends." This case was adapted in 1986 by CBS Television, and starred Peter Ustinov as Hercule Poirot.

"Three Blind Mice"

PUBLISHING HISTORY: First published by Dodd, Mead and Co., New York, 1950. This collection was not published in England.

CHARACTERS: Mrs. Boyle, Mrs. Casey, Giles Davis, Molly Davis, Detective Sergeant Kane, Mrs. Lyon, Major Metcalf, Mr. Paravicini, Inspector Parminter, Sergeant Trotter, Christopher Wren.

A tale of revenge and murder, "Three Blind Mice" follows the harrowing events at Monkswell Manor, where the residents are trapped by a snowstorm and find themselves stalked by a maniacal murderer. The killer is seeking vengeance for the abuse of three children at Longridge Farm during World War II, when they had been evacuees from the city during the German bombings.

The short story was never published in England at the specific request of the author, as she was already using the story to serve as the basis for a play. That play was *The Mousetrap* (see under Stage.)

Three Blind Mice and Other Stories

PUBLISHING HISTORY: First published by Dodd, Mead and Co., New York, 1950. This collection was not published in England.

CONTENTS:

"Three Blind Mice"
"Strange Jest" (Marple)
"The Tape-Measure Murder" (Marple)
"The Case of the Perfect Maid" (Marple)
"The Case of the Caretaker" (Marple)
"The Third Floor Flat" (Poirot)
"The Adventure of Johnnie Waverly" (Poirot)
"Four and Twenty Blackbirds" (Poirot)
"The Love Detectives" (Satterthwaite)

Three Blind Mice and Other Stories contains nine short stories—four featuring Miss Marple, three featuring Hercule Poirot, and one featuring Mr. Satterthwaite, as well as the famous short story "Three Blind Mice."

"The Thumb Mark of Saint Peter"

PUBLISHING HISTORY: First published by William Collins Sons and Co., Ltd., London, 1932, in the short story collection *The Thirteen Problems*. First published in the United States by Dodd, Mead and Co., New York, 1933, in the short story collection *The Tuesday Club Murders*.

CHARACTERS: Miss Jane Marple; Sir Henry Clithering, Mr. Denman, Geoffrey Denman, Mabel Denman, Joyce Lemprière, Mr. Pender, Mr. Pretherick, Raymond West.

At a meeting of the Tuesday Night Club, Miss Marple is told that it is her turn to tell a story, with the added command that her fellow members expect "something really spicy." She surprises them with a dark tale of murder: "You think that because I have lived in this out-of-the-way spot all my life I am not likely to have had any very interesting experiences."

Miss Marple's niece, Mabel, married a man of violent temper, Mr. Denman. After ten years of marriage, he died quite suddenly. Soon, the people in the village suspected Mabel of poisoning her husband, and the aspersions became so intense that she was on the verge of mental collapse. She writes to Miss Marple and asks her help. The old sleuth arrives and elicits a full recounting of Mabel's story, including the gruesome demise of her husband after he ate what was thought to be a plate of poisoned mushrooms. One of the few clues to the crime had been Denman's ramblings before his death about "a heap of fish." The solution, involving a fresh haddock—bearing black spots, or the marks of St. Peter's thumb, according to folk belief—and a strong poison, pilocarpine, proves that insanity did run in the Denman family, as had been rumored. The murderer in this case is caught, but not before laughing. Miss Marple describes it as "one of the most vicious laughs I have ever heard. I can assure you it made my flesh creep."

Towards Zero

PUBLISHING HISTORY: First published by William Collins Sons and Co., Ltd., London, 1944. First published in the United States by Dodd, Mead and Co., New York, 1944.

CHARACTERS: Mary Aldin, Miss Amphrey, George Barnes, Jane Barrett, Superintendent Battle, Sylvia Battle, Alice Bentham, Lord Cornelly, Allen Drake, Detective Sergeant Jones, Edward Latimer, Dr. Lazenby, Inspector James Leach, Andrew MacWhirter, Thomas Royde, Audrey Strange, Kay Strange, Nevile Strange, Mr. Trelawny, Lady Camilla Tressilian, Mr. Treves, Emma Wales.

Mr. Treves, an eighty-year-old lawyer, discusses with fellow lawyers the details of a recent and very sensational murder case. He argues that all murders begin slowly, with seemingly unrelated events that set off new actions, and finally climax at a "zero point," or murder. His assessment becomes important as the events at Gull's Point unfold.

There follows a set of apparently completely unrelated events. Andrew MacWhirter fails in a suicide attempt and is offered a job in South Africa. Superintendent Battle is summoned to his daughter Sylvia's boarding school and learns that she has confessed to stealing various items around the school, but then claims that she had confessed only to have an end to the headmistress's badgering. The tennis pro Nevile Strange plans a trip to see Lady Tressilian, even though he knows that his present wife and former wife will also be there. The only common thread in each of the stories is that the principals plan to journey to Saltcreek or the surrounding area.

Lady Tressilian, mistress of the seaside house of Gull's Point, near Easterhead Bay and Saltcreek, plans for guests with her secretary, Mary Aldin, with some trepidation. While she has no relatives, she has attracted over the years assorted houseguests, including Nevile Strange (the ward of her late husband, Sir Matthew Tressilian), Nevile's wives, and two former romantic interests of the two wives, Thomas Royde and Ted Latimer. She sees that it might be a stay fraught with high tension. She does not anticipate, however, that the visits will climax in murder—her own. She is found dead, beaten to death with a heavy object. Her murder is evidently without motive, thus posing quite a puzzle to Superintendent Battle, who is called into the case.

• • •

Towards Zero was organized by Christie in a manner different from that of her other novels. Instead of the usual numbered chapters, she divided the narrative into five parts, a prologue and four sections: "Open the Door and Here Are the People"; "Snow White and Rose Red"; "A Fine Italian Hand"; and "Zero Hour."

The book was dedicated to Robert Graves, the poet and novelist perhaps best known for the novel *I, Claudius*:

Dear Robert,

Since you are kind enough to say you like my stories, I venture to dedicate this book to you. All I ask is that you should sternly restrain your critical faculties (doubtless sharpened by your recent excesses in that line!) when reading it.

This is a story for your pleasure and not a candidate for Mr. Graves' literary pillory!

Your friend,

Agatha Christie

Agatha Christie adapted *Towards Zero* for the stage in 1956. It opened at the St. James' Theatre, London (for other details, see under Stage).

"The Tragedy of Marsdon Manor"

PUBLISHING HISTORY: First published by *Sketch* Magazine, London, 1923–1924; reprinted by John Lane Publishers, London, 1924, in the short story collection *Poirot Investigates.* First published in the United States by Dodd, Mead and Co., New York, 1925, in the short story collection *Poirot Investigates.*

CHARACTERS: Hercule Poirot; Captain Arthur Hastings; Chief Inspector James Japp; Dr. Ralph Bernard, Captain Black, Mr. Maltravers, Mrs. Maltravers.

An intriguing murder case that is narrated by Captain Arthur Hastings, "The Tragedy at Marsdon Manor" relates Poirot's investigation into a most puzzling death. Commissioned by the Northern Union Insurance Company to look into the death of Mr. Maltravers, Poirot takes on what seems a routine inquiry and uncovers a most simple yet ingenious crime. Maltravers had a sizable life insurance policy with the usual suicide clause. Soon after passing the company's physical exam, Maltravers was found dead on the grounds of his estate, Marsdon Manor, in Essex. A cursory examination found the cause of death to be a hemorrhage, given the profuse amount of blood in the mouth. As it was rumored that Maltravers was on the verge of bankruptcy, an inquiry into his demise seemed appropriate.

Poirot and Hastings make their way to Marsdon Leigh and question the persons closely related to the case—Mrs. Maltravers, Dr. Bernard, and a family friend, Captain Black. Poirot uncovers the murderer by using his proverbial "little grey cells" and a clever game of word association. The mur-

derer is actually caught as a result of the sudden appearance of Mr. Maltravers.

• • •

This case was adapted in 1991 by London Weekend Television for the series *Agatha Christie's Poirot* starring David Suchet.

"Triangle at Rhodes"

PUBLISHING HISTORY: First published by William Collins Sons and Co., Ltd., London, 1937, in the short story collection *Murder in the Mews.* First published in the United States by Dodd, Mead and Co., New York, 1937, in the short story collection *Dead Man's Mirror.*

CHARACTERS: Hercule Poirot; General Barnes, Miss Susan Blake, Commander Tony Chantry, Mrs. Valentine Chantry, Douglas Cameron Gold, Marjorie Gold, Miss Pamela Lyall.

While on vacation on the island of Rhodes, Hercule Poirot observes the flirtatious behavior of the well-known beauty Valentine Chantry. Thanks to her roving eye, a triangle has developed among Chantry, her swinish husband, Tony, and a young and virile husband, Douglas Gold, with whom Valentine is obviously much taken. The triangle becomes increasingly tense, especially given the long-suffering Mrs. Gold's apparent willingness to put up with her philandering husband. Poirot, however, senses great danger, and he urges Valentine to leave Rhodes. She fails to heed his warning and is murdered in a scheme that only Poirot can decipher.

• • •

This case served as the foundation for the 1941 novel *Evil under the Sun.* It was also adapted by London Weekend Television in 1989 for the series *Agatha Christie's Poirot* starring David Suchet.

The Tuesday Club Murders

See *The Thirteen Problems*

"The Tuesday Night Club"

PUBLISHING HISTORY: First published by William Collins Sons and Co., Ltd., London,

1932, in the short story collection *The Thirteen Problems.* First published in the United States by Dodd, Mead and Co., New York, 1933, in the short story collection *The Tuesday Club Murders.*

CHARACTERS: Miss Jane Marple; Milly Clark, Sir Henry Clithering, Mrs. Jones, Albert Jones, Joyce Lemprière, Gladys Linch.

One of the stories related by a member of the Tuesday Night Club and collected in *The Thirteen Problems,* this particular case is presented by Sir Henry Clithering, "that well-groomed man of the world" who had been until recently commissioner of Scotland Yard. He had also been a participant in the investigation and is thus aware of the real conclusion. Each member of the club, Miss Marple included, has an opportunity to offer his or her own explanation, but Miss Marple, of course, discerns immediately the full truth.

This case is concerned with an apparent bout of food poisoning—canned lobster and trifle—that afflicted three people; two recovered from the botulism but a third, Mrs. Jones, became worse and soon died. Her husband was, naturally, suspected, and growing suspicions force an autopsy. The exam reveals a lethal dose of arsenic. For Miss Marple, the solution is simple, and bears obvious similarities to her own experience with "old Hargraves who lived up at the Mount."

• • •

"The Tuesday Night Club" is notable because it contains the earliest written description of Miss Marple:

Miss Marple wore a black brocade dress, very much pinched in round the waist. Mechlin lace was arranged in a cascade down the front of her bodice. She had on black lace mittens, and a black lace cap surmounted the piled-up masses of her snowy hair.

Naturally, Miss Marple is much preoccupied throughout the story (and the collection) with knitting. The story predates by two years (at the time of its writing, not its publication) the first appearance of Miss Marple in the novel *The Murder in the Vicarage* (1930). (For other details about Miss Marple, please see Marple, Jane; see also the section in that entry on her appearance for the most common description of the sleuth.)

"The Unbreakable Alibi"

PUBLISHING HISTORY: First published by William Collins Sons and Co., Ltd., London, 1929, in the short story collection *Partners in Crime.* First published in the United States by Dodd, Mead and Co., New York, 1929, in the short story collection *Partners in Crime.*

CHARACTERS: Tommy Beresford; Tuppence Beresford; Una Drake, Mr. Montgomery Jones, Mr. Le Marchant, Mr. and Mrs. Oglander, Dicky Rice.

Young Mr. Montgomery Jones comes to the offices of Tommy and Tuppence with an intriguing problem for them to solve. His fiancée, the fickle Australian Una Drake, has made a wager with him: She claims that she can establish two airtight alibis at exactly the same time, one in Torquay and another in London, and wagers that he will be unable to shake either one. Knowing that Una is going to make her final decision on whether to marry him based on his success with this problem, Montgomery Jones turns to the Beresfords.

• • •

As is the custom with the Beresfords in the collection *Partners in Crime,* they solve this case by imitating the characters and methods of detectives of fiction. In this case, they imitate Inspector Joseph French, a Scotland Yard official created by Freeman Wills Crofts (d. 1957).

"The Under Dog"

PUBLISHING HISTORY: First published by Dodd, Mead and Co., New York, 1951, in the short story collection *The Under Dog and Other Stories.* First published in England by William Collins Sons and Co., Ltd., London, 1960, in the short story collection *The Adventure of the Christmas Pudding and a Selection of Entrées.*

CHARACTERS: Hercule Poirot; Lady Nancy Astwell, Sir Reuben Astwell, Victor Astwell, Dr. Cazalet, Miss Cole, George, Charles Leverson, Lily Margrave, Mr. Mayhew, Inspector Miller, Captain Humphrey Naylor, Owen Trefusis.

Young Lily Margrave, paid companion to Lady Astwell, visits Hercule Poirot on behalf of her employer in the hope that he will take up the case involving the murder of Sir Reuben Astwell and prove that the obvious suspect, Reuben's nephew, Charles Leverson, is innocent. All the evidence points to Leverson: He had a quarrel with his uncle on the night of the murder, he was heard leaving the Tower Room—where the corpse was found—and his bloody fingerprints were found on the corner of a chest in the room. Above all, Leverson was one of Sir Reuben's designated heirs. Despite all this, Lady Astwell is absolutely convinced that Leverson is not the murderer. Instead, she believes the real murderer is Sir Reuben's diminutive secretary, Owen Trefusis, even though the man has a seemingly airtight alibi.

Poirot heads to Sir Reuben's estate, Mon Regios, with his superb, useful, and perpetually unflappable butler, George. Not only does the detective find evidence salvaging the hopes of Leverson, but uncovers several potential suspects and a host of secret motives. George performs the role played by Captain Arthur Hastings in other cases, that of Poirot's sidekick, and displays a lack of imagination even more profound than that of the good captain. Nevertheless, the valet is instrumental in providing Poirot with several vital clues. Finally, with the help of the Harley Street physician Dr. Cazalet and his abilities with hypnosis, Poirot reveals who murdered Sir Reuben and how the crime was accomplished.

• • •

This case was adapted by London Weekend Television for the series *Agatha Christie's Poirot* starring David Suchet. George (or Georges) appeared in a number of Poirot cases, and always displays what Poirot consistently claims is very little imagination.

The Under Dog and Other Stories

PUBLISHING HISTORY: First published by Dodd, Mead and Co., New York, 1951. All the stories had been published previously in magazines in England between 1923 and 1926.

CONTENTS:
"The Under Dog"
"The Plymouth Express"
"The Affair at the Victory Ball"
"The Market Basing Mystery"
"The Lemesurier Inheritance"
"The Cornish Mystery"
"The King of Clubs"
"The Submarine Plans"
"The Adventure of the Clapham Cook"

The Under Dog and Other Stories contains nine Poirot stories in which Captain Arthur Hastings is also present. This collection was originally published only for an American audience. All the stories were published subsequently in book form in England.

"The Under Dog," "The Plymouth Express," "The Affair at the Victory Ball," "The Cornish Mystery," "The King of Clubs," and "The Adventure of the Clapham Cook" were adapted by London Weekend Television for the series *Agatha Christie's Poirot* starring David Suchet. The collection also offers several stories that were later expanded into longer and more complex cases: "The Submarine Plans" was lengthened into "The Incredible Theft," and "The Plymouth Express" became *The Mystery of the Blue Train*.

The Unexpected Guest

PUBLISHING HISTORY: Adapted from the 1958 play, *The Unexpected Guest,* by Charles Osborne and published by St. Martin's Minotaur, New York, 1999.

CHARACTERS: Henry Angell, Miss Bennett, Sergeant Cadwallader, Julian Farrar, Michael Starkwedder, Inspector Thomas, Mrs. Warwick, Jan Warwick, Laura Warwick, Richard Warwick.

The publication of *The Unexpected Guest* in 1999 marked the second adaptation of a Christie play into a novel. Both were undertaken by Charles Osborne, with the full cooperation of the Christie estate, and both represent an exciting chance for readers to enjoy the plots and characters from Christie plays that are now virtually impossible to find, even in published form. For this novel, Osborne transfers the successful 1958 play that had originally been staged in two acts, opening in London on August 12, 1958.

Michael Starkwedder, "a somewhat thick-set, sandy-haired man of about thirty-five," has driven his car off the road in a fog along a country road in South Wales, near the Bristol Channel. He seeks help at a nearby house and knocks at the french windows along the side of the building. As there is no response, he tries the handle and finds the door unlocked. Entering a dark room, he uses his flashlight to scan the well-appointed study, stopping at a wheelchair in which a man has apparently fallen asleep. When the man gives no reply, Starkwedder discovers that he is dead. Stunned at the discovery, Starkwedder searches for a light switch and turns on the lamps on the two nearby occasional tables. He is given a second shock when he sees an attractive woman about thirty and wearing a cocktail dress and matching jacket. She stands with her arms hanging limply at her side, but in one hand is a revolver.

Starkwedder is informed by the woman that she is named Laura Warwick and that her husband, shot dead in his wheelchair, was Richard Warwick. Learning from Laura that Richard was a monster, Starkwedder decides to help the apparent murderer by concocting a suitable alibi and possible other names of people who might have wanted Richard Warwick dead. The list is a long one, including Julian Farrar, a candidate for Parliament who has been having an affair with Laura; Miss Bennett, Richard's secretary; and Jan Warwick, Richard's mentally ill young half-brother. They settle, however, on an even more likely murderer—and one outside the family. Richard ran over a child with his car, and the father, a man named McGregor, swore revenge after Richard used his influence and charm to evade prosecution.

The concocted plan goes horribly awry when it is learned that McGregor could not possibly have committed the murder. He died two years before, meaning that the murderer was in the house all along. The police, under Inspector Thomas and Sergeant Cadwallader, conduct a thorough investigation, climaxing in another tragedy and a final, shocking revelation.

Unfinished Portrait

PUBLISHING HISTORY: First published by William Collins Sons and Co., Ltd., London, 1934. First published in the United States by Doubleday and Co., New York, 1934.

CHARACTERS: Aubrey, Miss Banks, Monsieur Barre, Madame Beauge, Jeanne Beauge, Miss Bennett, Celia, Marjorie Connell, Cyril, Major Johnnie Deburgh, Mary Denman, Dermot, Fanny, Gladys, Ralph Graham, Grannie, Mrs. Grant, Bernard Grant, Jim Grant, Gregg, The Gun Man, Mary Hayes, Judy, Kate, Monsieur Kochter, J. Larraby, Miss Leadbetter, Madame Lebrun, Miss Lestrange, Cousin Lottie, Mrs. Luke, Miss MacKintosh, Margaret MacRae, Janet Maitland, Captain Peter Maitland, Miss Mauhourat, Miriam, Janet Paterson, Maisie Payne, Margaret Priestman, Roger Raynes, Mrs. Rouncewell, Mr. Rumbolt, Mrs. Rumbolt, Mrs. Steadman, Susan, Sybil Swinton, Miss Tenterden, Bessie West.

J. Larraby, a former painter who has lost his hand, is visiting a Spanish island and notices a woman sitting in a spot that he enjoys overlooking the sea. He has a suspicion that she may have come to commit suicide and so invites her to dine with him in order to be able to talk to her. He subsequently becomes the narrator of her story, the life of Celia.

Celia had a happy childhood until she reached the age of ten, when her father died, leaving the family in difficult financial circumstances. As she grew older, she attracted many suitors and finally settled on Dermot, a handsome soldier, after a whirlwind courtship. Their early marriage was happy, but Dermot's bouts of jealousy and, finally, his infidelity destroyed their marriage. At the same time that she was divorced, Celia's mother died. Although she had derived some solace from writing, the shattering events in her personal life drove her to depression, a nervous breakdown, and, ultimately, attempted suicide.

• • •

Unfinished Portrait was the second novel written by Agatha Christie under the pseudonym of Mary Westmacott. According to Christie's husband, Max Mallowan, the novel was, perhaps more than anything Christie wrote, "a portrait of Agatha." Her main character, Celia, endures the breakup of her marriage, is forced to raise a daughter on her own, and suffers a nervous breakdown. Certainly, in a broad sense, the events mirror Christie's own life, culminating in Celia's marriage at the age of thirty-nine; this was the same age at which Christie wed Max Mallowan.

"The Veiled Lady"

PUBLISHING HISTORY: First published in *Sketch* magazine, London, in 1923–1924; reprinted by John Lane, London, 1924, in the short story collection *Poirot Investigates.* First published in the United States by Dodd, Mead and Co., New York, 1925, in the short story collection *Poirot Investigates.*

CHARACTERS: Hercule Poirot; Captain Arthur Hastings; Chief Inspector James Japp; Gertie, Mr. Lavington, Lady Millicent Castle Vaughan.

In another case of Poirot coming to the rescue of the aristocracy, the detective is consulted by Lady Millicent Castle Vaughan in the desperate hope that he will be able to save her engagement to the young duke of Southshire. At the age of sixteen, she had written a compromising and immature letter, and a blackmailer, Mr. Lavington, has come into possession of it. He demands the enormous sum of twenty thousand pounds or he will show the letter to her fiancé.

Poirot meets with Lavington and finds him as odious as Lady Millicent had predicted he would. As their conversation proves fruitless, Poirot decides upon the dramatic and unusual course of burglarizing the blackmailer's house. The burglary succeeds with typical Poirot-like brilliance, much to the joyous relief of Hastings—the sleuth sleeps late the following morning—although one of the detective's elegant suits is completely ruined. Lady Millicent is delighted with the results. Poirot, however, has not only retrieved the compromising letter but has a major surprise for the young noblewoman. The key clue to the story is a pair of significantly well-worn and cheap shoes.

• • •

A loose adaptation of this case was produced by London Weekend Television for the series *Agatha Christie's Poirot* starring David Suchet.

"A Village Murder"

See "The Tape-Measure Murder"

"The Voice in the Dark"

PUBLISHING HISTORY: First published by William Collins Sons and Co., Ltd., London, 1930, in the short story collection *The Mysterious Mr. Quin.* First published in the United States by Dodd Mead, and Co., New York, 1930, in the short story collection *The Mysterious Mr. Quin.*

CHARACTERS: Mr. Satterthwaite; Mr. Harley Quin; Mrs. Casson, Alice Clayton, Margery Gale, Marcia Keane, Mrs. Lloyd, Lady Barbara Stranleigh, Roley Vavasour

Mr. Satterthwaite is consulted by Lady Stranleigh, who is puzzled and worried by her daughter, Margery. It seems that Margery is hearing voices, leading Lady Stranleigh to assume that the house, Abbot's Mede, is haunted. Satterthwaite sets out and encounters Mr. Harley Quin on the train, which convinces Satterthwaite that he is destined to have an unusual experience. This is confirmed when he questions Margery and hears of her being awakened by a voice that hissingly proclaims: "You have stolen what is mine. This is death." Matters take an even darker turn when Lady Stranleigh receives a gift of a box of poisoned chocolates.

The mood of the supernatural continues when the family holds a séance, and the spirit of Lady Stranleigh's long-dead sister, Beatrice, makes her supposed presence felt. With Beatrice, Lady Stranleigh and a maid, Alice, had been involved in a shipwreck; Beatrice had died and was now seemingly speaking from beyond the grave, demanding, "Give back what is not yours." A short time later, Satterthwaite reads the shocking news: Lady Stranleigh had been found dead in her bath.

"Wasps' Nest"

PUBLISHING HISTORY: First published by Dodd, Mead and Co., New York, 1961, in the short story collection *Double Sin and Other Stories.*

CHARACTERS: Hercule Poirot; Molly Deane, John Harrison, Claude Langton.

With his customary sharpness and humility, Hercule Poirot observes: "If one can investigate a murder before it has happened, surely that is much better than afterward. One might even—a little idea—prevent it." This becomes his driving principle as he proceeds to prevent a murder in "Wasps' Nest." The detective pays a call on a friend, John Harrison, informing Harrison that he is there investigating a potential crime, the most serious possible—murder. Poirot is convinced that a murder will be committed unless the pair can prevent it.

Poirot observes a wasps' nest on Harrison's property and learns that a friend, Claude Langton, was going to put an end to it, supposedly with petrol. What is strange, though, is that in the poison book at the local chemist's in Barchester is the clear signature of Claude Langton, who had purchased cyanide of potassium. Deepening the strangeness of the situation is the interconnected history of Langton and Harrison: Harrison's fiancée, Molly Deane, was once engaged to Claude Langton and threw him over for Harrison. While her reasons were not entirely clear, the detective

supposes that Langton "has not forgotten or forgiven."

Poirot laments that the English are stupid. "They think they can deceive anyone but no one can deceive them." Using the skills taught to him by a pickpocket, he replaces a packet of poison in someone's pocket with washing soda and so prevents a murder. However, the detective does nothing to bring the attempted murderer to justice, for reasons that are clear to both Poirot and the would-be killer. Rather than gratitude tinged with bitterness, Poirot receives the absolute gratitude of a person whose very soul has been saved.

"'The Western Star,' The Adventure of"

PUBLISHING HISTORY: First published in *Sketch* magazine, London, 1923, reprinted by John Lane Publishers, London, 1924, in the short story collection *Poirot Investigates.* First published in the United States by Dodd, Mead and Co., New York, 1925, in the short story collection *Poirot Investigates.*

CHARACTERS: Hercule Poirot; Captain Arthur Hastings; Mary Marvell, Gregory Rolf, Lady Yardly, Lord Yardly.

In a case that displays all too clearly the shortcomings of Captain Hastings as a detective, Hercule Poirot is consulted by the actress Mary Marvell, "undoubtedly one of the most popular actresses on the screen," who is afraid that her prize jewel, the Western Star, will soon be stolen. She has been warned of its impending theft by three letters that say: "The great diamond which is the left eye of god must return whence it came." Each of the letters is more threatening than the last and more clear that the dire event is imminent, and includes the assurance: "At the full of the moon, the two diamonds which are the right and left eyes of the god shall return. So it is written." In fact, Mary Marvell and her movie costar husband, Gregory Rolf, are heading to the estate of Yardly Chase to stay with Lord and Lady Yardly. Lady Yardly is owner of the Star of the East, a companion gem to the Western Star. Lady

Yardly has also received threatening letters, and the presence of both diamonds together under the same roof would seem to be the perfect time for their joint theft.

Poirot and Hastings journey to Yardly Chase, and soon after their arrival Lady Yardly is robbed of her jewel by what she claims was "the China-man," the same Chinese man who was earlier seen delivering the alarming letters. Despite Hastings' concerns that Mary Marvell's jewel is also threat-ened, Poirot declines to act immediately. The next morning, the detective is informed of the theft of the Western Star. Poirot recovers the missing jew-els by relying upon several clues, including the let-ters, the mysterious Chinaman, and an article in *Society Gossip* magazine. Hastings, of course, reaches all the wrong conclusions and laments to Poirot, "You've made a perfect fool of me!"

• • •

"The Adventure of 'The Western Star' " was adapted in 1990 by London Weekend Television for the series *Agatha Christie's Poirot* starring David Suchet.

What Mrs. McGillicuddy Saw!

See *4.50 from Paddington*

"Where There's a Will"

See "Wireless"

"While the Light Lasts"

PUBLISHING HISTORY: First published in *Novel* magazine, London, 1923. First published in the United States by G. P. Putnam's Sons, New York, 1997, in the short story collection *The Harlequin Tea Set and Other Stories.*

CHARACTERS: Deirdre Crozier, George Crozier, Tim Nugent.

George and Deirdre Crozier travel across the sun-drenched African plain in search of a tobacco plantation that George has just purchased. Their progress over rocky roads in the heat is made even more intolerable for George because he knows his wife's thoughts. She is wrapped in memories of her first husband, a young, lean, and heroic man whom she had chosen over George at the start of World War I. Tim Nugent, however, had been killed in the fighting in West Africa, and George had won Deirdre's hand in marriage. Since that happy day for George, he has denied her nothing, not even a diamond from the Kimberley mines.

Finally reaching the plantation, the Croziers are greeted by the caretakers and are given a tour. The sun becomes too much for Deirdre, and she is taken back to the main house. While on her way, she hears a shocking voice call out her name. Whirling around, she sees the face of her dead husband. Tim is still alive, and Deirdre realizes with horror the choice she must make.

• • •

"While the Light Lasts" had never been pub-lished in the United States, nor had it been col-lected in any compilation, before appearing in *The Harlequin Tea Set and Other Stories.* Like other Christie stories, this one is concerned with war and its cost to the lives and loves of its partici-pants. It also deals peripherally with one of the largely forgotten theaters of operation during World War I, West Africa.

Why Didn't They Ask Evans?

PUBLISHING HISTORY: First published by William Collins Sons and Co., Ltd., London, 1934. First published in the United States by Dodd, Mead and Co., New York, 1934, under the title *The Boomerang Clue.*

CHARACTERS: Dr. George Arbuthnot, Thomas Askew, Henry Bassington-ffrench, Roger Bass-ington-ffrench, Sylvia Bassington-ffrench, Tommy Bassington-ffrench, Badger Beadon, Alan Car-stairs, Amelia Cayman, Leo Cayman, Lady Frances Derwent, Robert Jones, Reverend Thomas Jones, Lord Marchington, Dr. Jasper Nicholson, Moira Nicholson, Rose Chudleigh Pratt, Mrs. Rivington, Gladys Evans Roberts, John Savage, Frederick Spragge, Dr. Thomas, Inspector Williams.

Bobby Jones and a friend, Dr. Thomas, a mid-dle-aged physician, play a round of golf, and Jones slices his ball over the nearby edge of a hill. Going in search of the ball, Jones and Thomas discover something strange at the base of the cliff, "a dark heap of something that looked like old clothes." As they approach, they are shocked to see that the pile is actually a dying man. As he slips into final unconsciousness, the dying man cries out in a final gasp, "Why didn't they ask Evans?" In searching the dead man's pocket for a handkerchief to cover his face, Bobby finds a photograph of a "haunting" woman.

Several days later, Jones meets his childhood friend Lady Frances Derwent and relates his odd experience on the golf course. She then shows him an article about the dead man, Alex Pritchard, brother of Amelia Cayman. While an inquest gives a verdict of death by misadventure (or accident), Lady Frances admits that it would be far more exciting if Pritchard had been pushed.

Following the inquest, Amelia Cayman and her husband ask Jones if her brother had said anything before he died. Jones is unable at first to remember, but he later writes them with the odd declaration by Pritchard. A few days later, Jones is poisoned with morphine in a beer and is hospitalized. The murder attempt jars Jones's memory, and he realizes that the woman in the photograph was not Amelia. With Lady Frances at his side, Jones sets out to discover who Evans might be and why Pritchard was murdered to prevent anyone from finding out.

• • •

This novel features two characters who, like other ingenious but amateur sleuths, made a one-time appearance in a Christie mystery. Bobby Jones and Lady Frances Derwent are definitely not professional detectives, but they make a memorable duo. Like Mark Easterbrook, Dr. Calgary, and Lucy Eylesbarrow in other novels, the two never appeared again, and readers who took a shine to them could only regret that they were in just one case.

This novel was adapted by London Weekend Televsion in 1981.

"Wireless"

PUBLISHING HISTORY: First published by William Collins Sons and Co., Ltd., London, 1933, in the short story collection, *The Hound of Death and Other Stories.* Also titled "Where There's a Will."

CHARACTERS: Elizabeth, Mrs. Mary Harter, Mr. Hopkinson, Dr. Meynell, Charles Ridgeway.

Old Mrs. Harter is not in the best of health, but her doctor assures her that she will live for another five years if she avoids all sudden shocks and excitement. This seems likely given the old girl's quiet life, and she is much aided in her sedate life by her nephew, Charles Ridgeway, a young man who lives with her. She is so pleased with her nephew's attention that she changes her will, leaving her fortune to Charles instead of a niece.

In a kind gesture, Charles gives her a radio, but things take an odd turn when voices begin emanating out of the device. Mrs. Harter hears the voice of her long-dead husband. The dead man speaks to her and gives the shocking news that he is on his way to fetch her into the next world.

• • •

Also titled "Where There's a Will," "Wireless" was included in the collection *The Hound of Death and Other Stories,* a volume that featured tales of the supernatural (such as "The Hound of Death," "The Red Signal," and "The Lamp"). It should be added, of course, that the collection also boasts "Witness for the Prosecution" and "The Mystery of the Blue Jar." The story was adapted in 1983 by London Weekend Television.

"Within a Wall"

PUBLISHING HISTORY: First published in *Royal Magazine,* London, 1925. First published in the United States by G. P. Putnam's Sons, New York, 1997, in the short story collection *The Harlequin Tea Set and Other Stories.*

CHARACTERS: Alan Everard, Jane Haworth, Mrs. Lemprière, Isobel Loring.

A tale of love, of sacrifice, and of the many forms of slavery, "Within a Wall" traces the triangular relationship between the painter Alan Everard, his wife, Isobel Loring, and their friend Jane Haworth. Everard is a gifted artist, but an impoverished one. His first paintings, *Color* and *The Connoisseur,* earned him great praise, but his wife had expenses, as did their daughter, Winnie. Financial help is always supplied by Jane, a woman of complex motives who is described by Everard as "the most alive person" he has ever met. Jane's sacrifices of money, time, and support eventually end when she is swept away by an influenza outbreak. It is only then that Everard realizes the depth of her gifts, the freedom it had bought him, and the true nature of his wife.

• • •

"Within a Wall" had never been published in the United States, nor had it been collected in any compilation, before appearing in *The Harlequin Tea Set and Other Stories.*.

"Witness for the Prosecution"

PUBLISHING HISTORY: First published by William Collins Sons and Co., Ltd., London, 1933, in the short story collection *The Hound of Death and Other Stories.*

CHARACTERS: Emily French, George Harvey, Romaine Heilger, Janet Mackenzie, Mr. Mayherne, Leonard Vole.

Leonard Vole has been arrested for the murder of Emily French and, despite his assurances of his innocence, the case against him is quite impressive. Emily had become much infatuated with Vole, a man forty years her junior, and had even handed to him control of her finances. Soon after, she was found murdered.

Vole is certain that he will be saved by his mistress, Romaine, as she will testify that he had returned home before the time that the murder was taking place. To his shock, however, Romaine not only refuses to testify to such an alibi but expresses her seething hatred of Leonard. Not only does Romaine destroy Leonard's alibi, she testifies that he arrived home with his clothes stained with blood.

Faced with doom for his client, Vole's attorney, Mr. Mayherne, pulls victory out of the gloom when a priceless piece of evidence comes into his possession. He manages to win Leonard's acquittal, but that is only the start of some truly shocking surprises.

• • •

"Witness for the Prosecution" formed the basis for the 1953 stage play of the same name by Agatha Christie. The play became one of her most successful stage creations and was likewise used as the basis for the 1957 film *Witness for the Prosecution* by Billy Wilder. Another adaptation was made in 1982 for television.

Witness for the Prosecution and Other Stories

PUBLISHING HISTORY: First published by Dodd, Mead and Co., New York, 1948. This collection was not published in England.

CONTENTS:
"Witness for the Prosecution"
"The Red Signal"
"The Fourth Man"
"SOS"
"Where There's a Will"
"Sing a Song of Sixpence"
"The Mystery of the Blue Jar"
"Philomel Cottage"
"Accident"
"The Mystery of the Spanish Shawl"
"The Second Gong"

Six of the stories were originally published in the collection *The Hound of Death and Other Stories* (1933): "Witness for the Prosecution," "The Red Signal," "The Fourth Man," "SOS," "Where There's a Will" (titled "Wireless" in England), and "The Mystery of the Blue Jar." Four of the stories were published in the collection *The Listerdale Mystery* (1934): "Philomel Cottage," "Accident,"

"Sing a Song of Sixpence," and "The Mystery of the Spanish Shawl" (called "Mr. Eastwood's Adventure" in England). The last story, "The Second Gong," is a version of the longer "Dead Man's Mirror," which had been included in the collection *Murder in the Mews and Other Stories* (1937).

"The World's End"

PUBLISHING HISTORY: First published by William Collins Sons and Co., Ltd., London, 1930, in the short story collection *The Mysterious Mr. Quin*. First published in the United States by Dodd, Mead and Co., New York, 1930, in the short story collection *The Mysterious Mr. Quin*.

CHARACTERS: Mr. Satterthwaite; Mr. Harley Quin; Naomi Carlton-Smith, Alec Gerard, Henry Judd, the duchess of Leith, Rosina Nunn, Mr. Tomlinson, Mr. Vyse.

A romantic mystery set on the picturesque island of Corsica, "The World's End" challenges Mr. Satterthwaite to solve a crime and restore the hope of a young woman. While vacationing on Corsica with the authentic but rather shabby looking old lady the duchess of Leith, Satterthwaite meets her niece, Naomi, a young but depressed artist still reeling from the arrest and imprisonment of Alec Gerard, the man she loves, for the theft of an opal from the actress Rosina Nunn. Nunn is also on Corsica with friends, and the group goes for a picnic. During the meal, conversation comes around to the theft, and Rosina provides sufficient detail for Mr. Satterthwaite to discern the true events surrounding the theft of the opal. His solution offers Naomi renewed hope. Mr. Quin makes his usual enigmatic appearance, and his departure, similar to that in "The Man from the Sea," demonstrates Quin's less-than-earthly origins.

"Yellow Iris"

PUBLISHING HISTORY: First published by Dodd, Mead and Co., New York, 1939, in the short story collection *The Regatta Mystery and Other Stories*.

CHARACTERS: Hercule Poirot; Stephen Carter, Tony Chappell, Barton Russell, Lola Valdez, Pauline Weatherby.

Hercule Poirot receives an anonymous phone call that urges him to go to the Jardin des Cygnes and find a table decorated with yellow irises. He goes to the restaurant and encounters a party in progress, a memorial dinner in honor of the late Iris Russell, who died from poisoning exactly four years before. Her husband, Barton Russell, has organized this dinner as a precise re-creation of that terrible night, and has faithfully reproduced every tiny detail, such as the music and the lighting. As in the original murder, the lights go out suddenly. When the lights go back on, however, another guest at the party is apparently dead.

• • •

"Yellow Iris" was the basis for the novel *Sparkling Cyanide* (1945). It was also adapted in 1993 by London Weekend Television for the series *Agatha Christie's Poirot* starring David Suchet.

PART TWO

The Characters

It is no good thinking about real people—you must create your characters for yourself. Someone you see in a tram or a train or a restaurant is a possible starting point, because you can make up something for yourself about them.

—*Agatha Christie,* An Autobiography

Aarons, Joseph An expert in matters of the theater and a longtime friend of Hercule Poirot. He gives assistance to the detective in several published cases: *The Big Four, The Mystery of the Blue Train,* and *Murder on the Links.*

Abbot, Mr. Two characters in different mysteries. The first was an attorney in *Murder Is Easy.* He is a resident of Wychwood and is one of the early suspects in the brutal murders being committed in the village. The second Mr. Abbot was the owner of a grocery store in *Sad Cypress.* He is a friendly little man, but it is his store from which Mary Carlisle purchased the fish paste that was the main ingredient in a batch of fatal sandwiches.

Abdul An Arab servant in *Appointment with Death.* Abdul discovers the body of Mrs. Boynton, but he is not considered a likely suspect in her murder.

Abercrombie, Colonel A witness in *One, Two, Buckle My Shoe.* A patient of Dr. Morley, he is a former soldier and has retained all of his pomposity and smug British demeanor. Hercule Poirot finds him a terrible annoyance, so much so that he proclaims Abercrombie to be one of those "Englishmen who are altogether so unpleasing and ridiculous that they should have been put out of their misery at birth."

Abernethie, Helen A member by marriage of the Abernethie family in *After the Funeral.* She was widowed and went to extreme lengths to remain in the good graces of the Abernethie family. An observant woman, she notices some peculiar behavior by one of the suspects and attempts to pass along a vital clue to the attorney Mr. Entwhistle. Before she can do so, however, she is bludgeoned and sent to the hospital.

Abernethie, Maude An imperious member of the Abernethie family in *After the Funeral.* She is the very dominant wife of Timothy Abernethie, and uses her position to keep her husband completely under her control. It thus comes as a terrible blow to her when she breaks her ankle and is forced to employ the cook and

housekeeper, Mrs. Gilchrist, thereby losing a little control over her husband.

Abernethie, Timothy A member of the Abernethie family in *After the Funeral.* He is married to Maude Abernethie and is completely dominated by her, remaining a virtual invalid. This weak position has left Timothy a bitter and broken man, but he is determined to press home the claim of being head of the family upon the death of his brother. He is opposed to the involvement of Hercule Poirot in the investigation of murder in the family.

Ackroyd, Mrs. Cecil A member by marriage of the Ackroyd family and mother of Flora Ackroyd in *The Murder of Roger Ackroyd.* She is the widow of Cecil, the so-called black sheep of the Ackroyd family. Despite Cecil's death, she is permitted to live in the home of Roger Ackroyd, Fernly Hall, and moves to England from Canada. Although impoverished, she maintains the veneer of a grand lady. Her daughter, Flora, is the primary object of her attentions, as she is determined to arrange for her a suitable marriage.

Ackroyd, Flora The daughter of Mrs. Cecil Ackroyd and the niece of Roger Ackroyd in *The Murder of Roger Ackroyd.* Her mother is determined that she marry well, and her marriage is also of interest to Roger Ackroyd. The squire desires her to wed his stepson, Ralph Paton; by the end of the case, however, she is engaged to Hector Blunt.

Ackroyd, Roger The murder victim in *The Murder of Roger Ackroyd.* A wealthy retired manufacturer, Ackroyd settled into the life of a country squire at Fernly Hall, permitting his sister-in-law to reside there as well, along with his niece, Flora. His estate lies close to the home of Hercule Poirot, and Ackroyd has known the detective for some time. As is the custom in small villages, Ackroyd is the object of much local gossip, centering mainly on his relationship with Mrs. Ferrars. It is generally acknowledged that he will marry Mrs. Ferrars, but she commits suicide and he is brutally murdered before any verification can be found for the rumor.

Adams, Dr.   A country physician in a small Cornish village in "The Cornish Mystery." He was the physician to Mrs. Pengelly and was absolutely convinced that her complaint of illness was nothing more than gastritis. He holds firm to this diagnosis, even after Mrs. Pengelly dies, and he grows incensed that Poirot should suggest anything to the contrary. In time, of course, the remains of Mrs. Pengelly are exhumed, and it is discovered that she was, indeed, poisoned.

Adams, Carlotta   An actress and impersonator in *Lord Edgware Dies.* Adams was hired by the American actress Jane Wilkinson to impersonate her at a dinner held by Lord Edgware. For this relatively simple task, the actress pays her the enormous sum of ten thousand pounds. Adams, however, is found later, poisoned by an overdose of veronal. Her maid assures Hercule Poirot that Carlotta never took more than one veronal pill.

Addison, Thomas   The father of Lily Gilliat and Maria Horton in "The Harlequin Tea Set." Addison is also a friend of Mr. Satterthwaite. He suffers from gout and is color-blind, conditions that curb a life of action and sports.

Afflick, Dorothy   A wealthy and socially active woman in *Sleeping Murder.* She is married to Jackie Afflick, despite his crude manner and the considerable differences in their social circumstances. She met her husband on a cruise.

Afflick, Jackie   The husband of Dorothy Afflick in *Sleeping Murder.* He is a rather crude man, the proprietor of Afflick's Daffodil Coaches, a tour company that uses exceedingly brightly colored yellow buses. Given his manner and less than elegant occupation, his marriage to the socially distinguished Dorothy is a mystery. He met his wife on a cruise.

Agrodopolous, Mr.   An old friend of Aristide Leonides in *Crooked House.* He was given a copy of Leonides's will for safekeeping, with the instruction that upon Leonides's death he should deliver it to proper authorities.

Akibombo, Mr.   A student in *Hickory, Dickory, Dock.* Akibombo is from West Africa and stays in the youth hostel run by Mrs. Nicoletis. He has trouble adjusting to British food and British customs, and his perpetually upset stomach leads to the discovery of a vital clue; he searches for some bicarbonate of soda and finds instead a bottle of boracic acid.

Albert   An auto mechanic in *The Hollow.* He has responsibility over the care of Henrietta Savernake's automobile.

Alcadi   A handsome, capable pilot in *Destination Unknown.*

Aldin, Mary   A lady's companion in *Towards Zero.* Mary is an exceedingly intelligent woman with "a really first-class brain," according to her employer, Lady Tressilian. The only reason Mary serves in the capacity of lady's companion is because of financial circumstances beyond her control.

Alfred   A one-time footman at the Chimneys in *The Seven Dials Mystery.* He is hired away from Chimneys by Mr. Mosgorovsky after receiving the incredible offer of a salary three times his present one and a bonus of one hundred pounds. Alfred is also hired by Lady Eileen Brent to provide her with as much information as possible about the members of the Seven Dials Club.

Alfredge, Madame   The proprietor of a clothing store in *The Hollow.* She hires Midge Hardcastle to sell dresses, but her real purpose is to have Midge—who has many wealthy friends, despite her personal financial predicament—draw in potential customers.

Ali, Achmed   An Egyptian student in *Hickory, Dickory, Dock.* He stays at the youth hostel run by Mrs. Nicoletis and is considered a rather unsavory character; he is hostile and possesses a large amount of pornography.

Ali, Prince   The son of a Middle East leader in "The Theft of the Royal Ruby." Prince Ali journeyed to London to have a priceless ruby reset and then had the gem stolen from under his nose. Poirot is hired to recover the gem, and the prince—to whom the Belgian detective takes an instant dislike—admits with some chagrin that the ruby was most likely stolen by a young woman whom he had met and to whom he had, unwisely, shown the ruby. Prince Ali is almost certainly a thinly disguised literary version of King Farouk of Egypt.

Alice A housemaid in *The Mystery of the Blue Train.* She is a devoted employee to Katherine Grey.

Ali Yusef A thief in *Murder in Mesopotamia.* He is arrested for attempting to steal artifacts from the Tell Yarimjah site in Iraq.

Ali Yusef, Prince The prince and hereditary sheik of Ramat, a nondescript Middle Eastern country, in *Cat among the Pigeons.* A youthful, progressive ruler married to a young Englishwoman, he is toppled in a bloody coup and forced to flee in the middle of descending chaos. With a trusted pilot, Bob Rawlinson, he sets out by plane for freedom, but the craft never reaches its destination. Later, the wreckage of a plane is discovered with two burned corpses inside, presumed to be the remains of the prince and the pilot.

Allaby, Mr. A middle-aged man in "Next to a Dog." He is looking for a governess for his children for an upcoming trip to the Continent and hires Joyce Lambert for the job. He is a devoted dog owner and displays great sensitivity toward Joyce's dying dog, an act of kindness that endears the two people to each other.

Allen, Barbara A beautiful woman who is apparently murdered (and the crime disguised as a suicide) in "Murder in the Mews." She had lived in India and had been married to a man named Armitage; he was a drinker and had seemingly died, followed by their little daughter. At the time of her death, Barbara was engaged to be married to Charles Laverton-West, M.P., and had no obvious reason to commit suicide.

Allenson, Captain Jimmy A victim of a gunshot in "The Shadow on the Glass." A dashing thirty-year-old, he is murdered from afar while in the arms of Moira Scott in a garden.

Allerton, Major A man with a loathsome past in *Curtain.* He becomes involved with Judith Hastings, much to the grief of her father, Captain Arthur Hastings. A woman in Allerton's past had been so disgraced by him that she had killed herself, an event that Captain Hastings is determined will not happen to his daughter. So great is his fear that he actually launches a plan to poison Allerton.

Allerton, Mrs. One of the passengers on board the *Karnak* in *Death on the Nile.* She journeys to Egypt with her son, Tim, on whom she seemingly dotes. During the trip on the Nile, she develops a cordial association with Hercule Poirot and ultimately provides him with useful information in his investigations into the murders on board.

Allerton, Tim The son of Mrs. Allerton and a passenger on board the *Karnak* in *Death on the Nile.* He introduces himself to the subsequent murder victim Lynette Doyle as the cousin of an old friend of hers, Joanna Southwood, and becomes embroiled in the theft of pearls and the clever feat of replacing them with imitations. Cleared of suspicion in the murders on the boat, however, Tim proposes to young Rosalie Otterbourne.

Alloway, Lord A powerful government minister in "The Submarine Plans." He is almost certainly going to become the next prime minister of Britain and thus can ill afford a major scandal involving the theft of top-secret documents. He turns to Hercule Poirot to rescue him from what proves to be a case of blackmail by an agent of an enemy power. Lord Alloway is resurrected in "The Incredible Theft" under the name Lord Sir Charles McLaughlin Mayfield.

Altamount, Lord Edward A retired and once powerful government minister in *Passenger to Frankfurt.* He does not survive the events recounted in the novel.

Alton   A butler in *Lord Edgware Dies.* He disappears immediately after stealing one hundred pounds from his late employer, Lord Edgware.

Alverstoke, Lord   The former Lord Chief of Justice in *Destination Unknown.* Although no longer on the bench, and although he is quite old, feeble, and suffering from deafness and blindness, he still possesses a thirst for justice.

Amalfi   The head of an international ring of jewel thieves in "The Regatta Mystery." With his daughter-in-law, Maria Amalfi, he impersonates a wealthy American businessman and manages to become attached to the retinue of Isaac Pointz, a jewel magnate.

Amalfi, Maria   The daughter-in-law of the jewel thief Amalfi in "The Regatta Mystery." She impersonates a respectable member of society and manages to insinuate herself into the company of the diamond merchant Isaac Pointz. Once there, she steals the fabulous Morning Star diamond while in plain view of the entire company.

Amberiotis, Mr.   A blackmailer who is murdered in *One, Two, Buckle My Shoe.* He had worked in previous years as a spy, and, at the beginning of the novel, journeys to England, intending to blackmail someone. Before he can launch his scheme, however, he is poisoned in a dentist's office with a massive dose of procaine and anesthetic. He manages to return to his hotel before the fatal effects of the poison strike, and he is found dead some time later. His death proves a blow to Poirot's investigation into the murder of the dentist, Dr. Morley, for Amberiotis was a leading suspect. While the Morley death was originally ruled a suicide, it is later confirmed to be a murder, and Amberiotis's death is likewise a homicide because it would have been virtually impossible for Morley to have poisoned him accidentally.

Amery, Blanche   A young noblewoman in "Swan Song." She becomes embroiled accidentally in hidden events of the past and reveals the true identity of a long-forgotten woman.

Ames, Mr.   A real estate agent in "Philomel Cottage."

Ames, Dr. Robert   A physician who takes part in the archaeological expedition to uncover the tomb of King Men-her-Ra in "The Adventure of the Egyptian Tomb." Ames was "a capable-looking man of thirty-odd, with a touch of greying hair at the temples." As doctor to the expedition, he was given the unpleasant task of caring for the members of the team who died under strange and horrible circumstances.

Amphrey, Miss   The headmistress of a girls' school in *Towards Zero.* An educator who believes earnestly in the most modern methods of education, Miss Amphrey tends to rely too heavily on fads, including word games and psychological word association tests. She uses one game to trap Sylvia Battle into admitting stealing, even though the daughter of Superintendent Battle did not commit any such crime. This effort, however, proves helpful in solving the crimes in the case.

Anastasia, Grand Duchess   A beautiful young aristocrat of the European country of Catonia in "The Girl in the Train." Known diminutively as Alexa, she is the niece of the thoroughly unpleasant Prince Osric and is expected to wed the equally odious Prince Karl, her cousin. Through the events recounted in the story, she meets and falls in love with George Rowland.

Anchoukoff, Boris   A markedly devoted butler in *The Secret of Chimneys.* He serves Prince Michael Obolovitch of Herzoslovakia until the prince is murdered. So faithful was he to the prince that Boris vows bloody revenge upon the murderer. He subsequently enters the employ of Anthony Cade and proves to be an equally faithful butler to his new master.

Andersen, Dr.   A leader of a cult in "The Flock of Geryon." Andersen, who has adopted many aliases over the years, uses his good looks, charisma, and charm to win the trust of his followers, who, for the most part, are gullible and lonely middle-aged women who give him their money. In the scam presented in the story, Andersen pretends to be the Good Shepherd, the leader of his "flock." It is not mere coincidence that his followers frequently die from mysterious causes shortly after leaving all of their money to his "church."

Andersen, Thelma An actress who is hired by Hercule Poirot in "The Augean Stables." She is commissioned to impersonate a companion of an Argentine gigolo.

Anderson, Colonel A chief constable in *The A.B.C. Murders.* A man of some vigor, he is nevertheless quite pessimistic.

Anderson, Esther See Walters, Esther.

Anderson, Greta A formidable woman in *Endless Night.* She is described as "a super Valkyrie with shining golden hair." Greta also has a peculiarly close relationship with Ellie Guteman, which proves to be a major obstacle to Ellie's happiness with Michael Rogers.

Andras, Count A Hungarian diplomat stationed in the Hungarian embassy in London in *The Seven Dials Mystery.* He is also a participant in secret activities, adopting the enigmatic name No. 5.

Andre A member of the archaeological team in *They Came to Baghdad.* Andre serves as a French archaeological assistant, but his work is only a pretense used to disguise his real motives in assisting the dig.

Andrenyi, Countess Helena Maria A young, beautiful woman married to Count Rudolph Andrenyi in *Murder on the Orient Express.* She is considered one of the leading suspects in the murder of Ratchett, in large measure because of a monogrammed handkerchief that seemingly implicates her in the crime. Her exceptionally devoted husband goes to considerable lengths to hide her possible involvement in the murder and the potentially damning truth about her true, humble origins.

Andrenyi, Count Rudolph A suave Hungarian diplomat and aristocrat in *Murder on the Orient Express.* He is married to Helena Maria Andrenyi, to whom he is absolutely devoted, going to great lengths to shield her from possible suspicion in the murder of Ratchett. He is especially concerned about a monogrammed handkerchief and her passport; the latter is used by Hercule Poirot to demonstrate that Helena is a woman of far humbler origins than her elegance and aristocratic mien would indicate.

Andrew A grandson of Tommy and Tuppence Beresford in *Postern of Fate.* Fifteen years old at the time of the story, Andrew hopes to become a poet, but he also displays a small talent for detection.

Andrews, Squadron Leader A pilot in *Passenger to Frankfurt.* Andrews, a former member of the Royal Air Force, works as a pilot on secret air missions.

Andrews, Betsy A cook in *The Big Four.* She works for the unfortunate Jonathan Whalley.

Angelica One of the names used by Ann Shapland in *Cat among the Pigeons.* She is also known as Señora Angelica de Toredo.

Angelica de Toredo, Señora One of the names used by Ann Shapland in *Cat among the Pigeons.* She is also known simply as Angelica.

Angelique, Sister Marie A Belgian nun and refugee in "The Hound of Death." Sister Angelique possesses unique abilities and powers, which, along with her knowledge, are of great interest to an ambitious scientist. She submits to his careful investigation of the mysterious Sixth Sign, but she refuses to reveal its details and dies to make certain that no one will ever learn its secrets.

Angkatell, David A young man and scholar at Oxford University in *The Hollow.* He is heir to a fortune.

Angkatell, Edward A member of the Angkatell family in *The Hollow.* He is in love with Henrietta Savernake, but she refuses his offer of marriage. After a clumsy attempt at suicide, he finds a new and presumably lasting love with Midge Hardcastle.

Angkatell, Sir Henry The patriarch of the Angkatell family in *The Hollow.* He is a relatively young man, but his many cares have aged him prematurely. He also hosts a party at which Dr. John Christow is shot to death and at which, fortunately, Hercule Poirot is a guest.

Angkatell, Lady Lucy Wife of Sir Henry Angkatell and an often obsessive but charming hostess in *The Hollow.* She fusses about a party that turns tragic and later believes that she has solved the mystery. Concerned about where her knowledge will lead, she attempts to convince Poirot to drop the case. The Belgian detective, of course, refuses, but he remains fond of Lady Lucy nevertheless.

Angus A man who gave potentially vital information about arsenic to one of the suspects in *Dumb Witness.* Angus also witnessed the revision of a will, an event of some significance in the solution of the murder case.

Annesley, Gerard The husband of the unfortunate Mabelle Annesley in "The Bird with the Broken Wing." He claimed that he was completely oblivious to the fact that his wife was being strangled in an adjacent room.

Annesley, Mabelle The wife of Gerard Annesley in "The Bird with the Broken Wing." Described as ethereal, she is found dead in a room next to the one in which her husband was sitting, and the death is considered at first a suicide. It is subsequently learned that she was strangled to death with a ukelele string.

Annette A young woman in *The Secret Adversary.* She assists Tommy Beresford in escaping from a Bolshevik house in Soho and leaves quite an impression on the Englishman. Annette has a more complex personality and origins than are initially assumed.

Annie A parlor maid in "The Adventure of the Clapham Cook." In the service of Mrs. Todd, Annie proves of some value to Hercule Poirot in his search for the Clapham cook, despite the fact that she is convinced that the cook has been taken by "white slavers."

Ansell, Mr. A solicitor in *A Pocket Full of Rye.* He provides Miss Marple with very useful information pertaining to the will of Adele Fortescue.

Anstruth, Mrs. Bridget Conway's aunt in *Murder Is Easy.*

Anstruther, Mr. The narrator of the harrowing events of "The Hound of Death." He learns from an American reporter that a Belgian nun and refugee is now residing in the same small Cornish village where his sister lives. The nun had performed a peculiar and devastating miracle during World War I, and Anstruther becomes embroiled in the efforts by the ambitious Dr. Rose to learn the secret of her power.

Anthony, Mrs. See Merrowdene, Mrs.

Antoine, Monsieur See Leech, Andrew.

Antrobus, Dr. An associate of Mr. Parker Pyne in "The Case of the Rich Woman." Described as a doctor dressed in European clothes but possessed of a swarthy face and dark, oblique eyes, "with a peculiarly piercing power in their glance," he assumes the name Dr. Constantine for the case and offers an unusual diagnosis to the problem of unhappiness plaguing Amelia Rymer: "Your body is not sick . . . but your soul is weary. We of the East know how to cure that disease." Parker Pyne admits that the name Constantine is an assumed one, used by a friend with a talent for acting.

Appleby, Colonel A resident of Little Furze in *The Moving Finger.* He develops his own theory as to who is responsible for a series of poison-pen letters and a murder and attempts to give police the benefit of his wisdom and support.

Appledore A servant in *N or M?* Although he is a well trained and exceedingly capable domestic worker, he is curiously willing to work for very low wages.

Arbuthnot, Colonel One of the passengers on the Calais Coach in *Murder on the Orient Express.* A soldier in the Indian army, he is the only pipe smoker in the coach and thus falls under obvious suspicion when a pipe cleaner is found near the body of the murdered Ratchett. He dismisses any such notion of his involvement in the crime as absurd.

Arbuthnot, Dr. George A physician in *Why Didn't They Ask Evans?* A clever and resourceful person, he assists in some subterfuge involving the home of Sylvia Bassington-ffrench.

Archdale, Betty A parlor maid in *Sparkling Cyanide.* She has a habit of overhearing conversations and is able to provide some useful information to Colonel Race in his inquiries.

Archer, Mrs. See Davis, Jessie.

Arden, Enoch An alias used by Charles Trenton in *Taken at the Flood.*

Arden, Linda The one-time stage name used by a famous American actress in *Murder on the Orient Express.* She adopts an assumed name during the trip on the Calais Coach and plays a significant part in the events that transpire surrounding the murder of Mr. Ratchett.

Ardingly, David A young man in *The Pale Horse* who has a penchant for seeking young women whom he considers to be less than brilliant.

Ardley, Beatrice A young girl who attends the fateful gathering in *Hallowe'en Party.*

Arguileros, Karl A one-time actor in *Passenger to Frankfurt.* He claims to be the son of Adolf Hitler and has a swastika branded on his foot. In his impersonation of Hitler's son, he assumes the name Franz Joseph.

Argyle, Christina (Tina) A librarian in *Ordeal by Innocence.* An adopted child, she is of mixed descent. Her adoptive mother, Rachel Argyle, is murdered, but she is not considered a likely suspect. Nevertheless, as is the case with her adopted siblings, Christina did not feel any particular love for her mother.

Argyle, Hester A young woman who was adopted by Rachel Argyle in *Ordeal by Innocence.* She ran away because of her resentment toward Rachel and had a disastrous affair with a married man. She returns to Sunny Point just in time for Rachel to be murdered. Hester becomes one of the leading suspects, lamenting at one point that the entire family is consumed with mistrust. She does have the opportunity for genuine happiness at the end.

Argyle, Jack (Jacko) An adoptive son of Rachel Argyle in *Ordeal by Innocence.* When his mother is murdered, he is convicted of the crime and is sentenced to life in prison because of the amnesia of a key witness. He dies in prison of pneumonia, and his cause is taken up by Dr. Calgary (the key witness in the case). Ultimately, he is proven innocent of the crime.

Argyle, Leo The long-suffering husband of Rachel Argyle in *Ordeal by Innocence.* Leo is devoted to his wife even after she virtually ignores him in favor of her five adopted children. He falls in love with his secretary, but he will not leave his wife or consider an affair. After the murder of his wife and the clearing of his adoptive son Jacko of the crime, he displays little enthusiasm for discovering who really was responsible.

Argyle, Mary The wife of the paralyzed pilot Philip Durrant in *Ordeal by Innocence.* She is embroiled in the events surrounding the murder of Rachel Argyle, her adoptive mother, and is obsessed with keeping control over her husband. He, nevertheless, is also obsessed—with solving the murder and bringing the true criminal to justice.

Argyle, Michael (Micky) A haunted young man in *Ordeal by Innocence.* An adoptive son of Rachel Argyle, he learns that he was actually sold into adoption by his real parents for the sum of one hundred pounds, a fact that causes him deep personal trauma.

Argyle, Rachel The matriarch of the Argyle household in *Ordeal by Innocence.* The wife of Leo Argyle, she was never able to have children of her own and found caring for children in a nursery during the war to be so rewarding that she took steps to adopt. Her need for motherhood became so intense, however, that she even turned to illegal means to obtain more children. Having secured control of five children, she devotes herself wholly and absolutely to their care, sacrificing all thought for her husband. The raising of her children includes directing their futures, and she becomes so domineering and demanding that one of her charges murders her.

Aristides, Mr.   A fabulously wealthy megalomaniac in *Destination Unknown.* He uses his vast wealth to to establish a society of young, brilliant scientists who will assist him in influencing the financial destiny of the world. Aristides is a villain in the same mold as Blofeld in the novels of James Bond, although Aristides claims that he is laboring for purely humanitarian aims.

Aristopoulos   A supposedly expert jeweler from Athens who apparently assists Mr. Parker Pyne in "The Oracle at Delphi." Evidently summoned to Delphi at the request of Parker Pyne, he assists Mrs. Peters in recovering her son by crafting a set of artificial diamonds.

Armstrong, Dr. Edward George   One of the ten people brought to the island mansion in *And Then There Were None.* Dr. Armstrong's particular sin was that he operated on a patient while under the influence of alcohol. He managed to escape detection, but the patient died, a crime that was seemingly forgotten by all but the organizer of the murderous gathering on the island.

Arrichet, Françoise   A servant in *Murder on the Links.* Françoise has long worked at the Villa Genevieve.

Arundell, Charles   A member of the Arundell family in *Dumb Witness.* Charles was the nephew of Emily Arundell, on whom he relies for money. He is in constant need of funds and once supposedly told Emily that he would "bump her off" if she did not give him monetary assistance.

Arundell, Emily   An unmarried woman and head of the Arundell family in *Dumb Witness.* Emily is plagued in many ways by her relatives, all of whom want something from her, especially money. Concerned for her own safety after falling down a flight of stairs, she writes to Hercule Poirot and her solicitors. Before the detective can respond, however, Emily dies, giving a rambling speech about her faithful dog, Bob, his little rubber ball, and a wall picture being askew. Her letter takes two months to reach Poirot because it is not mailed until it is discovered in a blotter after Emily's death. Poirot takes the case and launches an investigation that reveals murder.

Dr. Armstrong (Walter Huston) and other doomed guests on Indian Island find another corpse in And Then There Were None. *(Photofest)*

Arundell, Theresa A niece of Emily Arundell in *Dumb Witness*. She is spoiled and looks forward to receiving her share of Emily's inheritance. Thus, after Emily dies, she is appalled to learn that her aunt had changed her will and left her money to her companion, Miss Lawson. Theresa leads the charge to have the will broken, declaring to Poirot that she is not at all averse to using underhanded methods to do it.

Ascanio, Signor A young Italian gentleman who arrived in London a mere two days before the murder of Count Foscatini in "The Adventure of the Italian Nobleman." Ascanio stayed at the Grosvenor Hotel and visited the count shortly before the murder, making him a logical suspect. His alibi seems airtight, however, as the Italian ambassador himself testifies that Ascanio had been with him all evening on the night of the crime.

Ascher, Alice A woman who owns a tobacco shop in *The A.B.C. Murders*. She becomes the first victim of the A.B.C. killer, dying from a blow to the head simply because her name bears the initials A. A. and she lives in Andover. An open copy of the *A.B.C Rail Guide* is found next to her body. She was married to Franz Ascher.

Ascher, Franz The husband of Alice Ascher in *The A.B.C. Murders*. He was abusive and cruel to his wife—as is discovered by the police after the death of Alice—but he was supposedly drinking in a pub at the time his wife was brutally beaten to death.

Ashby, Joan A houseguest in "The Second Gong." As a visitor to Lytcham Close, she finds its many habits and customs to be quite amusing. At the start of the story, she has a disagreement with Harry Dalehouse as to whether there had been one or two gongs sounded—the ceremonial summons to dinner.

Ashe, Old The gardener at Little Paddocks in *A Murder Is Announced*. He provides useful information to the police.

Ashley, Diana A strikingly beautiful woman in "The Idol House of Astarte." She is seen frequently in the society pages and is "dark and tall . . . her half-closed dark eyes set slantways in her head gave her a curiously piquant oriental appearance." Ashley appears at a fancy dress party dressed completely in black (as The Unknown) and becomes entranced with the Idol House, where she proclaims herself a priestess of Astarte moments before the death of Sir Richard Haydon from seemingly inexplicable causes.

Askew, Thomas A landlord in *Why Didn't They Ask Evans?*

Astor, Anthony See Wills, Muriel.

Astwell, Lady Nancy Wife of Sir Reuben Astwell in "The Under Dog." She stands to inherit Sir Reuben's estate and is possessed of remarkable intuition concerning his death.

Astwell, Sir Reuben A wealthy estate holder in "The Under Dog." He has made numerous enemies over the years as a result of his underhanded methods, so there is a long list of suspects after he is brutally bludgeoned to death.

Astwell, Victor A member of the Astwell family in "The Under Dog." Owing to his violent temperament, he is considered an obvious suspect in the bludgeoning death of Sir Reuben Astwell.

Atkinson, Colonel A former military officer in *Postern of Fate*. He is nicknamed Moustachio-Monty for the obvious reason, and plays a part in the events of murder and espionage that are recounted.

Atlas A reporter in "The Apples of the Hesperides." He gives assistance to Hercule Poirot in his efforts to recover the fabled Borgia goblet.

Austin, Celia A young student in *Hickory Dickory Dock*. She has a problem with kleptomania, an obsession revealed by Hercule Poirot. Another student, Colin McNabb, suggests that he would like to study her case by marrying her, but she is soon found dead from an apparent overdose of morphine. Poirot observes that her suicide note is not written in her hand and that she secured the drug from her place of work, St. Catherine's Hospital.

Babbington, Reverend Stephen A friendly minister and father of four in *Three-Act Tragedy*. He attends a party thrown by the retired actor Charles Cartwright and dies during the festivities after taking a drink and suffering a seizure. His murder is a genuine mystery, as he seemingly had no enemies.

Bacon, Inspector An officer of Scotland Yard who takes part in the investigation of the case presented in *4.50 from Paddington*. He assists Detective Inspector Dermot Craddock in his labors.

Badcock, Arthur The husband of Heather Badcock in *The Mirror Crack'd from Side to Side*. As a result of the investigation into Heather's death, it is revealed that Arthur is not quite who he claims to be and that he had an intimate connection to the actress Marina Gregg.

Badcock, Heather A gossipmonger and bit of a bore who sets off a series of murders in *The Mirror Crack'd from Side to Side*. Heather attends a benefit at Gossington Hall to raise money for the St. John's Ambulance Brigade and there meets the American movie star Marina Gregg. She confesses that she had met Gregg years before and had been such a big fan that she had violated a German measles quarantine just to see her. A short time later, Heather suffers a seizure and dies. It is determined that her death was caused by ingesting a massive dose of a sedative, Calmo.

Badgworth, Inspector A member of the Cornwall police in "Ingots of Gold." Badgworth was a passenger on the train carrying Raymond West to Cornwall; he was extremely well informed about the sinking of the ship *Otranto* off the Cornish coast. He subsequently heads the investigation into the kidnapping of John Newman and the resolution of the *Otranto* affair.

Badgworthy, Chief Inspector A police officer in *The Secret of Chimneys*. Badgworthy is a serious and dedicated investigator; he is determined to solve the murder of Prince Michael Obolovitch.

Bailey, Donovan A young man who is eager to wed the beautiful Patricia Garnett in "The Third Floor Flat." He and a friend, Jimmy Faulkener, assist Patricia, who is locked out of her apartment, by taking the coal lift to her kitchen. They accidentally miscount the floors and, instead of arriving at Patricia's fourth-floor flat, they enter the third-floor flat. Once inside, they discover the body of Mrs. Ernestine Grant.

Baker, Mr. and Mrs. A couple who act as caretakers at Crabtree Manor in "The Case of the Missing Will." A pleasant couple, they have an important role to play in helping Hercule Poirot to discover the location of a missing will. Mr. Baker is "gnarled and pink-cheeked, like a shriveled pippin"; his wife is "a woman of vast proportions and true Devonshire charm."

Baker, Mrs. Calvin A minion in the service of Mr. Aristides in *Destination Unknown*. She organizes the brain trust that has been assembled by Aristides and demonstrates a genuine efficiency.

Baker, Cherry A young woman who serves as cook and housekeeper for Miss Marple in *The Mirror Crack'd from Side to Side*. She brings to Miss Marple the first news of the murder of Heather Badcock and subsequently provides useful information about the events that transpired just before Mrs. Badcock's death. Recently married, Cherry feels rather ignored because of her husband's obsession with model airplanes. Eventually, in *Nemesis,* the couple moves into Miss Marple's house.

Baker, David A painter in *Third Girl*. He adopts the appearance of a bohemian artist to a ludicrously excessive degree, and even wears a velvet waistcoat. It is learned that Baker has a rather checkered past and has been bought off by several worried fathers who have taken steps to free their wealthy daughters from the grips of this ne'er-do-well. His present girlfriend, Norma Restarick, consults Hercule Poirot because she is worried that she may have committed a murder, but Baker is also, for a time, considered a suspect.

Baker, Jim Husband of Cherry Baker in *The Mirror Crack'd from Side to Side* and *Nemesis*. In

The Mirror Crack'd from Side to Side, he is obsessed with making model airplanes, much to the misery of his wife. In *Nemesis,* he and Cherry move into Miss Marple's house.

Baker, Richard (Owl) An archaeologist who becomes involved in the events described in *They Came to Baghdad.* While on his way to join Dr. Pauncefoot Jones on a dig, he meets the recently kidnapped Victoria Jones and gives her a most timely and fateful ride.

Baldock, Mr. (Baldy) A bachelor and scholar in *The Burden.* He dispenses some very useful advice to Laura Franklin about the diminishing value of self-sacrifice, especially at the cost of one's own life.

Baldwin, Superintendent A Scotland Yard official in *Dead Man's Folly.* He supervises the activities of Inspector Bland and demonstrates a firm grasp of details and procedure.

Ball, Mr. An innkeeper in *The A.B.C. Murders.* He is rather slow-witted.

Balsano, Giuseppe A waiter in *Sparkling Cyanide.* He has the dubious distinction of serving as waiter on the night that Rosemary Barton was poisoned by arsenic in champagne. A year later, when that fateful dinner is recreated, Balsano again serves as waiter.

Banks, Miss The owner of a flat in *Unfinished Portrait.* The newlywed couple Celia and Dermot consider renting the flat but decide against it, as they fear that Miss Banks will be a "tartar."

Banks, Gregory A chemist in *After the Funeral.* He is tormented by the memory of almost killing a customer many years before and confesses, erroneously, to the murder of Richard Abernethie. He is married to Susan Abernethie Banks.

Banks, Susan Abernethie Niece of Richard Abernethie in *After the Funeral.* A strong-willed woman, she is married to the tormented Gregory Banks and is a suspect in the murder of her uncle.

BANTRY, COLONEL ARTHUR A friend of Miss Marple, husband of Dolly Bantry, and one of the residents of St. Mary Mead. The owner of Gossington Hall, Bantry is a devoted country squire, made of stolid principles, but is rather unimaginative; when, for example, he is informed that a corpse has been discovered in his library, he at first concludes that his wife must have been dreaming. One of his closest friends is Colonel Melchett, chief constable of the county.

Colonel Bantry appears in several of Miss Marple's published cases. He is introduced in *The Thirteen Problems,* when he and Dolly first meet Miss Marple; they consider her at first "the typical old maid of fiction. Quite dear, but hopelessly behind the times." They invite her to dinner at the encouragement of Colonel Melchett and soon discover her talents as a sleuth. Bantry appeared again in *Sleeping Murder* and, of course, is the victim of a truly perverse prank in *The Body in the Library,* in which a corpse is dumped in his library and discovered the following morning. Between that case and the one recounted in *The Mirror Crack'd from Side to Side,* Colonel Bantry passed away, for Dolly is mentioned in the latter book as being a widow.

BANTRY, DOLLY A dear friend of Miss Marple and the wife of Colonel Arthur Bantry. Dolly and Arthur reside in Gossington Hall in St. Mary Mead. She is first introduced in *The Thirteen Problems,* in which she and Arthur are encouraged by their good friend Colonel Melchett to invite Miss Marple to dinner. Dolly's view of the old lady is that she is "the typical old maid of fiction. Quite dear, but hopelessly behind the times." Soon after actually meeting her, Dolly's view is radically changed. After many years of watching Miss Marple's capacity for sleuthing, she exclaims, "Why don't you come out boldly and call yourself a criminologist" (*The Mirror Crack'd from Side to Side*). When the Bantrys discover a corpse in their library, Dolly wastes no time telephoning Miss Marple, telling her outright: "Oh, I don't want comfort. But you're so good at bodies . . . you're very good at murders."

Dolly appeared in *The Thirteen Problems, Sleeping Murder, The Body in the Library,* and *The Mirror Crack'd from Side to Side.* By the time of her appearance in *The Mirror Crack'd,* she had become a widow. Following Arthur's death, she sold Gossington Hall, retaining for herself only a small section of the large estate, the East Lodge. As a fan of movies and movie stars, she is delighted at the rumor that Gossington Hall will be purchased by Marina Gregg, the film star in *The Mirror Crack'd.*

Barker, Sister   A nurse in *Nemesis.* She is not a charming woman and exudes an air of indifference.

Barley, Harley   The name given to a scarecrow in "The Harlequin Tea Set." He is of interest because his appearance bears a striking similarity to the mysterious Mr. Harley Quin.

Barling, Gregory   A financier in "The Second Gong." He is the subject of an odd codicil in the will of Hubert Lytcham Roche, which says that Diana Cleves will inherit all Lytcham Roche's money only if she marries Barling.

Barnaby, Sir George   The husband of Lady Vivien Barnaby in "The Sign in the Sky." His wife is murdered, but Sir George seems to have an airtight alibi: He was playing bridge at the time.

Barnaby, Lady Vivien   The wife of Sir George Barnaby in "The Sign in the Sky." She is murdered after having an affair, but her husband seems to have an airtight alibi.

Barnard, Major   A witness to the fateful events that took place on a golf course in "The Sunningdale Mystery." The major was the last person to see Captain Sessle alive before his murder on the links with a hat pin.

Barnard, Mr.   The father of Elizabeth "Betty" Barnard in *The A.B.C. Murders.* He is shattered with grief after his daughter's murder and cannot conceive of any possible motive for the crime.

Barnard, Mrs.   The wife of Mr. Barnard and mother of Elizabeth "Betty" Barnard in *The A.B.C. Murders.* She is crushed, like her hus-band, by the news of their daughter's murder. Mrs. Barnard is of Welsh descent.

Barnard, Elizabeth (Betty)   One of the victims of a serial killer in *The A.B.C. Murders.* A waitress, she was engaged to be married but had a flirtatious nature. Thus, when she is found strangled, her jealous fiancé is considered a likely suspect. However, her connection with the other A.B.C. murders becomes obvious when an opened *A.B.C. Rail Guide* is found next to her body

Barnard, Megan   The sister of Elizabeth Barnard in *The A.B.C. Murders.* After the murder of her sister by an apparent serial killer, she enlists to assist Hercule Poirot in tracking down the murderer.

Barnes, Mrs.   A landlady in "Next to a Dog." While she seems to have a gruff exterior, she is actually quite compassionate, especially when learning of the tragedy that strikes a beloved dog.

Barnes, George   The operator of a ferry in *Towards Zero.* He provides information to the police that is germane to the murder investigation.

Barnes, Reginald   A member of British intelligence in *One, Two, Buckle My Shoe.* He also operates under the code name QX912 and uses the alias Albert Chapman.

Barnett, Inspector   A policeman who investigates the death of Benedict Farley in "The Dream." He is of stern military bearing.

Barraclough, Raymond   A suave young man who has an affair with a married woman in *Death in the Clouds.* His dalliance leads to blackmail and scandal.

Barre, Monsieur   A teacher in a French finishing school in *Unfinished Portrait.*

Barrett, Jane   A maid in the household of Lady Tressilian in *Towards Zero.* An elderly woman, Barrett was drugged to prevent her from responding to the summons by her mistress on the night that Lady Tressilian was bludgeoned to death with a heavy object.

Barron, Barbara   See Stranleigh, Lady.

Barron, Beatrice   The name of one of the passengers on board a ship that sank many years before the events recounted in "The Voice in the Dark." After surviving the tragedy at sea, she lost her memory and lived for decades assuming she was someone else.

Barron, Dr. Louis A scientist in *Destination Unknown.* He is a dedicated bacteriologist who becomes a willing associate of the powerful Mr. Aristides.

Barrow, Miss One of the two female bodyguards assigned to protect Miss Marple in *Nemesis.* A most efficient professional, Miss Barrow works with Miss Cooke to insure that nothing untoward happens to Miss Marple during her investigation into the events surrounding the death of Elizabeth Temple.

Barry, Major A retired soldier in *Evil under the Sun.* He wants very much to be a ladies' man, but he lacks many of the requisite communication skills.

Bartlett, Mrs. A middle-aged woman in *The Body in the Library.* She takes in lodgers.

Bartlett, George One of the murder suspects in *The Body in the Library.* His car is stolen, but he does not report it missing for some time. When it is found, the police discover it burned. Inside is the charred corpse of Pamela Reeves, a revelation that Bartlett is at some pains to explain.

Barton, Emily One of the five Barton sisters in *The Moving Finger.* She owns a house that is rented by Jeremy and Joanna Burton. She also receives several of the vicious poison-pen letters that circulate throughout the village; the letters accuse her of poisoning several members of her family.

Barton, George One of the key figures in *Sparkling Cyanide.* He suffers the loss of his wife at her birthday party and discovers that she was murdered. In the hopes of catching the murderer, he reenacts the events of the birthday party one year later at the same restaurant with all of the same guests in attendance. He tells everyone that something important will happen at 9:30 P.M., and events seem to go well for Barton until the appointed time ar-

rives. Barton toasts his wife's memory and another tragedy strikes. Barton himself had a motive to kill his wife—he discovered that she had been having an affair.

Barton, Lady Laura One of the suspects in the theft of a pink pearl in "The Affair of the Pink Pearl." She is not considered a likely suspect, owing to her wealth and position, but it is eventually learned that she suffers from kleptomania.

Barton, Mary An English woman who apparently murders her companion, Amy Durrant, and then kills herself in "The Companion." Mary travels to the Grand Canary Island with Amy, and there she apparently drowns her poor companion. Later, while in Cornwall, she writes a suicide note, leaves her clothes on the beach, and walks into the water to drown herself.

Barton, Rosemary The wife of the wealthy George Barton in *Sparkling Cyanide.* She is a beautiful woman, but she is also unfaithful to her husband and amasses a list of enemies. Rosemary dies suddenly at her birthday party, and her death is believed by her husband to have been murder. Her sister, Iris Marle, thinks that she committed suicide.

Bassington-ffrench, Henry A member of the Bassington-ffrench family in *Why Didn't They Ask Evans?* He is a morphine addict.

Bassington-ffrench, Roger A member of the Bassington-ffrench family in *Why Didn't They Ask Evans?* He stays with the body of Alex Pritchard after its discovery at the base of a cliff. He is subsequently involved in the events of the investigation by Bobby Jones and Lady Frances Derwent. Roger is considered rather the black sheep of the family.

Bassington-ffrench, Sylvia A member of the Bassington-ffrench family in *Why Didn't They Ask Evans?*

Bassington-ffrench, Tommy A member of the Bassington-ffrench family in *Why Didn't They Ask Evans?* The heir to the family fortune, Tommy suffers several near-fatal accidents.

Batani An old African woman in *The Man in the Brown Suit.*

Bateman, Rupert (Pongo) A young man in *The Seven Dials Mystery.* He assists in the effort to determine the innocence of a suspect by hiding alarm clocks under a bed.

Bates, Annie A servant in the house of the Laceys in "The Adventure of the Christmas Pudding." She is touched by Hercule Poirot's courtesy and becomes concerned for his safety when she overhears a conversation that she interprets to be a plot to poison the detective. The detective is very grateful for her diligence and her concern.

Bateson, Leonard (Len) A medical student in *Hickory Dickory Dock.* He is rather dim-witted, but is considered a suspect when the police learn that his father is in a mental institution.

Batt, Albert The devoted assistant and butler to Tommy and Tuppence Beresford. He first appeared in *The Secret Adversary* as a fifteen-year-old elevator operator and then became one of their most useful minions. Over time, he became their butler, appearing in *Partners in Crime, N or M?, By the Pricking of My Thumbs,* and *Postern of Fate.* Tuppence pays him a great compliment by observing, "The comfortable thing about Albert was that he always accepted everything. Nothing ever had to be explained to him" (*By the Pricking of My Thumbs*). By the time of the case recounted in *By the Pricking of My Thumbs,* he was married to Milly Batt and had several children, including Elizabeth, Charlie, and Jean.

Batt, Elsie A maid in *Cards on the Table.* She provides some very helpful information to Hercule Poirot in the investigation into the murder of Mr. Shaitana.

Battersby, Miss The retired headmistress of a school in *Third Girl.* She provides Hercule Poirot with some valuable information about a particular girl.

BATTLE, SUPERINTENDENT A hardworking Scotland Yard official who appeared in five published cases: *Murder Is Easy, The Secret of Chimneys, The Seven Dials Mystery, Towards Zero,* and *Cards on the Table.* In *Cards on the Table,* Battle was teamed with three brilliant detectives, Colonel Race, Ariadne Oliver, and Hercule Poirot. In the four other cases, Battle solved the crimes himself, or at least took part in investigations related to the events of the case.

Battle was described as "a big, square, wooden-faced man" who adhered to the maxim "Never display emotion" and "never give in." He thus distinguished himself for his tenacity in solving thorny problems. This is not to imply that Battle was a plodder. Rather, he stayed with a problem until solving it, and he displayed a genuine talent for solving political cases that were both sensitive and essential for the public good.

Battle was married and the father of five children. One of his children, a daughter, Sylvia, became involved in the case recounted in *Towards Zero.* The youngest child of the Battles, Sylvia attended Miss Amphrey's school, near Maidstone, and was accused of thieving. Interrogated by Miss Amphrey, Sylvia became so tired of the headmistress's mind games that she confessed to the thefts just to have an end to the inquisition. The proceedings were of little amusement to her father.

Battle, Sylvia The daughter of Superintendent Battle in *Towards Zero.* Much to her father's chagrin, she is accused of stealing items from her boarding school. The inspector, however, becomes even more incensed when Sylvia informs him that she had confessed only to bring an end to her badgering at the hands of the headmistress, Miss Amphery.

Bauer, Carl A Russian spy who is assigned the task of uncovering a double agent in "The Adventure of the Sinister Stranger." He took on an assumed name when dealing with Tommy and Tuppence Beresford.

Bauer, John A footman at the Chimneys in *The Seven Dials Mystery.* He is an exceptionally capable worker.

Bauerstein, Dr. A London specialist and one of the world's experts on poisons who suffers a nervous breakdown and recuperates in the village of Styles St. Mary in *The Mysterious Affair at Styles.* There is much more to the good doctor than might appear. He also has a friendship with Mary Cavendish that proves dangerous for the young woman.

Bault, Felicie An unfortunate French woman who manages to kill herself by strangulation in "The Fourth Man." Suffering from the condition of having multiple personalities, she was so overcome with grief at the death of her friend Annette Ravel that she murdered herself.

Beadle, Alfred The real name of a man in *The Mirror Crack'd from Side to Side.* Under this name, he was once married to the actress Marina Gregg, an event that seems wholly unlikely, given his rather unprepossessing appearance.

Beadon, Badger A well-positioned young man in *Why Didn't They Ask Evans?* Curiously, he works in an automotive shop and invites his friend Bobby Jones to join him. When Jones and Lady Frances Derwent become embroiled in the events surrounding the murder of Alex Pritchard, Badger proves a faithful friend and assistant, even rescuing them from possible death.

Beatrice A maid in *The Sittaford Mystery.* Beatrice is less than attentive to her duties.

Beauge, Madame A dressmaker in *Unfinished Portrait.* Her daughter, Jeanne, departs France to work as the governess of an English child. Jeanne, however, is faithful in sending her pay home to assist her family.

Beauge, Jeanne The daughter of Mme. Beauge in *Unfinished Portrait.* She left her mother and France to work as a governess to an English child. Jeanne faithfully sent her money home to support her family, a devotion that greatly amused of the English servants in the household.

Beck, Colonel The head of Scotland Yard's special branch in *The Clocks.* He gives some excellent advice to special branch investigator Colin Lamb.

Beddingfeld, Anne The heroine in *The Man in the Brown Suit.* The pretty young daughter of an anthropologist, Anne is orphaned and left in poverty after her father dies unexpectedly. Dubbing herself Anna the Adventurous, she moves to London to seek her fortune, and it does not take long for her to become embroiled in a mystery. While on the platform of the Hyde Park Corner tube station, she witnesses a man fall onto the tracks and get electrocuted by the third rail. The tragedy becomes curious when a man in a brown suit claims to be a doctor, examines the body, and then hurries off, leaving behind a paper containing a seemingly vital clue. Convinced that adventure awaits, Anne takes the paper and sets out to solve the mystery.

Bell, Miss A typist in the service of Rex Fortescue in *A Pocket Full of Rye.* She witnesses his cruel death from poison and assumes at first that he has suffered from some kind of seizure. She also provides information to the police about Fortescue's involvement with the black market.

Bell, Sergeant A Scotland Yard officer who investigates the murders in *Hickory Dickory Dock.* What he lacks in skill he makes up for in enthusiasm.

Bellever, Juliet (Jolly) A nurse in *They Do It with Mirrors.* She is an ugly woman, but she is also dedicated to her work and is a genuinely kind person.

Belling, Mrs. J. The owner of a public house in *The Sittaford Mystery.* She is described as "fat and excitable," and she claims to have important information about the events surrounding the murder of Captain Trevelyan.

Beltane, The Honourable Eustace The uncle of the unfortunate Lord Cronshaw in "The Affair at the Victory Ball." He is a passionate collector and stands to inherit Cronshaw's large fortune after his nephew is stabbed to death.

Ben The son of a cook and a housekeeper in "Sing a Song of Sixpence." He has been in jail twice and his father "was a bad one." His mother, Martha, however, is devoted to him, going to some lengths to shield him from possible prying questions by the authorities following the death of Miss Crabtree.

Bence, Margot A photographer in *The Mirror Crack'd from Side to Side.* There is a detail from her past that makes her an obvious suspect in the events of the murder investigation. At the age of five, she was sold by her mother to a film star who could not have children. The actress subsequently abandoned her after four years.

Benfield, Charlotte A sixteen-year-old girl who is murdered in *Hallowe'en Party.*

Bennett, Miss A seamstress in *Unfinished Portrait.* She is quite poor, but she claims that in reality she is the illegitimate daughter of an aristocrat.

Bennet, Alice A maid in the service of Lord Edgware in *Lord Edgware Dies.* She discovers her employer's body one evening.

Benson, Mrs. One of the murder victims in *Cards on the Table.* She was killed by ingesting hat paint that she had assumed was syrup of figs.

Bent, Clifford The son of a wealthy oil magnate in *Passenger to Frankfurt.* He heads the Youth Movement.

Bentham, Alice A housemaid in *Towards Zero.* She is remarkably observant, and is described by Superintendent Battle as "the pop-eyed one."

Bentham, Mildred A member of a tour that is visiting famous houses and gardens of Britain in *Nemesis.* She is an elderly woman, much hobbled with infirmities, but she is also determined to enjoy life for as long as she can.

Bentley, James A rather unpleasant and unlucky man who is convicted of murdering his landlady in *Mrs. McGinty's Dead.* His story, however, is so peculiar that Superintendent Spence consults with Hercule Poirot in the hopes that the detective will investigate the case and prove that Bentley is actually innocent. Poirot subsequently learns that Bentley is most devoted to his mother, but he does not have many friends.

Bercy, Sir Ambrose The owner of Clodderham Court and the guardian of Sylvia Keene, who was apparently poisoned with foxglove in "The Herb of Death." He is described as "a very distinguished-looking old man—and not so very old really—not more than sixty, I suppose. But he was very delicate—he had a weak heart, could never go upstairs—had had to have a lift put in, and so that made him seem older than he was . . . He had beautiful white hair and a particularly charming voice."

Beresford, Betty The adopted daughter of Tommy and Tuppence Beresford. She is mentioned twice, in *Postern of Fate* and in *N or M?* A smart young woman, Betty heads off to Africa to work as a research anthropologist.

Beresford, Deborah One of the twin children, with Derek Beresford, of Tommy and Tuppence Beresford. Deborah makes three appearances in novels featuring her parents: in *N or M?,* in *By the Pricking of My Thumbs,* and in *Postern of Fate.* During World War II, she worked as a code-breaker for British intelligence. After the death of her husband, she moved into her parents' home with her three children. See also Betty Beresford.

Beresford, Derek One of the twin children, with Deborah Beresford, of Tommy and Tuppence Beresford. Derek appears in only one of the books featuring his parents, *N or M?* He served during World War II in the Royal Air Force.

BERESFORD, TOMMY Known in full as Lieutenant Thomas Beresford, Tommy was the husband of Tuppence Cowley Beresford and, like her, a fun-loving and adventurous detective. Tommy was orphaned while a young man and was taken in and raised by his uncle, Sir William Beresford. Sir William made him heir to the family fortune, but it would be many years before he could come in to the money. Tommy fought in World War I and was twice wounded. During a period of convalescence in England, he met a childhood friend, Tuppence Cowley, who was in a similar predicament to his: The end of the war brought little prospect of employment for either of them. To rectify the situation, the Beresfords formed the firm of Young Adventurers, Ltd. They decide to place an advertisement in the newspaper offering to go on any adventure on behalf of a client, as long as it is well-paying. Even before they can place the ad, however, they are embroiled in intrigue, an adventure recounted in *The Secret Adversary*.

Tommy had an excellent relationship with the mysterious Mr. Carter, head of British intelligence. For Carter and the service, Tommy—and Tuppence—took over Blunt's International Detective Agency in London, with the objective of trapping a dangerous foreign spy who was identified by the number sixteen. In the process of waiting for the spy, Tommy and Tuppence investigated a variety of other cases, documented in *Partners in Crime*. Further investigations were recounted in *N or M?*, *By the Pricking of My Thumbs,* and *Postern of Fate*.

Called affectionately Carrots and Carrot Top by his children, Tommy was tall and handsome, with bright red hair. He married Tuppence after the case of *The Secret Adversary* and then gave up the International Detective Agency after Tuppence announced that she was expecting. The couple eventually had three children, the twins Derek and Deborah and an adopted daughter, Betty.

Ever willing to serve their country, Tommy and Tuppence came out of retirement in World War II to work against German agents in *N or M?* They also became embroiled in mystery and murder even as they approached old age and retirement at the Laurels. These cases were recounted in *By the Pricking of My Thumbs* and *Postern of Fate*.

By nature, Tommy was the slower of the two, leaving much of the thinking to Tuppence. Whereas Tuppence was impetuous, Tommy was more plodding, applying common sense and restraining his wife's natural ten-dency to leap. His longtime boss, Mr. Carter, called Tommy "an ordinary clean-limbed, rather block-headed young Englishman. Slow in his mental processes. On the other hand, it's quite impossible to lead him astray through his imagination. He hasn't got any—so he's difficult to deceive."

BERESFORD, TUPPENCE Called Prudence Cowley Beresford in full, Tuppence was the longtime and much beloved wife of Tommy Beresford, a mother, grandmother, and often talented detective who adored adventure and excitement. The fifth daughter of Archdeacon Cowley of Little Missendell, she counted Tommy Beresford among her dearest friends in childhood. Possessed of a keen mind, she also had "no claim to

Tommy and Tuppence Beresford (James Warwick and Francesca Annis in London Weekend Television's Partners in Crime. *(Photofest; London Weekend Television)*

beauty, but there was character and charm in the elfin lines of her little face, with its determined chin and large, wide-apart grey eyes that looked mistily out from under straight black brows."

Throughout World War I, Tuppence worked in a hospital and came to recognize that she possessed little prospect for employment once the war was at an end. It was at the conclusion of the war that she met another person with poor hopes of employment: Tommy Beresford. She and her childhood friend decided to form Young Adventurers, Ltd, to find fun and employment. Their first case soon developed, recounted in *The Secret Adversary.* (For their subsequent cases, please see under Beresford, Tommy.)

Tuppence married Tommy soon after *The Secret Adversary* affair and became pregnant with the twins Derek and Deborah at the end of the assorted investigations collected in *Partners in Crime.* The couple also later adopted another daughter, Betty, and became happy grandparents.

Tommy was also the perfect match and foil for Tuppence, as he was blessed with common sense and such a lack of imagination that he was rarely prone to self-deception. Tuppence, meanwhile, had the much sharper mind, the more active and creative imagination, and a more pronounced proclivity toward impulsiveness. Her greatest failing, of course, was her complete lack of modesty, as she took great pleasure in pointing out her personal successes and her brilliant deductions.

Tuppence remained active in her later years, as demonstrated by her investigations in *By the Pricking of My Thumbs* and *Postern of Fate.* During these cases, Tommy and Tuppence were in their supposed retirement to the Laurels, with the added company of a Manchester terrier, Hannibal.

Tommy and Tuppence Beresford are unique in the Christie writings because they age in a logical fashion throughout the course of the published cases. Thus, they are quite young when first met in *The Secret Adversary* and are quite advanced in age by the time of the *Postern of Fate.* This stands in contrast to Miss Marple and Hercule Poirot, who were old when first introduced in their respective published cases and remained increasingly, even unbelievably, aged by the time of their last investigations.

Beresford, Sir William   The uncle of Tommy Beresford in *The Secret Adversary.* Sir William is a dedicated misogynist but a decent person nevertheless. He adopted the young orphan Tommy, raised him as his own, and made him the heir of his extensive fortune. Because he does not like women, there is concern that he will remove Tommy as his heir after the arrival in Tommy's life of the stunning Tuppence. She so charms the old fellow, however, that he readily agrees to have Tommy remain his heir.

Bernard, Dr. Ralph   The lone doctor in Marsdon Leigh, who performs the examination of the dead Mr. Maltravers and announces that he died from a hemorrhage in "The Tragedy of Marsdon Manor." He is "an elderly man, high-shouldered and stooping with a pleasant vagueness of manner"; Hastings considers him "rather an old ass."

Beroldy, Jeanne   The real name of a character in *Murder on the Links.* She conspired with her lover, George Conneau, to murder her husband. Forced to stand trial after Conneau fled the scene, she was acquitted of the crime and moved to southern France, where she changed her name.

Bessner, Dr. Carl   A German doctor on vacation in Egypt who takes part in the voyage of the *Karnak* in *Death on the Nile.* His presence on board proves timely, given the murders that take place, and he inadvertently provides Hercule Poirot with a vital clue to the solution of the crimes. Much to his surprise, the doctor wins the heart of a young woman.

Best, Grace   The second housemaid on the estate of Simeon Lee in *Hercule Poirot's Christmas.*

Betterton, Olive   The wife of Thomas Betterton in *Destination Unknown.* After the disappearance of her husband, Olive, his wife of six months, sets out for Morocco on a vacation. Her plane crashes, however, and she is mortally injured. Before her death, she imparts some important information to Hilary Craven, including the cryptic statements "Boris is dangerous" and "Snow, snow, beautiful snow. You slip on a lump and over you go." Her persona is subsequently adopted by Hilary Craven. Olive and her husband regularly played bridge with Dr. Evans and his wife.

Betterton, Thomas Charles (Tom) A ruthless and greedy scientist in *Destination Unknown*. He is widowed twice, the first time after the poisoning death of Elsa Mannheim and the second after the plane crash involving his second wife, Olive Betterton. The death of Elsa was no accident, and Dr. Betterton did not accidentally inherit the results of her valuable research into fission. Self-absorbed and avaricious, he joins forces with the maniacal Mr. Aristides, but he soon regrets his decision.

Betts-Hamilton, Mr. The husband of the loquacious Mrs. Betts-Hamilton in "The Affair of the Pink Pearl." He rarely says anything, leaving his more than talkative wife to handle most of their social activities. His wife loses a pink pearl from a pendant, a loss that is investigated by Tommy and Tuppence Beresford.

Betts-Hamilton, Mrs. The extremely talkative wife of Mr. Betts-Hamilton in "The Affair of the Pink Pearl." She talks so much that her husband rarely opens his mouth. A pink pearl in a pendant that she owns disappears, and the case is handled by Tommy and Tuppence Beresford.

Bex, Monsieur Lucien A French commissary of police in *Murder on the Links*. He has worked with Hercule Poirot in the past and thus welcomes his involvement in the case of Paul Renauld.

Big Charlotte The nickname given to the Grafin Charlotte von Waldsausen in *Passenger to Frankfurt*. She earned her nickname because of her staggering obesity.

Biggs, Abraham A name used by Robert Grant in *The Big Four*.

Biggs, Alfred A dental assistant in *One, Two, Buckle My Shoe*. He is not especially competent in his job, forgetting the names of patients and showing an excessive interest in detective fiction. As a result of the latter failing, however, Hercule Poirot is able to learn of an important clue in the murder of Dr. Morley.

Bill A laborer in *Three Blind Mice*. He reluctantly gives information to the police.

Billingsley, Mr. A solicitor in *A Pocket Full of Rye*. He is an exceedingly discreet attorney who is hesitant to reveal the terms of a will that had been dictated by the murdered Rex Fortescue.

Bindler, Horace An architect in "Greenshaw's Folly." He is a friend of Raymond West, the nephew of Miss Marple, and is taken to view the architectural "monstrosity" of Greenshaw's Folly. A murder soon takes place there.

Binion, Dr. A dental surgeon in *N or M?* He is a friend of Commander Haydock.

Binns, Edith A maid in *The Pale Horse*. She has an excellent eye for detail and provides very useful information to Mrs. Ariadne Oliver about one of the victims of murder.

Birell, Louise An older woman in *Third Girl*. She used several assumed names, was a heavy drinker, and believed that she was dying from cancer. She dies after being hurled from a seventh-story window.

Black, Captain A soldier who has recently returned from East Africa in "The Tragedy of Marsdon Manor." He was staying at the Anchor Inn at the time of Mr. Maltravers's murder, and he becomes a suspect when it is learned that he was once in love with the victim's widow, Mrs. Maltravers. His knowledge of rifles is a vital element in Poirot's solution of the crime.

Blacklock, Charlotte (Lotty) The daughter of a physician and sister of Letitia Blacklock in *A Murder Is Announced*. The fact that her sister will inherit the fortune of a former employer is the cause of much concern to Charlotte.

Blacklock, Letitia (Letty, Blackie) The daughter of a physician and sister of Charlotte Blacklock in *A Murder Is Announced*. She worked for many years as the secretary to the wealthy businessman Randall Goedler. He leaves his estate to his wife, but includes the provision that, upon his wife's death, Letitia will inherit the remainder. This becomes the source of much interest for Charlotte and is a vital element in solving the murder of Rudi Scherz.

Blair, Mrs. Suzanne A woman who becomes involved in the events of *The Man in the Brown Suit* when she accepts the invitation of Sir Eustace Pedler to join him on a trip to South Africa. She meets Anne Beddingfeld during the trip and shares in her adventures, serving as a support and a useful ally.

Blairgowrie, Duke of A proud and arrogant nobleman in "Blindman's Bluff." He tries unsuccessfully to murder Tommy Beresford. The duke is married to the daughter of a butcher from Chicago.

Blake, Basil A wild and infamous debaucher in the village of St. Mary Mead in *The Body in the Library*. He is nearly framed for murder by the real killer of Ruby Keene. When visited by Colonel Melchett, he is described as wearing "orange corduroy trousers and a royal-blue shirt." By profession, he is "about fifteen in the list of those responsible for set decorations at Lenville Studios, headquarters of British New Era Films."

Blake, The Honourable Elvira A headstrong young woman in *At Bertram's Hotel*. When she turns twenty-one, she will inherit a large trust fund, a fact that makes her a likely target for murder. At the time of the events recounted in the novel, she is involved romantically with the world-famous race-car driver Ladislaus Malinowski, who is also having an affair with Elvira's mother, Lady Bess Sedgwick.

Blake, Meredith Brother of Philip Blake and one of the suspects in *Five Little Pigs*. Even after many years, the mild-mannered Meredith feels responsible for the murder of Amyas Crale, because the poison that was used to commit the crime was stolen from his laboratory. He subsequently travels with Hercule Poirot in the detective's effort to solve the sixteen-year-old murder.

Blake, Philip Brother of Meredith Blake and one of the suspects in *Five Little Pigs*. A stockbroker, he was a friend of the murdered Amyas Crale—who had been poisoned some sixteen years before—and is of the view that Caroline Crale (who was originally convicted of the crime) is still responsible.

Blake, Susan A young woman in "Triangle at Rhodes." She is selfish and shallow, but she does manage to accomplish a remarkable feat: Hercule Poirot agrees to rub suntan lotion into her shoulders.

Blanche, Angele A French teacher in a girls' school in *Cat among the Pigeons*. She is not quite who she pretends to be, and her efforts to blackmail a murderer result in her own death.

Bland, Detective Inspector A chief constable who leads the police inquiries into the murder of Marlene Tucker at Nasse House in *Dead Man's Folly*. He is a thoroughly meticulous investigator and earns the praise of Hercule Poirot.

Bland, Josiah A neighbor of the murder victim in *The Clocks*. He practices the construction trade and is found to be notably corrupt. Neither he nor his wife, Valerie, heard anything of import on the fateful day when R. H. Curry was murdered. It is subsequently revealed, however, that his wife may have been a participant in the crime.

Bland, Valerie Wife of Josiah Bland in *The Clocks* and a neighbor to Millicent Pebmarsh, in whose apartment a corpse is found. Like her husband, she denies having seen or heard anything on the day when R. H. Curry was poisoned and stabbed, but it is later learned that she may have been involved in the crime, owing to a scheme to secure an inheritance.

Blatt, Horace One of the suspects in the murder of Arlena Marshall in *Evil under the Sun*. He is an unpleasant man and is suspected of being a heroin smuggler.

Bleibner, Mr. An American businessman and friend of George Chetwynd in *Giant's Bread.* He hires the amnesiac Vernon Deyre to serve as his chauffeur.

Bleibner, Rupert A member of the archaeological expedition to uncover the tomb of King Men-her-Ra in "The Adventure of the Egyptian Tomb." Convinced that he had contracted leprosy while in the Egyptian desert, Bleibner committed suicide, leaving an important note that helps Poirot to unmask a murderer.

Bletchley, Major A soldier in *N or M?* The major is an old-fashioned officer and is firmly convinced that the military in the new era is not worth a damn.

Bligh, Gertrude (Nellie) See Johnson, Mrs.; see also Mrs. Starke.

Blondin, Monsieur Gaston The owner of an exclusive restaurant in *Death on the Nile.* Thanks to Hercule Poirot, his reputation is saved from ruin.

Blore, William Henry One of the unhappy guests on Indian Island in *And Then There Were None.* Blore is one of the last survivors of the bloody game of cat and mouse that takes place on the island, but he, too, eventually succumbs to murder, as the eighth victim. He had been a member of British intelligence and had perhaps been responsible for a man's death. For that "crime" he was chosen to become a member of the doomed company on the island.

Blundell, Caleb (Pop) A rich American magnate whose daughter loses one of a pair of earrings supposedly worth $80,000 in "The Pearl of Price." Described as "stout and prosperous," Blundell seems obsessed with impressing his fellow travelers with his wealth, and asserts that he could buy three more such expensive pairs of earrings before noticing it in his bank account.

Blundell, Carol The daughter of the American magnate Caleb Blundell and the owner of a pair of expensive earrings in "The Pearl of Price." She is described as "pretty, spoiled, and

extremely sure of herself as the only woman among half a dozen men." While on a journey in the Jordanian desert, she loses an earring from a pair supposedly worth $80,000. The loss of the earring sparks a frantic search for it in the campsite and the unraveling of the theft by Mr. Parker Pyne.

Blunt, Alistair The head of one of England's foremost banks in *One, Two, Buckle My Shoe.* This wealthy financier also wields great political power, as is clear from the efforts of Inspector Japp and Hercule Poirot to investigate the murder of Poirot's dentist, Dr. Morley. Blunt was also one of Morley's patients and had seen him on the very day of the dentist's murder. A supreme patriot, he seems a more than unlikely suspect.

Blunt, Major Hector A one-time big game hunter and a friend of Roger Ackroyd in *The Murder of Roger Ackroyd.* Despite his prowess in the field, he remains painfully shy and thus nearly lacked the courage to ask Flora Ackroyd to marry him. Blunt inherits twenty thousand pounds following Roger's death, an inheritance that makes him a prime suspect in the murder.

Blunt, Admiral Philip A member of the British cabinet in *Passenger to Frankfurt.* He is an advocate among the ministers against any détente with Russia.

Blunt, Theodore The owner of Theodore Blunt's International Detective Agency in *Partners in Crime.* He is also a member of an international espionage ring in England and is picked up by the British secret service. Chief Carter, head of the secret service, requests that Tommy Beresford take over the identity of Mr. Blunt and that Tuppence Beresford assume the identity of his secretary. The couple readily accepts and takes over Blunt's offices at 118 Haleham Street, London. Under the guise of Blunt, Tommy—with Tuppence ever at his side—is engaged by assorted clients.

Bob The most unique witness in the many unusual cases presented by Agatha Christie, Bob is a devoted little terrier in *Dumb Witness.* He is at first blamed for the supposedly accidental fall of Emily Arundell down a flight of stairs, but her subsequent murder leaves the dog as the only true witness to the events surrounding her death. He develops a delightful relationship with Hercule Poirot, but in a rare show of determination, it is Captain Hastings who insists on assuming ownership of Bob after the conclusion of the investigation.

Bodlicott, Henry (Chuck)   A young gardener in *Postern of Fate.* The grandson of Isaac Bodlicott, he is hired to serve as the gardener at the estate owned by Tommy and Tuppence Beresford when his grandfather is found murdered. As Isaac was assisting the Beresfords in solving a murder, Henry joins them in his grandfather's stead.

Bodlicott, Isaac   A gardener in the house at Hollowquay in *Postern of Fate.* He cares for the grounds of the estate owned by Tommy and Tuppence Beresford and has served it for many years, since the death of the old gardener Alexander Parkinson. As events reveal, Parkinson was murdered, and Bodlicott is determined to help the Beresfords in uncovering why and how it happened. His efforts result in his murder, and his grandson, Henry, assists in solving the case with the Beresfords.

Bolford, Mr.   A partner of a tailoring firm in *They Came to Baghdad.* He prefers—owing to tradition—to cater almost exclusively to male clients, making his tailoring services available to women only on a limited basis.

Bollard, Mr.   The owner of a jewelry store in *At Bertram's Hotel.* He caters for the most part to the English upper classes.

Bond, James   A clever but temperamental hero in "The Rajah's Emerald." Bond is prone to bitterness about his financial situation, a tendency that surfaces when he goes on a seaside vacation with his girlfriend and they encounter some of her wealthy friends. His girlfriend stays at the fancy Esplanade Hotel, while he must take up lodging in a humble boardinghouse. During the stay, however, Bond becomes involved in an adventure surrounding the rajah's emerald, an escapade that brings him into contact with the highest levels of society.

Bond, Sergeant Percy   A police officer in *Cat among the Pigeons.* While generally a competent officer, he displays a curious reluctance to interrogate teachers, owing to a lifelong fear of instructors.

Bones, Billy   The nickname given to Sir William Ossington by his fellow Scotland Yard colleagues in *Murder Is Easy.*

Bonnington, Henry   A friend of Hercule Poirot in "Four and Twenty Blackbirds." He enjoys dining at the Gallant Endeavour restaurant in King's Road, Chelsea, and was a respected customer. One evening, while dining with the Belgian detective, he points out the peculiar behavior of a patron and sparks Poirot's interest to the point that the sleuth is hardly surprised to learn of the odd diner's death some three weeks later. Bonnington is later astonished at the skill of the detective in unraveling an entire mystery solely from one man's eating habits.

Borrow, Richard (Dick)   A "hardworking East End parson" in "The Call of Wings." He is a good friend of Silas Hamer, but he does not share his wealthy friend's refusal to believe in anything he cannot see or touch. After Hamer's mysterious adventures, however, Borrow is the unexpected recipient of an enormous donation, receiving the additional surprise of learning that Hamer has witnessed a vision.

Boscombe, Mr.   The owner of an art gallery in *Third Girl.* He impresses Hercule Poirot by informing the detective that art should speak for itself, a sentiment with which the sleuth agrees wholeheartedly.

Boscowan, Emma   The widow of the painter Tommy Boscowan in *By the Pricking of My Thumbs.* One of her husband's paintings becomes an important clue in the solution of a mystery by the Beresfords, and Emma provides vital information about the painting.

Bosner, Frederick   A one-time German spy who is nearly killed in a train crash. He survives the disaster, but his face is terribly disfigured. Given the damage, he uses the chance to leave his old life behind and assume the identity of a new person. He subsequently resurfaces as an archaeologist in *Murder in Mesopotamia.*

Bott, Police Constable   A police officer in *Hickory Dickory Dock.* He is a vigorous police official, but his competence is somewhat limited.

Bouc, Monsieur   The director of *La Compagnie Internationale des Wagons Lits* in *Murder on the Orient Express.* He is an old friend of Hercule Poirot and is delighted to learn that he will be traveling with the Belgian detective on the Orient Express to London. When, however, one of the passengers is found brutally murdered, Bouc insists that Poirot take the case. He subsequently assists the detective in his inquiry, but his lack of experience becomes obvious at times. Owing to his bias against Italians, he is certain that the Italian suspect, Antonio Foscarelli, is the murderer.

Bourget, Louise   A lady's maid in *Death on the Nile.* She is in the service of Linnet Ridgeway and accompanies her and her new husband on their whirlwind trip to Egypt. After the murder of her mistress, Louise discovers clues as to the identity of the murderer and makes an attempt at blackmail. For her efforts, she is brutally murdered.

Mr. Bouc (Martin Balsam, left) examines a vital clue in Murder on the Orient Express *(1974), with Poirot and Dr. Constantine. (Photofest)*

Bourne, Ursula A parlor maid in the household of the Ackroyds in *The Murder of Roger Ackroyd*. She is dismissed from service shortly after Roger Ackroyd is murdered.

Bower, Dr. Charles A supposed scientist in "The Adventure of the Sinister Stranger." He enlists the help of Tommy and Tuppence Beresford in guarding his research on alkaloids. There is, however, much more to Dr. Bower than the Beresfords at first assume.

Bower, John See Bauer, John.

Bowers, Miss A nurse and traveling companion in *Death on the Nile*.

Boyd Carrington, Sir William A friend of Captain Arthur Hastings and an acquaintance of Hercule Poirot in *Curtain*. His habits are the source of intense irritation to the Belgian detective.

Boyle, Mrs. A victim of murder in "Three Blind Mice." An annoying and thoroughly unpleasant woman, her death by strangulation (one of two in this case) comes as little surprise to those who knew and disliked her.

Boynton, Mrs. A remarkably evil villainess in *Appointment with Death*. Described as a woman whose eyes emitted "a wave of evil," Mrs. Boynton sits like "a distorted old Buddha" and rules her family with an iron fist. A onetime warden in a women's prison, she is analyzed by Dr. Gerard, a French psychiatrist, who sums her up by observing: "She does not love tyranny because she has been a wardress. Let us rather say that she became a wardress because she loved tyranny. In my theory it was a secret desire for power over the other human beings that led her to adopt that profession." Her ability to remember details about faces and people she had seen many years before leads to her murder, much to the relief of her now psychologically damaged family.

Boynton, Carol A stepdaughter of Mrs. Boynton in *Appointment with Death*. She feels like a prisoner of the dread matriarch of the Boynton family but lacks the strength to make a break for freedom.

Boynton, Ginerva (Jinny) The gentle daughter of Mrs. Boynton in *Appointment with Death*. She is starkly different from her evil mother. She is nicknamed Jinny.

Boynton, Lennox The weak-willed stepson of Mrs. Boynton in *Appointment with Death*. He has long been under the terrible control of his

The horrendous Mrs. Boynton (Piper Laurie), in Appointment with Death *(1988). (Photofest; Cannon/Golan Globus)*

stepmother and has obediently wed Nadine Boynton. Mrs. Boynton exercises the same ruthless control of the couple that she had exercised over her son, forcing them to live in her own house and to travel with her. His wife, however, struggles to free her husband from the clutches of his evil mother, but it is only in his mother's death that Lennox discovers his own strength and his love for his wife.

Boynton, Nadine The wife of Lennox Boynton in *Appointment with Death.* She married Lennox at the behest of Mrs. Boynton and soon discovered herself a virtual slave to the old woman's wishes, just as Mrs. Boynton's children were hostages to the matriarch's iron will. Nadine is studying, at Mrs. Boynton's command, to become a nurse, even as she struggles to free her husband from the evil woman's control.

Boynton, Raymond (Ray) A stepson of Mrs. Boynton in *Appointment with Death.* He hates his stepmother so much that he considers murdering her; when pondering the act, he admits that he would consider such a crime no more terrible than killing a mad dog.

Brabazon, Archdeacon A cleric in *Nemesis.* He remains plagued by guilt over the advice he gave a young woman many years ago concerning her proposed marriage. She was killed soon afterward, an event that Brabazon still feels was his fault. The archdeacon also conducts the funeral service for Miss Temple.

Bradburn, Cyrus G. An American millionaire in "At the 'Bells and Motley.'" He pays an enormous amount of money for a mansion and all of its contents.

Bradbury-Scott, Anthea One of three sisters in *Nemesis.* She is described by Miss Marple as "a mature Ophelia," and she is also considered more of a murder suspect than her sister Clotilde.

Bradbury-Scott, Clotilde One of three sisters in *Nemesis.* She lives with Anthea and Lavinia in an old house and speaks to Miss Marple about the young woman, Verity Hunt, who had been murdered years ago. She had raised

Verity after her parents had been killed in a plane crash and was extremely protective of her interests.

Bradley, C. R. A mysterious figure in *The Pale Horse* who seems to orchestrate the deaths of many individuals through occult means. He is consulted by people who wish someone to die; in return for large sums (such as five thousand pounds), he will make a wager that the person in question will not live past some appointed date. Bradley becomes a target for exposure by Mark Easterbrook, but proves a clever foe.

Brandon, Eileen A young woman in *The Pale Horse* who works as a waitress. She had previously conducted surveys for a living but gave up the position because she found it "unsavoury." As a matter of apparent coincidence, the people she surveyed died a short time later.

Breck, Dr. Alan A scientist in *They Came to Baghdad.* A physicist at the Harwell Atomic Institute, he examines a uranium specimen at the request of another character.

Brent, Clement Edward Alistair The indolent master of the Chimneys who appears in two novels, *The Secret of Chimneys* and *The Seven Dials Mystery.* Extremely wealthy and possessor of the title of ninth marquis of Caterham, he is expected to engage in politics but is far too lazy to undertake such an ambitious project. He has three daughters who become involved in assorted adventures: Daisy, Dulcie, and Eileen (Bundle).

Brent, Daisy (Guggle) One of three daughters, with Dulcie and Eileen, of Lord Clement Brent in *The Secret of Chimneys.* Daisy is twelve years old and is most energetic, a remarkable contrast to her indolent father.

Brent, Diana A schoolgirl who takes part in a fatal celebration in *Hallowe'en Party.*

Brent, Dulcie (Winkle) One of three daughters, with Daisy and Eileen, of Lord Clement Brent in *The Secret of Chimneys.* The youngest of Brent's daughters, Dulcie is a precocious ten-year-old.

Brent, Edna One of the victims in *The Clocks*. She is killed as a result of being confined to the office of a typing service because of a broken shoe heel.

Brent, Lady Eileen (Bundle) One of three daughters, with Daisy and Dulcie, of Lord Clement Brent in *The Secret of Chimneys* and *The Seven Dials Mystery*. The oldest daughter, she is also the wildest of Brents, proclaiming herself a "red hot socialist" and enjoying driving at ludicrously high speeds. She is a major participant in the events described in *The Seven Dials Mystery*.

Brent, Emily Caroline One of the unhappy guests of Indian Island in *And Then There Were None*. Brent was invited to the island because of her dark past, including the likelihood—at least in the murderer's mind—that she had once killed someone. She becomes the fifth victim of murder.

Brent, Gladys A maid in "The Tape-Measure Murder." Brent worked in the service of Mrs. Spenlow and had the day off at the time of her mistress's murder.

Brent, Marcia, Marchioness of Caterham The sister-in-law of Lord Clement Brent in *The Seven Dials Mystery*. The widow of Lord Brent's brother, Henry, she is quite fond of dispensing advice to her three nieces.

Bréon, Edouard A retired French opera star in "Swan Song." When a singer falls ill, he is pressed to take up the mighty role in *Tosca* in the other singer's stead. Little does Bréon realize that he is also the target of a murderer seeking revenge for a terrible wrong committed many years before.

Brett, Dr. A physician in "Murder in the Mews." Brett is sharp-eyed, for he notices the illogical placement of the pistol in the hand of Barbara Allen's corpse and thus deduces that her death was actually a murder disguised as a suicide.

Brewis, Amanda A secretary and housekeeper in *Dead Man's Folly*. She cares deeply for her employer and dislikes his wife intensely.

Brewster, Emily One of the suspects in the murder of Arlena Marshall in *Evil under the Sun*. She is one of the witnesses to discover the body, coming across it in a small cove while out on a boat ride with Patrick Redfern.

Brewster, Jim One of the members of the Youth Movement in *Passenger to Frankfurt*.

Brewster, Lola An actress in *The Mirror Crack'd from Side to Side*. She is possessed of a very wrathful temperament, to the point that she regularly threatens to shoot people. She is a suspect in the murder of Heather Badcock, especially when it seems that the real target of the murder was Marina Gregg, one of Brewster's rivals in the film industry.

Brice-Woodworth, Patricia A wealthy and most self-possessed woman who took part in the deadly birthday party in *Sparkling Cyanide*. On the terrible night in which George Barton recreates the party at which his wife died, a recreation at which he is himself murdered, Patricia remains astonishingly calm and collected.

Bridget A fifteen-year-old girl in "The Theft of the Royal Ruby." With two other members of the Lacey household, Bridget plans a fake murder for fun, but the play seemingly takes a deadly turn.

Brill, Inspector A police officer in *Sad Cypress*. Brill is quite capable and meticulous in his investigation, and he uncovers a clue that almost solves the case. Fortunately, Poirot is on hand to crack the entire puzzle.

Bristow, Frank An artist in "The Dead Harlequin." Aside from his many talents as a painter, Bristow is the creator of one painting in particular that catches the eye of Mr. Satterthwaite. The painting *The Dead Harlequin* offers a figure that strongly resembles Mr. Harley Quin.

Broad, Nora A young woman who disappears suddenly in *Nemesis*. Because she has a reputation as a person with rather loose morals, her disappearance is not considered sinister.

Broadribb, James A solicitor and senior partner of the law firm representing the interests of the dead Jason Rafiel in *Nemesis*. A shrewd attorney, he is responsible for presenting Miss Marple with many of the details of the mission she is sent on by Rafiel. He treats Miss Marple with considerable courtesy, but also with circumspection, given what he knows Rafiel wishes her to accomplish.

Brown, Mr. A mysterious and sinister figure in *The Secret Adversary.* Mr. Brown seems to be the leader of a group of conspirators intent on damaging England. During World War I, he promoted the peace movement and other propaganda efforts to undermine British morale. He becomes the target of the efforts of Tommy and Tuppence Beresford.

Brown, Geraldine Mary Alexandra A woman in *The Clocks.* She is especially useful to investigators because of her particular circumstances. Geraldine is forced to remain in her room (à la *Rear Window*) because of a broken leg. She uses her condition, however, to spy on her neighbors, one of whom is a murderer.

Brown, John An alias used by Cedric Crackenthorpe in *4.50 from Paddington.*

Brown, Laurence A tutor in the Leonides household and one of the suspects in *Crooked House.* Although a conscientious objector during World War I, he is nevertheless suspected of conspiring with Brenda Leonides to murder her husband, especially as it is common knowledge that she has a passion for Brown. Laurence, however, is appalled at the notion of being a suspect, protesting that the very idea of murder is a "nightmare."

Browne, Anthony An alias used by Tony Morelli in *Sparkling Cyanide.* He has a very checkered past.

Brun, Mademoiselle Geneviève One of the names used by the adventuress and former dancer Angele Mory in *The Secret of Chimneys.*

Brunston, Mrs. A cook in *The Burden.* She is a confidante of Laura Franklin, who comes to her for advice.

Bryant, Dr. Roger James One of the passengers on the deadly flight in *Death in the Clouds.* He is a suspect in the murder of Madame Giselle, both because he is a medical practitioner and because he plays the flute; both abil-

ities make him an obvious suspect because of the poisoned dart used to murder Giselle.

Buckle, Mrs. A woman in *Elephants Can Remember* who provides very useful information to Mrs. Aridane Oliver, particularly about four wigs that are a vital clue.

Buckley, Reverend Giles A clergyman in *Peril at End House.* He suffers the murder of his daughter but does little to advance the investigation. However, his wife, Jean Buckley, is quite vigorous in her pursuit of the murderer.

Buckley, Jean The wife of Reverend Buckley in *Peril at End House.* While her husband is more concerned with prayer and clichés than with hunting down the murderer of their daughter, Magdala, Jean is very active.

Buckley, Magdala Also known as Maggie, the daughter of Reverend and Mrs. Buckley in *Peril at End House.* She is murdered while wearing her cousin Nick's lacquer-red Chinese shawl. Her parents have very different responses to her death.

Buckley, Nick A young woman in *Peril at End House* who manages to survive five different attempts on her life before a murderer is finally brought to justice by Hercule Poirot. She first meets Poirot while he is on vacation in St. Loo, after she has already survived three accidents. While she sits with the detective, a fourth attempt is made: a bullet passes so close to her head that she thinks it is a wasp. Poirot knows better and notices a bullet hole in her hat. The cause for the murder attempts is simple: She has inherited the family home, End House, after the death of her brother. Poirot considers her fortunate, but he also thinks she is a "feather-head."

Bullard, Louise A parlor maid in "The Sign in the Sky." She provides important testimony to Mr. Satterthwaite, and tells him that she noticed a figure in the sky made of smoke on the fateful day of a murder. Her evidence assists in freeing a man charged with murder.

Bulmer, Sir Edwin The defense attorney for Elinor Carlisle in *Sad Cypress.* His efforts are generally viewed as a waste of time, as the case against Carlisle in the murder of Mary Gerrard seems virtually airtight.

Bulstrode, Honoria   The headmistress of the Meadowbank School in *Cat among the Pigeons*. Described as "tall, and rather noble looking," she is nearly single-handedly responsible for the success of the school. At the time of the events recounted in the novel, she is planning on retiring.

Bunner, Dora (Bunny)   A dear friend of Letitia Blacklock in *A Murder Is Announced*. She lives at Little Paddocks with her old school friend as a result of Letitia's generosity. Described as "painstaking but never competent," her mind tends to wander, and she has the habit of revealing more about the past than she should. When she has a seemingly innocuous visit with Miss Marple, her unreliability proves too much for a murderer. She is murdered with poisoned aspirin soon after a birthday party thrown in her honor.

Burch, Bessie   The niece of Mrs. McGinty in *Mrs. McGinty's Dead*. She is, in the view of Hercule Poirot, a straightforward Englishwoman, but he encounters much difficulty in questioning her because of her intense dislike of foreigners. Her husband is Joe Burch.

Burch, Joe   The husband of Bessie Burch in *Mrs. McGinty's Dead*. While his wife is reluctant to assist Poirot in his inquiries, owing to her dislike of foreigners, Joe is more than cooperative. His excessive zeal to be helpful is viewed with suspicion by Poirot, who becomes convinced that he is hiding something.

Burgess, William   A servant to Major Charles Rich in "The Mystery of the Spanish Chest." He finds the body of Arnold Clayton apparently stuffed into a chest in the major's living room, and provides damning evidence against his employer. As Burgess is rather shifty, however, he becomes a suspect.

Burgoyne   The manservant to Major Rich in "The Mystery of the Baghdad Chest." He discovers the body of Edward Clayton and subsequently provides apparently damning evidence against his employer. Hercule Poirot finds him of great help in examining the clues of the case.

Burnaby, Major John Edward   A onetime adventurer with his friend Captain Trevelyan in *The Sittaford Mystery*. The two remained friends throughout their lives, sharing many similar interests, including mountain climbing and big game hunting. One evening, while attending a séance, Burnaby learns the terrible news: TREVELYAN DEAD—MURDER. Burnaby calls the police, who rush to Trevelyan's house and find him beaten to death. Burnaby subsequently plays a major part in the investigation of the murder.

Burnaby, Mr.   The owner of the Three Crowns Pub in *Death on the Nile*. He is an excellent source of local news and gossip.

Burns, Charlie   A young shipping clerk in "The Face of Helen." He is the apparent victor in the contest to win the affections of a young woman. Her old suitor, however, has other plans, which are foiled by Mr. Satterthwaite.

Burrows, Godfrey   The private secretary to Lord Chevenix-Gore in "Dead Man's Mirror." He has a hidden background that is revealed by Hercule Poirot.

Burshaw, Miss   A schoolmistress in "The Girdle of Hippolyta." It is the source of some distress to her when one of her students goes missing and then mysteriously returns unharmed.

Burt, Dr.   A physician in "The House of Lurking Death." He is the attending physician to several people who have been poisoned by arsenic; two die before Tommy and Tuppence Beresford arrive on the scene to investigate.

Burt, Mr.   A member of the United States secret service in "The Adventure of the Cheap Flat." He has been tracking the elusive Elsa Hardt and some important missing documents.

Burt, James   A veterinarian in *The Rose and the Yew Tree*. He is married to Milly Burt and is a cruel and abusive husband.

Burt, Milly   The wife of James Burt in *The Rose and the Yew Tree*. A pretty and gentle woman, she is the victim of her husband's brutal and abusive habits.

Burton, Jerry and Joanna Brother and sister in *The Moving Finger* who settle in Little Furze so that Jerry can recuperate from wounds suffered in the war. The narrator of the case, Jerry, is a tall, handsome RAF pilot shot down during World War II and forced to endure a very long healing period. His sister is also good-looking and smart; both are chain smokers. After moving into the home they rent from Emily Barton, they become aware of the odd poison-pen letters spreading through the village and are themselves the target of one. Making the acquaintance of Miss Marple, they assist in the resolution of the problem. Jerry falls in love with young Megan Hunter, while Joanna falls for Dr. Griffith.

Burton-Cox, Mrs. A twice-widowed woman in *Elephants Can Remember.* She has a reputation for being extremely unpleasant and self-important. She dominates her stepson, Desmond Burton-Cox, and hides from him the fact that he will receive a large inheritance left to him by his natural mother when he turns twenty-five. It is Mrs. Burton-Cox who presses Mrs. Ariadne Oliver to look into the tragic details of Mrs. Oliver's goddaughter's family history. Mrs. Burton-Cox's interest is personal, for the goddaughter, Celia Ravenscroft, is desirous of marrying her stepson.

Burton-Cox, Desmond The natural son of Kathleen Fee and, after her death, the stepson of Mrs. Burton-Cox in *Elephants Can Remember.* He is dominated utterly by his stepmother and does not know that he stands to inherit a considerable amount of money when he turns twenty-five. He wishes to marry Celia Ravenscroft, Mrs. Ariadne Oliver's goddaughter.

Bury, Dr. An army doctor in *Giant's Bread.* He is both incompetent and arrogant.

Bury, Colonel Ned A onetime soldier in "Dead Man's Mirror." An old friend of the Chevenix-Gore family, he has a long, passionate, but unrequited love for Lady Vanda Chevenix-Gore.

Butler, Judith The mother of one of the party guests in *Hallowe'en Party.* Her daughter is the precocious twelve-year-old Miranda, whose mind impresses Hercule Poirot.

Butler, Miranda The twelve-year-old daughter of Judith Butler and one of the party attendees in *Hallowe'en Party.* She was a friend of one of the murder victims and impresses Hercule Poirot with her logical and orderly mind.

Butt, Johnnie The town paperboy in Chipping Cleghorn in *A Murder Is Announced.* He delivers the local paper, the *Gazette,* on October 29. The paper that day carries the very peculiar announcement: "A murder is announced and will take place on Friday, October 29 . . ."

Cabot, Mr. and Mrs. Elmer Two figures in the events depicted in *At Bertram's Hotel.* They are involved in the illegal activities in the hotel.

Cade, Anthony The hero of *The Secret of Chimneys.* A young adventurer, he is asked by his friend Jimmy McGrath to deliver the memoirs of Count Stylptitch to a publisher in return for 250 pounds. The supposedly simple task is soon complicated when Cade is threatened and attempts are made to bribe him, all for control of the manuscript. He faces other adventures and travels, culminating with his journeys to the Chimneys. There, he solves the mysteries that have plagued him from the start of the story and learns his own true identity. Cade also finds love in the person of Virginia Revel.

Cadwallader, Sergeant A local police officer in *The Unexpected Guest.* He is of Welsh descent and has a poetical nature, often quoting Keats.

Calder, Alice The twenty-five-year-old wife of the hereditary sheik of Ramat in *Cat among the Pigeons.* Even as Ramat sinks into chaos he is toppled from power, her husband manages to have Alice smuggled out of the country.

Calgary, Dr. Arthur The hero in *Ordeal by Innocence.* A geophysicist, he was a vital witness and could have provided an alibi for Jack Argyle following the murder of Jack's adoptive mother, Rachel Argyle, but on the very night that the murder took place Calgary was hit by a bus and suffered from amnesia. He subsequently recovered but then went on a research trip to Antarctica and learned of the terrible events only upon his return. Wracked with guilt because he could have been the means of freeing Jack (who died in prison), Calgary sets out to find the real murderer. By the end of the story, he plans to wed Hester Argyle.

Callaway, Michael   An artist in *Absent in the Spring.* He has an exceedingly unorthodox and reprehensible solution to easing the tension faced by Joan Scudmore.

Campion, Lord Edward   A sporting man in "The Rajah's Emerald." He is exceedingly wealthy, but he prefers comfortable and unpretentious clothes. As a result, he has his clothes taken accidentally by the young James Bond, setting off a series of misadventures.

Capel, Derek   A man haunted by his past in "The Coming of Mr. Quin." He shoots himself rather than face the possible consequences of an exhumation.

Capelli, Bianca   The original name of Madame Paula Nazorkoff in "Swan Song."

Capstick, Nurse   A nurse in *The A.B.C. Murders.* She cares for the dying Lady Charlotte Clarke.

Carbury, Colonel   A British officer in charge of law enforcement in the region around Amman in *Appointment with Death.* He first introduces Poirot to the case involving the death of Mrs. Boynton and is delighted but surprised to hear from Poirot that the case will be solved in twenty-four hours. As the case reaches its climax, Carbury asks Poirot to provide not only the solution but a list of the most significant facts, just as "the detective does in books."

Cardew Trench, Mrs.   A hotel guest in *They Came to Baghdad.* An extremely talkative Englishwoman, she is a severe annoyance to other guests.

Cardiff, Peter   A painter in *Third Girl.* The epitome of the worst example of modern youth, he is described by Mrs. Ariadne Oliver as "the dirtiest young man" she's ever seen.

Cardner, Mary   The daughter of a butcher in *Giant's Bread.* She volunteers for the Red Cross during World War II.

Cardwell, Susan   A friend of the Chevenix-Gore family in "Dead Man's Mirror." She was staying at the Chevenix-Gore home at the time of the murder of Sir Gervase Chevenix-Gore.

Carey, Richard   An architect who is working on an archaeological dig in *Murder in Mesopotamia.* He is the object of the excessive attentions of the unfaithful wife of the dig leader.

Carfax, Colonel Maurice   An old friend and confidante of Lord Listerdale in "The Listerdale Mystery." When Lord Listerdale disappears, Carfax is given power of attorney to act in his best interests, although some of his financial steps do not seem to be performed with Listerdale's best interests at heart.

Cargill, Rupert   A physician in *Absent in the Spring.* He is middle-aged and married to an invalid wife, and both factors influence his attraction to his pretty, unmarried, and, above all, young assistant. She, however, refuses to carry on their romance because it might wreck both their career and home life.

Carlisle, Charlie   A confidential secretary to Lord Mayfield in "The Incredible Theft." While he was away from the room containing a set of secret plans, having gone to assist a French maid, the plans were supposedly stolen by some unknown agent.

Carlisle, Elinor Katherine   A young woman accused of murdering Mary Gerrard, the new love of her onetime fiancé, Roderick (Roddy) Welman, in *Sad Cypress.* The case against her seems airtight, but she is saved from conviction by Hercule Poirot.

Carlo   A member of the Comrades of the Red Hand in *The Secret of Chimneys.* He serves as a rather inept sentry.

Carlton, Mrs.   A member of the house staff of The Elm School in *Hallowe'en Party.*

Carlton-Smith, Naomi A young artist in "The World's End." She is so devastated by the possibility that her fiancé is a jewel thief that she contemplates suicide. She is discouraged in this rash act by Mr. Harley Quin, whom she sketches.

Carmichael, Lady There were two Lady Carmichaels in the Christie writings. The first is a noblewoman and inveterate expert in gossip in "The Horses of Diomedes." She is consulted by Hercule Poirot, who receives valuable information from her concerning the events and personalities of his case. The second Lady Carmichael is a sinister woman in "The Strange Case of Sir Arthur Carmichael." Her stepson suffers from a kind of derangement of mind that has caused him to act like a cat, and she is herself attacked in the throat while she sleeps. Considered a powerful occult master, she dies most unexpectedly at precisely the same moment that her stepson recovers from his insanity.

Carmichael, Sir Arthur A young man in "The Strange Case of Sir Arthur Carmichael." He survives a murder attempt by his sinister stepmother but suffers an apparent breakdown in sanity that causes him to act like a cat. He recovers from this odd ailment after falling into the icy waters of a pond; at that precise same moment, his stepmother dies.

Carmichael, Henry A member of British intelligence in *They Came to Baghdad.* He is an expert in languages, especially those of the Middle East, and he speaks six regional languages as well as numerous mountain dialects. He is killed in the line of duty.

Carmichael, William A senior attorney in the law firm that represents the interests of Linnet Doyle in *Death on the Nile.* He is the uncle of James Fanthorp, who is sent out to Egypt to safeguard the financial health of the firm's client.

Carnaby, Amy A "plump, amiable-looking creature" who works as a lady's companion in "The Nemean Lion." The sister of Emily Carnaby, she provides details to Hercule Poirot concerning the disappearance of a Pekingese, Shan Tung, while she was taking the dog for a walk. The detective is exceedingly impressed with the woman, declaring that "there is nothing wrong with your brains or with your courage." Miss Carnaby later enlists Poirot's assistance in saving a friend from the clutches of a cult leader in "The Flock of Geryon." Once again, she displays her courage as well as her abilities as an actress.

Carnaby, Emily The sister of Amy Carnaby in "The Nemean Lion." She is a semi-invalid and is unable to work. Her support thus comes from Amy, who also has a deep fondness for her Pekingese, Augustus.

Carpenter, Mrs. A middle-aged lady's companion in *At Bertram's Hotel.* She is nicknamed The Carpenter.

Carpenter, Adelaide The companion of Sylvia Keene in "The Herb of Death." She is "a big soft white purry person . . . One of those widows left in unfortunate circumstances, with plenty of aristocratic relations, but no ready cash."

Carpenter, Dickie A young man in "The Gipsy." He is warned by a gypsy in a dream not to undergo an operation but does so anyway and dies. His death leaves his friend MacFarlane shaken.

Carpenter, Eve A onetime employer of Mrs. McGinty in *Mrs. McGinty's Dead.* She becomes a suspect in the death of Laura Upward after her perfume lingers in the room in which the corpse is discovered. She is obsessed with furthering her husband's political career.

Carpenter, Guy The husband of Eve Carpenter in *Mrs. McGinty's Dead.* A politically ambitious man, he is protected and encouraged by his obsessive wife and does much to keep details about their lives secret from investigators out of fear that they might hurt his political career.

Carpenter, Louise One of the names used by Louise Borell in *Third Girl.*

Carr, Lady Esther An English aristocrat who journeys to Shiraz, Persia, accompanied by her maid, Muriel King, in "The House at Shiraz." For some reason, Lady Carr remains in an elegant house at Shiraz, adopting Eastern dress and refusing to see anyone from Europe, especially any Englishmen. Mr. Parker Pyne had known Lady Carr's father, Lord Micheldever, and had met Lady Micheldever, "a noted Irish beauty" with black hair and violet-blue eyes. The appearance of Lady Carr's parents is a vital clue in Parker Pyne's solution of the mystery in the house at Shiraz. (See also King, Muriel.)

Carr, Sister   An army nurse in *Giant's Bread*. Although she is extremely popular, she suffers from a chronic inability to be punctual.

Carrege, Monsieur   A French examining magistrate in the murder investigation conducted into the death of Ruth Kettering in *The Mystery of the Blue Train*.

Carrington, Lady Adeline   See Clapperton, Lady Adeline.

Carrington, The Honourable Flossie   The daughter of the wealthy American industrialist Ebenezer Halliday and wife of the disreputable Rupert Carrington in "The Plymouth Express." She is murdered while traveling on a train and her expensive jewels are stolen.

Carrington, Air Marshal Sir George   A powerful figure in the armed forces in "The Incredible Theft." He was once in the navy and still retains "the bluff breeziness of the ex-Naval man." Concerned about the safety of a set of secret plans and the apparent involvement of his host, Lord Mayfield, with a possible spy, he journeys to Mayfield's house to confront the minister of armaments.

Carrington, Lady Julia   The wife of Air Marshal Sir George Carrington in "The Incredible Theft." She is exceedingly fond of bridge and is perpetually in a state of disapproval concerning her son, Reggie.

Carrington, Reggie   The son of Air Marshal Sir George Carrington and Lady Julia Carrington in "The Incredible Theft." He is twenty-one and most uninterested in any matters of government.

Carrington, The Honourable Rupert   The disreputable husband of Flossie Carrington and the much-disliked son-in-law of the wealthy American industrialist Ebenezer Halliday in "The Plymouth Express." As it is widely suggested that he married only for money, he is a likely suspect in the murder of his wife, especially as her jewels were stolen in the process.

Carruthers, Miss   A "horsey spinster who dropped her g's" in "Miss Marple Tells a Story." She "was about forty, wore pince-nez, had close-cropped hair like a man and wore mannish coats and skirts." With Mrs. Granby, she is one of the only possible suspects—albeit an unlikely one—in the murder of Mrs. Rhodes.

Carruthers, Nurse   A nurse who attended to the dying Emily Arundell in *Dumb Witness*. She testifies to Hercule Poirot that Miss Lawson has lied about the will left by Emily.

Carslake, Alan   Brother of Sylvia Carslake in *In a Glass Darkly*. He gives his sister a place to stay after she flees her violently jealous husband.

Carslake, Captain   A Conservative local political leader in *The Rose and the Yew Tree*. He is also an officer serving in the Home Guard and is an air raid warden during World War II.

Carslake, Sylvia   The sister of Alan Carslake in *In a Glass Darkly*. She is initially engaged to Charles Crawley, but breaks off the engagement and weds someone else. When he becomes violently jealous, Sylvia flees to the safety of her brother's house. Her husband, however, pursues her there and tragedy nearly strikes.

Carson   A butler in *Endless Night*. He was actually a bodyguard hired to protect Ellie Guteman.

Carstairs, Alan   A Canadian explorer, hunter, and naturalist in *Why Didn't They Ask Evans?* He is found dying at the base of a cliff by Bobby Jones and Dr. Thomas and asks the curious question, "Why didn't they ask Evans?" before dying from injuries suffered in his fall. In his pocket is a photograph of Moira Nicholson.

Carstairs, Dr. Edward   A psychologist in "The Strange Case of Sir Arthur Carmichael." He examines the unfortunate Arthur Carmichael and determines that he has suffered some kind of dementia in which he thinks of himself as a cat.

Carstairs, The Honourable Julia An elderly woman in a retirement home in *Elephants Can Remember*. Although partly deaf, she is able to recall very important details of a murder from many years before.

Carter, Detective Sergeant A police officer in "Mr. Eastwood's Adventure." He arrests Eastwood under the apparent belief that Eastwood is a wanted criminal, but his own activities, as Eastwood discovers, are themselves worth investigating.

Carter, A. The chief of British intelligence who appears in several mysteries featuring Tommy and Tuppence Beresford, including *The Secret Adversary, Partners in Crime,* and *N or M?* Described as tall, "with a lean, hawklike face and a tired manner," he has the awesome responsibility of protecting Britain from attack by enemy agents. He takes a particular interest in the Beresfords and finds them quite useful as operatives even under dangerous circumstances. In another milieu, he is actually Lord Easterfield.

Carter, Frank A young and generally unreliable employee in *One, Two, Buckle My Shoe*. He becomes embroiled in murder and emerges as a suspect after receiving employment as a gardener on the estate of Mr. Alistair Blunt, one of England's most powerful bankers.

Carter, Harry A thoroughly unpleasant owner of a pub who is drowned in *Murder Is Easy*. His daughter is Lucy Carter.

Carter, Lucy The daughter of the pub owner Harry Carter in *Murder Is Easy*. On the night of her father's death, she was out with a local chauffeur.

Carter, Stephen One of the members of the dinner party in "Yellow Iris." He was present on the night that Iris Russell was murdered and on the night that fateful gathering is re-created.

Carton, L. B. A participant, with his wife, in a diamond mine robbery in *The Man in the Brown Suit*. He frames two other men but is killed when he is pushed onto a subway track. The same day, his wife is stabbed to death in Mill House. A man in a brown suit pretends to be a doctor and rushes up to check his pockets. Inside is a piece of paper that contains the cryptic words "17–122 Kilmorden Castle."

Cartwright, Dr. A local physician in Market Basing. He is in the unpleasant position in two mysteries—*The Secret of Chimneys* and *The Seven Dials Mystery*—of being summoned to the Chimneys to examine the victims of murder or mysterious death.

Cartwright, Sir Charles A famous stage actor who suffers a nervous breakdown and is unable to perform for two years in *Three-Act Tragedy*. He thought about changing his name at one point to Ludovic Castiglione, a far different appellation from the one he bore originally, Charles Mugg. He hosts a dinner party at which Reverend Babbington imbibes a drink and drops dead.

Carver, Dr. a "world-renowned elderly archaeologist" who is conducted digs in the Jordanian desert in "The Pearl of Price." Dr. Carver is adamant in his assertion that there is no possible way for a sudden temptation to turn an honest man into a criminal. This belief has a direct bearing on the solution to the theft of an expensive earring. Of additional note is Carver's habit of walking with his eyes always downward, scanning the ground for small objects that may be of archaeological interest.

Cary, Frances A young part-time artist's model in *Third Girl*. She is a roommate of Norma Restarick.

Casey, Mrs. The landlady in "Three Blind Mice." Mrs. Lyon is strangled to death in her establishment.

Casey, Patrick A renowned cat burglar in "The Apples of the Hesperides." Casey is generally rumored to have stolen the infamous Borgia goblet.

Caspar, Mr. A participant in a tour of English homes and gardens along with Miss Marple in *Nemesis*. He views her behavior with considerable suspicion.

Caspearo, Señora de A guest with Miss Marple on the island of St. Honoré in *A Caribbean Mystery.* She is loud and outspoken in her views, especially when discussing the complete lack of charm in men over the age of thirty-five.

Cassell, Dr. A physician in Market Basing in *The Seven Dials Mystery.* He examines a man who had been apparently run over by Eileen Brent and was actually already dead from gunshot wounds.

Cassetti The real name of the vicious kidnapper of Daisy Armstrong in *Murder on the Orient Express.* He escaped justice in the murder of the little girl, but he was pursued across the world by those seeking revenge for his crime. Justice finally catches up with him on board the Calais Coach.

Casson, Mrs. An expert in the occult and the paranormal in "The Voice in the Dark." She summons a medium to assist in unraveling an apparent mystery.

Castiglione, Ludovic A name that the actor Sir Charles Cartwright had considered adopting in *Three-Act Tragedy.*

Castle, Mrs. The owner of the Jolly Roger Hotel on Smuggler's Island, Leathercombe Bay, Devon, in *Evil under the Sun.* She is a gorgon of a woman with flamboyantly colored hair. Her hotel is the site of the murderous events recounted in the novel.

Castelton, Harry One of the names used by Quentin Duguesclin in *The Clocks.*

Caterham, Lord The noble title borne by Alistair Edward Brent, ninth marquis of Caterham, in *The Secret of Chimneys* and *The Seven Dials Mystery.*

Cauldfield, Richard A former British officer hoping to find love and happiness in *A Daughter's a Daughter.* His first wife had died many years before, and Cauldfield is hopeful of marrying Ann Prentice, but Prentice's daughter is so opposed to the union that Prentice calls off their relationship. Cauldfield marries another woman, a wealthy younger woman. He remains secretly in love with Ann, however, and just how much they both regret the failure of their relationship becomes apparent when they speak again some time later.

Caux, Monsieur The commissary of police investigating the murder of Ruth Kettering in *The Mystery of the Blue Train.*

Cavendish, John A friend of Captain Arthur Hastings in *The Mysterious Affair at Styles.* He has known Hastings for forty-five years and so, when Hastings is required to convalesce after terrible experiences in World War I, Cavendish invites him to come and stay at his home, Styles Court, a country house near the village of Styles St. Mary in Essex. John resides at Styles Court with his family, including his wife, Mary, his brother, Lawrence, his stepmother, Emily Inglethorp, and her husband, Alfred Inglethorp. As money is controlled completely by his stepmother, John depends entirely upon her for his financial existence. When Emily is murdered, John—who had ample motive, given the financial circumstances—turns to Hastings for help; the good captain, in turn, seeks out an old friend and Belgian refugee, Hercule Poirot, who happens to be staying in a nearby town.

Cavendish, Lawrence Brother of John Cavendish in *The Mysterious Affair at Styles.* Younger than his brother by five years, the forty-five-year-old Lawrence is an aspiring poet. He used up his inheritance some time ago and thus resides at Styles Court with the rest of the Cavendish clan and is entirely dependent upon his stepmother, Emily Inglethorp, for his financial support.

Cavendish, Mary The wife of John Cavendish in *The Mysterious Affair at Styles.* A beautiful woman, she inspires Captain Hastings to find love for himself. Mary also has a friendship with Dr. Bauerstein that becomes both an embarrassment and a potential threat to her freedom. Mary's name reappears in "The Adventure of 'The Western Star,' " when Lady Yardly approaches the detective and tells him that Mary Cavendish had suggested she consult him.

Cawthorn, The Honourable Virginia See Revel, Virginia.

Cayley, Alfred A man in *N or M?* who suffers from assorted imaginary diseases in order to remain an invalid and retain virtual total control over his wife, Elisabeth.

Cayley, Elisabeth The wife of Alfred Cayley in *N or M?* She is a virtual prisoner of her husband, for he uses his host of imaginary ailments as a reason for her to wait on him.

Cayman, Amelia A dishonest young woman in *Why Didn't They Ask Evans?* Described as "a painted-up raddled bitch" by Frankie Derwent, she is married to Leo Cayman.

Cayman, Leo The husband of Amelia Cayman in *Why Didn't They Ask Evans?* A charming fellow, he is also a bigamist, because while he is married to Amelia, he is also married to Rose Emily Templeton under the name Edgar Templeton.

Cazalet, Dr. A friend and associate of Hercule Poirot in "The Under Dog." A likable and eminent practitioner with offices in Harley Street, he is called into a case by Poirot and hypnotizes a vital witness.

Célestine A French maid in "The Jewel Robbery at the Grand Metropolitan." When the pearl necklace of Mrs. Opalsen disappears, she is suspected immediately in the theft but is more than adamant about her innocence. The evidence seems absolutely damning when the police discover the necklace hidden in her bed. Hercule Poirot, however, has other ideas.

Celia The main character and narrator of *Unfinished Portrait.* She is a sensitive and caring creature who undergoes a transformative healing after contemplating suicide. Celia endures the end of her marriage to a soldier named Dermot and is forced to raise her daughter alone. She suffers an understandable breakdown but overcomes her many tragedies to mature and to find happiness with a new, loving husband.

The character of Celia bears a more than striking resemblance to Agatha Christie. For more details, see *Unfinished Portrait* (page 151).

Chadwick, Miss A stolid teacher in *Cat among the Pigeons.* She is known as "Faithful Chaddie"

to her friends, and she fulfills her title by giving up her life for someone else.

Challenger, Commander George A member of a cocaine ring in *Peril at End House.* He works with his uncle, a physician, to keep their friends and associates supplied with narcotics.

Chandler, Admiral Charles A proud former naval officer in "The Cretan Bull." He is the inheritor of a noble family tradition of service in the Royal Navy, dating back to the time of Queen Elizabeth I. It was a matter of course that his son, Hugh, should follow him into the service, but then Hugh is ordered inexplicably to leave the navy. Hugh begins displaying symptoms of madness—another, more dread family inheritance—and the admiral endures the torment of watching his son slowly deteriorate mentally.

Chandler, Hugh The son of Admiral Charles Chandler in "The Cretan Bull." He is the scion of a proud family and enters the Royal Navy in keeping with his family's expectations. He is instructed by his father, however, to depart the service and soon after begins to deteriorate mentally. His condition, which includes supposed blackouts and acts of unspeakable violence, reaches the point that Hercule Poirot is consulted by Hugh's devoted former fiancée, Diana Maberly.

Chantry, Commander Tony The husband of Valentine Chantry in "Triangle at Rhodes." Tony has been married to Valentine for only six months, but their marriage seems doomed, not only because of his loss of interest in her but also because of her considerably greater interest in Douglas Gold. Valentine, however, is murdered, and her husband becomes the obvious suspect. He is described as having a "touch of the primeval ape about him."

Chantry, Valentine The unpleasant wife of Commander Tony Chantry in "Triangle at Rhodes." She is described as "a tall woman very conscious of herself and her body." Known throughout the world for her beauty, she has been married five times and has enjoyed innumerable lovers, including an Italian count, an American steel magnate, and a tennis professional. All have died or been excised from her life by divorce. Recently, she married again, to Commander Chantry, but she begins showing greater interest in the handsome Douglas Gold. Valentine soon is murdered, and her brutish husband is the obvious suspect.

Chapman, Albert   See Barnes, Reginald.

Chapman, Nigel   Also called Nigel Stanley, a student of medieval history in *Hickory Dickory Dock.* He is immature and spoiled.

Chappell, Anthony   A young man and friend of Hercule Poirot in "Yellow Iris." He is a melancholy person who contemplates drinking poison because of the despair he feels over losing the beautiful Pauline Weatherby. He also provides Poirot with details about the different suspects in the death of Iris Russell.

Charles   A headwaiter in *Sparkling Cyanide.* On the night that Rosemary Barton was murdered, Charles was responsible for pouring the wine.

Charlton, Mr.   A solicitor in *Hercule Poirot's Christmas.* He is required to read the will of Simeon Lee to Lee's not-so-bereaved family and is reluctant to do so because of the responses that often greet the details of a testament. His fears are realized.

Charnley, Lady Alix   A grim and seemingly cursed widow in "The Dead Harlequin." She has lived with the torment of guilt over the suicide of her husband shortly after their marriage, in the assumption that it was done in the face of her unfaithfulness to him.

Charnley, Hugo   The brother of Lord Reggie Charnley in "The Dead Harlequin."

Charnley, Lord Reggie   The husband of Lady Alix Charnley in "The Dead Harlequin." He committed suicide shortly after his marriage, presumably because of his wife's infidelity.

Charpentier, Louise   A woman who uses several other names in *Third Girl.* She is hurled from a window.

Charteris, Mrs. Bigham   A widow in *The Rose and the Yew Tree.* She resides in St. Loo Castle.

Charteris, Isabella   A tall, aristocratic woman in *The Rose and the Yew Tree.* She lives in St. Loo Castle.

Chatterton, Lady Abbie   The wife of the otherwise unremarkable Lord Chatterton, who is an acquaintance of Hercule Poirot in "The Mystery of the Spanish Chest." She is considered by Poirot to be "one of the brightest jewels" in what he calls *le haut monde.* She invites him to a party to introduce him to Margharita Clayton and thus brings him into the case of the death of Clayton's husband.

Chatterton, Lady Alice   A powerful socialite in "The Mystery of the Baghdad Chest." She invites Hercule Poirot to a party with the express purpose of having him meet Marguerita Clayton, whose husband was brutally murdered. Lady Chatterton has been an admirer of Poirot since he solved a case involving the peculiar behavior of a Pekingese, which led to the capture of a burglar.

Checkheaton, Lady Matilda   A socially active older woman who insists on traveling and enjoying life, despite the concerns of her doctor. One of her favorite pastimes is squirreling out secrets from the lips of her many friends in high society.

Chelles, Monsieur   A traveling silk merchant in *The Secret of Chimneys.*

Chester, Adela   A domineering mother in "Problem at Pollensa Bay." She controls virtually every aspect of the life of her son, Basil.

Chester, Basil   The son of Adela Chester in "Problem at Pollensa Bay." He lives under the near total domination of his mother. While he actually enjoys the attention, he finds Adela's interference to become unacceptable when matters of the heart are involved.

Chetwynd, George   A wealthy American businessman in *Giant's Bread.* He falls in love with Nell Vereker, but she refuses to marry him because of his drinking. Years later, they meet again when he purchases an estate Nell inherits. This time, they wed, an event that becomes complicated when Nell's former husband, Vernon, turns up.

Chetwynd, Gordon An unpleasant man with many enemies in *Passenger to Frankfurt.*

Chevenix-Gore, Sir Gervase Francis Xavier A nobleman and victim of murder in "Dead Man's Mirror." Sir Gervase is a dyed-in-the-wool aristocrat with a pompous and overinflated view of himself and his family; he supposedly divides the world into two camps—the Chevenix-Gores and the other people. His unique personality has become eccentric over the years. One of his most peculiar rituals is the custom of requiring all family members to be present before the gong is sounded for dinner. His own absence at the sounding of the gong is the first indication that he has suffered some terrible fate.

Chevenix-Gore, Ruth The adopted daughter of Sir Gervase and Lady Vanda Chevenix-Gore in "Dead Man's Mirror." She is a very attractive girl "in the modern style." Even the mechanical Hercule Poirot must admit that she is one of the most beautiful women he has ever seen.

Chevenix-Gore, Lady Vanda Elizabeth The wife of Sir Gervase Chevenix-Gore in "Dead Man's Mirror." An attractive older woman, she is the longtime object of worship by Colonel Bury and Ogilvie Forbes; she is also as eccentric as her husband, believing that she is the reincarnation of an Egyptian queen and wearing amulets and scarabs in homage to its spirit.

Chichester, Reverend Edward One of the disguises and aliases used by Arthur Minks in the pursuit of information in *The Man in the Brown Suit.*

Chilcott, Mary One of the characters involved in the murderous events in "The House of Lurking Death." She attempts to maintain a facade of calm even as she lives in terror of death by poison.

Christow, Gerda The wife of Dr. John Christow in *The Hollow.* She is also mother of two children, including Zena, who predicts accurately, using cards, that Dr. Christow will die.

She is extremely concerned that her husband has a wandering eye.

Christow, Dr. John A physician with exceedingly wealthy clients in *The Hollow.* He is married to Gerda Christow and is the father of two, including Zena, a nine-year-old who accurately predicts his murder. Despite his commendable efforts in medical research, he is a reprehensible husband who is serially unfaithful. John is found shot to death near his swimming pool; his wife is found standing over him, revolver in hand, by Hercule Poirot.

Christow, Zena The nine-year-old daughter of Dr. John and Gerda Christow in *The Hollow.* She enjoys reading the future with cards and predicts with perfect accuracy the impending death of her father.

Chudleigh, Rose A household cook in *Why Didn't They Ask Evans?* She was a witness to the signing of a forged will.

Church, Miss The aunt of the dead girl, Amy Gibbs, in *Murder Is Easy.* She is firmly convinced that Amy could not have swallowed oxalic acid by accident.

Clancy, Daniel A writer of detective stories in *Death in the Clouds.* He is a passenger on the plane on which Madame Giselle is murdered. He is considered a likely suspect, especially as he owns a blowpipe—ostensibly for research on a book he is writing—that might have been used to fire the poisoned dart that killed Giselle.

Clapperton, Adeline The widow of Lord Carrington and wife of Colonel John Clapperton in "Problem at Sea." An extremely unpleasant woman, she manages to offend virtually everyone on board the cruise ship and publicly humiliates her husband in assorted ways, including reminding him of her former husband's considerable wealth. She is found in her cabin stabbed to death with a dagger.

Clapperton, Colonel John A former music hall entertainer who is now married to the dreadful Adeline Clapperton in "Problem at Sea." He wed her for money and is constantly reminded of the wealth of her first husband, Lord Carrington. Adeline is found stabbed to death in their cabin, but John seems to have an excellent alibi.

Clark, Sergeant A local policeman investigating the murder of Dr. John Christow in *The Hollow.* He is a competent officer who assists Poirot's inquiries.

Clark, Dr. Campbell A psychologist traveling on a train in "The Fourth Man." He provides many details pertaining to the death of a young, psychologically troubled girl.

Clark, Milly The companion of Mrs. Albert Jones in "The Tuesday Night Club." Mrs. Jones dies after a meal of canned lobster and trifle; three other people fell ill. Miss Clark is a pleasant, plump woman.

Clarke, Sir Carmichael The third victim in *The A.B.C. Murders.* A collector of Chinese art, he is found with his head battered and a copy of the *A.B.C. Rail Guide* opened and positioned next to his body. He resided at Churston, in Devon. Hercule Poirot is warned about Sir Carmichael's impending murder, but the letter giving him clues about Churston was apparently diverted and arrives too late to prevent the crime.

Clarke, Lady Charlotte The feeble wife of Sir Carmichael Clarke in *The A.B.C. Murders.* She is anxious for Hercule Poirot to find the murderer of her husband.

Clarke, Franklin The brother of Sir Carmichael Clarke in *The A.B.C. Murders.* He is a smart man who benefits from the death of his brother. Nevertheless, he volunteers to assist Poirot in finding the murderer.

Claythorne, Vera Elizabeth One of the unfortunate guests of Indian Island in *And Then There Were None.* She is considered worthy of inclusion in the murderous exercise taking place on the island because this former games mistress was accused—but never convicted—of killing a young boy.

Clayton, Arnold The jealous husband of the beautiful Margharita Clayton in "The Mystery of the Spanish Chest." He is found stabbed to

death. In the shorter version of this case recounted in "The Mystery of the Baghdad Chest," Arnold Clayton is renamed Edward Clayton.

Clayton, Edward See Clayton, Arnold.

Clayton, Elsie A young woman, "pretty in an old-fashioned style," in "The Stymphalean Birds." She travels with her mother, Mrs. Rice, and meets Harold Waring in Herzoslovakia. The cordial association with Waring takes a deadly turn when Elsie's abusive husband, Philip, arrives and instigates an incident of violence that climaxes in his apparent death. Elsie turns to Waring for help.

Clayton, Margharita A beautiful woman and wife of Arnold Clayton in "The Mystery of the Spanish Chest." Poirot considers her to be one of the most dangerous of all women, for her stunning beauty is sufficient to drive men wild, but she is virtually oblivious to that fact. When her husband is found brutally stabbed, she consults with Poirot in an effort to save her friend, Major Charles Rich, from conviction for the crime. In the version of this case recounted in "The Mystery of the Baghdad Chest," Margharita is renamed Marguerita Clayton.

Clayton, Marguerita See Clayton, Margharita.

Cleat, Mrs. A woman in *Moving Finger* who has the reputation for being a witch.

Clegg, Emmeline A gullible and easily led woman in "The Flock of Geryon." She falls under the spell of the Great Shepherd, Dr. Andersen, and enters the membership of the Flock, a cult whose adherents regularly give all of their money to Dr. Andersen and soon die. Clegg's best friend, Amy Carnaby, is so concerned for her welfare that she consults Hercule Poirot.

Clegg, Freda A young woman who comes to Mr. Parker Pyne in the hopes of relieving her loneliness and boredom in "The Case of the Discontented Soldier." In return for a certain sum of money, she is suddenly and unknowingly thrust into an adventure with Major Charlie Wilbraham involving a hidden treasure in East Africa. After facing several perils with the major, Freda finds a way to enliven her lonely life. (See also Wilbraham, Major Charlie.)

Clegg, Joe The husband of Maureen Clegg in *Ordeal by Innocence.* He married Maureen after the death of her first husband, Jacko Argyle, in prison, following his conviction for murder. Joe steadfastly refuses to believe that Jacko could have been innocent.

Clegg, Maureen The former wife of Jacko Argyle who marries Joe Clegg after her first husband's conviction for murder and his subsequent death in prison in *Ordeal by Innocence.*

Clement, Father See Gabriel, John.

Clement, Dennis The nephew of Reverend Leonard Clement and Griselda Clement in *Murder at the Vicarage.* He is a clever sixteen-year-old with a keen interest in detective work.

CLEMENT, GRISELDA The wife of Reverend Leonard Clement and a dear friend of Miss Marple. Griselda is twenty years younger than her husband, the vicar of St. Mary Mead; she is, not surprisingly, much more active than Len, and she raises their two sons. Clever and devoted to her husband, she proves her mettle when Colonel Protheroe is shot to death in Len's own vicarage. She has other appearances, too—in *The Body in the Library* and *4.50 from Paddington.* By the time of the events in *4.50 from Paddington,* she is a widow, but she remains living at the vicarage, which, by then, is "shabby." She assists Miss Marple in that case by providing maps, a request that strikes her son Leonard as very peculiar and suspicious.

CLEMENT, REVEREND LEONARD Called Len by his devoted wife, Griselda, Reverend Clement is the vicar of St. Mary Mead and a friend of Miss Marple. The vicarage sits next door to Danemead, Miss Marple's home, and thus the two get along very well as neighbors, and Clement relies on her for advice. At no time is she more valuable to him than during the crisis recounted in *The Murder at the Vicarage,* when Colonel Protheroe is shot to death and left in Clement's office.

Leonard was long thought a confirmed bachelor in St. Mary Mead and thus caused a storm of surprise when he announced his engagement—and was subsequently married—to Griselda, a woman twenty years younger and far more energetic than he. The couple proved extremely happy, however, and produced two sons, including Leonard, Jr. (who appears briefly in *4.50 from Paddington*). After an appearance in *The Body in the Library,* Clement unfortunately passed away. Griselda chose to remain at the vicarage after his death.

Cleveland, Jane The heroine in "Jane in Search of a Job." She is looking for work when she reads a fortuitous advertisement in the paper. Jane is hired to impersonate a duchess whose life is threatened, and she subsequently embarks upon a series of adventures.

Cleveland, Mortimer A psychic researcher who uses his training and his insight in "SOS." Forced to seek assistance from a family after his car breaks down, Cleveland meets the Dinsmeads and is soon embroiled in a mystery of death and attempted murder. Through his intuition, he prevents a murder and frees a young woman from danger.

Cleves, Diana A rather calculating woman in "The Second Gong." She desires to marry Captain John Marshall, a man considered most unsuitable by her adoptive father, Hubert Lytcham Roche, and to convince Hubert that she has lost her feelings for Marshall, Diana displays an interest in Geoffrey Keene. All of this becomes apparently academic when Hubert is found dead, but Diana is then surprised to learn that Hubert has left a provision in his will that allows Diana to inherit only if she weds Gregory Barling. Poirot notes that she is quite unaffected with grief over the death of her adoptive father.

CLITHERING, SIR HENRY A longtime dear friend and admirer of Miss Marple, Clithering is a onetime commissioner of Scotland Yard and a devoted full-time member of the Tuesday

Night Club. First introduced in *The Thirteen Problems,* he subsequently had parts to play in *The Body in the Library* and *A Murder Is Announced.* Clithering, "during his term as commissioner of the Metropolitan Police, had been renowned for his quick grip on essentials" (*The Body in the Library*). One of those abilities is the appreciation of little old ladies and their value to criminal investigations, in large measure because they are invaluable in providing details about local village or town life and the many quirky personalities therein. Above all little old ladies, of course, is Miss Marple: "She's just the finest detective God ever made. Natural genius cultivated in a suitable soil."

His involvement in the case of *The Body in the Library* is both professional and personal, as he is friends with three of the participants in the case, Conway Jefferson (who had made Ruby Keene his heir) and Dolly and Colonel Arthur Bantry (in whose library was discovered a corpse). Clithering also has a keen interest in the career of Inspector Dermot Craddock, his nephew, who likewise shares an appreciation of Miss Marple's mind for crime.

Cloade, Frances A member by marriage of the Cloade family of Warmsley Vale in *Taken at the Flood.* Like the other members of the family, she and her husband, Jeremy, are dependent upon Gordon Cloade for funds and generous extensions of loans. She will stop at nothing to protect her husband's interests.

Cloade, Gordon The wealthy head of the Cloade family of Warmsley Vale in *Taken at the Flood.* The sixty-two-year-old patriarch is the primary means of financial support for the other members of the family, so his sudden and entirely unexpected marriage to the young widow Rosaleen Underhay is greeted with genuine concern. This fear turns into terror when Gordon is killed during an air raid and his money passes to his widow.

Cloade, Jeremy A member of the Cloade family of Warmsley Vale in *Taken at the Flood.* The

brother of Gordon, Lionel, and Rowland Cloade, Jeremy is a successful solicitor.

Cloade, Katherine (Kathie) A member by marriage of the Cloade family of Warmsley Vale in *Taken at the Flood.* She is the wife of Lionel Cloade and the sister-in-law of Gordon, Jeremy, and Rowland Cloade and is quite disturbed by the prospect of Gordon's young widow inheriting the bulk of the Cloade estate. Her obsession is revealed in her dress, a fact noted by George, Hercule Poirot's valet.

Cloade, Dr. Lionel A member of the Cloade family of Warmsley Vale in *Taken at the Flood.* A physician, he is married to Katherine Cloade, who is fiercely concerned about the estate of the Cloades passing to Gordon's young widow. Lionel also examines the body of Enoch Arden, providing Poirot with details about the cause and time of death.

Cloade, Rosaleen The young widow of Gordon Cloade in *Taken at the Flood.* As Rosaleen Underhay, she met the wealthy Gordon Cloade while they crossed the Atlantic and married him after a whirlwind courtship. Soon after their arrival in England, however, Gordon is killed in an air raid and the considerable estate passes to her. This development is a nightmare to Gordon's family, especially his brothers. Her own apparent brother, David Hunter, is concerned about the Cloades and warns her to watch out for her own safety. A far greater threat, however, seems to come from the mysterious Enoch Arden, who threatens to reveal the details about Rosaleen's earlier marriage to Robert Underhay if she does not agree to his terms of blackmail.

Cloade, Rowland (Rowley) A member of the Cloade family in *Taken at the Flood.* A farmer, Rowley is also of a fiery temperament, demonstrating this passionate nature when he tries to strangle Lynn Marchmont after she breaks off her engagement with him. This rash act is stopped in time by Hercule Poirot.

Clode, Christobel A young woman who passed away in "Motive vs. Opportunity." Left an orphan when her father died in the war and her mother died in childbirth, she went to live with her grandfather, Simon Clode. He was utterly devoted to her and was thus crushed when she died at the age of eleven from pneumonia. In his grief, Simon turns to a medium, Eurydice Spragg, to make contact with his beloved dead granddaughter.

Clode, George The nephew of Simon Clode in "Motive vs. Opportunity." His father had died in poor circumstances, and George and his sisters, Grace and Mary, had been invited to live with their uncle. While not as beloved as Simon's granddaughter, Christobel, they were all given kindness and assistance. George was found employment in a nearby bank. Originally a beneficiary in Simon's will, along with his sisters, George was disappointed to learn that his uncle had fallen under the influence of the American medium Eurydice Spragg.

Clode, Grace The niece of Simon Clode and sister of George and Mary Clode in "Motive vs. Opportunity." When their father died in poor circumstances, she, George, and Mary went to live with their uncle. She later married a "clever young research chemist of the name of Philip Garrod."

Clode, Mary A niece of Simon Clode in "Motive vs. Opportunity." When their father died, Mary and her brother, George, and sister, Grace, went to live with their uncle. She devoted her days to taking care of Simon and was described as "a quiet, self-contained girl."

Clode, Simon—A wealthy elderly man in "Motive vs. Opportunity." A client of the lawyer Mr. Petherick, Clode lost a son in World War I, and after the death of his granddaughter's mother in childbirth, he brought little Christobel to live with him. He also invited his nephew, George Clode, and his nieces, Mary and Grace Clode, to share his house after their father died in poor circumstances. When

Christobel died suddenly from pneumonia, Simon was plunged into grief and fell under the influence of an American medium, Eurydice Spragg. So enthralled was Clode with the medium's apparent powers to contact the spirit of Christobel that he seemingly changed his will in her favor just before his death.

Clonray, Lady Susan The aunt of the Honourable Hermione Crane in "The Case of the Missing Lady." She defends the privacy of her niece, even in the face of an uproar surrounding Mrs. Crane's disappearance.

Cobb, Mr. The director of an art gallery in "The Dead Harlequin." He notes that Mr. Satterthwaite has excellent artistic taste.

Cocker, Mrs. A housekeeper and cook in *Sleeping Murder*. After she discovers a skeleton, she passes out and is given a brandy. Unfortunately, this act of kindness nearly kills her, for the brandy is poisoned.

Cocker, Doris A housemaid in *Three-Act Tragedy*. She waited on Reverend Babbington on the night that the cleric was poisoned to death. For this reason, she is initially considered a likely suspect for the crime.

Codders The nickname given to the Honourable George Lomax in *The Secret of Chimneys* and *The Seven Dials Mystery*.

Coggins A savage thug in "The Case of the Sinister Stranger" who tortures Tommy Beresford in an effort to gain some valuable information.

Coghan, Mr. A laborer in "The Case of the Missing Will." A "big, gaunt man with a grizzled mustache," he provides Hercule Poirot with details on a secret hiding spot in a fireplace; this information proves instrumental in solving the case.

Cohen, Sir Herman The name used for Sir Joseph Salmon by the actress Jane Helier in her recounting of "The Affair at the Bungalow."

Cole, Miss The "brusque manageress" of the Mitre Hotel in "The Under Dog." She provides Hercule Poirot with details about one of her guests, Captain Humphrey Naylor.

Cole, Mr. (Detective Inspector) A police officer and associate of Inspector Japp who goes undercover in "The Flock of Geryon." He impersonates a member of the Flock in the hopes of trapping the dangerous Mr. Andersen. Miss Carnaby meets him in his role as Dr. Cole and considers him seriously mentally ill.

Cole, Elizabeth See Litchfield, Elizabeth.

Coleman, Bill A British archaeologist in *Murder in Mesopotamia*. He is exceedingly unpopular in the archaeological dig in Mesopotamia because of his cloddish behavior.

Coleman, Monkey An alias used by Victor Drake in *Sparkling Cyanide*.

Coles, Dr. A physician in the Keston Spa Hydro who attends to the medical needs of Miss Marple during her visit in "A Christmas Tragedy."

Coles, Doris An associate of Mr. Satterthwaite in "The Bird with the Broken Wing." She assists Satterthwaite in solving the murder of Mabelle Annesley.

Colgate, Inspector The police official who investigates the murder of Arlena Marshall in *Evil under the Sun*. His methodical approach to solving the murder impresses Hercule Poirot.

Collins, Miss The secretary and companion to Mrs. Waverly in "The Adventure of Johnnie Waverly." Miss Collins has been with the Waverlys for a little more than a year, but the questions that arise about this capable young woman make her a leading suspect when young Johnnie Waverly is kidnapped.

Collins, Beryl The secretary and receptionist in the service of Dr. Christow in *The Hollow*. A very capable worker, she refuses to accept the notion that Gerda Christow shot her husband to death, despite the fact that Gerda was found standing over his corpse with a gun in her hand.

Collodon, Miss A researcher in *Postern of Fate*. The older woman assists Tommy Beresford in researching different matters.

Colonel The code name used by the sinister head of a criminal organization in *The Man in the Brown Suit*.

Combeau, Pierre A friend of Hercule Poirot in *The Big Four*.

Conneau, George The original name of Paul Renauld in *Murder on the Links*.

Connell, Marjorie A young secretary in *Unfinished Portrait*. She has an affair with Dermot, husband of Celia, and eventually marries him, thus destroying Celia's marriage and happiness.

Miss Connell and the events in which she takes part bear a striking resemblance to the sad events surrounding the doomed real-life marriage of Agatha Christie and Archie Christie.

Conrad, Mrs. A prominent and active socialite in "The Submarine Plans." Her beauty and social connections, however, belie the fact that she is a potentially dangerous woman with connections to Germany, spies, and blackmailers. Thus, when secret plans for a submarine disappear, she is immediately considered a suspect.

Constantine, Dr. A Greek physician in *Murder on the Orient Express*. He assists Hercule Poirot in his investigation into the murder of Mr. Ratchett, examining the victim's body. His careful observation determines that there are twelve stab wounds and that at least two people took part in the assault.

Constantine, Dr. Claudius The name used by Dr. Antrobus while assisting Mr. Parker Pyne in "The Case of the Rich Woman." (See Antrobus, Dr.)

Constantine, Dimitri A wealthy businessman in *Endless Night*. He is having a luxury house built and complains about the costs being run up by his unpleasant architect, Mr. Santonix.

Conway, Bridget An attractive young woman in *Murder Is Easy*. She is the cousin of Jimmy Lorrimer, through whom she meets Luke Fitzwilliam. He falls in love with her virtually from the moment they meet, which poses an intriguing problem because Bridget is unhappily engaged to the ruthless and unpleasant Lord Easterfield. Bridget, of course, develops an attraction to Fitzwilliam as she assists him in his pursuit of a murderer in Wychwood.

Bridget Conway (Lesley-Anne Down) and Lord Easterfield (Timothy West) in Murder Is Easy. *(Photofest)*

Conway, Sir George The home secretary who enlists Hercule Poirot's assistance in "The Augean Stables." Conway and the prime minister need the detective's help in suppressing a story about the former prime minister John Hammett. Conway is a complete politician who "had lost the art of simple narration."

Cooke, Miss A bodyguard in *Nemesis*. With Miss Barrow, she is hired to keep an eye on Miss Marple during her travels to the homes and gardens of England and during her investigation into an old murder.

Coombe, Alicia A dressmaker who has considerable trouble with a life-size doll in "The Dressmaker's Doll." She is unable to figure out what to do when a doll seems to change position on its own and even moves from one room to another. Her solution is rather extreme.

Coote, Lady Maria The wife of Sir Oswald Coote in *The Seven Dials Mystery*. An aging and lonely woman, she attempts to reverse her doldrums by renting out the estate the Chimneys and throwing a lavish party for young people. The event proves the catalyst for murder. Lady Coote is also fond of playing bridge, although she has a reputation for cheating.

Coote, Sir Oswald A very successful businessman in *The Seven Dials Mystery*. He started out as a mere bicycle shop owner and rose from one financial success to another until he became a steel magnate. Granted a peerage, he became one of England's most wealthy industrialists, but this did not prevent his wife from suffering from loneliness and regret over their success. To ease her ennui, he agrees to rent their estate, the Chimneys, and throw a party there for young people. The event is marred by murder.

Cope, Jefferson A young man in *Appointment with Death.* He is exceedingly fond of Nadine Boynton, who, as a physician observes, is dedicated to the notion of good rather than evil.

Copleigh, George and Liz A husband and wife who own a guest house in Sutton Chancellor in *By the Pricking of My Thumbs.* They are able to provide the Beresfords with few details in their investigation.

Copling, Nurse The nurse to the rather difficult Mrs. Pritchard in "The Blue Geranium." She was "a very good sort—a sensible woman to talk to." At her suggestion, the fortune-teller Madame Zarida is consulted by Mrs. Pritchard, with terrible consequences ensuing from her mysterious predictions for the future.

Corjeag, Ewan A nephew of Myles Mylecharane in "Manx Gold." He receives a letter from his late uncle's lawyers informing him of the chance to discover his uncle's treasure. The inheritance is buried in four chests at different spots on the Isle of Man. Ewan must compete with three other relatives in the search and dies during the hunt.

Cornelly, Lord An unusual nobleman in *Towards Zero.* He deliberately hires employees who are scrupulously honest to represent his business interests around the world. He hires Andrew MacWhirter for a job in South Africa.

Corner, Sir Montague A wealthy Englishman who enjoys hosting parties in *Lord Edgware Dies.* He is an avid collector of art and artifacts and provides Lady Edgware an unimpeachable alibi, as she was dining with him on the night that Lord Edgware was murdered.

Cornish, Inspector An officer of Scotland Yard in *The Mirror Crack'd from Side to Side.* He works with Inspector Craddock to find the murderer.

Cornworthy, Hugo The efficient private secretary to the millionaire Benedict Farley in "The Dream." Supposedly on behalf of his employer, he contacts Hercule Poirot and requests his presence for a meeting with Farley. The millionaire dies soon afterward from an apparent suicide.

Corrigan, Eileen The true name of a character in *Taken at the Flood.* She is approached by a ruthless blackmailer, Enoch Arden, who demands to share in an inheritance or he will reveal damaging secrets from her past. Arden is found dead a short time later.

Corrigan, Dr. Jim A police surgeon who examines Father Gorman's body in *The Pale Horse.* He is a friend of Mark Easterbrook, and his sister, Ginger Corrigan, serves as assistant to Easterbrook in his investigation into the connection between the Pale Horse Inn and the numerous deaths that have taken place.

Corrigan, Katherine (Ginger) The sister of Dr. Jim Corrigan in *The Pale Horse.* She is also a close friend of Mark Easterbrook, assisting him in the investigation of a series of murders and the connection that the Pale Horse Inn seems to have with them. Her labors, especially her impersonation of Mark's wife, make her a target for murder, and she is very nearly killed by poisoning.

Cortman, Mildred Jean A woman who plays the role of wife to the American diplomat Sam Cortman in *Passenger to Frankfurt.* She plays a number of other roles in the events described.

Cortman, Sam An American diplomat in *Passenger to Frankfurt.* He is sent to Britain to serve as ambassador to the Court of St. James, but a group of masked assassins shoot him down on the very steps of the American embassy.

Cosden, Anthony A young man with what he believes are only six months to live in "The Man from the Sea." He attempts unsuccessfully to kill himself, but he is saved from ending his life by Mr. Satterthwaite.

Courtenay, Coco A beautiful young actress in "The Affair at the Victory Ball." She dresses as

Columbine for the gala evening, but her mood is exceedingly foul as she quarrels with her beau, Lord Cronshaw. Soon after the ball, she is found dead from an overdose of cocaine.

Cowan, Mr. The business manager to Madame Nazorkoff in "Swan Song." He endures her temperamental personality with much aplomb.

Cowley, Prudence The former name of Tuppence Beresford. See Beresford, Tuppence, for other details.

Crabtree, Mrs. A patient of Dr. Christow in *The Hollow*. She is suffering from a rare disorder, Ridgeway's disease, and was receiving treatment through hormone injections.

Crabtree, Emily The wife of William Crabtree, the nephew of Lily Crabtree, in "Sing a Song of Sixpence." She had a bitter argument with Lily on the day that her husband's aunt was murdered.

Crabtree, Lily An unmarried elderly woman in "Sing a Song of Sixpence." She is an unpleasant person and is killed by a blow to the head. Her death is rather welcomed by her relatives, who stand to inherit a considerable estate.

Crabtree, William The husband of Emily Crabtree and the nephew of Lily Crabtree in "Sing a Song of Sixpence." At the time that Lily was bludgeoned to death, William claims to have been working on his stamp collection.

Crackenthorpe, Alfred A member of the Crackenthorpe family of Rutherford Hall in *4.50 from Paddington*. He is considered the least successful of the assorted children of the family—a sad statement, given the generally underachieving qualities of the other Crackenthorpes. In fact, Alfred is little better than an amateur hooligan. Unfortunately, he never has a chance to make good in his life, as he dies from arsenic poisoning. Before his death, he makes the offer of a job and marriage to Lucy Eylesbarrow.

Crackenthorpe, Lady Alice A member by marriage of the Crackenthorpe family of Rutherford Hall in *4.50 from Paddington*. She is married to Harold Crackenthorpe and lives a miserable existence, for she has chosen him solely to avoid poverty. Her husband is murdered by poison.

Crackenthorpe, Cedric A member of the Crackenthorpe family of Rutherford Hall in *4.50 from Paddington*. He is a deliberately bohemian painter who enjoys flaunting his unorthodox lifestyle in front of people. When supplying information to authorities as to whether he was on board the 4:50 from Paddington, he gives only vague replies.

Crackenthorpe, Emma A member of the Crackenthorpe family of Rutherford Hall in *4.50 from Paddington*. She is considered by Miss Marple to be one of the least likely of suspects, although the affection shown to her by Dr. Quimper may not be entirely genuine.

Crackenthorpe, Harold A member of the Crackenthorpe family of Rutherford Hall in *4.50 from Paddington*. He is married unhappily to Lady Alice Crackenthorpe. Like his siblings, he is not especially successful or a remarkably decent person. In fact, although he is a seemingly successful businessman, he is actually deeply, perhaps irretrievably, in debt. He also pays attention to Lucy Eylesbarrow, offering her a good-paying job in his business.

Crackenthorpe, Luther The patriarch of the Crackenthorpe family of Rutherford Hall in *4.50 from Paddington*. He is a tyrannical old man who enjoys humiliating his seven children, who rely on him for their financial support. Although his health is poor and he needs a companion, he is well enough to make cruel gibes at his family and make vulgar suggestions to his young attendant, Miss Lucy Eylesbarrow.

Crackenthorpe, Martine See Dubois, Martine.

Craddock, Mrs. The wife of Charles Craddock in *Cards on the Table*. She is consistently unfaithful to her husband, to the point that he plans on reporting one of her lovers, a doctor, to the General Medical Council. Both Mrs. Craddock and her husband die before that ever happens; she succumbs to an infection in Egypt.

Craddock, Charles   The understandably jealous husband of Mrs. Craddock in *Cards on the Table*. He is concerned about his wife's adulterous affairs, especially the one he suspects that she is conducting with a physician. He plans to report the doctor to the General Medical Board, but both he and his wife die before he has the chance. Charles succumbs to anthrax, which had been planted on his shaving brush.

Craddock, Chief Inspector Dermot Eric   Nephew of Sir Henry Clithering and a longtime friend and admirer of Miss Marple. Craddock was first introduced in *A Murder Is Announced*, during which he develops a keen appreciation for the detective skills of Miss Marple. He reappeared in the published cases *4.50 from Paddington,* "Sanctuary," and *The Mirror Crack'd from Side to Side*. He rises through the ranks of Scotland Yard until finally reaching the highest offices of Britain's police force. While investigating crimes in St. Mary Mead, he considers Miss Marple's house to be his "headquarters," and is never disappointed in her deductions. He is described as having both "brains and imagination" and "the self-discipline to go slow, to check and examine each fact and to keep an open mind until the very end of the case."

Craig, Dr. Donald   A physician in *Ordeal by Innocence*. He is very much in love with Hester Argyle, to the point that even if she did murder her mother he wants to take care of her.

Crale, Amyas   The victim of a murder that occurred sixteen years before the events recounted in *Five Little Pigs*. A well-known painter, Crale was poisoned, presumably by his wife, and perhaps for his numerous indiscretions. Hercule Poirot, however, sets out to prove that Caroline Crale could not have poisoned her husband.

Crale, Carla   Also known as Carla Lemarchant, the daughter of Caroline Crale in *Five Little Pigs*. She is unable and unwilling to marry until she knows for certain whether her mother was actually guilty of murdering Amyas Crale. She thus hires Hercule Poirot to uncover the truth.

Crale, Caroline   The wife of the painter Amyas Crale and the mother of Carla Crale in *Five Little Pigs*. She was convicted of poisoning her husband sixteen years before. Only her daughter has doubts about her guilt and retains Hercule Poirot to determine once and for all the truth of what actually happened so long ago.

Cram, Gladys   The secretary to Dr. Stone in *Murder at the Vicarage*.

Crane, The Honourable Hermione   A young widow in "The Case of the Missing Lady." She disappears quite suddenly, and it is up to Tommy and Tuppence Beresford to find her. She is engaged to Gabriel Stavansson.

Craven, Nurse   A scheming nurse in *Curtain*. She is involved with Major Allerton and at the same time attempts to gain the eye of Sir William Boyd.

Craven, Hilary   A suicidally depressed woman who becomes embroiled in espionage in *Destination Unknown*. After the death of her child and a messy divorce, Craven decides to kill herself, but is prevented by an operative of the Special Intelligence Unit. He suggests that instead of killing herself, she should consider giving her life for her country by taking part in a most dangerous espionage operation. Her task is to impersonate the dead Olive Betterton and insinuate her way into the Brain Trust.

Crawford, Mr.   An attorney in *Endless Night*.

Crawford, Joanna   A traveler with Miss Marple and others on a tour of English homes and gardens in *Nemesis*. While in the company of Emlyn Price, she witnesses Elizabeth Temple being crushed beneath a boulder, and sees the person who actually pushed the rock.

Crawley, Charles   A young man with a scar who is engaged to marry Sylvia Carslake in "In a Glass Darkly." She breaks off their engagement after receiving a warning about marrying a man with a scar.

Cray, Veronica   An actress in *The Hollow*. She had planned to win back the love of Dr. Christow after fifteen years. Cray had once been rejected by Christow, and she is reluctant to divulge any details to Hercule Poirot after the doctor is murdered.

Cregan, Pam   An eighteen-year-old girl in "Problem at Sea." She latches on to Colonel Clapperton and encourages him to vex his wife. Unfortunately, Mrs. Clapperton is murdered in her cabin.

Cresswell, Mrs.   The second wife of a brother-in-law to Mrs. Greenshaw in "Greenshaw's Folly." She lives and works on Mrs. Greenshaw's estate, called Greenshaw's Folly, for little money save room and board on the assumption that she will inherit the estate, despite having no particular claim to the property. The inheritance seems incontestable, however, after Mrs. Greenshaw apparently wills the estate to her and has the document legally witnessed.

Crispin, Angus   A member of British intelligence who is assigned to protect Tommy and Tuppence Beresford in *Postern of Fate.* His presence is a secret, and he assumes a useful alias. He manages to save Tommy's life after a third attempt is made to kill him.

Crockett   A servant in the house of Monica Deane in "The Clergyman's Daughter" and "The Red House." She is an elderly and very unpleasant woman who assumes that because her sister was successful in marrying above her station that she shares in the elevated status of her relative.

Croft, Bert   The presumably Australian husband of Milly Croft in *Peril at End House.* He attempts to appear friendly, open, and extremely Australian, but Hercule Poirot regards him with some suspicion.

Croft, Milly   The wife of Bert Croft in *Peril at End House.* Like her husband, she attempts to appear extremely Australian and is somewhat unconvincingly confined to a wheelchair. Inspector Japp, however, is fairly certain that he and Mrs. Croft have met before.

Crofton Lee, Sir Rupert   A well-known explorer and traveler in *They Came to Baghdad* who searches for a site in China where he knows that a secret weapon is being built. He is killed when he finds the location, but the information, fortunately, is passed along.

Croker   A nickname used by Mr. Lavington in "The Veiled Lady."

Crome, Inspector   A Scotland Yard investigator who is officially in charge of the inquiry into *The A.B.C. Murders.* He is the subject of a disagreement between Poirot and Hastings.

Cronshaw, Lord Conch   A young nobleman who is murdered in "The Affair at the Victory Ball." One fateful evening, he and his party were dressed as members of a harlequinade, and Cronshaw was disguised as Harlequin. Soon after an unpleasant exchange with his fiancée, Coco Courtenay, he is found stabbed to death. His uncle, the Honourable Eustace Beltane, inherits Cronshaw's title (not to mention his wealth) and is also mentioned in "The Adventure of 'The Western Star.' "

Crosbie, Captain   A police operative in *They Came to Baghdad.* He is described as having "protuberant eyes."

Crossfield, Superintendent   A very officious policeman who heads the investigation into the murder of Sir Bartholomew Strange in *Three-Act Tragedy.* He is most opposed to any civilian interference in his investigation.

Crossfield, George   A relative of the Abernethie family in *After the Funeral.* He is a poor investor and so is in desperate need of money, making him a leading suspect in the case.

Crotchet, Mr.   See Simpson, Mr.

Crowther, Sydney   A very close friend and associate of Hercule Poirot in *The Big Four;* he is officially designated the executor of the detective's will. He is also secretary of state for home affairs.

Crozier, Deirdre   The wife of George Crozier in "While the Light Lasts." She is happily married to George, but he was not her first choice of husbands. Deirdre originally married Tim Nugent, but he was supposedly killed in World War I during a campaign in Africa. It thus comes as a terrible blow to discover that Tim is still alive.

Crozier, George The husband of Deirdre Crozier in "While the Light Lasts." He has long loved Deirdre, but was not her first choice in marriage. That person was Tim Nugent. He died in World War I, however, and Deirdre consented to marry George. He has tried to provide her with everything she could want and more, including a diamond and a tobacco plantation.

Crump, Mr. A butler in *A Pocket Full of Rye.* He is married to the extremely talented cook Mrs. Crump, and relies on the popularity of his wife's food as a guarantee that he will keep his job, despite his own considerable failings as a butler.

Cunningham, Dr. Alice A young psychologist in "The Capture of Cerberus." She is engaged to Niki Rossakoff, son of Countess Vera Rossakoff, and enjoys spending a great deal of time in the celebrated nightclub Hell. Her habits are of particular interest to Hercule Poirot, who noted especially her peculiar attire—dowdy clothes with big pockets.

Curry, Inspector The chief investigating officer in the murder of Christian Gulbrandsen in *They Do It with Mirrors.* He is a discreet officer who does not seek headlines.

Curry, R. H. The mysterious name printed on business cards found in the possession of a murder victim in *The Clocks.* The victim is subsequently identified, and the coroner determines that he was first poisoned and then stabbed to death.

Curtain, Miss The chief of a hospital's ward maids (or nurses) in *Giant's Bread.* She is described as tall and thin, with "a face like a dreaming duchess."

Curtis, Inspector A police investigator in "The Love Detectives."

Curtis, Mr. A one-time gardener at Sittaford House in *The Sittaford Mystery.* Although married, to Amelia Curtis, he is a dedicated misogynist who believes that women talk too much and do not know "the truth of what they are talking about."

Curtis, Mrs. A Red Cross official in *Giant's Bread.* She is considered pompous and incompetent in the execution of her duties.

Curtis, Amelia A day servant in *The Sittaford Mystery.* She is quite observant and sees through the efforts of Enderby and Emily Trefusis to impersonate cousins while in a hotel. She is married to Mr. Curtis.

Curtis, Sir Ralph See Alloway, Lord.

Curtiss The successor to the esteemed manservant George (or Georges) to Hercule Poirot in *Curtain.* Although George is of the view that Curtiss is not quite up to the standards on which Poirot would normally insist, Curtiss must do, as George is off to take care of his ailing father. Curtiss' large build and physical strength are of use to Poirot, for the manservant must carry the dying detective each day to and from the garden.

Curtiss, Major A party guest in *The Mystery of the Baghdad Chest.* He was in attendance at the time that Edward Clayton was apparently murdered. He was a friend of both Edward Clayton and his beautiful wife, Marguerita Clayton.

Cust, Alexander Bonaparte The chief suspect in *The A.B.C. Murders.* Given a truly grand name by his late mother with the hopes that he would be inspired to great deeds, Cust proved terribly unequal to his namesakes. He is a weak-willed and very impressionable salesman and becomes convinced that he is involved in the A.B.C. murders. His fears seem confirmed when, returning to his hotel from a theater in Doncaster, he discovers blood on his cuff and a bloody knife in his pocket. The fourth victim of the A.B.C. murderer is soon found in the same theater, stabbed to death, with an open *A.B.C. Rail Guide* in his pocket. Fearing that he has lost his mind, Cust turns himself in to the police, who remand him for trial. Poirot, however, has doubts about Cust's guilt.

Cyril The brother of Celia in *Unfinished Portrait.* With his jovial personality, Cyril bears a striking similarity to Agatha Christie's own brother, Louis Miller, just as Celia is remarkably similar to Dame Agatha herself.

Czarnova, Countess   An aging noblewoman in "The Soul of the Croupier." She is a proud aristocrat who has enjoyed many lovers, but whose fortunes have taken a distinct turn downward. She also bears a secret from her past.

Dacre, Major   A young officer in the British army in *Giant's Bread.* He has little to offer because of his lowly rank and his lack of money.

Dacre, Denis   The name used by Denis Davis while engaged in his unusual activity in "The Bloodstained Pavement." He and his wife, Margery, have an apparently chance meeting with Carol Harding in the Cornish village of Rathole. Soon after, Margery Dacre is found dead from a suspicious drowning accident. One year later, he returns to Rathole with a new wife, Joan, and has another chance meeting with Carol.

Dacre, Joan   The second wife of Denis Dacre in "The Bloodstained Pavement." A year after the mysterious death by drowning of Margery Dacre in the Cornish village of Rathole, she and Denis return to the site in Cornwall and have a chance encounter with Carol Harding.

Dacre, Margery   The first wife of Denis Dacre in "The Bloodstained Pavement." She and Denis visit the Cornish village of Rathole and have a chance encounter with an old friend of Denis's, Carol Harding. Soon after, Margery dies from drowning under suspicious circumstances.

Dacres, Mr.   A solicitor in *The Sittaford Mystery.* He looks after the legal interests of Emily Trefusis and thus represents her fiancé, James Pearson, when he is accused of murdering his uncle, Captain Trevelyan. Dacres seems to hold little hope for his release, but he does believe that Pearson is innocent of the crime.

Dacres, Cynthia   A suspect in the murder of Sir Bartholomew Strange in *Three-Act Tragedy.* A dress designer, she is known to have a very fiery temper and was angry with Sir Strange, and is thus a suspect. She is married to Freddie Dacres.

Dacres, Captain Freddie   The husband of the fiery Cynthia Dacres in *Three-Act Tragedy.* He is devoted to racehorses.

Dakin, Mr.   An intelligence officer in *They Came to Baghdad.* He does little to impress his field agents at first because of his apparent lethargy—or even laziness—which he uses as a mask for his very sharp mind.

Dale, Sylvia   A young woman in "The Sign in the Sky." She is absolutely convinced that Martin Wylde is innocent of murdering Lady Barnaby, and she enlists the aid of Mr. Satterthwaite in proving it.

Dalehouse, Harry   The nephew of Sir Hubert Lytcham Roche in "The Second Gong." He resides at Lytcham Close and is thus very familiar with the nightly routine involving the sounding of gongs to announce that dinner is served. He thus expresses surprise when the routine is disrupted by the arrival of Hercule Poirot.

Danahan, Syd   The long-suffering and faithful manager to Olga Stormer in "The Actress." He makes suggestions to assist Olga out of a predicament with a blackmailer, but she chides him for not being subtle enough.

Dane Calthrop, Reverend Caleb   The vicar of Much Deeping, who appears in several cases with his wife, Maud. An elderly and scholarly cleric, he appears in *The Moving Finger* and *The Pale Horse.* He has the interesting ability to summon a perfect Latin quote for virtually any occasion. His scholarly habits and personality leave him rather scatterbrained, and he relies on Maud to maintain his orderly existence.

Dane Calthrop, Maud   The wife of Reverend Caleb Dane Calthrop, vicar of Much Deeping. Whereas her husband is scholarly and rather disorganized, Maud is very well organized and keeps her husband's affairs in excellent order. She appears with her husband in *The Moving Finger* and *The Pale Horse.*

Daniels, Captain   A former officer in the army

who served as secretary to the prime minister in "The Kidnapped Prime Minister." While little is known about him or his family, Daniels was chosen by the prime minister to serve as his secretary for a trip to France because of his remarkable linguistic skills. He is found gagged, bound, and chloroformed in the car that was carrying the prime minister and is thus a suspect in the kidnapping.

Darnley, Rosamund   A successful business-woman in *Evil under the Sun,* she runs a dress-making company called Rose Mond, Ltd. She is a longtime friend of Kenneth Marshall and is thus distressed to see him so unhappily married to Arlena Marshall. Rosamund becomes a suspect when Arlena is found dead, but she subsequently marries Kenneth Marshall and starts a new life with him and his daughter.

Darrell, Claud   A brilliant but mysterious figure in *The Big Four.* A onetime actor who abandoned the stage, Darrell becomes the target of Hercule Poirot's investigation, but he proves quite elusive, thanks to his ability to adopt completely different aliases and disguises. In the course of events, Darrell portrays a Russian chess master, a doctor, and a footman.

Darrell, Richard   The husband of the formidable Theodora Darrell in "Magnolia Blossom." He is employed by the firm Hobson, Jekyll, and Lucas, and comes home one day to inform his wife that the firm has gone under through illegal activities. In order to protect himself, Darrell asks Theodora to help him in a way that is reprehensible and shatters their marriage.

Darrell, Theodora   The wife of Richard Darrell in "Magnolia Blossom." She intends to leave her husband but is confronted by the news that he is involved in terrible legal trouble. To assist him, she embarks upon what Darrell thinks is the ultimate sacrifice of self-respect. Through allowing—even encouraging—Richard to ask her to undertake this act of help, Theodora finds great personal strength.

Dashwood, Everett   A young reporter in "The Augean Stables." He is determined to make his name in journalism and is willing to do anything to achieve his aims. He thus is delighted to help Hercule Poirot in his effort against a rival newspaper.

Da Silva, Mrs.   One of the aliases used by a member of a smuggling ring in *Hickory Dickory Dock.*

Daubreuil, Madame   A woman in *Murder on the Links* who has a very dark past. After her involvement in a crime for which she was acquitted, she changed her name to Madame Daubreuil and moved to southern France. She exudes great charm and beauty despite her advancing years, especially entrancing Captain Hastings. Her daughter is Marthe Daubreuil.

Daubreuil, Marthe   The twenty-two-year-old daughter of Madame Daubreuil and her late former husband in *Murder on the Links.* Like her mother, Marthe has an easy time enchanting Captain Hastings.

Daubreuil, Raoul   The fiancé of Madame Simone, a famous psychic, in "The Last Séance." He is concerned about Simone's determination to hold a séance despite her failing health.

Davenheim, Mr.   The senior partner of Davenheim and Salmon, "well-known bankers and financiers," in "The Disappearance of Mr. Davenheim." His sudden and inexplicable disappearance brings Hercule Poirot into the investigation, an involvement that leads to the uncovering of embezzlement and attempted murder.

Davenheim, Mrs.   The wife of Mr. Davenheim, senior partner of Davenheim and Salmon, in "The Disappearance of Mr. Davenheim." The fact that she and her husband ceased some time ago to sleep in the same room is a vital clue to Hercule Poirot.

Daventry, Mr.   The assistant to the administrator of St. Honoré Island in *A Caribbean Mystery.* Following the murder of Major Palgrave, Daventry is consulted by Dr. Graham.

Daventry, Vera (Socks)   An active young woman who is invited to the Chimneys by Lord and Lady Coote in *The Seven Dials Mystery.*

David, Lucy The cook in the household of Simon Clode in "Motive vs. Opportunity." She was "a fresh buxom young woman of thirty."

Davidson, Mrs. The wife of Chris Davidson in "The Affair at the Victory Ball." Attending the costume ball with her husband, she dresses as Pierette; Chris dresses as Pierrot. She is one of the party guests who discovers the remains of Lord Cronshaw.

Davidson, Chris The husband of Mrs. Davidson in "The Affair at the Victory Ball." He attends the costume party with his wife and the friends of Lord Cronshaw dressed as Pierrot; his wife dresses as Pierette.

Davis A steward on the flight during which Madame Giselle is murdered in *Death in the Clouds.*

Davis, Carol See Harding, Carol.

Davis, Denis See Dacre, Denis.

Davis, Giles The proprietor of the Monkswell Manor boardinghouse in "Three Blind Mice." A morose man, he is married to the beautiful Molly Davis and is firmly convinced that his wife is having an affair with Christopher Wren.

Davis, Jesse An employee of the *Customer's Reaction Classified* in *The Pale Horse.* She dies and has a minister summoned to her deathbed. As she expires, Jesse gives Father Gorman a list of nine names that prove very important in unraveling the secrets of the Pale Horse Inn.

Davis, Molly The young wife of Giles Davis in "Three Blind Mice." She runs, with her husband, the Monkswell Manor boardinghouse. Her husband is convinced that she is having an affair with Christopher Wren.

Davy, Chief Inspector Fred An avuncular officer at Scotland Yard who investigates the disappearance of Canon Pennyfeather in *At Bertram's Hotel.* He is a pleasant and popular detective at Scotland Yard, where he is known affectionately as Father. It does not take long for him to look into the events surrounding the disappearance of Pennyfeather and to come into

Inspector Davy (George Baker) in At Bertram's Hotel. *(Photofest)*

contact with Miss Marple—thereby deducing that things are not what they seem at Bertram's Hotel.

Dawes, Rhoda See Despard, Rhoda Dawes.

Dawlish, Lord The real name of one of the passengers traveling in Egypt in *Death on the Nile.* While at Oxford, he embraced communism and adopted a new name that he uses when abroad.

Deacon, Phillis The wife of a baronet in *Giant's Bread.* She enjoys indulging in the art of matchmaking.

Deane, Molly The "very charming . . . very beautiful girl" who is engaged to John Harrison in "Wasps' Nest." She was previously engaged to Claude Langton but left him for Harrison.

Deane, Monica The title character in "The Clergyman's Daughter." She inherits the Red House from her aunt and moves in with her mother. The two decide to convert the home into a guest house, but they are soon troubled

The stunning Molly Deane (Melanie Jessop), the object of two men's love, in "Wasps' Nest." (Photofest; London Weekend Television)

by apparent poltergeist activity. Monica turns to Tommy and Tuppence Beresford for help.

De Bathe, Colonel   One of the numerous aliases used by Major Eustace in "Murder in the Mews."

De Bellefort, Jacqueline   Known commonly as Jackie, the former fiancée of Simon Doyle and the onetime best friend of Doyle's new wife, Linnet Doyle, in *Death on the Nile*. Crushed by what she apparently sees as a perfidious betrayal by two people who have been most dear to her, Jackie pursues the new couple on their honeymoon in order to harass and inconvenience them. Her hunt reaches its climax in Egypt—despite the warning from Hercule Poirot that she should give up and go home—on board the steamer *Karnak* as it sails on the Nile. Jackie becomes drunk and accidentally shoots Simon. Later that night, someone uses the same pistol to murder Linnet Doyle and Jackie becomes an immediate suspect when the initial *J* is found scrawled in blood next to Linnet's body.

Debenham, Mary Hermione   One of the passengers aboard the Calais Coach in *Murder on the Orient Express*. She is heading from India to England via the Orient Express and is on board at the time of the murder of Ratchett. When

interviewed by Hercule Poirot, she unknowingly reveals details of her past, including the fact that she had been in America.

Debrugh, Major Johnnie   A wealthy middle-aged soldier in *Unfinished Portrait*. He asks Celia to marry him and attempts to sway her rather unmoved heart with a variety of gifts.

De Castina, Mrs.   The name used by a talented actress while adopting an alias in *The Man in the Brown Suit*. She is also known as the Russian dancer Nadina and a traveler named Mrs. Grey.

de Haviland, Edith Elfrida   The sister-in-law of Aristide Leonides in *Crooked House*. Her sister had been married to Aristide, and, after her sister's death, Edith agreed to assist him in raising his seven children. She never became fond of Aristide, however, and is appalled by Aristide's decision to wed a twenty-four-year-old former waitress.

Delafontaine, Henry   The husband of the domineering Mary Delafontaine in "How Does Your Garden Grow?" He is "a tall man with grizzled hair . . . it was plain that he expected her to take the lead in any conversation." Following his wife's lead, he is hostile to the Russian companion of his wife's aunt, Katrina, implying to Poirot that she might be involved with Bolsheviks.

Delafontaine, Mary The niece of Miss Barrowby in "How Does Your Garden Grow?" She is married to the weak-willed Henry Delafontaine and inherited her aunt's house and estate following her sudden death. Miss Barrowby wrote to Poirot and asked him to save her from murder, but he arrives too late.

Delangua, Paul A young man and friend of Sir James and Lady Dwighton in "The Love Detectives." He is known to be a libertine and is tossed out of the Dwighton house when Sir James finds him in an apparently compromising situation with Lady Laura Dwighton. When Sir James is found murdered, Delangua becomes a suspect and actually confesses. His apparent admission is discounted, however, because it is thought that he is protecting Lady Laura.

de la Roche, Comte Armand A supposed nobleman in *The Mystery of the Blue Train.* He is a successful blackmailer of young and wealthy women, seducing them to the point that they fall under his influence, at which time he reveals his true nature. He managed to win the confidence of Ruth Kettering and is on his way to meet her—and her fabulous Heart of Fire rubies—when she is murdered aboard the Blue Train.

de la Rochefour, Count Armand A disreputable nobleman in "The Plymouth Express." He managed to win the trust of the Honourable Flossie Carrington and was on his way to meet with her (and her jewels) when she was murdered and her jewels stolen on the Plymouth Express.

Demetrius the Black Browed The feared head of a group of Greek jewel thieves in "The Oracle at Delphi." He is a clever thief who adopts the alias of a gifted sleuth to separate wealthy women from their jewels.

Demiroff, Olga Also known as Olga Vassilovna, a Russian prostitute in *The Mystery of the Blue Train.* She has dealings with Comte Armand de la Roche and assists him in hiding stolen jewels.

Denby, Mr. The financial overseer of Styles Court in *The Mysterious Affair at Styles.* He provides Alfred Inglethorp with a seemingly unshakable alibi for the night that Emily Inglethorp was murdered.

Denman, Mr. The father of Geoffrey Denman in "The Thumb Mark of Saint Peter." He "was what is called 'not quite right in the head.' Quite peaceful and well-behaved, but distinctly odd at times." When his son dies under grim circumstances, members of the household are reluctant to inform him, as they are concerned about distressing him.

Denman, Anna The wife of John Denman in "Harlequin's Lane." She was originally named Anna Kharsanova and was once one of the world's greatest ballerinas. She gave up her career to wed Denman and adopt a quiet, ultimately despair-filled lifestyle in the English countryside. Through the intervention of Mr. Harley Quin, she is permitted one last magnificent performance.

Denman, Geoffrey Husband of Mabel Denman in "The Thumb Mark of St. Peter." He "was a man of very violent temper—not the kind of man who would be patient with Mabel's foibles." After a severe quarrel with his wife, Denman dies in agony from poisoning. He rambles incoherently before his death about what sounds like fish. His widow is soon suspected of the crime.

Denman, John A stolid and unimaginative Englishman who won the hand in marriage of the brilliant ballerina Anna Kharsanova in "Harlequin Lane." He lives in the English countryside with his wife, barely comprehending the despair that has gripped her.

Denman, Mabel A niece of Miss Marple who is rescued from suspicion of murder in "The Thumb Mark of Saint Peter." She married a violent man named Geoffrey Denman and took up residence with his household, including his increasingly senile father. Suddenly, after ten years of unhappy marriage, Geoffrey dies from apparent poisoning. Within a short time, Mabel is suspected of the crime and calls upon

Miss Marple to free her from the chains of suspicion. Her aunt describes her as "fond of being melodramatic and of saying a great deal more than she meant whenever she was upset."

Denman, Mary A housemaid in *Unfinished Portrait*. She remains with Celia's family despite their crushing financial hardships, but she departs their service when they become sound financially and decide to move to the country.

Depleach, Sir Montague A flamboyant and successful lawyer in *Five Little Pigs*. He takes up the challenge of defending Caroline Crale on the charge of murder, but he encounters stiff resistance from his own client, who refuses to assist him in defending her. Caroline Crale is subsequently convicted and dies after a year in prison.

Dering, Martin The husband of Sylvia Dering, niece of the murdered Captain Trevelyan in *The Sittaford Mystery*. A passably successful author, he claims that he was not present at the dinner and séance held during the time that Trevelyan was murdered.

Dering, Sylvia The wife of Martin Dering and the niece of the murdered Captain Trevelyan in *The Sittaford Mystery*.

Dermot A young, handsome man who wins the heart of Celia—much to her deep later sadness—in *Unfinished Portrait*. He proves an unfaithful and unsympathetic husband who enters into an affair while his wife is occupied with grief for her mother. Dermot subsequently leaves Celia to marry his secretary.

There is a close similarity between Dermot and Agatha Christie's first husband, Colonel Archibald Christie. (See page 1 for other details.)

Déroulard, Madame An old woman and the mother of the murdered Baron Paul Déroulard in "The Chocolate Box." She suffers from cataracts, uses atropine, and thus has very poor eyesight.

Déroulard, Monsieur le Baron Paul An eminent French deputy and politician in "The Chocolate Box." He was a rabid anti-Catholic and was rising rapidly in the government at the time of his sudden death. He had married some

years before and had used the money of his wife—who died in an accidental fall—to promote his political career. He had a passion for chocolate, a fact of some importance in discovering his murderer.

de Rushbridger, Margaret A victim of murder in *Three-Act Tragedy*. She is confined to a sanitarium for an uncertain reason but manages to send a communication to Hercule Poirot asking him to meet with her on a matter of some importance. Before he can meet with her, however, she is murdered by means of a box of poisoned chocolates.

Derwent, Lady Frances (Frankie) The adventurous young woman who joins Bobby Jones in his investigation into murder in *Why Didn't They Ask Evans?* The daughter of Lord Marchington, she finds her life of wealth and ease to be unfulfilling and is thus delighted to assist her childhood friend Jones in hunting down a murderer. A clever and energetic young woman, she shares a series of adventures with Jones and decides at the end to marry him and move to Kenya.

de Sara, Madeleine An associate of Mr. Parker Pyne who assists him whenever those cases require a skilled and beautiful actress to assume a variety of personae. Born Maggie Sayers, the fourth daughter of a hardworking family in Streatham, Madeleine is able to transform herself into such diverse characters as the Grand Duchess Olga ("The Case of the City Clerk"), the dancer Sanchia ("The Case of the Distressed Lady"), and Delores Ramone ("Problem at Pollensa Bay"). Parker Pyne acknowledges Madeleine's beauty and allure by calling her the Queen of Vamps.

Desjardeaux, Monsieur The premier of France in *The Big Four*. He is amazed when Hercule Poirot identifies a very surprising individual as a member of an international conspiracy threatening the stability of Europe.

Despard, Colonel John Hugh One of the four suspects in the murder of Mr. Shaitana in *Cards on the Table*. A military man, he is also an expert hunter and enjoys safaris. Eventually cleared as a suspect, he nevertheless provides valuable information to Hercule Poirot about Shaitana and saves Rhoda Dawes from drowning when she is hurled into a river by another suspect. The colonel marries Rhoda and retires to the country with his bride. He and Rhoda make another appearance, in *The Pale Horse,* in which they are shown to be living happily in Much Deeping.

Despard, Rhoda Dawes　The wife of Colonel John Despard in *Cards on the Table* and *The Pale Horse.* Rhoda is first introduced in *Cards on the Table,* in which she initially shares a flat with Anne Meredith. Suspected for a time in the murder of Mr. Shaitana, she is later saved from death by drowning when Colonel Despard jumps in a river to save her. She subsequently marries him and they move to Much Deeping, where they share an idyllic existence and are still happily married in *The Pale Horse.* Mark Easterbrook, the main character in *Pale Horse,* is her cousin.

Dessin, Armand　A prefect of the Paris police in *Death in the Clouds.* He assists Hercule Poirot in his investigation into the murder of Madame Giselle.

de Toredo, Señora Angelica　One of the names used by Ann Shapland, the cabaret dancer in *Cat among the Pigeons.*

Devereaux, Ronny　An intelligence operative in *The Seven Dials Mystery.* He is shot and then is accidentally run over by Lady Eileen Brent. Before he finally dies, however, Devereaux is able to whisper an important message to Lady Eileen. His code name is Number Two.

Deveril　The butler in the service of Sir Carmichael Clarke in *The A.B.C. Murders.* His employer is murdered by the A.B.C. killer.

Deverill, Christine　One of the aliases used by an accomplice to murder in *Evil under the Sun.*

Deyre, Myra　The mother of Vernon Deyre in *Giant's Bread.* She is married to the serially unfaithful Walter Deyre and endures severe heartbreak when Walter leaves her. The bitter fights between Myra and Walter are a source of lingering trauma for their son.

Deyre, Vernon　The son of Myra and Walter Deyre and a would-be composer in *Giant's Bread.* Raised in a household torn apart by the adultery of his father, Vernon grows into adulthood on his beloved estate, Abbots Puissants, and is confronted at the age of twenty-one with the prospect of losing his home. He secretly longs to compose music and is encouraged in his aspiration by Jane Harding and eventually marries Nell Vereker. Going off to war, Vernon is thought to have been killed in the trenches, but returns home with a case of amnesia. After a series of traumatic adventures, he recovers his memory with the help of Jane and ultimately is forced to choose between Jane and Nell in a matter of life and death.

Deyre, Walter　The father of Vernon Deyre and husband of Myra Deyre in *Giant's Bread.* He is a perpetually unfaithful husband who eventually leaves his family.

Digby, Captain　A friend of Lord Cronshaw in "The Affair at the Victory Ball." He discovers Cronshaw's body at the ball.

Digby, Mr.　The butler at Lytcham Close in "The Second Gong." Among his many duties, the most important is to ring the gong twice, summoning the members of the household to dinner.

Digby, Sir Stanley　The air minister for Britain in *The Seven Dials Mystery.* He is determined to secure control of a formula for a new type of metal.

Dinsmead, Mr.　The head of the Dinsmead household in "SOS." While outwardly friendly and open, Mr. Dinsmead actually harbors dark secrets. He is the husband of Maggie Dinsmead and the presumed father of Johnnie, Charlotte, and Magdalen Dinsmead.

Dinsmead, Charlotte　The presumed daughter of Mr. and Mrs. Dinsmead in "SOS." She senses that her life may be in danger and perhaps contacted the psychic investigator Mortimer Cleveland by writing "SOS." in the dust on a dressing table.

Dinsmead, Johnnie　The son of Mr. and Mrs. Dinsmead in "SOS." He has an interest in chemistry and welcomes the psychic investigator Mortimer Cleveland, whom he assists in solving the mystery in the Dinsmead household.

Dinsmead, Magdalen   A daughter of Mr. and Mrs. Dinsmead in "SOS." She may have summoned Mortimer Cleveland's help by scrawling "SOS." into the dust on a dressing table.

Dinsmead, Maggie   The wife of Mr. Dinsmead and the presumed mother of Johnnie, Charlotte, and Magdalen Dinsmead in "SOS." She is prone to extreme emotional outbursts.

Director, Herr   A talented speaker with a dominating personality in *Destination Unknown.* A onetime revivalist preacher, this hypnotic figure is hired by the villainous Aristides to serve as the chief organizer of the Brain Trust complex.

Dittisham, Lady   See Greer, Elsa.

Dittisham, Lord   A nobleman and the third husband of Elsa Greer in *Five Little Pigs.* He is the writer of "fantastical poetic dramas."

Dixon, Gladys   A maid in *The Mirror Crack'd from Side to Side.* She goes into hiding at the insistence of Miss Marple because she has seen too much and is thus in danger of being murdered.

Dobbs, Mr.   A gardener from King's Gnaton who has never left his little village in "The Four Suspects." He is one of the four people considered a possible suspect in the death of Dr. Rosen.

Dodge, Bernard   A member of the war cabinet in the government of Prime Minister David MacAdam and a close personal friend of the P.M. in "The Kidnapped Prime Minister." With Lord Estair, Dodge consults Hercule Poirot in the desperate hope that the detective will be able to recover the missing leader.

Dodo   The nickname of Iris Mullins in *Postern of Fate.*

Donaldson, Dr.   A young physician attending Lady Matilda Checkheaton in *Passenger to Frankfurt.* He has recently replaced Checkheaton's longtime doctor and finds himself struggling to establish a rapport with the gregarious older woman.

Donaldson, Dr. Rex   A physician in *Dumb Witness.* A clever and intelligent doctor, he lacks only the money to become a genuine success.

Donovan, Sheila   One of the many aliases used by an ingenious criminal and smuggler in *Hickory Dickory Dock.* She is also known as Mrs. Da Silva, Mrs. Gladys Thomas, Nina Le Mesurier, Olga Kohn, Mrs. Mahmoudi, Moira O'Neele, and Irene French.

Dortheimer, Lady Naomi   The wife of Sir Reuben Dortheimer in "The Case of the Distressed Lady." She is thoroughly charmed by the attentions of a young man who apparently intends to steal and replace the ring she wears.

Dortheimer, Sir Reuben   The husband of Lady Dortheimer in "The Case of the Distressed Lady." He falls under the charms of one of the many incarnations of the ravishing Madeleine de Sara.

Dove, Mary   The housekeeper of Yewtree Lodge in *A Pocket Full of Rye.* She is exceedingly efficient in her job and also maintains the accounts of the lodge.

Downes, Roger Emmanuel   A target for murder in *The A.B.C. Murders.* He was chosen to become the fourth victim of the A.B.C. murderer and was actually sitting in a movie theater in which the slaying was to take place. Fortunately for him and unfortunately for George Earlsfield, the theater was too dark for the killer to make a perfect identification just before striking.

Doyle, Linnet   A spoiled and extremely wealthy woman who is murdered while on a trip to Egypt in *Death on the Nile.* Linnet Ridgeway, a very affluent heiress, is originally engaged to Lord Charles Windlesham, but her engagement is broken abruptly when she meets and falls in love with Simon Doyle. As it turns out, he is the fiancé of Linnet's best friend, Jackie de Bellefort, who had pleaded with Linnet to give him a job. Marrying Simon after a whirlwind courtship, Linnet sets off with her new husband on a honeymoon that soon turns nightmarish when Jackie stalks them across the globe. While sailing up the Nile in the steamer *Karnak*, Linnet is shot in the head with a small pistol. As it turns out, most of the passengers had very good reasons for wanting her dead.

Doyle, Simon   The good-looking and charming husband of Linnet Doyle in *Death on the Nile*. He was originally a poor fellow who found work in the employ of the wealthy Linnet Doyle at the behest of his fiancée—and Linnet's best friend—Jackie de Bellefort. Within a short time of meeting Linnet, he is involved with her romantically and soon marries her, much to the chagrin of Jackie. The newlyweds set out on a honeymoon and find themselves pursued across the globe by the spiteful Jackie. Finally, while cruising on the Nile on board the steamer *Karnak*, Jackie becomes drunk and shoots Simon in the leg. Later that night, while he recuperates, the same pistol is used to shoot Linnet in the head.

Drage, Lady Cynthia   A friend of Mr. Satterthwaite who teaches young women social skills in "The Shadow on the Glass." She has a tendency to wear too much makeup.

Dragomiroff, Princess Natalia   One of the passengers on board the Calais Coach in *Murder on the Orient Express*. Hercule Poirot considers her to be one of the ugliest old women he has ever seen, possessed of a "yellow, toadlike face." Incredibly, this largely immobile aristocrat becomes a suspect in the murder of Ratchett when one of her handkerchiefs is found in the clue-laden compartment in which Ratchett was stabbed to death. Her companion is Fräulein Hildegard Schmidt.

Drake, Allen   The partner in a Malaysian plantation with Thomas Royde in *Towards Zero*. Whereas Royde is considered taciturn and unsociable, Drake is outgoing and loquacious.

Drake, Hugo   A victim in *Hallowe'en Party*. He was killed by a hit-and-run driver some time before the events recounted in the book. His widow is Rowena Drake.

Drake, Lucilla   The widow of a clergyman, aunt of Rosemary Barton, and mother of Victor Drake in *Sparkling Cyanide*. Her husband died twenty years before, but she continues to dress in mourning garb.

Drake, Rowena Arabella   The widow of Hugo Drake in *Hallowe'en Party*. Her husband was murdered some time before the start of the events recounted in the novel. The organizer of the Halloween party at which Joyce Reynolds is murdered, she displays such vigor when she meets Hercule Poirot that the detective barely knows what to do with her.

Drake, Una   An ingenious young woman in "The Unbreakable Alibi." She makes a wager with the wealthy Montgomery Jones, who is much enamored of her, that she can create an unshakable alibi by being two places at the same time with witnesses to prove it. Jones consults with Tommy and Tuppence Beresford to see if they can shatter Una's alibi.

Drake, Victor   A cousin of the murdered Rosemary Barton and the son of Lucilla Drake in *Sparkling Cyanide*. Also the son of a deceased clergyman, Victor was once a student at Oxford University but was dismissed for forging checks. After that, he moved from job to job, taking positions as a waiter, porter, and politician and adopting assorted aliases, including Monkey Coleman and Pedro Morales.

Draper, Mary   The aunt of the unfortunate Mary Gerrard in *Sad Cypress*. Considered by Poirot to be "a remorseless and unscrupulous woman," she has a long and very checkered past, including a stint as a nurse in New Zealand. Her previous husband died suddenly and mysteriously, leaving her with his considerable wealth.

Driver, Inspector   A Scotland Yard investigator in "Mr. Eastwood's Adventure." He interviews the unlucky Mr. Eastwood after his brush with another Scotland Yard officer.

Driver, Jenny   A friend of Carlotta Adams in *Lord Edgware Dies*. She runs a hat shop.

Drouet, Inspector   A police official and member of the Sûreté in "The Erymanthean Boar." He insinuates himself into the staff of a lodge perched atop the high mountain, Rochers Neiges, and assumes the position of a waiter. Later, he identifies himself to Poirot first as the waiter Gustave and then as Drouet.

Drower, Mary The niece of Alice Ascher, the first victim in *The A.B.C. Murders.* In order to catch the killer of her aunt, Mary enlists in Hercule Poirot's "Special Legion."

Dublay The leader of a gang of international thieves in "The Apples of the Hesperides." He and his group are accused of stealing the Borgia goblet.

Dubois, Martine A French woman who is thought to have been murdered and dumped in a sarcophagus on the estate of the Crackenthorpes in *4.50 from Paddington.* She is involved in the past events that spur the killer into action.

Dubois, Vivian A suave and clever blackmailer who preys on women married to older, feeble husbands in *A Pocket Full of Rye.* He succeeds in attaching himself to Adele Fortescue, who subsequently makes out her will and leaves her money to Dubois.

Dubosc, Colonel A "gallant Frenchman" on leave from service in Syria who is one of the travelers in the Jordanian desert in "The Pearl of Price." The colonel is of the view that honesty is relative; that it is a convention with different meanings in different countries and among different peoples. This view is one of several expressed in discussions surrounding the theft of an expensive earring and its recovery by Mr. Parker Pyne.

Dubosc, Lieutenant A young French officer who escorts Hercule Poirot to his awaiting train in Syria in *Murder on the Orient Express.*

Duguesclin, Quentin The real name of Mr. R. H. Curry in *The Clocks.* His corpse is discovered with only one source of identification: a business card bearing the name R. H. Curry.

Duke, Mr. A onetime chief inspector of Scotland Yard in *The Sittaford Mystery.* He has taken to believing in séances and the occult and attends the séance at which the death of Captain Trevelyan is reported through a medium.

Dundas, George A young man who desires the wealthy and beautiful Mary Montresor in "The Golden Ball." He is fired from his job by his uncle for failing to go after the "golden ball" of business and thus seemingly has little to offer Mary. She picks him up in her car and provides him with an extemporaneous means of impressing her sufficiently to win her hand.

Dunlop, Sister An army nurse in *Giant's Bread.* She is considered pleasant and rather docile.

Dunn, Eliza The title character in "The Adventure of the Clapham Cook." A good cook, she is lured away from her employment in the house of the unpleasant Mr. and Mrs. Todd for the possibility of her own house and yearly income. Her newfound fortune, however, comes with a price and is not what she thinks.

Dupont, Armand A French archaeologist in *Death in the Clouds.* He was a passenger on the flight on which Madame Giselle is murdered and is a suspect in her death because of the presence of Kurdish pipes in his luggage. Hercule Poirot, however, does not consider him to be a likely murderer, as his mind is not on the present but on events that took place in 5,000 B.C. His son is Jean Dupont.

Dupont, Jean The son of the French archaeologist Armand Dupont in *Death in the Clouds.* Like his father, Jean is considered a suspect in the airborne murder of Madame Giselle. He claims, rather flamboyantly, that he might consider killing a beautiful woman who had driven him mad with jealousy, but he would never kill such an ugly crone as Madame Giselle.

Durand, Sir George A solicitor in "The Fourth Man." He takes part in a grim discussion aboard a train about murder and death that also engrosses a doctor, a cleric, and a psychologist.

Durrance, Mr. A onetime photographer in *Postern of Fate.* Tuppence Beresford consults with him after finding a photograph album in the home she and Tommy purchase. He provides her with information about past events.

Durrant, Amy An English woman who apparently drowns in "The Companion." She had been a traveling companion to Mary Barton and had worked for her for around five months when they journeyed to the Grand Canary Island. There, she drowned. In investigating her death, Dr. Lloyd had been unable to discover much about her past other than that she had been orphaned at an early age, had been raised by an uncle, and had made her own living since the age of twenty-one. Adding to the mystery is the question of whether Miss Barton had deliberately drowned her companion. (See Barton, Mary.)

Durrant, Mary Two women who appeared in different novels. The first was the wife of the paralyzed former pilot in *Ordeal by Innocence*. She is obsessed with taking care of her husband and thus reduces him to a truly helpless cripple. Her adoptive mother, Rachel Argyle, was murdered, and her husband undertakes to discover her killer. The second Mary Durrant was a young woman who transports a case of expensive miniatures in "Double Sin." She claims to be working for her aunt, Elizabeth Penn, an antiques dealer in Ebermouth, and has the miniatures stolen from her luggage while traveling by bus. Captain Hastings is drawn to her auburn hair.

Durrant, Philip A paralyzed former pilot in *Ordeal by Innocence*. Stricken with polio, he is confined to a wheelchair and receives such attentive care from his wife that she is perhaps unconsciously trying to reduce him to an utter cripple. Despite his infirmities and his wife's excessive and obsessive care, he undertakes to discover who murdered his mother-in-law, Rachel Argyle.

Dutch Pedro A thief and blackmailer in *The Secret of Chimneys*. He gives to Jimmy McGrath a set of what he believes are love letters in gratitude for McGrath's saving his life.

Duval, Aristide One of the names used by the stage actor Sir Charles Cartwright in *Three-Act Tragedy*.

Duveen, Bella The sister of Dulcie Duveen in *Murder on the Links*. She and her twin sister are American-born former vaudeville performers who find themselves in Europe, caught up in events surrounding the murder of Paul Renauld.

Duveen, Dulcie See Hastings, Dulcie Duveen.

Dwighton, Sir James A thoroughly unpleasant man in "The Love Detectives." He terrorizes and abuses his wife, Lady Laura Dwighton, and fires his butler on a flimsy pretext without giving him references. To no one's surprise or particular grief, he is found dead in his library with his head battered in by a bronze statue.

Dwighton, Lady Laura The abused and long-suffering wife of Sir James Dwighton in "The Love Detectives." Owing to her dress and overall appearance, she looks like "a visitor from another world." Her husband is found in his library with his skull smashed by a bronze statue.

Dyer A "broken-down European" in "The Lost Mine." He is seemingly implicated in the murder of the Chinese businessman Wu Ling because of his known involvement with the Chinese underworld.

Dymchurch, Detective Inspector A supposed police officer in "The Adventure of the Sinister Stranger." He brings an apparent warning of danger to Tommy and Tuppence Beresford.

Dyson, Greg An American botanist in *A Caribbean Mystery*. He and his wife, Lucky, visit the island of St. Honoré each year with their friends Colonel and Evelyn Hillingdon, but this year's visit ends in tragedy. Lucky is found drowned. Although he loves his wife, Dyson does have a habit of flirting with other women. Also, the medicine he takes for his heart condition is found in the room of one of the other victims.

Dyson, Lucky The second wife of the American botanist Greg Dyson in *A Caribbean Mystery*. She is loved very much by her husband, but she won his proposal of marriage through manipulation and with the help of a family friend, Colonel Hillingdon, with whom she once had an affair. Traveling to the island of St. Honoré with her husband on their annual vacation with Colonel Hillingdon and his wife, Lucky is drowned in a creek.

Eardsley, John One of the many aliases adopted by Harry Redburn in *The Man in the Brown Suit.*

Earl, William An assistant gardener in *The Mysterious Affair at Styles.* He is instructed to witness the will drawn up by Emily Inglethorp on the day before she dies.

Earlsfield, George One of the victims in *The A.B.C. Murders.* He is stabbed to death in a movie theater, but his murder is considered by Poirot and the police to have been a mistake. The reason for this assumption is that his name ends with an *E,* and the next logical target for murder was someone whose last name began with a *D.* It is thus presumed that the killer struck Earlsfield down in the dark theater by accident.

Easterbrook, Doreen The married name of Katherine "Ginger" Corrigan in *The Pale Horse.*

Easterbrook, Mark A young archaeologist and friend of Ariadne Oliver in *The Pale Horse.* He is also a cousin of Rhoda Despard and the godson of Lady Hesketh-Dubois, the person through whom he becomes embroiled in the murderous events in Much Deeping. He decides to investigate the many mysterious deaths in the area. Easterbrook attends a church social with Ariadne Oliver and is trying to finish work on a book on Mogul architecture.

Easterfield, Lord A wealthy newspaper publisher in *Murder Is Easy.* He is engaged to Bridget Conway, who does not love him and has consented to be his wife only for financial reasons. That is hardly surprising, for while Easterfield wields considerable power and influence, he has clawed his way to the top—his original name was Gordon Ragg—from obscurity by the successful operation of his as-

sorted publications, described as "nasty little weekly newspapers." He is a suspect in the multiple murders that have taken place in Wychwood, and is seemingly directly tied to the death of Lavinia Fullerton through his Rolls Royce, which was used to run her down. He seems to add to the likelihood of his guilt when he threatens Luke Fitzwilliam and Bridget after they reveal that they have fallen in love.

Eastley, Alexander The son of Bryan Eastley and hence a prospective heir to the Crackenthorpe estate in *4.50 from Paddington.* A clever and precocious lad, he treats Bryan more like a brother than a father, knowing that Bryan has never recovered from the death of his wife (Alexander's mother) or from his sudden transition to civilian life after a heroic career in the RAF during World War II. Alexander desires his father to remarry, taking the initiative in suggesting a union between Bryan and the eminently marriageable Lucy Eylesbarrow.

Eastley, Bryan The father of Alexander Eastley and a member of the Crackenthorpe family by marriage (his late wife was the daughter of old Luther Crackenthorpe) in *4.50 from Paddington.* A distinguished pilot during World War II, he has encountered trouble in adjusting to civilian life and to being a widower. His clever son senses this and thus is quite protective of his father.

Eastney, Phil A young and spiteful man in "The Face of Helen." He works in a glass factory and is also genuinely skilled in music. He puts these two abilities to fiendish use, creating a diabolical if not highly improbable means of exacting revenge upon Gillian West for spurning his romantic aspirations.

Easton, Vincent The lover of Theodora Darrell in *Magnolia Blossom.* Easton hopes to run away with Theodora to South Africa, but his plans are cut short when she discovers that her husband faces total financial ruin. Easton, however, proves of critical importance to both Theodora and her husband when it is learned that he possesses papers that could lead to Richard Darrell's imprisonment.

Eastwood, Anthony The title character in "Mr. Eastwood's Adventure." A mystery writer who suffers from writer's block, he is unable to concoct a suitable plot for a story with the rather unpromising title of "The Mystery of the Second Cucumber." He is saved from literary panic by a mysterious phone call that sets him on a series of adventures, climaxing in encounters with two sets of police officers.

Ebenthal, Bertha The real name of a German operative in "The Kidnapped Prime Minister."

Eberhard, Herr A crude but clever inventor who creates a desirable formula for strengthening steel in *The Seven Dials Mystery.* Although he is an obnoxious, nail-biting scientist, Eberhard has managed to create steel wire with the strength of a bar of steel, an invention of the greatest interest to the British government as well as to the secret society that assembles at the Seven Dials.

Eccles, Mr. Two men who appeared in different cases. The first is the supposed brother of Pam Eccles in "Sanctuary." He and his sister appear quite conveniently to identify as a relative the body of the man who died on the steps of a church in Chipping Cleghorn. They subsequently display an inordinate interest in a particular piece of luggage. The second Mr. Eccles was a lawyer in *By the Pricking of My Thumbs.* He is an example of looks being most deceiving, as his cautious and seemingly proper appearance belies a sly and brilliant criminal mind.

Eccles, Pam The supposed sister of Mr. Eccles in "Sanctuary." With her brother, she arrives very conveniently in Chipping Cleghorn to identify as a relative a man who died on church property.

Eckstein, Professor A chemicals expert who is consulted by members of the government in *Passenger to Frankfurt.*

Edge, Bella The wife of the local chemist in "The Case of the Caretaker." Bella was once romantically linked—like many others—to the previously disrespectable Harry Laxton.

Edge, Mr. The local chemist in "The Case of the Caretaker." His wife was once romantically involved with the recently returned Harry Laxton, but Mr. Edge seems to greet his presence with considerable calm.

Edgerton, Sir James Peel A talented amateur criminologist and political figure in *The Secret Adversary.* He becomes involved in the investigation undertaken by Tommy and Tuppence Beresford and, despite the risk of scandal or harm to his rapidly rising political career, he proves most willing to assist them in their adventure.

Edgware, the Fifth Baron, Lord The formal title borne by Captain Ronald Marsh in *Lord Edgware Dies.*

Edgware, the Fourth Baron, Lord The formal title borne by the unfortunate George Alfred St. Vincent in *Lord Edgware Dies.*

Edith A servant in the household of Ann Prentice in *A Daughter's a Daughter.* She remains in Ann's employ for many years out of faithful devotion to the family.

Edmunds, Alfred A managing clerk in a law office in *Five Little Pigs.* He performs a service for Hercule Poirot and thus assists the detective's inquiries into a murder that took place sixteen years before.

Edmundson, John A secretary at the British embassy in Ramat during the turbulent collapse of its government in *Cat among the Pigeons.* He is a good friend of the ill-fated Bob Rawlinson.

Edna Two young women who become involved in mysteries. The first was Miss Marple's maid in "The Case of the Perfect Maid." She informs Miss Marple about her friend Gladys Holmes, who had lost her position as a maid over suspicions of theft. Her concern first brings Miss Marple into the case, which ends with multiple thefts and a disappearance. The second Edna was a young woman, not too bright, who becomes involved with a married man in *Mrs.*

McGinty's Dead. She is a frequent visitor to Mrs. Sweetiman's post office and candy store. She later admits that on the night that she was cheating on her boyfriend with the married man—the night that Mrs. Upward was murdered—she saw a fair-haired woman entering the house.

Egerton, Richard A partner in the law firm that oversees the trust for Elvira Blake in *At Bertram's Hotel.* He is more than happy to dispense his extensive knowledge about the law to his clients.

Elise The French maid in the service of Madame Paula Nazorkoff, an internationally renowned but tyrannical opera star, in "Swan Song."

Elizabeth The maid to Mrs. Harter in "Where There's a Will." She is exceedingly devoted to her mistress.

Ellen The name of four maids who appeared in different mysteries. The first was in the household of Emily Arundell in *Dumb Witness.* While cleaning out the effects of her late mistress, she comes across a letter addressed to Hercule Poirot and sends it to him. Its dispatch sets in motion the detective's inquiry into murder. A second Ellen was at the White House in "The Man in the Mist." When a murder takes place, she suffers from a severe case of hysteria. The third Ellen was a maid and cook to Amelia Viner in *The Mystery of the Blue Train.* Ellen's real name is Helen, but Amelia changes it to Ellen, which Amelia thinks sounds more appropriate for a person of Ellen's station. The fourth Ellen was in the household of the Fortescues in *A Pocket Full of Rye.* She provides Inspector Neele and Sergeant Hay with the potentially useful information that Rex Fortescue would have divorced his wife, Adele, had he not been poisoned to death.

Elliot, Mrs. One of the discoverers, with the local baker, of the body of Mrs. McGinty in *Mrs. McGinty's Dead.*

Elliot, James A young man who, with his wife, a "flashy piece of goods," is suspected of in-

volvement in the kidnapping of Winnie King in "The Girdle of Hippolyta." He may have a record of previous criminal activity, but kidnapping is not considered his kind of crime.

Elliot, Lady Noreen A flamboyant and wild young aristocrat in "The Manhood of Edward Robinson." She has the habit of stealing expensive jewelry, wearing it for a brief time, and then returning it. Edward Robinson stumbles into the middle of one of her romps.

Ellis A maid in the service of Jane Wilkinson in *Lord Edgware Dies.* She is completely trusted by her employer, so much so that Jane sends her to Paris to accomplish the delicate task of retrieving a very expensive box of gold and rubies.

Ellis, Miss Two women in separate cases. The first was a secretary to Harold Crackenthorpe in *4.50 from Paddington.* The second Miss Ellis was a clever woman in *Passenger to Frankfurt* who adopts several aliases, including Miss Ellis, nurse to Robert Shoreham.

Ellis, Big Jim The common-law husband of Victoria Johnson in *A Caribbean Mystery.* The father of her two children, Ellis is also considered a suspect in Victoria's stabbing death after she tries to blackmail the owner of a bottle of pills.

Ellis, Joe A carpenter in the village of St. Mary Mead in "Death by Drowning." He is considered "a quiet fellow . . . Close." He had been in love with Rose Emmott and had hoped that she would return to him for marriage even though she was carrying another man's child.

Ellis, John A butler in the employ of Sir Bartholomew Strange in *Three-Act Tragedy.* He disappears shortly after the murder of his employer, but the recently hired servant leaves behind evidence of blackmail and the suggestion that he knows dark secrets concerning Sir Strange. His real identity is subsequently revealed.

Ellis, Lou A buxom and fiery-tempered young woman in *The Pale Horse.* She has a nasty hair-pulling fight with Thomasina Tuckerton in an espresso bar that is witnessed by Mark Easterbrook. He reads in the paper the following week that Miss Tuckerton has died suddenly.

Ellsworthy, Mr. One of the chief suspects in the multiple murders striking down residents of Wychwood in *Murder Is Easy.* Ellsworthy is a dedicated member of a witches' coven and has an intense interest in two of the victims. He is described as having "a womanish mouth, long black hair and a mincing walk."

Elsa An Italian woman who first met her husband, James Folliat, after he deserted from the British army in Italy during World War II in *Dead Man's Folly.* She subsequently married him and then worked with him under an assumed name to secure control of his family's estate.

Elsie A maid in the service of Madame Simone in "The Last Séance." A devout Catholic, Elsie does not approve of her mistress's plan to hold a séance. At the dramatic conclusion of the séance, she discovers the horribly desiccated remains of Madame Simone.

Elspeth A woman who oversees the work of the dressmakers in "The Dressmaker's Doll."

Emlyn, Miss The headmistress of the Elm School in Woodleigh Common in *The Hallowe'en Party.* She provides some assistance to Hercule Poirot and Mrs. Ariadne Oliver concerning the background of the unfortunate Joyce Reynolds and the earlier death of a teacher in the school.

Emmott, David An American archaeologist who works as an assistant in an archaeological dig in *Murder in Mesopotamia.* Although he is a submissive person, he is also an excellent judge of character. At the end of the story, he is planning to marry Sheila Reilly.

Emmott, Rose A young woman in the village of St. Mary Mead who is murdered in "Death by Drowning." She becomes pregnant by Rex Sandford, but another man, Joe Ellis, wishes to marry her nevertheless. Unfortunately, she dies in a river at the hands of an unknown killer. Her father, Tom Emmott, is convinced that the murderer is Rex Sandford.

Emmott, Tom The father of Rose Emmott in "Death by Drowning." He is the proprietor of the Blue Boar and is convinced that his daughter was murdered by Rex Sandford.

Enderby, Charles A young newspaper reporter in *The Sittaford Mystery.* An ambitious young man, Enderby becomes an ally of Emily Trefusis and works with her to solve the murder of Captain Trevelyan in return for an exclusive on the story.

Enrico A Cuban cook in *A Caribbean Mystery.* He is a possible witness to murder, for he sees a guest carrying a knife just before Victoria Johnson is stabbed to death.

Entwhistle, Miss The sister of Mr. Entwhistle in *After the Funeral.* While she is loyal to her brother, she is also stubborn and rude in her attempts to convince her brother to cease his involvement in the affairs of the unfortunate members of the Abernethie family.

Entwhistle, Mr. An attorney in *After the Funeral.* He is an old friend of the unfortunate Richard Abernethie, so much so that even after retirement he continues to have a major part in organizing Abernethie's affairs. Following his client's death, he consults with Hercule Poirot and introduces the detective to the murder case. He faces resistance in this matter from his opinionated and stubborn sister, who dislikes his involvement in the affairs of the Abernethies.

Ericsson, Torquil A brilliant young Norwegian scientist in *Destination Unknown.* He is naively idealistic and becomes convinced that only science has all the answers to human progress and that scientists should consequently be given a superior position in society. He finds like-minded allies in the Brain Trust.

Erskine, Major Richard Setoun A former soldier in *Sleeping Murder.* He once had an affair with Helen Halliday but did not pursue any long-term relationship with her because of his of love for his wife and children. Erskine's wife, however, has remained bitter over the affair for years.

Esa The matriarch of the ancient Egyptian family in *Death Comes As the End.* She warns her son,

Imhotep, against marrying and is thus not delighted when he attaches himself to a concubine, Nofret. She urges him to take Nofret with him when he travels north because of the obviously rancorous feeling within the family toward her. Esa's fears are confirmed when Nofret is found dead. The matriarch soon has reason to fear for her own life, but her many precautions are to no avail.

Estair, Lord The leader of the House of Commons who, with Mr. Bernard Dodge, requests the urgent help of Hercule Poirot in recovering the missing prime minister David MacAdam in "The Kidnapped Prime Minister." He is reluctant to speak about the details of the disappearance in front of Hastings.

Estcourt, Mervyn (Bugler) A friend of Tommy and Tuppence Beresford in "The Man in the Mist." He is dating the actress Gilda Glen when he encounters the Beresfords in a restaurant.

Estravados, Pilar The real name of Conchita Lopez in *Hercule Poirot's Christmas.*

Ethel A maid who has a brief appearance in *The Burden.*

Eustace, Major A rather odious former soldier in "Murder in the Mews." He is considered "a doubtful character" by Charles Laverton-Smith, but knew the late Barbara Allen while she was in India. Revealed to be a blackmailer, he is the obvious suspect in her murder, and several important clues left at the crime scene apparently seal his fate. He has used several aliases, including Colonel De Bathe.

Evans A secret service agent who gives assistance to Tommy Beresford in "The Man Who Was No. 16."

Evans, Dr. A scientist in *Destination Unknown.* Evans and his wife play bridge with Olive and Thomas Betterton.

Evans, Inspector A clever retired detective in "Accident." A friend of Captain Haydock, he takes a special interest in Haydock's neighbors, the Merrowdenes, especially Margaret Merrowdene, whom he recognizes as a woman once acquitted of murdering her husband. Evans is able to work out the details of a fiendish plot, although he overlooks one small but very significant detail.

Evans, Albert A young man with murder on his mind in *A Pocket Full of Rye.* He courts Gladys Martin, the half-witted former maid to Miss Marple, and enlists her aid in murder. Once having used Gladys, Albert disposes of her through strangulation and then cruelly attaches a clothespin to her nose. Unbeknownst to him, Gladys was so pleased with her supposed beau that she sent a photograph of herself with him to Miss Marple.

Evans, Charles The fourth husband of Lady Rosalie Tamplin in *The Mystery of the Blue Train.* He is considered by Lady Tamplin's daughter, Lenox Tamplin, to be nothing more than "an expensive luxury."

Evans, Doris The love of the murdered Captain Sessle in "The Sunningdale Mystery." She was summoned to join him in Sunningdale for the purposes of a romantic liaison and, after he is found stabbed to death with a hat pin, she is the prime suspect in his death.

Evans, Gladys A onetime parlor maid whose name is mentioned on the dying breath of a murder victim, Alan Carstairs, in *Why Didn't They Ask Evans?* She is in the service of the of the vicar of Marchbolt and lives under the married name of Roberts.

Evans, Rebecca The wife of Robert Evans in *The Sittaford Mystery.* Her husband works in the home of Captain Trevelyan as his manservant. Despite the fact that she is an excellent cook, Rebecca is not hired by Captain Trevelyan, as he refuses to hire any woman for work in his house.

Evans, Robert Henry A onetime sailor who is hired to work as a manservant in the home of Captain Trevelyan in *The Sittaford Mystery.* His wife, Rebecca Evans, is an excellent cook, but Trevelyan refuses to hire any woman for his household, an unwillingness that creates some tension.

Everard, Alan A gifted painter and husband of

Isobel Loring in "Within a Wall." Genuinely talented, Everard earned high regard as an artist for his early work. Gradually, however, he settled into the comfortable existence of a portrait painter, setting aside his true creative potential. How that sad turn of events developed is the thrust of the story.

Everard, Mrs. The aunt of Captain Daniels in "The Kidnapped Prime Minister." She plays a significant role in the recovery of the missing prime minister, David MacAdam.

Everett, Mr. An actor and acquaintance of Hercule Poirot in "The Tragedy of Marsdon Moor." He is hired by the detective to assist him in solving the murder of Mr. Maltravers; Everett specializes in theatrical makeup.

Eversleigh, Bill One of the members of the Seven Dials organization in *The Secret of Chimneys* and *The Seven Dials Mystery.* Known in the group by the code name Number 3, he meets and eventually becomes engaged to Eileen Brent.

Eversleigh, Mrs. Violet A guest in the home of Claire Trent in "The Red Signal." She participates in the séance during which it is announced that someone is in great danger. Soon after, one of the guests is murdered.

Evesham, Lady Laura Keene A woman in "The Coming of Mr. Quin" who suffers from assorted superstitions. She expresses the hope that a dark man will be the first to cross her doorstep on New Year's Day, as it is thought to bring luck. Her husband, Tom Evesham, relates a story of suicide that is of much interest to Mr. Satterthwaite.

Evesham, Tom The husband of Lady Laura Keene Evesham in "The Coming of Mr. Quin." He attends a gathering at which he relates a tale of suicide, much to the interest of Mr. Satterthwaite and Harley Quin.

Exe, Madame An obsessed and grieving mother in "The Last Séance." Exe is consumed with the need to contact her dead daughter and so consults Madame Simone, a gifted medium, in an effort to materialize the poor deceased

girl. The séance proves horrific, but Madame Exe has her wishes fulfilled.

Eylesbarrow, Lucy One of the most competent assistants in the unorthodox service of Miss Marple, Lucy appears in only one reported case, *4.50 from Paddington,* but she has since remained a truly memorable amateur sleuth. Lucy is a graduate of Oxford University (where she earned first honors in mathematics), but she prefers to have money and so, "to the amazement of her friends and fellow scholars," she enters into domestic service. Such is her intelligence and vigor that she soon develops a reputation for excellence, allowing her to choose the situations that best suit her whims. She first meets Miss Marple when she is hired by Miss Marple's devoted nephew, Raymond West, to help his aunt recover from a bout of pneumonia. The two develop an immediate rapport. Thus, when Miss Marple needs someone with brains and skill to discreetly investigate the events in the Crackenthorpe household, she turns to Lucy. Once established in the midst of the extremely dysfunctional Crackenthorpes, Lucy becomes indispensable, receiving amorous attentions from the patriarch, Luther Crackenthorpe, and proposals of assorted kinds from other male members of the family. Much to the regret of fans, Lucy never appeared again in Christie's writings.

Fairborough, Lady Muriel The aunt of Henry Glyn-Edwards in *The Burden.* An eccentric old woman, she is easily manipulated by others, especially her nephew.

Fane, Eleanor The despotic and controlling matriarch of the Fane household in *Sleeping Murder.* A widow, she has focused all her attention on keeping her sons subservient to her will, and even tries to direct their choices in love and marriage.

Fane, Geoffrey A pompous professor of archaeology in *A Daughter's a Daughter.* He has a not-very-serious relationship with Ann Prentice; it is doomed, especially as she has too many personal troubles and actually cares for Richard Cauldfield.

Fane, Walter The much oppressed son of Eleanor Fane in *Sleeping Murder*. Walter's mother is a cruelly domineering woman who seeks to maintain control over the lives of her sons, even with regard to their romantic interests. Suffering under this repression, Walter flares out from time to time, and even attacks his brother with a poker. He was once in love with Helen Halliday and leaves England for Ceylon when he is rejected.

Fanshaw, Ada The eighty-three-year-old aunt of Tommy Beresford in *By the Pricking of My Thumbs.* Much disliked by her relatives for being impossible, imperious, and altogether unpleasant, Aunt Ada has been confined to the Sunny Ridge retirement home. There, she is visited by Tommy and Tuppence. She displays the same disagreeable temperament that they remember and goes so far as to insult Tuppence, referring to her as "that type of woman" and mentioning that her name is better suited to a parlor maid. Aunt Ada dies soon after their visit, but she leaves a set of clues about the retirement home so curious that Tuppence begins investigating a mystery.

Fanthorpe, James Lechdale A British attorney in *Death on the Nile*. He is sent by his firm to keep a watchful eye on Linnet Doyle during her honeymoon in Egypt. His very presence on board the steamer *Karnak* is a source of interest to Hercule Poirot, for Fanthorpe is clearly not the kind of person who would journey to Egypt purely for enjoyment.

Faraker, Juan A young man in "Manx Gold" who sets out with his cousin, Fenella Mylecharane, to discover buried treasure on the Isle of Man. Their uncle, Myles Mylecharane, dies and leaves them the promise of his fortune if they can find it. The inheritance is in the form of four buried boxes hidden in various spots on the island. They must decipher four sets of clues and outrace two other relatives to the gold. Juan is also the narrator of the adventure.

Farley, Benedict The eccentric and close-fisted millionaire in "The Dream." He seemingly summons Hercule Poirot for a meeting, reveals details about a recurring dream, and then dismisses the great detective. A short time later, Farley apparently commits suicide under the exact circumstances in his dream. A man of regular and peculiar habits, Farley eats a daily dinner of cabbage soup and caviar.

Farley, Joanna The rebellious daughter of Benedict Farley in "The Dream." She hates her father with a passion, disliking him even more after he has her fiancé fired. When interviewed by Hercule Poirot, she expresses no regret of any kind that her father is dead.

Farley, Louise The wife of Benedict Farley in "The Dream." She is not in the least upset by the murder of her husband.

Farquhar, Esmée A very beautiful young woman who consults Hercule Poirot in "The Million Dollar Bond Robbery." She is the fiancée of Philip Ridgeway, an officer of the London and Scottish Bank and a leading suspect in the amazing theft of the one million dollars' worth of Liberty bonds from the ship *Olympia.* She is convinced that Philip is innocent.

Farr, Stephen The name used by Stephen Grant while traveling in *Hercule Poirot's Christmas.*

Farraday, Lady Alexandra Catherine (Sandra) The wife of Stephen Farraday in *Sparkling Cyanide.* She is ruthlessly devoted to her husband and his political career as a Tory member of Parliament. She is a very likely suspect when Rosemary Barton, mistress to her husband, is murdered.

Farraday, Stephen A member of Parliament for the Tories and the husband of Lady Alexandra Farraday in *Sparkling Cyanide.* An ambitious politician, he lives in fear of his indiscretions becoming public, especially his affair with Rosemary Barton. Fortunately for him, Barton is murdered.

Farrell, Detective Inspector An officer of Scotland Yard in "Jane in Search of a Job." He is assigned the task of capturing a clever American thief.

Fat Ikey One of the nicknames used by Herman Isaacstein in *The Secret of Chimneys.* He is also known as Ikey Hermanstein and Nosystein.

Faulkener, Jimmy There were two characters named Jimmy Faulkener in the Christie writings. The first was a young man of good society in "The Crackler." He unwittingly passes counterfeit bills to others of his social standing. The second Jimmy Faulkener was a friend of Donovan Bailey and a would-be suitor of Patricia Garnett in "The Third-Floor Flat." When Patricia Garnett is locked out of her fourth-floor flat, Jimmy and Donovan use a coal lift to enter her apartment. However, they mistakenly enter the third-floor flat and discover the body of Ernestine Grant.

Faulkner, Leslie A confused young playwright in "The Affair at the Bungalow." He had written a play and had sent a copy to the actress Jane Helier. The reply he receives, however, is apparently not from Jane; lured to a bungalow in Riverbury, he meets a woman whom he assumes is Jane but then passes out and wakes up dazed along the road. The police arrest him under suspicion of burglarizing the very bungalow he had just visited.

Fausett, Dr. A physician in *Five Little Pigs.* He examines the body of Amyas Crale and determines the cause of death.

Fayll, Dr. A cousin of Myles Mylecharane in "Manx Gold." He receives a letter from his late cousin's lawyers informing him of the chance to find Myles's buried treasure. The inheritance is contained in four chests located at different spots on the Isle of Man. He was unknown to his cousin Myles and thus proves a dark horse in the race among family members to unearth the treasure.

Félice A maid in the household of Paul Déroulard in "The Chocolate Box." She was suspected of stealing a bottle of heart medicine.

Fellows-Brown, Mrs. A very heavyset woman in "The Dressmaker's Doll." Although she is frightened by the lifelike doll in Alicia Coombe's dress shop, she finds shopping in the establishment rewarding, for the clothing there does much, she says, "to minimize my behind."

Fenn, Ardwyck A movie producer in *The Mirror Crack'd from Side to Side.* In the view of Inspector Craddock, he becomes a suspect in the murders committed in the case.

Fenn, Kathleen The birth mother of Desmond Burton-Cox in *Elephants Can Remember.* As the mistress of Mr. Burton-Cox, Desmond's father, she allowed Desmond to be adopted by Mrs. Burton-Cox, as she had little prospect of raising him properly. She became a successful entertainer, however, and left Desmond a considerable sum of money at her death. This fact was hidden from him by his adoptive mother.

Feodor, Count See Paul, Prince of Maurania.

Ferguson, Dr. A physician in *Hallowe'en Party.* He is Joyce Reynolds's physician, and when she is found drowned in a tub of water used for bobbing for apples, he insists that her death is an accident.

Ferguson, Mr. A supporter of communism and other radical political ideas in *Death on the Nile.* He enjoys shocking other passengers with his views, even referring to Hercule Poirot as one those "dressed-up, foppish good-for-nothings." His especially bitter comments about Linnet Doyle make him a suspect in her murder. In truth, Ferguson is Lord Dawlish, a very wealthy member of the British aristocracy.

Ferrarez, Carmen A beautiful and apparently Spanish woman in "Mr. Eastwood's Adventure." She is not who she appears to be, as Mr. Eastwood discovers after rescuing her from possible harm.

Ferrars, Mrs. A widow in *The Murder of Roger Ackroyd.* She was someone in whom Roger Ackroyd had a romantic interest, but she dies of an apparent overdose of veronal. The cause of her suicide, it is rumored, was remorse over murdering her husband with poison. It is subsequently learned that she was being blackmailed.

Ferrier, Dagmar The wife of Prime Minister Edward Ferrier and the daughter of the former

P.M. John Hammett in "The Augean Stables." She is as popular as her father and her husband with the English people and is considered "the popular ideal of English womanhood . . . a most valuable asset to the party." She becomes a target of a vicious scandal sheet and is seriously besmirched. Her vindication by Poirot helps to extricate her husband and father from a potentially ruinous political scandal.

Ferrier, Edward   The prime minister of Great Britain in "The Augean Stables." He comes to Hercule Poirot in the hope that the detective will prevent the explosion of a political scandal involving Ferrier's father-in-law and predecessor as P.M., John Hammett. Poirot takes the case solely on the basis of the opinion of a friend concerning Ferrier: "He's a sound man." While he is neither a staggeringly charismatic leader nor an eloquent speaker, Ferrier is a firm and capable P.M.

Ferrier, Lesley   A solicitor's clerk in the law firm of Fullerton, Harrison, and Leadbetter and possibly a forger in *Hallowe'en Party*. She was stabbed to death before the events recounted in the case, and her death was attributed to a jealous husband or boyfriend to whom she was being unfaithful. Her death, however, was much more than that.

Finch, Sally   One of the students living in Mrs. Nicoletis's boardinghouse in *Hickory Dickory Dock*. An American, she proposes to Len Bateson.

Finn, Jane   A young woman and passenger on board the doomed liner *Lusitania* in *The Secret Adversary*. She loses her memory after a series of dangerous adventures in espionage and is registered in the hospital as Janet Vandemeyer. Her situation becomes of interest to Tommy and Tuppence Beresford when Tuppence uses the name by accident in a conversation and finds herself embroiled in dangerous intrigue.

Finney, Major   Chief constable of the police investigating the murder of Rachel Argyle in *Ordeal by Innocence*. He is at first firmly convinced that Jacko Argyle is the murderer, but, by the end of the case, Dr. Calgary has succeeded in changing his mind.

Fish, Hiram   An American visitor to the Chimneys in *The Secret of Chimneys*. He claims to have a keen interest in paintings and rare books, but after just a rudimentary discussion, it becomes clear that he is ignorant about both. His presence at the Chimneys thus becomes quite suspicious.

Fitzroy, Mr.   The secretary to Lord Alloway in "The Submarine Plans." He is in charge of the secret submarine plans, and when they disappear under mysterious circumstances he is, naturally, considered a suspect.

Fitzwilliam, Luke   The amateur sleuth in *Murder Is Easy*. After years as a policeman in the Mayang Straits, Luke returns to England and finds himself on the connecting train from Dover to London. Sharing a compartment with Miss Fullerton, he learns that there are some odd and rather murderous events going on in her little village of Wychwood. The next day, Luke reads that Miss Fullerton was killed by a hit-and-run driver. One week later, a newspaper carries a story about another untimely death in Wychwood. Determined to investigate Miss Fullerton's death, Luke sets out for Wychwood and learns that murder seems to be stalking the inhabitants. Consulting with Superintendent Battle, Luke catches the killer and falls in love with Bridget Conway.

Like several characters of some interest and potential, Luke Fitzwilliam appears in only one Christie novel. Other characters who might have made excellent detectives in other settings include Lucy Eylesbarrow and Dr. Calgary.

Flavelle, Hippolyte   A servant in *The Mystery of the Blue Train*.

Flavelle, Marie   The wife of Hippolyte Flavelle in *The Mystery of the Blue Train*. She works as a cook.

Fleetwood, Mr.   A ship's engineer in *Death on the Nile*. Like many other people, Fleetwood has a reason to murder Linnet Doyle. The heiress revealed to Fleetwood's mistress, her maid, Marie, that he is married and has three children.

Luke Williams (Bill Bixby) bids a permanent farewell to Lavinia Fullerton (Helen Hayes) in Murder Is Easy. *(Photofest)*

Flemming, Mr.   Two men who take part in separate cases. The first was a solicitor in *Giant's Bread.* He convinces Vernon Deyre to depart Abbots Puissant. The second Mr. Flemming was an amateur anthropologist and full-time solicitor in *The Man in the Brown Suit.* He makes the charitable decision to invite the daughter of his deceased client, Professor Beddingfield, to live with him and his wife in London. She is unable to accept.

Flemming, Mrs.   The wife of the solicitor Mr. Flemming in *The Man in the Brown Suit.* Like her husband, she agrees that they should do something kind for the daughter of a late client of her husband's, Professor Beddingfeld. When called upon to put the charitable impulse into action, however, Mrs. Flemming is reluctant. Nevertheless, she makes the hesitant offer to Anne Beddingfeld to come and work for the Flemmings as a governess to their children. Fortunately for Mrs. Flemming, Anne declines their offer.

Fletcher, Sergeant   An officer of the local constabulary in Chipping Cleghorn in *A Murder Is Announced.* He assists Inspector Craddock in his investigation into the murder of Rudi Scherz.

Fletcher, Agnes   A parlor maid in *One, Two, Buckle My Shoe.* She dislikes the police and thus delays in reporting some seemingly vital information to them.

Fletcher, Nat   The supposed nephew of Miss Greenshaw in "Greenshaw's Folly." He appears suddenly after Miss Greenshaw is murdered and seems poised to make a claim to her estate on the basis of her declaration that he was her nephew, despite the absence of any blood relationship. Owing to the ambiguity of his claim, he is a suspect in her murder, even though he was supposedly some distance away at the time of her death.

Florence   A onetime parlor maid to Emily Barton in *The Moving Finger.* She is devoted to Emily, even though she blames the rest of the Barton family for her present circumstances, namely the fact that she must operate a boardinghouse.

Fogg, Quentin The Crown attorney in the trial to bring the murderer of Amyas Crale to justice in *Five Little Pigs.* He provides Hercule Poirot with extensive details about the trial and the case against Caroline Crale.

Folliat, Amy The mother of James Folliat in *Dead Man's Folly.* She resides in a small cottage on the estate of Sir George Stubbs and enjoys working in the garden. Her casual manner, preference for tweeds, and seemingly inoffensive nature do not sit well with Hercule Poirot.

Folliat, James The son of Amy Folliat in *Dead Man's Folly.* He was a soldier in World War II who deserted and subsequently married an Italian woman named Elsa. With his mother, Folliat schemes to gain control of a fortune.

Folliott, Mrs. Richard A member by marriage of the Folliott family, she is the wife of Captain Richard Folliott in *The Murder of Roger Ackroyd.* She is anxious that no one learn of her relationship with Ursula Bourne, the former parlor maid in the Ackroyd household.

Forbes, General An old and old-fashioned retired soldier in "Problem at Sea." He has an impossible time accepting the notion that the former music hall entertainer John Clapperton has in any way earned the title that he uses, Colonel. This matter weighs heavily upon General Forbes, who tries to relieve his frustration by circling the ship deck forty-eight times every day.

Forbes, Ogilvie A lawyer and longtime friend of the Chevenix-Gores in "Dead Man's Mirror." Forbes shared with Colonel Bury a long and unrequited love for Lady Vanda Chevenix-Gore.

Ford, Monica A name used by Aspasia Glen in "The Dead Harlequin."

Fortescue, Adele The second wife of Rex Fortescue in *A Pocket Full of Rye.* Young, beautiful, and sensual, Adele makes clear her love of money and is thus a logical suspect in the murder of her husband. Her guilt becomes less likely, however, when she is found dead from cyanide poisoning.

Fortescue, Elaine The lone daughter of Rex Fortescue in *A Pocket Full of Rye.* Like many others, she had a motive to murder her father. Rex destroyed her marriage plans to Gerald Wright by announcing that Wright was unsuitable for her because of his leftist ideas.

Fortescue, Jennifer The daughter of Helen MacKenzie and wife of Percival Fortescue in *A Pocket Full of Rye.* Originally named Ruby MacKenzie and raised by her mother to hate the Fortescues for some old wrong they committed, she decided, nevertheless, to wed Percival Fortescue, much to the chagrin of her mother. Taking the name Jennifer, she first met Percival while working as a nurse and cared for him during his recovery from pneumonia. Like many other people, she hated Rex Fortescue, her father-in-law, for his vicious opinion that Percival had married far beneath him.

Fortescue, Lancelot A son of Rex Fortescue in *A Pocket Full of Rye.* Rather a black sheep, he was forced to leave England after forging a check. He went to East Africa, where he met his wife, Patricia. When he returns to England, his hopes for the future are renewed.

Fortescue, Patricia The wife of Lancelot Fortescue in *A Pocket Full of Rye.* The daughter of an Irish peer, she met her husband in East Africa and considers herself an unlucky woman; she has already been twice widowed.

Fortescue, Percival A son of Rex Fortescue in *A Pocket Full of Rye.* Nicknamed Val and "Prim Percy," he married Ruby MacKenzie, a union of which his father did not approve, as Rex felt she was beneath his son. The logical heir to the many business interests of the family, Percival disagreed with his father on numerous occasions about investments.

Fortescue, Rex The tyrannical patriarch of the Fortescue family in *A Pocket Full of Rye.* Described as "a large flabby man . . . less impressive than he should have been," Rex heads the offices of Consolidated Investments Trust, a financial powerhouse. His domestic life is not a happy one, as his sons are disappointments to him. He is also twice married, to Elvira—mother of Lancelot, Elaine, and Percival Fortescue—and to the glamorous Adele. Much hated, he is poisoned by taxine, an alkaloid of a substance found in the leaves and berries of the yew tree. After dying horribly, Rex is found with a handful of rye grain in his jacket pocket.

Foscarelli, Antonio   A onetime chauffeur and passenger on the Calais Coach in *Murder on the Orient Express*. A naturalized American citizen, he is nevertheless exceedingly Italian, abusing the English language repeatedly in his long-winded theorizing about the probable murderers of Ratchett.

Foscatini, Count   A presumed Italian nobleman who is brutally murdered in "The Adventure of the Italian Nobleman." Foscatini is in fact not the possessor of a legitimate title, and it is discovered after his death that he was a blackmailer of the first order.

Fothergill, Sir Hugo   A friend of Mrs. Ariadne Oliver in *Elephants Can Remember*. Mrs. Oliver visits him to learn some information about the case, but Fothergill can provide few details.

Fournier, Monsieur   A member of the Sûreté in *Death in the Clouds*. He gives generally competent assistance to Hercule Poirot and Inspector Japp.

Fowler, Mrs.   A witness to the events surrounding the death of Alice Ascher in *The A.B.C. Murders*. She receives five pounds from the detective in return for revealing the details.

Fox, Sybil   A fabric cutter in the dressmaking shop owned by Alicia Coombes in "The Dressmaker's Doll." She becomes obsessed with the lifelike doll in the store.

Frances, Nurse   The nurse who is hired to care for Vernon Deyre after he breaks his leg in *Giant's Bread*. She proves to be a very compassionate caregiver and actually helps Vernon to deal with the many issues left over from his youth.

François   A butler in the household of Paul Déroulard in "The Chocolate Box." He provides Hercule Poirot with vital information concerning Paul Déroulard's habits, in particular his absolute passion for consuming chocolates.

Franklin, Angela and Arthur   The parents of Laura, Shirley, and Charles Franklin in *The Burden*. They are shattered by the early death of Charles from polio and thus withdraw their affections from Laura, an emotional collapse that leaves their daughter scarred for life. Any chance of repairing their relationship with Laura is destroyed by their hasty conception of a child to replace Charles in their affections and then by their deaths in a plane crash while on vacation.

Franklin, Barbara (Babs)   The wife of Dr. John Franklin in *Curtain*. She is a feeble and ailing woman who is virtually bedridden. When others complain that she is a hypochondriac, Mrs. Franklin has little chance to justify her infirmities, for she is poisoned when a Calabar bean is put in her coffee. Her unsympathetic husband wastes no time after her death in marrying his assistant.

Franklin, Charles   The young son of Angela and Arthur Franklin and brother of Laura Franklin in *The Burden*. He died in his youth from polio, a demise that left his parents emotionally shattered, as he was their favorite and was considered superior in every way. His death thus had terrible ramifications for his sister.

Franklin, Dr. John   A physician and expert on tropical diseases in *Curtain*. A callous researcher, he comments that he would not mind killing a large number of people, especially as "about eighty percent of the human race *ought* to be eliminated." He has little sympathy for his frail wife, and, after her murder, he wastes little time in marrying his assistant.

Franklin, Laura   The main character in *The Burden*. Laura is the daughter of Angela and Arthur Franklin and the sister of Charles Franklin. The early death of Charles from polio damaged forever the emotional condition of her parents, so they withdrew from their commitment to her and considered her unequal to the lost ideal of their dead son. Just as Laura has hopes of establishing a relationship with her parents, they confound her by conceiving another child to replace Charles. Laura at first was insanely jealous of Shirley and prayed that her younger sister would die. When, however, the house catches on fire, Laura saves her eleven-year-old sister. Laura then becomes utterly devoted to Shirley, but she is unable to guarantee Shirley happiness.

Franklin, Shirley The daughter of Angela and Arthur Franklin and sister of Laura Franklin in *The Burden.* Conceived as a replacement after the early death of her brother, Charles Franklin, from polio, Shirley spent her early childhood much hated by her jealous sister. This changed after Laura rescued Shirley from a burning house, after which she was ever under Laura's watchful eye. Shirley was married twice, first to a serial adulterer and then to an adventurer. Both marriages ended in unhappiness, however, and Shirley took to drinking and eventually killed herself.

Fraser, Donald The violent fiancé of Elizabeth Barnard in *The A.B.C. Murders.* He threatened that he would kill Elizabeth if she spent time with any other men, making him a possible suspect when she is murdered by the A.B.C. killer.

Freebody, Miss The actual name of Mary Debenham in *Murder on the Orient Express.*

French, Emily The victim of murder in "Witness for the Prosecution." A lonely older woman, she fell under the charms of Leonard Vole, a man forty years her junior. Soon after she turned control of her financial affairs over to Leonard, Miss French was murdered.

French, Irene One of the names used by Valerie Hobhouse in *Hickory Dickory Dock.*

Frobisher, Colonel George The oldest friend of Admiral Chandler in "The Cretan Bull." The godfather of Hugh Chandler, Frobisher is aware of the increasing mental instability of the old admiral's son, but he seems reluctant to involve himself in the family tragedy, at least openly. He is, however, a good and devoted friend to both the admiral and Hugh.

Fullerton, Jeremy A partner in the respected law firm of Fullerton, Harrison, and Leadbetter in *Hallowe'en Party.* He is interviewed by Hercule Poirot concerning several deaths, including that of a former client of the firm, Mrs. Llewellyn-Smythe, and a former employee, Lesley Ferrier. The detective is also curious about Olga Seminoff, an au pair who had apparently forged a codicil to Mrs. Llewellyn-Smythe's will and then disappeared before the case could be brought to court. The attorney tries to be evasive, but Poirot learns more than Mr. Fullerton suspects.

Fullerton, Lavinia A charming little old lady from the village of Wychwood who meets Luke Fitzwilliam on a train in *Murder Is Easy.* Lavinia is deeply concerned about the deaths befalling the residents of her village and is headed to London and Scotland Yard to express her suspicions. Before she can reach the Yard, however, she is killed by a hit-and-run driver. Fitzwilliam learns of her death and sets out to find the killer.

Gabriel, John A British politician in *The Rose and the Yew Tree.* He is initially extremely ambitious and cruelly manipulative, using anyone and anything as long as it will advance his career. Finally, however, he undergoes a near total transformation, becoming Father Clement and giving his life over to aiding the poor and suffering.

Gaigh, Lady Elizabeth An important player in the events recounted in "The Girl in the Train." The daughter of a marquis, she bears a striking resemblance to the grand duchess Anastasia and even impersonates her to permit the elopement of her brother with the real Anastasia. Lady Elizabeth subsequently marries George Rowland, a match that is perfectly acceptable to both families. She is pleased with George's money—permitting her to spend freely—and George's family likes very much the title she brings to the family.

Gaitskill, Mr. An old solicitor and friend of Aristide Leonides in *Crooked House.* He has long been associated with the legal affairs of Mr. Leonides and is thus insulted grievously when he learns that Leonides substituted a different version of his will for the original.

Galbraith, Mr. An eighty-year-old partner in a real estate firm in *Sleeping Murder.* He once served in India but later suffered a stroke and is plagued by infirmities. He also has a habit of repeating stories.

Gale, Margery A young woman in "The Voice in the Dark." As the heiress to the Stranleigh title, she is approached by several suitors, including one who has a claim of his own to the family title.

Gale, Norman One of the suspects in the murder of Madame Giselle in *Death in the Clouds.* Known as James Richards in South America, he is a dentist who is returning to England and thus becomes embroiled in the murder on board the plane. He gives assistance to Hercule Poirot, in part because it allows him to spend time with his beloved, Jane Grey. Under the name John Robinson, Gale impersonates a blackmailer to assist Poirot in his investigation.

Ganett, Miss A woman in *Murder Is Easy.* She is a neighbor of Caroline and Dr. Sheppard and plays mah-jongg with them on a regular basis.

Gapp, Florence (Flossie) One of the names used by Merlina Rival in *The Clocks.*

Garcia, Dr. Alan A pathologist who works as an analyst for the Home Office. A respected doctor, he appears in two Poirot cases, *Sad Cypress* and "The Lernean Hydra," and is always eager to provide gruesome details of autopsies. He refers to Poirot as "the man who is always right."

Gardener, Carrie An American woman in *Evil under the Sun.* She is exceedingly loquacious and is the cause of boredom in virtually everyone who meets her. Her husband, too, is apparently bored with her.

Gardiner, John The secretary to Hugo Lemesurier in "The Lemesurier Inheritance." He has apparently served the Lemesuriers with

dedication, but he has also had an affair with Hugo's wife and marries her after Hugo's death.

Gardner, Mrs. A woman who assists Mr. Parker Pyne in "The Case of the Rich Woman." Parker Pyne once saved her only son from penal servitude, leaving her perpetually grateful. She provides a valuable service in Parker Pyne's unusual plan to relieve the unhappiness of Amelia Rymer.

Gardner, Jennifer The wife of the invalid Captain Robert Gardner in *The Sittaford Mystery.* She is distinctly hostile to her husband's nurse and is also estranged from her brother, the unfortunate Captain Trevelyan. A beautiful woman, she also has a dominating personality, even as she ministers to the weaknesses of her husband.

Gardner, Captain Robert The husband of the beautiful Jennifer Gardner in *The Sittaford Mystery,* he is also the brother-in-law of the unfortunate Captain Trevelyan. Gardner is an invalid, but not from any physical malady. Rather, he suffers psychological problems and lives every day enjoying the attentions of his wife and his nurse.

Garfield, Michael One of the victims of murder in *The Hallowe'en Party.* Garfield is a young architect who inherits property upon the death of a client and then is himself murdered soon afterward. Before his death, he irreverently calls Hercule Poirot Señor Mustachios; he also pokes fun at Poirot's patent-leather shoes, especially because, even though they are refined, they are most painful to wear.

Garfield, Ronald The rather pathetic nephew of Caroline Percehouse in *The Sittaford Mystery.* He is deliberately subservient to the whims of his aunt, all in the hopes of becoming the heir to her vast fortune upon her death. Sadly, his aunt sees through his efforts and actually wishes that he would be more assertive in their relationship.

Garnett, Patricia (Pat) A woman who loses her apartment key in "The Third-Floor Flat." A friend of Mildred Hope and the object of the affections of Jimmy Faulkener and Donovan Bailey, Patricia discovers the loss of her key upon returning to her flat after a party. Jimmy and Donovan attempt to enter her apartment via a coal lift; they miscalculate, however, and instead of entering her fourth-floor flat, they break into the third-floor flat. Once inside, they stumble across a corpse.

Garrod, Grace The niece of Simon Clode in "Motive vs. Opportunity." She lives in dread of being disinherited. Her husband, Philip Garrod, is also deeply worried about the inheritance.

Garrod, Philip The husband of Grace Garrod in "Motive vs. Opportunity." He is deeply concerned about her receiving her inheritance from Simon Clode, and goes so far as to put a plan into motion to guarantee her the money.

Garroway, Chief Superintendent The chief investigating officer into the deaths of General and Lady Ravenscroft in *Elephants Can Remember.* Although the general view is that they had committed suicide, Garroway is firmly convinced that they were murdered.

Gascoigne, Henry An eccentric former artist who was estranged from his twin brother in "Four and Twenty Blackbirds." He was a man of precise habits, dining in the same restaurant on specific nights every week—Tuesday and Thursday—and never varying in his diet over the course of a decade. It is thus a source of great interest and importance to Hercule Poirot that the artist, called Old Father Time by the staff at the restaurant, should appear on a Monday night and order a radically different meal from his usual fare. Soon after, Gascoigne fell down a flight of stairs and was killed.

Gaskell, Mark A scoundrel in *The Body in the Library.* He has been twice married, but he strives to maintain the secrecy of his second marriage in order to inherit his first wife's estate. Being married again, of course, has not impeded his romantic adventures.

Gaunt, Emma The housemaid to Simon Clode in "Motive vs. Opportunity." She was "a tall middle-aged woman who had been in service there for many years and who had nursed Clode

devotedly." With the cook, Lucy David, she witnessed Simon Clode's revised will.

George The elderly gardener to the Martins in "Philomel Cottage." He is talkative and provides some very useful information to Alix King Martin about the activities of her husband.

GEORGE (GEORGES) The superb and impeccable gentleman's gentleman in the service of Hercule Poirot. Such are the credentials of this perfect valet that he consents to enter into Poirot's employ only after the Belgian detective was received at Buckingham Palace.

Known variously as George and Georges (depending upon the specific case), George made his first appearance in *Murder on the Links,* following the departure of Poirot's longtime friend Captain Arthur Hastings for Argentina and wedded bliss. From that time, until the last published Poirot case, *Curtain,* George was a permanent fixture in the daily routine of the great detective. In *Curtain,* the detective, seemingly inexplicably, sends George away to care for his ill father and engages the highly unsuitable Curtiss during what prove to be the sleuth's last days. Given the unusual nature of Poirot's life, George's many talents always came in handy, especially his extensive (Jeeves-like) knowledge of the English aristocracy, their eccentricities, and habits. Poirot is often forced to confess that George lacks much of an imagination, but his declared disappointment normally follows some effort on his part to elicit information from George that falls outside his clearly delineated boundaries. As Hastings observed, "He was a competent, matter-of-fact man, with absolutely no imagination. He always stated things literally and took them at their face value" (*Curtain*).

George appears in numerous published cases, including "The Apples of the Hesperides," *Cat among the Pigeons,* "The Lernean Hydra," "The Nemean Lion," and "The Under Dog." When, at the end of *Curtain,* he is informed of Poirot's death, "He was distressed and grieved and managed very nearly to conceal the fact."

George, Uncle The old, white-haired uncle of Jack Hartington in "The Blue Jar." He is the owner of a priceless blue jar that becomes the focus of a spiritual adventure undertaken by his nephew.

Georges See George

Gerard, Ted A member of a religious organization called the Oxford Group in "The Tape-Measure Murder."

Gerard, Dr. Theodore A well-known psychologist who vacations in the Middle East in *Appointment with Death*. He visits Jerusalem at the same time as the Boynton family and is thus well positioned to make a thorough psychological assessment of the extremely dysfunctional brood. He eventually is suspected in the murder of Mrs. Boynton when it is discovered that a hypodermic needle and some digitoxin are missing from his medical bag. Dr. Gerard also gives Poirot an insightful look into Mrs. Boynton's mental state, an analysis that actually helps the detective to solve the murder.

Geronimo A servant in *Hickory Dickory Dock*. A native Italian, he has a habit of eavesdropping that proves most helpful to investigators.

Gerrard, Ephraim The caretaker on the Welman estate in *Sad Cypress*. He and his wife have raised Mary Gerrard as their own daughter in return for money, but he comes to resent Mary because of the continuing involvement of her birth mother, who provides money for her education.

Gerrard, Mary The foster daughter of Ephraim Gerrard in *Sad Cypress*. Mary was raised in the household of the Gerrards, but she was actually the illegitimate daughter of Sir Lewis Rycroft and Laura Welman. Her birth mother remains active in her upbringing, including supplying money for her education. Mary's possibilities for the future are cut short, however, when she is found dead after eating a fish paste sandwich laced with morphine.

Gertie A jewel thief in "The Veiled Lady."

While she pretends to be an aristocrat, Poirot sees through her disguise.

Gibbs, Amy A maid in the service of Lord Easterbrook in *Murder Is Easy*. She is both impudent and considered morally unsuitable by Lord Easterbrook, who fires her. Soon after, however, she is found dead after drinking red hat paint that had been substituted for her red cough syrup. Her death is initially considered a suicide, but further investigation reveals a far more murderous event.

Gibson, Old Mother A crotchety old woman who owns an antique glassware store in "Mr. Eastwood's Adventure." She permits the Patterson gang to rent out the rooms above her store for their nefarious schemes.

Gilbey, Miss The headmistress of St. Anne's School in *Absent in the Spring*. She is stern and demands discipline from her students.

Gilchrist, Miss The housekeeper and companion to Cora Lansquenet in *After the Funeral*. She is Cora's longtime companion, and she is very much an old maid. Her service to Cora ends when she dies after eating a piece of wedding cake laced with arsenic.

Gilchrist, Dr. Maurice The physician who cares for the movie actress Marina Gregg in *The Mirror Crack'd from Side to Side*. He believes that Gregg would be far better off seeing a psychologist instead of a physician, but he ministers to her many needs and moods anyway.

Giles, Dr. A physician in the town of Market Basing in "The Market Basing Mystery." He is exceedingly competent and, after his examination of the victim, Walter Prothero, he introduces such doubts into the ruling of suicide that Poirot proceeds with a murder investigation.

Gilles, Monsieur A French policeman in *Death in the Clouds*. He serves as the chief of the detective force of the Sûreté and works with Hercule Poirot in his investigation into the death of Madame Giselle.

Gilliat, Beryl The second wife of Simon Gilliat in "The Harlequin Tea Set." She is determined to secure Thomas Addison's inheritance for her son and to defeat her stepson, Timothy Gilliat, in his bid for the inheritance. Beryl is a ruthless and unscrupulous schemer.

Gilliat, Lily Addison The first wife of Simon Gilliat in "The Harlequin Tea Set." Prior to events recounted in the story, she was killed in a car accident in Kenya. Her death makes possible Simon's marriage to the scheming Beryl Gilliat and places her son in grave danger.

Gilliat, Roland (Roly) The son of Beryl Gilliat and stepson of Simon Gilliat in "The Harlequin Tea Set." Born Roland Eden, he assumes the name of his stepfather and poses as the grandson of Thomas Addison in the hope of becoming his heir. His mother, a scheming woman, labors to displace Timothy Gilliat, Roland's half brother, as the heir.

Gilliat, Simon A onetime World War II pilot and squadron leader in the RAF in "The Harlequin Tea Set." His first wife, Lily, was killed in a car accident in Kenya, making possible his marriage to Beryl Gilliat. Simon is unaware of Beryl's relentless scheme to displace Simon's son, Timothy, in favor of her own son, Roland, in the anticipated inheritance of Thomas Addison's estate (Addison is Simon's former father-in-law).

Gilliat, Timothy The son of Simon Gilliat and the late Lily Gilliat in "The Harlequin Tea Set." Timothy has long suffered from the schemes of his stepmother, Beryl Gilliat, to supplant him in virtually every way with her own son, Roland. Timothy, however, can lay claim to his legitimate place in the Addison bloodline (and thus can claim the right to a large estate) for several reasons, including the fact that he has the traditional Addison attribute of severe color blindness.

Gince, Miss A rather homely woman in *The Moving Finger*. She works in a local law firm as a clerk, but she is forced to leave her job when she is accused by a poison-pen letter of having an affair with her boss.

Giraud, Monsieur A member of the Paris branch of the Sûreté who serves as an investigating officer in the murder recounted in *Murder on the Links*. He is a self-professed man of action, relying upon vigorous searches for clues and careful methodology, rather in the fashion of Sherlock Holmes. He has an immediate conflict with Hercule Poirot over method, especially disagreeing with the Belgian detective's preference for a more cerebral approach to crime detection. Poirot, meanwhile, dismisses Giraud as a mere "human foxhound." In the end, Poirot demonstrates the superiority of the cerebral method.

Giselle, Madame A moneylender and blackmailer who is murdered in *Death in the Clouds*. An ugly woman, both in her appearance and her personality, she is murdered by one of her victims while on a flight from Paris to England. Her murder is accomplished by shooting her with a poisoned dart dipped in the venom of the boomslang snake. There are numerous suspects in the crime, including her daughter, who receives an estate of more than one hundred thousand pounds amassed through criminal activity.

Giuseppe A butler in the service of the actress Marina Gregg in *The Mirror Crack'd from Side to Side*. Suave, clever, and handsome, this Italian butler is the object of the affections of most of Gregg's domestic staff, but he has other ambitions. He tries to blackmail someone and is shot to death for his greed.

Gladys There are several maids in Christie's works who are named Gladys, and they normally play a minor but often useful role in the solution of crimes. One Gladys is a maid in *Unfinished Portrait*. A second is a kitchen maid in the service of Colonel Protheroe in *Murder at the Vicarage*. Also called Gladdie, she is described as a "shivering rabbit." A third Gladys is a servant in the Astwell household in "The Under Dog." She provides Poirot with some useful information about a woman's dress. Yet another Gladys is a feather-brained servant questioned by Hercule Poirot in "The Lernean Hydra." Finally, there is the Gladys serving as a maid in "The Case of the Perfect Maid." Although she is a decent person, she is falsely accused of being a thief.

Glen, Aspasia   A talented woman in "The Dead Harlequin" who works as a governess under the name of Monica Ford. She also impersonates several ghosts in the course of Mr. Satterthwaite's investigation.

Glen, Gilda   A gorgeous British actress in "The Man in the Mist." Actually from humble origins, she is desperate to divorce her husband, a policeman, in order to free herself for better prospects. This proves a deadly gambit.

Gldyr, Major Boris Andrei Pavolv   A talented and energetic investigator with the FBI in *Destination Unknown.* The nephew of the scientist Professor Mannheim, he is determined to discover the reason scientists are disappearing across the globe. His inquiry takes him into the dark world of Mr. Aristide and the Brain Trust, which he infiltrates under an assumed name. During the course of his secret and dangerous work, he falls in love with Hilary Craven, a romantic distraction that places him in even greater danger.

Glyn-Edwards, Henry   A serial adulterer in *The Burden.* He makes the life of his wife, Shirley Franklin, absolutely miserable because of his habitual infidelity and his profligate spending, which keeps them forever on the verge of bankruptcy. Henry, however, contracts polio and degenerates into an invalid. His torment of his wife comes to an end when he is given a double dose of a sleeping draught.

Glynne, Lavinia Bradbury-Scott   One of the three sisters who become a source of great interest to Miss Marple in *Nemesis.* Unlike her sisters, Anthea and Clotilde Bradbury-Scott, Lavinia is noted by Miss Marple to be a good person, one highly unlikely to have committed murder.

Goby, Mr.   A generally competent private detective to whom Hercule Poirot turns on several occasions for assistance. The Belgian relies on him in *Elephants Can Remember, After the Funeral,* and *Third Girl.* Goby is also hired by the wealthy Rufus van Aldin in *The Mystery of the Blue Train.* Goby's primary value is his ability to ferret out obscure and unusual information. His talent for his work is often hard to comprehend, for Goby is quite unsocial, avoiding any eye contact with his clients and remaining always out of the limelight.

Goedler, Belle   The widow of Randall Goedler in *A Murder Is Announced.* She inherits a vast estate upon the death of her husband and takes up a happy existence in Scotland. Randall's will, however, includes the unusual provision that, upon Belle's death, his remaining estate should pass to his former secretary, Letitia Blacklock.

Goedler, Randall   A wealthy businessman in *A Murder Is Announced.* He dies and leaves his extensive estate to his wife, Belle, but the will also contains the unusual provision that upon Belle's death the remaining estate should pass to his former secretary, Letitia Blacklock.

Goedler, Sonia   The sister of Randall Goedler in *A Murder Is Announced.* She is the mother of Pip and Emma and would have left them the bulk of her share of her brother's estate if she had not entered into a bitter quarrel with him.

Gold, Douglas Cameron   The husband of Marjorie Gold in *Triangle at Rhodes.* He is a decent chap, but he is also not extremely bright. Douglas is framed for the murder of Mrs. Valentine Chantry, with whom he was apparently infatuated. Poirot must clear him of the crime.

Gold, Marjorie   The seemingly mild-mannered and long-suffering wife of Douglas Gold in "Triangle at Rhodes." Only Hercule Poirot recognizes that Marjorie disguises her true personality, a perception on his part that is essential to the solution of the murder of Valentine Chantry and the vindication of Douglas Gold.

Goodbody, Mrs.   A witch and psychic in *Hallowe'en Party.* Mrs. Goodbody is also a housekeeper at Woodleigh Common, providing Hercule Poirot with such insightful information on the members of the Reynolds family that the detective is able to advance considerably his investigation of murder. A self-professed witch, Mrs. Goodbody does not accept the notions of black magic.

Goodman, Adam A member of the Special Branch (a special department of the police) who works as a gardener at the Meadowbank School in *Cat among the Pigeons*. He is much aided in his role by having worked previously as a gardening columnist for newspapers.

Gordon Leigh, The Honourable Hermione The object of much concern from several people in "The Case of the Missing Lady." While preparing for her marriage to the explorer Gabriel Stavansson, Hermione suddenly disappears, and her continued absence so worries the explorer that he consults with Tommy and Tuppence Beresford in the hopes that they might be able to find her.

Goring, Edward A onetime RAF fighter pilot during World War II in *They Came to Baghdad*. He opens a coffee shop called the Olive Branch. The shop serves as the secret base of operations for subversive activities. He is manipulative and uses Victoria Jones for his own devices.

Gorman, Father A Presbyterian minister in *The Pale Horse*. The minister of St. Dominic's Church, he visits the deathbed of the widow of a small-time criminal and receives from her a list of names that she assures him is of great importance. For safekeeping, he places the list in his shoe, an act that proves providential. Soon after leaving the widow's side, Father Gorman is struck on the head and dies. He is found by Mark Easterbrook.

Gorman, Michael (Mickey) The commissionaire and doorman in *At Bertram's Hotel*. A shady character, he was once married to Lady Bess Sedgwick, the internationally famous socialite who has been married several times since she and Mickey parted company. When chance brings Lady Bess to the hotel, Mickey reminds her of their marriage—which is still legal, rendering all her other marriages illegitimate. Soon after receiving a warning from Lady Bess, Mickey is shot to death.

Michael Gorman (Brian McGrath) in At Bertram's Hotel. *(Photofest)*

Gorringe, Miss The receptionist in *At Bertram's Hotel*. A shrewd and cunning woman, she has an uncanny ability to remember details about the tastes and needs of the hotel's guests. Her response to the interrogation by Chief Inspector Davy is a masterpiece of evasion, but it nevertheless convinces the policeman that all is not as it seems in the hotel.

Gottlieb, Professor John An operative in *Passenger to Frankfurt*. He is cursed with the physical appearance and mannerisms of a monkey, an affliction that makes him virtually unforgettable. He carries with him a letter from the president of the United States and uses it to secure a meeting with Countess Renata Zerkowski.

Grace The object of young James Bond's affections in "The Rajah's Emerald." Grace is a spoiled young woman who takes great delight in the fact that Bond is of such limited financial means. Thus, when she is invited for a vacation, she stays in an upscale hotel while Bond is forced to reside in a modest boardinghouse. By the end of the story, however, James has completely reversed their fortunes.

Grace, Inspector   A Scotland Yard investigator in "The Ambassador's Boots." He works with Tommy and Tuppence Beresford on their case.

Grace, Patience   A cocaine addict in "The Horses of Diomedes." She has gone through several husbands and moved on to a shabby boyfriend named Hawker. When she and Hawker have a quarrel, she takes a shot at him with a pistol. Her pathetic story is the immediate cause for Poirot's involvement in the case.

Graham, Dr.   A physician living at the Golden Palm Hotel in *A Caribbean Mystery.* He encounters Miss Marple and has a chat with her under the assumption that she is a lonely old bird. Later, of course, he recognizes her real skills. Graham also launches the investigation into the death of Major Palgrove, another guest in the hotel.

Graham, Jennifer   A young woman in *A Daughter's a Daughter* who has the physical appearance and mannerisms of a horse. When she laughs, she whinnies.

Graham, Ralph   A young man in *Unfinished Portrait.* He is a tea planter in Ceylon.

Graham, Roger   A young man in "The Bird with the Broken Wing." He is initially engaged to Madge Keeley, but he becomes infatuated with Mabelle Annesley. He soon considers leaving Madge for Mabelle, but then reconsiders.

Grainger, Dr.   The physician to Emily Arundell in *Dumb Witness.* Although a well-liked medical man, he does little to display his competence when he misses the signs of Emily's murder by phosphorous poisoning. One major reason for the error is the fact that he has lost all sense of smell, due to an illness he suffered some time before.

Granby, Mrs.   A suspect in the murder of Mrs. Rhodes in "Miss Marple Tells a Story." An Anglo-Indian widow, she "had reddish hair rather untidily done, was sallow-faced and about fifty years of age. Her clothes were rather picturesque, being made mostly of native silks, etc." With Mrs. Carruthers, she is one of the few suspects in the murder of Mrs. Rhodes other than Mr. Rhodes.

Grandier, Madame   The ravishing but perpetually grief-stricken widow in "The Erymanthian Boar." Each year she returns to the resort of Rochers Neige to commemorate her husband's passing. Her ritual is so important to her that she allows nothing to distract her; even after the hotel suffers from a bitter storm and is cut off from the world below the high mountains, she remains utterly focused on her grief.

Grandier, Elise   The personal maid to Madame Giselle in *Death in the Clouds.* She journeys on the same flight as her employer and is thus present when Giselle is murdered by a dart dipped in poison. As her loyalty to Madame Giselle ends with her death, Elise is able to give Poirot a valuable notebook concerning Giselle's activities.

Grange, Inspector   A chief inspector from Scotland Yard investigating the murder of Dr. John Christow in *The Hollow.*

Grannie   The paternal grandmother of the main character in *Unfinished Portrait.* She is in her eighties and is eager to impart much of her wisdom to her granddaughter, especially about men—indeed, she has been married and widowed three times and is still the object of their affections. Her advice is simple: "Never leave your husband alone."

The grandmother in this story bears a striking resemblance to Agatha Christie's own grandmother, who gave her similar advice about men—advice that Agatha should have heeded when dealing with her first husband, Archie.

Grant, General   The patriarch of the Grant clan in "The Horses of Diomedes." He is a former colonial officer who has retired and apparently suffers from gout. Poirot has his doubts about the general's infirmities and tests his theory by "accidentally" tripping and grabbing the general's supposedly sore foot.

Grant, Mr.   A member of British intelligence in *N or M?* who recruits Tommy Beresford to work for him. As is the case with other Tommy and Tuppence adventures, Mr. Grant soon discovers that Tuppence will be involved regardless of his own hopes. Grant surrenders to circumstances and uses both of the Beresfords in his operation.

Grant, Mrs.   A charming woman considered by the main character of *Unfinished Portrait* to be "the loveliest thing" she has ever seen. Despite her private belief that her son is making a most unsuitable marriage, she does not interfere, respecting his right to make his own decisions.

Grant, Bernard   A friend of the main character in *Unfinished Portrait.* He is described as a jolly, big man.

Grant, Ernestine   The tenant of a third-floor flat and a victim of murder in "The Third-Floor Flat." Grant lives directly below Patricia Garnett and writes a letter to Patricia requesting a meeting. Before the two can meet, however, Grant is murdered. Her body is discovered, apparently by accident, when friends of Patricia wander into the wrong flat.

Grant, Gerda   A onetime actress and the first wife of the powerful Alistair Blunt in *One, Two, Buckle My Shoe.* She figures in the events described in the mystery.

Grant, James   A friend and suitor of Ann Prentice in *A Daughter's a Daughter.* He has known Ann for twenty-five years and is determined to marry her.

Grant, Jim   A young man in *Unfinished Portrait* who meets the main character in France. They become engaged, but Grant calls off the proposed wedding when he decides that they are not well matched.

Grant, Pam   A beautiful and seemingly good person in "The Horses of Diomedes." She is apparently the daughter of General Grant and sister of Sheila Grant.

Grant, Robert   A manservant in the employ of Jonathan Whalley in *The Big Four.* Also called Abraham Biggs, he is a former convict and a most unpleasant-looking man.

Grant, Sheila   The apparent sister of Pam Grant and daughter of General Grant in "The Horses of Diomedes." She is also known as Sheila Kelly and has a history of shoplifting and cocaine use. Nevertheless, she attracts the attentions of Dr. Michael Stoddart, who decides that he will help her overcome her addiction.

Grant, Stephen   Two young men in different cases. The first was a caretaker hired by Captain Harwell to oversee his horses at Ashley Grange in "At the 'Bells and Motley.' " He is suspected in the disappearance of Harwell, but the police can find no evidence of foul play on his part. The second Stephen Grant was a son of Simeon Lee in *Hercule Poirot's Christmas.* He flies from South Africa to England under the name Stephen Farr to meet with his father and is suspected in Simeon's murder. Hercule Poirot, however, has other ideas and, when he is cleared of the crime, he asks Conchita Lopez for her hand in marriage.

Graves, Constable   A local policeman in Sittaford who takes part in the early investigation into the death of Captain Trevelyan in *The Sittaford Mystery.* With Major Burnaby and Dr. Warren, he breaks into Trevelyan's bungalow.

Graves, Dr.   The physician who treats Henry Glyn-Edwards for his polio in *The Burden.* He prescribes the sleeping potion that is used to kill Glyn-Edwards.

Graves, Inspector   A London-based police investigator who assumes command of the inquiry into the events involving the village of Lymstock in *The Moving Finger.* He specializes in anonymous letters and is thus considered the ideal officer to investigate a series of poison-pen letters. His admiration of the quality of the letters is the source of some amusement to the people in Lymstock.

Graves, Mr.   The valet/butler of Count Foscatini in "The Adventure of the Italian Nobleman." He is "an agitated middle-aged man" who provides many useful details about his murdered master to Hercule Poirot.

Graves, Sir Ronald   The assistant commissioner of Scotland Yard in *At Bertram's Hotel.* He has a habit of doodling during his meetings with other officials, but this serves only to concentrate his faculties rather than to dissipate them. In the course of his labors in the case involving the hotel, he must organize a meeting between Chief Inspector Davy and the mysterious Mr. Robinson.

Gray, Dr.   A physician who cares for Aristide Leonides in *A Crooked House.*

Grayle, Lady Ariadne   An extremely wealthy woman who fears for her life, with much justification, in "Death on the Nile." Lady Grayle was forty-eight and had suffered since the age of sixteen "from the complaint of having too much money . . . She was a big woman, not bad-looking as regarded features, but her face was fretful and lined, lavish make-up she applied only accentuated the blemishes of time and temper . . . She was overdressed and wore too much jewelry." While on a journey down the Nile on the S.S. *Fayoum,* the unpleasant woman attempts to enlist the aid of Mr. Parker Pyne because she fears that her husband, George, is trying to kill her. She soon dies from what is deduced to be strychnine poisoning, and Parker Pyne undertakes an investigation to find her murderer.

Grayle, Sir George   The long-suffering husband of Lady Ariadne Grayle in "Death on the Nile." An impoverished baronet, Sir George had married Lady Ariadne to solve his financial problems, including racing debts and pressing creditors. He subsequently spent the next ten years enduring the constant complaints and miseries of his wife. While on a journey up the Nile on the S.S. *Fayoum,* Lady Ariadne dies from strychnine poisoning, and Sir George is immediately suspected, especially as his late wife had tried to enlist the services of Mr. Parker Pyne to confirm her suspicions that George was poisoning her.

Grayle, Pamela   The niece of Sir George Grayle and Lady Ariadne Grayle in "Death on the Nile." She relies on them for financial assistance and

adores her uncle, whom she calls "Nunks." As for her aunt, Pamela finds her unbearable and believes her many medical ailments to be feigned. Pamela is also in love with Basil West, a relationship that does have a bearing on the investigation into the murder of Lady Ariadne.

Green, Cyril   A witness to the murder of Rachel Argyle in *Ordeal by Innocence.* He is quite unreliable, and advances the improbable claim that she was killed by Russians who had landed in their "sputniks."

Green, George   The name assumed by Vernon Deyre in *Giant's Bread* during the time that he suffers from amnesia.

Greene, Netta   A young understudy to the actress Jane Helier who assists with a scheme to expose the affair between Sir Joseph Salmon and the wife of Jane's first husband, Claude Averbury, in "The Affair at the Bungalow."

Greenholtz, Mr.   One of the partners in the firm of Greenholtz, Simons, and Lederbetter in *They Came to Baghdad.* Devoid of any sense of humor, he fires Victoria Jones for acting out a humorous impersonation of his wife.

Greenshaw, Katherine Dorothy   The owner of the Greenshaw estate in "Greenshaw's Folly." A rather eccentric but shrewd old woman, she convinces her housekeeper that she will leave her money to her in lieu of pay. Miss Greenshaw apparently does change her will, leaving everything to her housekeeper, and the will is actually witnessed by Raymond West, Miss Marple's novelist nephew. She also hires Laura, the niece of West's wife, to edit her grandfather's diaries for publication. During Laura's labors, Miss Greenshaw is murdered with an arrow that was shot through her neck.

Greer, Elsa   The wife of Lord Dittisham and a onetime mistress of the artist Amyas Crale in *Five Little Pigs.* Greer has been married a total of three times, but her relationship with Crale left the greatest impression, especially after he was poisoned and his wife died in prison after being convicted of the crime. As Crale's wife,

Caroline, supposedly committed the murder out of fear that Amyas was preparing to leave with Greer, the entire incident has destroyed Greer emotionally.

Gregg   A parlor maid in *Unfinished Portrait.*

Gregg, Betty   The fiancée of Basil Chester in "Problem at Pollensa Bay." She is considered to be most unsuitable by Basil's mother, especially since she dresses inappropriately, drinks, and even uses foul language.

Gregg, Ernie   One of the delinquents in the home run by Christian Gulbrandsen in *They Do It with Mirrors.* He is murdered because he is able to identify the killer of Gulbrandsen.

Gregg, Marina   A famous actress and film star who is apparently the target for murder in *The Mirror Crack'd from Side to Side.* While at a party to celebrate her current film project, she is reintroduced to several important people from her past (including a child she had adopted and several ex-husbands, whom she does not even remember). Her past comes back to haunt her throughout the succeeding days, and she is offered a terrible reminder of the young child she lost to German measles many years before. While talking to Heather Badcock, Miss Gregg seemingly escapes being poisoned, as her drink ends up in Heather's hand and Heather dies soon after drinking it. This proves to be only the first of several murders of people associated with Marina and her past.

Gregson, Garry   A writer of detective stories in *The Clocks.* He once had in his employ one of the suspects in the case, and an unpublished manuscript of his proves to be of very great importance to Hercule Poirot.

Greta   The secretary to Sir Joseph Hoggin in "The Nemean Lion." It is clear to Hercule Poirot that Greta has clear plans to become Sir Joseph's next wife, a possibility that Poirot urges Sir Joseph to reject.

Grey, Detective Sergeant   A policeman in the Berkshire constabulary in "The Lernean Hydra." He discovers a compact full of white powder that seems to utterly damn one of the suspects. In fact, the discovery permits Hercule Poirot to wrap up the case and find the real murderer.

Grey, Mrs.   One of the names used by Anita Grunberg in *The Man in the Brown Suit.*

Grey, Jane   A clever and attractive young woman who assists Hercule Poirot in *Death in the Clouds.* The winner of the Irish Sweepstakes and a onetime hairdresser, Jane is on board the flight during which Madame Giselle is murdered. She assists Poirot by serving as secretary to Jean Dupont, catching Dupont's eye. She is, however, in love with Norman Gale.

Grey, Katherine   A self-possessed young woman who serves as companion to Miss Amelia Viner in *The Mystery of the Blue Train.*

Grey, Mary   A saleslady who proves of great help to Megan Hunter in *The Moving Finger.* When Megan undergoes a complete makeover, thanks to the generosity of Jerry Burton, Miss Grey oversees the transformation.

Grey, Thora   A beautiful young woman in the employ of Sir Carmichael Clarke in *The A.B.C. Murders.* Hastings finds her to be a true stunner, but Clarke's wife does not agree. It is learned that Sir Carmichael had planned to ask Thora to marry him after the eventual death of his wife, but such plans are cut short by Sir Carmichael's murder. Mrs. Clarke wastes little time in firing Thora once her husband is out of the way.

Grey, Thyrza   An enigmatic occultist in the village of Much Deeping in *The Pale Horse.* She is able to give advice and encouragement to Mark Easterbrook as he investigates the strange goings-on in Much Deeping that seemingly involve black magic.

Griffin, Dr.   A physician in Chipping Cleghorn in "Sanctuary." He is summoned to attend to the dying Walter St. John on the steps of the local church.

Griffin, Mrs.   A ninety-three-year-old woman in *Postern of Fate.* She still has an excellent memory and is able to provide Tuppence Beresford with useful details about events that took place decades before.

Griffith, Miss   The head typist for sixteen years in the offices of Consolidated Investments Trust in *A Pocket Full of Rye*. She calls the police when her boss, Rex Fortescue, is taken suddenly and violently ill after drinking some poisoned tea. Despite her cool and efficient demeanor, she has a secret desire for the rascal Lance Fortescue.

Griffith, Aimee   The sister of Dr. Owen Griffith in *The Moving Finger*. An overly passionate, jealous, and domineering woman, she controls most of her brother's life, even as she is overwhelmed by her passion for Richard Symmington. This love is unrequited, and Aimee becomes the object of one of the fiendish poison-pen letters circulating in the village.

Griffith, Dr. Owen   The brother of Aimee Griffith in *The Moving Finger*. As the local doctor, he is a competent physician, but his sister dominates much of his life. This changes, however, when he meets Joanna Burton; the two eventually marry.

Griffiths, Walter   One of the last witnesses (with two others) to see Thomas Betterton before he disappeared in *Destination Unknown*.

Grosjean, Monsieur le President   The leader of France during the crisis recounted in *Passenger to Frankfurt*. He summons other world leaders to a conference to discuss the problem of student unrest across the globe and what can be done to quell it.

Grosvenor, Irene   The "incredibly glamorous blonde" secretary to Rex Fortescue in *A Pocket Full of Rye*. She customarily serves Rex a cup of his special blend of tea and does so on the fateful morning of his death. To her horror, Rex takes a sip, grabs his throat, and cries out in agony before dropping dead. It is subsequently learned that her glamour and sartorial splendor are merely a pretense; Irene is, in fact, from the lower class, as her accent reveals when she endures great stress.

Groves, Mrs.   A cleaning lady in "The Dressmaker's Doll." She is especially uncomfortable in the presence of the life-size doll in the dressmaker's shop.

Grunberg, Anita   A talented South African–born actress in *The Man in the Brown Suit*. Most likely of Hungarian descent, she is active in criminal activities and uses a variety of names and disguises. Among her aliases are Mrs. Grey, Mrs. De Castina, and Nadina. While posing as Mrs. De Castina, Grunberg is murdered.

Gudgeon, Mr.   A butler to Lady Angkatell in *The Hollow*. He is an exceedingly protective and faithful servant.

Gulbrandsen, Christian   A trustee of the Gulbrandsen Institute in *They Do It with Mirrors*. He arrives unexpectedly at the reformatory called Stonygates and begins asking some rather uncomfortable questions of Miss Marple and others. Soon after dinner, he is shot to death in his room, to which he had retired to compose a mysterious letter.

Gun Man, The   A mysterious figure who troubles the dreams of the main character in *Unfinished Portrait*. During times of intense emotional stress, the main character dreams of a shadowy figure who is remembered most for having stumps instead of hands.

The figure of The Gun Man was based on Agatha Christie's own experiences. When she was a young girl, she suffered from nightmares in which the Gun Man, as she called him, appeared.

Gustave   A waiter at the resort of Rochers Neige in "The Erymanthian Boar." He demonstrates his skills as a waiter by complaining that the altitude wreaks havoc with his effort to make a proper cup of coffee. Nevertheless, Gustave may not be the waiter he seems.

Guteman, Ellie   See Rogers, Ellie.

Guthrie, Alexander   An art critic and advisor to Cora Lansquenet in *After the Funeral*. He frequently assisted her in her purchases of art, but he notes that virtually all of her art collection is worthless, save for one truly intriguing piece that he notices only after she has been murdered.

Gwenda A clerk in *Postern of Fate*. She works in the Hollowquay post office and is able to provide useful information about local lore to Tuppence Beresford.

Haggard, Blanche A onetime schoolmate of the main character in *Absent in the Spring*. She has been married five times and has two children, but these attachments have never proven a hindrance to her personal commitment to enjoying life on her own terms.

Hale, Captain Bingo An unscrupulous houseguest of Lady Vere Merivale and her husband, Sir Arthur Merivale, in the connected short stories "Finessing the King" and "The Gentleman Dressed in Newspaper." Despite being a guest of Sir Arthur, he embarks upon a tawdry affair with Lady Vere. After she is murdered, however, he claims to have received a note warning him about meeting her at the Ace of Spades on the night she was killed. He also provides the title for the second story (in which the murder is solved) by dressing as "the gentleman dressed in newspaper" from *Alice in Wonderland*.

Hall, Dr. The operator of a nursing home in Bournemouth in *The Secret Adversary*. He provides care to the amnesiac Jane Finn.

Halliday, Mr. A British scientist in *The Big Four*. He has been experimenting with wireless energy and disappears on a trip to Paris to meet with Madame Olivier. His wife is Mrs. Halliday.

Halliday, Mrs. The wife of Mr. Halliday in *The Big Four*. She is quite alarmed because her husband has disappeared on a trip to Paris.

Halliday, Arthur An unpleasant suitor of Joyce Lambert in "Next to a Dog." He pursues Joyce relentlessly, even though he knows that she does not love him. He is thus quite pleased when she finally reaches a point of such financial distress that she accepts his offer of marriage. This triumph, however, proves short-lived.

Halliday, Ebenezer The steel king of America who consults with Hercule Poirot in "The Plymouth Express" concerning the murder of his daughter, Flossie. Described as "a large, stout man with piercing eyes and an aggressive chin," he had benefited from Poirot's expertise some years before in a matter of bearer bonds. His current task, however, is far more grave. Halliday swears to spend his last cent to catch the murderer and relies upon Poirot "to deliver the goods."

Halliday, Flossie The daughter of Ebenezer Halliday in "The Plymouth Express." (See Carrington, Mrs. Rupert, for other details.)

Halliday, Helen Spenlove Kennedy The stepmother of Gwenda Reed in *Sleeping Murder*. She was a stunning beauty who was the object of the attentions of virtually every man and the target of hatred by many women in her day. She disappeared twenty years ago, after her marriage to Major Halliday, and was never seen alive again. Her death is the source of deepseated emotional trauma for Gwenda, who unknowingly purchases the old house in which they lived.

Halliday, Major Kelvin The father of Gwenda Reed and the husband of Helen Halliday in *Sleeping Murder*. Major Halliday was married twice. His first marriage produced his daughter, Gwenda, and his second, to Helen, ended in disaster. When the philandering Helen disappeared, he sent Gwenda to be raised in New Zealand and checked himself into an insane asylum on the assumption that he somehow had murdered his wife. His psychiatrist disagreed strenuously with this assumption, but the major's guilt was such that he finally committed suicide.

Halliwell, Clare A thirty-two-year old woman in "The Edge" who, while not beautiful, nevertheless "looked fresh and pleasant and very English." She had been a close friend of Sir Gerald Lee since childhood and fully expected to marry him. Her expectations are shattered by Gerald's marriage to Vivien Lee, an event that spurs Clare to develop a pathological dislike for the other woman.

Hamer, Silas A millionaire and dedicated materialist in "The Call of Wings." After assuring his friend, an East End cleric named Richard Borrow, that he could not possibly accept any notion of the spiritual world, Hamer undergoes a profound spiritual transformation. His conversion culminates with his decision to give away all his money to a mission for the poor. Shortly after this act of charity, Hamer meets his fate while rescuing a little girl from death on a subway track.

Hamilton Clipp, Mrs. A very talented intelligence operative in *They Came to Baghdad.* She and her associate and "husband," George Hamilton Clipp, seem an unlikely pair for espionage, especially given her diminutive appearance. Nevertheless, she has a long career of "jumping from boats into aeroplanes and from aeroplanes into trains." She makes possible the hiring of Victoria Jones as her traveling companion by pretending to have a broken arm.

Hamilton Clipp, George An American intelligence agent in *They Came to Baghdad.* He works with his associate and "wife," Mrs. Hamilton Clipp. Like her, he bears little resemblance to the dashing agents of literature.

Hammond, Mr. The solicitor to Roger Ackroyd in *The Murder of Roger Ackroyd.* A small man to whom the years have not been kind, he nevertheless is possessed of a keen mind, revealed by his "sharp grey eyes."

Hannah A maid in "The House of Lurking Death." She is a zealously religious woman, and her deep beliefs drive her to attack one of the suspects in the murder of her employer.

Hardcastle, Detective Inspector The police official in charge of the investigation in *The Clocks.* A meticulous detective, he also has an excellent memory and a face that never reveals his true thoughts to a suspect.

Hardcastle, Mrs. An unpleasant-looking woman in *A Pocket Full of Rye.* A middle-aged personal secretary who is soon called Horseface Hetty and the Gorgon behind her back, she replaces the stunning Miss Grosvenor in the firm of the late Rex Fortescue.

Hardcastle, Claudia The half sister of Rudolf Santorix in *Endless Night.* She dies a short time after Ellie Rogers because she has learned too much about Ellie's death.

Hardcastle, Midge A relative of Lucy Angkatell in *The Hollow.* As she is in financial straits (despite her relative's wealth), she takes a job in a dress shop. She also breaks off her engagement with Edward Angkatell, despite the fact that she does love him. Nevertheless, she saves him from committing suicide.

Harden, Grete An intelligence operative in *They Came to Baghdad.* She fails in her mission, however, and is captured.

Harding, Carol The name used by Carol Davis while visiting the Cornish village of Rathole in "The Bloodstained Pavement." She has a chance encounter with Denis Dacre—supposedly an old friend—and his wife, Margery. Soon after, Margery is found dead from drowning. A year later, Carol returns to Rathole and has another chance meeting with Denis and his new wife, Joan.

Harding, Jane A friend and advisor to Vernon Deyre in *Giant's Bread.* She plays an important part in shaping Vernon's future, going so far as to sacrifice her own potentially brilliant career to assist him in launching his first opera. She also provides him financial, social, and personal assistance. In the end, however, she pays the ultimate price for her devotion.

Hardman, Cyrus Bethman An American detective traveling on the Calais Coach in *Murder on the Orient Express.* He journeys in the guise of a typewriter ribbon salesman, but subsequently reveals that he was hired to protect someone on board the train. Poirot spots him immediately—thanks to his dreadful attire and his coarse habits—as an example of "the true Western spirit of hustle."

Hardman, Marcus A wealthy collector of jewels and jewelry described as an "elderly social butterfly" in "The Double Clue." He is robbed of a priceless emerald necklace during a party and has difficulty believing that any of his very socially prominent guests might have been involved. He thus asks Poirot to undertake a discreet investigation.

Hardt, Elsa A clever and elusive spy who creates the circumstances investigated by Hercule Poirot in "The Adventure of the Cheap Flat." She impersonated a singer in New York until coming into the possession of a set of secret documents and then fled to Europe to sell the secrets to the highest bidder.

Harfield, Jane An elderly and wealthy woman in *The Mystery of the Blue Train.* She leaves her extensive estate to her companion, Katherine Grey, a decision vehemently opposed by her cousin, Mary Anne Harfield, and other relatives. (See also Harrison, Dr. Arthur.)

Harfield, Mary Anne A cousin of Jane Harfield in *The Mystery of the Blue Train.* A dreadful woman whose cruel personality is matched only by her greed, Mary Anne refuses to accept the terms of Jane Harfield's will and tries to overturn it to win control of the estate for herself.

Hargraves, Laura See Upward, Laura.

Hargreaves, Mrs. The wife of the local church organist in *Hallowe'en Party.* She offered to provide a large green plastic pail for apple dunking at the doomed party. Had her offer been accepted, it is unlikely that Joyce Reynolds would have died in quite the gruesome manner that she did.

Hargreaves, Lois A victim of murder in "The House of Lurking Death." She is deeply frightened that someone is trying to poison her—especially after narrowly escaping death in the form of a box of poisoned chocolates—and contacts Tommy and Tuppence Beresford for help. Before they can arrive on the scene, however, Lois is murdered by means of a poisoned sandwich.

Harker, Captain A bad sort who tries to kidnap Tuppence Beresford in "Blindman's Bluff."

Harmon, Diana (Bunch) The favorite godchild of Miss Marple and the wife of Reverend Julian Harmon. Appearing in only two published cases (*A Murder Is Announced* and "Sanctuary"), Bunch proves both her devotion to her godmother and her impressive intelligence, although she at times seems to be a bit vacuous. She helps Miss Marple solve both cases, one of which ("Sanctuary") starts on the steps of her husband's church. Diana's cat is named Tiglath-Pileser.

Harmon, Reverend Julian The vicar of Chipping Cleghorn and husband of Diana "Bunch" Harmon. Julian is a superbly educated vicar and his vast storehouse of knowledge extends beyond matters ecclesiastical or theological. Given his position and his other interests, he does not become especially involved in the two cases in which he appears (*A Murder Is Announced* and "Sanctuary"), leaving the fun of assisting Miss Marple's investigation to Diana.

Harper, Mr. A young man who serves as secretary to the doomed Rupert Bleibner during the ill-fated archaeological expedition to uncover the tomb of King Men-her-Ra in "The Adventure of the Egyptian Tomb." He is "a pleasant, lean young man wearing the national insignia of horn-rimmed spectacles."

Harper, Superintendent A clever officer in the Glenshire police force who investigates the murder of Ruby Keene in *The Body in the Library.* He uses very subtle methods in questioning suspects and witnesses.

Harris, Myrna A waitress at the Royal Spa Hotel in *A Murder Is Announced.* She dated the unfortunate Rudy Scherz and was thus able to provide important information to police. Based on her testimony, the official cause of Scherz's death was changed to murder from suicide.

Harrison, Mrs. The landlady of the murdered Mabelle Saints-Bury Seale *in One, Two, Buckle My Shoe.* An older woman, Mrs. Harrison is very cooperative and gives her assistance to

Hercule Poirot and Inspector Japp when they search Saints-Bury Seal's flat.

Harrison, Nurse The nurse who cares for the dying Mrs. Oldfield in "The Lernean Hydra." She falls in love with Dr. Oldfield and is quite certain that he will marry her after Mrs. Oldfield finally dies. When, however, Dr. Oldfield displays no interest in her, Nurse Harrision becomes embittered and spreads vicious rumors about her employer and Jane Moncrief.

Harrison, Dr. Arthur A physician who cared for Jane Harfield in *The Mystery of the Blue Train.* He gives his professional opinion that Jane was entirely of sound mind at the time she made out her will and left everything to her companion, Katherine Grey. The doctor assures Miss Grey that Jane's greedy relatives have no claim of any kind to her estate.

Harrison, John A young friend of Hercule Poirot in "Wasps' Nest." He is visited by Poirot and given encouragement not to act on a plan he has in mind for another good friend and for his own fiancée, Molly Deane. Of much importance to Poirot is the fact that Harrison has been having problems with wasps near his house.

Harry A young man in *The Mirror Crack'd from Side to Side.* He fails to come to his fiancée's help when she almost falls out a window, a failure that is of great interest to Miss Marple.

Harter, Mary An elderly and eccentric widow in "Where There's a Will." She is difficult with other people and tolerates only her doting nephew, Charles Ridgeway. Soon after changing her will in his favor, she begins hearing her dead husband's voice in a radio and is convinced that she does not have long to live.

Hartigan, Tom A witness in *The A.B.C. Murders.* He notices that Alexander Bonaparte Cust has been present during each of the murders by the A.B.C. killer and reports it to the police. This information proves of great importance to the police in tracking down the person they believe is responsible for the crimes.

Hartington, Jack A golf enthusiast in "The Mystery of the Blue Jar." While golfing each morning, he hears the cry of "Murder—help! Murder" and decides to investigate. The investigation leads him into a series of what seem to be supernatural events that climax with the summoning of spirits through a priceless blue jar.

Hartnell, Amanda The next door neighbor of Miss Marple in St. Mary Mead. Miss Marple considers her to be of rather dubious credibility. She nevertheless plays a minor role in several cases: "The Case of the Perfect Maid," "The Tape-Measure Murders," *The Body in the Library,* and *Murder at the Vicarage.* Reverend Clement describes her as "weather-beaten and jolly and much dreaded by the poor."

Harvey, George A friend of Leonard Vole's in "Witness for the Prosecution." It was Harvey who first revealed to Vole the extent of Emily French's wealth.

Harvey, Jim The fiancé of Amy Gibbs in *Murder Is Easy.* He and Amy quarreled a short time before she was found dead.

Harwell, Eleanor A supposedly Canadian woman, the wife of Captain Harwell in "At the 'Bells and Motley.'" Her husband apparently deserted her soon after they returned from their honeymoon.

Harwell, Captain Richard See Mathias, John.

Hassan An Egyptian servant to Sir John Willard in "The Adventure of the Egyptian Tomb." He is a devoted servant, and so, when his master is murdered, he assists Hercule Poirot in uncovering the murderer.

HASTINGS, CAPTAIN ARTHUR, O.B.E. The faithful friend, associate, assistant, and sometime chronicler of the cases of Hercule Poirot. For many years, Hastings was an invaluable companion to the great Belgian detective, serving in much the same capacity as did the redoubtable Dr. John Watson for Sherlock Holmes. In a kind of compliment, reminiscent of Holmes speaking of Watson, Poirot summed up Hastings's value by declaring: "As in a mirror I see reflected in your mind exactly what

The best of all the Hastingses (Hugh Fraser), in Agatha Christie's Poirot. *(Photofest; London Weekend Television)*

the criminal wishes us to believe. That is terrifically helpful and suggestive."

While the event is, regrettably, not documented, Hastings first met Hercule Poirot some time before World War I. He was working at the time for Lloyd's of London, and Poirot was already a so-called private inquiry agent, with most of Europe as his field of activity. They met again during the Great War. During a period of convalescence in 1916 from wounds received in combat, Hastings found himself at the country estate of Styles Court, which belonged to the family of a friend. While there, he saw Hercule Poirot, who had been forced by the war into the role of refugee. When murder struck down Emily Inglethorp, Hastings remembered the detective's genius and recruited him to solve the case. Not long afterward, he and Poirot were involved in the potentially disastrous kidnapping of Prime Minister David MacAdam, a case recounted in "The Kidnapped Prime Minister."

After this brilliant beginning, Hastings

gladly took rooms with Poirot in London, at 14 Farraday Street. Poirot once more began work as a private detective, with Hastings as his chief assistant. While generally kind to his friend, Poirot had little regard for Hastings' intellect and even less for his skills as a detective. Once, he lamented that Hastings was often a complete imbecile. Nevertheless, this lack of ability was of use to Poirot, for Hastings had "a knack of stumbling over the truth unaware without noticing it himself." This gave to Poirot a truly valuable sounding board for his thoughts and let him see the aforementioned reflection of a criminal's intention. It is true that Hastings lacked much ability in trying to solve cases on his own. This was made manifest in such cases as "The Disappearance of Mr. Davenheim" and "Double Sin."

It was while on a case with Poirot that Hastings met his wife, Dulcie Duveen. He had always taken note of attractive women, and Poirot had even poked gentle fun at his friend's attraction to women with auburn hair in "Double Sin." First told that she was named Cinderella, Hastings learned her full name and wasted little time in marrying Dulcie and then moving with her to Argentina to manage a ranch for the Renauld family. He returned occasionally to England to meet his friend and then took part in several memorable cases with the detective, most notably Poirot's war against an international criminal organization, the Big Four. By the time of Hastings' last published case with Poirot, *Curtain,* Hastings was the proud father of two unnamed sons and two daughters, Grace and Judith. Hastings was also the brother of two unnamed sisters. In *Curtain,* it is revealed that Dulcie had died, and Hastings was deeply troubled about the prospects for his daughter, to the point that he was willing to commit murder.

Agatha Christie created Hastings with a deliberate purpose in mind: "I quite enjoyed Captain Hastings. He was a stereotyped creation, but he and Poirot represented my idea of a detective team. I was still writing in the Sherlock

Holmes tradition—eccentric detective, stooge assistant, with a Lestrade-type Scotland Yard detective, Inspector Japp . . ."

Her opinion had changed between *The Mysterious Affair at Styles* and *Murder on the Links.* "This time I provided a love affair for Hastings. If I had to have a love interest in the book, I thought I might as well marry off Hastings! Truth to tell, I think I was getting a little tired of him. I might be stuck with Poirot, but no need to be stuck with Hastings too."

While there have been a few Hastingses in film, the most memorable has been Hugh Fraser, appearing in the London Weekend Television series *Agatha Christie's Poirot* starring David Suchet.

Hastings, Dulcie Duveen   The wife of Captain Arthur Hastings. Originally born in America, she grew up in England with her twin sister, Bella, with whom she starred in vaudeville as the Dulcibella Kids. She first meets Hastings in *Murder on the Links,* playing a game of mistaken identity with her sister but eventually forming a deep attachment to him. By the end of the novel, she is in love with him and finally punctures his reserved nature to win his hand in marriage. After their marriage, she moves to Argentina with him (as reported in *Curtain*) and they raise two sons and two daughters, including Judith Hastings, an accomplished specialist in tropical diseases. After many years of happiness, Dulcie dies, and Hastings returns to England for one last case with Hercule Poirot.

Hastings, Judith   The favorite daughter of Captain Hastings and his beloved wife, Dulcie. According to information in *Curtain,* Judith is a research assistant in tropical diseases. Her boss is Dr. John Franklin, whom she eventually marries and accompanies to Africa. Captain Hastings admits that, while she has always been his favorite child, Judith remains a mystery in her outlook and interests.

Hautet, Monsieur   An examining magistrate in *Murder on the Links.* His incompetence is the source of much frustration to Hercule Poirot.

Havering, Roger   The second son of the fifth Baron Windsor and heir to a substantial fortune in "The Mystery of Hunter's Lodge." He goes to Hercule Poirot for aid following the murder of his uncle, Harrington Pace, in Derbyshire. Havering is himself a suspect, as he is heavily in debt, but the evidence seems to point in a different direction. Later, with the murderer still at large, Havering and his wife are killed in a plane crash.

Havering, Zoe   The wife of Roger Havering in "The Mystery of Hunter's Lodge." She is a stage actress determined to clear her husband of any suspicion of murdering his uncle, Harrington Pace. She and her husband do manage to inherit Pace's extensive estate, but they are both subsequently killed in a plane crash.

Hawker, Dr.   A physician in "The Adventure of the Italian Nobleman." Hawker is a bachelor who lives in a gloomy old house close to Hercule Poirot's flat; he is also counted among the many friends and acquaintances of Poirot and Captain Hastings. While Poirot and Hastings are dining at the doctor's residence, the physician is informed by his housekeeper that Count Foscatini telephoned and cried out that he was being murdered. This shocking event launches Poirot upon an investigation into blackmail and murder.

Hawker, Anthony   A shabby and unscrupulous boyfriend of Patience Grace in "The Horses of Diomedes." He is shot at by Patience while she is under the thrall of cocaine, drugs that Hawker provided.

Hawkes, Mr.   A new curate in the vicarage of St. Mary Mead in *Murder at the Vicarage.* He has definite views on the Anglican church and fasting, but he does little to win the trust of Reverend Leonard Clement, the vicar of St. Mary Mead. Clement finds him a rather dubious figure, and it is highly possible that Hawkes is guilty of embezzlement.

Haworth, Mrs. Alistair   A stunningly beautiful gypsy woman in "The Gipsy." She has inherited her mother's innate ability to predict the future and foretells several events of importance. Mr. Macfarlane is confident in her abilities, so when she tells him that he will never see her again, he readily assumes that she is predicting his death.

Haworth, Jane   The devoted friend to Alan Everard and Isobel Loring in "Within a Wall." She is extremely devoted to Winnie, the daughter of Everard and Loring, and will do almost anything for the little girl. It is revealed that she is also the source of essential revenue, and the motive for her fidelity becomes known only after her death from influenza.

Hay, Sergeant   A redoubtable if somewhat unimaginative sergeant who works with Inspector Neele in *A Pocket Full of Rye*. Hay discovers the curious presence of rye in the pocket of the murdered Rex Fortescue.

Haydock, Captain   A friend of Inspector Evans in "Accident." He tries unsuccessfully to convince Evans not to pursue his inquiry into Mrs. Merrowdene.

Haydock, Commander   A shadowy figure in *N or M?* He assumes several aliases, including Dr. Binion. As the latter personality, he questions Tuppence Beresford rather menacingly.

Haydock, Dr.   The police surgeon in St. Mary Mead and the next door neighbor, personal physician, and good friend of Miss Marple. The reliable Dr. Haydock appears in several published cases, including "The Case of the Caretaker," "Death by Drowning," *Murder at the Vicarage, The Body in the Library, The Mirror Crack'd from Side to Side,* and *Sleeping Murder.* Dr. Haydock was a physician in whom Miss Marple had complete confidence, as is demonstrated by the length of time that she relied on him to care for her health. He was also a source of invaluable information about medical aspects of cases and murders. In *The Mirror Crack'd from Side to Side,* he prescribes "a nice juicy murder" for Miss Marple when she is low in spirits. Naturally, his prescription is filled. By the time of the Heather Badcock murder in that particular case, Haydock is semiretired and giving most of his patient load to his new partner, Dr. Sandford. Miss Marple, naturally, does not at all approve of the younger physician.

Haydon, Elliot   The cousin of Sir Richard Haydon in "The Idol House of Astarte" and a poor struggling barrister. He discovers his cousin dead and is stabbed in the shoulder during the bizarre events at the Idol House. Years later, despite inheriting all of his cousin's property and wealth, he sets off for the South Pole on an expedition and dies there.

Haydon, Sir Richard   The wealthy purchaser of the property Silent Grove, in Dartmoor, which contains the mysterious house in "The Idol House of Astarte." He hosts a fancy dress party, during which he is murdered under peculiar circumstances near the Idol House. It is learned that he was stabbed through the heart.

Hayes, Sergeant   The police officer in charge of the investigation into the death of Walter St. John in "Sanctuary."

Hayes, Mary   A somewhat slow-witted woman who is hired to serve as the companion to the main character in *Unfinished Portrait.*

Haymes, Phillipa (Pip)   A widow who works as an assistant gardener in Chipping Cleghorn in *A Murder Is Announced.* She is in a position to inherit, with her sister Emma Stamfordis, the estate of Letitia Blacklock.

Hayward, Sir Arthur   Assistant commissioner of Scotland Yard in *Crooked House.* Known as the old man, he is also the father of Charles Hayward and is thus concerned about his son's involvement with Sophie Leonides, a suspect in the murder of Aristide Leonides.

Hayward, Charles   The son of Sir Arthur Hayward in *Crooked House.* A onetime diplomat, Charles met and fell in love with Sophie Leonides while serving with her in Egypt. When Aristide Leonides is murdered, Sophie is, naturally, one of the suspects, and Charles is determined to prove her innocence. His actions are the source of much concern to his father, assistant commissioner of Scotland Yard.

Hazy, Lady Selina A very elderly old lady and guest in *At Bertram's Hotel.* She has journeyed to London to consult with her Harley Street physicians about her chronic arthritis and her bad eyes. Her deteriorating vision is the source of some consternation to other guests, as Lady Hazy habitually mistakes them for friends of hers.

Hearn, Detective Inspector A British policeman in "The Girdle of Hippolita" who is also a friend and associate of Hercule Poirot. The detective uses Hearn to communicate with the French police, especially as Hearn has established a good rapport with them.

Heath, Dr. An admirer of Hercule Poirot and a physician in *Lord Edgware Dies.* He is summoned to examine the body of Carlotta Adams.

Heavyweather, Sir Ernest An infamous and theatrical defense attorney in *The Mysterious Affair at Styles.* He is retained to defend John Cavendish on the charge of murder, and uses his typical egotistical, abrasive, and rude behavior to badger witnesses and intimidate the jury on behalf of his client.

Heilger, Romaine See Vole, Romaine.

Helier, Jane Also called Jane Helman, a popular British actress who is the narrator of the story related in "The Affair at the Bungalow." Jane also has a brief appearance in "Strange Jest," in which she encourages a young couple to consult with Miss Marple about a very odd case.

Hellin, Marie An unpleasant young woman whom Poirot visits in the hopes of tracking down an elusive maid in "The Arcadian Deer." The detective hopes that she might be a maid formerly in the service of Katrina Samoushenka, but he soon determines that she could not possibly be that charming young woman who had won the heart of Ted Williamson.

Helman, Jane See Helier, Jane.

Hemming, Mrs. An eccentric woman in *The Clocks.* She keeps twelve cats and is known for her habit of speaking to them with as much enthusiasm as she uses in speaking to humans.

She also lives next door to the house in which a murder takes place.

Hemmingway, Gerald A young actor and associate of Hercule Poirot in *Cards on the Table.* For the detective, he impersonates a window washer named Stephens in order to encourage Dr. Roberts to make an important admission.

Henderson, Dr. The bishop of Northumbria in "The Augean Stables." He plays an important part in Hercule Poirot's campaign against a tabloid newspaper, the *X-Ray News,* by coming forward to testify that during the time Dagmar Ferrier was supposedly engaged in her adulterous liaison with an Argentine gigolo she was, in fact, with him and his wife.

Henderson, Deidre A homely young woman in *Mrs. McGinty's Dead.* She is the recipient of a sizable sum of money from her aunt; this allows her to control the finances of her mother and stepfather.

Henderson, Ellie A passenger on board the same ship as Hercule Poirot in "Problem at Sea." She is willing to freely discuss her age and her other weaknesses, such as an obsession with scandals. Ellie is also captivated by Colonel Clapperton, becoming, briefly, a possible suspect when Clapperton's wife is murdered.

Hendon A butler at Nasse House in *Dead Man's Folly.* He is an especially active ringer of the dinner gong.

Henet The housekeeper to Imhotep in *Death Comes As the End.* She is murdered by being suffocated by linen.

Hengrave, Mrs. A widow in *Sleeping Murder* who is noted for her exceedingly peculiar tastes in decorations for the home.

Henry A member of the staff in *At Bertram's Hotel.* This butler is remarkably efficient and able to anticipate the needs of the guests

Hensley, Mr. A quiet man who is employed by the public works department of Baghdad in "The Gate of Baghdad." A man of few words, he becomes a suspect in the murder of Smethurst, his best friend, while they are taking a trip across the desert to Baghdad. Hensley is suspected in part because he sat behind the victim and in part because sand, presumably from the sandbag that is thought to be the murder weapon, is found in his spare socks, which had been kept in the pocket of his overcoat. Mr. Parker Pyne, in fact, uses the presence of the sand to discover the murderer.

Henson, Reverend Eustace A young curate in *The Burden*. He presides over the christening of Shirley, the third child of the Franklins.

Hermanstein, Ikey See Isaacstein, Herman.

Heroulde, Monsieur A suspicious character in "The Crackler" who hides his disreputable nature beneath a veneer of respectability.

Hersheimmer, Julius P. A wealthy American cousin of Jane Finn in *The Secret Adversary*. When Jane disappears, he offers a reward of one million pounds to find her. A typical American, he carries a pistol, named Little Willie, and uses such quaint American phrases as "put me wise." He also becomes quite taken with Tuppence Beresford, going so far as to make her a half-serious offer of marriage.

Hetherington, Janet An intelligence operative in *Destination Unknown*. She hides her real activities in Spain and Morocco by impersonating a gossiping, middle-aged Englishwoman who is always careful to associate only with a certain class of English and American visitors.

Higgins, Bill A deep-sea diver who is commissioned by John Newman to search for the sunken cargo from the old *Juan Fernandez* in "Ingots of Gold."

Higgins, Mary See Skinner, Emily.

Higgs, William A Cockney dog trainer who is in charge of the enormous and dangerous guard dog Cerberus in "The Capture of Cerberus." A small, ferret-like man, he is virtually alone in his ability to control to Cerberus, using methods that he is reluctant to discuss in front of a lady. While seemingly successful in his work, Higgs is not the only person to have mastery over the hound; Hercule Poirot also displays a certain talent.

Higley, Milly A waitress in the Ginger Cat with the second victim, Elizabeth Barnard, of the A.B.C. killer in *The A.B.C. Murders*. Hercule Poirot questions her with much skill, playing upon her vanity and obvious physical endowments to gather more information than she realizes she is imparting.

Hill, Mr. The piano accompanist to the singer Jane Harding in *Giant's Bread*. He is described as having the appearance of a white worm.

Hill, Florence A onetime maid in the service of Miss Marple. After some time, she left Miss Marple's employ to run a lodging house. Nevertheless, she is very fond of Jane Marple and is quite happy to fill in as maid when Lucy Eylesbarrow is sent on assignment to Rutherford Hall in *4.50 from Paddington*.

Hill, Gladys A parlor maid in "The Affair of the Pink Pearl." She very conveniently finds the pendant with the missing pearl.

Hill, Mary A chambermaid in the Crown Hotel in Barnchester in "Miss Marple Tells a Story." She comes from the area and has served in the hotel for ten years. Mary is also the last person to see Mrs. Rhodes alive and has, apparently, no motive for murdering the woman.

Hillingdon, Colonel Edward A botanist, adulterer, and husband to Evelyn Hillingdon in *A Caribbean Mystery*. A friend of the Dysons, he had an affair with Lucky Dyson and was instrumental in bringing about her marriage to Greg Dyson as a replacement for Dyson's first wife. The Hillingdons travel to the West Indies each year with the Dysons, but this particular trip proves disastrous, as Lucky is drowned.

Hillingdon, Evelyn The wife of Colonel Hillingdon in *A Caribbean Mystery*. Like her husband, she is a botanist and a friend of the Dysons, with whom she and her husband travel once a year to the West Indies. She is aware of the fact that her husband once had an affair with Lucky Dyson—at a time when she trusted Lucky completely—and is determined to make her marriage successful. Nevertheless, the trip to St. Honoré is marred by Lucky's drowning.

Hinchcliffe, Miss A strong and rather grim woman who lives on a pig and poultry farm in *A Murder Is Announced.* She shares the farm with her companion, the dim-witted Amy Murgatroyd, and is prodded into attending the peculiarly announced murder party by her enthusiastic friend. The event embroils the pair in murder, and Miss Hinchcliffe is devastated when Amy also falls prey to the same killer.

Hobhouse, Valerie The daughter of Mrs. Nicoletis in *Hickory Dickory Dock.* She is a clever and ruthless young woman who adopts a variety of aliases, including Mrs. Da Silva, Sheila Donovan, Miss Irene French, Mrs. Olga Kohn, Miss Nina Le Mesurier, Madame Mahmoudi, Miss Moira O'Neele, and Mrs. Gladys Thomas.

Hod A medical orderly in *Peril at End House.* While he is well-meaning, Hod is not especially bright. Thus, when he is given responsibility to take care of Nick Buckley, he brings her, by accident, a box of poisoned chocolates.

Hodgson, Mr. One of the attorneys in the firm that has the honor of representing the legal interests of Hercule Poirot. Appearing in *The Big Four,* Mr. Hodgson is willing to handle some of Poirot's odder requests, including interviewing assorted individuals who reply to an advertisement placed by the detective concerning Claud Darrell.

Hoffman, Robert A diamond merchant in *At Bertram's Hotel.* He and his brother own a seemingly above-board diamond business, but it is eventually learned that there is more to their enterprise than meets the eye.

Hogben, Superintendent The alias of a man who impersonates a police officer in "Three Blind Mice."

Hogg, Doris A member of the staff at the Meadowbrook School in *Cat among the Pigeons.* She is notably uninformed and uninformative when interviewed by the police about events at the school, especially the murder of Miss Springer.

Hogg, Frederick A young boy and self-important witness in the death of Mrs. Allen in "Murder in the Mews." He provides some useful but misleading details to Hercule Poirot and Inspector Japp concerning the activities of Major Eustace on the day that Mrs. Allen died.

Hogg, Mrs. James The wife of the chauffeur to the residents of number 18, the Mews, in "Murder in the Mews." She provides information to Hercule Poirot and Inpector Japp concerning the household shared by the late Mrs. Allen and Miss Plenderleith.

Hoggin, Sir Joseph The husband of Lady Milly Hoggin in "The Nemean Lion." He is bullied by his wife into hiring Hercule Poirot to find Shan Tung, a kidnapped Pekingese. He does so with great reluctance, but he comes to have a radically different view of the detective by the conclusion of the case. Poirot notes immediately that Hoggin is having an affair with his secretary; the detective gives him a veiled warning not to go through with a possible plot to supplant his wife with a new one.

Hoggin, Lady Milly The unpleasant wife of Sir Joseph Hoggin in "The Nemean Lion." She is described as a "stout, petulant-looking woman with dyed henna red hair." Her obnoxious personality is matched only by her preference for her dog over virtually any other form of companionship. Thus, when her beloved Pekingese, Shan Tung, is kidnapped and the kidnapper threatens to clip the dog's ears and tail off if the ransom demands are not met or if she goes to the police, Lady Milly forces her reluctant husband to consult Hercule Poirot.

Hohenbach Salm, Princess Sasha An enigmatic Russian noblewoman who convinces Joan Scudamore to confront her personal feelings in *Absent in the Spring.*

Hollaby, Mr. The last person to see Anthony Sessle alive in "The Sunningdale Mystery." He is a partner in Sessle's Porcupine Assurance Company and testifies to the odd behavior of Anthony Sessle on the golf course.

Holland, Desmond One of the suspects in the murder of Joyce Reynolds in *Hallowe'en Party.* He seems a likely prospect as a murderer because of his psychiatric troubles. Poirot, however, finds him to be quite interesting (not to mention innocent), and enjoys the young man's agreement with his status as a suspect. Holland suggests several other likely suspects, however, offering very imaginative reasons for their possible guilt. Poirot comes to trust Holland to such a degree that he assigns him the task—with Nicholas Ransome—of protecting a target of the real murderer.

Holland, Elsie An inhabitant of the village of Little Furze in *Moving Finger.* Like others, she is a recipient of a poison-pen letter. Elsie is considered one of the most beautiful woman in the area, save for her "flat" voice.

Holmes, Mr. See Obolovitch, Prince Michael.

Holmes, Mr. The personal butler to the eccentric magnate Benedict Farley in "The Dream." He is meticulous in following his master's orders, including the seemingly peculiar ones.

Holmes, Gladys A maid in "The Case of the Perfect Maid" who falls under suspicion of theft. The temporary disappearance of a brooch convinces Gladys's employers that she is dishonest, even though they have no proof. This rumor soon spreads throughout St. Mary Mead, and Gladys has some difficulty finding a new employer. Miss Marple vouches for her honesty, despite noting Gladys's "adenoidal accents."

Honeycott, Mrs. A bigoted woman in "The Man in the Mist" who owns the house in which Gilda Glen is murdered. A venomous anti-Catholic, she refers to the Catholic church as "The Scarlet Woman."

Hood, Miss A governess to the main character's family in *Unfinished Portrait.*

Hope, Evelyn See Upward, Robin.

Hope, Evelyn A woman accused of murder in *Mrs. McGinty's Dead.* After being cleared of the charge of murder in the Craig trial, she moves to Australia and changes her name.

Hope, Mrs. Gerald The mother of one of the girls in the Meadowbrook School in *Cat among the Pigeons.* She is angry that her daughter will not be allowed to leave in the middle of the term for a family vacation, but Miss Bulstrode is able to play on her vanity (complimenting her designer suit) and so defuses the situation.

Hope, Mildred A friend of Patricia Garnett in "The Third-Floor Flat." She was given a spare key to Patricia's flat but somehow misplaced it. It was thus necessary for Jimmy Faulkener and Donovan Bailey to use unusual means to gain entry into the apartment. Along the way, they discover a corpse.

Hopkins, Jessie A district nurse who develops considerable interest in the estate of Laura Welman in *Sad Cypress.* Her claim to have been stabbed in the finger by a rose thorn in the garden of Hunterbury Hall is proven impossible by Alfred Wargraves, an expert on roses.

Hopkinson, Mr. An attorney and legal advisor to Mary Harter in "Where There's a Will." He assists her in drafting her various wills.

Horbury, Lady Cicely One of the passengers on board the flight from France to England during which Madame Giselle is murdered in *Death in the Clouds.* A former chorus girl now married to Lord Horbury, she is an acute embarrassment to her husband because of her gambling and cocaine addictions. He wants to get a divorce, but she refuses to give him one.

Horbury, Lord Stephen A nobleman who is living in agony over his faithless wife, Lady Cicely Horbury, in *Death in the Clouds.* He wed Cicely, a former chorus girl, and soon regretted it, after becoming aware of her gambling and cocaine addictions. She refuses, however, to give him a divorce. In order to avoid giving his wife the upper hand in any legal proceedings, Lord Horbury refuses to admit his deep feelings for Venetia Kerr.

Horbury, Sydney A creepy and furtive male nurse to Simeon Lee in *Hercule Poirot's Christmas.* He confounds the other members of the

Lee family with his habit of lurking in shadows and watching goings-on in the house.

Horder, Mr. A retired gardener in *The Burden*. He still performs tasks for Laura Franklin in her garden because he respects her considerable skills as a gardener.

Hori An important friend and counselor to Imhotep in *Death Comes As the End*. He plays a vital role in discovering a murderer in the royal household and actually saves the life of Imhotep's daughter, Renisenb; for his achievement, he is rewarded with her hand in marriage.

Horlick A young gardener in *Sad Cypress* who hopes soon to be married. He asks Elinor Carlisle to give him a recommendation as gardener to the new owner of Hunterbury Hall after she sells the estate. He has a curious physical attribute; his Adam's apple moves up and down his neck as he carries on a conversation.

Horriston, Dr. A physician who runs a weight-reducing clinic in "The Case of the Missing Lady." He is viewed with much suspicion by Tommy Beresford.

Horsefall, Pamela A reporter in *Mrs. McGinty's Dead*. She is a virtual parody of the tough female reporter: hard-talking, hard-drinking, and hard-smoking, with a rough manner. She writes an article about women and murder cases that makes at least one person very nervous.

Horsefield, Sir Roderick An elderly soldier who consults Hercule Poirot in the hopes that he might retrieve some politically scandalous papers in *Third Girl*. Despite his poor health and warnings from his doctors, Horsefield always enjoys a strong whiskey.

Horsham See Crispin, Angus.

Horsham, Henry A member of a British government security department in *Passenger to Frankfurt*. Horsham enjoys access to highly sensitive documents and knows numerous leaders in the British intelligence service. He thus knows much about Project Benvo.

Horton, Dr. A physician in "The Harlequin Tea Set." He is consulted by Mr. Satterthwaite and is asked to perform an analysis of a possible poison in a teacup. His daughter is Inez Horton, and his late wife was Maria Horton, daughter of Thomas Addison.

Horton, Major A onetime British soldier in India with a stiff mustache and bulging eyes in *Murder Is Easy*. Although retired for some years, he still maintains a firmly regimented life and prefers to be under the command of a superior. His new superior is his wife, Lydia Horton, who nags him about virtually everything. As the major puts it, a husband needs his wife to keep him in line, "Otherwise he gets slack—yes, slack." Lydia dies unexpectedly from gastroenteritis.

Horton, Inez The granddaughter of Thomas Addison and the daughter of Dr. Horton in "The Harlequin Tea Set." Her mother, Maria Horton, died while giving birth to her, and she lives with her father in the house next to her grandfather.

Horton, Lydia The domineering wife of Major Horton in *Murder Is Easy*. Much to her husband's apparent satisfaction, Mrs. Horton runs her household as though it were a military post, nagging her husband and controlling virtually every aspect of his life. A thoroughly unpleasant woman, she is despised in the neighborhood and runs through household help to the tune of fifteen cooks and maids in less than a year. She dies suddenly and unexpectedly from gastroenteritis.

Horton, Maria The late wife of Dr. Horton and the daughter of Thomas Addison in "The Harlequin Tea Set." She died in childbirth while bringing Inez Horton into the world.

Hoskin, Robert (Bob) A local policeman in *Dead Man's Folly*. He is always careful to keep copious notes of his interviews and his examinations of crime scenes.

Howard, Evelyn (Evie) The companion to Emily Inglethorpe in *The Mysterious Affair at Styles*. Known commonly as Evie, she provides a great deal of emotional stability and common sense in the Inglethorpe household and even receives the praise of Hercule Poirot, who refers to her as "an excellent specimen of well-balanced English beef and brawn."

Howell, Mrs. A housekeeper at the Chimneys in *The Seven Dials Mystery.* An exceedingly solemn woman, she makes her employer, Lady Coote, rather uncomfortable, but Lady Eileen Brent is able to charm her completely and to puncture her dignified exterior. Mrs. Howell knows a great deal about the household at the Chimneys.

Hubbard, Mrs. The sister of Felicity Lemon, secretary to Hercule Poirot, in *Hickory Dickory Dock.* Whereas Miss Lemon is thin and of severe appearance, Mrs. Hubbard is soft and round-faced. She also lacks Miss Lemon's sharp mind. After living for years in Singapore, the widowed Mrs. Hubbard returns to England and takes a position as the manager of Mrs. Nicoletis's youth hostel. When the hostel is plagued by a series of thefts, she turns to Hercule Poirot for help.

Hubbard, Caroline Martha A retired famous stage actress who is traveling on the Calais Coach in *Murder on the Orient Express.* She claims to be journeying on the train to visit her daughter and son-in-law, who teaches at the American University in Smyrna. Poirot and the other passengers find her loud and brash, but the detective also finds her to be a natural leader among the peculiar gathering of travelers in the Calais Coach. Miss Hubbard's real name is Linda Arden.

Hudd, Gina The stunningly beautiful wife of Walter Hudd in *They Do It with Mirrors.* She is very much aware of her good looks and has used them to catch the eye of most of the male residents at Stonygates, much to the chagrin of her husband.

Hudd, Walter (Wally) The American husband of Gina Hudd in *They Do It with Mirrors.* He is unhappy with the fact that his wife flaunts her beauty and is such a flirt with the men of Stonygates. His real hope is to take her back with him to America.

Huish, Superintendent A police superintendent who is in charge of the Argyle murder case in *Ordeal by Innocence.* He is especially fond of

magic tricks and jokes and is thus very popular at children's parties.

Humbleby, Jessie Rose The widow of Dr. John Humbleby in *Murder Is Easy.* She is devastated when her husband dies unexpectedly, and tells Luke Fitzwilliam that the village of Wychwood is harboring a great evil. Her daughter is Rose Humbleby.

Humbleby, Dr. John Ward A country doctor in *Murder Is Easy.* He dies quite suddenly from septicemia, leaving behind a grief-stricken widow, Jessie Humbleby, and a daughter, Rose. While his death is not unambiguously a murder, everyone in the village of Wychwood knows that his death is one of many that have occurred recently.

Humbleby, Rose The daughter of Dr. John and Jessie Rose Humbleby in *Murder Is Easy.* She falls in love with her father's medical partner, Dr. Thomas, but acquiesces to her father's wishes that she not have a relationship with him. This changes upon her father's death, although she decides to wait an appropriate amount of time before the wedding.

Humfries, Mr. The manager of Bertram's Hotel in *At Bertram's Hotel* who is adroit at anticipating the needs and whims of guests and who has the added skill of adapting his own conversation to match the interests of a guest. He is the object of a great deal of suspicion on the part of Chief Inspector Davy, who sees him as a "smarmy sort of chap" and who suspects him of being more than a mere hotel manager.

Hunt, Verity A supposed victim of murder who sparks Miss Marple's involvement in *Nemesis.* After her parents died in a plane crash in Spain, she was raised by her appointed guardian, Clothilde Bradbury-Scott, a friend of her parents. It was assumed that she was murdered—by Michael Rafiel—when a disfigured body, presumed to be hers, was found in a quarry.

Hunter, David The supposed brother of Rosaleen Cloade in *Taken at the Flood.* He enjoys a favored position in the Cloade household, thanks to his sister's marriage to the late Gordon Cloade and her assumption of control over the family's estate. It becomes increasingly clear, however, that David and Rosaleen are not brother and sister, and the two face a troublesome blackmailer in the enigmatic Enoch Arden. When Arden is murdered, Hunter is charged with the crime, and his position seems to sink even further when Rosaleen dies in her sleep. Poirot, however, turns his "little grey cells" in a different direction.

Hunter, Megan A gangly and ungraceful young girl in *The Moving Finger*. She discovers the corpse of Agnes Woddell and is instrumental in bringing a murderer to justice at the risk of her own life. She undergoes a transformation of sorts from an awkward youth into a beautiful young woman when she is taken on a trip to London by Jerry Burton and patronizes the dressmaker and hairdresser used by Burton's sister. By the solution of the case, she has given her heart to Jerry.

Hurst, Jim Secretary to the American magnate Caleb Blundell in "The Pearl of Price." Hurst has a checkered past, having once been caught attempting to steal from Blundell. At the request of Blundell's daughter, Carol, the magnate gave Hurst a second chance. The young man more than made good with his opportunity, earning Blundell's trust and proving a reliable confidante. Because of his past, however, Hurst is immediately suspected of stealing an expensive earring when the jewel goes missing.

Imhotep A mortuary priest in the service of the Temple of Meripath in *Death Comes As the End*. A widower, he stuns his family, especially his four children, when he brings into the household a nineteen-year-old concubine, Nofret, whom he declares to be his heir. This liaison creates chaos for the family, and shortly after her arrival murders start occurring that threaten everyone.

Inch The name used in St. Mary Mead for the local cab company, Inch's Taxi Service. The name remains Inch despite the fact that the company no longer is owned by Mr. Inch and is operated by a Mr. Roberts. Miss Marple travels "in Inch" in *The Mirror Crack'd from Side to Side* and *Nemesis*.

Ingles, John An expert in Chinese political affairs in *The Big Four*. Soon after setting sail from Marseilles on board the S.S. *Shanghai,* Ingles disappears and his Chinese servant is murdered. This event takes place shortly after Ingles was consulted by Hercule Poirot about the possibility that the Big Four might have been connected to the Chinese underworld and the opium trade.

Inglethorp, Alfred The recently acquired much younger husband of Emily Inglethorp in *The Mysterious Affair at Styles*. The former secretary to Emily, he is considered a very poor choice for marriage by her family and is even called a fortune hunter. Nevertheless, he seems to be devoted to his wife until she dies from strychnine poisoning. Alfred is then arrested on the charge of murder and put on trial. Hercule Poirot considers him to be "a man of method."

Inglethorp, Emily Agnes The seventy-year-old-matriarch in *The Mysterious Affair at Styles*. She is devoted to using her wealth to support a variety of causes and charities, including an effort to house Belgian refugees during World War I at Leastways Cottage. One of her boarders is thus the refugee Hercule Poirot. Emily decides to marry her much younger secretary, Alfred Inglethorp, a union strenuously opposed by her family, who considers Alfred to be a gold digger. She seems happy for a time, but she eventually succumbs to strychnine poisoning. Poirot is determined to bring the murderer of his patron to justice.

Inglewood, Sir Mortimer A formidable attorney and orator who prosecutes the libel suit against the *X-Ray News* in "The Augean Stables." He uses appeals to patriotism, national security, and the threat that fascism and communism pose to democracy in his appeal against the paper.

Instow, Jean A woman in "The Blue Geranium" who is in love with George Pritchard. She has an intense dislike for Mary Pritchard and wants her to die so that she can become George's new wife.

Ipy One of the four children of Imhotep in *Death Comes As the End*. A clever lad, he nevertheless falls prey to murder; his body is found face down in a stream.

Isaacstein, Herman Also called Ikey Hermanstein, Fat Ikey, and Noseystein, a financier in *The Secret of Chimneys*. Described as one of the "strong, silent, yellow men of finance," he agrees to assist Prince Michael Obolovitch of Herzoslovakia in return for certain concessions. The prince is murdered, however, and Isaacstein is seemingly implicated when the murder weapon is discovered in his suitcase.

Ivanovitch, Boris A mysterious ratlike man who appears in *The Mystery of the Blue Train* and *The Secret Adversary*. In *The Secret Adversary,* he pretends to be Count Stepanov and a member of a gang of Bolsheviks; in *The Mystery of the Blue Train,* he impersonates Monsieur Krassine and lays his hands on the Heart of Fire rubies.

Ivanovitch, Sergius See Oranoff, Prince Sergius.

Jackson, Arthur A male nurse, masseur, and all-around personal valet to Jason Rafiel in *A Caribbean Mystery*. He proves useful to Miss Marple in that he worked previously in the pharmaceuticals industry and thus knows a great deal about the assorted drugs found in the cosmetics collection of Molly Kendall.

Jacobs, Miss An elderly woman who rings the police after the discovery of the body of David Baker in *Third Girl*.

Jacques One of the staff members of the Hotel Rochers Neiges in "The Erymanthean Boar." Jacques is both surly and unprofessional.

James See Darrell, Claude.

James, Caroline The wife of an incompetent gardener in *The Man in the Brown Suit*. Caroline is a superb cook, so much so that the man who employs both Caroline and her husband, Sir Eustace Pedler, will not fire her husband for fear of losing her.

Jameson, Commissionaire The chief police officer in the area around Doncaster in *The A.B.C. Murders*. He discovers the body of George Earlsfield in a movie theater seat, with a copy of the A.B.C. *Rail Guide* beneath the seat.

Jameson, Mrs. A hair stylist in *The Mirror Crack'd from Side to Side*. She has a faithful group of clients comprised almost entirely of aging women who never deviate from their preferred hair styles. She gives assistance to Miss Marple in her investigation into the death surrounding Marina Gregg by providing the old sleuth with copies of movie magazines.

Jameson, Richard One of the participants in a tour of famous houses and gardens of Great Britain in *Nemesis*. He is of great annoyance to his fellow tourists because of his superior attitude and his ceaseless lectures about architecture. Even Miss Marple has her patience strained by his tedious discourses.

Jane A friend of Tuppence Beresford in "The Unbreakable Alibi." She provides Tuppence with four photographs in an effort to break the seemingly unshakable alibi of Una Drake.

Janet There are three Janets in the Christie writings. The first is the eleven-year-old granddaughter of Tommy and Tuppence Beresford in *Postern of Fate*. The second is a maid in "The Love Detectives" who lives in dread that her lover, a valet, will somehow be implicated in murder. The third Janet is an elderly maid at Enderby Hall in *After the Funeral*. She has a curious friendship with the ninety-year-old butler, Lanscombe, with whom she enjoys assorted disagreements; they are in firm agreement, however, over the inappropriate behavior of the younger generation of servants.

JAPP, CHIEF INSPECTOR JAMES An officer serving in Scotland Yard who is best known for his long association with Hercule Poirot. Described as "a little, sharp, dark, ferret-faced man," Japp was also one of the few detectives or police officers of any kind in Christie's writings who received a promotion from one case to the

A grand Inspector Japp (Philip Jackson), in Agatha Christie's Poirot. *(Photofest; London Weekend Television)*

next. Hercule Poirot liked Japp, even though he often thought little of the policeman's methods and results: "Japp is the 'younger generation knocking at the door.' And *ma foi!* They are so busy knocking that they do not notice that the door is open!"

Despite Poirot's low opinion of the policeman's abilities, the two had a generally cordial and lengthy professional relationship. They first met in 1904, when Poirot was still working in the Belgian police force and Japp was with Scotland Yard. They were both involved in the unpublished Abercrombie forgery case and the matter involving Baron Altara. It is unknown if that was the last case before World War I, but Poirot and Japp again met during *The Mysterious Affair at Styles*. Once Poirot was firmly established as a London detective, the two were frequently working on the same case, with "Moosier Poirot" invariably solving the crime or mystery first. His tendency to mispronounce Poirot's name was deliberate. Japp was also an amateur botanist and was married.

In the London Weekend Television series *Agatha Christie's Poirot* starring David Suchet,

the role of Inspector Japp was played throughout by Jackson. One other notable Inspector Japp appeared in the television feature *Thirteen for Dinner*, starring Peter Ustinov as Hercule Poirot. There, Japp was played by David Suchet, who went on to play Poirot.

Jarrold, Detective Inspector A Scotland Yard officer who has the difficult task of following a spy named Mardenberg in "The Girl in the Train." He is aided in his work unexpectedly by the appearance of George Rowland.

Jarrow, Dorothea The twin sister of Molly Ravenscroft in *Elephants Can Remember.* She was the recipient of the attentions of General Alistair Ravenscroft even before her sister was.

Jeanne The dresser to Madame Nadina, the famous Parisian dancer in *The Man in the Brown Suit.*

Jefferson, Adelaide A widow and overly devoted mother in *The Body in the Library.* She is very concerned about guaranteeing that her son, Peter Carmody, remains the heir to Conway Jefferson, his step-uncle. Part of this worry has to do with her own financial difficulties, which resulted from the severe losses on the stock market she sustained after her late husband mismanaged the funds. She is also the object of the affections of Raymond Starr and Hugo McLean.

Jefferson, Conway A wealthy and intellectually vigorous man who is confined to a wheelchair after a plane crash that also claimed his wife, son, and daughter in *The Body in the Library.* He falls under the influence of Ruby Keene and plans to adopt her formally and make her his heir. This is a most unwelcome development in the view of his relatives, especially Adelaide Jefferson and her son, Peter Carmody, Conway's step-nephew. The inheritance becomes a moot point, however, as Ruby Keene is murdered.

Jeffries, Edward A young American whose wife, Elsie, is aided by Mr. Parker Pyne in "Have You Got Everything You Want?" Described by his wife as straitlaced and of Puritan ancestry, he is tormented by an indiscretion that took place before his marriage and that now threatens the happiness of his union. He receives some advice from Parker Pyne concerning how to deal with women, including the amazing suggestion, "It is a fundamental axiom of married life that you must lie to a woman. She likes it!"

Jeffries, Elsie A young American woman who is helped by Mr. Parker Pyne in "Have You Got Everything You Want?" Surprised to encounter Parker Pyne on the Simplon Express, she knows of him from his famous newspaper advertisement and asks his assistance. She fears some threat to her life or well-being while on the train, a fear that is seemingly fulfilled when her jewels are stolen. While she is initially very disappointed in Parker Pyne, Elsie is delighted by his swift recovery of the jewels. (See also Subayska, Madame.)

Jenkins, Miss A seemingly dim-witted and certainly homely secretary in the firm of Gable and Stretcher in *Dumb Witness*.

Jenkins, Sister An army hospital nurse in *Giant's Bread*. She is a very pessimistic person.

Jennings A valet in "The Love Detectives." He is in the service of Sir James Dwighton and, given his background (Jennings was once dismissed for stealing), Jennings is considered a suspect in Dwighton's murder. Jennings is given some protection by one of the maids in the household, but her efforts prove fruitless.

Jennson, Miss A severe and unattractive woman who works for Mr. Aristide in *Destination Unknown*. She is an important figure in the operations of the Brain Trust and thus becomes a target of Andrew Peters.

Jesmond, Mr. A member of the British foreign office who enlists the assistance of Hercule Poirot in "The Theft of the Royal Ruby." He has the difficult task of requesting the aid of Poirot in locating the stolen ruby belonging to Prince Ali. As this will mean that Poirot will have to spend Christmas at the Kings Lacey estate, Mr. Jesmond assures Poirot that he will have all modern conveniences at his disposal during his stay there, in an effort to assuage Poirot's many concerns about his personal comfort.

Jessop, Mr. A member of a British intelligence unit in *Destination Unknown*. He prevents Hilary Craven from committing suicide and then recruits her to assist his operation against Mr. Aristide and the Brain Trust.

Jethroe, Johnny A photographer's assistant in *The Mirror Crack'd from Side to Side*. He makes an obvious observation to Inspector Dermot Craddock that a murder case is very much like a photograph, in that it "develops."

Jim One of the children who were evacuees during World War II and who became victims of abuse while in the care of the Lyons couple in "Three Blind Mice." He schemes to exact revenge upon all of those who did him and his fellow children harm during their time in the war. He impersonates several people in the accomplishment of murder and vengeance.

Jobson, Mr. A cab driver in *Lord Edgware Dies*. He is a gruff old fellow, with a hoarse voice, glasses, and a seedy mustache. Nevertheless, he proves instrumental in destroying the alibis of Geraldine and Ronald Marsh.

John There are three Johns in the Christie writings. The first is a medium in "The Bird with the Broken Wing." He owns a Ouija board that is used by Mr. Harley Quin to send a useful message concerning Madge Keeley to Mr. Satterthwaite. A second John is a young squadron leader in *Murder in Mesopotamia*. He gives Nurse Leatheran information concerning the American expedition laboring at Tell Yarimjah. He was once much attracted to Mrs. Leidner, but his view of her is now radically different. The third John is the father of the main character in *Unfinished Portrait*. He dies when the main character is eleven years old, and his death leaves the family in terrible financial condition.

Johnson The butler in the employ of Sir Alington West in "The Red Signal." He testifies that he overheard an argument between Dermot West and Sir Alington shortly before he discovered his employer shot through the heart.

Johnson, Colonel The name of the chief constables in two different cases. The first Colonel Johnson is chief constable for the village of Middleshire in *Hercule Poirot's Christmas.* He is consulted by Hercule Poirot after the brutal murder of Simeon Lee. The second Colonel Johnson is chief constable of Yorkshire and a friend of Mr. Satterthwaite. He is in charge of investigating the events in *Three-Act Tragedy.*

Johnson, Constable A constable in the area around Market Basing in *The Secret of Chimneys.* Johnson assists Inspector Badgworthy and expresses much excitement at the prospect of his first murder investigation ending with a hanging.

Johnson, Miss Two characters in separate Christie works. The first Miss Johnson is a school matron in *Cat among the Pigeons.* She is very fond of the Meadowbank School and considers the establishment to be her home. The second Miss Johnson is a young, heavyset woman who works in the Crown and Feathers in Croydon in *Death in the Clouds.* She is involved with Albert Davis, the second steward on the *Prometheus,* the plane that carried Madame Giselle to her death.

Johnson, Mrs. See Bligh, Gertrude.

Johnson, Mrs. See Willett, Mrs.

Johnson, Anne A member of the American expedition at Tell Yarimjah in *Murder in Mesopotamia.* She provides an important clue to Hercule Poirot but is then murdered soon afterward. She dies after drinking hydrochloric acid that had been poured into her glass in place of water.

Johnson, Elizabeth One of the boarders in the home of Mrs. Nicoletis in *Hickory Dickory Dock.* She is called Black Bess by her fellow boarders because of her dreadful personality, her ego (said to equal that of Napoleon), and her membership in the Communist party.

Johnson, Victoria A maid at the Golden Palms Hotel in *A Caribbean Mystery.* She discovers who took the bottle of pills from Major Palgrave's room and decides to try her hand at blackmail. This backfires terribly, and she is stabbed to death.

Joliet, Madame The all-powerful manager of the Ballet Maritski in Paris in *4.50 from Paddington.* She is contacted by the police for information on Anna Stravinska. Madame Joliet has little patience for the police and makes the caustic observation that her biggest enemies are men, for they are constantly robbing her of dancers.

Jonathan, Caleb The head of a firm of attorneys who represent the legal interests of the Crale family in *Five Little Pigs.* He is an old-fashioned lawyer and has a personality that is much to the liking of Hercule Poirot.

Jones The valet to Lord Edward Campion in "The Rajah's Emerald." He is present at the time when the rajah's fabulous emerald goes missing and plays a part in the events that follow, especially those concerning young James Bond.

Jones, Detective Sergeant A policeman who takes part in the investigation of the murder of Lady Tressilian in *Towards Zero.* He is instrumental in bringing the murderer to justice.

Jones, Miss The spectacled secretary to Olga Stormer in "The Actress." She handles the actress's affairs with considerable alacrity.

Jones, Mr. A bank manager in the village of Wychwood in *Murder Is Easy.* He provides information to Luke Fitzwilliam concerning the whereabouts of two suspects on the day that Lavinia Fullerton was murdered in London; Jones helps establish that the two were not in Wychwood on the fateful day.

Jones, Mrs. A rather nondescript woman of forty-five whose death is recounted in "The Tuesday Night Club." She was murdered, but her death was initially and incorrectly attributed to eating canned lobster tainted with botulism. Her husband is Albert Jones.

Jones, Albert The husband of Mrs. Jones in "The Tuesday Night Club." He is a salesman for a chemical manufacturing company and inherits eight thousand pounds after his wife dies from apparent botulism poisoning after eating canned lobster. It becomes increasingly clear that not only is he an insincere grieving widower but that he has a dark past to keep secret.

Jones, Policewoman Alice A female police officer in *Dead Man's Folly* who assists in proving that Lady Hattie Stubbs could have died from drowning while a tour boat was meandering past her very location.

Jones, Gwyneth A children's companion in *The Burden* who was ordered by her doctor not to work with children because of her tendency to suffer seizures. She disregards the physician's imperative and suffers a seizure while sitting with several young ones. Her episode leads to a fire that nearly kills the children.

Jones, Mary The fiancée of Stephen Grant and the daughter of the innkeeper "At the 'Bells and Motley.' " She is absolutely convinced that Grant is innocent of the crimes of which he has been accused and hopes that Mr. Satterthwaite will be able to help him.

Jones, Montgomery A hopeful young man who comes to Tommy and Tuppence with an odd request in "The Unbreakable Alibi." He asks the sleuths to prove that Una Drake does not have an absolutely unbreakable alibi, an effort that would assist him in winning her affections.

Jones, Queenie A kitchen maid in the household of the doomed Simeon Lee in *Hercule Poirot's Christmas.*

Jones, Robert (Bobby) The fourth son of the vicar of Marchbolt in *Why Didn't They Ask Evans?* He discovers a corpse while playing golf and becomes—with the help of assorted friends, including Lady Frances Derwent, the woman he hopes to marry—the primary investigator into the murder. A clever and vigorous young man, he assumes several disguises (including a chauffeur and a lawyer) in pursuit of

the murderer. After bringing the killer to justice, he moves with his love to Kenya to manage a coffee plantation.

Jones, Reverend Thomas The vicar of Marchbolt and father of Robert Jones in *Why Didn't They Ask Evans?* Although he has several sons, the one called Robert—or Bobby—is his chief concern, because of his wild ways and his equally wild friends. He tries to bear the discomfort caused by his son with stoic acceptance, but this does not prevent his stomach from causing him much agony.

Jones, Victoria A clever and beautiful young woman who takes part in a series of adventures in *They Came to Baghdad.* Miss Jones is fired from her job after doing an all-too-realistic impersonation of her employer's wife and subsequently has a chance meeting with Edward Goring while she is eating lunch in a park. She falls for him immediately and then, on a wild whim, decides she wants to follow him to Baghdad. She concocts a suitable past for herself (claiming that she is related to a bishop and a famous archaeologist) and is hired as a nurse-companion to Mrs. Hamilton Clipp, who is journeying to Baghdad for reasons of her own. Once in Baghdad, Miss Jones is swept up in international intrigue and espionage, and eventually finds herself working for the mysterious Mr. Dakin and British intelligence itself.

Jones, William The proprietor of the inn in "At the 'Bells and Motley' " and father of Mary Jones. He provides a full account of the disappearance of Captain Harwell to Mr. Harley Quin and Mr. Satterthwaite.

Jordan, Mary A member of British intelligence in *Postern of Fate.* She was murdered many years before the investigation by Tommy and Tuppence Beresford into her death. She met her demise while making inquiries about potentially dangerous political goings-on in the village of Hollowquay during World War I; she supposedly died by accident after eating lethal foxglove that had been tossed into a salad.

Joseph, Franz   See Arguileros, Karl.

Josephine   A cat, also called Jehoshaphat, who is used by the main character in *The Burden* to smother a baby. The cat, however, is most unwilling to go along with the plot.

Juanita   See Cortman, Mildred Jean.

Judd, Henry   The doting husband of the actress Rosina Nunn in "The World's End." He becomes involved with a group of strangers who are stranded together while waiting for a sudden snowstorm to end. The time of waiting proves very revealing.

Judy   The daughter of Celia in *Unfinished Portrait*. She suffers because she and her mother were abandoned by her father, and Celia dedicates herself to making up for any damage to Judy that might have been caused.

Jules   The maitre d'hotel in the *Chez Ma Tante* in *Death on the Nile*. He is a most distinguished and well-known figure who is also quite familiar with the gastronomic needs, caprices, and refined tastes of Hercule Poirot. To please his patron, Jules organizes a special meal for the detective that is described as "positively a poem" by the restaurant's proprietor.

Kait   The wife of Sobek and the daughter-in-law of Imhotep in *Death Comes As the End*. She has a most jaundiced opinion of men, especially her acutely unfaithful husband. Her opinion sours even further when Imhotep returns home with a new concubine and proclaims that the woman is his new heir, thus supplanting Kait's children.

Kameni   A suitor to Renisenb in *Death Comes As the End*. He bears a striking resemblance to Renisenb's late husband, but this in itself fails to move her heart.

Kane, Eva   See Hope, Evelyn.

Kane, Norton   One of the passengers on board the motor coach in "Double Sin." He is an immediate suspect in the theft of a set of expensive miniatures. Hercule Poirot, however, finds him of interest because of his poor mustache, which seems even more pathetic compared to the detective's far more impressive version.

Karl, Prince   A nobleman in "The Girl in the Train" who expects to wed his cousin, the grand duchess Anastasia. Described as "a horrid, pimply person," he pursues Anastasia across Europe and is finally incommoded by George Rowland. When George refuses to duel him, Prince Karl tweaks his enemy's nose, whereupon George launches into a fistfight with him. Karl does not come out victorious, and he never does gain Anastasia's hand.

Kate   A cook in *Unfinished Portrait* who is noted for her refusal to follow recipes.

Keane, Marcia   A friend of Margery Gale in "The Voice in the Dark." She differs with her friend over the question as to whether a ghost is haunting Abbot's Mead. In order to bring the matter to a close, Marcia takes part in a séance.

Keble, Ellen   The companion to Mrs. Samuelson in "The Nemean Lion." While she was taking Mrs. Samuelson's beloved Pekingese, Nanki Poo, for a walk, she stopped to admire a baby in a carriage and had the little dog kidnapped right from under her nose.

Keeley, David   A mathematician in "The Bird with the Broken Wing." He shows Mr. Satterthwaite the body of Mabelle Annesley and is of the view that she committed suicide. His daughter is Madge Keeley.

Keeley, Madge   The daughter of David Keeley in "The Bird with the Broken Wing." She is quite different from her father, for where he is dull and plodding, she is energetic and enthusiastic. She also loves her fiancée, Roger Graham, but becomes alarmed when he becomes attached to Mabelle Annesley, who soon dies.

Keen, Dr.   A doctor in *Giant's Bread*. The young physician is wounded during World War I.

Keene, Sergeant   The head of local police in Kingston Bishop in *Endless Night*. He is remarkably knowledgeable about local lore, especially when it concerns the gypsies. He thus provides valuable details to Michael Rogers about Gipsy's Acre.

Keene, Geoffrey The retiring and rather dull secretary to Hubert Lytcham Roche in "The Second Gong." While he is definitely attracted to Diana Cleves, she uses him to convince her father that she has lost interest in another man of whom her father disapproves.

Keene, Ruby An eighteen-year-old platinum blond dancer in *The Body in the Library.* Born Rosy Legge, she grew up under harsh financial circumstances and was determined to find a way to secure a wealthy patron. She acquires one in Conway Jefferson, who goes so far as to name her his heir and adopt her. Before she can enjoy her new position, however, Ruby is murdered and her body is at first presumed to have been dumped in the library in the home of Arthur Bantry. In fact, Ruby's charred corpse was placed in the stolen automobile belonging to George Bartlett.

Keene, Sylvia The ward of Sir Ambrose Bercy and the fiancée of Jerry Lorimer in "The Herb of Death." Sylvia dies after eating an excess of poisonous foxglove. Initially considered an accident—especially as she had picked the foxglove and sage herself—her death is later found to have been murder.

Kellett, Billy A pickpocket who served three months in prison in "The Disappearance of Mr. Davenheim." He becomes a leading suspect in the presumed kidnapping and murder of Mr. Davenheim.

Kelly, Sheila See Grant, Sheila.

Kelsey, Detective Inspector The officer in charge of the inquiry into the murder at the Meadowbank School in *Cat among the Pigeons.* He has worked with Hercule Poirot previously and shares with the detective the desire to be as efficient as possible.

Kelsey, Inspector A police officer in *The A.B.C. Murders* who works with Inspector Crome to find the A.B.C killer. He has an un-

canny ability to mimic the idiosyncrasies of assorted witnesses.

Kelsey, Major The husband of Mary Kelsey and a member of the expedition to Tell Yarimjah in *Murder in Mesopotamia.* He and his wife hire Miss Leatheran to assist in the care of their newborn child.

Kelsey, Mary The wife of Major Kelsey in *Murder in Mesopotamia.* She has recently given birth to a baby and thus encourages her husband to hire a nurse to assist her while they are on the expedition to Tell Yarimjah.

Kelvin, Mr. The owner of the Three Amigos pub in the Cornish village of Polperran. He is described as "a remarkable man, dark and swarthy, with curiously broad shoulders." Because of his prison record, his training as a diver, and his reputation for illegal behavior, he is the obvious suspect in the kidnapping of John Newman and the theft of the bullion from the sunken ship *Otranto.*

Kemp, Chief Inspector The Scotland Yard official who works with Colonel Johnny Race to find the murderer in *Sparkling Cyanide.*

Kench, Joan A maid in the household of Simeon Lee in *Hercule Poirot's Christmas.*

Kendall, Molly The co-owner of the Golden Palm Hotel in *A Caribbean Mystery.* She is a lovely and kind woman in her twenties who is plagued by hallucinations, memory loss, and nightmares. The cause of these maladies becomes clear and is tied to murder. Her husband is Tim Kendall.

Kendall, Tim The co-owner of the Golden Palm Hotel and husband of Molly Kendall in *A Caribbean Mystery.* He is young and good-looking, but he must follow his wife's suggestions and pay close attention to female guests. Miss Marple receives some of his special charm, although she is too smart to succumb to such obvious blandishments.

Kennedy, Helen Spenlove See Halliday, Helen Spenlove Kennedy.

Kennedy, Dr. James The physician in the village of Dillmouth in *Sleeping Murder.* He takes a dim view of his half sister's twenty-year absence. He is a competent physician, but he somehow misses the clues that point to the fact that Helen Spenlove Kennedy Halliday was actually murdered.

Kent, Captain A member of the secret service who is sent by the United States government to investigate the disappearance of Mr. Halliday in *The Big Four.* He is so stern-faced that it appears as if his visage was carved out of wood rather than flesh.

Kent, Charles The illegitimate son of Roger Ackroyd's housekeeper in *The Murder of Roger Ackroyd.* Kent claims that on the night of Ackroyd's death, he was in the house, but he was visiting his mother, Mrs. Russell.

Kent, Dr. Marcus The physician to the pilot Jerry Burton in *The Moving Finger.* He suggests that Burton, who is recovering from war wounds, find a small, out-of-the-way spot to recuperate. Burton's choice proves anything but restful.

Kerr, Dr. The police surgeon in *The A.B.C. Murders* who is summoned to examine the first victim of the A.B.C. killer, Amy Ascher. He is of the view that the killer is probably not a woman, as this murder is not a typical crime for a woman to commit.

Kerr, Allegra A friend of Maisie Wetterman in "The House of Dreams." She becomes attracted to John Segrave, but her family history of insanity makes her more than reluctant to wed anyone. In the end, she becomes caught up in John's recurring dream of a perfect white house.

Kerr, Mary The name used by Jane Helier in "The Affair at the Bungalow" to refer to an actress who is having an affair with the actor Claud Leason.

Kerr, The Honourable Venetia Anne A highly socially prominent woman in *Death in the Clouds.* She is deeply in love with Lord Horbury and considers his wife "a little tart." Hopeful that Horbury will eventually be able to divorce his wife, she is stunned to see Lord Horbury appear with his wife after the death of

Madame Giselle, but her aspirations are more than fulfilled with the timely help of Hercule Poirot.

Kettering, Derek The husband of Ruth Kettering and son-in-law of the wealthy American Rufus van Aldin in *The Mystery of the Blue Train.* He is habitually unfaithful and chronically in need of money. Nevertheless, he has prospects of inheriting of the family title of Lord Leaconbury. His precarious financial situation and his dependence on his wife do not keep him from continuing to cheat on her.

Kettering, Ruth The daughter of the wealthy American Rufus van Aldin and the unhappy wife of Derek Kettering in *The Mystery of the Blue Train.* She wed Derek in order to secure the eventual possibility of his inheriting the title of Lord Leaconbury. Encouraged to divorce him by her father, she finally agrees and apparently embarks on an affair of her own with Count Armand de la Roche. She is, in fact, on her way to see him when she is murdered on board the Blue Train. Her murder comes only after her father has given her the Heart of Fire rubies.

Kharsanova, Anna See Denman, Anna.

Khay The late husband of Renisenb in *Death Comes As the End.*

Kidd, Gracie See Mason, Gracie.

Kidd, Kitty See Mason, Ada.

Kiddell, Mrs. A housekeeper in *Mrs. McGinty's Dead.* She takes a certain peculiar pride in the fact that she is working in a house in which a murder took place. Her pride appalls Hercule Poirot.

Kidderminster, Lady Victoria (Vicky) A socially prominent woman with a horsey face in *Sparkling Cyanide.* She and her husband, Lord William Kidderminster, consider their son-in-law, Stephen Farraday, to be acceptable despite his philandering because of his political usefulness and ambition. When Farraday's mistress turns up dead, Lady Kidderminster believes her daughter to be more than capable of committing the crime.

Kidderminster, Lord William A politically powerful figure and husband of the equally prominent Lady Kidderminster in *Sparkling Cyanide.* He is well suited to the ruthless life he shares with his wife. They both approve of their habitually unfaithful son-in-law, Stephen Farraday, because of his political ambition.

Killer Kate See Lancaster, Julia.

Kimble, Lady Abbot A onetime parlor maid to Helen Spenlove Kennedy Halliday in *Sleeping Murder.* She is contacted by Gwenda Reed, who is seeking information about Helen, and eagerly supplies details. Despite the objections of her husband, she sets out to meet with Dr. Kennedy, Helen's half brother and is murdered on her way to the meeting.

King, Alix See Martin, Alix.

King, Amelie A onetime debutante in *Giant's Bread.* She married for love rather than money and ended up in difficult financial circumstances.

King, Beatrice The housekeeper in the service of Mrs. Oldfield in "The Lernean Hydra." She is fired almost immediately following Mrs. Oldfield's death.

King, Muriel A maid who accompanied Lady Esther Carr to Persia in "The House at Shiraz." She suffered at the hands of her increasingly unstable mistress and supposedly fell to her death from a high ledge while carrying a breakfast tray. Her death was a severe blow to Herr Schlagal, a German pilot. The fact that Muriel King had "flashing dark eyes" is a vital clue in Parker Pyne's unraveling of the mystery in the elegant house at Shiraz. (See also Carr, Lady Esther.)

King, Sarah A young woman who has just completed her medical studies and is touring Jerusalem in *Appointment with Death.* She takes a professional interest in the eminently dysfunctional Boynton family and is summoned to determine the time of death in the murder of Mrs. Boynton. Sarah's interest in Raymond Boynton eventually becomes more than professional.

King, Winnie A young student in Miss Pope's school for girls in Neuilly, France, in "The Girdle of Hippolyta." She disappears from a train in France, but no ransom is ever demanded by the kidnappers. She then is returned unharmed with no ransom ever paid.

Kingston Bruce, Beatrice The daughter of Colonel and Mrs. Kingston Bruce in "The Affair of the Pink Pearl." She enlists the help of Tommy and Tuppence Beresford at the International Detective Agency in her effort to locate a pink pearl that has apparently been stolen from her houseguest, Mrs. Betts-Hamilton. She is also romantically connected to Mr. Rennie, a leftist of whom her parents strongly disapprove.

Kingston Bruce, Colonel Charles and Mrs. The parents of Beatrice Kingston Bruce in "The Affair of the Pink Pearl." They own an estate called the Laurels and are convinced that Beatrice's deadbeat leftist boyfriend, Mr. Rennie, is responsible for the theft of a pink pearl from one of their houseguests, Mrs. Betts-Hamilton.

Kirkwood, Frederick One of the partners in the law firm of Walters and Kirkwood in *The Sittaford Mystery.* Kirkwood served as Captain Trevelyan's solicitor and is thus responsible for taking care of the assorted legal details when Trevelyan in murdered.

Kleek, Sir James (Jamie) A friend of Lord Edward Altamount in *Passenger to Frankfurt.* He is a nervous and rather suspicious-looking young man.

Knight, Miss A nurse companion hired by Raymond West for his aunt, Miss Marple, in *The Mirror Crack'd from Side to Side.* Miss Knight is an acutely irritating caregiver, and Miss Marple works hard to send her away on complicated errands so that she can then set out on her own to investigate mysteries. She is described as "a big, rather flabby woman of fifty-six with yellowing grey hair very elaborately arranged, glasses, a long thin nose, and below it a good-natured mouth and a weak chin."

Knighton, Major   The secretary to Rufus van Aldin in *The Mystery of the Blue Train*.

Knox, Dr. Llewellyn   A missionary in *The Burden*. He embraced the religious life at an early age but eventually—after many years—suffers a nervous breakdown. He has also beheld a lingering vision of a dark-haired woman.

Kochter, Monsieur   A piano teacher in *Unfinished Portrait*. He tells the main character that she will never be good enough to be an accomplished concert pianist.

Kohn, Olga   See Hobhouse, Valerie.

Kramenin   A revolutionary leader, socialist, and anarchist in *The Secret Adversary*. He is seemingly mild-mannered and most unprepossessing, but beneath this placid exterior lurks the heart of a true fanatic. Known in his organization as Number One, he is credited with fomenting deadly social anarchy, including no less an upheaval than the Russian Revolution.

Kranin, Colonel   A serious and threatening-looking nobleman who first interviews Jane Cleveland in "Jane in Search of a Job." It is Kranin who determines whether Jane is suitable to be sent on to Count Stylptitch, who decides finally whether she will then go to see Grand Duchess Pauline.

Krapp, Charlotte   See Von Waldsausen, the Grafin Charlotte.

Krassine, Monsieur   See Ivanovitch, Boris.

Lacey, Colin   The fifteen-year-old grandson of Colonel Horace Lacey in "The Theft of the Royal Ruby." He will inherit the Lacey estate at the time of his grandfather's death. A precocious youth, he schemes to play a joke on Hercule Poirot during the detective's visit over Christmas.

Lacey, Em   The wife of Colonel Horace Lacey in "The Theft of the Royal Ruby." She is concerned about the future of her granddaughter, Sarah Lacey, and enlists the assistance of Hercule Poirot in making certain that a fortune hunter, Desmond Lee-Wortley, does not win her heart.

Lacey, Colonel Horace   The patriarch of the Lacey clan of the Kings Lacey estate in "The Theft of the Royal Ruby." A onetime soldier, he disapproves strongly of Desmond Lee-Wortley and his efforts to win the heart of Lacey's granddaughter, Sarah Lacey.

Lacey, Sarah   The granddaughter of Colonel and Mrs. Lacey in "The Theft of the Royal Ruby." She is described in detail by her grandmother, who notes that she "wears these funny clothes that they like to wear, and black stockings or bright green ones," and lives in "two rather unpleasant rooms in Chelsea down by the river." Sarah is involved with a greedy fortune hunter, Desmond Lee-Wortley, a man of whom her grandparents disapprove very strenuously.

Laidlaw, Major   A suspected counterfeiter who enlists the assistance of Tommy and Tuppence Beresford in "The Crackler." He is believed by Scotland Yard to be involved in a counterfeiting ring. His wife is Marguerite Laidlaw.

Laidlaw, Marguerite   Wife of Major Laidlaw in "The Crackler." A Frenchwoman, she is suspected by Scotland Yard of being involved with counterfeiters after she is found on three separate occasions with funny money.

Lake, Captain John   An estate agent for Sir Gervase Chevenix-Gore in "Dead Man's Mirror." While he believes that Chevenix-Gore was mad as a hatter, Captain Lake does not accept any notion that he might have committed suicide.

Lal, Chandra   One of the students in Mrs. Nicoletis's hostel in *Hickory Dickory Dock*. Of Indian extraction, he feels much put upon by the other students and has an obsessive interest in politics.

Lal, Ram   A young student from India who makes an attack on the prime minister in *One, Two, Buckle My Shoe*. He is considered "a bit excitable but he feels the wrongs of India very keenly."

Lamb, Detective Sergeant   A local police official in *Crooked House*. He has considerable doubts, but he proceeds with the arrest of Brenda Leonides and Lawrence Brown for the murder of Aristide Leonides.

Lamb, Colin A special government agent in *The Clocks*. He impersonates a police constable and during the investigation falls in love with one of the suspects, Sheila Webb. They subsequently wed, and Lamb becomes a marine biology instructor in a university in Australia.

Lambert, Joyce A financially struggling young widow in "Next to a Dog." Although left alone by the death of her husband in the war, Joyce is perhaps best remembered for her absolute devotion to her dog, Terry, an old half-blind terrier who was a gift from her husband. Facing financial ruin, she considers the possibility of marrying the wealthy but odious Arthur Halliday. Her entire world collapses when Terry dies, and Joyce is suddenly confronted with a host of new opportunities.

Lancaster, Mrs. A widow with a young son who purchases a new home in "The Lamp." She soon encounters the ghost of a young boy who becomes increasingly involved in the fate of her own child, Geoffrey.

Lancaster, Geoffrey The young son of Mrs. Lancaster and the grandson of Mr. Winburn in "The Lamp." When his mother and grandfather move him into a new house, he meets the ghost of a young boy. The two become attached and come eventually to share a similar fate.

Lancaster, Julia An elderly woman in *By the Pricking of My Thumbs* who has a very dark past. The daughter of an unwed mother who committed suicide soon after giving birth, Julia grew up with serious mental problems and blossomed into the often deranged gangster called Killer Kate, who, with fellow gang members, led a life of crime. She eventually married a nobleman who was forced to commit her to assorted rest homes. She is the object of investigation by Tuppence Beresford, who finally finds her in a retirement home in Watermead; Julia has little chance to speak of her past, for she is poisoned soon after meeting Tuppence.

Lane, Patricia One of the boarders in Mrs. Nicoletis's hostel in *Hickory Dickory Dock*. Patricia is a homely archaeology student, and she is robbed of a diamond solitaire ring. She is also knocked unconscious with a blow from a paperweight wrapped in a sock.

Lane, Reverend Stephen A clergyman much troubled with concerns of the devil in *Evil under the Sun*. He observes that the devil is quite busy in his neighborhood, "especially the Devil in the guise of a woman—scarlet woman—whore of Babylon." He notes that the doomed Arlena Marshall embodies all the "evil under the sun."

Lang, Dr. An army surgeon, very popular with the nurses, in *Giant's Bread*. His popularity is considerable despite his sarcastic personality.

Langdon, Miss The manager of the Golf Hotel in "The Under Dog." She becomes quite flustered when Hercule Poirot enters her establishment.

Langton, Claude A friend of John Harrison and onetime fiancé of Molly Deane in "Wasps' Nest." He is enlisted by Harrison to remove a nest of wasps.

Lanscombe The ninety-year-old butler to the Abernethie family in *After the Funeral*. He is utterly dedicated to the family and to Enderby Hall, but he also enjoys sharing with the maid Janet his stern disapproval of modern domestic help.

Lansquenet, Cora Abernethie The sister of the late Richard Abernethie in *After the Funeral*. A widow, she makes a chance remark that her brother was murdered. Her comment sparks an investigation and leads directly to her own murder.

La Paz, The Mistress of An enigmatic woman in "The Man from the Sea." She is the source of fascination and personal happiness for Mr. Satterthwaite despite her dark past, which includes a marriage to a cruel Englishman who died under catastrophic circumstances.

Larkin, Mrs. A woman in *The Clocks* who has the appearance of a gypsy.

Larkin, Beryl A friend of Anthony Hawker in

"The Horses of Diomedes." She hosts parties at which cocaine is distributed freely.

La Roche, Mademoiselle An eminently fashionable woman in *Destination Unknown*. She has worked for years in the fashion industry in France and labors to provide the women scientists of the Brain Trust with some sense of fashion. This is a difficult task, as "these scientific ladies often take very little interest in *la toilette*."

Larraby, Dr. A physician in *After the Funeral*. He steadfastly refuses to accept any notion that Richard Abernethie may have been murdered.

Larraby, J. The narrator—but not the main character—of *Unfinished Portrait*. He was a brilliant painter until World War I, when he lost his hand, and has since had to make do with a mere stump. Despite his many problems, he prevents the main character from taking her own life.

Latimer, Edward (Ted) A ruthless character in *Towards Zero*. He tries to use charm to cover up his dark personality.

Laurier, Henri A supposed French commercial agent in *Destination Unknown*. In fact, Laurier is a representative of the Brain Trust, fronting for the sinister organization and recruiting new members.

Laverton-West, Charles A member of Parliament and a man with a bright political career ahead of him in "Murder in the Mews." He was engaged to be married to Barbara Allen, a victim of apparent murder—at least in the opinion of Laverton-West, who can think of no reason for her to commit suicide. Rather imperious and "good-looking in a well-bred way," he considered Miss Allen to be beneath him socially. By marrying her, he would thus elevate her to a higher position than she had enjoyed previously.

Lavigny, Father See Menier, Raoul.

Lavington, Mr. A blackmailer and jewel thief in "The Veiled Lady." Using the aliases Croker and Reed, he is supposedly in possession of a compromising letter from Lady Millicent Vaughan, which Poirot is commissioned to recover. He has hidden the valuable item in a Chinese puzzle box and secured it in a safe location in his house.

Lavington, Dr. Ambrose A "doctor of the soul" in "The Mystery of the Blue Jar." A guest at the Stourton Heath Hotel, he is an expert in the paranormal and recommends a séance to investigate the claims of another guest that voices can be heard every morning at 7:25 A.M. It is possible, he claims, to make contact with the spirit of a woman who was murdered at Heather Cottage.

Lawes, Esther The fiancée of Dickie Carpenter in "The Gipsy." She inexplicably severs their engagement after Carpenter's return from the sea. Her sister is Rachel Lawes.

Lawes, Rachel The sister of Esther Lawes in "The Gipsy." She is the "truer and sweeter" of the two sisters, with "honest brown eyes."

Lawson, Edgar The illegitimate son of Lewis Serrocold in *They Do It with Mirrors*. It is claimed that he suffers from schizophrenic paranoia. He moves to his father's estate and is drowned.

Lawson, Wilhelmina (Mina) A spiritualist and beneficiary of Miss Arundell's will in *Dumb Witness*. She served Miss Arundell with great devotion for many years and attempted to dissuade her from changing her will right before her death. She is astonished when Miss Arundell's will is revealed and the estate is left to her, an event of some surprise and horror to Miss Arundell's relatives.

Laxton, Harry A young man who returns to his little village as a kind of prodigal son in "The Case of the Caretaker." The son of a major, he was a savage youth—"broken windows, robbed orchards, poached rabbits"—and had run up a considerable debt before being sent off to Africa. There, he had made good, eventually marrying an Anglo-French girl, the possessor of a considerable fortune, and returning to his village to settle down. Tragedy comes to the couple, however, and Harry becomes a widower.

Laxton, Louise The Anglo-French wife of Harry Laxton in "The Case of the Caretaker."

The possessor of a vast fortune, she married Harry and settled with him in his little English village. She has trouble adjusting to life in England and is especially troubled by the curses and cruelty of the old caretaker of Kingsdean House, Mrs. Murgatroyd. The curse seems to come to pass, for Louise is thrown from her horse and dies, apparently from the fall.

Lazarus, Jim The co-owner, with his father, of an art gallery on Bond Street in *Peril at End House*. He is also a friend of Nick Buckley.

Lazenby, Dr. A police surgeon in *Towards Zero* who provides details about how Lady Tressilian was murdered. He determines that the murderer was a left-handed person and used a golf club.

Lazenby, Cedric The prime minister of England during the tumultuous events recounted in *Passenger to Frankfurt*. He is forced to deal with the problem of the Youth Movement and attempts to publicly maintain a spirit of optimism.

Leach, Inspector James The nephew of Superintendent Battle and an officer of Scotland Yard in *Towards Zero*. He is involved, with his uncle, in the investigation into the death of Lady Tressilian.

Leadbetter, Mr. One of the witnesses to the fourth murder committed by the A.B.C killer in *The A.B.C. Murders*. He greets the horrific event with annoyance rather than any sense of distress.

Leadbetter, Ephraim The uncle of George Dundas in "The Golden Ball." He fires his nephew for failing to go after the "golden ball." This is an act he comes to regret.

Leaman, Harriet A cleaning lady in the employ of Mrs. Llewellyn-Smythe in *Hallowe'en Party*. She was a witness to the signing of the codicil to her employer's will and takes details of the event to Mrs. Ariadne Oliver.

Leason, Claud See Averbury, Claud.

Leatheran, Amy A buxom and faithful companion to Lady Matilda in *Passenger to Frankfurt* who is described as "a nice faithful, kindly sheep."

Leatheran, Nurse Amy A smart young nurse in *Murder in Mesopotamia* who is hired to care for the newborn baby of the Kelseys and then to assist in the care of the unstable Mrs. Leidner. She at first considers Hercule Poirot to be a rather comical figure, but this opinion is changed radically when Mrs. Leidner is murdered and the detective displays his customary genius. Amy subsequently becomes a useful assistant to the Belgian as he brings a killer to justice.

Leathern, Miss An inveterate gossip and busybody in "The Lernean Hydra." Her vicious gossipmongering is used to brilliant effect by Hercule Poirot, who, through her, circulates an erroneous rumor of an exhumation to smoke out a killer.

Leathern, Eve A supposed teenager in "The Regatta Mystery." At a dinner party, she makes a wager that she can cause a diamond necklace to disappear. Things go awry, however, when the stone really does vanish. Suspicion does not fall on Eve but on someone else. Her father is a wealthy American businessman, Samuel Leathern.

Leathern, Samuel An apparently wealthy American businessman in "The Regatta Mystery." He and his daughter, Eve Leathern, take part in a dinner at which a most expensive diamond necklace goes missing.

Leblanc, Monsieur A French agent who is given the task of finding and eradicating the Brain Trust that has been established by Mr. Aristides in *Destination Unknown.*

Lebrun, Madame A piano teacher in *Unfinished Portrait*. She is described as having white hair and hands like claws.

Leckie, Martha A faithful cook in the household of Sir Bartholomew Strange in *Three-Act Tragedy*. She considers the police methods being used to investigate the death of Sir Strange to be reprehensible.

Lecky, Mr. The last person to see Captain Sessle alive in "The Sunningdale Mystery." Sessle was stabbed in the heart with a hat pin.

Le Conteau, Eleanor A member of a troupe of acrobats who work as thieves and steal valuable art and other objects in "At the 'Bells and Motley.' "

Lee, Adelaide The late wife of Simeon Lee in *Hercule Poirot's Christmas.* She is reported to have died from a broken heart over her husband's ceaseless adulteries.

Lee, Alfred The oldest son of Simeon Lee in *Hercule Poirot's Christmas.* Married to Lydia Lee, who hates Simeon, he nevertheless lives with his father and seemingly devotes himself entirely to caring for the old man. He is despised by both his father and his brother Henry for his weakness.

Lee, David The youngest son of Simeon Lee in *Hercule Poirot's Christmas.* He has lived away from his father's house for twenty years, bitterly angry at his father for his many adulteries—which, David believes, caused his mother's death from a broken heart. David is married to Hilda Lee; she is troubled by David's obsessive tendencies concerning his dead mother.

Lee, Dinah The platinum-blond mistress of Basil Blake in *The Body in the Library.* She delights in shocking Blake's neighbors and the folk in St. Mary Mead by her seemingly wanton life with Blake. In fact, she and Blake are married.

Lee, Esther A much-feared old woman in *Endless Night.* Known as Old Mother Lee, she is a fortune-teller and a reputed witch who gives dire warnings of future events at Gipsy's Acre. After she falls under suspicion of sending anonymous messages, she is discovered dead in a quarry a short time after the murder of Ellie Rogers.

Lee, George The second son of Simeon Lee in *Hercule Poirot's Christmas.* Dull and dim, he is a member of Parliament who maintains a facade of affection for his father. His wife, Magdalene, is much younger than he is and is chronically unfaithful.

Lee, Sir Gerald A wealthy country squire in "The Edge." He is the lifelong friend of Clare Halliwell, who has expectations of marrying him. Gerald, however, decides to wed the young redhead Vivien. Gerald remains quite oblivious to the seething hatred in Clare for Vivien and the infidelity of his wife.

Lee, Henry Also called Harry, the third son of Simeon Lee in *Hercule Poirot's Christmas.* Henry departed England years before because he forged his father's signature on a check and has since roamed the world. Summoned home by his father, Henry is reconciled with Simeon and learns, to his surprise, that his father has left his entire estate to him.

Lee, Hilda The wife of David Lee in *Hercule Poirot's Christmas.* A chunky, middle-aged woman, she is forceful and tries with patience to deal with her husband's seeming obsession with the memory of his long-dead mother.

Lee, Lydia The wife of Alfred Lee in *Hercule Poirot's Christmas.* Described as a "lean greyhound of a woman," she disdains her father-in-law because of his cruel and contemptuous treatment of her husband. Simeon Lee, however, finds her quite remarkable.

Lee, Magdalene The young, attractive, and platinum-blond wife of George Lee in *Hercule Poirot's Christmas.* She is considerably younger than her husband and has a wandering eye. She enjoys the company of other men, and lived with a lover prior to her marriage to George. Her previous activities are difficult to learn about because of the mask of serenity she tries to maintain.

Lee, Simeon The curmudgeonly patriarch of the Lee clan in *Hercule Poirot's Christmas.* He is the master of his household, not only dominating the lives of his four legitimate sons and daughter but inviting the participation of his two illegitimate sons in his life as well. All his family members, as well as numerous business acquaintances, harbor bitter grudges against him. His family especially despises him because of his tyranny, and for having driven his wife, Adelaide, to an early death through his ceaseless affairs and mental cruelty. When he summons his children for Christmas, the anger finally erupts into violence. Simeon Lee is brutally murdered.

Lee, Vivien   The young, elfin, red-haired beauty who married Sir Gerald Lee in "The Edge." Although she cares about her husband, she has a hard time adjusting to quiet country life and has an affair. Knowledge of the event falls into the hands of Clare Halliwell, who decides to use it in a diabolically ruthless fashion.

Leech, Andrew   The owner of a beauty salon in *Death in the Clouds.* Known as Monsieur Antoine, he is also called "the old devil." Jane Grey is one his employees.

Lee-Wortley, Desmond   A young and unscrupulous fortune hunter in "The Theft of the Royal Ruby." He is determined to win the heart of Sarah Lacey, but her family is convinced that he is interested only in her wealth. Thus, when Lee-Wortley arrives at Kings Lacey for Christmas, Hercule Poirot is enlisted to keep an eye on him.

Legge, Alec   An atomic scientist in *Dead Man's Folly* who, despite his moodiness (especially toward his wife, Sally), is determined to use his knowledge to rectify all the injustice in the world.

Legge, Rosy   See Keene, Ruby.

Legge, Sally   The long-suffering wife of Alec Legge in *Dead Man's Folly.* She has long endured her husband's moodiness and unpleasantness, and, in the end, she leaves him. Sally is a university graduate who once owned an art studio in Chelsea.

Legge, Sir Thomas   An assistant commissioner in the service of Scotland Yard in *And Then There Were None.* He investigates the bizarre deaths of ten people on Indian Island and considers it all "fantastic—impossible."

Leicester, Marjory   A friend and roommate to Una Drake in "The Unbreakable Alibi." She assures Tommy and Tuppence Beresford that, on one particular night, Una was home all evening.

Leidner, Dr. Eric   A notable archaeologist and the head of the expedition to Tell Yarimjah in *Murder in Mesopotamia.* He is truly devoted to his wife, Louise, and grows increasingly concerned about her mental health. He thus hires Nurse Leatheran to care for her. Leidner has a secret past that is revealed during the murderous events at the dig.

Leidner, Louise   The wife of Dr. Eric Leidner in *Murder in Mesopotamia.* She is considered "a mass of affection" but she is also a "champion liar." She also has a somber past, having turned her first husband, Frederick Bosner, over to the authorities when she discovered that he was a German spy responsible for the deaths of many people. Louise subsequently married Dr. Leidner, who is as obsessively devoted to her as her first husband. After spending weeks in terror resulting from the receipt of threatening letters, and apparently evidencing considerable mental instability, she is murdered by having her head smashed.

Leith, Duchess of   An elderly noblewoman who charms Mr. Satterthwaite in "The World's End." She wears expensive diamond brooches pinned haphazardly on her dresses. Satterthwaite finds her delightful and even agrees to travel from Cannes to Corsica with her.

Lejeune, Inspector   A capable, quiet, unostentatious police inspector in *The Pale Horse.* He diligently pursues a murderer in his own methodical way.

Lemaitre, Charles   See Martin, Gerald.

Leman, Anne Morisot   See Morisot, Anne.

Lemarchant, Carla   A young woman who enlists the help of Hercule Poirot in *Five Little Pigs.* She lives in dread uncertainty about whether her mother was actually a murderer, and she is unable to marry until she has this terrible question resolved once and for all.

Le Marchant, Jimmy   A witness interrogated by Tommy and Tuppence Beresford in "The Unbreakable Alibi." He swears that Una Drake had dinner with him on a certain night, but he adds that a friend of his also saw her in Torquay on the same day, a feat that should be impossible.

Le Marquis, Monsieur The name used by an internationally feared jewel thief in *The Mystery of the Blue Train.* He is intent on stealing jewels of historical importance and sets his sights on the Heart of Fire rubies. He adopts an alias to bring himself into closer proximity to the jewels.

Lementeuil, Commissionaire A Swiss commissionaire of police and an old friend of Hercule Poirot in "The Erymanthian Boar." He provides his friend with details about the murderer Marrascaud and arrives at Rochers Neige by helicopter to arrest the wanted criminal. Hercule Poirot, of course, is quite happy to deliver the killer into his old friend's hands.

Lemesurier, Hugo A member of the apparently cursed Lemesurier family in "The Lemesurier Inheritance." He is quite concerned about the curse and tries to take steps to reverse its deadly effects upon his firstborn son, Ronald.

Lemesurier, Major Roger A member of the Lemesurier family in "The Lemesurier Inheritance." As he is a distant cousin to the family, he is not considered a likely candidate for the terrible curse that claims the family's firstborn male heir. He does, however, relate details of the curse to a most interested Hercule Poirot.

Lemesurier, Ronald The eight-year-old son of Hugo Lemesurier in "The Lemesurier Inheritance." He is the heir to the Lemesurier fortune and thus falls under the dread family curse. He thus begins to suffer from assorted suspicious accidents, but his murder is prevented by Hercule Poirot.

Lemesurier, Sadie The unhappy wife of Hugo Lemesurier in "The Lemesurier Inheritance." She finds herself trapped in a miserable marriage and bears a dark secret about her son's true lineage. After the death of her husband, she marries John Gardiner, her husband's secretary.

Lemesurier, Vincent The nephew of Hugo Lemesurier in "The Lemesurier Inheritance." He is a soldier recovering from shell shock incurred during the fighting in World War I, and his mental health is further strained by his growing concerns over the family curse that claims the firstborn heir.

Lemoine, Monsieur A supposed inspector with the Sûreté in Paris who is involved in an investigation in *The Secret of Chimneys.* He wears a black beard and absurd clothes—ridiculous enough that the discerning eye grows suspicious about his authenticity. He is, in fact, a different kind of character altogether.

LEMON, FELICITY The incredibly efficient but singularly ugly secretary first to Mr. Parker Pyne and then to Hercule Poirot. Miss Lemon first appeared in the position of secretary to Parker Pyne in "The Case of the Middle-Aged Wife" and "The Case of the Distressed Lady." She subsequently left his employ and entered into the service of Hercule Poirot. This post she held for many years, taking part in at least eight published cases: "How Does Your Garden Grow?" "The Nemean Lion," "The Capture of Cerberus," "The Mystery of the Spanish Chest," *Hickory Dickory Dock, Dead Man's Folly, Third Girl,* and *Elephants Can Remember.*

A memorable Miss Lemon (Pauline Moran), in Agatha Christie's Poirot. *(Photofest; London Weekend Television)*

As noted: "Miss Lemon was unbelievably ugly and incredibly efficient. To her Poirot was nobody in particular—he was merely her employer. She gave him excellent service. Her private thoughts and dreams were concentrated on a new filing-system which she was slowly perfecting in the recesses of her mind." Also, "She had a passion for order almost equalling that of Poirot himself, and though capable of thinking, she never thought unless told to do so." Thus, her relationship with Poirot was largely limited to maintaining his office and correspondence in perfect order and supplying him with useful information when possible. An excellent example of the latter was her ability to reply swiftly and without comment to Poirot's inquiry concerning the location of Hell in "The Capture of Cerberus."

While the efficiency of Miss Lemon was remarked upon in virtually every description of her, so, too, was her ugliness. She was "composed entirely of angles—thus satisfying Poirot's demand for symmetry." "Her general effect was that of a lot of bones flung together at random."

Virtually nothing is known about Miss Lemon's private life and family. Indeed, it is known that she had a sister, Mrs. Hubbard, only because it is relevant to the case recounted in *Hickory Dickory Dock.* The existence of Miss Lemon's relation was first revealed after Poirot found several mistakes in a letter that she had typed. Only a disaster of truly gigantic dimensions could cause such inefficiency, especially as she normally "typed with the speed and precision of a quick-firing tank."

The most memorable of the Miss Lemons in film and television is Pauline Moran, who has played the secretary since 1989 on the London Weekend Television series *Agatha Christie's Poirot,* starring David Suchet as Hercule Poirot.

Lempriére, Joyce   An artist who appears in several mysteries in the short-story collection *The Thirteen Problems*: "The Tuesday Night Club," "The Idol House of Astarte," "Ingots of Gold,"

"The Bloodstained Pavement," and "The Thumb Mark of Saint Peter." She is described as having a "close-cropped black head and queer hazel-green eyes." Joyce narrates the events of murder and swindling in "The Bloodstained Pavement."

Lempriére, Mrs.   A gossiping socialite in "Within a Wall." She has assorted comments to make about the paintings of Alan Everard.

Leonides, Aristide   The patriarch of the Leonides clan in *Crooked House.* A wealthy Greek businessman, he is described as "a gnome—ugly little fellow—but magnetic." A thoroughly unpleasant man, he rules his family with a cruel hand, knowing that his children, their spouses, and his grandchildren rely upon him for their financial survival. It thus comes as a grim surprise when he marries a waitress nearly half a century his junior, whom he met in one of his restaurants. He further confounds his heirs by naming his granddaughter Sophia to be his sole beneficiary. Soon after, Aristide is murdered; his insulin is replaced with eserine.

Leonides, Brenda   A twenty-four-year-old waitress who worked in one of the restaurants owned by Aristide Leonides in *Crooked House.* Described as "a big purring lazy cat," she is the source of great surprise to the Leonides family when the old man marries her. She takes up an awkward place in the Leonides household and develops a passion for Laurence Brown, the family tutor. Thus, when Aristide is murdered, she becomes one of the obvious suspects.

Leonides, Clemency   The wife of Roger Leonides in *Crooked House.* She is a scientist in her own right, studying radiation and its effects, but she is also utterly devoted to her husband, who "made up her whole existence." Indeed, save for her limitless devotion and love for him, Clemency leads a remarkably austere existence.

Leonides, Eustace   The sixteen-year-old grandson of Aristide Leonides in *Crooked House.* The son of Philip and Magda Leonides, he suffers a severe limp from polio and compensates by being arrogant and irascible. He also resents having to be tutored with his younger sister, Josephine.

Leonides, Josephine The eleven-year-old granddaughter of Aristide Leonides in *Crooked House.* The daughter of Philip and Magda Leonides, she actually bears a more striking resemblance to her grandfather than to her parents, and she certainly carries her grandfather's intelligence. Josephine is the person best informed as to what occurs in the Leonides household. She apparently knows too much about someone, as three attempts are made to murder her.

Leonides, Magda The wife of Philip Leonides and mother of Josephine, Sophia, and Eustace Leonides in *Crooked House.* A stage actress who goes by the name Magda West, she is increasingly concerned about her fading career on the stage. As an actress, she is prone to excessive displays of emotion, especially when she enters and leaves a room. She is one of the few members of the household who was genuinely fond of her father-in-law, the gruesome Aristide Leonides, but her own preoccupation with her career leads her to be unconcerned with finding his murderer.

Leonides, Philip A son of Aristide Leonides and the husband of Magda West in *Crooked House.* Philip is also the father of Josephine, Eustace, and Sophia Leonides and is unlike other members of the family in that he is not utterly dependent upon his father for his survival; Aristide had given him a large sum years before. Nevertheless, Philip is emotionally retarded, struggles to maintain his confidence, and secretly longs for his father's approval.

Leonides, Roger The oldest son of Aristide Leonides and the husband of Clemency Leonides in *Crooked House.* Although he is a decent and kind person, Roger has absolutely no capacity for business and thus stands as a poor choice to succeed his father in his many financial and business affairs. His wife, Clemency, is completely devoted to him and defends him with fierce loyalty when Roger is attacked by other resentful family members.

Leonides, Sophia The oldest daughter of Philip and Magda Leonides and granddaughter of Aristide Leonides in *Crooked House.* An intelligent, capable, and courageous young woman, she works for the British government and is serving in Egypt when she meets her future fiancé, Charles Hayward. The two fall in love and agree to wed, but her life is soon overshadowed by family events. Her grandfather announces that he has left control of his vast estate to her because he believes her to be the only heir who is capable of managing the complicated tangle of his money and investments with discretion and skill. This news comes as a complete surprise to Sophia, as does her grandfather's murder soon after. She is considered a leading suspect and is saved only by the "little grey cells" of Hercule Poirot.

Leonie Two coquettish French maids in similar cases of theft and espionage. The first Leonie is in the service of Mrs. Vanderlyn in "The Incredible Theft." She screamed at a most inopportune moment while in the Mayfield household, claiming that she had seen a ghost. When pressed by Hercule Poirot, however, she admitted that her scream had been caused by the sudden and unexpected kiss she received from Reggie Carrington. Leonie admits further that were Poirot to meet her on the stairs, she would not scream.

The second Leonie is in the service of Mrs. Conrad in "The Submarine Plans." She screamed on the stairs at a most inconvenient time and claimed that she had seen a ghost. She later admits to Hercule Poirot that her cry of alarm resulted from the fact that Leonard Weardale suddenly kissed her.

Lessing, Ruth The secretary to George Barton in *Sparkling Cyanide.* She is a capable and loyal secretary, and her calm facade belies a profoundly passionate interior.

Lester, Charles A young bank clerk in "The Lost Mine." He traveled on the same ship, the

S.S. *Assunta,* as the murdered Mr. Wu Ling and was considered a leading suspect in the crime.

Lestrange, Miss   A pleasant woman who rents an apartment to a newlywed couple in *Unfinished Portrait.*

Lestrange, Mrs.   A mysterious woman in the village of St. Mary Mead in *Murder at the Vicarage.* She is virtually unknown by the residents and is thus the source of intense speculation. In fact, she was previously married to Colonel Protheroe and is the mother of the troubled young woman Lettice Protheroe. The fact that she met with her former husband on the night before his murder makes her one of a large number of suspects.

Letardeau, Raoul   One of the travelers in a train compartment in "The Fourth Man." He journeys with three talkative English passengers and listens with interest to their tale of love and psychological dysfunction. At the end, he is able to provide them with vital clues about the case of Felice Bault.

Leverson, Charles   The chief suspect in the murder of Sir Reuben Astwell in "The Under Dog." The nephew of Sir Reuben, he had a bitter argument with his uncle a very short time before the murder.

Levinne, Mr. and Mrs.   A Jewish couple in *Giant's Bread.* They purchase an expensive estate and are confronted with the pervasive anti-Semitism of their neighbors. Their son, Sebastian Levinne, is especially victimized.

Levinne, Sebastian   The son of Mr. and Mrs. Levinne in *Giant's Bread.* He is victimized by the vicious anti-Semitism of his neighbors, but he also befriends Vernon Deyre. The two remain close ever after, and Sebastian assists him financially in writing his music.

Levitt, Jake   A petty and shabby blackmailer in "The Actress." While attending a stage performance, Jake discovers that the actress Olga Stormer is actually someone he recognizes from his past, Nancy Taylor. Knowing details about Nancy's background and that their revelation could destroy her career and her possible happi-

ness with Sir Richard Everard, M.P., Jake sets out to blackmail her. His plans go awry, however, when he finds himself set against an equally desperate and clever opponent.

Li Chang Yen   The leader known simply as Number One in *The Big Four.* Hercule Poirot considers this mysterious and dangerous Chinese mastermind to have "the finest criminal brain ever known." The detective sets out to destroy Li Chang Yen's vast empire of murder and crime.

Linch, Gladys   A young maid in "The Tuesday Night Club." She died in childbirth after her lover, Albert Jones, deserted her; her tale is recounted by one of the members of the Tuesday Night Club.

Lindstrom, Kirsten (Kirsty)   A Swedish nurse and masseuse who worked in the nursery run by Rachel Argyle during the war in *Ordeal by Innocence.* She was very devoted to Rachel and remained on as a housekeeper after the murder of her employer.

Lingard, Miss   An assistant to Sir Gervase Chevenix-Gore in "Dead Man's Mirror." She was hired to assist in the writing of the Chevenix-Gore family history, but she also has a past that is revealed by Hercule Poirot.

Lionel, Sir   The assistant commissioner of the central intelligence division of Scotland Yard in *The A.B.C. Murders.* He is deeply concerned about the murderous activities of the A.B.C. killer, especially when he ponders the prospect that the murderer will be able to continue killing until he reaches the letter *Z.* He is also determined that, when the killer is finally captured, there will be no possibility of his being declared insane and thereby escaping true justice.

Lippincott, Andrew   The solicitor to Ellie Rogers in *Endless Night.* He grows concerned for her safety and hires two detectives to keep an eye on her.

Lippincott, Beatrice   The manager of an inn in Warmelsy Vale in *Taken at the Flood.* In her inn, the mysterious Enoch Arden blackmails David

Hunter, and Beatrice gives a report of their meeting to Rowley Cloade.

Lipscomb The assistant and faithful minion to Dr. Andersen in "The Flock of Geryon." Lipscomb is a rough and unpleasant man whose presence helps to reveal Dr. Andersen's true demeanor.

Liskeard, Professor An unassuming archaeologist who serves as a historical consultant to Countess Vera Rossakoff and her nightclub, Hell, in "The Capture of Cerberus." The professor assists the countess in making the club as authentic as possible in its depiction of the hoary underworld. The professor is also blithely unaware of events transpiring in the club.

Listerdale, Lord A wealthy nobleman who disappears mysteriously in "The Listerdale Mystery." He is a selfish and unpleasant person until the day he simply disappears. Soon after, Listerdale's house is rented to a widow and her family of limited financial means. The widow pays astonishingly little rent, and the arrangement includes a devoted butler who seems to know a great deal about his former employer.

Litchfield, Elizabeth See Cole, Elizabeth.

Littledale, James Arthur A chemist in *Sad Cypress.* He is able to identify the drug used to poison Mary Gerrard.

Littleworth, Mr. See Sanders, Jack.

Livingstone, Miss A secretary to Mrs. Ariadne Oliver in *Elephants Can Remember.* She replaced Mrs. Oliver's former secretary, Miss Sedgwick, but proves unequal to the task. Miss Livingstone cannot maintain the standards expected by Mrs. Oliver.

Llewellyn, Evan A writer who becomes an obvious suspect in the theft of a diamond in "The Regatta Mystery." He wins a large amount of money at the racetrack on the same day that the diamond is stolen, and he has a hard time explaining his good fortune.

Llewellyn-Smythe, Mrs. One of the victims of murder in *The Hallowe'en Party.* She is a wealthy woman who dominated her family by threatening to disinherit her relatives. One family member, Hugo Drake, a nephew, has a bitter fight with her, and she disinherits him. Soon after, both she and her nephew are dead. A codicil to the will that seemingly names an au pair her heir is determined to be a forgery.

Lloyd, Dr. A physician and member of the Tuesday Night Club. He recounts the story of "The Companion." Dr. Lloyd is putting on weight, and it is noted that his waistcoat is, of late, uncomfortably tight. He also participated in the solution of the stories "The Herb of Death" and "The Affair at the Bungalow."

Lloyd, Mrs. A wondrous-looking and flamboyant medium who conducts a séance in "The Voice in the Dark." She is dressed in an appropriately supernatural fashion, with rings and moonstones; she also eats only fruit before holding a séance.

Lloyd, Gerald The suitor of Sarah Prentice in *A Daughter's a Daughter.* He is generally considered a weak-willed person, but his abiding love for Sarah prompts him to become stronger and more assertive.

Lloyd, Stanford An investment banker in *Endless Night.* He manages an investment portfolio for Ellie Rogers until he begins discovering certain financial peculiarities and is fired by her husband.

Loftus, Squadron Leader A murder suspect in "The Gate of Baghdad," Loftus is a squadron leader traveling from Damascus to Baghdad. In the brief investigation of the murder of Smethurst, Loftus is helpful to Mr. Parker Pyne; this cooperation proves instrumental in the solution to the case.

Logan, Miss The onetime companion to Lady Radclyffe in "The House of Lurking Death." She subsequently takes up the post of housekeeper to Lois Hargreaves, Lady Radclyffe's niece. Miss Logan dies of shock following an attempt to commit arson.

Lolopretjzyl, Baron (Baron Lollipop) A nobleman from Herzoslovakia in *The Secret of Chimneys.* He attempts to secure the manuscript of the memoirs of the late Count Stylptitch, which could be the source of much scandal if published.

Lomax, The Honourable George The undersecretary of state for foreign affairs in *The Secret of Chimneys* and *The Seven Dials Mystery*. Nicknamed Codders because of his bulging, fishlike eyes and his generally ugly appearance, he is much disliked by his staff; one assistant describes him as "a disgusting windbag, an unscrupulous, hypocritical old hot-air merchant—a foul, poisonous self-advertiser."

Lombard, Captain Philip One of the guests of Indian Island in *And Then There Were None*. He stands accused of massacring twenty-one members of an East African tribe during his bloody days as a soldier of fortune. He becomes the ninth victim of remorseless justice on the island.

Lonely Lady A young woman in her twenties "in a shabby black coat and skirt that had seen their best days" in "The Lonely God." She becomes entranced by the pathetic little idol from Mexico in the British Museum and discovers that another visitor to the museum, Frank Oliver, is also a kind of "worshiper." They develop a peculiar relationship, and both are freed from their loneliness through the battered Mexican god.

Long, Samuel A defaulted financier whose insolvency amounted to three million pounds and who is finally captured in "The Gate of Baghdad." Rumored to have escaped to South America, he actually turns up in disguise as a member of the party with whom Mr. Parker Pyne is journeying from Damascus to Baghdad. Long murders a friend whom he had known years before at Eton and who was going to turn him in to the authorities. While confessing his guilt, he argues that his talents "lie in quite another direction."

Longman, Professor A scientist who specializes in paranormal studies in "Motive vs. Opportunity." He is called in to investigate the suspicious spiritualist Eurydice Spragg and, if possible, expose her as a charlatan.

Lonsdale, Susan The mistress of a married man in *The Burden*. She impudently confronts the wife of her lover and demands that the poor woman grant a divorce to her husband.

Lopez, Conchita A young woman who impersonates her friend and attempts to win an inheritance in *Hercule Poirot's Christmas*. She is exposed by Poirot, who notes that her brown eyes would have been impossible if, as she claims, both of her would-be parents possessed blue eyes. She becomes a suspect in the brutal murder of Simeon Lee.

Lord, Dr. Peter A physician in *Sad Cypress*. He enlists the help of Hercule Poirot in clearing Elinore Carlisle of suspicion of murder. Lord is also a remarkably compassionate doctor who is determined to aid as many people as possible.

Lorimer, Jerry The fiancé of the unfortunate Sylvia Keene in "The Herb of Death." Before Sylvia's demise, he is seen kissing Maud Wye, making him an obvious suspect in Sylvia's death by poisoning.

Loring, Isabel The scheming, malicious, and ruthless wife of Alan Everard in "Within a Wall." She was considered the most beautiful of the debutantes in her time, but her family was not well-to-do. It was thus a shock when she decided to marry the impoverished painter Everard. As the years go by, Isabel reveals her ambitions for him, and her husband demonstrates a skill in portrait painting.

Lorrimer, Mrs. One of the guests at the dinner hosted by the mysterious Mr. Shaitana in *Cards on the Table*. She becomes one the four suspects in his murder, but she is herself subsequently murdered by an overdose of evipan.

Lorrimer, Dr. George A physician and a nephew of Anthony and Henry Gascoigne in "Four and Twenty Blackbirds." He becomes involved in the investigation by Hercule Poirot into the peculiar deaths of the two older men.

Lowen, Mr. A financial speculator in "The Disappearance of Mr. Davenheim." He had a meeting with Davenheim shortly before the banker disappeared and was thus considered a prime suspect in Davenheim's presumed kidnapping and murder.

Lucas, Harry One of the victims of the unscrupulous and scheming Anita Grunberg in *The Man in the Brown Suit*. He worked as a diamond prospector until he was conned by Grunberg. Having lost his reputation and honor, he fled to the army and was killed attempting to win back his personal dignity.

Lucas, Dr. Mark A research chemist in *Destination Unknown*. He was one of three people to have last seen Thomas Betterton alive before his disappearance.

Luke, Mrs. The dowager of local society in *Unfinished Portrait*. Her particular area of interest is in matchmaking.

Luscombe, Colonel Derek The manager of the trust belonging to Elvira Blake in *At Bertram's Hotel*. He is a decent and kind person who wants only the best for the often headstrong young woman. He thus did his best to raise Elvira and to prepare her financial future after her father died. Unfortunately, she is too obstinate and he is too old-fashioned to be able to reach her.

Luttrell, Claude An associate of Mr. Parker Pyne who appears in two of his published cases and is considered for use in a third. A handsome, semi-reformed lothario, Claude has quite a checkered past, including several "brazen" affairs on the Riviera and the "notable and callous" exploitation of Mrs. Hattie West, the wife of the Californian Cucumber King. He uses his charms on behalf of Parker Pyne in "The Case of the Middle-Aged Wife," but he also expresses remorse at his lifestyle, causing Pyne to observe: "Interesting vestiges of a conscience noticeable in hardened Lounge Lizard." Claude also played the sensational dancer Jules in "The Case of the Disturbed Lady" and was a candidate for Parker Pyne's scheme in "The Case of the Rich Woman."

Luttrell, Daisy The wife of Colonel Luttrell in *Curtain*. She owns and operates Styles Court, and her nasty, unpleasant manner prompts Hercule Poirot to declare that were she his wife he would take a hatchet to her. She saves the most vicious aspects of her personality for her husband—whom she humiliates at every opportunity—and for playing bridge, which she plays without mercy or concern for the rules. Her personality undergoes a remarkable transformation after she is "accidentally" shot by her husband, who claims that he was aiming for a rabbit.

Luttrell, Colonel George A long-suffering retired military officer in *Curtain*. He was once stationed in India and now runs Styles Court. His days are filled with seemingly endless humiliations at the hands of his wife until, one day, he shoots her. She survives, and he claims that he was actually aiming at a rabbit, but the shooting brings about a complete change—in his view, for the better—in Mrs. Luttrell.

Luxmore, Mrs. A widow in *Cards on the Table*. She believes—quite erroneously—that her husband was shot by John Despard because he was desperately in love with her. In fact, it is she who was attracted to Despard.

Lyall, Captain A pilot in the RAF in "The Kidnapped Prime Minister." He is picked to fly the rescued prime minister, David MacAdam, to the court of Versailles and an important conference that will shape the future course of the war against Germany.

Lyall, Pamela One of the guests staying at a hotel in Rhodes in "Triangle at Rhodes." A devoted gossipmonger, she notes the curious and adulterous goings-on between Douglas Gold and Valentine Chantry.

Lyon, Maureen One of the victims of murder in "Three Blind Mice." In a former life—as Maureen Gregg—she was a defendant in a scandal involving criminal neglect of children who had been entrusted to her care as evacuees during the war. She is strangled to death and called by the murderer "The Farmer's Wife."

Lytcham Roche, Hubert The oppressive and often cruel patriarch of the family in "The Second Gong." He demands, among other things, that all family and guests come to the dinner table on time each evening or be banished from the table forever. He seemingly commits suicide by shooting himself in the head; a note, bearing the simple declaration "Sorry," is found beside him.

Lytton Gore, Hermione (Egg) The daughter of Lady Mary Lytton Gore in *Three-Act Tragedy*. Known as Egg because of her shape as an infant, she is a strong-willed and intelligent young woman who becomes involved in the investigation by Sir Charles Cartwright and Mr. Satterthwaite into the murder of Bartholomew Strange. Egg pretends to be attracted to Sir Charles, but she is actually in love with Oliver Manders.

Lytton Gore, Lady Mary The widowed mother of Hermione Lytton Gore in *Three-Act Tragedy*. She is concerned with virtually every aspect of her daughter's affairs, especially her love life.

M See Sprot, Millicent.

Maberly, Diana The fiancée of Hugh Chandler in "The Cretan Bull." She is perplexed when Chandler suddenly and inexplicably calls off their engagement and consults with Hercule Poirot in the hopes that the detective might be able to unravel the mystery.

MacAdam, David The prime minister of England during the difficult period of World War I in "The Kidnapped Prime Minister." The P.M. is abducted while on his way to France to address a conference of the Allies. Known as Fighting Mac, MacAdam was a stout leader for the country during the war and was considered more than prime minister—"He *was* England." His kidnapping causes powerful members of the government to seek out the help of Hercule Poirot in the desperate hope that he might be able to recover the prime minister before disaster befalls the country.

MacAllister, Dr. A physician in *Peril at End House*. He is also the uncle of Commander George Challenger.

MacAndrews, Dr. A physician in "Four and Twenty Blackbirds." He assists Hercule Poirot in his investigation into the death of Henry Gascoigne and thereby helps Poirot solve a murder and prosecute a criminal impersonation.

MacArthur, General John Gordon, C.M.G., D.S.O. One of the unfortunate guests on Indian Island in *And Then There Were None*. Like his fellow prisoners, he harbors a dark and murderous secret about his past, but, unlike most of the other guests, he has long been tormented about it and thus is quite willing to meet his grim fate at the hands of an unknown murderer. He becomes the third victim on the island when his skull is crushed by a heavy object.

Macatta, Mrs., M.P. A member of Parliament and a guest in the Mayfield house on the night that a set of secret plans was stolen in "The Incredible Theft." A great authority on housing and infant welfare, she "barked out sentences rather than spoke them and was generally of a somewhat alarming aspect."

Mace, Albert A young chemist's assistant in *The Mysterious Affair at Styles*. He originally testified that he had sold Alfred Inglethorp a quantity of strychnine, but later admitted that he had in fact never met the man.

Macfarlane, Mr. A "dour Scot, with a Celtic imagination hidden away somewhere," in "The Gipsy." He possesses second sight, a talent that comes to the fore in the story.

MacKenzie, Helen A severely embittered woman in *A Pocket Full of Rye*. She is convinced that her deceased husband was cheated out of his money by Rex Fortescue and so developed a pathological hatred for the man that was passed on to her children. She makes all her children promise that somehow they will murder Fortescue in revenge. As for Mrs. MacKenzie, she voluntarily surrenders herself to the Pinewood Private Sanitarium.

MacKenzie, Janet The maid to the unfortunate

Emily French in "Witness for the Prosecution." A very elderly woman, she was devoted to her murdered mistress and is firmly convinced that Leonard Vole killed her. She thus testifies against him at the trial and tries to assure the jury that Miss French was perfectly competent in managing her financial affairs and did not need the help of Vole, as he claimed.

MacKenzie, Ruby The daughter of the bitter Helen MacKenzie in *A Pocket Full of Rye*. She was raised to hate Rex Fortescue—her mother believes him to be responsible for the financial ruin and death of Ruby's father—but Ruby refuses to follow through with her promise to murder Rex in revenge. Instead, she horrifies her mother and marries Percival Fortescue.

MacKintosh, Miss The head of a dancing school in *Unfinished Portrait*. She is considered a dominating and formidable woman.

MacMaster, Dr. A retired friend of Dr. Calgary in *Ordeal by Innocence*. When Calgary begins a serious investigation into the death of Rachel Argyle, MacMaster gives him useful advice.

MacNaughton, Elsie The traveling companion and nurse to Lady Ariadne Grayle in "Death on the Nile." She is described as "an efficient creature" and "a dark horse" by Pamela Grayle, and she tells Mr. Parker Pyne that Lady Ariadne was not troubled by any real ailments. "A few floors to scrub every day and five or six children to look after" would leave her healthy and happy. However, lately Elsie has become convinced that Lady Ariadne is being poisoned, and suspects Lady Ariadne's husband, Sir George.

MacQueen, Hector Willard Private secretary to Samuel Ratchett and one of the passengers on the Calais Coach in *Murder on the Orient Express*. He has traveled with Ratchett for some time and is able to report a number of curious incidents involving his murdered employer. He at first mistakes Hercule Poirot for "a woman's dressmaker." Poirot subsequently learns that MacQueen was actually connected to the dreadful Armstrong kidnapping through his

father, who was the district attorney in charge of the case.

MacRae, Margaret A childhood friend of the main character in *Unfinished Portrait*. She has a distinct lisp because of several missing front teeth.

MacWhirter, Andrew A "damned pig-headed Scot" who once tried to kill himself but who nevertheless proves useful to Lord Cornelly in *Towards Zero*. He is able to clear Audrey Strange in the murder of Lady Tressilian.

Madeleine See Morisot, Anne.

Mahew, George A solicitor who has two appearances in Poirot cases. The first is in *Five Little Pigs* and the second is in "The Under Dog." He is a clever and resourceful attorney whose appearance belies his intelligence.

Mahmoud The dragoman (guide or interpreter) for the trip that is taken by the Boynton family in *Appointment with Death*.

Mahmoudi, Madame See Hobhouse, Valerie.

Maine, Inspector The Scotland Yard officer in *And Then There Were None*. He conducts extensive background checks into the victims that are discovered on Indian Island.

Maitland, Captain The captain of the local police near the Tell Yarimjah archaeological dig in *Murder in Mesopotamia*. He assumes command of the investigation into the deaths of Anne Johnson and Louise Leidner. Fortunately, Hercule Poirot is present to assist him in his duties.

Maitland, Ellie The wife of Peter Maitland in *Unfinished Portrait*. She stands more than six feet tall and was married to Peter for ten years until he left her for a woman he met on a cruise.

Maitland, Peter The husband of Ellie Maitland in *Unfinished Portrait*. Described as "a merry little fellow," he leaves Ellie after ten years of marriage to run off with a woman he met on a cruise.

Malinowski, Ladislaus An adventurous, unscrupulous, and dashing world champion race car driver in *At Bertram's Hotel*. He enjoys the company of women and conducts affairs with Lady Bess Sedgwick and her daughter, Elvira

Hector MacQueen (Anthony Perkins) is interrogated by Poirot (Albert Finney) in Murder on the Orient Express *(1974). (Photofest)*

Blake, at the same time. His handgun is used to murder Micky Gorman.

Mallaby, Mrs. A friend of Lord Cronshaw in "The Affair at the Victory Ball." She discovers Lord Cronshaw's body at the ball.

Maltravers, Mrs. A widow whose husband was murdered in a unique manner in "The Tragedy of Marsdon Manor." She is around "twenty-seven or eight, and very fair, with large blue eyes and a pretty pouting mouth."

Manders, Oliver A leading suspect—especially in the opinion of Hercule Poirot—in the murders of Sir Bartholomew Strange and Stephen Babbington in *Three-Act Tragedy*. A dedicated Communist, he suffers from the handicaps of being foreign-born and of having a serious inferiority complex.

Manelli, Giuseppe A member of the Comrades of the Red Hand, an anarchist group, in *The Secret of Chimneys*. He is given the task of stealing the memoirs of Count Stylptitch and attempts to blackmail Virginia Revel. For his efforts, Manelli is murdered.

Mannheim, Professor The father-in-law of Thomas Betterton in *Destination Unknown*. He is also a research chemist. His daughter is Elsa Mannheim.

Mannheim, Elsa The daughter of Professor Mannheim and the wife of Thomas Betterton in *Destination Unknown*. Like her father, she is a research chemist, and she is murdered for the knowledge she possesses and the secrets she holds.

Manning Two old gardeners appearing in separate mysteries. The first is the venerable head gardener at Styles Court in *The Mysterious Affair at Styles*. He is called as a witness to the signing of Emily Inglethorp's new will. The second Manning is a seventy-five-year-old gardener in *Sleeping Murder*. He is asked to take up the curious post of assistant to the even older gardener—who is eighty—at Hillside House. Manning's other task is to gather useful information about the Kennedys.

Marbury, Lily The daughter of the landlady to Napoleon Bonaparte Cust in *The A.B.C. Murders*.

March, Cicely The owner of a beauty salon in "The Ambassador's Boots." She responds to an advertisement placed by Tommy and Tuppence Beresford and asks them to help her locate Eileen O'Hara. The Beresfords soon discover that there is much more to Cicely March than meets the eye.

Marchaud, Felice The occupant of a cottage in "The Mystery of the Blue Jar." She comes to believe that the cottage is haunted by the spirit of a dead woman.

Marchington, Lord The father of Lady Frances "Frankie" Derwent in *Why Didn't They Ask Evans?* Lord Marchington is gout-ridden, but he is also quite wealthy and liberal with his daughter's allowance.

Marchmont, Adela The widowed sister of Gordon Cloade in *Taken at the Flood.* She and her daughter, Lynn, relied entirely upon her brother for their financial survival and had expected to inherit his estate after his death. Instead, Adela is stunned to learn that Cloade's estate will pass to his new wife, Rosaleen Underhay. Adela thus must go to Rosaleen and her brother, David Hunter, to ask for a loan.

Marchmont, Lynn The daughter of Adela Marchmont in *Taken at the Flood.* She is engaged to Rowley Cloade but breaks their plans for marriage after developing an almost uncontrollable passion for the mysterious David Hunter. This news comes as a terrible shock to Rowley, and he nearly strangles her to death.

Mardenberg A German spy in "The Girl in the Train." He becomes involved by accident in the adventure of George Rowland and Grand Duchess Anastasia, thus throwing his own plans into chaos. His actual objective is to smuggle secret plans of Portsmouth Harbor back to his bosses in Germany.

Margaret, Sister One of the volunteers at Town Hospital in *Giant's Bread.* Although she is considered a competent nurse, she is also called "a holy terror."

Margrave, Lily The companion to Lady Nancy Astwell in "The Under Dog." She becomes a suspect in the murder of Sir Reuben Astwell after Hercule Poirot learns her true identity and her real reason for entering into service in the Astwell household.

Marguerite See Vandemeyer, Rita.

Marie A former maid in the service of Linnet Doyle in *Death on the Nile.* She is told by Doyle that the man she loves, a ship's engineer named Fleetwood, is actually married and has three children. The news is enough for Fleetwood to make threats against Doyle, who is murdered soon after.

Marks, Miss The attractive secretary and dental assistant to Dr. Pengelley in "The Cornish Mystery." She is described by Mrs. Pengelley as "the yellow-haired hussy." Miss Marks is also the object of considerable gossip in the local community after the death of Mrs. Pengelley, and the announcement of her engagement to Dr. Pengelley hastens his arrest on the charge of murder.

Marle, Iris The chief suspect in the death of her sister, Rosemary Marle, in *Sparkling Cyanide.* She has long thought that Rosemary committed suicide, but it is learned that her sister was actually murdered. Once it becomes certain, Iris falls under suspicion; her future husband, Anthony Browne, however, has a very different view of things.

MARPLE, MISS JANE

"I am in my own way an emissary of justice."

The venerable spinster sleuth of St. Mary Mead, Miss Jane Marple was a born detective and possessed one of the most ideal minds for criminal investigative work ever depicted in fiction. Such was her virtually ruthless ability as an "emissary of justice" that Jason Rafiel gave her the name Nemesis. Another character called Miss Marple "The most frightening woman I have ever met." Miss Marple appeared in twelve published novels and twenty short

The ultimate Miss Marple, Joan Hickson. (Photofest)

stories, in which she solved a variety of mysteries. Her most formidable talents were reserved for murder, as noted by Dolly Bantry in *The Body in the Library:* "But you're so good at bodies . . . you're very good at murders."

BIOGRAPHY: Unfortunately, very little is known with certainty about the early life of Miss Marple, save for a few tantalizing bits provided in offhand remarks. She first appeared when she was between the ages of sixty-five and seventy in *Murder at the Vicarage.* The image first established of her in that case became the one that was forever connected to her. Miss Marple herself acknowledged that it was difficult for others to picture her as "young and pigtailed and struggling with decimals and English literature." Still, she could remember her youth in some detail:

"I was, I think, well educated for the standards of my day. My sister [a relative who does not figure in the cases at all] and I had a German governess—a Fräulein. A very sentimental creature. She taught us the language of flowers."

She rarely spoke of her father and mother, but it is clear from various references that her grandmother left her with a definite impression of what it meant to be a lady. Several significant events are noted in the writings. One was her visit to London at the age of fourteen with her Aunt Helen and Uncle Thomas, including a stay at Bertram's Hotel. A second was her trip at the age of sixteen to spend time at a school in Florence. While there, she met Carrie Louise and Ruth Martin, two American girls who became her good friends and remained so after many years. Miss Marple helped solve a murder in the estate owned by Carrie Louise in *They Do It with Mirrors.*

While Carrie Louise and Ruth Martin were married a total of six times between them, Miss Marple never married and became a classic model for the village spinster. In her youth, she did have several suitors, but not one could capture her heart forever. It can be deduced that she was also fond of dancing, as noted in *A Caribbean Mystery.*

Aside from a fleeting reference to her "long experience of nursing," next to nothing is to be found about the long decades between her active youth and her career as a detective. She laments, however, that "one *is* alone when the last one who *remembers* is gone. I have nephews and nieces and kind friends—but there's no one who belongs to the old days. I've been alone for quite a long time now."

RELATIVES: Aside from her well-remembered grandmother, Miss Marple had a number of other relatives to whom she made assorted references. There was a great aunt Fanny; an aunt Helen; a great uncle Thomas (a retired admiral); an uncle Henry, who hid money in large amounts in his library behind volumes of sermons; an uncle Thomas, a canon of Ely; an unnamed uncle who was canon of Chichester Cathedral; and cousins Anthony, Gordon, Fanny, and Ethel.

Perhaps her best-known relative was her favorite nephew, Raymond West. A successful novelist and poet (in the modern style), West displayed much concern for his aunt, paying for several of her vacations, including a trip to the Caribbean and a stay at Bertram's Hotel.

Miss Marple's Published Cases

NOVELS
At Bertram's Hotel
The Body in the Library
A Caribbean Mystery
4.50 from Paddington
The Mirror Crack'd from Side to Side
The Moving Finger
The Murder at the Vicarage
A Murder Is Announced
Nemesis
A Pocket Full of Rye
Sleeping Murder
They Do It with Mirrors

SHORT STORIES
"The Affair at the Bungalow"
"The Bloodstained Pavement"
"The Blue Geranium"
"The Case of the Caretaker"
"The Case of the Perfect Maid"
"A Christmas Tragedy"
"The Companion"
"Death by Drowning"
"The Four Suspects"
"Greenshaw's Folly"
"The Herb of Death"
"The Idol House of Astarte"
"Ingots of Gold"
"Miss Marple Tells a Story"
"Motive vs. Opportunity"
"Sanctuary"
"Strange Jest"
"The Tape-Measure Murder"
"The Thumb Mark of Saint Peter"
"The Tuesday Night Club"

DESCRIPTION: Perhaps the best description of Miss Marple was given in *A Pocket Full of Rye*. She was "a tall elderly lady wearing an old-fashioned tweed coat and skirt, a couple of scarves and a small felt hat with a bird's wing. The old lady carried a capacious handbag and an aged but good-quality suitcase reposed by her feet." This contrasts sharply with the description of Miss Marple as a very Victorian old lady in "The Tuesday Club Murder," and is supported by several other accounts, most notably the one in *Nemesis*: "She sat there, upright as was her habit. She wore a light tweed suit, a string of pearls and a small velvet toque."

The overall description that emerges is of a little old lady with white or light gray hair, a pink, wrinkled face, and delicate teeth. She is graced with light blue eyes and a distant, innocent, and unremarkable visage that was, obviously, quite deceptive, especially to criminals. Her clothing was at best dowdy, replete with tweeds, scarves, fleecy coats, and sensible shoes. She carried a large bag, an umbrella, and a shopping bag. Hats were always present. There were very few adornments, save for a string of pearls and "pale blue enamel watch that she wore pinned to one side of her dress."

HABITS AND PERSONAL LIFE: Given her age and background, Miss Marple's daily activities were limited to domestic pastimes. There is frequent mention of her fondness for knitting. This she also used as a convenient blind while interrogating a witness. She also enjoyed gardening and bird-watching, both of which proved useful as a means of observing her neighbors and keeping an eye on the goings-on in the village.

Her activities were limited in many ways by an assortment of infirmities. She suffered from chronic bronchitis and pneumonia, and only recovered from the latter by following a prescription from her longtime physician, Dr. Haydock—a nice juicy murder. Medical problems prompted her nephew Raymond West to find assorted diversions for her, such as a trip to

A fun Miss Marple, Margaret Rutherford, with Inspector Craddock (Charles Tingwell), from Murder, She Said *(1962). (Photofest)*

the Caribbean, and to hire a housekeeper for her. Miss Marple disliked one of her nurses, Miss Knight. Two other very memorable attendants were Cherry Baker and the redoubtable Lucy Eylesbarrow.

For someone who confronted death on a regular basis and actually placed her own life in danger on numerous occasions, Miss Marple had a remarkable sense of justice and a belief in prayer. In bringing a murderer to justice, she was relentless and quite free of mercy. Her ability to follow the path of justice wherever it might lead was precisely why Jason Rafiel sought her out posthumously to investigate the possibility that his son might be a murderer after all. She also went to extreme lengths to catch killers, normally being in on the climax of the case or catching the murderer in the very act of striking again.

Given her cold-blooded application of justice, it is surprising that she actually did have a softer side. She could give encouragement and almost loving advice to friends and relatives and earned their trust and admiration. She was close to Dr. Haydock, Dolly Bantry, and Griselda Clement, and was much admired by Colonel Melchett and Inspector Craddock.

METHODS: Miss Marple was not a detective by profession. As Raymond West observed: "Some commit murder, some get mixed up in murder, others have murder thrust upon them. My Aunt Jane comes into the third category." Hers was a natural genius for criminal detection. Sir Henry Clithering informed Inspector Craddock: "Remember that an elderly unmarried woman who knits and gardens is streets ahead of any detective sergeant. She can tell you what might have happened and what ought to have happened and even what actually *did* happen. And she can tell you why it happened!"

Miss Marple possessed several vital prerequisites for solving crime. She was able to use her age and appearance as powerful camouflage. She

St. Mary Mead

Miss Marple solved murders in the Caribbean, London, and in a few spots around England, but she is forever linked with the quaint, tiny village that she called home for most of her life: St. Mary Mead. It was, in part, through her intimate knowledge of the village's inhabitants—including their dark secrets and numerous foibles—that she was able to become such an expert on human nature and such a superb detective.

The village of St. Mary Mead was located in the county of Downshire, about twenty-five miles south of London and twelve miles north of the coast. It was ideally suited for travel in and out of the great metropolis, as well as to and from the nearby resort town of Danemouth. The village itself evolved naturally along the High Street, with its collection of shops, the railroad station, and the church, of which Reverend Leonard Clement was the beloved vicar.

Miss Marple lived in the cottage of Danemead, just off the High Street. Her neighbors were Dr. Haydock (her longtime friend and personal physician), Miss Hartnell, Miss Wetherby, and Miss Price Ridley (the chief gossipmonger of the village). She also lived next to the vicarage and was thus close to Reverend Clement and his lovely wife, Griselda. Living next to the vicarage proved
of great importance in the solution to the murder of Colonel Protheroe in Murder at the Vicarage.

Several other locations in St. Mary Mead deserve mention. First, there was Gossington Hall, the home of Miss Marple's friends Colonel and Dolly Bantry. Second, there was Old Hall, the home of Colonel Protheroe until his death, after which it became a block of four flats. Finally, there was the Development, a late addition to the village (mentioned in The Mirror Crack'd from Side to Side) *that was a symbol of the relentless march of progress, even in the sedate and unchanging landscape of St. Mary Mead.*

According to Jane Marple's chief biographer, Anne Hart (in The Life and Times of Miss Jane Marple), *the village was, over the course of four decades, the site of sixteen murders (five poisonings, two shootings, two drownings, two strangulations, and five murders from undetermined causes) as well as four attempted murders. There were also eight embezzlements, five robberies, and a host of crank calls, poachings, blackmailings, and poison-pen letters. While this did not reach the subsequent gold standard of mayhem set by Cabot Cove, Maine, in the television series* Murder, She Wrote, *which featured the sleuth Jessica Fletcher, it certainly was an impressive environment in which a brilliant sleuth like Miss Marple could apply her talents.*

also had a superb eye for the obvious. Finally, she knew the most intimate details of human nature because she knew St. Mary Mead.

It was very easy to underestimate Miss Marple. She could appear to be a dotty old spinster asking innocuous questions as she interrogated a suspect. In her daily activities—knitting, gardening, shopping, having tea, and bird-watching—she found the means of divining clues, asking questions, and probing witnesses. Once she had assembled clues, she noted their significance and logically organized them, thus giving herself almost everything she needed to solve the crime.

A final solution was possible once Miss Marple analyzed the human aspect of the case. As she once said, "You simply cannot afford to believe everything that people tell you. When there's anything fishy about, I never believe anyone at all." Operating from this assumption, Miss Marple could then turn to her source for all information about human nature—St. Mary Mead. She found in the village a perfect microcosm of the criminal world, a place where every crime and criminal had a perfect counterpart. As she observed: "There is a great deal of wickedness in village life."

In her autobiography, Agatha Christie cred-

A fey Miss Marple, Angela Lansbury, from The Mirror Crack'd *(1980). (Photofest)*

ited the creation of Miss Marple to her earlier work on *The Murder of Roger Ackroyd* (1926): "I think it is possible that Miss Marple arose from the pleasure I had taken in portraying Dr. Sheppard's sister in *The Murder of Roger Ackroyd*. She had been my favourite character in the book—an acidulated spinster, full of curiosity, knowing everything, hearing everything: the complete detective service in the home." Christie added: "Miss Marple was born at the age of sixty-five to seventy—which, as with Poirot, proved unfortunate, because she was going to have to last a long time in my life. If I had had any second sight, I would have provided myself with a precocious schoolboy as my first detective; then he could have grown old with me."

After her debut in 1930, Miss Marple appeared again two years later in the short story collection *The Thirteen Problems*, but did not appear in a novel again until 1942's *The Body in the Library*. As she became a rival to Hercule Poirot

in popularity, the number of cases featuring her increased during the next decades. It is an oft-noted reality that in terms of chronological time, rather than the nebulous literary time of books, Miss Marple would have been well over 110 years old by the time of her last published case. As Christie liked Miss Marple more than Poirot, it was fitting that the last of her published novels, *Sleeping Murder* (1976), should feature the spinster from St. Mary Mead.

Miss Marple has enjoyed a wide popularity in film, on television, and on the stage, with a number of memorable performers taking on the demanding role of the sleuth in assorted adaptations of Christie works. Without question, the two most memorable performances were by Margaret Rutherford and Joan Hickson. Rutherford played Miss Marple in four films from 1962 to 1964, while Hickson earned well-deserved praise as the foremost Miss Marple for her work in the BBC television productions made between 1985 and 1992. Helen Hayes also played Miss Marple in two American television films made during the 1980s. (For further details, please see part three.)

Marquis, Monsieur le An international jewel thief in *The Mystery of the Blue Train*. He has a long and nefarious history of jewel thefts and has set out to steal the Heart of Fire rubies that have been given by Rufus van Aldin to his daughter.

Marrascaud A supremely dangerous and cunning murderer in "The Erymanthian Boar." He is described as "a wild boar, ferocious, terrible, who charges in blind fury," a portrait that appeals to Hercule Poirot and challenges him to attempt another of his Herculean labors. Marrascaud has eluded authorities in Europe for some time, but Poirot learns of his presence at the Swiss resort of Rochers Neige, a secluded mountaintop hotel where the criminal plans to gather his feared gang. The detective and Marrascaud enter into a battle of wits in the high mountain air when an avalanche cuts off the hotel from the outside world. The Belgian detective, of course, proves victorious.

Marriot, Inspector A Scotland Yard detective who is involved in several cases featuring Tommy and Tuppence Beresford. He enlists their help in bringing to justice a clever counterfeiting ring in "The Crackler" and subsequently works with them in "The Unbreakable Alibi," "The Adventure of the Sinister Stranger," and "The Affair of the Pink Pearl."

Marsden, Chief Inspector An officer of Scotland Yard who has an unshakable belief in the guilt of Elinor Carlisle in *Sad Cypress.* He remains convinced that he has arrested the right person, despite the efforts of Hercule Poirot to prove otherwise.

Marsdon, Antony (Tony) An operative in British intelligence in *N or M?* He is especially skilled in breaking codes.

Marsh, Andrew An eccentric and old-fashioned wealthy country farmer in "The Missing Will." A kind man, he willingly took in and raised his niece as though she were his own daughter, but he disapproved of her modern ways, especially her university education. So, when he died, he set up a challenge for her by hiding his will, thus forcing her to find it somewhere in Crabtree Manor.

Marsh, George Alfred St. Vincent, the fourth Baron Edgware The cruel, sadistic, and altogether reprehensible nobleman and murder victim in *Lord Edgware Dies.* He is much hated by friends and family, especially his daughter, whom he has long mistreated. When he is murdered, there are no tears for him, and his daughter actually expresses gratitude to the killer.

Marsh, Geraldine (Dina) One of the suspects in the death of Lord Edgware in *Lord Edgware Dies.* Because of her difficult childhood, during which she was abandoned by her mother and mistreated by her father, she has little affection for her father and grieves not at all upon his death. She tells Hercule Poirot that she is actually grateful to the murderer for his deed.

Marsh, Captain Ronald, the fifth Baron Edgware The nephew of the fourth Baron Edgware in *Lord Edgware Dies.* He stands in sharp contrast to his uncle, for he is friendly, considerate, and rather forgettable.

Marsh, Violet A young woman with a businesslike manner who enlists Hercule Poirot's assistance in "The Missing Will." The heir to the estate of her uncle, Andrew Marsh, she disagreed with his old-fashioned ways and was determined to seek a university education. For her obstinacy, her uncle left her his estate, but he hid his will and challenged her to find it somewhere in Crabtree Manor.

Marshall, Andrew The legal advisor to the Argyle family in *Ordeal by Innocence.* He has little sympathy or affection for his scheming and unpleasant clients, observing that they embody the name of the home in which they dwell: Viper's Point.

Marshall, Arlena A selfish, shallow, and petty actress in *Evil under the Sun.* Known previously as Helen Stuart, she has enjoyed a glittering stage career and has amassed both wealth and influence; she has also acquired a new husband, Captain Kenneth Marshall, as well as a host of enemies. While visiting the Jolly Roger Hotel, she proves to be a horrid wife and ceaselessly flirts with other men, in particular Patrick Redfern. Many guests have their own private reasons to hate her, and soon she is found strangled on the beach.

Marshall, Edward John A former resident of New Zealand in *Sad Cypress.* He serves as a witness in the trial of Elinor Carlisle.

Marshall, Captain John A friend of Hubert Lytcham Roche in "The Second Gong." He is much attracted to Diana Cleves—and she to him—but any romance between them is considered completely unacceptable to her adoptive father, Mr. Lytcham Roche. After Lytcham Roche's death, of course, there is no obstacle between them.

Marshall, Captain Kenneth The husband of the wealthy and beautiful but dreadful Arlena

Marshall in *Evil under the Sun.* A good man and devoted father, Marshall also has the unfortunate habit of "making unfortunate marriages." Perhaps the worst of these unions is with Arlena Marshall; she may be glamorous and wealthy, but she is also shallow, cruel, and flirtatious. His daughter, Linda, especially despises her stepmother. After the terrible events recounted in the book, Marshall marries his longtime friend Rosamund Darnley.

Marshall, Linda The daughter of Captain Kenneth Marshall and the stepdaughter of Arlena Marshall in *Evil under the Sun.* Linda truly hates her stepmother and secretly wishes her to die. This wish comes to pass after Linda creates a voodoo doll and sticks a pin into it, whereupon Arlena Marshall is found dead on a beach. Stricken with guilt, Linda tries to kill herself.

Marston, Anthony James (Tony) The first of ten victims of murderous revenge in *And Then There Were None.* Like the other guests on Indian Island, Marston is guilty of some crime from years before; in his case, he ran down two young people with his car and has absolutely no remorse for the deed.

Martha The faithful housekeeper and cook to Lily Crabtree in "Sing a Song of Sixpence." When her mistress is murdered, she is the last person to see her alive and thus provides important details about events leading to her death. While she is quite devoted to Miss Crabtree, Martha is not without her own secrets.

Martin, Miss The secretary to Abe Ryland in *The Big Four.*

Martin, Alix A young and intelligent woman in "Philomel Cottage" who decides to throw her usual caution to the wind and wed Gerald Martin, despite knowing surprisingly little about him. With this act, she casts aside the attentions of a longtime suitor, Dicky Windyford, who wanted to wait until he could earn a suitable fortune before marrying. Her hasty marriage soon becomes a troubling one, as she begins to uncover small but disturbing bits of information

Alix Martin (Ann Harding) in Love from a Stranger *(1937), based on "Philomel Cottage." (Collection of the author)*

about her husband's past. Her concerns only deepen after speaking with the gardener. Gradually, she fears for her life and must find a way out of the seemingly lethal situation in the house.

Martin, Brian An actor in *Lord Edgware Dies.* He is tossed over by Jane Wilkerson for the far wealthier Duke of Merton and suffers terrible heartache over the loss.

Martin, Elizabeth An American tourist in "The Soul of the Croupier." An acquaintance of Mr. Satterthwaite, she is " 'doing Europe' in a stern conscientious spirit." Satterthwaite finds her presence desirable at a party in Monte Carlo.

Martin, Gerald The husband of Alix Martin in "Philomel Cottage." He has swept her off her feet, and she weds him without knowing much at all about his past. Slowly, bits of his disturbing history are revealed over the first days of their marriage. Most peculiar is his collection of newspaper clippings and photographs concerning Charles LeMaitre, a man who had supposedly murdered several women in America. The man in the photographs bears a striking resemblance to Gerald Martin. These revelations seemingly confirm Alix's worst fears, and she must concoct some way to escape apparent death at Gerald's hands.

Martin, Gladys   A half-witted former maid to Miss Marple in *A Pocket Full of Rye*. After working for Miss Marple, Gladys found employment in the Fortescue household. There, she was clumsy but earnest and there, too, she attracted the attention of "Bert Evans." This would-be "suitor" cruelly uses Gladys to act as his accomplice in a murder and then, just as brutally, strangles her, maliciously placing a clothespin on her nose. Unfortunately for the murderer, Gladys sent a photo of herself with her beau to Miss Marple.

Martindale, Hilda   See Bland, Valerie.

Martindale, Katherine   The proprietor of the Cavendish Secretarial and Typing Bureau in *The Clocks*. Even though she is an impressive and rather dominating figure, the employees refer to her as Sandy Cat behind her back.

Marvel, Sir Donald   A member of Parliament and "a tired-looking English politician" who is traveling through the Jordanian desert with a group of people (including Mr. Parker Pyne) in "The Pearl of Price." He is desirous of marrying Carol Blundell, daughter of the American magnate Caleb Blundell, but she considers him nothing more than a "stuffed fish."

Marvell, Mr.   The attorney who represents James Reilly in "The Man in the Mist." He must defend a client accused of murder.

Marvell, Mary   An American film star in "The Adventure of 'The Western Star.' " She is married to the American film actor Gregory Rolf and is the owner of a fabulous diamond, the Western Star.

Mary   A housemaid in "A Christmas Tragedy." She worked at the Keston Spa Hydro until she died under curious circumstances from what seemed to be a mildly infected finger.

Mary Ann   See Zerkowski, Countess Renata.

Mason, Ada Beatrice   Also known as Kitty Kidd, an actress and accomplice to Monsieur Le Marquis in *The Mystery of the Blue Train*. With him, she plans on stealing the Heart of Fire rubies from Rufus van Aldin and his daughter, Ruth Kettering.

Mason, Jane   Also known as Gracie Kidd, an impersonator and thief who targets the jewels of The Honourable Flossie Carrington in "The Plymouth Express."

Massingham, Mrs.   A woman in *A Daughter's a Daughter* who spent many years in India and is generally referred to as the Mem Sahib.

Massington, Mrs.   One of the friends of Iris Wade in "The Case of the Discontented Husband." Like Iris, she is married to a seemingly rather dull fellow who is concerned chiefly with "stocks and shares and golf alternately."

Masterman, Edward Henry   The personal valet, or gentleman's gentleman, to Samuel Ratchett in *Murder on the Orient Express*. During the investigation into the murder, Poirot discovers that Masterman had served previously as an aide to the doomed Colonel Armstrong during World War I and thus had a motive to kill Ratchett. The valet, however, has a seemingly airtight alibi: he shared a compartment with Antonio Foscarelli, an Italian who never ceased talking, and was also troubled by a toothache.

Masterton, Connie   One of Poirot's unofficial witnesses in *Dead Man's Folly*. She is described by Hercule Poirot as looking like a bloodhound, with a "full underhung jaw and large, mournful, slightly bloodshot eyes." She is the reason her husband is so successful politically, and her sharp wit proves of value to the detective throughout his investigation.

Matcham, Mrs.   The old nanny to Mrs. Ariadne Oliver in *Elephants Can Remember*. She proves of much assistance to Mrs. Oliver in her investigation, especially as she provides details about the twins Dolly Jarrow and Molly Ravenscroft.

Mathias, John A member of a traveling acrobatic troupe in "At the 'Bells and Motley.' " He puts his acting abilities to use in several felonious ways throughout the events recounted in the case.

Maud The fiancée of Edward Robinson in "The Manhood of Edward Robinson." She is a demanding, practical, and obstinate young woman who is also "always right about everything." Her attributes are the source of some consternation to her fiancé, especially as he longs for a more carefree existence.

Mauhourat, Mademoiselle A prospective tutor to the main character in *Unfinished Portrait*. She is not acceptable to the main character and so is not hired.

Maverick, Dr. The chief psychiatrist at the home for delinquent boys in *They Do It with Mirrors*. Miss Marple disagrees severely with the psychiatrist's views, considering him "distinctly abnormal." She is most opposed to his notion that "We're all mad . . . That's the secret of existence."

Mayerling, Mr. A British agent in the secret service in *The Big Four*. He has been missing for five years in the Soviet Union and surfaces at last to provide Hercule Poirot with useful information on the master criminal organization called the Big Four. Mayerling dies soon after getting the information to Poirot.

Mayfield, Lord (Sir Charles McLaughlin) The minister of armaments in "The Incredible Theft." He is in charge of a set of secret plans that are stolen from his library, much to the alarm of other members of the government. He is "a big man, square-shouldered, with thick silvery hair, a big straight nose and a slightly prominent chin." Mayfield has also apparently succumbed to the charms of the dangerous Mrs. Vanderlyn.

Mayherne, Mr. The defense attorney for Leonard Vole in "Witness for the Prosecution." Mayherne is firmly convinced that his client is entirely innocent in the murder of Emily French. He thus leaves no stone unturned and no witness unharassed in the pursuit of Vole's acquittal. He proves especially capable in destroying the potentially fatal witness against his client—Vole's wife, Romaine.

Mayhew, Mr. The solicitor who claims Charles Leverson as a client in "The Under Dog." His client becomes a suspect in the murder of his uncle, Reuben Astwell. Mayhew is considered a "dry, cautious gentleman."

McGillicuddy, Elspeth A vital witness to murder in *4.50 from Paddington*. While on her way to visit Miss Marple in St. Mary Mead after a full day of Christmas shopping, Mrs. McGillicuddy witnesses what she is certain is a murder on board a train traveling in the opposite direction from the one she is riding. She relates the event to Miss Marple, who not only believes her but undertakes the hunt for the murderer. Mrs. McGillicuddy subsequently departs for Ceylon but continues to assist in the investigation; at the end of the case, she makes a direct identification of the murderer, thanks to the brilliant connivance of Miss Marple.

McGinty, Mrs. The title character and victim of brutal murder in *Mrs. McGinty's Dead*. A cleaning lady and washerwoman, she was murdered by being beaten in the back of the head with a heavy object. James Bentley is convicted of the crime, but Hercule Poirot is convinced of Bentley's innocence.

McGrath, Jimmy An old friend of Anthony Cade in *The Secret of Chimneys*. He agrees to transport a manuscript and some letters from Africa to England on Cade's behalf.

McKay, Elspeth The widowed sister of the former police superintendent Spence in *Hallowe'en Party*. Elspeth is as sharp as her brother and makes several useful observations to Hercule Poirot.

McLaren, Commander Jock An old friend of Margharita and Arnold Clayton in "The Mystery of the Spanish Chest." While he pretends to be merely a friend of the couple, it becomes

Charles Laughton as Sir Wilfrid Robarts, based on Mr. Mayherne in Witness for the Prosecution. *(Photofest)*

clear that he is also deeply attracted to Mrs. Clayton romantically.

McLaughlin, Sir Charles   See Mayfield, Lord.

McLean, Hugo   A "tall, middle-aged man with a thin, brown face" in *The Body in the Library.* He is deeply in love with Adelaide Jefferson and wants to marry her; his hopes are fulfilled by the end of the story.

McNabb, Colin   A student and would-be fiancé to Celia Austin in *Hickory Dickory Dock.* He is a resident in Mrs. Nicoletis's student hostel and is studying for a graduate degree in psychiatry. On the very night that he proposes to Celia, she is murdered.

McNaughton, Mrs.   A supposed witness in *The Clocks.* She claims to have seen the murdered

man, R. H. Curry, and tries to provide important details to the police. Unfortunately, the police, under Detective Inspector Hardcastle and special branch investigator Lamb, recognize immediately that she is an unreliable witness who "just wants to think she's seen him" when she has not really done so. Her husband is Angus McNaughton.

McNaughton, Angus   A retired professor in *The Clocks.* He and his wife live next door to the house in which the body of R. H. Curry is discovered. While his wife is rather a busybody, he is quite content to remain in his garden.

McNeil, Mr.   One of the partners in the law firm of McNeil and Hodgson in *The Big Four.* His firm represents the legal interests of Hercule Poirot.

McNeil, Sir Andrew   A prison governor in *Nemesis*. He is firmly convinced that Michael Rafiel could not be the murderer of Verity Hunt and thus should not have a cloud of suspicion hanging over him.

McRae, Detective Constable   A capable but lighthearted police officer in *Hickory Dickory Dock*. He heads the investigation into the disappearances at the Hickory Road Hostel.

Meadows, Detective Inspector   An investigator from Scotland Yard who takes charge of the investigation into the murder of L. B. Carton in *The Man in the Brown Suit*.

Meadows, Dr.   An army doctor in *Giant's Bread*.

Meadows, Inspector   A Scotland Yard officer in charge of the English end of the investigation into the Whalley case in *The Big Four*.

Meauhourat, Mademoiselle Zellie   A French governess in *Elephants Can Remember*. She is able to assist Hercule Poirot in his investigation into the deaths of General Alistair and Lady Molly Ravenscroft.

Melchett, Colonel   The chief constable for Radfordshire who appears in several cases involving Miss Marple. Melchett resides in Much Benham, but one of the villages within his jurisdiction is St. Mary Mead. Thus, his investigations often bring him into contact with Miss Marple, of whom he has a very high opinion. He is a "dapper little man who had a habit of snorting suddenly and unexpectedly." He takes part in the cases recounted in *The Body in the Library, Murder at the Vicarage,* "The Tape-Measure Murder," and "Death by Drowning."

Melford, Mildred   The guardian of Elvira Blake and cousin of Colonel Derek Luscombe in *At Bertram's Hotel*. She is a witness to a crime, but her value to the police is quite limited because she also suffers from the handicap of being "fearfully easy to deceive."

Melrose, Colonel   Chief constable for the part of England that includes Market Basing and King's Abbot; he is thus the local police official in charge of the investigations at the Chimneys, especially as he is a friend of Lord Chatterham. Colonel Melrose appears in three cases: *The Secret of Chimneys, The Seven Dials Mystery,* and "The Love Detectives."

Menier, Raoul   A thief who targets museums and art collections and who is caught in Baghdad in *Murder in Mesopotamia*. He is arrested along with a colleague, but only after successfully impersonating a member of the group at Tell Yarimjah. During his time there, he was able to substitute electroplated copies for several important archaeological finds.

Merall, Major   A police officer who takes over the investigation into the murder of Marlene Tucker in *Dead Man's Folly*.

Mercado, Joseph   A member of the Tell Yarimjah expedition in *Murder in Mesopotamia*. He is serving in his second year with the expedition, but his ability to work, let alone function, is increasingly threatened by his overwhelming addiction to narcotics. His wife, Marie Mercado, assists him in hiding his terrible addiction.

Mercado, Marie   The wife of Joseph Mercado in *Murder in Mesopotamia*. She is an excessively protective woman who goes out of her way to help Joseph hide his increasingly suicidal narcotics addiction.

Merdell   An elderly dockworker in *Dead Man's Folly*. The ninety-two-year-old Merdell is murdered when someone pushes him into the river.

Meredith, Anne   One of the guests at the dinner party hosted by Mr. Shaitana in *Cards on the Table*. She thus becomes a suspect in Shaitana's death, but she drowns while attempting to kill Rhoda Dawes.

Merivale, Sir Arthur   The husband of the murdered Lady Merivale in "The Gentleman Dressed in Newspaper." He attends the Three Arts Ball dressed, ironically, in the garb of a seventeenth-century executioner. His wife is soon murdered and Sir Arthur becomes an obvious suspect. The likelihood of his being the killer only increases when it is learned that his wife has been manifestly unfaithful.

Merivale, Lady Vere   The victim of murder and the unfaithful wife of Sir Arthur Merivale in "The Gentleman Dressed in Newspaper." She is murdered while on her way to meet with her lover. A jeweled dagger is stabbed into her heart.

Merrion, Miss   The manager of the Ginger Cat café in *The A.B.C. Murders.* She has a piercingly shrill voice.

Merrowdene, George   The hopelessly naive husband of Margaret Merrowdene in "Accident." A former chemistry professor, he seems happily married and thus does not suspect any possible danger when his wife encourages him to take out a large life insurance policy.

Merrowdene, Margaret   The seemingly charming wife of George Merrowdene in "Accident." She is a woman with a dark past who was once charged and tried for the poisoning of her first husband with arsenic. While acquitted of the charge, she certainly seemed to have acted most suspiciously, as she encouraged her husband to take out a large life insurance policy just before his accidental death. Now, years later, she pushes her new husband, George, to do the same thing.

Merrypit, Mrs.   A woman who runs a wool shop in Carristown in *Nemesis.* She assists Miss Marple in matching yarn, but she also provides the old sleuth with details about the death of Verity Hunt.

Mersu, Divine Father   A physician in ancient Egypt in *Death Comes As the End.* He tries valiantly but unsuccessfully to save the life of the poisoned Sobek.

Merton, the Dowager Duchess of   A dominating and thoroughly unpleasant woman in *Lord Edgware Dies.* Described by Hercule Poirot as someone who seeks "to arrange the universe to her manner of thinking," the dowager duchess attempts to hire Poirot to terminate the relationship between her son and Jane Wilkinson, a romance she feels is most inap-propriate. Her son, the duke of Merton, resents bitterly his mother's interference in his affairs.

Merton, duke of   The son of the dowager duchess of Merton in *Lord Edgware Dies.* Described as more like a "weedy young haber-dasher than like a duke," he is a curious bag of inconsistencies: His supposed deep religious beliefs prevent him from marrying a divorcée, but he leaps into a romance with the wildly in-appropriate Jane Wilkinson, a relationship of which his mother disapproves heartily. She thus tries to enlist Hercule Poirot to sever the romantic entanglement, and the duke grows even more resentful toward his mother.

Merton, Mrs.   A witness to events in *One, Two, Buckle My Shoe.* Wearing a memorable hairdo, she is interviewed by Hercule Poirot and In-spector Japp and gives them details about the enigmatic Mr. Chapman.

Merton, Milly   See Croft, Milly.

Mesnard, Virginie   A poor cousin of Paul Déroulard in "The Chocolate Box." She lived in the Déroulard household because of her finan-cial situation and was thus a witness to the tragic events that took place. She had a motive for killing Paul Déroulard after he made a pass at her, but she also consulted Hercule Poirot because she was convinced that Déroulard's death was no accident.

Metcalf, Dr.   A physician in *The Body in the Li-brary.* His patient is the wealthy recluse Con-way Jefferson, and he advises him to stop being obsessed with death and to enjoy the life that he has left.

Metcalf, Major   See Tanner, Inspector.

Meynell, Dr.   A physician in "Where There's a Will." Mrs. Harter was one of his patients, and he reveals after her murder that she had only a few months to live and would have died soon had someone not killed her.

Michael   One of the members of a traveling repertory theater in *Mrs. McGinty's Dead.* He told Maude Williams about Evelyn Hope, an Australian playwright.

Michel, Pierre A competent and popular train conductor who appears in several cases involving Hercule Poirot. He is the conductor on the fateful journey recounted in *Murder on the Orient Express.* He discovers the murdered body of Mr. Ratchett and becomes one of the key witnesses in Poirot's subsequent investigation. Pierre is also present on the Blue Train in *The Mystery of the Blue Train.* Once again, he discovers the body of the murder victim. In this case, he finds the strangled corpse of Ruth Kettering.

Miklanova, Anna See Denman, Anna.

Miles The butler of Dwighton Manor in "The Love Detectives."

Miller, Inspector A Scotland Yard inspector who crosses paths on several occasions with Hercule Poirot. Although he is competent, he nevertheless evinces a certain tension in dealing with the Belgian detective, especially because, in most situations, he has fingered the wrong person as the murderer. He appears in "The Lost Mine," "The Disappearance of Mr. Davenheim," "The Under Dog," and "The Mystery of the Spanish Chest."

Milly A maid in the service of Mrs. Ariadne Oliver in *The Pale Horse.*

Milray, Mrs. An enormously overweight woman in *Three-Act Tragedy.* An "immense dumpling of a woman," she uses her corpulence as a psychological weapon to dominate and enslave her long-suffering daughter, Violet. She grudgingly grants an interview to Hermione Lytton Gore and Sir Charles Cartwright about the murder of Reverend Babbington.

Milray, Violet The long-suffering daughter of Mrs. Milray in *Three-Act Tragedy.* She has worked for the retired actor Sir Charles Cartwright for six years and is considered by him to be "the perfect robot." In truth, she is passionately in love with him. Violet has long been under the oppressive control of her mother, who uses her vast corpulence as a kind of cruel weapon of domination.

Minks, Arthur A clever impersonator who assumes various disguises and personae in *The Man in the Brown Suit.* In the course of gaining the confidence of other people and hence winning from them valuable information, he becomes the Reverend Edward Chichester, Miss Pettigrew, and Count Sergius Paulovitch.

Minton, Sophia An older woman in *N or M?* Called "the *compleat* British spinster," she is also appallingly bad at bridge.

Mirabelle The newest mistress of the king of Bosnia in "The Soul of the Croupier." She appears with a mighty flourish in Monte Carlo and causes a considerable stir among high society. She also generates great jealousy in the Countess Czarnova, the king's former mistress.

Mirelle A dancer and the mistress to Derek Kettering in *The Mystery of the Blue Train.* It is perhaps only a coincidence that she is on the same train as Ruth Kettering and that Ruth should be strangled while on board.

Miriam A devoted mother in *Unfinished Portrait.* She is willing to give up everything to care for her daughter and to make certain that she has a comfortable, safe, and loving environment in which to grow up.

Mitchell, Henry Charles The chief steward on board the plane *Prometheus* during the fateful flight from Paris to England in *Death in the Clouds.* He discovers the corpse of Madame Giselle on board.

Mitchell, Ruth A woman in *Death in the Clouds* who has some rather original ideas about the death of Madame Giselle. She expresses the belief that Giselle was killed by a Communist plot and that the crime had the additionally vicious aspect of being arranged to take place on a British airplane.

Mitzi The emotionally overwrought foreign maid and cook to Miss Blacklock in *A Murder Is Announced.* When learning that a murder has been announced in the local newspaper, Mitzi is immediately certain that her life is in danger. She remains frightened even after the apparent gunman, Rudi Scherz, is killed, and she seems to be hiding important details from the police as a result of some unknown dread. Her nerves become even more strained after she bakes a chocolate cake for Dora Bunner's birthday and Patrick Simmons calls it "delicious death." Despite her many emotional problems, Mitzi proves indispensable to Miss Marple in setting a trap for the murderer.

Mohammed An elevator operator in *Destination Unknown*. In return for various incentives, including being established in his own business in Chicago, Mohammed offers to assist Andrew Peters in securing a disguise and escaping.

Molly The very observant and pleasant waitress in the *Gallant Endeavour* in "Four and Twenty Blackbirds." She notes the peculiar changes in the routine and dietary habits of Henry Gascoigne, a solitary and regular customer for years. For ten years, he dined in the restaurant each Tuesday and Thursday evening, always ordering the same simple meal. To her surprise, however, he arrived one Monday night and ate a rich dinner, including suet pudding and blackberries. Her story fascinates Poirot and sets him off on the trail of a murderer.

Monckton, Colonel One of the witnesses on the night that Lord Reggie Charnley inexplicably committed suicide in "The Dead Harlequin." He expresses the view that it was "damned bad taste" for Charnley to have killed himself just as guests were arriving at his home. He thus agrees with Mr. Satterthwaite that the circumstances were sufficiently odd for the whole matter to be viewed with much suspicion.

Moncrieffe, Jean A capable and extremely virtuous young woman in "The Lernean Hydra." She has been working as a pharmaceutical dispenser to Dr. Oldfield for three years and is thus shocked to hear rumors circulating in the town that he may have murdered his wife. When he proposes to her, however, she declines, precisely because of the possibility that the rumors might actually be true. At that point, Jean herself becomes a suspect.

Monro, Flossie A potentially important witness to Hercule Poirot in *The Big Four*. A

"somewhat lurid-looking lady no longer in her first youth," Miss Monro helps Poirot to identify the elusive Claud Darrell and even offers to provide him with a photograph of Darrell. Before she is able to get the photo into the detective's hands, however, she is run down by an automobile.

Montresor The last name used by Jane Cleveland when she impersonates a reporter from New York in "Jane in Search of a Job."

Montresor, Mary A beautiful, wealthy, and very strong-willed young woman in "The Golden Ball." She picks up the recently fired George Dundas—whom she loves but about whom she is still not quite sure—and takes him for a drive. Her seemingly reckless ways land them in danger, and George comes to her rescue. Pleased with his courage and resourcefulness, she agrees to marry him.

Montu The so-called Divine Father of the Temple of Hathor in *Death Comes As the End*.

Moody, Elizabeth A onetime theater dresser in *By the Pricking of My Thumbs*. By the time that Tommy and Tuppence Beresford meet her, she is a resident in a retirement home. Soon after observing that she may have recognized someone from her past, she is murdered with an overdose of morphine.

Mooney, Kitty A young woman in "Problem at Sea" who, with Pam Cregan, makes a deliberate effort to help Colonel Clapperton enjoy himself, despite his wife's many unpleasant demands.

Moorhouse, Hannah The name given to the wealthy Amelia Rymer in "The Case of the Rich Woman" when she becomes a simple, poor farm servant, as promised by Mr. Parker Pyne.

Morales, Pedro One of the names used by Victor Drake in his work as a confidence man in *Sparkling Cyanide*.

Morelli, Tony The real name of Anthony Browne in *Sparkling Cyanide*.

Morisot, Anne The daughter of Madame Giselle and George Leman in *Death in the Clouds*. A clever twenty-four-year-old woman, she adopts assorted names and identities for work and other activities until she is murdered on a train.

Morisot, Marie Angelique One of the names used by the unpleasant moneylender and blackmailer Madame Giselle in *Death in the Clouds.*

Morley, Georgina The sister of the murdered dentist Henry Morley in *One, Two, Buckle My Shoe.* Heavyset and prone to using her weight to her advantage, she blames the death on her brother's alcoholic partner.

Morley, Dr. Henry Hercule Poirot's dentist, who is murdered in *One, Two, Buckle My Shoe.* On the very evening after Poirot receives treatment from the dentist, the detective is informed by Inspector Japp that Morley has apparently killed himself. Poirot sets out to learn the details and gradually determines that Morley was murdered.

Morris, Dr. Two physicians who appear in different cases. The first Dr. Morris makes an examination of the remains of Mabelle Annesley in "The Bird with the Broken Wing." He determines that she had been strangled and then hanged in her room to make it look like a suicide. The second Dr. Morris is the physician to Luther Crackenthorpe in *4.50 from Paddington.* He questions the mental stability of Luther's mother and informs authorities about his doubts.

Morris, Isaac An agent hired to prepare Indian Island for its doomed guests in *And Then There Were None.* He makes certain that the island is purchased, all provisions are ready, and that the mysterious invitations are sent out to the condemned guests. He dies from a drug overdose just before the victims set foot on the island.

Morton, Inspector An officer of Scotland Yard in *After the Funeral.* He assumes control of the investigation into the death of Cora Lansquenet.

Mory, Angele A dancer and adventuress in *The Secret of Chimneys.* A onetime performer in the Folies Bergère, she is hired by a secret organization to attract the attention of the king of Herzoslovakia and trap him into a scandalous affair. Instead, she falls utterly in love with him

and marries him, becoming Countess Popoleffsky. Among her other adopted names are Virginia Revel and Genevieve Brun.

Moscomb, Beatrice The third housemaid on the estate of Simeon Lee in *Hercule Poirot's Christmas.*

Mosgorovsky, Mr. A Russian emigré and the proprietor of the Seven Dials Club in *The Seven Dials Mystery.* He operates a legal dancing club, but he also enjoys the benefits of having illegal tables for gambling on the premises.

Moss, Edwin The supposed brother-in-law of Walter St. John in "Sanctuary." He attempts to retrieve a suitcase containing expensive gems from Bunch Harmon.

Moss, Mary A onetime dancer who worked under the name Zobeida in "Sanctuary." She died in prison and left emeralds sewn into a costume in the hope that they would be used to care for her little daughter, Jewel St. John.

Mountford, Mrs. The wife of a confectioner in Dillmouth in *Sleeping Murder.* She is interviewed about what she might know concerning the missing Helen Spenlove Halliday.

Mugg, Charles See Cartwright, Charles.

Mullins, Iris An assistant gardener hired by Tommy and Tuppence Beresford in *Postern of Fate.* She is mistrusted by their beloved terrier, Hannibal.

Mundy, Mrs. A woman in Chipping Cleghorn who has the responsibility for raising Jewel St. John, the daughter of Walter St. John and Mary Moss. Jewel's father dies on the church steps in Chipping Cleghorn.

Murchison, Bianca The wife of Dr. Simon Murchison and a member of the Brain Trust in *Destination Unknown.* An Italian-born intellectual, she is honored in her own right for her talents, and gives lectures in economics and commercial law for the other members of the Brain Trust, established by Mr. Aristides.

Murchison, Dr. Simon A research chemist and the husband of Bianca Murchison in *Destination Unknown.* He is a "thin, anaemic-looking man of about twenty-six," but he is also a talented researcher and a member of the Brain Trust, established by Mr. Aristides.

Murdoch, Cynthia One of the residents at Styles Court in *The Mysterious Affair at Styles.* She works at the Red Cross Hospital pharmacy and stays at Styles Court through the kindness of Emily Inglethorpe.

Murgatroyd, Mr. and Mrs. An elderly couple who had been caretakers of Kingsdean House for many years in "The Case of the Caretaker." When Harry Laxton returns from abroad and tears down the estate, the couple is forced to retire. Mrs. Murgatroyd refuses to accept the situation and curses Laxton and his young bride. Tragedy follows when Louise Laxton is killed in a riding accident.

Murgatroyd, Amy A dim-witted, fat, and amiable woman in *A Murder Is Announced.* She responds enthusiastically to the newspaper announcement that a murder will take place at Little Paddocks and attends the occasion with much excitement. In the ensuing bloody events, during which Rudi Scherz is murdered, Amy notices something important but realizes it only later. Before she can inform anyone, however, she is herself murdered. Amy lives on a small poultry and pig farm with Miss Hinchcliffe, who is absolutely devastated by her death.

Murray, Dr. The physician in the retirement home in which Elizabeth Moody lived in *By the Pricking of My Thumbs.* He performs an autopsy, which reveals that she died of morphine poisoning.

Mylecharane, Fenella A young woman in "Manx Gold." She and her cousin, Juan Faraker, set out to discover buried treasure on the Isle of Man. Their uncle, Myles Mylecharane, dies and leaves them the promise of his fortune if they can find it. The inheritance is in the form of four buried treasures hidden in various spots on the island. They must decipher four sets of clues and outrace two other relatives to the gold.

Nadina See Grunberg, Anita.

Nancy A secretary in "The Case of the Middle-Aged Wife" who schemes to catch the eye of her boss, George Packington. She deliberately wears revealing clothing and pays careful attention to her boss in the hopes of winning his affection. Her actions are the source of much concern in Mrs. Packington.

Narracott, Fred The police official in charge of investigating the murder of Captain Trevelyan in *The Sittaford Mystery.* He is not prone to displays of emotion, but he is highly detail-oriented.

Narracott, Gladys A maid at the Jolly Roger Hotel in *Evil under the Sun.* When an empty pill bottle is found, she is asked to identify the owner.

Nasby, Lord The wealthy owner of the *Daily Budget* newspaper in *The Man in the Brown Suit.* He hires Anne Beddingfeld to investigate the mystery of the man in the brown suit after she convinces him that she can deliver the goods and give him a great story.

Nash, Superintendent The county supervisor for the criminal investigation department of Scotland Yard in *The Moving Finger.* He is assigned to investigate the rash of poison-pen letters in the area, and approaches the problem with calm and confident efficiency.

Naylor, Captain Humphrey One of the suspects in the murder of Sir Reuben Astwell in "The Under Dog." He has a very good reason to wish Sir Reuben dead: The captain was cheated out of a lucrative share in a gold mine in Africa by Sir Reuben. Captain Naylor also had the opportunity to kill Sir Reuben, as he was staying at a nearby hotel at the time of the murder.

Naylor, Lily The sister of Captain Humphrey Naylor in "The Under Dog." He sends her to act as a spy in the Astwell household by having her forge her references and take up a position as a lady's companion.

Nazorkoff, Paula The real name of a brilliantly successful opera star in "Swan Song."

Neasdon, Dr. The police surgeon for the area around the Jolly Roger Hotel and the Devon coast in *Evil under the Sun.* He is called to examine the remains of Arlena Marshall after she is strangled to death.

Needheim, Helga   One of the members of Mr. Aristides's Brain Trust in *Destination Unknown*. A noted endocrinologist, she also has a rather distorted outlook on the world, and chooses fascism as her preferred form of government. She thus fits in well with Mr. Aristides.

Neele, Chief Inspector   An old friend of Hercule Poirot and an officer of Scotland Yard in *Third Girl*. He takes over the investigation into the events befalling the Restarick family and subsequently looks into other murderous doings in the case.

Neele, Inspector   An official of Scotland Yard in *A Pocket Full of Rye*. He takes over the investigation into the death of Rex Fortescue.

Neilson, Dr.   The deputy director of the Brain Trust in *Destination Unknown*. He works for Mr. Aristides and is respected for his intelligence and meticulousness.

Neuman, Lisa   A lab assistant and secretary to Robert Shoreham in *Passenger to Frankfurt*. Not only is Lisa a devoted employee and associate, she is hopelessly in love with Shoreham.

Neville, Gladys   The office secretary at the dental practice of Morley and Reilly, Hercule Poirot's dentists, in *One, Two, Buckle My Shoe*. She is considered absolutely invaluable to the company, and her honesty and diligence are beyond reproach. She is thus not ranked as a suspect in the murder of Dr. Morley. Rather, the police and Poirot accept as entirely true that she was called away from the office by a fake telegram on the day of the murder and that she was in no way an accomplice.

Newman, John   A "man of intelligence and independent means" who searches for sunken treasure in "Ingots of Gold." He invites his friend Raymond West to the Cornish village of Polperran to take part in the search for the sunken ship *Juan Fernandez*. He is apparently kidnapped by local smugglers and found lying on a motor vehicle in the road leading from the village to the coast.

Nicholas V, Prince   One of the names used by Anthony Cade in *The Secret of Chimneys*.

Nicholson, Dr. Jasper   A physician in *Why Didn't They Ask Evans?* He runs a clinic that treats people suffering from addictions and assorted forms of stress. His wife is Moira Nicholson.

Nicholson, Moira   The wife of Dr. Jasper Nicholson in *Why Didn't They Ask Evans?* Shadowed by a somewhat murky past, she was once known as Rose Emily Templeton and was the beneficiary of the will forged by Roger Bassington-ffrench.

Nicoletis, Mrs.   The seemingly upright and honest proprietor of a student hostel in *Hickory Dickory Dock*. The calm of her establishment is shattered when her students begin to notice that items are being stolen from their rooms. Subsequently, one student, Celia Austin, is found dead from an apparent overdose of morphine. When the police want to obtain a search warrant to rummage through the hostel, Mrs. Nicoletis becomes even more concerned. Her worries are short-lived, however, for she dies from morphine poisoning. Subsequent investigations reveal that there was much more going on in the hostel than met the eye. Her daughter is Valerie Hobhouse.

Nina, Aunt   The aunt of Vernon Deyre in *Giant's Bread*. She has a terrible reputation because of her inability to control herself when it comes to men.

Nofret   The much-hated concubine of Imhotep in *Death Comes As the End*. Upon her arrival with Imhotep at his family home, she manifests immediately the great influence she wields over him. Instantly disliked and viewed as a threat by other family members, Nofret is murdered when someone pushes her off a cliff.

Norreys, Hugh   The narrator in *The Rose and the Yew Tree*. He relates the details of the story to readers, providing a picture of himself as well. He commences the story after being confined to a wheelchair as a result of a bus accident.

Norris, Inspector An agent in British intelligence in *Postern of Fate*. In disguise, he is assigned to take up a protective post at the Laurels.

Norris, Sister A nurse in *Giant's Bread*. She is infamous for her razor-sharp tongue and temper.

Norton, Stephen A victim of murder in *Curtain*. An amateur naturalist, he witnesses something important through his binoculars and dies soon afterward from a gunshot wound in the forehead.

Nugent, Tim A young man who loves and marries Deirdre Crozier in "While the Light Lasts." Tim went off to fight in the African campaign during World War I and was reported killed. Several years later, it comes as a shattering surprise to Deirdre, who remarried, that Tim was not killed and is working in a tobacco plantation that has just been purchased by Deirdre's husband.

Nunn, Rosina An actress in "The World's End." She is not as young as she used to be and uses her weakness as a formidable weapon to control those around her and hold their attention.

Nye, Sir Stafford An official in the Foreign Office in *Passenger to Frankfurt*. He has "failed to fulfill his early promise," and thus, despite considerable connections and associations in British politics, he will not advance in the government.

Obolovitch, Prince Michael The heir to the throne of Herzoslovakia in *The Secret of Chimneys*. He flees across Europe to escape the terrible burdens of office and duty and assumes several identities, including Mr. Holmes and Count Stanislaus. Finding his way to the apparent sanctuary of the Chimneys, he is murdered while staying there.

Obolovitch, Nicholas Sergius Alexander Ferdinand One of the aliases used by Anthony Cade in *The Secret of Chimneys*.

O'Connor, Sergeant An officer of Scotland Yard who takes part in the investigation in *Cards on the Table*. He has earned the nickname the Maidservant's Prayer because of his winning ways with female servants whom he might interview in the course of his work.

O'Connor, Derek A messenger in *Cat among the Pigeons* who brings to Joan Sutcliffe news about the death of her brother, Bob Rawlinson. He also provides details about the jewels that her brother was smuggling.

Oglander, Miss One of the members of the Oglander family in "The King of Clubs." A younger daughter, she assists in taking care of Valerie Saintclair after she staggers into the Oglander house and collapses on the floor. Of the members of the household, Hercule Poirot finds her far and away the least imaginative.

Oglander, Mr. and Mrs. The next-door neighbors to Henry Reedburn in "The King of Clubs." They claim that on the night of Reedburn's murder they were playing bridge with other family members when Valerie Saintclair staggered into their house, cried out, "Murder," and collapsed on the floor. They took care of the girl and put her in one of their rooms until she could recover fully from the shock of the terrible murder. Hercule Poirot finds the Oglanders to be of considerable interest to his investigation and determines that they share a secret that could destroy them all.

O'Hara, Eileen A young woman in "The Ambassador's Boots." She pretended to fall ill outside the cabin used by an ambassador as part of her scheme to assist an organization of drug smugglers. Tommy and Tuppence Beresford attempt to locate Miss O'Hara, placing an advertisement in the newspaper asking if anyone can provide details about her. Cicely March responds to the ad and offers some deviously helpful information.

Ohlsson, Greta A Swedish missionary and school matron in *Murder on the Orient Express*. She is the last person to see Mr. Ratchett alive. In questioning her, Hercule Poirot learns of her past connection to the Armstrong family; she served as the nurse to Daisy Armstrong, giving her a motive to commit murder.

Olde, Sir Malcolm An attorney in "Miss Marple Tells a Story." He is consulted by Mr. Petherick on behalf of his client Mr. Rhodes, the chief suspect in the murder of Mrs. Rhodes. According to Petherick, Olde has some ideas about the defense, but he is a specialist and thus he "may ignore completely what is . . . the vital point."

Oldfield, Dr. Charles A widowed physician in "The Lernean Hydra." He hires Hercule Poirot in the hopes that the detective will be able to clear his reputation; since the death of his wife, local townspeople have spread rumors that he killed his her. The fact that he is in love with Jean Moncrieffe, his dispenser, and has asked her to marry him has only added to the hot speculation about his possible criminal tendencies.

Olga, Grand Duchess See de Sara, Madeleine.

OLIVER, MRS. ARIADNE An eminently successful mystery writer and the creator of the popular Finnish detective Sven Hjerson, Mrs. Ariadne Oliver was also a capable sleuth who most often found herself involved in investigations with either Hercule Poirot or, less frequently, with Mr. Parker Pyne. Described as "handsome in a rather untidy fashion, with fine eyes, substantial shoulders, and a large quantity of rebellious gray hair with which she was continually experimenting," Mrs. Oliver was first introduced in "The Case of the Discontented Soldier" and "The Case of the Rich Woman." Both scenarios demonstrated Mrs. Oliver's skill in plotting and her understanding of human nature. It is little wonder, then, that by the time of her association with Parker Pyne, she was the author of "forty-six works of fiction, all best sellers in England and America, and freely translated into French, German, Italian, Hungarian, Finnish, Japanese, and Abyssinian." Mrs. Oliver was also addicted to eating apples until young Joyce Reynolds was found drowned in a bucket used for bobbing for apples in *Hallowe'en Party.*

Hallowe'en Party was one of the cases that Mrs. Oliver solved in the company of Hercule Poirot. With the Belgian detective, Mrs. Oliver was involved in six cases: *Dead Man's Folly, Cards on the Table, Elephants Can Remember, Hallowe'en Party, Mrs. McGinty's Dead,* and *Third Girl.* In *Cards on the Table,* Mrs. Oliver investigated the murder of the cryptic Mr. Shaitana, along with Poirot, Colonel Johnny Race, and Superintendent Battle. Mrs. Oliver also worked with young Mark Easterbrook to solve the string of murders that were centered around the eponymous inn in *The Pale Horse.*

Mrs. Ariadne Oliver served two very useful purposes for Agatha Christie. First, she provided Christie with a suitable foil for Hercule Poirot, especially in the later Poirot novels. At a time when Christie had lost interest in the Belgian sleuth, Mrs. Oliver helped to inject new life and a certain enjoyable repartee into his cases. In *Third Girl,* for example, both Mrs. Oliver and Poirot are able to lament their ages and expound upon their dislike for modern culture.

Mrs. Oliver was also the literary alter ego of Dame Agatha. Through Mrs. Oliver, Christie articulated many of her frustrations as an author. Mrs. Oliver expressed a passionate dislike for her fictional detective, Sven Hjerson, observing, "If I ever met that bony, gangling vegetable-eating Finn in real life, I'd do a better murder than any I've ever invented." Christie, of course, harbored the same attitude toward Poirot.

Mrs. Oliver also detested public gatherings, cocktail parties, gala luncheons, and author receptions. In *Five Little Pigs,* Mrs. Oliver dreads attending a gathering where readers come up to her and tell her how much they love her books. Christie, likewise, loathed public events.

Oliver, Frank "A man just over forty" who has spent the last eighteen years of his life in Burma and has recently returned to England in "The Lonely God." Oliver is desperately lonely and spends much of his time in the British Museum. While there, he encounters a battered little idol from Mexico that he dubs the Lonely God. He also meets and falls in love with another "worshiper" of the idol, a woman he calls the Lonely Lady.

Olivera, Jane   The American niece of the powerful banker Alistair Blunt in *One, Two, Buckle My Shoe.* She is involved in a relationship with Howard Raikes, a leftist and, in the view of her uncle, a wholly unsuitable young man. Jane shares Raikes's left-wing views.

Olivera, Julia   A relative by marriage of the powerful banker Alistair Blunt in *One, Two, Buckle My Shoe.* A thoroughly unpleasant woman, she is often rude and condescending.

Olivier, Madame   A brilliant French chemist who is suspected of being the criminal agent called Number Three in *The Big Four.* She is described as "one of the most prominent personalities of the day." Hercule Poirot takes considerable interest in her alleged criminal doings.

O'Murphy   An Irishman from County Clare who is also a member of the criminal investigation department of Scotland Yard in "The Kidnapped Prime Minister." When Prime Minister David MacAdam travels to France to attend a conference of Allies during World War I, O'Murphy is assigned the job of chauffeur. He prevents one apparent assassination attempt, but then disappears in London almost immediately after dropping off the P.M. at Charing Cross. Because of his ties to Ireland and his disappearance, he is immediately suspected of being a conspirator in the kidnapping of MacAdam.

O'Neele, Moira   One of the aliases used by Valerie Hobhouse *in Hickory Dickory Dock.*

O'Neill, Captain   One of the aliases used by King Victor in *The Secret of Chimneys.*

Opalsen, Mrs.   The wife of a wealthy man who is an acquaintance of Captain Hastings in "The Jewel Robbery at the Grand Metropolitan." She encounters Hastings and Poirot at the Grand Metropolitan Hotel in Brighton. She has a special passion for jewelry and is eager to display her prized pearls. The strand has been stolen, however, and she implores Poirot to undertake its recovery.

Opalsen, Ed   A wealthy stockbroker who has made a fortune in a recent oil boom in "The Jewel Robbery at the Grand Metropolitan." His wife has a strand of pearls stolen from her room and implores the aid of Hercule Poirot in recovering it. When the detective succeeds, Mr. Opalsen writes a check in thanks; the amount is so pleasing that the detective offers to return to Brighton with Captain Hastings, this time at the sleuth's expense.

Oranoff, Prince Sergius   A Russian dancer and émigré in "Harlequin's Lane." He is contracted to perform in the harlequinade and discovers among the troupe a beloved fellow Russian dancer whom he had last seen a decade before. Their reunion becomes a touching element in the story.

O'Rourke, Flight Lieutenant   A member of the party traveling with Mr. Parker Pyne from Damascus to Baghdad in "The Gate of Baghdad." The officer assists Parker Pyne with his investigation into the murder of Smethurst.

O'Rourke, Mrs.   A calamitously heavy woman in *N or M?* who is described as being "like an ogress dimly remembered from early fairy tales." She takes obsessive note of the details and goings-on in the Sans Souci Hotel.

O'Rourke, Terence   Secretary to the air minister Sir Stanley Digby in *The Seven Dials Mystery.* As part of his duties, he takes part in the negotiations that are held concerning a secret metal formula and is subsequently drugged and robbed of all relevant documents.

Orwell, Robert   A onetime partner of Andrew Restarick in *Third Girl.* Orwell once worked with Restarick in a prospecting operation in Africa, and, after Restarick dies, he returns to England and attempts to defraud Norma Restarick of her inheritance.

Osborne, Zachariah   A chemist in *The Pale*

Horse. He is described as "a small, middle-aged man with a bald domed head." Osborne also owns the Customer's Reactions Classified, a market research firm that proves of great importance in unraveling the pattern of deaths in Much Deeping.

Osric, Prince The uncle and guardian to Grand Duchess Anastasia in "The Girl in the Train." An unimaginative and disagreeable figure, he arranges a marriage between the grand duchess and Prince Karl, but he proves incapable of convincing his niece to accept the proposed union. He is soon forced to roam across Europe searching after her.

Otterbourne, Rosalie The daughter of Salome Otterbourne in *Death on the Nile.* She is an utterly miserable young woman, in large measure because of the stress of caring for her alcoholic and erratic mother. When she meets Linnet Doyle, Rosalie finds her utterly monstrous, expressing the desire to "stamp on her lovely, arrogant, self-confident face." She thus becomes a suspect when Doyle is murdered. During the course of the investigation, she falls in love with Tim Allerton.

Otterbourne, Salome The mother of Roslaie Otterbourne in *Death on the Nile.* An alcoholic—despite claiming publicly not to drink any liquor—and prone to erratic and unstable behavior, she is the author of assorted torrid novels. Salome figures out who murdered Louise Bourget, but before she can inform Hercule Poirot she is herself murdered.

Owen, Ulick Norman One of the names used by the mysterious host of the doomed guests on Indian Island in *And Then There Were None.*

Owen, Una Nancy One of the names used by the mysterious host of the doomed guests on Indian Island in *And Then There Were None.*

Oxley, Louise The niece of Joan West in "Greenshaw's Folly." Through the efforts of her aunt, she is able to secure a position as editor of Nathaniel Greenshaw's diaries, working at the Greenshaw estate. She becomes a seemingly important witness to the murder of Miss Greenshaw; while she is locked in the library, she sees Miss Greenshaw shot by an arrow.

Pace, Harrington A wealthy American and the uncle of Roger Havering in "The Mystery of Hunter's Lodge." He resides in Derbyshire with his nephew and his nephew's wife, Zoe. His murder precipitates the events investigated by Captain Arthur Hastings, who acts as a proxy for the ailing Hercule Poirot.

Packard, Miss The manager of the Sunny Ridge nursing home in *By the Pricking of My Thumbs.* Miss Packard is so efficient that everything she does is carefully measured and organized, including her emotions. Thus, when the beloved Ada Fanshawe dies, Miss Packard "was an expert in the exact amount of condolence which would be acceptable."

Packington, George The husband of the much distressed Mrs. Maria Packington in "The Case of the Middle-Aged Wife." He has become obsessed with a much younger woman, a typist who is described as a "nasty made-up little minx, all lipstick and silk stockings and curls." Mrs. Packington describes her husband as stout and bald, a man who dances in a style from twenty years ago. He is brought back to his wife through the scheming of Mr. Parker Pyne.

Packington, Mrs. Maria A client of Mr. Parker Pyne in "The Case of the Middle-Aged Wife." Distraught over the wandering eye of her husband, George, she comes to Parker Pyne for help, lamenting that "I've always been a good wife to George. I worked my fingers to the bone in our early days . . . I've never looked at any other man." The source of her distress is her husband's involvement with a typist, "a nasty made-up little minx, all lipstick and silk stockings and curls." Parker Pyne's solution costs her two hundred guineas, but proves ideal. (See also Luttrell, Claude.)

Pagett, Edith The sister-in-law of the confectioner of Dillmouth in *Sleeping Murder.* She is interviewed by Gwenda Reed.

Pagett, Guy The secretary to Sir Eustace Pedler, M.P., in *The Man in the Brown Suit.* Competent and efficient, Pagett nevertheless is the source of some frustration to Sir Eustace because of his ethical habits. He is also hiding from his employer the fact that he has a wife and four children, a condition that would have prevented his employment.

Palgrave, Major A former British colonial who becomes a victim of murder in *A Caribbean Mystery.* A guest at the Golden Palm Hotel, he is described as being "purple of face, with a glass eye, and the general appearance of a stuffed frog." He regales a very patient Miss Marple with stories of his days in Kenya. He finally sparks her genuine interest when he asks if she would like to see a photograph of a murderer. Palgrave looks over her shoulder, however, sees someone, and changes the subject. Major Palgrave dies that night, and the photograph disappears.

Palgrove, Edward (Ted) An office clerk in "A Fruitful Sunday." He purchases an old car and takes his girlfriend, Dorothy Pratt, for a drive one beautiful Sunday. On this particular outing, they purchase a basket of fruit and discover a necklace worth a fortune.

Palk, Constable One of the local law enforcement officers in St. Mary Mead. He participates in two published cases: *The Body in the Library* and "The Tape-Measure Murder."

Palliser, Sir Edward A retired attorney in "Sing a Song of Sixpence." Once one of the foremost barristers of his generation, Sir Edward agrees to come out of retirement and honor an old promise to Magdalen Vaughan. She asks him to investigate the death of Lily Crabtree, and he succeeds in his quest.

Palmer, Mabel A member of the vast criminal organization in *The Big Four.* A "pleasant-faced woman of middle-age," she impersonates a nurse for the Lark Sisterhood, in which capac-

ity she involves Hercule Poirot in the affairs of the Templetons.

Papopolous, Aristide A headwaiter described as "a lean Mephistopheles" in "The Capture of Cerberus." Aristide works in the popular but suspicious nightclub called Hell, and is suspected by the police of being involved in a drug-dealing ring.

Papopolous, Demetrius A gifted diamond cutter in *The Mystery of the Blue Train.* He was assisted by Hercule Poirot some years before and is in debt to Poirot for his past kindness. Thus, when Papopolous receives the Heart of Fire rubies, he gives Poirot important information that assists the detective in solving the murder of Ruth Kettering. His daughter is Zia Papopolous.

Papopolous, Zia The daughter of Demetrius Papopolous in *The Mystery of the Blue Train.* She disagrees with her father's involvement in illegal activities and so informs Hercule Poirot that he is in possession of the Heart of Fire rubies. This revelation proves of great importance in solving the murder of Ruth Kettering.

Pardoe, William Reuben A cousin to Ellie Rogers in *Endless Night.* He pays a call on Ellie's husband, Michael, after her death to offer his deepest condolences.

Pardonstenger, Amy A name used by Bella Wallace in the course of her work as a dangerous gangster's moll in "The Golden Ball."

Parfitt, Canon One of the passengers on a train in "The Fourth Man." He is a cleric well known for his "scientific sermons" and takes a particular theological position in the discussion about Annette Ravel; he disagrees with the position of Dr. Clark.

Parker The butler in the Ackroyd estate in *The Murder of Roger Ackroyd.* He is described as having a "fat, smug, oily face." He becomes a suspect in the death of Roger Ackroyd, especially as he has been in service for only one year.

Parker, Mr. and Mrs. A dangerous pair of blackmailers in "The Market Basing Mystery." They attempt to blackmail Walter Protheroe.

Parker, Bernard One of the suspects in the theft of the Medici necklace in "Double Clue." An associate of Marcus Hardman, he has a "white, effeminate face and affected lisping speech." He also seemingly left behind an incriminating bit of evidence at Hardman's home, making him a likely suspect in the theft of the necklace.

Parker, Gerald An old friend of Captain Arthur Hastings in "The Adventure of the Cheap Flat." He throws a party at which Mrs. Robinson relates the curious story of how she and her husband were able to rent an amazingly cheap flat in a swanky London building. The story reaches the ears of Hercule Poirot, who senses, correctly, that the couple is in great danger.

Parker, Harry One of the aliases used by Harry Rayburn in *The Man in the Brown Suit*.

PARKER PYNE, CHRISTOPHER An unusual kind of detective, Mr. Parker Pyne does not regularly investigate murder or other nefarious crimes. Rather, he undertakes to provide his many clients with happiness in return for a fee that may be as little as five pounds or as much as one thousand pounds.

Little is known in detail about Parker Pyne's early life save what he said himself: "You see, for thirty-five years of my life I have been engaged in the compiling of statistics in a government office. Now I have retired, and it has occurred to me to use the experiences I have gained in a novel fashion." Establishing himself in offices at 17 Richmond Street, London, Parker Pyne acquires clients through an advertisement:

ARE YOU HAPPY? IF NOT, CONSULT MR. PARKER PYNE, 17 RICHMOND STREET.

As Parker Pyne explained in "The Case of the Middle-Aged Wife":

Unhappiness can be classified under five main heads—no more, I assure you. Once you know the cause of a malady, the remedy should

not be impossible. I stand in the place of the doctor. The doctor first diagnoses the patient's disorder, then he proceeds to recommend a course of treatment. There are cases where no treatment can be of any avail.

Applying his statistical knowledge, he places his clients on one of the five schedules and then provides them with the perfect solution to their particular dilemma. The solutions can be fairly simple, such as the use of a pretty or handsome face to spark jealousy and win back the attention of a wandering wife or husband. Others might involve a mysterious physician from the East or hidden treasures in East Africa.

Parker Pyne is supported in his work by a small, effective network that includes, at various times, the ever-reliable Miss Felicity Lemon; the renowned mystery writer Ariadne Oliver; the beautiful "Queen of Vamps," Madeleine de Sara; and the "lounge lizard" Claude Luttrell, among other invisible or anonymous associates.

While apparently limited to a special kind of investigation, Parker Pyne does also possess genuine skills as a criminal detective. His abilities in police-type detection—à la Poirot—are on display in several published cases, such as "Death on the Nile" (1934), "The Gate of Baghdad" (1934), and "Have You Got Everything You Want?" (1934). These cases also provide a demonstration of the considerable, albeit somewhat limited, success of his detective agency. He is able to embark upon a lengthy vacation that includes trips to Egypt, Iraq, Persia, Greece, and Jordan, but his funds are not inexhaustible. Hence, he accepts an offer of one hundred pounds from Lady Ariadne Grayle in "Death on the Nile," as he has found Egypt more expensive than anticipated.

Parkinson, Alexander A young boy and victim of murder in *Postern of Fate*. Parkinson was murdered because he knew too much, but before his death he left a vital clue by underlining a message in a book. The tome finds its way to

Tuppence Beresford, and she embarks on an investigation into murder.

Parminster, Inspector An official of Scotland Yard in "Three Blind Mice." He is in charge of the investigation into the brutal strangulation of Maureen Lyons.

Parsons The butler at the estate of Sir Reuben Astwell in "The Under Dog." He is considered an impeccable butler.

Parsons, Olive One of the students at the school operated by Miss Amphrey in *Towards Zero*. A charming young girl with wide eyes, she is also a thief.

Partridge, Mr. James A witness in *The A.B.C. Murders*. He was the last person to see Alice Ascher alive, just before she became the first victim of the A.B.C killer.

Paton, Captain Ralph The stepson of Roger Ackroyd in *The Murder of Roger Ackroyd* and, according to Hercule Poirot, an "unusually good-looking" man "for an Englishman." He had departed the Ackroyd estate after a bitter disagreement with his stepfather. On the night of Ackroyd's murder, however, he was in the area and thus becomes a suspect.

Patterson, Elsie The sister of Gerda Christow in *The Hollow*. Following the murder of Gerda's husband, Dr. John Christow, Elsie moves into Gerda's house to assist in running her affairs. This act comes at a cost for Elsie, as she is not especially fond of Gerda.

Patterson, Janet A fifteen-year-old girl in *Unfinished Portrait*. She is the object of envy by the main character because of her figure.

Patterson, Phyllis The fiancée of Arthur Carmichael in "The Strange Case of Sir Arthur Carmichael." She is exceedingly devoted to Carmichael and remains with him during his time of troubles, especially when he is apparently possessed by the spirit of a Persian cat.

Paul, Prince of Maurania A gallant and honorable nobleman in "The King of Clubs." He is in love with Valerie Saintclair and turns to Hercule Poirot and his legendary "grey cells"—as

well as his discretion—to save Valerie from a potentially disastrous scandal. The prince sometimes uses the alias of Count Feodor.

Pauline, Grand Duchess The supposed noblewoman who is in need of someone to impersonate her in "Jane in Search of a Job." She apparently approves Jane Cleveland as her double and stand-in when she is threatened by assassins. As events unfold, however, Jane learns that the duchess may not be entirely what she seems.

Paulovitch, Count Sergius One of the aliases used by the brilliant impersonator Arthur Minks in *The Man in the Brown Suit*.

Pauncefoot Jones, Dr. John Also called Pussyfoot, the senior archaeologist on the dig in the city of Murik in *They Came to Baghdad*.

Pavlovitch, Count Alexis An old nobleman and friend of Hercule Poirot in "The Arcadian Deer." The detective relies upon the count to provide him with information about the art world and its varied population.

Payne, Maisie A young American girl at the same French finishing school as Celia in *Unfinished Portrait*. She has a distinct American drawl and helps Celia to become comfortable with her surroundings.

Paynter, Mr. A writer, traveler, and researcher who stumbles across details about the criminal organization in *The Big Four*. He prepares a manuscript detailing their secret activities in China and is killed. The manuscript disappears immediately after his death. His nephew is the artist Gerald Paynter.

Paynter, Gerald The nephew of Mr. Paynter in *The Big Four*. He is an artist by profession, and on the night that his uncle was murdered, he had an unshakable alibi.

Peabody, Caroline A friend of Emily Arundell in *Dumb Witness*. She is able to provide Hercule Poirot with extensive information about the other members of the Arundell household.

Pearson, Mr. One of the directors of a prominent bank in "The Lost Mine." He is interested in investing in a recently discovered mine in Burma and arranges to meet with a representative, Mr. Wu Ling, in Southampton. As fog delays his train, however, he is unable to meet Wu Ling's boat and follows him to London. There, he learns that Wu Ling has been murdered, whereupon he calls Scotland Yard. Pearson soon becomes unhappy with their progress, however, and calls in Hercule Poirot.

Pearson, Mrs. Hercule Poirot's landlady at 14 Farraway Street in *The Big Four.* She is known as Mrs. Funnyface.

Pearson, Brian The younger brother of James Pearson and a nephew of Captain Trevleyan in *The Sittaford Mystery.* He has resided for years in Australia and returns to England a short time before his uncle is murdered.

Pearson, James The older brother of Brian Pearson and a nephew of Captain Trevleyan in *The Sittaford Mystery.* He is considered by his attorney, Mr. Dacres, to be a rather dishonest sort and falls under suspicion when his uncle is murdered.

Pebmarsh, Millicent A blind schoolteacher in *The Clocks.* It is her unfortunate lot to have discovered in her house the body of R. H. Curry. The scene is made even more odd by the presence of an assortment of clocks, including a Dresden china clock, a French gilt ormolu clock, and a silver clock, none of which Miss Pebmarsh owns. All the clocks have been stopped at 4:13. Much is learned about Miss Pebmarsh in the course of the investigation by Hercule Poirot.

Pedler, Sir Eustace, M.P. An often dubiously legitimate member of Parliament and the owner of Mill House in *The Man in the Brown Suit.* Gruff and sociable, he becomes involved in the adventure of Anne Beddingfield, especially her pursuit of the elusive criminal mastermind called the Colonel. Some of the narrative in *The Man in the Brown Suit* is comprised of an extract from Sir Eustace's own journal.

Sir Eustace is notable as being one of the few characters in a Christie novel who is almost certainly modeled after a personal acquaintance of the author. In this case, the real-life counterpart is Major Ernest R. Belcher, who was described by Christie as a man full of "bluff"; she added that "how much of Belcher's stories was invented and how much was true, we never knew." Christie came to know Belcher very well during a world tour she took with him when he was the director of the British Empire Mission (a much sought-after and very comfortable job requiring travel around the globe on behalf of the British Empire). Unfortunately, over time, the strain of traveling with him became unbearable and a mighty row erupted. Relations were eventually repaired, and Christie even gave in to Belcher's pleas that he be included in one of her books. The result is a somewhat unflattering but reasonably close depiction.

Pendar, Dr. An elderly cleric in St. Mary Mead and a friend of Miss Marple in *The Thirteen Problems.* As a member of the Tuesday Night Club, he takes part in the presentations of mysteries and the efforts on the part of the members to find a solution.

Pengelly, Mrs. The victim of foul play in "The Cornish Mystery." A little old lady convinced that her husband is poisoning her, Mrs. Pengelly turns to Hercule Poirot for help. Before the detective can arrive in Cornwall, however, she is dead and rumors are already flying that she was murdered, despite the absolute and unwavering assurance by the local doctor that she has died from gastritis. As was inevitable, her body is exhumed and arsenic is found. Her husband is soon arrested for her murder, but Poirot is not so certain of his guilt.

Pengelly, Edward A dentist and the husband of Mrs. Pengelly in "The Cornish Mystery." Suspected by his wife of trying to poison her, Pengelly becomes the subject of numerous rumors after his wife dies exactly as she had feared. The rumors become a full firestorm when Pengelly soon thereafter marries his beautiful assistant.

When, at last, Mrs. Pengelly's remains are exhumed, arsenic is found in her system, and Dr. Pengelly is arrested for her murder.

Penn, Elizabeth The owner of an antiques store in Ebermouth in "Double Sin." She sends her niece, Mary Durrant, on a special assignment for her. Mary must transport a set of miniatures to the collector J. Baker Wood. The miniatures never reach their destination.

Penn, Major General Sir Josiah A retired general and a respected member of the International Union of Associated Security in *By the Pricking of My Thumbs*. He was also once a suitor to Tommy Beresford's aunt Ada and might very well have married her had he not decided to put his career first and head out to India. By the time of the events described in the novel, the general is a very old man of large girth, who is also "extremely deaf, half-blind, crippled with rheumatism."

Pennington, Andrew The American attorney and trustee of the vast estate of Linnet Doyle in *Death on the Nile*. He journeys to Egypt to meet with Mrs. Doyle on her honeymoon with Simon Doyle. He ostensibly desires to discuss business with her, but his true intention is to have her sign papers that will assist him in the continued embezzlement of her fortune. He thus becomes a suspect in her murder on the S.S. *Karnak*. His business partner is Sterndale Rockford.

Pennyfeather, Canon A scatterbrained cleric in *At Bertram's Hotel*. A brilliant albeit absent-minded scholar and expert in Hebrew and Aramaic, he journeys to London to attend a conference on the Dead Sea Scrolls but arrives on the wrong day. He then reaches his hotel room and is knocked unconscious by an unknown assailant, whereupon he disappears for five days. Pennyfeather is found on a country road by the Wheelings. His housekeeper is Mrs. MacRae.

Pennyman, Major A retired army officer living in Baghdad in *Murder in Mesopotamia*. He finds the archaeological dig at Tell Yarimjah to be most inconvenient, but he also notes that things are not quite right at the dig: "They all pased the butter to each other too politely." His observation proves correct.

Penrose, Dr. A psychiatrist and the superintendent of the Saltmarsh House nursing home in *Sleeping Murder*. He is consulted by Gwenda Reed concerning the suicide of her father, Major Kelvin Halliday, a former patient under Dr. Penrose's care. After meeting with him, Gwenda comes to suspect that Penrose is himself suffering from mental illness.

Pentemian, Mrs. An Armenian woman traveling with her son from Damascus to Baghdad in "The Gate of Baghdad."

Percehouse, Caroline A wealthy older woman who is also the possessor of a vast estate in *The Sittaford Mystery*. She uses the vague promise of an inheritance as a means of controlling her relatives, especially her weak-willed nephew Ronald Garfield. Caroline is far more fond of her five cats than of her family.

Perenna, Eileen The manager of the Sans Souci guest house in *N or M?* As the widow of a member of the IRA, she is suspected by authorities of involvement in terrorist or subversive activities. Her daughter is Sheila Perenna.

Perenna, Sheila The daughter of Eileen Perenna in *N or M?* She disagrees strenuously with the activities of her father, a slain member of the IRA, and is against any form of patriotic fervor. It is thus a heavy blow to her when the man she loves is arrested for conspiring to commit sabotage.

Perrot, Jules An airline employee in *Death in the Clouds*. He is interrogated by Hercule Poirot and cracks under the withering questions of the detective, admitting that he had accepted a bribe to delay the departure of the plane that carried Madame Giselle to her death.

Perry, Alice and Amos The peculiar couple in *By the Pricking of My Thumbs* who took care of the dying Julia Lancaster. They are an odd couple, as Tommy and Tuppence Beresford discover; Amos is mentally ill and his wife has the curious appearance of a witch, with "a kind of steeple hat perched on her head."

Perry, Percy The infamous editor of the *X-Ray News* scandal sheet in "The Augean Stables." Perry's paper specializes in advancing stories of scandal and gossip, especially about government officials and leaders. He claims that his sleazy work is actually for the public good, for he seeks always to clean up government and Parliament by unleashing what he calls a "purifying flood of public opinion."

Peters, Andrew A name used by Major Boris Andrei Pavlov in *Destination Unknown.*

Peters, Mrs. Willard J. A doting and adoring mother who travels to Greece to indulge her son in "The Oracle at Delphi." She really despises Greece, with its rugged terrain and poor hotels, preferring instead the many comforts and first-class amenities of Paris, London, and the Riviera, her "spiritual homes." While in Delphi, she suffers the even greater misfortune of having her son kidnapped by the Greek bandit Demetrius the Black Browed, who demands the ransom of her diamond necklace. Mrs. Peters is assisted twice by Parker Pyne, once in a less-than-honorable endeavor and the second time to rescue her son and her necklace.

Peters, Willard J., Jr. An eighteen-year-old boy who is kidnapped for a mighty ransom in "The Oracle of Delphi." A "thin, pale, spectacled and dyspeptic" lad, he despises the appellation Junior and drags his mother on a tour of Greece, including Athens, Olympia, Corinth, Mycenae, and, finally, Delphi. While visiting the Byzantine mosaics in the area, he is captured by Demetrius the Black Browed and held for the ransom of his mother's diamond necklace.

Petherick, Mr. A solicitor who was responsible for Miss Marple's legal affairs and who brought to her attention several intriguing cases. A friend of Miss Marple and a member of the Tuesday Night Club, he was described as "a dried-up little man with eyeglasses which he looked over and not through" ("The

Tuesday Night Club") and "a very shrewd man and a really clever solicitor" ("Miss Marple Tells A Story"). Aside from appearing in "The Tuesday Night Club" and "The Idol House of Astarte," Petherick narrates the events in "Motive vs. Opportunity." After his death, his legal matters were assumed by his son. Miss Marple does not have quite the same confidence in the son that she had in old Mr. Petherick.

Pettigrew, Miss One of the aliases used by Arthur Minks in *The Man in the Brown Suit.*

Phelps, Hayward An American journalist in *The Seven Dials Mystery.* He becomes the object of the intense scrutiny of Lady Eileen Brent, and she watches him with much interest at the meeting held at the Seven Dials.

Phillips, Sergeant A local police officer in *Evil under the Sun.* He assists Hercule Poirot in his investigation into the murder of Arlena Marshall.

Phillpot, Major One of the most influential residents of Kingston Bishop in *Endless Night.* Called "God" locally, he is a friend of Ellie and Michael Rogers as well as Claudia Hardcastle and the gypsy woman Old Mother Lee. His wife is the invalid Gervase Phillpot.

Phillpot, Gervase The wife of Major Phillpot in *Endless Night.* An invalid, she displays a keen interest in the knowledge of Michael Rogers concerning social matters.

Pierce, Constable A young constable and murder victim in *The Clocks.* He is murdered soon after suggesting that a potential female witness should speak with his superior. His death plays an important part in the events of the mystery.

Pierce, Mrs. Two married women appearing in different mysteries. The first was the manager of a tobacco and stationery store in Wychwood in *Murder Is Easy.* One of her eight children, Tommy, has recently died, and she is interviewed by Luke Fitzwilliam, who is investigating the assorted deaths in the area in recent weeks. The second Mrs. Pierce was a cleaning lady in "Murder in the Mews." She cares for the flat shared by Barbara Allen and Jane Plenderleith, but she is generally unreliable, frequently arriving late for her job and thereby reducing her value as a witness to the events that surround the death of Mrs. Allen.

Pierce, Amabel A tourist in Jerusalem in *Appointment with Death.* She has a great fear of heights and becomes embroiled in the death of Mrs. Boynton. She is interviewed by Hercule Poirot and provides him with essential information concerning a small but key piece of evidence.

Pierce, Tommy The son of Mrs. Pierce in *Murder Is Easy.* One of eight children, he becomes involved with a cult of Satan worshipers and dies after falling from a third-story window while ostensibly washing windows in Wych Hall. His death is only one of many that have occurred in Wychwood.

Pierre A sixteen-year-old waiter at the expensive and exclusive Luxembourg restaurant in *Sparkling Cyanide.* He is the nephew of the headwaiter and is a "frightened white rabbit" when starting out on the job. His nervousness leads to a most significant event. He accidentally places Iris Marle's purse in the wrong chair at a table and so forces everyone to move over one seat. As someone at the table is the target of murder, the adjustment proves a fateful one.

Pike, Albert and Jessie The two witnesses to the official and valid will of Andrew Marsh in "The Case of the Missing Will."

Pikeaway, Colonel Ephraim The head of Special Branch Intelligence of the police who appears in several cases, including *Cat among the Pigeons, Passenger to Frankfurt,* and *Postern of Fate.* He specializes in those cases involving espionage or international intrigue.

Plenderleith, Jane A smart young woman and close friend of the unfortunate Barbara Allen in "Murder in the Mews." She disapproved of the two men in Mrs. Allen's life, Major Eustace and

Charles Laverton-Smith, and she refuses to believe that her friend could have committed suicide. Her peculiar behavior in the days after Mrs. Allen's death is of much interest to Hercule Poirot, especially her destruction of a set of golf clubs.

Pointz, Isaac A wealthy diamond merchant in "The Regatta Mystery." He enjoys the ill-advised habit of carrying with him a diamond worth some thirty thousand pounds as a good luck charm. His affectation nearly proves incredibly costly, for he is conned into a bet and the gem is stolen. Fortunately, it is retrieved by Mr. Parker Pyne. His partner is Leo Stein.

Poirot, Achille The brother of Hercule Poirot, who has only one appearance, in *The Big Four.* He is also given an important mention in the introduction to the collection *The Labours of Hercules.* Achille Poirot, who lives in Spa, Belgium, was never mentioned by Hercule Poirot to his good friend Captain Hastings until *The Big Four,* when the Belgian detective declares it necessary for his brother to be brought into the case. Hastings displays the same surprise as Dr. John Watson does when he learns from Sherlock Holmes after many years of friendship that Holmes has a brother, Mycroft. Interestingly, Achille has many of the same characteristics as Mycroft Holmes:

> *You surprise me, Hastings. Do you not know that all celebrated detectives have brothers who would be even more celebrated than they are were it not for constitutional indolence? . . .{Achille} does nothing. He is, as I tell you, of a singularly indolent disposition. But his abilities are hardly less than my own . . . He is not nearly so handsome and he wears no moustaches."*

Following what he believes to be the death of Hercule Poirot, Hastings actually meets Achille, who is in the company of Countess Vera Rossakoff. Achille is very much like Poirot, save that his eyes are darker, his voice is different, and the mustache that he wears is proven by the countess to be a fake, hiding beneath it a scar on his upper lip. He is last seen by Hastings in the Felsenlabyrinth just as the mountain explodes. When Hastings next awakens, he finds Hercule very much alive and Achille gone. Poirot then declares: "Brother Achille has gone home—to the land of myths. It was I all the time." He claims to have darkened his eyes with belladonna, changed his voice a little, and have given himself a scar two months before.

The claims of Hercule that Achille Poirot did not really exist were apparently supported by a comment made in *The Labours of Hercules.* When speaking with Poirot about why his parents had named him Hercule, Dr. Burton asks "If I remember rightly—though my memory isn't what it was—you also had a brother called Achille, did you not?" Poirot replies simply, "Only for a short space of time."

POIROT, HERCULE

"The true work, it is always done from within. The little grey cells—remember always the little grey cells, mon ami."

One of the preeminent detectives in the history of literature, Hercule Poirot is also one of the most popular, well-defined, and easily recognized. With his fastidious habits, lack of humility, patent-leather shoes, and, above all, magnificent mustaches, Poirot is unique. He is also one of the most widely known sleuths by virtue of the sheer volume of writings featuring him: In all, there are thirty-four novels and fifty-five short stories.

BIOGRAPHY: The life of Hercule Poirot is better known than many other detectives, thanks to the large number of cases he solved, his willingness to speak of his earlier days, and the fact that his death was recorded in the last of his investigations, *Curtain* (1975).

As he mentioned frequently, Hercule Poirot was a patriotic Belgian. Born sometime in the nineteenth century to conservative Catholic parents, he grew up near the town of Spa. It is not known what he did during his formative years, but it can be guessed that he studied at a university and was well educated in the classics. The latter is assumed by his many references to classical literature, as in *The Labours of Hercules* (1947), in which he displays a thorough knowledge of the events in the life of his legendary namesake, Hercules.

As he entered adulthood, Poirot moved to Brussels and joined the Belgian police force. His intelligence, diligence, and immediate success helped him to advance swiftly and to become the most respected member of the force. It was while still a member of the Belgian police that Poirot first met Inspector Japp of Scotland Yard. Both officers were investigating the Abercrombie forgery case in Brussels.

Around 1904, Poirot resigned for unknown reasons from the Belgian police force and embarked on a career as a private agent. He subsequently established himself as a celebrated detective in Europe and beyond. He encountered Inspector Japp once more on the Altara case, in Antwerp. He also first met Captain Arthur Hastings in the years before World War I, when both were involved in an investigation on behalf of Lloyd's of London, for whom Hastings was then working.

With the eruption of World War I and the invasion of Belgium by the German army, Poirot was forced to become a refugee in England. Through the kindness of the wealthy Emily Inglethorpe, Poirot and other Belgians were given comfortable shelter at Leastways, a cottage in Styles St. Mary. While there, Poirot and Hastings ran into each other again—Hastings was recovering from wounds suffered in the fighting on the western front—and they soon became an investigative duo, tracking down the murderer of Mrs. Inglethorpe in the case recounted as *The Mysterious Affair at Styles.*

Perhaps the greatest of all cinematic Poirots, Albert Finney, in Murder on the Orient Express *(1974). (Photofest)*

As they were fast friends and worked well together, Poirot and Hastings took rooms in London at 14 Farraway Street. Hastings served as Poirot's chronicler and assistant. Several years later, after the conclusion of the case recounted in *Murder on the Links,* Hastings married Dulcie Duveen and went off to Argentina. Henceforth, Hastings returned only intermittently, assisting his friend in major cases, such as his campaign against the international criminal organization, the Big Four.

Bored with his cases, Poirot retired to the country to devote himself to growing vegetable marrows. He settled at The Larches, King's Abbot, and developed a rapport with his neighbors, in particular Dr. James Sheppard and his sister, Caroline, and Roger Ackroyd. Even in self-proclaimed retirement, Poirot could not escape using his skills as a detective. Roger Ackroyd was murdered, and in one of his most challenging and shocking cases, Poirot brought the murderer to justice.

The Belgian realized that retirement was not to his taste, and so he went back to London and active detective work. He took up new quarters at Whitehaven Mansions, choosing the flat because of its symmetry and exact proportions. (There is some question as to the exact address, as it is also called 28 Whitehouse Mansions in some cases—for example, in *Cat among the Pigeons.*) To fulfill his clerical needs, he hired an equally angular secretary, Miss Felicity Lemon, who had previously worked for Mr. Parker Pyne. Poirot also organized his personal needs by hiring a valet, the unflappable and devoted George. George remained with Poirot right up to the detective's last days. Poirot's telephone number was Trafalgar 8137, and he rented his flat under the unlikely name of Mr. O'Connor.

Poirot spent the succeeding decades as one of the foremost detectives in the world, solving cases throughout Europe and in the Middle East, and enjoying the favor and attention of the highest levels of society and royalty. As a Belgian transplant in England, he was a perpetual outsider, a position that insulated him from many of the traditional impediments to social interaction in British society and that provided him with the ability to act as an impartial observer. His friendship with Captain Arthur Hastings and Mrs. Ariadne Oliver only furthered his social access. As Gillian Gill noted in *Agatha Christie: The Woman and Her Mysteries,* "Captain Hastings' correct affiliations are implicit in his very name and rank . . . and Ariadne Oliver, for all her shyness, knows the right people. Through these two friends, Poirot will gain access to the drawing rooms and upstairs corridors of places like Styles Court and thus be in a situation to get the upper-class suspects to betray themselves in conversation."

Poirot solved a number of his later cases with Mrs. Ariadne Oliver, finding in her a supportive friend and colleague and also someone with whom he found much common ground in their disdain for modern life (in the 1960s). This is made clear in *Third Girl,* in which Poirot disapproves very strongly of contemporary culture. Such cases also made Poirot feel increasingly out of sync with the world, a sense of isolation that climaxed with his last case,

Curtain. Always vain, the aging detective insisted on dyeing his thinning hair and wearing the same anachronistic costume that he had favored for so long and that had gone out of fashion decades before. Finally, in *Curtain,* Hastings makes the depressing last call on his friend at Styles Court, the site where they had enjoyed their first triumph. He finds the dying Poirot pathetically confined to a wheelchair from arthritis: "I can still feed myself, but otherwise have to be attended to like a baby." Nevertheless, despite his impending death, Poirot solves his last murder case and pushes away the very pills that could prolong his life. He bids farewell to his longtime friend:

> "Goodbye, cher ami, I have moved the amyl nitrate ampules away from beside my bed. I prefer to leave myself in the hands of the bon Dieu. May his punishment, or his mercy, be swift!
> "We shall not hunt together again, my friend. Our first hunt was here—and our last.
> "They were good days.
> "Yes, they have been good days."

The death of Hercule Poirot was announced in *The New York Times* on August 6, 1975. The headline declared:

Hercule Poirot Is Dead; Famed Belgian Detective

APPEARANCE: The now well-known image of Hercule Poirot was first established by Captain Hastings in *The Mysterious Affair at Styles*: "Poirot was an extraordinary looking little man. He was hardly more than five feet, four inches, but carried himself with great dignity. His head was exactly the shape of an egg, and he always perched it a little on one side. His moustache was very stiff and military. The neatness of his attire was almost incredible. I believe a speck of dust would have caused him more pain than a bullet wound."

Fastidious, even obsessively neat, Poirot also

insisted on wearing patent-leather shoes, even in the country, where a different kind of shoe was highly recommended. The shoes caused him pain on several occasions when he was forced to walk great distances. He also traditionally wore a magnificently tailored striped suit and waistcoat, and carried a family heirloom, a "big turnip-faced watch." As he devoted no time to exercise—even his methods of detection eschewed physical exertion—he was quite out of shape, preferring to conserve all his energy for the "little grey cells."

Poirot seemed to revel in his peculiar appearance. With every smirk thrown his way, every raised eyebrow, and every joke made about him, Poirot smiled inside and observed that the account of him "would provide entertainment for many winters to come." He was also practical about his appearance. In *Cat among the Pigeons,* he "prepared himself to beat down any insular prejudice that a headmistress (in this case, the formidable Miss Bulstrode) might have against aged foreigners with pointed patent leather shoes and large moustaches." He was Hercule Poirot, and the world must accept him as he was, in all of his grandeur.

PERSONAL HABITS: Order, for Poirot, was everything. He built his world and his profession around order and method. Thus, his daily routine and his activities were well organized and carefully planned. His residence at Whitehaven (or Whitehouse) Mansions was chosen precisely because he approved of its symmetry. His clothes were acceptable for their neatness and disposition, and he hired Miss Lemon because she was efficient and appropriately angular.

When things did not proceed according to the efficient method that Poirot desired, he became most unhappy. In "The Arcadian Deer," Poirot is annoyed that his expensive car, a Messaro Gratz, "had not behaved with that mechanical perfection which he expected of a car. His chauffeur, a young man who enjoyed a handsome salary, had not succeeded in putting things right." When it

is suggested that he should hire a car to continue on his journey, he is appalled. "His Latin thrift was offended. Hire a car? He already had a car—a large car—an expensive car."

Admittedly, Poirot's obsession with his appearance and neatness were a form of absurd vanity. He admits to Superintendent Spence in *Hallowe'en Party* that he has no gray hairs despite his age because "I attend to that with a bottle." In his visit to the Jolly Roger Hotel on the Devon coast in *Evil under the Sun,* he insists on wearing an immaculate white suit with a

A superb Poirot, David Suchet, from London Weekend Television's Agatha Christie's Poirot. *(Photofest; London Weekend Television)*

Panama hat and is concerned chiefly that his mustache will droop in the heat and that his hair dye will run onto his collar.

Poirot also has a memorable habit of abusing the English language. He mixes French phrases into his everyday speech, so that in *The Mysterious Affair at Styles,* he declares, *"En voilà, une table! . . .* Ah, my friend, one may live in a big house and yet have no comfort." Even more peculiar is his use of odd sentence constructions and his often paternal way of addressing people. He insists, for example, that some people, usually young women, refer to him as Papa Poirot, and he frequently calls his associates *mon ami.* Above all, Poirot was infamous for his complete lack of humility, to the point that he himself made note of it and even joked about it with friends.

ASSOCIATES AND RELATIVES: Poirot was respected and liked by many different classes of people and professions. Given his work on cases spanning many decades, he developed an excellent rapport with Scotland Yard and local police officials. He was once a policeman himself, and his associations with such officers as James Japp and Superintendent Battle gave him instant access to crime scenes and the willing cooperation of investigators, things that were given only grudgingly to someone like Miss Marple. Poirot did have his opponents, of course, such as Inspector Crome in *The A.B.C. Murders* and especially Giraud of the Sûreté in *Murder on the Links.* His results spoke for themselves, however, and police opponents shrank away in the face of his long line of successes.

As Poirot was known to the rich and powerful, he was seen frequently in the finest hotels and restaurants (witness his journey on the Orient Express) and in the company of royalty and the very wealthy. As he solved many cases for the upper classes and was a model of discretion, he was someone they could trust with even the most delicate problems, such as the rescue of Prime Minister MacAdam in "The Kidnapped Prime Minister" or solution to the murder of

Ruth Kettering and the recovery of the Heart of Fire rubies in *The Mystery of the Blue Train.* He also hobnobbed with the likes of the indescribably wealthy Mr. Shaitana, Sir Henry Angkatell, Lord Edgware, and Simeon Lee, and investigated their very often well-deserved murders.

Poirot had few friends. He had long acquaintances with George (his dealings with him were *never* casual), Miss Lemon (she saw him as little more than her employer), and the detective Mr. Goby (who was sometimes used by Poirot as a kind of subcontractor), but they could hardly be called friends. He also knew and got along quite well with Colonel Johnny Race, Superintendent Battle, and Inspector Japp. They lacked a real closeness, however. Ultimately, only three people ever earned the honor of being a true friend.

Poirot was fond of Mrs. Ariadne Oliver, solving many cases with her as his able companion in crime detection. They had much in common and a relative closeness in ages that permitted a similar world view. An even better friend was Captain Hastings, who was loyally with Poirot right at the end and was his most devoted chronicler. Finally, there was Countess Vera Rossakoff, the only woman who actually captured the Belgian's heart. (For details, see under Rossakoff, Countess Vera; see also Poirot, Achille.)

METHOD: Just as Poirot's private life was dominated by order and method, so, too, was his entire career as a detective. For Poirot, order was everything. As Hastings wrote in *Murder on the Links*: " 'Order' and 'Method' were his gods. He had a certain disdain for tangible evidence, such as footprints and cigarette ash, and would maintain that, taken by themselves, they would never enable a detective to solve a problem. Then he would tap his egg-shaped head with absurd complacency, and remark with great satisfaction, 'The true work, it is always done from *within. The little grey cells—remember always the little grey cells, mon ami.' "*

Poirot stood in firm opposition to such other

A larger than life Poirot, Peter Ustinov, in Death on the Nile *(1982). (Photofest)*

notable detectives as Sherlock Holmes, who relied upon vigor and the careful examination of fingerprints, dropped cigarette ash, the imprint of a booted foot, or a broken twig. These were useful to Poirot in setting the scene of a crime in his own mind, but they did not lead straight to a criminal. Instead, once he had assembled his clues, Poirot would sit in a comfortable chair and apply his "little grey cells." At times misinterpreted as inactivity or indolence, Poirot's method was just as active as any

policeman's who crawled along a floor looking for clues. His energy was internal, in the mind.

There were several superb examples of his method yielding formidable results. In one of his most celebrated cases, the murder of Ratchett on the Orient Express, Poirot was faced with a room stuffed with apparently incriminating clues that seemed to point to almost everyone in the Calais Coach. Using the clues as a starting point, Poirot preferred to concentrate his investigation on the careful interroga-

Hercule Poirot's Published Cases

NOVELS

The A.B.C. Murders
After the Funeral
Appointment with Death
The Big Four
Black Coffee (adapted from the 1930 play)
Cards on the Table
Cat among the Pigeons
The Clocks
Curtain
Dead Man's Folly
Death in the Clouds
Death on the Nile
Dumb Witness
Elephants Can Remember
Evil under the Sun
Five Little Pigs
Hallowe'en Party
Hercule Poirot's Christmas
Hickory Dickory Dock
The Hollow
Lord Edgware Dies
Mrs. McGinty's Dead
Murder in Mesopotamia
The Murder of Roger Ackroyd
Murder on the Links
Murder on the Orient Express
The Mysterious Affair at Styles
The Mystery of the Blue Train
One, Two, Buckle My Shoe

Peril at End House
Sad Cypress
Taken at the Flood
Third Girl
Three-Act Tragedy
The Unexpected Guest (adapted from the 1958 play)

SHORT STORIES

"The Adventure of Johnnie Waverly"
"The Adventure of the Cheap Flat"
"The Adventure of the Christmas Pudding"
"The Adventure of the Clapham Cook"
"The Adventure of the Egyptian Tomb"
"The Adventure of the Italian Nobleman"
"The Adventure of 'The Western Star' "
"The Affair at the Victory Ball"
"The Apples of the Hesperides"
"The Arcadian Deer"
"The Augean Stables"
"The Capture of Cerberus"
"The Case of the Missing Will"
"The Chocolate Box"
"The Cornish Mystery"
"The Cretan Bull"
"Dead Man's Mirror"
"The Disappearance of Mr. Davenheim"
"The Double Clue"
"Double Sin"
"The Dream"
"The Erymanthian Boar"
"The Flock of Geryon"

tion of the passengers, and then reached his remarkable and correct conclusion. In *Five Little Pigs,* Poirot unraveled a murder mystery that had occurred sixteen years before. There were few clues, and the entire case was solved solely by a thorough examination of the perspectives of the different witnesses. It was an entirely rational deduction.

The most amazing of all Poirot's feats was his recovery of the missing Prime Minister David MacAdam in "The Kidnapped Prime Minister." During the case, he proclaims: "It is not so that a good detective should act, eh? . . . He must be full of energy. He must rush to and fro. He should prostrate himself on the dusty road and seek the marks of tires through a little glass. He must gather up the cigarette-end, the fallen match?" Instead, Poirot sits for five hours in a hotel, "motionless, blinking his eyelids like a cat, his green eyes flickering and becom-

"Four and Twenty Blackbirds"
"The Girdle of Hippolita"
"The Horses of Diomedes"
"How Does Your Garden Grow?"
"The Incredible Theft"
"The Jewel Robbery at the Grand
    Metropolitan"
"The Kidnapped Prime Minister"
"The King of Clubs"
"The Lemesurier Inheritance"
"The Lernean Hydra"
"The Lost Mine"
"The Market Basing Mystery"
"The Million-Dollar Bond Robbery"
"Murder in the Mews"
"The Mystery of Hunter's Lodge"
"The Mystery of the Baghdad Chest"
"The Mystery of the Spanish Chest"
"The Nemean Lion"
"The Plymouth Express"
"Problem at Sea"
"The Second Gong"
"The Stymphalean Birds"
"The Submarine Plans"
"The Theft of the Royal Ruby"
"The Third-Floor Flat"
"The Tragedy of Marsdon Manor"
"Triangle at Rhodes"
"The Under Dog"
"The Veiled Lady"
"Wasps' Nest"
"Yellow Iris"

ing steadily greener and greener." The result is a complete triumph.

Still, others doubted his abilities. To prove the genius of his method, Poirot bet Inspector Japp that he could solve "The Disappearance of Mr. Davenheim" without leaving the comfort of his flat. Using Hastings as his useful go-between, Poirot correctly deduced the truth of the matter and won his bet.

This is not to say that Poirot was entirely

unwilling or unable to be a man of action. Just as Holmes did not rely exclusively on the examination of clues but likewise spent days in deep thought, so, too, did Poirot rouse himself to go forth and capture criminals with some energy. The finest hour for this was his brilliant effort against the international crime organization the Big Four. There was also his clever trapping of a murderer in *Black Coffee* and his heroic capture of a murderer and his gang in "The Erymanthian Boar." Poirot was imaginative, flexible, and more determined than the murderers he hunted.

Agatha Christie's genius was clearly displayed in Hercule Poirot even in her first published novel, *The Mysterious Affair at Styles,* in 1920. At the age of twenty-five, she began work on what she hoped would be a detective story. After fleshing out a few of the details, she began the important task of giving life to her detective. She was quite familiar with Sherlock Holmes and wanted someone just as memorable:

> I settled on a Belgian detective. I allowed him slowly to grow into his part. He should have been an inspector, so that he would have a certain knowledge of crime. He would be meticulous, very tidy . . . A tidy little man. I could see him as a tidy little man, always arranging things . . . He would have a rather grand name—one of those names that Sherlock Holmes and his family had . . . Hercules: a good name. His last name was more difficult. I don't know why I settled on the name Poirot . . . It went well not with Hercules but Hercule—Hercule Poirot. That was all right—settled, thank goodness."

The retired policeman was born and remained essentially unchanged for the next half century, save for a few minor touches added later on, such as a preference for modern art, the hobby of growing vegetable marrows, and the practice of driving about in a fancy automobile. Christie lamented, however, that she had started out with Poirot too old, a mistake she realized after *Murder on the Links:* "Now I saw what a terrible mistake I had made in starting with Hercule Poirot so *old*—I ought to have abandoned him after the first three or four books, and begun again with someone much younger."

The popularity of Poirot prevented any such crime against the Belgian, and Christie was stuck with the persistent detective right to the end. She grew very tired of him over the years and even introduced Mrs. Ariadne Oliver as a means of spicing things up and inserting in a literary way some of the frustrations that the real-life author was feeling about Poirot. Mrs. Oliver says about her creation, Detective Sven Hjerson, what Christie thought about Poirot: "If I ever met that bony, gangling vegetable-eating Finn in real life, I'd do a better murder than any I've ever invented . . . They say how much they love my awful detective Sven Hjerson. If they knew how I hated him! But my publisher always says I'm not to say so."

Perhaps some of her yearning to be rid of him was alleviated during World War II, when she wrote *Curtain,* the brooding account of Poirot's last horrible days. Having written his demise, she was able to put the manuscript (along with *Sleeping Murder,* Miss Marple's last published case) into a bank vault and let it sit for some thirty years. In between, Poirot became her most popular sleuth, eclipsing all her detectives, even Miss Marple, with the sheer volume of his cases.

Hercule Poirot was given added popularity in stage, film, and television adaptations. He was the first Christie character to be brought to life on stage, in the 1928 production of *Alibi,* an adaptation of The *Murder of Roger Ackroyd* starring Charles Laughton. Three years later, Poirot again set a precedent with the film version of *Alibi,* starring Austin Trevor (minus the mustache) in the first film adaptation of a Christie work. Forty-three years later, Poirot was the star attraction in the most successful Christie film

adaptation ever, *Murder on the Orient Express* (1974), which was nominated for six Academy Awards and is remembered for, among other things, the magnificent performance of Albert Finney as Poirot. *Murder on the Orient Express* sparked a Poirot renaissance, with new adaptations of Poirot novels and stories being released ever since. At the start of the new century, Poirot is still going strong on television, in the series produced by London Weekend Television starring David Suchet, one of the finest of all Poirots and a more than worthy successor to Laughton, Trevor, Finney, and Ustinov.

Poli, General An Italian general who becomes involved in the murder investigation described in "The Gate of Baghdad." He first meets Mr. Parker Pyne on the boat from Brindisi to Beirut and subsequently travels from Damascus to Baghdad. He does not comprehend fully the subtleties of English humor and is rather curious about Parker Pyne taking over the murder inquiry with such authority, as the latter had never been a soldier.

Pollard, Constable A police officer in the town of Market Basing in "The Market Basing Mystery." He reluctantly approaches Hercule Poirot and Inspector Japp while they are on holiday to ask their assistance with a murder investigation.

Pollock, Sergeant A police officer in the Sittaford area who takes part in the murder investigation in *The Sittaford Mystery.* He has a cautious personality and moves very slowly assembling evidence, refusing to give any theories or suppositions until the matter is well in hand.

Pollock, Alfred The lazy, illegitimate half cousin of Miss Greenhsaw in "Greenshaw's Folly." He becomes the immediate and obvious suspect in Miss Greenshaw's murder, but he is saved from the gallows by his incurable laziness and lack of diligence toward work.

Polonska, Vanda An unfortunate Polish refugee in *N or M?* After arriving penniless in England, she is forced to sell her young daughter in order to survive. Later, when she tries to recover her child, she is shot through the head.

Pope, Lavinia   The overpowering headmistress of a most exclusive girls' school in Neuilly, France, in "The Girdle of Hippolyta." She oversees every aspect of life in the school and is thus most incommoded when young Winnie King goes missing while on a train. She gives her cooperation to Hercule Poirot and actually helps him recover a stolen painting.

Popoleffsky, Countess Varaga   One of the names used by Angele Mory in *The Secret of Chimneys*.

Poporensky, Princess Anna Michaelovna   A supposed lady-in-waiting to Grand Duchess Pauline in "Jane in Search of a Job."

Portal, Alec   A worried husband in "The Coming of Mr. Quin." He is described as being of "the usual good, sound English stock." He is also concerned that his wife may have murdered her first husband, even though she was acquitted of the crime "more through the lack of evidence against her than from any overwhelming proof of innocence." Mr. Harley Quin is able to ease his worries.

Portal, Eleanor   The deeply troubled wife of Alec Portal in "The Coming of Mr. Quin." Eleanor was arrested years before for the murder of her first husband after her lover committed suicide and her husband's body was exhumed and found to contain strychnine. She was acquitted, but her freedom was won "more through the lack of evidence against her than from any overwhelming proof of innocence." She has spent the subsequent years living under the shadow of suspicion and has even considered suicide. Her new husband, Alec, is also concerned that the allegations might actually be true.

Porter, Major George Douglas   A retired army officer who belongs to the Coronation Club in *Taken at the Flood*. Known as the club bore, he is a sober and unimaginative soldier who nevertheless bears a terrible secret. The burden of his secret ultimately proves too terrible for him

and he shoots himself. Before his death, however, he provides useful information to Poirot about Gordon Cloade and his recent marriage to Rosaleen Underhay.

Porter, Major John, D.S.O.   A onetime army officer and game hunter in Africa in "The Shadow on the Glass." Years earlier, he and a friend, Richard Scott, had been on safari and had both fallen in love with Iris Staverton. Now, with a reunion imminent, he is deeply concerned about how emotions will play out in the confining quarters of Scott's home, Greenways House.

Potts, Gladys   A Red Cross volunteer in *Giant's Bread*. She is much hated by her fellow volunteers, especially as she steals their food rations.

Power, Emery   A wealthy art and antiquities collector in "The Apples of the Hesperides." He attempts to secure an infamous chalice that reportedly was once in the possession of the Borgias, but his fruitless efforts compel him to enlist the help of Hercule Poirot. Aware of the dark past of the elaborately decorated chalice, Poirot recovers the precious object and then convinces Power to be free of its possible malign influence.

Pratt, Dorothy Jane   An adventurous young woman in "A Fruitful Sunday." She enjoys going for Sunday drives with her boyfriend, Edward Palgrove, and on one of them they purchase a basket of fruit at a roadside stand. In the basket, they discover a diamond necklace and are immediately confronted with the question of what to do with it.

Prentice, Ann   The main character in *A Daughter's a Daughter*. A forty-one-year-old widow, she has spent sixteen years raising her daughter, Sarah, since the death of her husband and has developed a close relationship with her. The time has come, she knows, for both of them to become more independent. This becomes of some importance to Ann after she meets Richard Cauldfield, a former British army officer who eventually asks her to marry him. She then faces the long and ultimately futile effort to be her own authentic person and to find true happiness.

Prentice, Sarah The daughter of Ann Prentice in *A Daughter's a Daughter*. Stubborn, selfish, and jealous of anyone who might take away her mother's full attention, Sarah opposes Ann's betrothal to Richard Cauldfield and ultimately manages to wreck their planned marriage and her mother's future happiness. She then marries the dissolute and unreliable drug addict and aristocrat Lawrence Steene. The marriage proves a disaster, and Sarah is soon reduced to alcoholism and addiction to cocaine. To her rescue comes an old flame, Gerry Lloyd, who offers her the chance of full recovery and possible happiness with him in Canada. The question is, will she accept a second chance and will she ever recognize the pain she has caused her mother?

Prescott, Joan The sister of a cleric in *A Caribbean Mystery*. She refuses to admit it—and is even firm in her denials—but she has a fascination with gossip and relates to Miss Marple the story of Molly Kendall's apparent mental instability.

Preston, Hailey The assistant to Jason Rudd in *The Mirror Crack'd from Side to Side*. Described by Chief Inspector Craddock as "an efficient and voluble gas bag," Preston holds a variety of jobs under Rudd, including press agent, private secretary, and personal assistant. He is thus privy to virtually all of Rudd's private affairs and maintains an elegant air about himself.

Price, Emlyn A traveler on a tour of the gardens and houses of Great Britain, along with Miss Marple, in *Nemesis*. He is one of two witnesses to the murder of Elizabeth Temple when stones rain down on her from a cliff.

Price, Lily A young woman who is planning to marry her fiancé, Harry, and goes house shopping in *The Mirror Crack'd from Side to Side*. While looking out of a second-story window, she nearly falls to her death and is stunned to see that Harry does not react to help her. Miss Marple considers this to be of some importance and cautions Lily to reconsider her marriage, as "You want someone whom you can rely upon if you're in danger."

Price Ridley, Martha The queen of gossips and busybodies in St. Mary Mead. Much hated by those she injures with her gossip and sanctimonious air, she appears in two of Miss Marple's cases, *Murder at the Vicarage* and *The Body in the Library*.

Priestman, Marguerite An American girl in *Unfinished Portrait*. She speaks with a distinctive American accent.

Primer, Detective Inspector A police official in *Sleeping Murder*. He investigates the murder of Lily Kimble, who was killed while on her way to meet with Dr. Kennedy about Helen Spenlove Kennedy Halliday. Primer is courteous and self-effacing, and notes his deep admiration for Miss Marple and her skills as a detective.

Pritchard, George The long-suffering husband of Mary Pritchard in "The Blue Geranium." He endures the endless complaints and whining of his wife, bearing all with surprising patience but refusing to believe that her many ailments are real. It comes as a surprise, then, when his wife dies suddenly. While he cares a great deal for another woman, he does nothing about his feelings after Mary's death because of his concerns about obvious public suspicion.

Pritchard, Mary Wife of George Pritchard in "The Blue Geranium." According to Colonel Bantry, she "was one of those semi-invalids—I believe she really had something wrong with her, but whatever it was, she played it for all it was worth. She was capricious, exacting, unreasonable. She complained from morning to night." Visited by the fortune-teller Zarida, Mrs. Pritchard becomes obsessed with the future and grows absolutely terrified about her impending fate, which, according to Zarida, will be revealed at the sign of the blue geranium. She is found dead in her room, beneath a geranium in the wallpaper that has turned from pinky-red to deep blue.

Proctor, Dr. A physician in *After the Funeral*. Much to his displeasure, he is summoned to examine Miss Gilchrist, who is nearly poisoned to death with arsenic baked into a piece of wedding cake.

Protheroe, Anne The young wife of Colonel Lucius Protheroe and stepmother to Lettice Protheroe in *Murder at the Vicarage*. She has come to share the opinion of most people in St. Mary Mead concerning her husband—that he is a "pompous old brute"—and she has thus turned elsewhere for comfort. She presumably finds happiness in the arms of the painter Lawrence Redding. Thus, when her husband is murdered, she confesses to the crime.

Protheroe, Lettice The daughter of Colonel Lucius Protheroe and stepdaughter of Anne Protheroe in *Murder at the Vicarage*. She is considered "something of a minx" and causes her father to create a "shemozzle" when he learns that she has been posing for a portrait by the painter Lawrence Redding wearing only a bathing suit. It is widely rumored that she and Redding are involved, a story much discounted by Miss Marple. Lettice despises her stepmother and tries to have her blamed for her father's murder.

Protheroe, Colonel Lucius The master of Old Hall in St. Mary Mead and the local magistrate and churchwarden in *Murder at the Vicarage*. A "pompous old brute," Protheroe was disliked by virtually everyone in the village. Even the vicar, Leonard Clement, confesses that "any one who murdered him would be doing the world at large a service." A special dislike for him is harbored by Anne Protheroe, his wife, and Lettice Protheroe, his daughter. One afternoon, Reverend Clement arrives back at the vicarage for a meeting with the colonel and finds him sprawled across the vicarage desk, shot through the head.

Protheroe, Walter A onetime lieutenant in the Royal Navy in "The Market Basing Mystery." He becomes the target of blackmailers who have discovered a secret about his past.

Pryce, Netta Described as the youngest and most charming of the "tourist race," Miss Pryce is a member of the party traveling from Damascus to Baghdad in "The Gate of Baghdad."

She is making the journey with her aunt, a stern woman "with the suspicion of a beard and a thirst for Biblical knowledge."

Pugh, Eric A friend of Sir Stafford Nye in *Passenger to Frankfurt*. He knows a great deal more than people realize but he says nothing about what he knows, out of discretion and personal habit.

Purdy, Professor An elderly archaeologist in *The Clocks*. He hires Sheila Webb from the Cavendish Secretarial and Typing Bureau to assist him with his typing and other secretarial duties. These prove far more demanding than the bureau has anticipated, and Sheila is regularly kept late to finish the day's work.

Purvis, William A partner in the law firm of Purvis, Purvis, Charlesworth, and Purvis in *Dumb Witness*. This particular Purvis represents the legal interests of Emily Arundell. He advises against but does not stop the revision of her will shortly before her death.

Pye, Mr. A wealthy collector of antiques in *Moving Finger*. Derisively described as a "lady-like plump little man" with a high-pitched voice, he is a recipient of one of the vicious poison-pen letters that circulate through the town of Little Furze.

Quant, Esther A maid in "The House of Lurking Death." She is murdered when she eats a sandwich containing poisoned figs.

Quentin The name of the butler in the service of Lord Listerdale in "The Listerdale Mystery." He not only serves in the estate of Lord Listerdale, who disappeared mysteriously some years before, but also provides capable assistance to Mrs. St. Vincent and her family when they move in to the house at a remarkably low rent. Rupert St. Vincent, however, has his doubts about Quentin and sets out to discover the secrets of this mysterious servant.

Quimper, Dr. The physician to the Crackenthorpe family of Rutherford Hall in *4.50 from Paddington*. He is a seemingly competent doctor and provides the police with details about the family and its history, especially the fact that Luther Crackenthorpe's gastritis attacks bore a striking similarity to arsenic poisoning. He is subsequently caught up in the events that terrorize Rutherford Hall, including the fatal poisonings of Luther and Bryan Crackenthorpe. The celebration of Dr. Quimper's birthday is the setting for Miss Marple to unmask the murderer.

QUIN, HARLEY Without question, the most unusual and mysterious figure in the entire body of Christie's writings. Harley Quin's place in the mind of Agatha Christie is best revealed by the fact that she dedicated the collection *The Mysterious Mr. Quin* (1930) to him—the only time she honored a character in so obvious a fashion. The dedication reads: "To Harlequin, The Invisible."

Like the Harlequin, the most famous figure in the *commedia dell'arte* (along with Columbine, Pierrot, Pierrette, Punchinello, and Punchinella), Mr. Harley Quin has a kind of magical influence upon people and situations, affecting their lives in a very direct way, both for good and for ill. He appears swiftly, unexpectedly, and even inexplicably, wields his influence, and then is gone as quickly as he came—leaving behind changed lives, the memory of an elusive character, and the vision of moving, harlequin-like splashes of color, visible in his clothing, through a reflection of light in stained glass, in the flames of a fireplace, or in a rainbow.

The manner in which Quin affects people is equally subtle. He sets the stage for events that follow and then uses other people as his chief instrument. The most commonly used agent is his friend Mr. Satterthwaite, the urbane, snobbish bachelor. Satterthwaite gathers all the pieces together, but the picture is not clear. Quin arrives and asks a few, pointed questions. With an added comment, such as "You have seen with your own eyes," Quin makes the solution obvious. Once his work, or his magic, is accomplished, Quin disappears and is not seen again until the next mysterious moment. Mr. Satterthwaite acknowledged Quin's odd abilities when

he declared that he had "a power—an almost uncanny power—of showing you what you have seen with your own eyes, of making clear to you what you have heard with your own ears."

While never declared outright to be the Harlequin or a figure of magic and the supernatural, Quin's characteristics and abilities are certainly magical in their own right. This is driven home by his manner of departing in several stories. In "The Man from the Sea" and "The World's End," Quin walks away toward a cliff and literally disappears into the night.

The creation of Harley Quin by Agatha Christie can be attributed directly to her interest in the Harlequin of the *commedia dell'arte.* Indeed, the very origins of the character were obvious in 1924, with the publication of Christie's first volume of poetry, *The Road of Dreams.* Containing a set of poems on the *commedia dell'arte,* the book included "Harlequin's Song," a poem about the "Happy go lucky Harlequin."

RACE, COLONEL JOHNNY An agent working for the British secret service, Race is notable among the characters in Christie's writings for being one of the few who actually ages over the course of the different cases recounted. Thus, by his last appearance, in *Sparkling Cyanide,* Race has aged some four decades. A capable operative for the British government, Race was often sent out on troublesome, difficult, or sensitive missions and was usually found in one of the outposts of the Empire where trouble was brewing. Race was also the heir to Sir Laurence Eardsley.

In the accomplishment of his tasks, he came into contact with other capable detectives, most notably Hercule Poirot and Mrs. Ariadne Oliver. Race was one of four sleuths who collaborated to catch a murderer in *Cards on the Table* (along with Poirot, Ariadne Oliver, and Superintendent Battle). Race also worked with Poirot in solving the murder of Linnet Doyle and others in *Death on the Nile.* Colonel Race

Colonel Johnny Race (David Niven, left), from Death on the Nile *(1978). (Photofest)*

also participated in two other cases: *The Man in the Brown Suit* and *Sparkling Cyanide.* In *Brown Suit,* Race proposed to Anne Beddingfield and was rejected. He subsequently never married.

Radclyffe, Dennis The third victim of poison in "The House of Lurking Death." Deeply in debt, he was considered a likely suspect in the previous murders, because he was disinherited by his aunt in favor of Lois Hargreaves. Lois, however, includes him in her will. Soon after, Dennis is murdered with a poisoned cocktail.

Raddish, Mr. A real estate agent in "The Lamp." He rents a house to Mrs. Lancaster and is reluctant to tell her about the presence of a ghost because she likes the house so much.

Radley, General A retired soldier and a guest in *At Bertram's Hotel.* He is interviewed by Inspector Davy concerning the disappearance of Canon Pennyfeather.

Radmaager, Herr A well-known composer in *Giant's Bread.* He is so impressed with the music composed by Vernon Deyre that he encourages the young man to pursue his work in music.

Radnor, Jacob The assumed fiancé of Freda Stanton in "The Cornish Mystery." Radnor first becomes involved in the death of Mrs. Pengelley by virtue of knowing Freda Stanton, her niece. However, details emerge about his deeper association with Mrs. Pengelley, including the surprising revelation that Mrs. Pengelley had a passion for him.

Radzky, Countess Anna An alias used by Babe St. Maur in *The Seven Dials Mystery.*

Rafiel, Jason A wealthy old man who went once a year to the West Indies and who came to have a deep respect for the abilities of Miss Marple as a detective. Rafiel was "semi-paralyzed and looked like a wrinkled old bird of prey." He also derived his primary pleasure by "denying robustly anything that anyone else said." Never-

theless, he forms an odd, practical alliance with Miss Marple to solve the murders at the Golden Palm Hotel in *A Caribbean Mystery.* Rafiel never forgot Miss Marple, and, after his death, he made arrangements in his will for the old sleuth to solve one more mystery for him. In *Nemesis,* he provides a generous amount of money for her to investigate whether his son, Michael Rafiel, was truly guilty of murdering Nora Broad.

Rafiel, Michael The son of Jason Rafiel in *Nemesis.* A difficult young man, Michael was ar-

Jason Rafiel (Barnard Hughes), with Miss Marple (Helen Hayes), in A Caribbean Mystery *(1983). (Photofest)*

rested and imprisoned for the murder of his fiancée, Verity Hunt. Jason Rafiel, however, is convinced that his son is innocent. To prove it, he leaves provision in his will for Miss Marple to investigate the true circumstances of the murder and to prove that his son is guiltless.

Ragg, Gordon   The original name used by Lord Easterfield in *Murder Is Easy.*

Raglan, Inspector   One of the police officials in *The Murder of Roger Ackroyd.* He is not especially liked and is called "a horrid . . . little man."

Raglan, Inspector Henry Timothy   The chief of police in Woodleigh Common, who heads the investigation into the death of Joyce Reynolds in *Hallowe'en Party.* He is aware of the many skills of Hercule Poirot and actually suggests that the detective be consulted in the case.

Raikes, Mrs.   A young woman described as being "of gypsy type" in *The Mysterious Affair at Styles.* She has several meetings with Alfred Inglethorpe that become the source of much gossip after he is arrested for the murder of Emily Inglethorpe.

Raikes, Howard   The boyfriend of Jane Olivera in *One, Two, Buckle My Shoe.* Raikes is an American leftist whose ideas are most unacceptable to Miss Olivera's relative, the powerful conservative banker Alistair Blunt.

Ramone, Delores   One of the aliases used by Madeleine de Sara, the "Queen of Vamps," in her work for Mr. Parker Pyne in *Parker Pyne Investigates.*

Ramsay, Ted and Bill   Brothers in *The Clocks* who have energetic imaginations. They discover a Czechoslovakian coin in the garden of Mrs. Pebmarsh and immediately assume that there is some kind of Communist connection with the events that took place in her house.

Ramsbottom, Effie   The eccentric sister-in-law of Rex Fortescue in *A Pocket Full of Rye.* She lives with Rex and his family even though her sister died and Rex subsequently remarried.

Randolph, Myrna   A young woman in *Absent in the Spring.* She is rumored to have been on intimate terms with Rodney Scudamore.

Ransome, Nicholas (Nicky)   A young man on whom Hercule Poirot depends during his investigation in *Hallowe'en Party.* Although he is reliable, Nicky does have an overactive imagination. He assumes, for example, that sex is at the bottom of the murder of Joyce Reynolds because "there's always got to be a sex background to these things." The detective asks Nicky and another friend to watch over Miranda Butler.

Ratchett, Samuel Edward   An American traveler and businessman in *Murder on the Orient Express.* Encountering Ratchett on the Calais Coach, Hercule Poirot takes an immediate interest in the wealthy American and finds something seriously amiss about him, although "all seemed to speak of a benevolent personality. Only the eyes belied this assumption." Ratchett soon approaches Poirot and expresses his desire to hire the detective as a bodyguard. Threats have been made against the American's life, and Ratchett offers Poirot "big money" if he takes the job. The detective declines, observing, "If you will forgive me for being personal—I do not like your face." The following morning, Ratchett is found dead in his compartment, the victim of multiple stab wounds. In the ensuing investigation, Poirot determines Ratchett's true identity. He is actually a criminal called Casetti, a vile kidnapper, extortionist, and murderer, as well as the brains behind the cruel kidnapping and death of little Daisy Armstrong. After his arrest, Casetti was acquitted and fled America. Justice finally caught up with him, however, and Poirot is faced with a train coach full of suspects.

Rathbone, Dr.   A distributor of books in foreign locales for the enrichment of the native peoples in *They Came to Baghdad.* He relies upon charitable donations and assorted grants to fund his work, but he also sometimes uses the money for another, more important charity—namely, himself. This activity makes him liable to blackmail.

Rathbone, Dennis   A young man who desires strongly to marry Ann Shapland in *Cat among* *the Pigeons.* As she finds him far too dull, she never ceases to reject his suit.

Rattery, John The fiancé of Carla Lemarchant in *Five Little Pigs.* Carla's mother, Caroline Crale, was imprisoned for murdering her father, Amyas Crale, and Carla is obsessed with proving her mother's innocence, especially as she is concerned that her husband will always look upon her with suspicion.

Ravel, Annette A woman who becomes the subject of an intense conversation on a train in "The Fourth Man." She was one of several children raised at Miss Slater's home for indigent children and grew up to become a famous singer named Annette Ravelli. She is the central figure in unraveling the mysterious personality of Felice Bault. Her secret is finally revealed by Raoul Letardeau.

Ravelli, Annette The name used by Annette Ravel in her singing career in "The Fourth Man."

Ravenscroft, General Alistair A retired officer and the father of Celia and Edward Ravenscroft in *Elephants Can Remember.* Years before, he fell in love with Dolly Jarrow, but circumstances led him instead to marry her sister, Molly. In a great tragedy, the general and Molly were found dead, the victims of an apparent murder-suicide, but the question remains who killed whom and why. The deaths of her father and mother haunt their daughter for many years.

Ravenscroft, Celia The daughter of General Alistair Ravenscroft and Lady Margaret Ravenscroft in *Elephants Can Remember.* When she was twelve, her parents died in an apparent murder-suicide, and the tragedy has haunted her for many years. She can provide few details to her godmother, Mrs. Ariadne Oliver, because she was away at school at the time, but the event is of such importance to her that the mother of her fiancé, Mrs. Burton-Cox, asks Mrs. Oliver to discover, if she can, the true nature of events.

Ravenscroft, Lady Margaret (Molly) The wife of General Alistair Ravenscroft and the mother of Celia and Edward Ravenscroft in *Elephants Can Remember.* A onetime schoolmate of Ariadne Oliver, she wed Genral Ravenscroft after he had already fallen in love with her sister, Dolly. She and the general died in an apparent murder-suicide, with much question remaining as to what exactly happened. In the events leading up to her death, four wigs became of great importance and prove essential to revealing the secret of her and her husband's deaths.

Rawlinson, Dr. The physician to the Denmans in "The Thumb Mark of Saint Peter." He is both old and incompetent, and is described by Miss Marple as "so short-sighted as to be pitiful, slightly deaf and, withal, touchy and sensitive to the last degree." It is little surprise, then, that Rawlinson misses vital clues related to a murder.

Rawlinson, Squadron Leader Bob The private pilot to Prince Ali Yusef of Ramat in *Cat among the Pigeons.* When the royal government is overthrown by revolution, Rawlinson assists the prince by attempting to smuggle half a million pounds of jewels out of the country. Rawlinson, however, dies when his plane crashes.

Rayburn, Harry A mysterious man seen by Anne Beddingfield in *The Man in the Brown Suit.* The son of Lord Eardsley, Harry has a checkered past and has spent years trying to clear his name. After school at Cambridge, he journeyed to British Guyana with a friend, Harry Lucas, and became a diamond prospector. When they discovered a fabulous diamond deposit, they were cheated out of it, and Rayburn was framed with the charge of stealing diamonds from the DeBeers company. The charges were suppressed by his father, but Harry's honor was seemingly irretrievably damaged. He enlisted and served in World War I with Lucas and was given a second chance at regaining his honor when Lucas was killed while wearing Rayburn's identification tags. Presumed dead, Rayburn began a long quest for justice that includes wandering the globe in search of the elusive criminal mastermind called the Colonel. Along the way, Harry adopts assorted aliases, including Harry Parker, Harry Lucas, and John Eardsley. He also meets the inquisitive and beautiful Anne Beddingfield and falls in love with her.

Raymond, Geoffrey The private secretary to Roger Ackroyd in *The Murder of Roger Ackroyd*. He has served as secretary for two years and is thus privy to the many secrets of his employer. Following Ackroyd's death, Raymond receives five hundred pounds from Ackroyd's will.

Raynes, Roger A corpulent singer in *Unfinished Portrait*. He falls in love with Celia and asks her hand in marriage.

Read, Miss Vera The personal secretary to the domineering and larger-than-life opera diva Madame Nazorkoff in "Swan Song." She is thus the recipient of Madame Nazorkoff's many temperamental outbursts.

Redcliffe, Hermia A friend of Mark Easterbrook in *The Pale Horse*. She would very much like to be more than a friend to Easterbrook, but he eventually falls in love with Katherine Corrigan. Nevertheless, Miss Redcliffe proves a faithful friend and assistant in his investigation into the mysterious Pale Horse inn.

Redding, Lawrence A painter "in the modern style" in *Murder at the Vicarage*. He is decidedly bohemian, renting a studio on the grounds of the vicarage and painting Lettice Protheroe in her bathing suit. Colonel Protheroe creates quite a "shemozzle" over Lettice's posing, and Redding confesses freely that he wishes the colonel were dead. He seemingly gets his wish when Protheroe is found murdered. Adding to the apparent likelihood of Redding's involvement is the discovery by Reverend Leonard Clement, the vicar of St. Mary Mead, of Redding in a passionate embrace with Anne Protheroe, Colonel Protheroe's wife.

Redfern, Christine The extremely pale and seemingly shy wife of Patrick Redfern and a guest at the Jolly Roger Hotel in *Evil under the Sun*. She takes great care to protect herself from the sun and suffers growing agony over the behavior of her Adonis-like husband. Patrick is very attractive to women, and one woman in particular, Arlena Marshall, is drawn to him immediately. Christine becomes angry over her husband's apparent lack of fidelity and becomes a suspect in the murder of Arlena Marshall.

Redfern, Patrick The handsome and unfaithful husband of Christine Redfern in *Evil under the Sun*. A man who knows that he is attractive to women, Redfern apparently cruelly neglects his long-suffering wife and spends much of his time in the company of another guest at the Jolly Roger Hotel, Arlena Marshall. Hercule Poirot, meanwhile, takes an almost instant dislike to him, observing that he is an "adventurer" who preys on women.

Reece-Holland, Claudia The secretary to Andrew Restarick in *Third Girl*. Claudia is the first of the girls to rent the flat that is eventually shared with Frances Cary and Norma Restarick, the daughter of her boss.

Reed An alias used by the blackmailer Mr. Lavington in "The Veiled Lady."

Reed, Giles The husband of Gwenda Reed and a distant relative of Joan West, wife of Raymond West, Miss Marple's favorite nephew, in *Sleeping Murder*. Giles brings his new wife from New Zealand to England, and they move into a seemingly unfamiliar house. Soon after, Gwenda begins experiencing odd sensations and memories about the home. These are of some interest to Giles, especially as he is a fan of detective stories. He thus helps his wife through her memories and troubles, proving himself a faithful and loving husband.

Reed, Gwenda The wife of Giles Reed and a catalyst for unraveling a long-forgotten mystery in *Sleeping Murder*. A newlywed, Gwenda moves from New Zealand to England and settles into a home that she is sure she has never seen before but that seems oddly familiar. She experiences strange sensations and memories that compel her to try and find her stepmother, who had deserted her father some sixteen years before. She also tries to uncover details about her father, who committed suicide in an asylum while grieving for his dead wife. At the urging of Miss Marple, Gwenda discovers that she was in England a long time before and that she somehow witnessed a murder and had suppressed the memory. With Miss Marple's help, Gwenda threads her way through an ancient murder mystery and frees herself and her house from the tormenting memory of death.

Reedburn, Henry A famous and powerful impresario in "The King of Clubs." While influential and wealthy, Reedburn is also ruthless and cruel. He blackmails the rising star Valerie Saintclair and is then brutally murdered in his own house, with "the back of his head cracked open like an eggshell." As the murder may drag Miss Saintclair into a scandal, Prince Paul of Maurania, who is in love with Saintclair, asks Poirot to render his assistance and identify the murderer.

Rees-Talbot, Mary An old friend of Colonel Johnny Race in *Sparkling Cyanide*. She hired Betty Archdale for the position of parlor maid. Archdale had once worked for the murdered Rosemary Barton and thus might be able to provide a few useful details about the dead woman.

Reeves The butler in the service of Colonel Protheroe in *Murder at the Vicarage*. He is pompous and arrogant beneath a veneer of serene professionalism, and his relationship with Colonel Protheroe is far from peaceful.

Reeves, Inspector The police officer in charge of the investigation into the death of Hubert Lytcham Roche in "The Second Gong." He seems completely satisfied with the initial determination of suicide, and Hercule Poirot has a hard time convincing him otherwise.

Reeves, Emily The cook in the household of Simeon Lee in *Hercule Poirot's Christmas*.

Reeves, Pamela (Pamie) A victim of murder in *The Body in the Library*. A member of the Girl Guides, she is approached by a stranger and invited to be in the movies. Soon after setting off with the stranger, Pamie is murdered and her body is dumped in a location chosen by the killer to create confusion and to mislead.

Reichardt, Dr. The head of an insane asylum in *Passenger to Frankfurt*. He has a number of patients who are convinced that they are Adolf Hitler. Ironically, the doctor believes that one of his mad patients might actually be Hitler.

Reid, Major A British army officer stationed in Iraq in *Absent in the Spring*. He becomes involved with Barbara Wray and thus launches a scandal.

Reilly, Mr. The alcoholic partner of Dr. Morley in *One, Two, Buckle My Shoe*. He was the last person to see Morley alive on the day of the dentist's murder, but he is not considered a likely suspect, as there is no known reason why he would want to see his partner dead.

Reilly, Dr. Giles One of the members of the archaeological team at Tell Yarimjah in *Murder in Mesopotamia*. Following the death of Louise Leidner, Reilly announces that Hercule Poirot will be passing through the area, and that the team should enlist his assistance in solving the murder. His daughter is Sheila Reilly.

Reilly, James The chief suspect in the murder of Gilda Glen in "The Man in the Mist." He becomes the chief suspect in large part because of his appearance; he has "flaming red hair, [a] pugnacious jaw and appallingly shabby clothes." Gilda was also his onetime lover.

Reilly, Sheila The daughter of Dr. Giles Reilly in *Murder in Mesopotamia*. An attractive and intelligent young woman, Sheila is the center of attention for the male archaeologists on the dig at Tell Yarimjah. She settles her own attentions on David Emmott.

Reiter, Carl A photographer at the archaeological dig at Tell Yarimjah in *Murder in Mesopotamia*. He is infatuated with Louise Leidner, but she rewards his aspirations by humiliating him publicly in the camp and by poking fun at his poor social skills. He is thus a suspect in her subsequent murder.

Renauld, Madame The wife of the murdered Paul T. Renauld and the mother of Jack Renauld in *Murder on the Links.* A formidable presence to investigators, especially Captain Arthur Hastings, Madame Renauld testifies that on the night of her husband's murder, she was seized by two intruders, tied, and gagged. They then took her husband out of the house, murdered him, and left his corpse in an open grave. Although a suspect, she actually assists Hercule Poirot in catching the murderer.

Renauld, Paul T. A wealthy businessman in *Murder on the Links.* He sent a request for assistance to Hercule Poirot but is murdered before the detective can arrive. According to his wife, Renauld was abducted from his own house by two sinister men, taken outside, stabbed to death, and dumped in an open grave. In his investigation, Poirot uncovers dark secrets from Renauld's past, one of which caught up with him and led to his death.

Rendell, Dr. A physician in *Mrs. McGinty's Dead.* He was the employer of Mrs. McGinty, the murder victim. He also receives an anonymous letter telling him that the death of his first wife was not an accident. He is currently married to his second wife, Shelagh Rendell.

Rendell, Shelagh The second wife of Dr. Rendell in *Mrs. McGinty's Dead.* She grows alarmed when Hercule Poirot begins making inquiries into the death of Mrs. McGinty, as she assumes the detective suspects that Rendell's first wife did not die accidentally.

Renisenb The daughter of Imhotep and the mother of Teti in *Death Comes As the End.* A young widow, she is the object of the attentions of several men, including Hori and Kameni. Kameni seemingly has the advantage because he looks like Renisenb's late husband, but she chooses Hori instead.

Rennie, Mr. A leftist and radical who is in love with Beatrice Kingston Bruce in "The Affair of the Pink Pearl." She reciprocates his affections, but this may only be because of the intense displeasure her associations with Rennie cause her parents. Rennie only adds to their discomfort by his obnoxious behavior.

Restarick, Alexis An actor and playwright in *They Do It with Mirrors.* He is able to figure out in approximate terms who the murderer of Christian Gulbrandsen might be, and his guess proves a little too close for comfort for the murderer. Restarick actually takes nail clippings from Carrie Louise to be analyzed, an act that prompts the murderer to act against Restarick. He is found in the school theater with Ernie Gregg; both are dead, their skulls crushed.

Restarick, Andrew The father of Norma Restarick in *Third Girl.* He goes off to Africa with a partner, Robert Orwell, and apparently returns to England. He tells Hercule Poirot that he suspects that his daughter, Norma, is slowly poisoning his second wife and that she might be losing her mind.

Restarick, Mary The supposed second wife of Andrew Restarick in *Third Girl.* Her husband tells Hercule Poirot that he suspects that his daughter, Norma, is slowly poisoning her. Poirot, however, discovers there is more to the couple than meets the eye.

Restarick, Norma The daughter of Andrew Restarick and a possible victim, in her own mind, of insanity in *Third Girl.* Norma is convinced that she has caused someone's death, and she goes to Mrs. Ariadne Oliver for advice. The writer and amateur sleuth encourages her to go to Hercule Poirot, but Norma finds the detective "too old." The Belgian, meanwhile, is thoroughly unimpressed by the overly thin girl with "long straggly hair" and eyes that bear "a vacant expression." Norma departs Poirot's apartment and disappears, embarking upon a series of grim adventures that nearly climax in her own death. In the course of events, she meets and becomes involved with Dr. Stillingfleet.

Revel, Virginia In full, the Honourable Mrs. Timothy Revel, the widowed daughter of an English aristocrat in *The Secret of Chimneys*. She is a stunningly attractive woman, with "an indescribable mouth." She takes part in the effort to secure control of the memoirs of Count Stylptitch.

Reynolds, Mrs. The mother of two murder victims in *Hallowe'en Party*. She loses both Joyce and Leopold Reynolds to a vicious killer. Her older daughter, Ann, survives the murderous events of the case.

Reynolds, Ann The older sister of Joyce Reynolds and Leopold Reynolds in *Hallowe'en Party*. She survives the terrible events of the case, but her two siblings do not. The sixteen-year-old is described as tall and lithe.

Reynolds, Joyce A thirteen-year-old girl who becomes the victim of murder in *Hallowe'en Party*. Joyce is obnoxious and loud, irritating to virtually everyone who knows her. One of these unfortunates is Mrs. Ariadne Oliver, to whom Joyce proclaims that she had once witnessed a murder. Someone overhears their conversation and drowns Joyce a short time later in a tub of water that was to be used for bobbing for apples.

Reynolds, Leopold The brother of Ann Reynolds and the murdered Joyce Reynolds in *Hallowe'en Party*. He figures out who the murderer might be and makes a ludicrous effort at extortion. For his greed, Leopold is murdered in a similar fashion to his sister. He is drowned in a stream.

Rhodes, Mr. A man whose fate is placed in the hands of Miss Marple in "Miss Marple Tells a Story." He was staying with his wife in the Crown Hotel in Barnchester when, incredibly, his wife was somehow stabbed to death in their room. He was the obvious suspect, as the bedroom was accessible only from the room in which he was working; the door leading to a corridor was bolted from the inside and the window was closed and latched. Furthermore, the chambermaid was the only person to have been in the room other than Mr. Rhodes. As he expects to be arrested any minute for the crime, Rhodes turns to the solicitor Mr. Petherick, who brought the case to Miss Marple.

Riccovetti One of the thieves responsible for the theft of the Borgia goblet in "The Apples of the Hesperides." During the commission of the crime, he drove the getaway car.

Rice, Inspector An officer of Scotland Yard who takes part in the investigation into the death of Ernestine Grant in "The Third-Floor Flat."

Rice, Mr. A cocaine addict and the abusive husband of Frederica Rice in *Peril at End House*. He is killed by police after attempting to murder his wife.

Rice, Mrs. One of two manipulative and ruthless extortionists in "The Stymphalean Birds." She and her accomplice nearly succeed in blackmailing Harold Waring.

Rice, Dicky A witness in "The Unbreakable Alibi." He testifies to Tommy and Tuppence Beresford that Una Drake was in Torquay at the same moment she was also seen in London having lunch with Jimmy Le Marchant in the Savoy.

Rice, Frederica (Freddie) The wife of Mr. Rice and the best friend of Nicky Buckley in *Peril at End House*. Frederica gives Nicky a supply of cocaine and is also the beneficiary of Nicky's sizable will. As if this were not enough to make her an obvious suspect in the "accidents" that have been befalling Nicky recently, a gun is found in Freddie's pocket, the same weapon used to kill Maggie Buckley, Nicky's cousin. Frederica is also shot and wounded by her estranged and desperate drug-addicted husband.

Rich, Major Charles The chief suspect in the murder of Arnold Clayton in "The Mystery of the Spanish Chest." Although a friend of both Arnold and Margharita Clayton, Rich is also secretly in love with Margharita. Thus, when Arnold is found stabbed to death in a Spanish chest in Rich's own living room, Rich becomes the obvious and seemingly damned suspect.

Rich, Eileen One of the teachers at the Meadowbank School in *Cat among the Pigeons.* She is one of the best teachers in the school, although she took a one-term leave for personal reasons. Upon the retirement of the formidable Miss Bulstrode, Miss Rich becomes headmistress of the entire school.

Rich, Major Jack The chief suspect in the murder of Edward Clayton in "The Mystery of the Baghdad Chest." Although a friend of both Edward and Marguerita Clayton, Rich is also secretly in love with Margeurita. Rich becomes, inevitably, the obvious suspect when Edward is found stabbed to death in a Baghdad chest in Rich's own living room.

Richards The valet to Ambassador Ralph Wilmott in "The Ambassador's Boots." A most attentive servant, he provides Tommy and Tuppence Beresford with very useful details concerning Eileen O'Hara and a certain missing attaché case.

Richards, Ernestine The former secretary to Lady Naomi Dortheimer in "The Case of the Distressed Lady." She is described as a "fair-haired young lady" who is not married and who is not named Daphne St. John. The last fact is of some importance to Mr. Parker Pyne, who unravels a plot to steal a diamond ring from Lady Dortheimer. The mastermind of a plot to steal a diamond ring, Miss Richards is permitted to escape justice, but she does not take her defeat with grace. (See also St. John, Daphne.)

Richards, James The name used by Norman Gale while he was in South America in *Death in the Clouds.*

Richetti, Signor Guido A supposed Italian archaeologist who becomes involved in the events described in *Death on the Nile.* He earns the suspicion of Hercule Poirot because "he was almost too word perfect in his role."

Riddell, Albert A witness to the murder of Alice Ascher in *The A.B.C. Murders.* He was the first person to enter Ascher's tobacco shop shortly after her brutal death.

Riddle, Major The chief constable of Westshire in "Dead Man's Mirror." A "tall, spruce-looking man," Riddle is called in to investigate the death of Sir Gervase Chevenix-Gore and immediately accepts the notion that Sir Gervase killed himself. Poirot's belief that the man was murdered is the source of frustration to the chief constable.

Ridgeway, Dr. A physician who resides near Hercule Poirot and Captain Hastings in *The Big Four.* Following a violent explosion, he gives medical attention to the detective, Hastings, and the unfortunate Mr. Mayerling.

Ridgeway, Charles The nephew to Mary Harter in "Where There's a Will." Charles is seemingly a devoted relative to the old and eccentric widow, but he secretly harbors desperate hopes of her swift death so that he can inherit her estate. He thus decides to hurry things along in a subtle manner.

Ridgeway, Linnet See Doyle, Linnet.

Ridgeway, Philip An officer of the London and Scottish Bank in "The Million-Dollar Bond Robbery." Ridgeway was in charge of transporting one million dollars' worth of Liberty Bonds from London to New York aboard the *Olympia* and apparently had the bonds stolen straight out of his cabin. He is the obvious suspect, but his devoted fiancée, Esmée Farquhar, enlists the aid of Hercule Poirot to prove him innocent.

Rieger, Katrina The companion to Miss Barrowby in "How Does Your Garden Grow?" A Russian émigré, Miss Rieger becomes a suspect in the murder of Miss Barrowby and seems all but convicted when a cache of strychnine is discovered under her mattress. She is much disliked by the Delafontaines, Miss Barrowby's relatives, especially because she stands to inherit a large sum of money from her deceased employer. Hercule Poirot, however, is convinced that she is innocent.

Rigg, Dr. A physician in *The Clocks.* He is pressed into service as a coroner and oversees the inquest into the death of R. H. Curry.

Riley, Mary The maiden name of Mary Draper in *Sad Cypress*.

Rival, Merlina A victim of murder in *The Clocks*. A friend of Miss Martindale, she identifies the remains of the mysterious R. H. Curry as those of her former husband and is soon stabbed to death in Victoria Station.

Rivers, Mr. One of the victims of the ambitious murderer in Wychwood in *Murder Is Easy*. Rivers serves as the chauffeur to Lord Easterfield, but eventually becomes the murderer's seventh victim. He dies because he might be able to provide details about the driver of the car that killed Lavinia Fullerton.

Rivington, Mrs. Described as "a woman of more looks than brains," she is a witness in the murder investigation of John Savage in *Why Didn't They Ask Evans?*

Robbins, Miss A nursery governess in *Giant's Bread*.

Robert An expert in art who is consulted by Tommy Beresford in *By the Pricking of My Thumbs*. He is able to name a particular artist after examining a painting brought to him by Beresford.

Roberts, Dr. One of the four bridge players in *Cards on the Table* and thus one of the four suspects in the murder of Mr. Shaitana. A pleasant and friendly physician, he nevertheless has a dark past that comes to light as a result of the investigation into Shaitana's murder.

Roberts, Mr. A forty-eight-year-old government employee who consults Mr. Parker Pyne in "The Case of the City Clerk." For the fee of five pounds, Parker Pyne provides Roberts with an escapade, thus helping the bored clerk out of his rut. Roberts departs for the Continent while his wife and two children are away visiting her mother. Parker Pyne arranges for him to assist the Grand Duchess Olga in a dangerous adventure involving espionage and the Russian crown jewels aboard the Geneva-Paris express. For his bravery and resourcefulness, Roberts is awarded the Order of St. Stanislaus,

tenth class, with laurels. (See also de Sara, Madeleine.)

Roberts, Gladys A onetime parlormaid whose former surname is Evans in *Why Didn't They Ask Evans?* She subsequently marries and enters the household of the vicar of Marchbolt. She is a central witness to the events surrounding the death of Alan Carstairs.

Robinson, Mr. One of the most mysterious figures in the whole of Christie's writings, Mr. Robinson is consulted by Hercule Poirot, Miss Marple, and the Beresfords, as well as by members of Scotland Yard, for his expertise in international finance, but his exact role and title are never explained fully. Robinson appears in *At Bertram's Hotel, Cat among the Pigeons, Passenger to Frankfurt,* and *Postern of Fate,* describing himself as "a man who knows about money." While it is clear that he wields considerable influence, the only clue as to his activities is a reference to his membership in the Arrangers, an elusive organization that seeks to maintain control of international finance in a positive sense. He is described as "fat and well-dressed, with a yellow face, melancholy dark eyes, a broad forehead, and a generous mouth."

Robinson, Edward A kindhearted, hardworking, and rather unimaginative young man in "The Manhood of Edward Robinson." Secretly longing for more excitement, he wins five hundred pounds in a newspaper contest and spontaneously spends it on a new, flashy sports car. This step is a radical one for the normally frugal Robinson, but it also goes against his regular practice of consulting his extremely sensible fiancée, Maud, before he takes action of any kind. His decision sets him on a course of adventure that changes the direction of his life.

Robinson, John The name used by Norman Gale while assisting Hercule Poirot in *Death in the Clouds*.

Robinson, Stella A "charming little bride" in "The Adventure of the Cheap Flat." She and her husband attend a party held by Gerald Parker at which she relates a peculiar story about the inexpensive flat she and her husband are able to rent in a fashionable London building. The story reaches Hercule Poirot, who suspects that a dark business lurks at the bottom of the tale.

Robson, Cornelia Ruth The traveling companion of Mrs. van Schuyler in *Death on the Nile.* A poor American who travels with Mrs. van Schuyler, a relative, out of the latter's kindness, Miss Robson journeys to Egypt and becomes caught up in the events on board the Nile steamer *Karnak* and in the murder of Linnet Doyle. While on board, she meets Dr. Bessner, and the two form a lasting attachment.

Rockford, Sterndale A partner of Andrew Pennington and an American trustee of Linnet Doyle's estate in *Death on the Nile.* He works with Pennington to defraud Mrs. Doyle of her estate, and they agree to send Pennington to Egypt to advance the plan.

Rogers, Captain A former military officer who, with his wife, attends a fancy dress party in "The Idol House of Astarte." They are described as "hard riding, weather-beaten people."

Rogers, Mrs. The mother of Michael Rogers in *Endless Night.* She has a "mouth like a rattletrap and eyes that [are] eternally suspicious."

Rogers, Ellie The wife of Michael Rogers in *Endless Night.* A young American heiress originally named Ellie Guteman, she meets Michael on the supposedly cursed plot of land called Gipsy's Acre and elopes with him without consulting her relatives. While their marriage is seemingly happy at first, strains soon develop, in large measure because of the presence of Ellie's old friend Greta. The curse of Gipsy's Acre seems to befall Ellie, climaxing in her death while riding, leaving Michael as her sole beneficiary.

Rogers, Ethel and Thomas Two of the doomed guests on Indian Island in *And Then There Were None.* Hired to serve as butler and cook for the other guests, they are not spared the brutal fate of all who set foot on the island. Thomas is hacked to death with a hatchet, and Ethel dies from an overdose of sleeping potion.

Rogers, Michael A charming and good-looking young man who marries the wealthy American heiress Ellie Guteman in *Endless Night.* Described as having no interests other than "seeing the world, and getting off with good-looking girls," Michael works as a chauffeur and meets Ellie one day on the supposedly cursed plot of land called Gipsy's Acre. He is warned about the Acre by an old gypsy woman named Lee and is told that if he stays on the land he will be doomed. In a whirlwind romance, Michael marries Ellie, who buys Gipsy's Acre for them so that they can build their dream house. Their marriage is initially happy, but the curse seems to make itself felt when Ellie suffers minor mishaps. Tension mounts as Ellie's old friend Greta begins influencing the house. The curse reaches its full horror when Ellie dies from a fall, leaving Michael the sole beneficiary of a massive estate.

Rolf, Gregory B. An American actor married to the film star Mary Marvell in "The Adventure of 'The Western Star.'" He supposedly purchased the fabulous diamond called the Western Star for his wife—the same jewel that becomes the target of a robbery and that bears a striking similarity to its companion gem, the Eastern Star.

Ronnie The name used by Adam Goodman while working at the Meadowbank School as a gardener in *Cat among the Pigeons.*

Rosalie The daughter of Deborah Beresford and the granddaughter of Tommy and Tuppence Beresford in *Postern of Fate.* Like her mother, Rosalie is a smart and precocious child.

Roscari, Signor An opera star in "Swan Song." He is scheduled to sing the role of Scarpia in *Tosca* with his fellow star Paula Nazorkoff in a private performance for Lady Rustonbury, but he falls ill on short notice from a mild case of food poisoning. As a result, Edouard Bréon is asked to take his place. It becomes a fateful substitution.

Roscheimer, Lady A wealthy but determined philanthropist in "Harlequin's Lane." She sponsors a special ballet performance to benefit the local village and thus makes possible the comeback performance of Anna Denman. The ballet proves to be a fateful one, for Anna Denman is reunited with the man she loved and lost years before.

Rose, Dr. An investigator into the paranormal and the village physician for Folbridge, Cornwall, in "The Hound of Death." He becomes obsessed with the strange case of Sister Marie Angelique, the nun who was apparently responsible for blowing up her own convent by summoning the hound of death. Rose manages to unlock the secrets of the nun, but his house is destroyed—with him in it—in an avalanche that sweeps his cottage into the sea.

Rosen, Dr. A German counterintelligence agent in "The Four Suspects." He has penetrated the inner circles of the secret terrorist organization called the *Schwarze Hand* in Germany and has been responsible for its collapse. A hunted man, he flees to England and settles in the small village of King's Gnaton, where he lives in deliberate obscurity. His enemies, however, track him down and murder him.

Rosen, Greta The niece of Dr. Rosen in "The Four Suspects." She is suspected of murdering her uncle on behalf of the secret German terrorist organization the *Schwarze Hand.* At the time of his death, however, she was supposedly in the garden planting some bulbs.

Rosentelle, Madame The owner of the London hair salon called Eugene and Rosenstelle in *Elephants Can Remember.* She sold four wigs to the person who is believed to have been Molly Ravenscroft, a fact of some importance in the resolution of the case.

Ross, Donald An actor who is invited as the thirteenth guest at the fateful dinner party of Sir Montagu Corner in *Lord Edgware Dies.* Al-

though he is self-centered, he is also a clever observer, taking note that another guest makes a significant slip in confusing the city of Paris with the Greek mythological figure of Paris. When the murderer realizes the significance of this error, it is not long before Donald Ross is himself murdered.

Rossakoff, Countess Vera A "whirlwind in human form" and a Russian émigré who may or may not be an authentic Russian countess, Vera Rossakoff holds a special place in the life of Hercule Poirot. She is the only woman known to have captured the heart of the Belgian detective and to have earned from him the complimentary appellation, "a remarkable woman."

Vera Rossakoff first meets Poirot in the case recounted in "The Double Clue," when she visits his offices in the hopes of clearing her friend Bernard Parker of the charge of theft. She swept into Poirot's rooms, "bringing with her a swirl of sables (it was as cold as only an English June day can be) and a hat rampant with slaughtered ospreys. Countess Vera Rossakoff was a somewhat disturbing personality."

At the end of "The Double Clue," Poirot predicts that they will meet again. His words prove prophetic during the Belgian's violent war against the vast criminal organization called the Big Four. Countess Rossakoff is found working as Madame Olivier's secretary under the name Inez Veroneau. The detective thus finds her in the heart of the Big Four and receives further confirmation of the fact—already well established in "The Double Clue"—that the countess has associations with and even membership in various nefarious societies in the criminal underworld. This does not prevent Poirot, of course, from returning Vera's son, Niki, to her, nor does it bring any lessening of his esteem and fondness for her. Indeed, the countess proved of great help to Hastings and Achille Poirot in bringing down the Big Four. At the end of the novel, it is intimated

Countess Vera Rossakoff (Kika Markham) and her great love, Hercule Poirot (David Suchet), in "The Double Clue." (Photofest; London Weekend Television)

that Poirot and the countess will eventually marry, although this does not happen.

Some years pass without any contact between Poirot and the countess. It thus comes as quite a shock to the Belgian to chance upon the countess in London while they are riding escalators going in opposite directions and to learn that he might find her in a place called Hell in "The Capture of Cerberus." Thanks to the ingenuity of Miss Lemon, it is determined that Hell is a trendy nightclub and that the countess is a part owner of it, along with the shady figure Paul Varesco. Once again, Poirot shatters a criminal conspiracy to which the countess has become an appendage, although in this case her complicity is quite without her knowledge. As ever, Poirot is there to ensure that she remains free of any possible legal entanglements. The last known communication between the two

ill-fated lovers is the announcement that Niki will wed. The detective sends her roses, but only partly as a token of congratulations to her son.

The relationship of Hercule Poirot and Countess Vera was dramatized elegantly and touchingly by London Weekend Television in the series *Agatha Christie's Poirot* starring David Suchet. In "The Double Clue," the role of Countess Vera is played beautifully by Kika Markham.

Rossiter, Edward   A young, "fair-haired, amiable young giant" who consults with Miss Marple in "Strange Jest." He is planning to wed his cousin, Charmian Stroud, and is relying upon a promised inheritance from their eccentric Uncle Mathew. When, however, Mathew dies, they discover that the well-to-do estate has no obvious tangible value. Desperate to find the inheritance, Edward and Charmian turn to Miss Marple.

Rouncewell, Mrs. (Rouncey) An acquaintance of the main character in *Unfinished Portrait*. She devotes much effort to cooking.

Rouselle, Mademeoiselle (Maddy) The one-time governess to Celia Ravenscroft and Dolly Jarrow in *Elephants Can Remember*. She is interviewed by Hercule Poirot and reveals to him that one of her former wards was prone to severe jealousy.

Rowan, Miss One of the instructors at the Meadowbank School in *Cat among the Pigeons*. She refuses to accept that Miss Springer could have been murdered, insisting that the gunshot was a suicide, despite the fact that the bullet was fired from a distance of more than four feet.

Rowe, Janet (Nannie) One of the members of the Leonides household in *Crooked House*. Called Nannie, she is firmly convinced that Aristide Leonides was murdered by either Catholics or Communists. Her theory is proven wrong when she drinks by accident a cup of cocoa intended for Sophia Leonides and dies from digitalin poisoning.

Rowland, George A young man seemingly down on his luck when he is fired by his uncle for laziness in "The Girl in the Train." George is soon embroiled in international intrigue when he meets the Grand Duchess Anastasia on a train and assists her in escaping the clutches of her evil relatives. George also aids his own country by recovering important plans of English harbor defenses from a spy. For his efforts, he wins the hand of a beautiful and wealthy noblewoman.

Rowlandson, Mr. The manager of the Royal Hotel Spa in *A Murder Is Announced*. The slain Rudi Scherz was one of his employees, and Rowlandson is able to provide details about the victim to the police.

Royde, Thomas The partner of Allen Drake in a Malaysian plantation in *Towards Zero*. He is called Taciturn Thomas and Silent Thomas because of his quiet and reserved manner; thus,

most of the socializing for the firm is conducted by Drake. Royde is also called the Hermit Crab because of the sideways motion he uses to walk, the result of an injury sustained during an earthquake.

Rubec, Dr. One of the members of the Brain Trust established by Mr. Aristides in *Destination Unknown*. A psychologist, he is in charge of giving psychological tests to all new employees and making profiles of them for the Trust.

Rudd, Jason (Jinks) The fifth husband of film star Marina Gregg and a movie director in *The Mirror Crack'd from Side to Side*. He is notably unattractive but apparently devoted to his wife.

Rudge, Franklin An American tourist in Monte Carlo in "The Soul of the Croupier."

Rumbolt, Mr. A gardener in *Unfinished Portrait*. Subject to severe depression, he becomes so distraught when his adultery is discovered that he hangs himself in the stable. His wife, unable to find him, asks for the help of the other members of the household.

Runcorn, Lady One of the suspects in the theft of a priceless necklace from the safe of Marcus Hardman in "The Double Clue." Lady Runcorn was present at the party hosted by Hardman on the night of the theft and was absent for a sufficient amount of time to be considered a suspect.

Russell, Miss The housekeeper in the Ackroyd household in *The Murder of Roger Ackroyd*. Extremely efficient, she is mentioned in the will of Roger Ackroyd and is left one thousand pounds. She is described as having "pinched lips and an acid smile."

Russell, Barton The widower husband of Iris Russell in "Yellow Iris." One evening, at a gathering of friends, his wife was poisoned while sitting at the dinner table. Russell reenacts the fateful evening four years later with surprising results.

Russell, Iris The wife of Barton Russell in "Yellow Iris." She is poisoned with strychnine one evening while dining with friends. Her husband re-creates the crime down to the very same entertainment four years later in order to try and catch the murderer. It is up to Hercule Poirot, however, to bring the murderer to justice.

Rustington, Janet   One of the guests at Isaac Pointz's party in "The Regatta Mystery." A writer of "high brow" literature, she attracts the attentions of Evan Llewellyn.

Rustonbury, Lady   A wealthy philanthropist in "Swan Song." She is responsible for organizing a special performance of *Tosca* and convinces the opera stars Paula Nazorkoff and Signor Roscari to sing. The festival is marked by a minor disaster and then a grand episode of revenge.

Ryan, William P.   A former war correspondent who reveals to Mr. Anstruther the first details about the mysterious Sister Marie Angelique in "The Hound of Death."

Rycroft, Mr.   An "elderly, dried-up man" and spiritualist in *The Sittaford Mystery.* A member of the Psychical Research Society, Rycroft takes part in the séance that reveals the murder of Captain Trevelyan. Rycroft lives in a bungalow on the Sittaford estate and thus feels responsible for finding Captain Trevelyan's murderer.

Ryder, Hank P.   A wealthy American in "The Crackler." He falls in love with Marguerite Laidlow.

Ryder, James Bell   The head of a company on the verge of bankruptcy who is flying to Paris to arrange a loan for his seemingly doomed company in *Death in the Clouds.* On board the flight, he sits in the seat directly in front of Madame Giselle. He sells his "eye-witness" account to reporters and uses the financial windfall to save his company from ruin.

Rydesdale, Chief George   The chief constable of Middleshire who takes part in the investigation into the murder of Rudi Scherz in *A Murder Is Announced.*

Ryland, Abe   One of the wealthiest men in the world, "richer even than Rockefeller," in *The Big Four.* Known as the Soap King, Ryland is also a member of the Big Four, an international criminal organization. His symbol is the dollar sign with a star and two stripes. He hires Hercule Poirot to assist his business interests in Rio de Janeiro, but the detective is able to perceive his real intentions.

Rymer, Amelia   Also known as Mrs. Abner Rymer, a wealthy widow who comes to Mr. Parker Pyne for advice in "The Case of the Rich Woman": "If you're any good at all you'll tell me how to spend my money!" A onetime worker in a farmhouse, Amelia wed Abner Rymer—a workman in the mills in the area— and helped him become a success despite the many hardships they endured, including the death of all four of their children. Abner eventually died from a weak chest at the age of forty-three. Despite her very considerable wealth, Amelia is miserable and desires a change. For the fee of one thousand pounds, payable in advance, Parker Pyne transforms Amelia into Hannah Moorhouse, a simple farm laborer. To her surprise, Amelia grows to love her new life. (See also Constantine, Dr.)

Sainsbury Seale, Mabelle   The third victim of murder in *One, Two, Buckle My Shoe.* She had previously worked in India as a teacher but had also been an actress. She knows too much from the past, for which she is brutally murdered, and her body dumped in a flat at King Leopold Mansions. The buckle on her shoe is of great importance to the resolution of the case by Hercule Poirot.

Saint Alard, Monsieur de   A wealthy Belgian aristocrat and ardent defender of the Catholic faith in "The Chocolate Box." He had both the means and the opportunity to murder Paul Déroulard and was thus a leading suspect, in the view of Hercule Poirot.

Saintclair, Valerie   A rising dancer and the fiancée of Prince Paul of Maurania in "The King of Clubs." She becomes embroiled in murder during a visit to the home of the impresario Harry Reedburn. She apparently discovers him dead and staggers to the home of his next-door neighbors, the Oglanders, where she collapses on their floor. As the murder might scandalize her career, Prince Paul asks Poirot to undertake an investigation.

Salmon, Sir Joseph   The real name of Sir Herman Cohen in "The Affair at the Bungalow." He is having an affair with the wife of Jane Helier's former husband.

Samoushenka, Katrina   A brilliant dancer from Russia in "The Arcadian Deer." The daughter of a Leningrad taxi driver, Katrina traveled the world as a famed performer, but she eventually retired from public life when she contracted tuberculosis. Hercule Poirot paid her an important visit during his search for the lost love of Ted Williamson, brining the dancer a chance for hope and happiness. She had an affair with Sir George Sanderfield.

Sampson, Mr.   The oldest resident of St. Mary Mead. Sampson is ninety-six years old and takes enormous pride in being the most venerable person in the village. In *The Mirror Crack'd from Side to Side,* he notes, with remarkable accuracy, that the fund-raiser for the St. John's Ambulance Brigade at Gossington Hall will be marked by "a lot of wickedness." In fact, the gala is marked by murder.

Samuelson, Mrs.   A dog owner in "The Nemean Lion." Mrs. Samuelson has her beloved Pekingese, Nanki Poo, kidnapped and then pays the demanded ransom. In a clever trick, the parcel containing her money is replaced by the dognappers with a similar one stuffed not with money but with blank sheets of paper.

Sanchia   One of the names used by Madeleine de Sara in her role as "Queen of the Vamps." (See de Sara, Madeleine.)

Sandbourne, Mrs.   The tour guide for visitors to the gardens and houses of Britain in *Nemesis.* She is capable in her job, but she also devotes a great deal of effort to making certain that all participants in the tour, including Miss Marple, feel that they are actually taking part.

Sandbourne, William   See St. John, Walter Edmund.

Sandeman, Sir Edwin   A Harley Street physician in *A Pocket Full of Rye.* He is summoned to the offices of Rex Fortescue when the effects of poison begin to manifest themselves. Alas, he arrives too late to be of any possible help to Fortescue.

Sanderfield, Sir George   A man of great wealth who has an affair with Katrina Samoushenka in "The Arcadian Deer." He is "a short square man with dark coarse hair and a roll of fat in his neck." He is also an unpleasant personality, and Katrina does not love him.

Sanders, Gladys   The wife of Jack Sanders in "A Christmas Tragedy." She is a young woman utterly devoted to her husband, much to the concern of Miss Marple, who is convinced that Jack has dark and sinister plans for her. Within a short time, Gladys is brutally murdered, but her husband has an apparently airtight alibi.

Sanders, Jack   The husband of Gladys Sanders in "A Christmas Tragedy." Miss Marple becomes instantly suspicious of him: "Mr. Sanders was a big, good-looking, florid-faced man, very hearty in his manner and popular with all. And nobody could have been pleasanter to his wife than he was. But I knew! He meant to make away with her." Exactly as predicted, Mrs. Sanders is soon murdered, but Jack has an airtight alibi, and even Miss Marple is hard-pressed to shatter it.

Sandford, Dr.   A young physician in *The Mirror Crack'd from Side to Side.* He joins the practice of Dr. Haydock and attempts to bring a dose of modernity to the care of patients in the village. This earns the stern disapproval of Miss Marple, who complains that Sandford is the same as all young doctors: "Medicine nowadays is just like a supermarket—all packaged up."

Sandford, Rex   A young architect from London who spent time in St. Mary Mead in "Death by Drowning." During that time, he had a romance with Rose Emmott and became the father of her child. The pregnant young woman, however, is found drowned, and Rex is considered the prime suspect. Sir Henry Clithering describes him as "a tall young man, very fair and very thin. His eyes were blue and dreamy, his hair was untidy and rather too long. His speech was a little too ladylike." He was also afraid that his fiancée in London would learn of his affair, giving Rex an obvious motive for the crime.

Sanseverato, Rebecca The second wife of Alistair Blunt in *One, Two, Buckle My Shoe.* She receives a variety of surprises in the course of Hercule Poirot's investigation into the murders of Dr. Morley and others.

Santonix, Rudolf A very popular architect in *Endless Night.* He is in high demand for his work, but he maintains strict control over the choice of projects he will undertake. His last project proves perhaps his greatest accomplishment—the house on Gipsy's Acre for Ellie and Michael Rogers. The house is completed just before his death, and is inhabited with happiness for only a brief amount of time.

San Veratrino, Marchese di The original owner of the infamous Borgia goblet in "The Apples of the Hesperides." The goblet is stolen from his estate by a gang of thieves and delivered into the possession of Emery Power.

Sarah The name of two women appearing in mysteries. The first is a young student of the occult in "The Bird with the Broken Wing." She oversees a memorable session with the Ouija board that also involves Mr. Satterthwaite and Mr. Harley Quin. Through her efforts, Satterthwaite is contacted by Harley Quin and sent out on an important mission. The second Sarah is a family cook in *Unfinished Portrait.* She is utterly devoted to the family and carries with her to the grave the truth about a daughter to whom she gave birth six decades before.

Satipy The wife of Yahmose in *Death Comes As the End.* An attractive woman in "a hard, commanding kind of way," she nevertheless possesses a fearsome personality and is ever eager to find fault. She becomes the second victim of a murderer.

SATTERTHWAITE, MR. An urbane, sophisticated, and snobbish connoisseur of the arts who is also a friend of Hercule Poirot and a frequent agent and assistant of the mysterious Mr. Harley Quin. Satterthwaite describes himself as having "neither chick nor child" and is an avowed bachelor; his one well-established relative is his goddaughter, Lillian Gilliat. Satterthwaite enjoys the company of his many friends, especially those of social prominence, but he has a special fondness for Hercule Poirot and Harley Quin. Among his most cherished hobbies are music, amateur photography, the arts, fine dining, and writing; he authored the book *Homes of My Friends.* His favorite restaurant is Arlecchino.

Satterthwaite is primarily known for his association with Hercule Poirot and Quin. Poirot said of him: "He has the playgoer's mind; he observes the characters, he has the sense of atmosphere." Satterthwaite assisted Poirot at least twice, in *Three-Act Tragedy* and "Dead Man's Mirror."

His relationship with Harley Quin is far more complex: "His role was that of the looker on, and he knew it, but sometimes, when in the company of Mr. Quin, he had the illusion of being an actor—and the principal actor at that." In the cases involving Harley Quin, Satterthwaite plays a primary role as the instrument of the elusive Quin. Normally, Satterthwaite is brought into a situation by circumstances that are subtly and curiously arranged by Quin. Satterthwaite then uses his knowledge of people, his attention to detail, and his willingness to be guided and informed by Quin to solve assorted murders, mysteries, and long-standing personal tragedies. In each instance, however, Harley Quin is the catalyst of the involvement and is there at the end to congratulate the investigator, to frame the events philosophically, and to impart one final bit of magic. Satterthwaite is always rather in awe of Quin, but he is never overawed.

Invariably, Quin's arrival in a case is perfectly timed to coincide with the discovery of the last of the puzzle pieces by Satterthwaite. It takes Quin, of course, to ask a few well-placed questions before Satterthwaite can pull all of the clues together and discover for himself the solution to the case, which has been known by Quin all along.

Saunders, Doris A sculptor's model in *The Hollow*. Although she is attractive, she is also "a common mean spiteful little piece." She poses for Henrietta Savernake, but the creations for which she models are destroyed by the artists out of frustration.

Savage, John A wealthy but terminally ill cancer patient in *Why Didn't They Ask Evans?* He apparently commits suicide, as there is no hope of recovery, but his old friend Alan Carstairs has a difficult time accepting the idea that Savage might have died by his own hand. The questions asked about Savage's will prove important to the resolution of the case, especially the eyewitness account provided by the onetime parlor maid Gladys Evans, who found Savage's body.

Savaronoff, Dr. One of the aliases assumed by Claud Darrell in *The Big Four*. As Savaronoff, Darrell pretends to be a Russian chess champion.

Savernake, Henrietta A moody and frustrated sculptress in *The Hollow*. She specializes in *avant-garde* pieces as well as more traditional styles, using the nasty Doris Saunders as her model. Distraught over the death of John Christow, however, she is prone to mood swings, including the destruction of her own creations.

Sayers, Maggie The true name of the "Queen of the Vamps," Madeleine de Sara, in *Parker Pyne Investigates*. As her name would indicate, she is from a middle-class English family rather than the exotic parentage implied by her adopted name.

Scheele, Anna The sister-in-law of Dr. John Pauncefoot and the private secretary to Otto Morganthal in *They Came to Baghdad*. She undertakes to investigate a group of subversives in the area.

Scherz, Rudi The first victim of murder in *A Murder Is Announced*. Described as "a very ordinary pleasant young chap," Rudi is also suspected of stealing from his place of employment, the Royal Spa Hotel. Scherz is shot to death at Little Paddocks soon after placing an advertisement in the Chipping Cleghorn *Gazette* announcing that a murder would take place at 6:30 P.M. at Little Paddocks. His death is only the first of several murders.

Schlagal, Herr A German-born pilot in "The House at Shiraz." He is working for an air service in Baghdad and meets Mr. Parker Pyne in Tehran. His description of the peculiar events surrounding the two English ladies in Shiraz, Lady Esther Carr and her maid, Muriel King, are important factors in Parker Pyne's subsequent visit to Shiraz and his curiosity about the beautiful house occupied by the elusive English ladies. Part of the German's acute interest in the English ladies is his love for Muriel King, the doomed maid.

Schlieder, Anna and Freda A Dutch mother and daughter in *Giant's Bread*. They give help—at the risk of their own lives—to Vernon Deyre, who has recently escaped from a prison camp.

Schmidt, Fraulein Hildegarde The maid and companion to Princess Dragomiroff in *Murder on the Orient Express*. As Poirot investigates the murder of Ratchett, it is learned that Fraulein Schmidt has a connection to the doomed Armstrong family. She had worked as a cook in the Armstrong household.

Schneider, Mr. An American archaeologist and the representative of New York's Metropolitan Museum on the expedition to uncover the tomb of King Men-her-Ra in "The Adventure of the Egyptian Tomb." He becomes one of the victims of that ill-fated effort, dying in agony from tetanus.

Schuster, Mr. One of the attorneys in the law firm representing the interests of Jason Rafiel in *Nemesis*. He is involved in the execution of Rafiel's will and thus comes into contact with Miss Marple. He confesses that the provisions strike him as strange, especially the ones relating to Miss Marple. However, Mr. Broadribb, the senior partner, has a different view.

Schwartz, Mr. An American tourist who finds himself at the mountain resort of Rochers Neiges at the worst possible time in "The Erymanthian Boar." He proves of great value to Hercule Poirot, even saving the life of the detective when the members of the Marrascaud gang attempt to murder him.

Schwartz, Gertrud The old German servant in the employ of Dr. Rosen in "The Four Suspects." She has been in the service of Dr. Rosen for nearly forty years; nevertheless, she is a suspect in his murder. She claims to have been in the kitchen with the door closed at the time of his death and that thus she heard nothing.

Scott, Moira O'Connell The newlywed wife of Richard Scott in "Shadow on the Glass." She has beautiful red hair that "stood out round her small face like a saint's halo." Moira journeys to Greenways House with her husband for a visit that is marked by tragedy when she becomes a victim of murder. She is shot to death in the garden while in the embrace of another man.

Scott, Richard An adventurer and hunter who travels for a visit to Greenways House in "Shadow on the Glass." Scott arrives with his new, young, and beautiful wife, Moira, but he is also concerned about the tension level at the gathering, as there are dark and grim memories from the past that come to the surface. His concerns are seemingly confirmed when Moira is shot to death in the garden while in the arms of another man.

Scudamore, Joan The main character in *Absent in the Spring*. A domineering and grasping middle-aged woman, she journeys to Iraq to visit her daughter and then finds herself stranded for several days at Tell Abu Hamid, near the Turkish border. There, forced to do nothing but wait, she reviews her life and her actions, realizing that she has long controlled the lives and happiness of her husband, Rodney, and her children. The days alone with her thoughts spark a determination to change her ways, and she returns to England a new person. Her resolve to be different, however, proves tragically short-lived.

Scudamore, Rodney The long-suffering husband of Joan Scudamore in *Absent in the Spring*. An attorney by profession, Rodney would give virtually anything to be free of his job, as he hates being a lawyer; he would much rather be a farmer. His wife, of course, will not permit him to realize his dreams. When Joan is stranded in Mesopotamia and reflects on her life, she realizes that Rodney was more than relieved to see her depart.

Scudamore, Tony The son of Joan and Rodney Scudamore in *Absent in the Spring*. His mother attempts to dominate his life, as she has done with everyone else in the family, but he proves too determined for Joan. Against his mother's wishes, Tony moves to South Africa and runs an orange grove.

Scuttle, Mr. The head of the real estate firm for which James Bentley once worked in *Mrs. McGinty's Dead*. He is visited by Hercule Poirot as the detective investigates details about Bentley, and initially believes the Belgian to be a hotel manager or the owner of a restaurant.

Sedgwick, Miss The former secretary to Mrs. Ariadne Oliver in *Elephants Can Remember*. She is replaced by Miss Livingstone and is much missed by her employer, as the new secretary displays none of Miss Sedgwick's efficiency or flair for organization.

Sedgwick, Lady Bess The mother of Elvira Blake and a devoted adventuress in *At Bertram's Hotel*. A well-known figure, Lady Sedgwick has been married three times, but only one of her

Lady Bess Sedgwick (Caroline Blakiston) in At Bertram's Hotel. *(Photofest)*

marriages was legitimate. She has also had little to do with her daughter over the years, as she could not bring herself to settle down and commit herself to motherhood. Nevertheless, she loves Elvira and grows concerned about the sudden appearance of Michael Gorman—one of her former husbands—and the impact it might have on Elvira. Soon after his appearance, Michael is shot to death. Lady Sedgwick herself dies in a suitably melodramatic fashion.

Sedley, Amelia Mary   A witness at the trial of Elinor Carlisle in *Sad Cypress*. She reveals details about Mary Draper.

Segrave, John   A young man whose story is recounted in "The House of Dreams." The son of Sir Edward Segrave, John is visited by a recurring dream about a white house, a perfect place that beckons him but slowly corrodes his relationships with others and wrecks any true chance for happiness. When he goes off to Africa, he succumbs to fever and has, at last, a chance to enter the white house of his dreams.

Seminoff, Olga   The au pair in the service of Mrs. Llewellyn-Smythe in *Hallowe'en Party*. She forged a codicil to Mrs. Llewellyn-Smythe's will and continued to insist that she was owed money even after the codicil was declared a forgery. Olga disappeared soon afterward.

Serakis, Catherine   An employee of the Olive Branch in *They Came to Baghdad*. She serves as secretary to the company and is also romantically attached to Edward Goring.

Serrocold, Carrie Louise   The wife of Lewis Serrocold, the sister of Ruth van Rydock, and a longtime friend of Miss Marple in *They Do It with Mirrors*. Louise resides at Stonygate, in Market Kimble, where her husband has converted their estate into a reform school for delinquent boys. Her life on the estate is far from happy, however, as her own health is failing and the school seems on the verge of financial collapse. Miss Marple is asked by Ruth to visit Carrie Louise and determine if she is in any danger. Carrie Louise is seemingly oblivious to the potential disasters threatening the school.

Serrocold, Lewis   The husband of Carrie Louise Serrocold in *They Do It with Mirrors*. Always hoping to help society, Lewis manages to turn their estate at Stonygate, in Market Kimble, into a reform school for delinquent boys. There is growing question, however, as to the financial health of the institution, and Serrocold faces a stern series of tests from the trustees, especially Christian Gulbrandsen. Adding to the difficulty of the situation is the deteriorating health of his wife, a potentially fatal situation that draws the attention of Miss Marple, an old friend of Carrie Louise.

Sessle, Captain Anthony   A partner in an insurance firm and the victim of murder in "The Sunningdale Mystery." A onetime soldier, he is murdered by having a hat pin thrust into his heart and is found dead on the seventh tee. His death is investigated by Tommy and Tuppence Beresford.

Settle, Dr. The physician to Arthur Carmichael in "The Strange Case of Sir Arthur Carmichael." He attempts to treat the unusual Arthur Carmichael, who suffers from a form of dementia that makes him manifest the characteristics of a cat. In order to advance his care of Carmichael, Settle consults the psychiatrist Dr. Edward Carstairs.

Shaista, Princess A woman who claims to have been engaged to Prince Ali Yusef of Ramat in *Cat among the Pigeons*. Her claim is put to the test when her uncle, Emir Ibrahim, arrives for a visit. Curiously, she disappears just before her uncle's arrival.

Shaitana, Mr. The enigmatic and rather menacing victim of murder in *Cards on the Table*. Shaitana is a man "of whom nearly everybody was a little afraid," in large measure because he "knew a little too much about everybody." Nevertheless, he throws parties that are normally very well attended, "large parties, small parties, macabre parties, respectable parties, and definitely queer parties." He meets Hercule Poirot at an exhibit of snuffboxes at Wessex House and invites the detective to dinner, offering an absolutely irresistible incentive: In attendance, Shaitana assures him, will be four murderers, all of whom successfully eluded justice. Poirot attends the gathering and is thus on hand when one of the four criminals calmly murders Shaitana while everyone else is playing bridge. Shaitana is found sitting in a chair by the fire stabbed to death with a dagger decorated with jewels.

Shane, Michael The husband of Rosamund Abernethie Shane in *After the Funeral*. Although he is married, he is not faithful, and prefers the attentions of Sorrell Dainton.

Shane, Rosamund Abernethie The wife of the unfaithful Michael Shane in *After the Funeral*. An actress described as "not conspicuous for brains," Rosamund is nevertheless clever enough to observe that Hercule Poirot is impersonating Monsieur Pontarlier.

Shannon, Christine A beautiful but remarkably vapid blonde in *Sparkling Cyanide*. Described as "dumber than you'd believe possible except where money is concerned," she is a guest at the fateful party at the Luxembourg restaurant hosted by George Barton and was seated next to him.

Shapland, Ann The secretary to Miss Bulstrode at the Meadowbank School in *Cat among the Pigeons*. She is skilled in the field of dancing and was a very successful cabaret performer under the name of Señora Angelica de Toredo. Dennis Rathbone is almost desperate to marry her, but she declines his repeated offers, as she finds him "very dull."

Sharpe, Inspector An official of Scotland Yard in *Hickory Dickory Dock*. He proves very cooperative with Hercule Poirot in investigating the bloody events at the youth hostel operated by Mrs. Nicoletis.

Shaw, Dr. The local physician for the community surrounding Gipsy's Acre in *Endless Night*. Known as Leave-it-to-Nature-Shaw, he is very old-fashioned in his ways, preferring to let nature takes its course in healing a patient. He is called upon twice to treat Ellie Rogers. The first time, he examines her sprained ankle, but the second time he must determine the hour of her death.

Shaw, Mr. One of the joint managers of the London and Scottish Bank in "The Million-Dollar Bond Robbery." He was supposed to be responsible for transporting a million dollars' worth of bonds from London to New York on board the *Olympia*. Unfortunately, a case of severe bronchitis incapacitated him on the very day that the he was to sail; Philip Ridgeway took the bonds instead, and the securities were stolen.

Sheldon, Rose A chambermaid in *At Bertram's Hotel*. She is interviewed by the police concerning the disappearance of Canon Pennyfeather. Miss Sheldon was an actress before taking a position in the hotel.

Sheppard, Caroline The sister of Dr. James

Sheppard in *The Murder of Roger Ackroyd.* She is an intelligent and inquisitive young woman who becomes fascinated with the goings-on in the little village of King's Abbot, especially the death of Mrs. Ferrars and the murder of Roger Ackroyd. Her brother is determined not to encourage her, but he admits that she "can do any amount of finding out sitting placidly at home." It thus comes as a genuine pleasure to Caroline that her next-door neighbor should be none other than Hercule Poirot. Caroline provides the detective with valuable information throughout the case.

Sheppard, Dr. James The brother of Caroline Sheppard and a friend and physician to the doomed Roger Ackroyd in *The Murder of Roger Ackroyd.* Dr. Sheppard also serves as the narrator of the events recounted in the novel. He details the tragedies that occur in the village of King's Abbot, including the deaths of two of his patients, Mrs. Ferrars and Roger Ackroyd. He discourages the intense curiosity of his sister about the deaths, proclaiming her theories concerning Mrs. Ferrars to be nonsense. Sheppard also has frequent dealings throughout the investigation with Hercule Poirot, his next-door neighbor, and is fortunate enough to have a close-up view of the Belgian detective's "little grey cells" at work.

Sherston, Captain Charles An employee of a bank in *Absent in the Spring.* He is sent to prison for embezzling money. His wife is Leslie Sherston.

Sherston, Leslie The wife of the embezzler Captain Charles Sherston in *Absent in the Spring.* She is criticized by Joan Scudamore for being unpunctual, but Rodney Scudamore considers her a distinctly courageous woman in facing the hardship of having her husband sent to prison. Leslie dies from cancer.

Shoreham, Robert (Robbie) A physicist in *Passenger to Frankfurt.* He develops a unique gas that completely changes the personalities of those who inhale it, making them become kind and generous. Rather than allow it to be mis-used, Shoreham gives the gas, under the title of Project Benvo, to the British government.

Shrivenham, Lionel An official of the British embassy in Baghdad in *They Came to Baghdad.* He is in danger of being fired because of his incompetence.

Simmons, Archdeacon A clergyman and friend of Canon Pennyfeather in *At Bertram's Hotel.* He grows alarmed when the canon fails to arrive as expected. Eventually, he realizes that the chronically absentminded cleric is not merely lost but is actually missing.

Simmons, Julia The name used by Emma Stamfordis when she tries to insinuate herself into the social circle to which Letitia and Charlotte Blacklock belong in *A Murder Is Announced.*

Simmons, Patrick An engineering student and a cousin of Letitia Blacklock in *A Murder Is Announced.* He lives at Little Paddocks while attending college and becomes a suspect in the murder of Rudi Scherz.

Simone, Madame The most successful psychic of her time in "The Last Séance." For many years, she has demonstrated enormous skill in conducting séances and serving as a medium. These have come at a fearsome cost, however, and she is worn out. Nevertheless, she is engaged to undertake one last séance, for Madame Exe, in the hopes of contacting Exe's dead daughter. The séance proves a shocking one.

Simpson, Mr. One of the lodgers in the home of Mr. and Mrs. Todd in "The Adventure of the Clapham Cook."

Simpson, Lieutenant Alec, R.N. An officer in the Royal Navy in "The Plymouth Express." He makes the gruesome discovery of the strangled corpse of Flossie Carrington under his seat in the train compartment.

Simpson, Alexander The owner of an art gallery in "The Girdle of Hippolita." He requests the assistance of Hercule Poirot when a fabulously expensive Rubens painting is stolen from his gallery. The detective manages to recover the painting and to solve one other interesting mystery that is also part of the theft.

Sims, Inspector A police officer in charge of the investigation into the murder of Miss Barrowby in "How Does Your Garden Grow?" He cooperates with Hercule Poirot and expresses a certain sympathy for the difficult position of Katrina Rieger, the Russian exile and chief suspect in the crime.

Sims, Mr. An interior decorator in *Sleeping Murder*. He is hired by Gwenda Reed to decorate the home that she recently purchased. He has a sultry, nearly hypnotic voice.

Sims, Doris One of the models hired by Ambrosine, Ltd., in *Three-Act Tragedy*. She provides information to Hercule Poirot about the dressmaking company and its owner, Cynthia Dacres.

Skillicorn, Mrs. The housekeeper to Myles Mylecharane on the Isle of Skye in "Manx Gold." She is a grim woman who nevertheless provides the first clues to Juan Faraker and Fenella Mylecharane in their hunt to locate their late uncle's treasure.

Skinner, Emily The sister of Lavinia Skinner in "The Case of the Perfect Maid." She is rarely seen by others because of the supposedly precarious state of her health, and she stays in bed for much of the time. She is "a thin, indecisive-looking creature, with a good deal of grayish yellow hair untidily wound around her head and erupting into curls, the whole thing looking like a bird's nest of which no self-respecting bird could be proud."

Skinner, Lavinia The sister of Emily Skinner in "The Case of the Perfect Maid." She is "a tall, gaunt, bony female of fifty" and has a "gruff voice and an abrupt manner." Lavinia fires Gladys Holmes from her position as maid over a missing brooch and considers herself wildly fortunate to have found Mary Higgins, an apparently perfect domestic servant.

Slack, Inspector An overly officious police inspector who handles cases that, in published form, also involve Miss Marple. Slack heads up or takes part in the investigations recounted in "The Case of the Perfect Maid," *The Murder at the Vicarage, The Body in the Library,* and "The Tape-Measure Murder."

A member of the Much Benham police department, he makes little effort to conceal his general dislike of Miss Marple, relying at times on her skillful deductions but giving her little thanks or appreciation. As for Miss Marple, she sums him up by observing that "Inspector Slack—well, he's exactly like the young lady in the boot shop who wants to sell you patent leather because she's got it in your size, and doesn't take any notice of the fact that you want brown calf." One case that especially demonstrated Slack's habits and efforts to show that he "determinedly strove to contradict his name" was the murder of Colonel Protheroe in *The Murder at the Vicarage*.

Inspector Slack is one of the primary police officials used in the television adaptations of Miss Marple mysteries, especially those starring Joan Hickson. He is played with considerable vigor by David Horovitch in those productions.

Slicker, Mr. The partner of Mr. Lovebody in the Market Basing real estate firm of Lovebody and Slicker in *By the Pricking of My Thumbs*. He is visited by Tuppence Beresford and provides her with assorted bits of information about the house that is featured in the painting, *House by a Canal*. He is a relatively young man dressed in tweed, with "horsy checks."

Smethurst, Captain A member of the party traveling from Damascus to Baghdad in "The Gate of Baghdad." Described as "a young man of somewhat slow intellect," he recognizes the hunted criminal financier Samuel Long and is murdered before he can report him to authorities in Baghdad.

Smith, Ivor An investigator and friend of Tommy Beresford in *By the Pricking of My*

Thumbs. He assists Tommy with information concerning Mr. Eccles.

Smith, Nurse Janet   An old friend of Tuppence Beresford in "A Pot of Tea." She worked with Tuppence during World War I as a nurse. Years later, she works in Madame Violette's hat shop and desires the hand in marriage of Lawrence St. Vincent. Nurse Smith inexplicably disappears, and St. Vincent turns to Tommy and Tuppence Beresford to find her. The matter is an easy one for Tuppence, but Tommy goes to extraordinary and ultimately unnecessary lengths.

Snell   A butler to the Chevenix-Gore household in "Dead Man's Mirror." He is of "imposing proportions," and displays a large measure of pomposity in the execution of his duties.

Sobek   The second-oldest son of Imhotep in *Death Comes As the End.* He is married to Kait, but he also proves relentlessly unfaithful. Thus, when he dies from a cup of poisoned wine, Kait displays no remorse about his murder.

Solomon, Mr.   The apparent proprietor of a bookstore in *The Clocks.* He is elderly, "with a flat face like a stuffed fish." He is not quite what he seems, however, for the store he runs is actually a front for operations conducted by the special branch of British intelligence.

Somers, Miss   A typist in the Consolidated Investments Trust owned by Rex Fortescue in *A Pocket Full of Rye.* A recent hire, she displays little skill in typing.

Sonia   Secretary to Sir Roderick Horsefield, a soldier, in *Third Girl.* She is supposed to assist Sir Roderick with his memoirs, but she is suspected of espionage when some sensitive papers disappear. By the end of the story, she has accepted the soldier's hand in marriage.

Sopworth, Claud   Described as someone possessed "of no moral worth whatsoever," he is a rival to James Bond in "The Rajah's Emerald." He pursues Bond's girlfriend, Grace, with considerable enthusiasm and seemingly has an insuperable advantage over Bond because of his wealth.

Southwood, The Honourable Joanna   The cousin of Tim Allerton and a longtime friend of Linnet Doyle in *Death on the Nile.* Her name is used by Allerton to introduce himself to Doyle in Egypt. Miss Southwood is a wealthy but very bored socialite who is utterly faithless when disasters of any kind strike her friends. She was also once involved in some robberies, but only because she was so incredibly bored.

Spalding, Caroline   The name used by Caroline Crale before her marriage to Amyas Crale in *Five Little Pigs.*

Speeder, Carol   A member of a group associated with the United Nations in *Destination Unknown.* She is one of the last people to see the physicist Thomas Betterton before his disappearance.

Spence, Mrs.   One of the guests at the party hosted by Major Rich in "The Mystery of the Baghdad Chest." At that party, Edward Clayton was murdered and placed in a chest in Rich's living room—the same room where the guests are dancing and drinking.

Spence, Superintendent   The chief police officer of the Oatshire branch in *Taken at the Flood.* He heads up the investigation into the murder of Enoch Arden. He should not be confused with Superintendent Bert Spence.

Spence, Superintendent Bert   The head of the Kilchester police and a longtime associate and friend of Hercule Poirot. Spence had worked with Poirot on a number of earlier, albeit unreported, cases and took part with the Belgian in the investigations recounted in *Hallowe'en Party, Elephants Can Remember,* and *Mrs. McGinty's Dead.* In the latter case, Spence approached Poirot in the hopes that the detective might help clear the convicted and condemned James Bentley, as Spence was convinced that he had not murdered Mrs. McGinty. Upon his retirement, he went to live with his sister in Woodleigh Common. Spence was described as a "good honest police officer of the old type. No graft. No violence. Not stupid either. Straight as a die."

Spence, Jeremy The husband of Linda Spence in "The Mystery of the Spanish Chest." He and his wife attend a party hosted by Major Rich, the owner of a Spanish chest. Unbeknownst to the guests, the chest contains the corpse of Arnold Clayton.

Spence, Linda The wife of Jeremy Spence in "The Mystery of the Spanish Chest." She and her husband attend a party thrown by Major Rich. In the room where the guests are making merry is the Spanish chest, which contains the corpse of Arnold Clayton. Linda is a sharp woman, and makes several keen observations to Hercule Poirot. She intimates that Rich and Mrs. Clayton were having an affair, but, even more important, she expresses the view that the whole situation reminds her of *Othello*. This idea proves of great importance to Poirot.

Spender, Mr. A friend of Jack Sander in "A Christmas Tragedy." He is able to give testimony to the police regarding Sander's whereabouts at the time of his wife's death.

Spenlow, Mrs. A victim of murder in "The Tape-Measure Murder." She previously owned a flower shop in London but moved to St. Mary Mead with her husband. Not long after, she was strangled to death. Her husband is Arthur Spenlow.

Spenlow, Arthur The husband of Mrs. Spenlow in "The Tape-Measure Murder." He moved with his wife from London to St. Mary Mead, giving up his profession as a jeweler to spend his days as a gardener. This is found to be most doubtful in Miss Marple's opinion, and, when his wife is murdered, Arthur becomes an obvious suspect.

Spenser, Miss A counselor at Guildric's Agency in *They Came to Baghdad*. On the basis of her entirely fraudulent references and résumé, Victoria Jones is advised by Miss Spenser about the availability of positions as a woman's companion in the Middle East.

Spent, Gladys The head of the maids in the household of Simeon Lee in *Hercule Poirot's Christmas*.

Spiess, Herr Heinrich The chancellor of Germany in *Passenger to Frankfurt*. He attempts to put an end to the massive student unrest in Germany that is part of a wider plot of social upheaval.

Spragg, Absalom The husband of the American medium Eurydice Spragg in "Motive vs. Opportunity." He is "a thin, lank man with a melancholy expression and extremely furtive eyes."

Spragg, Eurydice An American spiritualist in "Motive vs. Opportunity." She "a stout woman of middle age, dressed in a flamboyant style. Very full of cant phrases about 'our dear ones who have passed over,' and other things of the kind." As a result of her apparent ability to contact Simon Clode's dear granddaughter beyond the grave, she gains near complete ascendancy over the old man and is named his principal heir in a new will.

Spragge, Frederick A senior partner in a law firm in *Why Didn't They Ask Evans?* A smooth and cunning attorney, Spragge is able to finagle details about the private lives of his clients, especially the members of the aristocracy.

Sprig, Mr. A real estate agent in *By the Pricking of My Thumbs*. An elderly curmudgeon, he is interviewed by Tuppence Beresford concerning Watermead House, and expresses his personal opinion on the "foolishness of women."

Springer, Grace The first of three victims of murder at the Meadowbank School in *Cat among the Pigeons*. The director of Meadowbank's department of physical education, she was known and much disliked by the other faculty for having the "manners of a pig." She takes particular delight in tormenting her fellow teachers, and especially enjoys revealing humiliating secrets from their pasts. She is shot to death inside the school's sports pavilion.

Sprot, Betty The original name of Betty Beresford, the adopted daughter of Tommy and Tuppence Beresford in *N or M?* and *Postern of Fate*. She had a tragic childhood; the daughter of a Polish refugee, she was sold to another woman after arriving penniless in England. Betty comes close to death in *N or M?* after her real mother is shot in the head, but she survives and is adopted by Tommy and Tuppence. (For other details, see Beresford, Betty.)

Sprot, Millicent   An Englishwoman in *N or M?* who is apparently the adoptive mother of Betty Sprot. She is a seemingly devoted mother, but, as the case progresses, it becomes clear that in many ways Millicent is not the person she claims to be.

Stamfordis, Emma Jocelyn   The sister of Pip and the great-niece of Belle Goedler in *A Murder Is Announced.* She stands to inherit a sizable estate after the eventual death of Letitia Blacklock. Should Letitia die before Emma's great-aunt Belle, Emma and her sister will each inherit one half of the estate. In order to keep an eye on the other relative mentioned in the will, Emma manages to insinuate herself into the Blacklock household at Little Paddocks under an assumed name. When murder strikes in the house, Emma's secret is revealed and she becomes a suspect in the crimes.

Stamfordis, Pip   See Haymes, Phillipa.

Stamfordis, Sybil Diana Helen   One of the sinister characters in *The Pale Horse.* Sybil is a purported psychic, "with dark, rather greasy hair, a simpering expression, and a fish-like mouth." She lives at the Pale Horse inn with the medium Thyrza Grey and the self-proclaimed witch Bella Webb. Sybil and the others are investigated by Mark Easterbrook.

Stanislaus, Count   One of the names used by Prince Michael Obolovitch in *The Secret of Chimneys.*

Stanley, Nigel   One of the student boarders in the youth hostel run by Mrs. Nicoletis in *Hickory Dickory Dock.* Known to the other students as Nigel Chapman, he is studying the Bronze Age and medieval and Italian History. In actual fact, Nigel is the son of Sir Arthur Stanley, and Nigel bears a dark secret about his son.

Stanton, Freda   The niece of Mrs. Pengelley in "The Cornish Mystery." She becomes engaged to Jacob Radnor, a happy event that is greeted, inexplicably, with horror and anger by her aunt. The cause of Mrs. Pengelley's anger is thought to have been her oddly placed passion for Radnor.

Stanwell, Molly   A young dancer in "Harlequin's Lane." She is encouraged by John Denman to dance the role of Pierrette in the Harlequinade.

Starke, Sir Philip   A seventy-two-year-old botanist, author, and magnate in *By the Pricking of My Thumbs.* Although he is quite distinguished and reserved, he is nevertheless very fond of children. It is thus a devastating blow when he falls under the suspicion of murdering a child.

Starr, Raymond   A tennis pro and dancer who works for the amusement of the guests at the Majestic Hotel in *The Body in the Library.* Tall, handsome, and charming, his attractiveness to wealthy female guests is increased by his intimation that he is an aristocrat who has fallen upon hard economic times. At the Majestic, he dances regularly with Ruby Keene and her cousin Josephine Turner. He thus provides some useful details about Ruby to investigators. Starr has hopes of marrying the very wealthy widow Adelaide Jefferson.

Stavansson, Gabriel   An internationally known explorer who consults Tommy and Tuppence Beresford in "The Case of the Missing Lady." He has been away for two years at the North Pole and returns from his expedition to discover that his fiancée, the Honourable Hermione Crane, has disappeared suddenly and inexplicably.

Staverton, Iris   One of the guests at Greenway House on the fateful weekend described in "Shadow on the Glass." A onetime lover of Richard Scott, Iris is said to be "the sort of woman who'd stick at nothing." When she is discovered holding the revolver used to shoot Moira Scott (Richard's wife) and Jimmy Allenson, she becomes the obvious suspect in their deaths.

Steadman, Mrs.   A friend of the main character in *Unfinished Portrait.* She gives very useful housekeeping instructions to that character shortly after her marriage.

Steene, Lawrence The husband of Sarah Prentice in *A Daughter's a Daughter*. A handsome, dissolute, and thoroughly reprehensible nobleman, Steene is also a drug addict, alcoholic, and serial adulterer. He weds Sarah and leads her down his path of dissipation. Soon, she is also a drug addict in failing health. Finally, she divorces Steene and finds one last chance at happiness.

Stein, Leo A diamond merchant and the partner of Isaac Pointz in "The Regatta Mystery." He is a member of the party that witnesses the disappearance of Pointz's expensive gem.

Stella The sister of Betty Gregg in "The Problem at Pollensa Bay." She is married to an artist and a member of the bohemian community at Pollensa Bay.

Stepanov, Count The name used by Boris Ivanovitch in *The Mystery of the Blue Train*.

Stepanyi, Count Paul The name used by an agent of Mr. Parker Pyne in "The Case of the City Clerk." Under the name Count Stepanyi, the agent brings to Mr. Roberts the Order of St. Stanislaus.

Stephens A window washer in *Cards on the Table*. He is actually an assistant to Hercule Poirot in trapping a murderer.

Stevens, Mr. A manservant to Jimmy Thesiger in *The Seven Dials Mystery*. Married to the household cook, Stevens makes an effort to improve his mind by taking numerous correspondence courses.

Stillingfleet, Dr. John A physician and friend of Hercule Poirot. Stillingfleet appears in two of Poirot's cases. First, he involves the detective in the curious affair of Benedict Farley in "The Dream." Later, he assists Poirot in the investigation of *Third Girl*. He meets Norma Restarick, falls in love with her, and moves with her to Australia.

Stirling, Pamela (Poppy) A girlfriend of David Ardingly and a friend of Mark Easterbrook in

The Pale Horse. She is described as being "extremely silly." She makes the important observation that by going to the Pale Horse inn, one might find a witch who could place a deadly curse on one's enemies.

St. John, Daphne A young woman who comes to Mr. Parker Pyne for help in "The Case of the Distressed Lady." She is in dire need of rescue from a situation involving an expensive diamond ring. Parker Pyne not only solves the dilemma with the aid of his assistants Madeleine de Sara and Claude Luttrell but also exposes the true plot concerning the ring, which has been masterminded by Ernestine Richards. (See also Richards, Ernestine.)

St. John, Jewel (Jill) The daughter of Mary Moss and Walter St. John in "Sanctuary." She is raised by Mrs. Mundy in Chipping Cleghorn. Her father's last wish was for his daughter to receive a packet of emeralds that had been in Mary's possession before her death.

St. John, Walter Edmund The victim of a gunshot wound who is discovered, dying, by Diana Harmon on the steps of the little church of Chipping Cleghorn in "Sanctuary." St. John escapes from prison, where he was serving a sentence for jewel theft, and tries to make his way to Chipping Cleghorn to bring a special gift to his daughter, Jewel St. John. There follows an effort to come into possession of the luggage carried by St. John at the time of his death.

St. Loo, Lady Adelaide The aunt of Rupert St. Loo in *The Rose and the Yew Tree*. An aged and poor noblewoman, she sits in melancholy remembrance of the days of the "old ruling class" in England.

St. Loo, Rupert The nephew of Lady Adelaide St. Loo in *The Rose and the Yew Tree*. An impoverished nobleman, Rupert serves as a soldier in World War II, taking part in the campaigns in Burma. He inherits the castle of St. Loo.

St. Maur, Babe A member of the Seven Dials in *The Seven Dials Mystery*. An actress, Miss St. Maur becomes involved in international intrigue and eventually gains membership in the Seven Dials under the name Countess Radzky. She becomes quite prominent in the organization, eventually earning the title of Number One.

Stoddard, Dr. Michael A physician and friend of Hercule Poirot in "The Horses of Diomedes." A young, talented, and industrious doctor, he is summoned to the party of Patience Grace to attend to a gunshot victim. While there—in the midst of cocaine addicts and excess—Stoddard meets Sheila Grant and determines to reform her.

Stoddart-West, James The son of Lady Martine Stoddart-West in *4.50 from Paddington.* He resides at Rutherford Hall when he is not away at school. During one eventful vacation, he and a friend, Alexander Eastley, have a chance to see the corpse lying in a sarcophagus in Rutherford Hall.

Stoddart-West, Lady Martine The mother of James Stoddart-West and wife of Sir Robert Stoddart-West in *4.50 from Paddington.* She has a key role to play in the events that haunt the Crackenthorpe family, and her sudden appearance assists in the resolution of the murder investigation.

Stokes, Dr. A physician in *At Bertram's Hotel.* He is summoned to care for Canon Pennyfeather when the Wheelings find the clergyman dazed and wandering on a country road. He loses his license to practice medicine when he is caught performing illegal abortions.

Stone, Dr. A reputed archaeologist in *The Murder at the Vicarage.* He is believed to be perfectly respectable, but Raymond West, nephew to Miss Marple, has his doubts and sets out to prove him a fraud.

Stonor, Gabriel The personal secretary to Paul Renauld in *Murder on the Links.* He has served Renauld for two years.

Stormer, Olga A very successful stage performer in "The Actress" who also has a dark secret in her past that could destroy her. Born Nancy Taylor, she has put her past behind her and hopes to marry Sir Richard Everard, M.P., and to continue her thriving career. All of these dreams are placed in jeopardy when a blackmailer, Jake Levitt, threatens her with exposure unless she gives in to his extortion. Olga instead comes up with a more clever and permanent solution to her problem.

Strange, Audrey The onetime wife of Nevile Strange in *Towards Zero.* She was married to Nevile for eight years, until they were divorced suddenly through the malign influence of Kay Strange, Nevile's second wife. At a certain time each year, Audrey visits Lady Tressilian, widow of Nevile's old guardian, at Gull's Point. This year, however, Nevile plans to arrive with Kay at the same time as Audrey, in the hopes that the two women might become friends. His plans go awry when Lady Tressilian is murdered, and Audrey becomes a suspect in her death.

Strange, Sir Bartholomew (Tollie) A friend and personal physician to Sir Charles Cartwright in *Three-Act Tragedy.* Friendly, compassionate, and intelligent, Strange is a guest at a party hosted by Sir Charles during which the Reverend Babbington is murdered. Sir Bartholomew himself is later murdered by nicotine poisoning.

Strange, Kay The second wife of Nevile Strange in *Towards Zero.* A ruthlessly manipulative woman, she connived to have Nevile divorce his first wife, Audrey, and marry her. Her scheme succeeds perfectly, but Nevile remains convinced that Kay and Audrey should become friends. He brings them together at Gull's Point, a gathering that ends in disaster. Lady Tressilian, widow of Nevile's old guardian, is murdered and Nevile, despairing of any joy in his marriage, asks Kay for a divorce.

Strange, Nevile A famous athlete and tennis player in *Towards Zero.* Nevile was married for eight years to Audrey Strange, ultimately divorcing her as a result of the machinations of Kay, his second wife. Never quite recovering from the dissolution of his first marriage,

Nevile decides that Audrey and Kay should be friends. He thus brings them together at Gull's Point, the home of Lady Camilla Tressilian, the widow of his late guardian, Sir Matthew Tressilian. Lady Tressilian is also the guardian of the trust that will pass to Nevile upon her death, which comes suddenly when Lady Tressilian is fatally beaten.

Stranleigh, Lady The mother of Margery Gale in "The Voice in the Dark." After asking Mr. Satterthwaite to investigate the possibility of ghostly activity in her house, Lady Stranleigh is murdered in her bath.

Stravinska, Anna A onetime ballet dancer in *4.50 from Paddington*. Anna becomes a victim of murder when she refuses—on the basis of her Catholic faith—to grant her husband a divorce. After she is strangled on a train, her body is taken and hidden in a sarcophagus on the Rutherford estate. Unfortunately for the murderer, there was a witness to the crime on another train.

Streptitch, Count Feodor Alexandrovitch The supposed secretary to Grand Duchess Pauline in "Jane in Search of a Job."

Strete, Mildred The daughter of Carrie Louise Serrocold and widow of Canon Strete in *They Do It with Mirrors*. Owing to the death of her husband and the peculiar transformation of the family estate into a home for delinquent boys, Mildred is both unhappy and bitter.

Stroud, Charmian A young woman, "slim and dark," who comes to Miss Marple with her fiancé and cousin, Edward Rossiter, for help in "Strange Jest." The couple had been anticipating an inheritance from their eccentric Uncle Mathew. When he died, however, they were stunned to discover that the estate had no tangible assets. Eager to find the promised inheritance, they turn to Miss Marple and her genius for unraveling mysteries.

Stroud, Matthew An eccentric great-great-uncle to Edward Rossiter and Charmian Stroud in "Strange Jest." He was their only relation, and was always fond of them; so he declared that when he died he would name them his

heirs. Toward the end, however, he grew suspicious of losing his money and failed to tell the couple before he died exactly what he had done to protect their inheritance. His only clue was to assure them that all would be well, tap his right eye, and wink.

Stuart, Arlena The stage name of Arlena Marshall in *Evil under the Sun*.

Stubbs, Lady Hattie Wife of Sir George Stubbs in *Dead Man's Folly*. Mrs. Stubbs is apparently a dim-witted wife of such vindictiveness and incompetence that her servants have a hard time believing that she is a real person. Questions about her mount throughout the investigation into the death of Marlene Tucker. When her cousin, Etienne da Sousa, arrives at Nasse House, Lady Stubbs disappears and is presumed dead by Hercule Poirot. The Belgian detective eventually reveals the fate of Lady Stubbs.

Stubbs, Sir George The supposed owner of Nasse House who is married to the mentally challenged Lady Hattie in *Dead Man's Folly*. He hosts a staged murder mystery for a charity event that turns deadly when Marlene Tucker is found strangled during a search for Lady Stubbs. Hercule Poirot takes up the investigation and reveals not only the murderer but the true nature of Sir George.

St. Vincent, Mrs. A widowed and impoverished member of the upper class who stumbles on an apparent windfall in "The Listerdale Mystery." Desperately seeking an affordable place for her and her family to live, Mrs. St. Vincent discovers the old town house of Lord Listerdale to be available at a more than affordable rent. Although the mystery of the missing Lord Listerdale hangs over the house, the St. Vincents find their new home more than acceptable, and Mrs. St. Vincent becomes attracted to the urbane butler, Quentin.

St. Vincent, Barbara The daughter of Mrs. St. Vincent in "The Listerdale Mystery." She is much concerned about her family's financial situation, especially as it threatens any chance of that she might find a good husband of her own class. It thus comes as a special surprise that the St. Vincents are able to rent the old town house of Lord Listerdale at a remarkably reduced rate. Barbara is soon engaged to a young man she met while visiting Egypt with her cousin.

St. Vincent, Lawrence   The wealthy heir to an earl in "A Pot of Tea." When his girlfriend, Janet Smith, disappears, he consults Tommy and Tuppence Beresford in their capacity as directors of the International Detective Agency. The matter is resolved easily by Tuppence, and St. Vincent proposes marriage to Janet immediately after their reunion. Tommy and Tuppence ask St. Vincent's assistance in the subsequent case of "The Crackler."

St. Vincent, Rupert   The son of Mrs. St. Vincent in "The Listerdale Mystery." He becomes suspicious when the family is able to lease the old town house of Lord Listerdale for an insanely affordable rent. The focus of his concern is the disappearance of Lord Listerdale and the curious activities of the efficient and urbane butler, Quentin.

Stylptitch, Count   A brilliant statesman and nobleman who was involved throughout his long career in a host of intrigues involving his native country of Herzoslovakia in *The Secret of Chimneys.* In pondering his long years of adventures and schemes, Count Stylptitch decides to write his memoirs, a tome that is of immediate concern to certain parties, especially in Herzoslovakia. The Count entrusts to Jimmy McGrath—who once saved the count's life—the transfer of his memoirs to his publisher. Jimmy soon discovers the lengths to which certain parties will go to gain control of the memoirs.

Subayska, Madame   A woman with a Slavic face whom Mr. Parker Pyne suspects is involved in the theft of Elsie Jeffries' jewels in "Have You Got Everything You Want?" When their train is stopped by a fire—which turns out to be a smoke bomb—Madame Subayska is found in Elsie's compartment. When Elsie's

jewels turn up missing, however, a search reveals that Madame Subayska does not have them. Nevertheless, Parker Pyne suspects her.

Sugden, Superintendent   The superintendent of the Middleshire police in *Hercule Poirot's Christmas.* He is called in to investigate the murder of Simeon Lee and is seemingly very cooperative with the Belgian detective. Sugden's superior, Colonel Johnson, chief constable for Middleshire, considers the officer to be bereft of imagination. Poirot, however, is far more concerned with the distinctive features of Sugden's face, which remind him of someone.

Summerhayes, Superintendent   A police official from Scotland Yard in *The Mysterious Affair at Styles.* He undertakes with Inspector Japp the investigation into the murder of Emily Inglethorpe and oversees the inquiry against Alfred Ingethorpe.

Summerhayes, Major John (Johnnie)   A onetime army officer and the husband of Maureen Summerhayes in *Mrs. McGinty's Dead.* The major has converted his old and dilapidated estate into a guest house.

Summerhayes, Maureen   The wife of Major John Summerhayes in *Mrs. McGinty's Dead.* She and her husband convert their shabby estate into a guest house. This proves quite a challenge for both of them, especially Mrs. Summerhayes, who is virtually incapable of cooking or cleaning the rooms.

Sutcliffe, Angela (Angie)   An actress and a suspect in the murders committed in *Three-Act Tragedy.* Known as Angie, she once had a torrid affair with Sir Charles Cartwright and likes to assure virtually everyone that she is "indiscreet."

Sutcliffe, Jennifer   The daughter of Joan Sutcliffe and niece of Bob Rawlinson in *Cat among the Pigeons.* A student at the Meadowbank School, Jennifer was the unwitting bearer of a cache of jewels that were smuggled out of Ramat in her tennis racket. As Rawlinson did not trust either his sister or his niece to remain discreet, he hid the jewels in Jennifer's tennis racket without saying a word to anyone.

Sutcliffe, Joan The sister of Bob Rawlinson in *Cat among the Pigeons.* Without Joan's knowledge, Rawlinson uses her and her daughter, Jennifer, to assist him in smuggling a cache of jewels belonging to Prince Ali Yusef out of Ramat. Rawlinson hides the jewels in Jennifer's tennis racket and then fails to tell anyone, as he does not consider his sister or his niece to be capable of discretion.

Sweeny, Mrs. A woman who has possession of the keys to Moat House in *The Secret Adversary.* She is visited by Tommy Beresford during his search for the missing Tuppence Beresford.

Sweetiman, Mrs. The owner of a sweet shop and the postmistress in Broadhinny in *Mrs. McGinty's Dead.* Her establishment makes Mrs. Sweetiman a virtual expert on the life and goings-on in the village. This makes her absolutely indispensable to Hercule Poirot when he needs to uncover details about the different residents. Among the useful bits of information given to Poirot is the fact that, on the day before her murder, Mrs. McGinty purchased a bottle of ink.

Swettenham, Edmund A young, somber, struggling writer "with an anxious face" in *A Murder Is Announced.* Swettenham also becomes one of the witnesses in the murder of Rudi Scherz when his mother forces him to go Little Paddocks and take part in the "murder" that was announced in the local newspaper. As a result of the investigation, he falls in love with Phillipa Haymes.

Swinton, Sybil A young girl in *Unfinished Portrait.* While she has an interest in art, she is also considered exceedingly dull.

Symmington, Brian The son of Mona and Richard Symmington and the half brother of Megan Hunter in *The Moving Finger.* He and his brother, Colin, were the children of Mona's second marriage.

Symmington, Mona The wife of Richard Symmington and the mother of Brian Symmington, Colin Symmington, and Megan Hunter in *The Moving Finger.* An unpleasant and selfish woman, she dies in what is at first considered a suicide. It is later determined that she was murdered.

Symmington, Richard The husband of Mona Symmington and the father of Colin and Brian Symmington in *The Moving Finger.* A partner in the law firm of Galbraith, Galbraith, and Symmington, Richard is the target of one of the poison-pen letters that circulate in the village of Little Furze. The letter accuses him of having an affair with his secretary, Miss Ginch. This is considered highly unlikely, as Richard is "not one to set the pulses madly racing."

Tamplin, The Honourable Lenox The daughter of Rosalie Tamplin in *The Mystery of the Blue Train.* Her mother was expecting a visit from Katherine Grey, a passenger on the same train as Ruth Kettering. Lenox makes a comment to Hercule Poirot about the case that proves of vital importance to the detective's final resolution of the mystery. She does not always get along with her mother, in part because of her mother's numerous marriages and her own rather abrasive personality.

Tamplin, Lady Rosalie The mother of Lenox Tamplin and a prominent socialite in *The Mystery of the Blue Train.* Lady Rosalie has been married four times, although she is quick to point out that only three of them count, as the first was merely a mistake. Her second husband was a button manufacturer (he died after three years), her third was Viscount Tamplin (she married him only for the title), and her fourth is Charles "Chubby" Evans, to whom she is presently married. Rosalie's relationship with her daughter is often strained, not only because of Lenox's overbearing personality but also because of Rosalie's many marriages.

Tanios, Bella The perpetually unhappy wife of Dr. Jacob Tanios in *Dumb Witness.* The mother of two and the niece of Emily Arundell, Bella can find no happiness because of her constant longing for what she does not have.

Tanios, Dr. Jacob   A Greek-born physician and the husband of Bella Tanios in *Dumb Witness.* Although he is amiable and suave, Dr. Tanios is much disliked by the other members of the Arundell family because of his foreign origins. His wife, Bella, is also perpetually unhappy in their marriage because of his poor financial judgment and his lack of real ambition. He becomes a suspect in the poisoning death of Emily Arundell because of the prescriptions he had given her.

Tanner, Inspector   An officer of Scotland Yard in "Three Blind Mice." He undertakes the investigation into murder and mayhem at Monkswell Manor by going undercover.

Tavener, Chief Inspector   The Scotland Yard official in charge of the investigation into the death of Aristide Leonides in *Crooked House.* He works with Detective Sergeant Lamb throughout the case. Tavener also makes the decision to arrest Brenda Leonides for the murder; Hercule Poirot disagrees strenuously with the decision.

Teeves, Dr.   A physician in the service of the Templetons in *The Big Four.* He is also an operative for the international criminal organization called the Big Four.

Temple, Miss   A maid in the service of Sir Charles Cartwright in *Three-Act Tragedy.* She served what is presumed to be a poisoned cocktail to Reverend Babbington during a dinner party hosted by her employer. As part of Hercule Poirot's investigation, she is asked to reenact her steps on that fateful evening.

Temple, Elizabeth   One of the participants in a tour of famous houses and gardens of England in *Nemesis.* She becomes friendly with Miss Marple and reveals that she had been a teacher and that one of her students was Verity Hunt, a young woman murdered years before, presumably by Michael Rafiel. Curiously, she says that Verity had been engaged to Michael Rafiel but had died of "love." Soon after, Miss Temple is

caught beneath a shower of falling rocks and lapses into a coma from which she never recovers. Miss Marple considers her death to be most significant and attends the funeral with much anticipation of seeing who else might be in attendance.

Templeton, Mr. and Mrs.   A couple who work for an international criminal organization in *The Big Four.* Their activities are the means by which Hercule Poirot first becomes embroiled in his struggle with the organization. Mr. Templeton is dying, and is attended to by Dr. Teeves. Their equally suspicious "son" is the brilliant impersonator Claud Darrell.

Templeton, Charles   An undercover operative working for Sir Henry Clithering in "The Four Suspects." He is assigned the role of secretary to Dr. Rosen in order to protect him from the looming threat posed by the secret German society the *Schwarze Hand,* which had sworn vengeance upon Dr. Rosen for his work against it. In the words of Sir Henry Clithering, Templeton is "a gentleman, he speaks German fluently, and he's altogether a very able fellow." Nevertheless, he is suspected of possible complicity in the murder of Dr. Rosen after it is learned that he has relatives in Germany.

Templeton, Edgar   One of the names used by Leo Cayman in *Why Didn't They Ask Evans?*

Templeton, Micky   One of the aliases used by the clever and lethal operative Claud Darrell in *The Big Four.* He pretends to be the son of the equally dubious Templetons.

Tenterden, Miss   A dance instructor in *Unfinished Portrait.* She is a gifted dancer, but she lacks any kind of personality.

Theodofanous, Daphne   An alias used by Countess Renata Zerkowski in *Passenger to Frankfurt.*

Therese, Sister   An ally and associate of Edward Goring in *They Came to Baghdad.* She travels on the same plane as Victoria Jones.

Thesiger, Jimmy   The best friend of Gerald Wade in *The Seven Dials Mystery.* With another friend, Ronny Devereaux, Jimmy discovers Gerry Wade dead in his room at the Chimneys from an overdose of chloral. Soon after, Ronny is also murdered, and dies with the words, "Seven dials—tell Jimmy Thesiger." With the help of Eileen "Bundle" Brent and Loraine Wade, Gerald's stepsister, Jimmy sets out to discover the secret of the Seven Dials and to bring a murderer to justice.

Thibault, Alexandre The French attorney for Madame Giselle in *Death in the Clouds*. After her murder, he is summoned to identify her body and offers information about her life and activities.

Thomas, Dr. A witness to the death of Alex Pritchard in *Why Didn't They Ask Evans?* While he was playing golf with Bobby Jones, Dr. Thomas discovers the body of Pritchard at the base of a cliff and hears the curious dying question, "Why didn't they ask Evans?" As a physician, Thomas conducts an examination of the dead man and is later called to the inquest to give testimony.

Thomas, Gladys One of the aliases used by Valerie Hobhouse in *Hickory Dickory Dock*.

Thompson, Dr. A psychiatrist consulted by the police after the start of the gruesome alphabet murders in *The A.B.C. Murders*. He renders the professional opinion that while it is distinctly possible that the alphabet connection could be mere coincidence, there is a greater likelihood that the killer has what he calls an "alphabet complex." His assessment seems confirmed with the subsequent murders.

Thompson, Mr. A "plump, middle-aged man" in "The Oracle at Delphi." Thompson is not who he appears to be and is an instrumental figure in the case involving the kidnapping and ransom of young Willard Peters.

Thompson, Mrs. A gifted medium and spiritualist in "The Red Signal." She conducts a séance for a group of party guests and shocks the participants with her bloodcurdling scream of "Danger! Blood!" Her words of warning are

soon fulfilled with the death of Alington West, a psychiatrist who was supposed to determine which of the guests was suffering from severe mental illness.

Tiddler, Detective Sergeant William (Tom) One of the police officers investigating the murders in *The Mirror Crack'd from Side to Side*. He assists Detective Inspector Craddock and earns his superior's admiration for his competence. Tiddler also proves useful because of certain connections he has to the movie industry, associations of much value in this particular investigation.

Tiglath-Pileser The family cat belonging to Reverend Julian and Diana "Bunch" Harmon in *A Murder Is Announced*. Given an Assyrian name by his extremely well-educated owners, Tiglath-Pileser provides Miss Marple with a vital clue in the solution to the murders at Little Paddocks.

Tio, Marcus A friendly but evasive hotel manager in *They Came to Baghdad*. He has a habit of speaking in such a way that no conversation with him ever seems to get anywhere. Victoria Jones finds this especially annoying, observing that "every topic found them returning to the point of departure."

Todd, Mr. and Mrs. A couple in Clapham who enlist the services of Hercule Poirot to find their missing cook in "The Adventure of the Clapham Cook." As Mrs. Todd observes, "A good cook's a good cook—and when you lose her, it's as much to you as are pearls to a fine lady." From the start of the case, the Todds are an annoyance to the detective and ultimately infuriate him when they terminate his services and pay him the humiliating fee of one guinea. Poirot decides to carry on the investigation and not only recovers the cook but catches a clever bank embezzler. Satisfied that he has enjoyed the last laugh, Poirot frames the one guinea as a reminder of the case. The Todds reside at 88 Prince Albert Road, Clapham.

Tomlinson, Mr. One of the members of the stranded picnic party in "The World's End." A retired judge in India, Tomlinson plays an important part in the recovery of Rosina Nunn's missing opal.

Tomlinson, Jean One of the boarders in the youth hostel run by Mrs. Nicoletis in *Hickory Dickory Dock*. A physiotherapist, she professes a firm support for justice, a sentiment seemingly out of place at the hostel, where crimes of theft and murder have been committed.

Tosswill, Dr. One of the members of the ill-fated Men-her-Ra expedition in "The Adventure of the Egyptian Tomb." He disagrees firmly with Hercule Poirot's stated position on magic and superstition. Tosswill also works in the British Museum.

Tredwell The butler in the service of Lord Caterham at the Chimneys. A magnificent example of the perfect butler, Tredwell appears in two published cases, *The Secret of Chimneys* and *The Secret Adversary*.

Trefusis, Emily The fiancée of James Pearson and a talented amateur sleuth in *The Sittaford Mystery*. Miss Trefusis wants to marry Pearson—despite his many shortcomings—because she will be able to "make something of him." Unfortunately, before she can do that, she must clear him of suspicion in the murder of his uncle, Captain Trevelyan. With skill and determination, Emily proves Pearson innocent and assists in bringing the real murderer to justice.

Trefusis, Owen The secretary to Sir Reuben Astwell in "The Under Dog." He is a mild-mannered and proper young man, but this does not keep him from becoming a suspect in Sir Reuben's murder.

Trelawny, Mr. The attorney representing the estate of Lady Camilla Tressilian in *Towards Zero*. He is visited by Superintendent Battle and informs the policeman of the unusual terms of her will.

Trent, Claire The object of Dermot West's love in "The Red Signal." A woman of surpassing beauty, described as "a thing of gold and ivory and pale-pink coral," she is also suspected by

West of being mentally ill and capable of murder. She is married to Jack Trent.

Trent, Hugo The nephew of Sir Gervase Chevenix-Gore in "Dead Man's Mirror." He is an orphan, but he also has expectations of inheriting the bulk of Sir Gervase's vast estate.

Trent, Jack The husband of Claire Trent and the host of an ill-fated dinner party in "The Red Signal." He has a complex personality and is just as likely as his wife to be mentally unbalanced, although Dermot West focuses his suspicions on Claire.

Trenton, Charles A blackmailer and con artist in *Taken at the Flood*. Under an alias, he tries to blackmail David Hunter and Rosaleen Cloade with a dark secret about their past. He soon ends up dead, murdered in his room at the Stag Inn by an unknown hand.

Tressilian The butler to the household of Simeon Lee in *Hercule Poirot's Christmas*. He has served the family for more than forty years and is extremely devoted to his employer, despite Lee's many deficiencies.

Tressilian, Lady Camilla The widow of Sir Matthew Tressilian in *Towards Zero*. Despite her advanced years, Lady Camilla is active mentally and remains a woman of very decided opinions. She is also in control of the trust that will come to Nevile Strange—a trust of which her late husband had been guardian—and attempts to give Nevile some sage advice about his marriages. Lady Camilla has invited Nevile and a group of friends to stay at the her estate, Gull's Point, where a certain tension develops, most so between Kay and Audrey Strange, Nevile's present and former wives. The unease is finally shattered when Lady Camilla is beaten to death in her own bed, a crime that seems bereft of any motive.

Trevelyan, Captain Joseph Arthur The owner of Sittaford House in *The Sittaford Mystery*. He is an elderly retired Royal Navy officer who still enjoys hearty physical exercise and sports, especially with his longtime best friend, Major Burnaby. Trevelyan is also a dedicated misogynist and is called "a regular philistine in every way—devoted to sport." One other attribute proves of some importance. His extreme frugality moves him to rent out Sittaford House during the winter, forcing him to take more spartan quarters in a rented cottage at Hazelmoor, in Exhampton. There, he remains isolated, especially after a rare blizzard strikes the area. Concern for Trevelyan's safety is sparked by the results of a séance held at Sittaford House, during which the ominous message TREVELYAN DEAD is announced by a series of rappings on a table. Major Burnaby hurries to Exhampton to check on his friend and discovers him beaten to death with a sandbag.

Treves, Mr. An attorney, a close friend of Lady Tressilian, and a specialist in crime in *Towards Zero*. Treves opens the account of the events in *Towards Zero* by having a conversation with other lawyers about crime. He insists that any crime can be said to have originated some time, perhaps even years, before it is committed, and so any murder mystery does not really begin with the murder. Instead, events build up to the crime, converging at Zero Point. Treves becomes an example of his own theory when he is killed. He suffers a fatal heart attack by being forced to walk up three flights of stairs because an elevator is falsely marked as being out of order. He dies soon after a discussion with a fellow guest at Lady Tressilian's home, Gull's Point, about the justice system, especially as it pertains to the curious tale of the death of a child at the hands of another child while playing bows and arrows. His inexplicable death is followed closely by the murder of Lady Tressilian herself.

Tripp, Isabel and Julia The Tripp sisters, two spiritualists in *Dumb Witness* who conduct a seemingly ominous séance in which a "luminous haze" appears around Emily Arundell. Isabel and Julia are described as "vegetarians, theosophists, British Israelites, Christian Scientists, spiritualists, and enthusiastic amateur photographers." They also enjoy holding séances; at the one during which they beheld the "luminous haze," it is later determined, Miss Arundell was dying from a fatal dose of phosphorus.

Tucker, Marlene One of the participants in the staged murder mystery organized by Mrs. Ariadne Oliver in *Dead Man's Folly*. Marlene agrees to play the role of a murder victim for the charity event, but she is soon actually murdered, strangled with a piece of clothesline during the game. The crime is at first apparently without motive, but Hercule Poirot subsequently learns from her sister, Marilyn, that Marlene was a small-time blackmailer who learned secrets about others by spying on them and then secured assorted gifts from the victims to remain quiet.

Tucker, Marilyn The sister of Marlene Tucker in *Dead Man's Folly*. After her sister becomes a victim of genuine murder during a staged murder mystery, Marilyn is visited by Hercule Poirot. She divulges to him that Marlene was a kind of blackmailer, ferreting out secrets about others and then taking gifts to remain quiet.

Tuckerton, Thomasina Ann (Tommy) One of the members of the "Chelsea group" in *The Pale Horse* and a fiery, hot-tempered, red-haired heiress. She has a fight with Lou Ellis in a Chelsea espresso bar that is witnessed by Mark Easterbrook, and within a week dies of what is called by the coroner an acute case of encephalitis. Hers is only one of numerous deaths that take place and that become the object of Easterbrook's investigation.

Turner, Mrs. A onetime occupant of Heather Cottage in "The Mystery of the Blue Jar." She disappears suddenly, and it is the opinion of Felice Marchaud that the terrible cries of "Murder—help!" that are heard by Jack Harrington are being produced by her ghost.

Turner, Josephine (Josie) The cousin of the murdered Ruby Keene in *The Body in the Library*. She is a dancer at the Majestic Hotel and was able to secure a similar position for Ruby not long before her death. Miss Marple is quite impressed with Josie's intelligence, but the sleuth observes that she has "one of those shrewd, limited minds that never do foresee the future and are usually astonished by it."

Tyler, Fred The owner of a fish shop in *A Murder Is Announced.* He is an acquaintance of Miss Marple, who questions him about certain details pertaining to the events at Little Paddocks. Through her shrewd questioning, she is able to learn far more from Fred than he realizes.

Underhay, Captain Robert The husband of Rosaleen Cloade in *Taken at the Flood.* While serving in Nigeria, he understands that his wife is having difficulty living there and so agrees to her request for a divorce. She subsequently remarries, this time to Gordon Cloade, on the assumption that Underhay has died. Her new husband dies as well, and Rosaleen stands to inherit a sizable estate, at least until someone arrives and tells her that her first husband may not be dead after all.

Unkerton, Mrs. Wife of Ned Unkerton in "The Shadow on the Glass." She and her husband are proud of their estate, Greenways House, but without her husband's knowledge she replaces a supposedly haunted windowpane. This attempt at home improvement proves of great importance in the execution of a murder.

Unkerton, Ned The owner of Greenways House in "The Shadow on the Glass." Proud of his home, Unkerton makes the serious mistake of inviting Richard Scott and his new wife, Moira, for a visit along with Iris Staverton, Richard's old lover. The faux pas creates an atmosphere of tension that climaxes in a murder. Mrs. Unkerton's decision to replace a haunted windowpane plays a critical role in the murder.

Upjohn, Mrs. Mother of Julia Upjohn and a onetime member of British intelligence during World War II in *Cat among the Pigeons.* Retired and happy to be the mother of a schoolgirl, Mrs. Upjohn reverts to her old training and form when she spots a dangerous operative

whom she had first seen in the war. Her daughter also clearly shares her mother's skill and keen sense of observation.

Upjohn, Julia The daughter of Mrs. Upjohn and a student at the Meadowbank School in *Cat among the Pigeons.* Julia clearly has inherited her mother's intelligence and keen eye, for she discovers a cache of jewels hidden in the tennis racket of her friend Jennifer Sutcliffe and informs Hercule Poirot.

Upward, Laura A onetime actress and the adoptive mother of Robin Upward in *Mrs. McGinty's Dead.* One of the employers of the murdered cleaning lady Mrs. McGinty, Laura is an invalid who nevertheless makes every effort to remain socially prominent. She is strangled one evening while her son is at a show with Mrs. Ariadne Oliver.

Upward, Robin The adoptive son of Laura Upward in *Mrs. McGinty's Dead.* A talented young man, he becomes an associate and friend of Mrs. Ariadne Oliver and assists her in adapting one of her novels for the stage. Robin's adoptive mother is strangled one evening while he is with Mrs. Oliver at a show.

Valdez, Lola A fiery and extravagant Peruvian dancer in "Yellow Iris." She was in attendance at the party held at the Jardin de Cygnes during which Iris Russell was poisoned to death. Hercule Poirot surprises Lola by asking her to dance, prompting the dancer to exclaim, "You're the cat's whiskers, Monsieur Poirot."

Van Aldin, Rufus The father of Ruth Kettering in *The Mystery of the Blue Train.* An American millionaire, he gives his daughter the Heart of Fire rubies and soon loses both his daughter and the jewels. Stunned at the murder of his daughter, van Aldin enlists the services of Hercule Poirot to recover the jewels and bring the murderer to justice.

Vandel, Ambrose A set designer in "The Arcadian Deer." He designed the set used in the ballet performed by Katrina Samoushenko. He gives details about Sir George Sanderfield to Hercule Poirot.

Vandemeyer, Janet The name under which Jane Finn is registered at the hospital following her fateful voyage on the *Lusitania* in *The Secret Adversary.*

Vandemeyer, Marguerite Supposedly the aunt of Jane Vandemeyer in *The Secret Adversary.* She was once involved with Sir James Peel Egerton, a future prime minister. Marguerite is also involved in espionage and dies after consuming a dose of chloral.

Vanderlyn, Mrs. A clever and dangerous spy in "The Incredible Theft." She has been married several times—to an Italian, a German, and a Russian—and has made a number of useful contacts that she has apparently put to good use in matters of espionage. There is concern in some quarters of British security that she has attracted the attentions of the powerful Lord Mayfield. When a set of secret plans disappears from Lord Mayfield's library, Mrs. Vanderlyn is the prime suspect.

Vane, Clarice A friend of Harry Laxton who has also been in love with him for some time in "The Case of the Caretaker." Despite her feelings for him, she becomes a devoted friend to both Harry and his new wife, Louise. Thus, when Louise dies from a fall, she defends Harry against the accusation of murder that is rumored throughout the village.

Van Heidem, Paul The public spokesman for Mr. Aristide and the Brain Trust in *Destination Unknown.* He is a ruthless and coldly unpleasant man who considers it cynically amusing to use a leper colony as a front for the activities of the Brain Trust.

Van Rydock, Ruth The sister of Carrie Louise Serrocold in *They Do It with Mirrors.* Ruth is an old school friend of Miss Marple and thus had the unique chance to know Miss Marple from the days of her youth. She has also been married three times, enjoying financial windfalls from each divorce. Remembering her days with Miss Marple, Ruth goes to her for help when she becomes concerned that Carrie Louise is slowly being poisoned.

Van Schuyler, Marie One of the passengers on board the *Karnak* in *Death on the Nile.* She is an elderly and temperamental kleptomaniac who swiftly alienates virtually everyone on board with her acerbic and unpleasant personality. She becomes a suspect in the death of Linnet Doyle because of her penchant for stealing things. Cornelia Ruth Robson travels with her as a companion.

Vansittart, Eleanor A schoolmistress at the Meadowbank School in *Cat among the Pigeons.* She is beaten to death with a sandbag.

Van Snyder, Mrs. Cortland A "middle-aged fashionably dressed woman from Detroit" who claims to have been kidnapped by the same assailant who goes after Tuppence Beresford in "The Man Who Was No. 16." Her true identity is revealed in the course of the investigation.

Van Stuyvesant, Cora The stepmother of Ellie Rogers in *Endless Night.* Her position is an unpleasant one, as she depends entirely upon her stepdaughter for her allowance. She also suffers the dislike of her stepson-in-law, Michael Rogers, but tries to win his favor.

Varaga, Queen of Herzoslovakia One of the names used by Angele Mory in *The Secret of Chimneys.*

Varesco, Paul The sinister financial backer of the wildly successful nightclub called Hell in "The Capture of Cerberus." Varesco gives support to Countess Vera Rossakoff, but he also has other uses for the club of which the countess is unaware.

Varez, Paul de An associate of No. 16 in "The Man Who Was No. 16." He impersonates a French cripple to assist the escape of his comrade from a hospital.

Vassilievitch A presumed Russian agent in "The Case of the City Clerk." Mr. Parker Pyne arranges for the malevolent Vassilievitch to menace Mr. Roberts.

Vassilovna, Olga Another name used by the Russian prostitute Olga Demiroff in *The Mystery of the Blue Train.*

Vaucher, Jeanne The original name of Countess Czarnova in "The Soul of the Croupier." She was once married to Pierre Vaucher.

Vaucher, Pierre A onetime French jeweler and husband of Jeanne Vaucher in "The Soul of the Croupier." He eventually went to work as a croupier in Monte Carlo. Fate makes it possible for him to meet his estranged wife once again, years after despairing of finding her.

Vaughan, Gwenda The secretary to Leo Argyle in *Ordeal by Innocence.* She is madly in love with her employer and has hopes of marrying him.

Vaughan, Magdalen The sister of Matthew Vaughan and a grandniece of Lily Crabtree in "Sing a Song of Sixpence." She and her brother become suspects in the murder of their great aunt.

Vaughan, Matthew The brother of Magdalen Vaughan and grandnephew of Lily Crabtree in "Sing a Song of Sixpence." He and Magdalen become suspects in the murder of their great aunt.

Vaughan, Lady Millicent Castle A supposed English noblewoman who enlists the help of Hercule Poirot in overcoming the cruel machinations of a blackmailer in "The Veiled Lady." She is in desperate need of recovering an indiscreet letter from the blackmailer Lavington, who has hidden the missive in a Chinese puzzle box. Poirot accepts the case, but he takes careful note of the fact that Lady Millicent's shoes are shabby while her clothes are expensive.

Vavasour, Mr. One of the comanagers of the London and Scottish Bank in "The Million-Dollar Bond Robbery." He has grown old and gray in the service of the bank and is the uncle of Philip Ridgeway, who had been responsible for transporting a million dollars' worth of Liberty bonds from London to New York. The funds are stolen, and Philip is the obvious suspect, a bitter blow to Vavasour.

Vavasour, Roley One of the heirs to the Stran-

leigh title in "The Voice in the Dark." He follows Margery Gale in the line of succession to the title. Margery thinks little of him, thinking that he is merely "out for what he can get."

Venables, Mr. An ostensibly wealthy world traveler and collector in *The Pale Horse.* He is confined to a wheelchair, owing to a bout of polio, and is thus not considered a prominent suspect in the series of deaths plaguing the area around the Pale Horse. Mark Easterbrook, however, sees him as "predatory" and determines that he may actually have been involved in the murder of Father Gorman.

Vera The twin sister of Una Drake in "The Unbreakable Alibi." She proves to be a most amenable associate to her sister in Una's effort to win a bet with a certain young man.

Vereker, Nell A character in *Giant's Bread* who first meets Vernon Deyre when they are both children. She proves to be a dull playmate for Vernon because she is always so overdressed. In later years, she is a charming young woman who decides to marry a poor soldier instead of the rich husband she had always expected to find.

Veroneau, Inez The name used by Countess Vera Rossakoff during her period of employment by Madame Olivier in *The Big Four.*

Verrall, Detective Inspector Joe A presumed member of the local constabulary in "Mr. Eastwood's Adventure." He is assisted by Detective Sergeant Carter in his "investigation" into the odd happenings involving Mr. Eastwood.

Verrier, Monsieur A French archaeologist who visits the dig in *Murder in Mesopotamia.* He arrives just after the death of Mrs. Leidner and gives hurried condolences to Dr. Leidner before continuing on his own journey.

Vicar, the Two English clergymen who appear in separate cases. The first sends Tuppence Beresford to search for the tombstone of Lily Waters in *By the Pricking of My Thumbs.* The second takes over the duties of Reverend Leonard Clement as vicar of St. Mary Mead after that popular cleric's demise. In *The Mirror*

Crack'd from Side to Side, he attends the charity event at Gossington Hall and overhears a very important conversation between Marina Gregg and Heather Badcock.

Victor, King An internationally known jewel thief in *The Secret of Chimneys.* Based in Paris, he assumes an impressive array of aliases: Monsieur Chelles, a traveling silk salesman; Monsieur Lemoine of the Sûreté; Captain O'Neill; and Prince Nicholas. His last incarnation proves to be his most dangerous and his least successful.

Vinegar, Mrs. The nickname given by Miss Marple to the postmistress of Carristown in *Nemesis.* She describes the woman as "middle-aged . . . with a vinegar face," and assumes her best impersonation of a dim old lady to shrewdly question her about the destination of a package sent from the Carristown post office. Her ruse succeeds brilliantly, for "Mrs. Vinegar" comes away from the conversation with the view that Miss Marple is "scatty as they make them, poor old creature."

Viner, Amelia A very old woman and an important witness in *The Mystery of the Blue Train.* She is interviewed by Hercule Poirot and gives him a vital newspaper clipping concerning a jewel robbery some years before. She confesses to the detective that she has managed to live for so long because every day she eats a slice of brown bread and spices up her meals with a "little stimulant."

Vitelli, Signor The representative of the Italian government to the international conference held to discuss student unrest in *Passenger to Frankfurt.* He is not as concerned as the other delegates about the disquiet, in large measure because he sees the troubles as a product of nature, made worse by the level of corruption throughout Europe.

Vladiroffsky, Prince A brilliant agent and impersonator in "The Man Who Was No. 16." He is able to adopt disguises and personalities of a dazzling variety, including those of assorted languages and cultures as well as both sexes.

One of his more successful disguises is that of Mrs. Cortland Van Snyder.

Vole, Leonard The chief suspect in the murder of Emily French in "Witness for the Prosecution." He was a friend, confidante, and financial advisor to Miss French, who came to trust him completely. Such was her faith in him that she named him her heir. Soon afterward, Miss French was murdered, and Vole was arrested for the crime. The trial goes against him, thanks to the damning evidence given against him by Romaine Vole, his mistress, but he is ultimately acquitted through the talents of his lawyer, Mr. Mayherne, and a certain Mrs. Mogson.

Vole, Romaine The Austrian-born mistress of Leonard Vole in "Witness for the Prosecution." She is a former actress named Romaine Heilger who had worked in Vienna but who had also spent time in an Austrian mental institution. Although she is Vole's mistress, not his wife, she insists on using his last name. During Leonard's trial for the murder of Emily French, she gives damning evidence against him. Nevertheless, he is acquitted because her testimony is torn to shreds by Mr. Mayherne, Leonard's attorney, with the help of the mysterious Mrs. Mogson.

von Deinim, Carl A British agent in *N or M?* He impersonates a German refugee and chemist and pretends to undertake the man's research. His impersonation is soon discovered.

von Waldsausen, the Grafin Charlotte An enormously and grotesquely heavy woman in *Passenger to Frankfurt.* Called Big Charlotte and Charlotte Krapp, she is vastly wealthy, and is also referred to as "a great, big, cheesy-looking woman, wallowing in fat." She also provides large amounts of money to the Youth Movement.

Vyse, Mr. A stage producer and minion of the actress Rosina Nunn in "The World's End." He had originally planned to produce a play authored by Alec Gerard, but the play was rejected after Gerard was convicted of stealing an opal from Miss Nunn.

Vyse, Charles A cousin of Nick Buckley in *Peril at End House.* A member of the law firm of Vyse, Trevanion, and Wynnard, he is a stern and inscrutable lawyer.

Wade, Gerald An employee of the British Foreign Office in *The Seven Dials Mystery.* During a visit to the Chimneys, he is the subject of a prank when his friends place eight alarm clocks—set for 6:30 A.M.—in his room as a reminder that he is perpetually late in rising. On that same night, he is murdered. His death is the first significant murder in the case and is the spark for the investigation by Jimmy Thesiger.

Wade, Iris The wife of Reginald Wade in "The Case of the Discontented Husband." She has become estranged from her husband after nine years of marriage and asks for a divorce in order to be able to remarry. Nevertheless, Iris gives Reginald six months, in return for his promise that if she is of the same mind at the end of that period of time, he will step aside. The man with whom she has become involved is described by Reginald Wade as a "nasty long-haired chap." As a result of Mr. Parker Pyne's solution to the situation, Iris once more desires her husband, but there is an unexpected result to the case. (See also Wade, Reginald.)

Wade, Loraine The stepsister to Gerald Wade in *The Seven Dials Mystery.* After the murder of her brother, she sets out with Jimmy Thesiger and Eileen Brent to find the killer.

Wade, Reginald A taciturn and athletic man who comes for assistance to Mr. Parker Pyne in "The Case of the Discontented Husband." Described as "a tall, broadly built man with mild, pleasant blue eyes and a well-tanned complexion," he is desperate for aid in dealing with his wife, who desires a divorce so that she can marry another man. Mr. Parker Pyne's solution to the difficulty does have its desired effect in winning back the affections of Reginald's wife, but it produces an unforeseen development that marks the case as perhaps the most disas-

The formidable Romaine Vole (Marlene Dietrich), in Witness for the Prosecution *(1957). (Photofest)*

trous of Parker Pyne's career. (See also de Sara, Madeleine.)

Wagstaffe, Inspector An official of Scotland Yard who investigates the theft of the Borgia goblet in "The Apples of the Hesperides." He consults with Hercule Poirot about the case and boasts that he speaks "a bit of Italiano."

Wainwright, Derek A friend of Sylvia Carslake in "In a Glass Darkly." She turns to him for help when her fiancé, Charles, drives her away because of his insane jealousy.

Waite, Josephine (Joe) A young woman in *Giant's Bread* who suffers emotional trauma when her mother abandons her to run off with her lover, a married sculptor.

Wake, Alfred The vicar of Wychwood in *Mur-*

der Is Easy. He provides useful information to Luke Fitzwilliam about the local goings-on and the assorted residents of the village.

Wales, Emma A housemaid in the service of Lady Tressilian at Gull's Point in *Towards Zero*. Called a "tall thin bit of vinegar," she testifies to Inspector Battle that she overheard a fierce argument between the murdered Lady Tressilian and Nevile Strange on the night that Lady Tressilian was beaten to death.

Wallace, Bella and Rube Two friends of Mary Montresor in "The Golden Ball." They help Mary in determining the potential worthiness of George Dundas as a husband.

Walters, Esther A onetime secretary to Jason Rafiel in *A Caribbean Mystery* and *Nemesis*. In *A*

Caribbean Mystery, she makes the mistake of falling in love with Tim Kendall, a married man. When Miss Marple takes steps to make certain that nothing comes from their relationship, Esther is resentful. In *Nemesis,* she finally finds happiness, with Edmund Anderson.

Wanstead, Professor   One of the participants in a tour of famous houses and gardens of Britain in *Nemesis.* Wanstead serves as a confidential advisor to the Home Office and an associate of Jason Rafiel. Rafiel instructs Wanstead to take the same tour as Miss Marple, for the purpose of keeping an eye on the old sleuth. Like Jason, Wanstead believes firmly that Michael Rafiel, Jason's son, is innocent of murder.

Warburton, Captain Jim   A self-proclaimed soldier whose secret is revealed in *Dead Man's Folly.* He is a supporter of the Masterton family's political ambitions.

Wargrave, Alfred James   An expert in roses in *Sad Cypress.* He is called in to testify against the claim by Jessie Hopkins that she has pricked herself on a rose thorn. Wargrave is able to prove that the roses around Hunterbury Hall are actually free of any thorns.

Wargrave, Mr. Justice Lawrence John   A formidable and merciless judge in *And Then There Were None.* Called Ulick Norman Owen and Una Nancy Owen (or simply U.N. Owen), he earned for himself a fierce reputation as "a hanging judge," and brings the same legal viewpoint to the horrible events on Indian Island.

Waring, Harold   An undersecretary to the prime minister of England in "The Stymphalean Birds." He goes on vacation to Herzoslovakia and becomes the target of two conniving blackmailers after he performs what seems a heroic and chivalrous deed. His political future seems on the verge of ruin, but he is rescued by Hercule Poirot.

Warren, Dr.   The local physician in *The Sittaford Mystery.* He attends the party at which a séance is held that predicts the murder of Captain Trevelyan. When the threat is con-

firmed, Warren is given the grim task of examining the body and determining the cause and the time of death.

Warren, Angela   The half sister of Caroline Crale in *Five Little Pigs.* She believes her sister to have been innocent of the murder of Amyas Crale and assists Hercule Poirot in his investigation into the grim events that took place sixteen years before. She provides a vital clue to the detective when she relates a practical joke she played on her brother-in-law.

Waterhouse, Edith   The sister of James Waterhouse in *The Clocks.* She bullies her brother and is much disliked by everyone who knows her.

Waterhouse, James   The brother of Edith Waterhouse in *The Clocks.* He lives with his sister and is completely under her control.

Waverly, Ada   The mother of the missing boy in "The Kidnapping of Johnnie Waverly." She is deeply concerned about the threats made against her son's safety and insists that her husband, Marcus, consult with Hercule Poirot. She is unaware of her husband's financial situation.

Waverly, Johnnie   The son of Marcus and Ada Waverly in "The Kidnapping of Johnnie Waverly." His parents receive threats of his impending seizure from an unknown person, and the warning comes to fruition with the boy's sudden disappearance. Hercule Poirot is able to retrieve Johnnie, but he decides against bringing the kidnapper to justice.

Waverly, Marcus   The father of Johnnie Waverly and the husband of Ada Waverly in "The Kidnapping of Johnnie Waverly." He consults Hercule Poirot at his wife's insistence in the hopes that the threatened kidnapping of his son can be prevented.

Waynflete, Honoria   The librarian and caretaker of the museum at Wych Hall in *Murder Is Easy.* She provides assistance to Luke Fitzwilliam in his investigation of the numerous deaths in the area and gives Luke the advice not to reveal his true identity to too many people in the village. Years before, she was engaged to be married to Lord Easterfield, but broke off their betrothal because, she claims, he had a homicidal and uncontrollable rage.

Weardale, Sir Harry   An admiral in "The Submarine Plans." He visits the home of Lord Alloway and becomes quite concerned when a set of top secret plans for a submarine is stolen. His son, Leonard, becomes the chief suspect in the theft. The admiral is married to Lady Juliet Weardale.

Weardale, Lady Juliet   Wife of Sir Harry Weardale and the mother of Leonard Weardale in "The Submarine Plans." She and her husband visit the home of Lord Alloway, and one evening the top secret plans to a submarine are stolen from right under Lord Alloway's nose. Lady Juliet, however, suspects that the culprit is her own son.

Weardale, Leonard   The son of Sir Harry and Lady Juliet Weardale in "The Submarine Plans." When a set of top secret submarine plans is stolen from the possession of Lord Alloway, Leonard becomes the chief suspect.

Weatherby, Pauline   The younger sister of Iris Russell in "Yellow Iris." Her sister was murdered at a dinner party four years before from a dose of potassium cyanide, and Pauline takes part in a commemorative dinner organized by her brother-in-law, Barton Russell. During the macabre festivities, Pauline grabs her throat and collapses, seemingly dead, in a manner exactly like that of her late sister.

Webb, Bella   A resident of the inn in *The Pale Horse,* with Sybil Stamfordis and Thyrza Grey. Bella provides the cooking for the inn, but she considers herself first and foremost to be a practicing witch. Her touch is described as "cold and boneless . . . like a slug."

Webb, Sheila Rosemary   An employee of the Cavendish Secretarial and Typing Bureau in *The Clocks.* She is sent to the home of the blind former schoolteacher Miss Pebmarsh to perform secretarial tasks and is instructed to let herself in should Miss Pebmarsh not be at home. Webb ends up instead discovering the corpse of R. H. Curry. Fleeing the house, she runs right into the arms of Inspector Colin Lamb. At the conclusion of the case, Miss Webb marries the inspector.

Weekes, Miss   A governess in *The Burden.* She is a most uninteresting person.

Welman, Laura   The widow of Henry Welman, the mother of Mary Gerrard, and the aunt of Elinor Carlisle and Roderick Welman in *Sad Cypress.* She suffers a stroke and requires two nurses to care for her. While recovering, she is visited by Elinor and Roderick, who have reason to believe that someone has been trying to gain influence over Laura so that she will redraft her will and disinherit her niece and nephew. Shortly after the visit, she is poisoned with morphine, and her will remains intact. Evidence seems to finger Elinor as the murderer of both her aunt and of Mary Gerrard.

Welman, Roderick   Called Roddy, the boyfriend of Elinor Carlisle and nephew of Laura Welman in *Sad Cypress.* He is engaged to be married to Elinor but breaks their planned marriage when he falls in love with Mary Gerrard. Mary is soon murdered, and Elinor becomes the chief suspect in the deaths of both Mary and Laura Welman. A romantic young man, he refers to Elinor as "la Princesse Lontaine" and Mary as "Atalanta."

Welsh, Joe   A simple but good-natured farmhand in "The Case of the Rich Woman." He falls in love with Hannah Moorhouse, who is actually the very wealthy Amelia Rymer.

Welwyn, David   A young man in "The Theft of the Royal Ruby" who is very much in love with Sarah Lacey. At the Christmas gathering at King's Lacey, he is supposed to be a dinner companion for someone else, but he has eyes only for Sarah and views the charms of Desmond Lee-Wortley as a genuine threat.

Wendover, Mr.   A name once used by Walter Protheroe in "The Market Basing Mystery."

West, Sir Alington   A famous Harley Street psychiatrist in "The Red Signal." He has a bitter disagreement with his nephew, Dermot, and is soon shot in the heart. His nephew is the lone suspect in the crime.

West, Basil Private secretary to Sir George Grayle in "Death on the Nile." West has a disarming smile and sufficient charm to be the only person in the household not subject to the unpleasant outbursts of Lady Ariadne Grayle. West and Pamela Grayle, Sir George's niece, supposedly have an understanding, although Lady Ariadne is also convinced that Basil is in love with her instead.

West, Bessie A friend of Celia in *Unfinished Portrait.* She tries unsuccessfully to convince her friend to become a nurse.

West, Chloe Elizabeth An actress in *Sparkling Cyanide.* She is hired by George Barton to impersonate his dead wife, Rosemary, at a party thrown in her honor. The dinner ends, as did the original party, in disaster.

West, David The second son of Joan and Raymond West and the grandnephew of Miss Marple in *4.50 from Paddington.* He works for British Railways and is able to assist Miss Marple's investigation by providing schedules for all trains that might have passed the one carrying Mrs. McGillicuddy, who witnessed a murder on a train that was running parallel to the one she was riding.

West, Dermot The nephew of Sir Alington West in "The Red Signal." Dermot possesses the odd ability to foretell impending danger, a skill he calls the "red signal." During a séance at the home of Claire Trent and her family, he has a flash of the "red signal." A short time later, after a disagreement with his uncle, Dermot finds himself accused of Alington's murder.

West, Gillian A stunningly beautiful young woman in "The Face of Helen." She has a long history of being connected with tragedy and it is in that condition that she is found by Mr. Satterthwaite. Two young would-be suitors, Philip Eastney and Charles Burns, are rivals for her affections. Possessed of a face that drives men wild with devotion, Gillian becomes a catalyst for murder when she rejects one of the suitors.

West, Joan Originally named Joyce Lemprière, she is an artist, a member of the Tuesday Night Club, and the wife of the novelist Raymond West, the favorite nephew of Miss Marple. Whereas her husband is a successful writer, Joyce is a flourishing artist, creating paintings that are described by Miss Marple as "remarkable pictures of square people with bulges on them." The cousin of Giles Reed and the aunt of Louise Oxley, Joyce is also the mother of two sons. She makes appearances in *The Thirteen Problems,* "Miss Marple Tells a Story," "Greenshaw's Folly," and *Sleeping Murder.* (See also West, Raymond.)

West, Magda The stage name used by Magda Leonides in *Crooked House.*

West, Maureen One of the employees of the Cavendish Secretarial and Typing Bureau in *The Clocks.* She holds her employer, Miss Martindale, in utter contempt. Miss West is described as having hair that "suggested she'd been out in a blizzard lately."

West, Raymond The favorite nephew of Miss Marple, the husband of the artist Joan West (née Joyce Lemprière), the father of two sons, and a celebrated novelist and poet. West enjoys great success as a writer, so much so that he and his wife are able to afford many treats and holidays for their aunt, including two very memorable trips, to Bertram's Hotel in London (recounted in *At Bertram's Hotel*) and to the Caribbean (in *A Caribbean Mystery*). Despite this generosity, West remains a relatively little-known figure in the published cases of Miss Marple, with few details ever provided about his life. Reverend Leonard Clement said of him: "He is, I know, supposed to be a brilliant novelist, and has made quite a name as a poet. His poems have no capital letters in them, which is, I believe, the essence of modernity. His books are about unpleasant people leading lives of surpassing dullness." Aside from *At*

Bertram's Hotel and *A Caribbean Mystery,* West is mentioned in *The Murder at the Vicarage, The Thirteen Problems,* "Miss Marple Tells a Story," "Greenshaw's Folly," and *Sleeping Murder.*

Westchester, bishop of   A "handsome and well-gaitered" cleric in *At Bertram's Hotel.* He is a longtime friend and admirer of Miss Marple and continues to refer to her as Aunt Jane, even after rising to his current level of episcopal dignity.

Westhaven, Sister   A nurse in *Giant's Bread.* She bears a permanent look of disapproval on her face.

Westholme, Lady   A member of Parliament in *Appointment with Death.* An American, she married an English country squire and managed to have herself elected to Parliament. Although very popular politically, she is much disliked by her fellow politicians—as well as those who know her personally—because of her boorish manners and her loud, annoying, and pushy personality. Nevertheless, she expects to be given a post as an undersecretary in the next general election and is determined to let nothing stand in the way of her advancement.

Weston, Colonel   The chief constable for the area around the Devon coast in *Evil under the Sun.* He heads the investigation into the death of Arlena Marshall and brings Poirot into the case. The bulk of the fieldwork is undertaken by Inspector Colgate. Weston also works with Poirot in *Peril at End House.*

Wetherby, Miss   The postmistress of St. Mary Mead in "The Case of the Perfect Maid." She is a friend of Gladys Holmes and is thus most upset when Miss Holmes's former employers, Emily and Lavinia Skinner, give her references but conspicuously neglect to mention that she is an honest employee.

Wetherby, Mr.   The stepfather of Deirdre Henderson and the husband of Mrs. Wetherby in *Mrs. McGinty's Dead.* He views his stepdaughter with "cold dislike," in large measure because she has control over his and his wife's finances.

Wetherby, Mrs.   The mother of Deirdre Henderson and the wife of Mr. Wetherby in *Mrs. McGinty's Dead.* She is an invalid who relies on her daughter for financial survival because of the terms of an inheritance. Mrs. Wetherby has a fear of open windows.

Wetherby, Caroline   An elderly woman in the village of St. Mary Mead who is declared by Reverend Leonard Clement to be "a mixture of vinegar and gush" and who is also one of the worst gossipmongers in the area. She lives two doors down from Miss Marple and appears in two of her cases, *The Murder at the Vicarage* and *The Body in the Library.*

Wetterman, Maisie   The daughter of the powerful businessman Rudolf Wetterman in "The House of Dreams." She is attracted to John Segrave, but her affections prove misplaced.

Weyman, Michael   An architect who is hired by Sir George Stubbs in *Dead Man's Folly.* He is commissioned to design a new indoor tennis court and also meets an old flame, Sally Legge, whom he eventually convinces to leave her unhappy marriage and begin a relationship with him.

Whalley, Jonathan   An associate of John Ingles in *The Big Four.* He tells Ingles of his deep fear of the vast criminal organization called the Big Four but is killed before he can arrange with Hercule Poirot for protection.

Wharton, Colonel   A intensely stressed British intelligence operative in *Destination Unknown.* He paces and babbles almost incoherently with "machine-gun abruptness."

Wheeling, Emma   A woman who, with her husband, finds Canon Pennyfeather lying unconscious along a country road in *At Bertram's Hotel.* She gives the canon badly needed assistance, including broth, until he can regain his strength and return to the hotel from which he disappeared.

Whistler, Dr. James   A police surgeon who examines the remains of Madame Giselle in *Death in the Clouds.* Although he is able to determine the time of death, he is unable to to pinpoint the nature of the poison in her system.

White, Janet A victim of murder in *Hallowe'en Party*. She was a teacher at the Elm School and was strangled while on her way home. Her murderer is never found, but it is known that she had received threats from a onetime boyfriend. Unfortunately, no one can remember his name or any other pertinent details that would help pinpoint his whereabouts.

Whitfield, Dr. An attorney in *Peril at End House*. He represents the interests of Sir Matthew Seton and Captain Michael Seton and is consulted by Hercule Poirot. The attorney is able to provide important details about the provisions in the wills of the Setons.

Whitstable, Dame Laura A psychologist and radio personality in *A Daughter's a Daughter*. She is a friend of Ann Prentice and served as godmother to Sarah Prentice.

Whittaker, Elizabeth A teacher at the Elm School in *Hallowe'en Party*. A woman devoid of humor and good will, she nevertheless helps to organize the party at which Joyce Reynolds is murdered.

Whittington, Edward A Bolshevist agent who is involved in the Draft Treaty case in *The Secret Adversary*. He is despised by Julius Herscheimer and is described by him as "the skunk, with his big sleek fat face."

Wickham, Claude A composer in "Harlequin's Lane." He is commissioned by Lady Roscheimer to compose the accompanying music to a new production of the harlequinade.

Wilburn, Mrs. A friend of Jane Wilkinson in *Lord Edgware Dies*. She hosts a party at which Jane is a guest; during the party, Jane makes a serious slip when she confuses the city of Paris with the Paris who was the prince of Troy in Greek mythology.

Wilbraham, Dr. An army doctor in *Giant's Bread*.

Wilbraham, Major Charlie A soldier who has recently returned to England after many years of service in East Africa, Wilbraham asks Mr. Parker Pyne for help in overcoming his boredom in "The Case of the Discontented Soldier." The Major has little in the way of material goods besides his pension and a cottage near Cobham, but he is unmarried, does not hunt or fish, and finds no interest in the "endless tittle-tattle about petty village matters" by his neighbors, who "are all pleasant folk, but they've no ideas beyond this island." For fifty pounds payable in advance, Parker Pyne agrees to relieve the Major's boredom. The Major soon becomes embroiled in an adventure involving Miss Freda Clegg and a hunt for a hidden treasure. (See also Clegg, Freda and de Sara, Madeleine.)

Wilding, Sir Richard A writer and adventurer in *The Burden*. He has journeyed the world on adventures and spends much of the year in retreat on an island. His experience does not extend to women, however, and his two marriages are both unsuccessful. His first wife commits adultery, and his second wife is unhappy in their union.

Wilkinson, Jane A successful and genuinely talented American actress in *Lord Edgware Dies*. She was married to George Alfred St. Vincent Marsh and was thus the stepmother of Geraldine Marsh and the aunt of Captain Ronald Marsh. Her marriage to Lord Edgware is a miserable one, however, and she is desperate to bring an end to it so that she might wed her "dreamy monk," the duke of Merton. She thus asks Hercule Poirot to approach her estranged husband and secure his willingness to grant her a divorce. Poirot becomes intrigued by the entire matter when Lord Edgware readily grants her request and is murdered soon afterward, apparently by Jane.

Willard, Lady The wife of Sir John Willard and the mother of Sir Guy Willard in "The Adventure of the Egyptian Tomb." Her husband dies sudenly while on an archaeological expedition, and the deaths that claim other members of the team convince her that her son is also in danger, as he has gone out to take up his father's labors. She enlists the help of Hercule Poirot to save her son from disaster.

Willard, Sir Guy   The son of Sir John Willard and a member of the archaeological expedition to uncover the tomb of the ancient Egyptian king Men-her-Ra in "The Adventure of the Egyptian Tomb." Sir Guy joined the expedition soon after graduating from Oxford, and, after the sudden death of his father, he is determined to carry on the work in the desert. As the expedition is clearly cursed—its members are dying horribly—Sir Guy's mother enlists Hercule Poirot to save her son from the same fate.

Willard, Sir John   A well-known English archaeologist who heads an expedition to uncover the tomb of the ancient Egyptian king Men-her-Ra in "The Adventure of the Egyptian Tomb." Shortly after the remarkable discovery of the tomb, the public is shocked to learn of Sir John's sudden death from heart failure. His death is only the start of tragedy for the members of the ill-fated archaeological expedition. His widow seeks the help of Hercule Poirot to protect her son from the same curse that claimed her husband.

Willett, Mrs.   The woman who rents Sittaford House from Captain Trevlyan in *The Sittaford Mystery.* She and her daughter, Violet, take the Captain's house during the winter and host assorted gatherings for their neighbors. Their primary enjoyment is found in séances, including an especially memorable one at which the death of Captain Trevelyan is prophesied. Mr. Rycroft notes that the Willetts are boorish, "Colonial, of course. No real poise." Inspector Narracott, meanwhile, views Mrs. Willett as "an exceedingly clever woman," and uncovers some very important secrets from her past.

Willett, Violet   The daughter of Mrs. Willett in *The Sittaford Mystery.* She and her mother rent Sittaford House from Captain Trevelyan for the winter and use the home to host assorted gatherings, including séances. At one of the séances, the death of Captain Trevelyan is prophesied.

Williams, Constable   A young police officer who takes part in the investigation into the bludgeoning death of Lady Tressilian in *Towards Zero.* Williams discovers a seemingly incriminating bundle of bloody clothes in the closet of Nevile Strange.

Williams, Inspector   A friend of Lady Derwent in *Why Didn't They Ask Evans?*

Williams, Cecilia   A poor elderly woman in *Five Little Pigs.* She was permitted to reside in the home of Amyas Crale at the time of his murder sixteen years before. She testifies that she saw Caroline Crale wipe fingerprints off of a beer bottle. She did not inform anyone of this at the time of the murder because she considered Amyas's death to be fully justified.

Williams, Maude   A woman in *Mrs. McGinty's Dead* who gives assistance to Hercule Poirot in his investigation. She takes a job in the much troubled Wetherby household to learn more about the residents. She visits Laura Upward on the very night that Laura is murdered, when her son, Robin Upward, is out with Mrs. Ariadne Oliver. Maude has a "full buxom figure [of which] Poirot approved."

Williamson, Flight Lieutenant   An air force officer traveling from Damascus to Baghdad in "The Gate of Baghdad." During the journey, he overhears a conversation that proves of some importance in the investigation into the murder of Smethurst.

Williamson, Ted   A garage mechanic in "The Arcadian Deer." He provides some assistance to Hercule Poirot and, despite his coarse manners, the detective agrees to assist him in finding the lost woman of his heart, the otherwise mysterious maid named Nita.

Willoughby, Dr.   A physician in *Elephants Can Remember.* He is consulted by Hercule Poirot in the hopes that he might be able to provide details about the personality of Dorothea Jarrow.

Wills, Muriel A sharp, acerbic, and ruthless playwright published under the pseudonym Anthony Astor in *Three-Act Tragedy.* She has a mild appearance that belies the dangerous, razor-sharp mind beneath. She also is present at the murders of Reverend Babbington and Sir Bartholomew Strange, making her a suspect in both cases.

Wilmott, Ambassador Randolph The ambassador from the United States to the Court of St. James in "The Ambassador's Boots." He consults the detectives Tommy and Tuppence Beresford when his bag is accidentally exchanged with that of an American senator.

Wilson, Detective Sergeant One of the police officials investigating the death of Madame Giselle in *Death in the Clouds.* In the course of the search for the blowgun used to murder Giselle, Wilson discovers it underneath the seat that had been occupied by Hercule Poirot during the fateful flight. On the basis of this discovery, Wilson pushes for the inquest to mount a charge of willful murder against the detective. This charge is so ludicrous, however, that the coroner refuses to accept it; the cause of death is subsequently amended to read "murder by persons unknown." The accusation made against Poirot is nevertheless a powerful inducement for the detective to solve the case.

Wilson, Ellen The housekeeper at End House in *Peril at End House.* She and her husband act as witnesses to the will written by Nick Buckley.

Wilson, John An Englishman and friend of Paul Déroulard in "The Chocolate Box." Described as "a regular John Bull Englishman, middle-aged and burly," he suffers from a heart condition and takes medication for it; his medicine is of great importance in unmasking the murderer of Déroulard.

Wimbourne, Mr. The attorney who cares for the legal interests of the doomed Crackenthorpe family in *4.50 from Paddington.* He is consulted by Miss Marple and provides copious and very valuable information about the nature of the family's inheritance.

Winburn, Mr. The grandfather of Geoffrey Lancaster and the father of Mrs. Lancaster in "The Lamp." Winburn takes part in many of the events recounted in the story, and, at the end, he hears Geoffrey leaving the house with a friend.

Windlesham, Mr. Charles The first fiancé of the doomed Linnet Ridgeway in *Death on the Nile.* He had hoped to wed the wealthy heiress, but she throws him over when she falls completely in love with Simon Doyle.

Windyford, Dicky An inordinately proud young man in "Philomel Cottage." He has long harbored hopes of marrying Alix King, but he is determined to make his fortune before establishing a lifelong commitment with someone. As a result, Alix—much out of character–does not wait and weds the more available and eager Gerald Martin. Dicky is later summoned by Alix to help her in a moment of great danger.

Winnie A nursemaid in *Giant's Bread.* After she becomes involved with her employer, she is banished from the house.

Winterspoon, Henry An expert in rare poisons in *Death in the Clouds.* Although he has a vague expression on his face, he is actually both intelligent and genuinely practiced in his profession. He identifies the poison that killed Madame Giselle as the venom of the boomslang, or tree snake.

Withers, Jessie The nurse to Johnnie Waverly in "The Adventure of Johnnie Waverly." She is fired by Johnnie's father after the discovery of several incriminating ransom notes in her possession before the actual kidnapping.

Wizell, Fred The gardener in the service of the Ravenscrofts in *Elephants Can Remember.*

Woddell, Agnes A maid in the household of the Symmingtons in *The Moving Finger.* She is troubled by something and knows that she should tell someone about her suspicions. Unfortunately, she is murdered before she can unburden herself.

Wood, J. Baker An American millionaire in "Double Sin" who plans on buying the miniatures that are stolen from the luggage of Mary Durrant. He is stereotypically loud and bombastic.

Woolmar, Janet A parlor maid in the Leonides household in *Crooked House.*

Wray, Barbara A young woman in *Absent in the Spring.* She marries the patient William Wray not out of love but because she is so desperate to escape the clutches of her domineering mother. She has an affair with an army major that comes close to destroying her marriage.

Wray, William The husband of Barbara Wray in *Absent in the Spring.* An exceedingly patient and forgiving man, he helps to rebuild his shattered marriage after his wife's affair with an army major nearly destroys it.

Wright, Alfred The director of the Northern Union Insurance Company in "The Tragedy of Marsdon Manor." He enlists the assistance of Hercule Poirot to investigate the sudden death of Mr. Maltravers, a policyholder who is on the verge of bankruptcy.

Wright, Gerald A young schoolteacher in *A Pocket Full of Rye.* Although he claims to have Socialist leanings, it turns out that he is far more interested in the money of his fiancée than in adhering to any political principles.

Wu Ling A Chinese businessman in "The Lost Mine." Wu Ling represents a Burmese mine seeking investors in England and so travels there on board the S.S. *Assunta.* His family possesses records and maps of the mine, but before he can meet with bankers, he is murdered and the information is stolen.

Wyatt, Captain A former soldier in *The Sittaford Mystery* who lives in a bungalow on the Sittaford estate. The only consistent company he keeps is that of Abdul, a servant from India. Curmudgeonly and utterly unsociable, he refuses to visit or see anyone unless he feels like it.

Wycherly, Nina A loquacious acquaintance of Mr. Parker Pyne in "The Problem at Pollensa Bay." She destroys his efforts at remaining anonymous by announcing the grand exploits of the detective for all to hear.

Wye, Maud A young woman in "The Herb of Death." She is "one of those dark ugly girls who manage to make an effect somehow." Maud is also a suspect in the poisoning death of Sylvia Keene, especially as she was seen the night before the murder in the arms of Sylvia's fiancé, Jerry Lorimer.

Wylde, Martin A young man falsely accused of the murder of Lady Barnaby in "The Sign in the Sky." He is saved from execution only by the timely intervention of Mr. Satterthwaite and Mr. Harley Quin. He is in love with the faithful but dim Sylvia Dale.

Wynwood, Professor A brilliant code-breaker in *The Secret of Chimneys.* He breaks the code used in the Revel-O'Neill letters all before lunch. He believes that "a banana and a water biscuit" are sufficient food for "any sane and healthy man . . . in the middle of the day."

Yahmose The oldest son of Imhotep and the husband of Satipy in *Death Comes As the End.* His marriage is not a happy one, and he is killed when he is impaled by an arrow.

Yardly, Lord A financially strapped nobleman in "The Adventure of 'The Western Star' " who is married to the lovely Lady Yardly. The tenth Viscount Yardly, he is "a cheery, loudvoiced sportsman with a rather red face." Unable to keep pace with his many expenses, he desires to sell his wife's magnificent diamond, the Eastern Star, but it is the target of a thief.

Yardly, Lady Maude A noblewoman married to Lord Yardly in "The Adventure of 'The Western Star.' " She is "tall, dark, with flashing eyes, and a pale proud face—yet something wistful in the curves of the mouth." She lived for several years in California and there met the American actor Gregory Rolf. Lady Yardly comes to Hercule Poirot for help in preventing the theft of her diamond, the Eastern Star.

Yoaschbim An internationally famed opera star

in "The Face of Helen." He is described as "a Yugoslav, a Czech, an Albanian, a Magyar and a Bulgarian," and he has a voice like that of Caruso—able to shatter glass. This ability becomes the centerpiece of a plot to murder a rival for a woman's love.

Zara   A fortune-teller in "Accident." She gives a warning to the retired police inspector Evans that he will soon face a dangerous situation and must be careful; her words prove prophetic.

Zara, Madame   A psychic in "The King of Clubs." She gives a warning to Valerie Saintclair that she faces danger, adding the ominous declaration: "Beware the King of Clubs."

Zarida   The name of a "psychic reader of the future" in "The Blue Geranium." She visits Mrs. Pritchard and makes a series of disturbing predictions, which culminate in Mrs. Pritchard's death.

Zerkowski, Countess Renata   The daughter of an aristocratic English father and a Greek mother who works as an agent for Sir Stafford Nye in *Passenger to Frankfurt.* In the course of her work, she impersonates Daphne Theodofanous and Mary Ann. The primary target of her efforts is the dangerous Youth Movement.

Zeropoulos, Monsieur   The owner of an antiques store in *Death in the Clouds.* He is consulted by Hercule Poirot concerning the blowgun used to murder Madame Giselle. Zeropoulos is able to provide the detective with the name of the person who purchased it, along with the dart that was the actual murder weapon.

Zielinsky, Ella   The social secretary to Marina Gregg in *The Mirror Crack'd from Side to Side.* She suffers from a host of allergies and uses an atomizer to ease her chronic congestion. She is murdered when she inhales from her atomizer and discovers too late that someone has added a dose of prussic acid to the medicine.

Ziyara, Sheik Hussein el-   A longtime friend of Henry Carmichael in *They Came to Baghdad.* He is a much-beloved sheik, known as "a Holy Man and a poet." The sheik gives Carmichael invaluable assistance when he receives an important roll of microfilm with photographs of a secret weapon site in Asia.

Zobeida   The original name used by Mary Moss when she worked as an exotic dancer in "Sanctuary."

Zuleika, Madame   A fortune-teller in *Dead Man's Folly.* She wears "flowing black robes, a gold tinsel scarf wound round her head and a veil across the lower half of her face." Zuleika reads the fortune of Hercule Poirot, but the detective is able to penetrate her disguise and recognizes the familiar person beneath it.

PART THREE

Film, Television, Stage, and Actors

Agatha herself has always been allergic to the adaptation of her books by the cinema . . .

— *M.E.L. Mallowan,* Mallowan's Memoirs

Film

Die Abenteuer, G.m.b.H. (1928)

DIRECTOR: Fred Sauer

CAST: Carlo Aldini (Tommy Beresford), Eve Gray (Tuppence Beresford).

An otherwise forgotten film that is distinguished as the first adaptation of a book by Agatha Christie for the screen. In this case, the original source material was the Tommy and Tuppence Beresford novel *The Secret Adversary* (1922). The translation of the title, *Die Abenteuer, G.m.b.H.,* means *The Adventure, Inc.,* a reference to the lighthearted company formed by the Beresfords to investigate crime.

Alibi (1931)

DIRECTOR: Leslie Hiscott

CAST: Austin Trevor (Hercule Poirot), Harvey Braban (Inspector Davis), Franklin Dyall (Roger Ackroyd), J. H. Roberts (Dr. Sheppard).

The first Christie film to be released with sound, *Alibi* was based on the 1928 play *Alibi* (which was itself adapted from the 1926 Christie

One of the earliest Christie movies, Alibi *(1931). (Photofest)*

novel *The Murder of Roger Ackroyd*). The director, Leslie Hiscott, was also the author of the screenplay for *The Passing of Mr. Quinn* (1928). One other notable aspect of the film was the presence of Austin Trevor as Hercule Poirot, the first of three films that featured Trevor as the Belgian detective. Critics note that Trevor was a little too young to play the detective, and he committed the extreme blasphemy of portraying Poirot without his fabled mustache. (See also *Black Coffee* and *Lord Edgware Dies.*)

The Alphabet Murders (1966)

DIRECTOR: Frank Tashlin
CAST: Tony Randall (Hercule Poirot), Anita Ek-

berg (Amanda Beatrice Cross), Robert Morley (Hastings), Maurice Denham (Japp), Guy Rolfe (Duncan Doncaster), Sheila Allen (Lady Diane), James Villiers (Franklin), Julian Glover (Don Fortune).

A lavish MGM production that is, at times, far too comical (especially given the tense moments that dominate the original novel, *The A.B.C. Murders*) and is often sacrilegious in the way it pokes fun at the Belgian detective and takes liberties with the plot. The screenplay uses a host of red herrings, gags, virtually screwball chases, and asides in poor taste—usually made by Poirot as he surveys a crime scene and notices assorted clues left by the killer.

Tony Randall plays Poirot with a painful deter-

Hercule Poirot (Tony Randall, right) points out an important clue to a rather rotund Captain Hastings (Robert Morley), in The Alphabet Murders *(1966). (Photofest)*

The poster for And Then There Were None *(1945). (Collection of the author)*

mination to accentuate the eccentricities of the sleuth, and his physical appearance is curious but in keeping with an extreme characterization of the detective. Ultimately, the film is disappointing in its lack of fidelity to the original material. There is a memorable cameo by Margaret Rutherford as Miss Marple (the screenplay was the work of David Pursall and Jack Seddon, who had also written the assorted Miss Marple films starring Rutherford for MGM).

Film historians note the fact that *The Alphabet Murders* did not start out as a Tony Randall movie. Instead, according to Philip Jenkinson, writing in the essay "The Agatha Christie Films" (in *Agatha Christie: First Lady of Crime,* 1977), the original version of the film, to be called *The A.B.C. Murders,* cast Zero Mostel as Poirot. Intended to be a very loose adaptation of the novel, and including a truly horrifying bedroom scene for Poirot, the project was given a merciful death by Dame Agatha.

And Then There Were None (1945)

DIRECTOR: René Clair

CAST: Barry Fitzgerald (Judge Quincannon), Walter Huston (Dr. Armstrong), Louis Hayward (Philip Lombard), Roland Young (Detective Blore), June Duprez (Vera Claythorne), Mischa Auer (Prince Nikki Starloff), C. Aubrey Smith (General Sir John Mandrake), Judith Andersen (Emily Brent), Richard Haydn (Rogers, the butler), Queenie Leonard (Mrs. Rogers), Harry Thurston (Boatman).

Generally considered the finest of the early adaptations of an Agatha Christie mystery, *And Then There Were None* was based on the novel *Ten Little Indians* (1939). Produced by Twentieth Century Fox, the screenplay was authored by Clair and Dudley Nichols, with sets by Ernst Fetge and costumes by René Hubert.

Stylish, fast-paced, and suspenseful, even for those who have seen the film before or who are familiar with the original novel, *And Then There*

Were None captures perfectly the eerie atmosphere of Indian Island and the sense of hopelessness felt by the guests, who realize they are inmates, trapped and facing a remorseless killer. Adding to the film are the performances by Barry Fitzgerald and Walter Huston as Judge Quincannon and Dr. Armstrong respectively. Unable to trust each other, the two guests perform a delightful dance of mutual suspicion.

The ending of the film was deliberately chosen by René Clair to mirror not the climax of the original novel but Christie's 1943 stage adaptation. The author adjusted the grim ending of the novel to achieve a happier, romantic conclusion, more satisfying to audiences and also more surprising for readers of the novel. That ending, based on the poem "Ten Little Indians" by Septimus Winner, 1868 was likewise adopted by Clair. Critics pointed out that Clair had thus violated the spirit and the letter of the novel's ending, but Christie herself had already altered the original story in her adaptation for the stage.

Appointment with Death (1988)

DIRECTOR: Michael Winner
CAST: Peter Ustinov (Hercule Poirot), Lauren Bacall (Lady Westholme), Carrie Fisher (Nadine Boynton), John Gielgud (Colonel Carbury), Piper Laurie (Emily Boynton), Hayley Mills (Miss Quinton), Jenny Seagrove (Dr. Sarah King), David Soul (Jefferson Cope), Nicholas Guest (Lennox Boynton), Valerie Richards (Carol Boynton), John Terlesky (Raymond Boynton).

The last major big-screen outing for Hercule Poirot (all the subsequent cinematic productions featuring the detective have been made for television), *Appointment with Death* marks the third cinematic appearance by Peter Ustinov as the great Belgian and the sixth overall, including television. Adapted for the screen by Anthony Shaffer, this film version of the original novel features the well-deserved murder of the former prison warden and matriarchal tyrant Mrs. Boynton. Shaffer also

wrote the screenplay for *Death on the Nile* (1978) and *Evil under the Sun* (1982), although he is best known for his brilliant *Sleuth*.

Appointment with Death was a box-office disappointment, despite possessing all the necessary ingredients for success, including an exotic location, lavish attention to costumes and sets, and a stellar cast. Unfortunately, poor directing and editing could not bring all the elements together, and the entire project pales in comparison with the two earlier Ustinov-Poirot films, *Death on the Nile* and *Evil under the Sun*.

Unlike *Murder on the Orient Express* (1974), in which the performances remain stunningly faithful to the original characters, with all their eccentricities, the performances in *Appointment with Death* seem at times uncertain and handicapped by a pedestrian script. Ustinov is comfortable in the role of Poirot—after other excellent performances in film and on television—and brings his customary vigor to the role of the detective. He generally has a lighter touch than other Poirots (especially Albert Finney). Two other significant casting coups were Lauren Bacall and Sir John Gielgud; both also appeared in *Murder on the Orient Express*.

Black Coffee (1931)

DIRECTOR: Leslie Hiscott
CAST: Austin Trevor (Hercule Poirot), Adrienne Allen, Melville Cooper, Richard Cooper, C. V. France.

A film version, produced by Twickenham Studio, of the Christie play of the same title, which had first debuted in 1930 in London. *Black Coffee* marked the return of Trevor Austin as Hercule Poirot (he had played Poirot previously in *Alibi,* 1931), a performance that is hampered severely by the fact that Trevor bears so little physical similarity to the literary Poirot. Above all, the viewer definitely misses Poirot's mustache. Director Leslie Hiscott had worked previously on *The Mysterious Mr. Quin* (1928), *Alibi* (1931), and *Lord Edgware Dies* (1934).

Death on the Nile (1978)

DIRECTOR: John Guillermin

CAST: Peter Ustinov (Hercule Poirot), Jane Birkin (Louise Bourget), Lois Chiles (Linnet Ridgeway), Bette Davis (Mrs. Van Schuyler), Mia Farrow (Jacqueline de Bellefort), Jon Finch (Jim Ferguson), Olivia Hussey (Rosalie Otterbourne), George Kennedy (Andrew Pennington), Angela Lansbury (Salome Otterbourne), Simon McCorkindale (Simon Doyle), David Niven (Colonel Race), Maggie Smith (Miss Bowers), Jack Warden (Doctor Bessner), Harry Andrews (Barnstable), I. S. Johar (manager of the *Karnak*).

Following the success—the Academy Award–winning success—of *Murder on the Orient Express* (1974), EMI-Paramount was eager to bring to life another of Christie's mysteries. The result was *Death on the Nile,* based on the 1937 novel and adapted for film by Anthony Shaffer, the author of the screenplays for *Evil under the Sun* (1982) and *Appointment with Death* (1988). As was true with *Murder on the Orient Express*—but with less opulence—*Death on the Nile* boasts a stellar cast, a gorgeous location (Egypt during the 1920s), and exquisite attention to costume detail. Particularly notable are the costumes worn by Mia Farrow and Angela Lansbury, two extremes of sartorial grandeur. Lansbury's costumes (like her delightfully over-the-top characterization of Salome Otterbourne, an alcoholic, oversexed writer) stand out as an example par excellence of the excesses of a bygone era.

Death on the Nile is aided considerably by the

The suspects assemble in Death on the Nile *(1978). (Photofest)*

performances of the entire cast, including Bette Davis, the ever-reliable Maggie Smith, David Niven, and Mia Farrow as the clever Jacqueline de Bellefort. Peter Ustinov appears for the first time as Hercule Poirot, filling the shoes (and mustache) of Albert Finney (for further details, please see under Ustinov, Peter).

Death on the Nile was followed by five more portrayals of Poirot by Ustinov in film and on television: *Evil under the Sun* (1982); *Thirteen at Dinner* (1985); *Dead Man's Folly* (1986); *Murder in Three Acts* (1986); and *Appointment with Death* (1988). Although *Death on the Nile* did not fare as well at the box office as *Murder on the Orient Express* (1974), it did well enough to guarantee the production of another Christie adaptation—*The Mirror Crack'd,* with Angela Lansbury as Miss Marple.

Desyat negrityat (1987)

DIRECTOR: Stanislav Govorukhin

CAST: Vladimir Zeldin, Tatyana Drubich, Aleksandr Kajdanovsky, Aleksei Zharkov, Anatoli Romashin, Lyudmila Maksakova, Mikhail Gluzsky, Aleksei Zolotnitsky, Irina Tereshchenko, Aleksandr Abdulov.

A Russian film adaptation of *Ten Little Niggers,* produced by the Odessa Film Studios. Virtually unknown in the West, the film was adapted from the original novel by Stanislav Govorukhin, the director.

Endless Night (1971)

DIRECTOR: Sidney Gilliat

CAST: Hywel Bennett (Michael), Britt Ekland (Greta), Hayley Mills (Ellie), David Bauer (Uncle Frank), Peter Bowles (Reuben), Patience Collier (Miss Townsend), Windsor Davies (Sargeant Reene), Walter Gotell (Constantine), David Healy (Jason), Helen Horton (Aunt Beth), Lois Maxwell (Cora), George Sanders (Lippincott), Ann Way (Mrs. Philpott).

A United Artists adaptation of Christie's 1967 romantic mystery novel, *Endless Night* was a major disappointment in England and was never even released in theaters in the United States. This was a sad fate for a version of one of Christie's favorite novels. As has been true with other adaptations, *Endless Night* is considered by most critics surprisingly lifeless and tends to creep along at a maddeningly slow pace. Savaged by English critics, the film was soon forgotten and is now seen—albeit rarely—on late-night television or on video.

Evil under the Sun (1982)

DIRECTOR: Guy Hamilton

CAST: Peter Ustinov (Hercule Poirot), Diana Rigg (Arlena Marshall), Jane Birkin (Christine Redfern), Nicholas Clay (Patrick Redfern), Maggie Smith (Daphne Castle), Colin Blakely (Sir Horace Blatt), Roddy McDowall (Rex Brewster), Sylvia Miles (Myra Gardener), James Mason (Odell Gardener), Dennis Quilley (Captain Marshall), Emily Hone (Linda Marshall).

The fourth adaptation by EMI of a Christie novel for the big screen (after *Murder on the Orient Express,* 1974; *Death on the Nile,* 1978; and *The Mirror Crack'd,* 1980), *Evil under the Sun* is based on the 1941 book. Whereas the first three films were largely faithful to the original material, this film chose to move the location from the Devon coast and the converted Georgian mansion called the Jolly Roger Hotel, located on Smuggler's Island, Leathercombe Bay, to a more exotic Mediterranean island, where nasty remarks can be made about the ignorant and lazy locals. The spot is nevertheless quite beautiful and adds considerably to the visual appeal of the film.

As with its predecessors, *Evil under the Sun* relies upon two primary ingredients for its success: the overall production values and the stellar cast, which populates an otherwise crowded plot. Stylish and lavishly costumed, the film is a joy to watch for its attention to detail and its array of outfits. *Evil under the Sun* also boasts some sharp dialogue, especially the biting exchanges between

Hercule Poirot (Peter Ustinov) questions a suspect, Sir Horace Blatt (Colin Blakely), in Evil under the Sun *(1982). (Photofest)*

the two former stage performers Arlena Marshall and Daphne Castle (dripping with vicious sarcasm and insincere flattery), portrayed by Diana Rigg and Maggie Smith respectively. As in the novel, virtually everyone has a reason to murder Arlena Marshall, and the rock-solid performers all imbue their characters with such life that any one of them is a believable suspect. Special notice goes to Jane Birkin (who also appeared in *Death on the Nile*) as the pale and long-suffering Christine Redfern. At the end of the film, she makes a truly memorable and dazzling descent down a staircase, an event that leaves her fellow guests gasping for air. Also notable is the presence of Colin Blakely and Denis Quilley, who both appeared previously in *Murder on the Orient Express.*

In his second outing as Hercule Poirot, Peter Ustinov has considerable fun, and takes Poirot to new cinematic heights, even performing a magic trick. Most arresting is his version of Poirot at the beach. At the film's climax, the murderer manages to accomplish a feat on behalf of all criminals captured by the detective: Poirot is punched in the nose.

Kiken-na Onna-tachi (1985)

DIRECTOR: Yoshitaro Nomura

CAST: Koji Ishizaka, Shinobu Otake, Kimiko Ikegami, Mariko Fuji, Yuko Kazu, Eitaro Ozawa, Tanie Kitabayashi, Akira Terao, Kunihiko Mitamura

A Japanese film adaptation of the original novel, *The Hollow*, *Kiken-na Onna-tachi (Dangerous Women)* is virtually unheard of outside of Japan. The adaptation was written by Juichiro Takeuchi and Motomu Furuta.

Lord Edgware Dies (1934)

DIRECTOR: Henry Edwards

CAST: Austin Trevor (Hercule Poirot), Jane Carr, Richard Cooper, John Turnbull.

This adaptation of the Christie novel *Lord Edgware Dies* (1934) was released by Real Art Studios and produced by Julius Hagen (who had worked on such previous Poirot films as *The Mysterious Mr. Quin*, 1928, and *Alibi*, 1931). The film marked the third and last appearance of Austin Trevor as Hercule Poirot, an appearance characterized once again by the absence of the famed Poirot mustache—a continued source of frustration for viewers.

Love from a Stranger (1937)

DIRECTOR: Rowland V. Lee

CAST: Ann Harding (Carol Howard), Basil Rathbone (Gerald Lovell), Jean Cadell (Aunt Lou), Donald Calthrop (Hobson), Binnie Hale (Kate Meadows), Joan Hickson (Emmy), Eugene Leahy (Mr. Tuttle), Bryan Powley (Doctor Gribble), Bruce Seton (Ronald Bruce).

This adaptation by Frances Marion of the 1936 play *Love from a Stranger,* by Frank Vosper, was itself based on an original short story by Christie, "Philomel Cottage." Filmed by Trafalgar Studios and released in the United States by United Artists, the film boasts several performers who went on to long and distinguished careers, including Basil Rathbone and Ann Harding.

Love from a Stranger (1947)

DIRECTOR: Richard Whorf

CAST: Sylvia Sidney (Cecily Harrington), Frederick Worlock (Inspector Hobday), John Hodiak (Manuel Cortez), Phyllis Barry (Waitress), Billy Bevan (Taxi Driver), Colin Campbell (Bank Teller), David Cavendish (Policeman), Charles Coleman (Hotel Doorman), Bob Corey (Taxi Driver), Ernest Cossart (Billings), Abe Dinovitch (Man), Isobel Elsom (Auntie Loo-Loo), John Howard (Nigel Lawrence), Ann Richards (Mavia), Philip Tonge (Dr. Gribble).

A remake of the generally well-received 1937 film of the same name, *Love from a Stranger* was originally released in the United States and then in England that same year under the title *A Stranger Passes.* Filmed by the independent company Eagle-Lion Films and produced by James J. Geller, *Love from a Stranger* was adapted for the screen by Philip MacDonald, who made a number of changes in the character names and the overall story line.

As is often the case with sequels and remakes (especially a remake of a film from only ten years before), it was difficult for audiences and critics to

Love from a Stranger *(1947), the second adaptation of "Philomel Cottage." (Photofest)*

embrace this version of *Love from a Stranger.* The production's value was undermined further by the absence of any big box-office draw in the cast. Subjected to harsh reviews by critics, the film failed and never escaped from the shadow of the first version.

The Mirror Crack'd (1980)

DIRECTOR: Guy Hamilton
CAST: Angela Lansbury (Miss Jane Marple), Edward Fox (Inspector Craddock), Elizabeth Taylor (Marina Gregg), Geraldine Chaplin (Ella Zielinsky), Kim Novak (Lola Brewster), Rock Hudson (Jason Rudd), Wendy Morgan (Cherry), Margaret Courtenay (Mrs. Bantry), Charles Gray (Bates, the Butler), Maureen Bennett (Heather Badcock), Eric Dodson (the Major), Charles Lloyd-Pack (the Vicar), Richard Pearson (Doctor Haydock).

The third adaptation of a Christie work by EMI Films (following the successful Poirot films *Murder on the Orient Express,* 1974, and *Death on the Nile,* 1978), *The Mirror Crack'd* marked a change of atmosphere for this studio's previous lavish productions. Instead of another Poirot mystery—and instead of staying with the demonstrated box-office success of the Belgian detective—EMI chose to produce a Miss Marple feature based on the novel *The Mirror Crack'd from Side to Side* (1962), the plot of which partly concerns itself with the acting profession and thus possesses intriguing casting possibilities. Most unusual of all, however, was the choice of actress for the role of Miss Marple.

Instead of casting an older actress to play the beloved spinster-sleuth, the producers chose Angela Lansbury, who had already appeared in the vigorous role of Mrs. Otterbourne in *Death on the Nile.* Lansbury was decades too young to play the aged sleuth, and it was thus necessary for her to be given added years with the help of extensive makeup. She was also facing an immediate uphill struggle with audiences because of the still-lingering popularity of Margaret Rutherford, who played Miss Marple during the 1960s. In the end,

Lansbury's interpretation and the presence of a genuinely heavy cast could not capture the magic of the previous two EMI outings.

Two primary difficulties emerged in the adaptation of *The Mirror Crack'd from Side to Side.* First, the cast of notables never gels together, as it did in what became the model for such adaptations, *Murder on the Orient Express.* Second, Lansbury's interpretation of Miss Marple is enjoyable, but of dubious fidelity to the original. As did Helen Hayes, Lansbury chose to make Miss Marple far more likable and sweet-natured than the detective of literature. She is also, at times, a bit daffy, with a vacant stare, and she is also possessed of a light sense of humor, albeit a gallows one. While beautifully acted—Lansbury never gives a bad performance—there is just not enough of the real Miss Marple.

The Mirror Crack'd was not as successful as *Death on the Nile* and was no match for the success of *Orient Express.* It was thus a turning point in the history of Christie on film, beginning a gradual process of diminishing returns and a movement that relegated Christie adaptations to the exclusive realm of television. *The Mirror Crack'd* was produced by John Brabourne and Richard Goodwin, with a screenplay by Jonathan Hales and Barry Sandler.

Murder at the Gallop (1963)

DIRECTOR: George Pollock
CAST: Margaret Rutherford (Miss Marple), Robert Morley (Hector Enderby), Flora Robson (Miss Milchrest), Charles "Bud" Tingwell (Inspector Craddock), Katya Douglas (Rosamund Shane), Stringer Davis (Mr. Stringer), James Villiers (Michael Shane), Gordon Harris (Sergeant Bacon), Robert Urquhart (George Crossfield), Duncan Lamont (Hillman), Finlay Currie (Old Enderby).

The second MGM film featuring Margaret Rutherford as Miss Marple, *Murder at the Gallop* was adapted for the screen by David Pursall and Jack Seddon, with assistance from James Ca-

Miss Marple
(Margaret Rutherford)
at work in Murder at
the Gallop *(1963).*
(Photofest)

vanagh, from the original Christie novel *After the Funeral* (1953). As the original novel was a Poirot mystery, the film obviously supplanted the book's main character, a change of which Agatha Christie disapproved strongly, calling the idea "awful." While the swapping of detectives did nothing to change Christie's already low opinion of film adaptations of her works, she was forced to acquiesce, as rights to several of her books had been sold to MGM in England (see *Murder, She Said* for other details).

Following loosely the general plot of *After the Funeral, Murder at the Gallop* is generally considered the best of the MGM Rutherford projects, in large measure because of the terrific interplay between Rutherford and Morley, in the role of Hector Enderby. Rutherford is also assisted ably by her husband, Stringer Davis, as Mr. Stringer, an assistant of sorts to Miss Marple. Definitely the high point of the MGM series of Marple films, *Murder at the Gallop* was followed by the far less successful *Murder Most Foul* (1964) and *Murder*

Ahoy! (1964). One especially memorable scene features Miss Marple on horseback.

Murder Most Foul (1964)

DIRECTOR: George Pollock

CAST: Margaret Rutherford (Miss Jane Marple), Ron Moody (Clifford Cosgood), Charles "Bud" Tingwell (Inspector Craddock), Andrew Cruickshank (Justice Crosby), Megs Jenkins (Mrs. Thomas), Stringer Davis (Mr. Stringer), Francesca Annis (Sheila Upward), Pauline Jameson (Maureen Summers).

This film marked the third time Margaret Rutherford played Miss Marple for MGM, following the two previous successful releases *Murder, She Said* (1962) and *Murder at the Gallop* (1963). As was the case with *Murder at the Gallop, Murder Most Foul* was adapted by David Pursall and Jack Seddon from an original Christie novel, in this case *Mrs. McGinty's Dead* (1952); this meant that, as with *Murder at the Gallop* (based on *After the Funeral*), what was originally a Poirot mystery was converted to a Miss Marple adventure. The plot bears only a passing similarity to the original story and definitely misses the presence of Poirot and Mrs. Ariadne Oliver (who was actually more similar to Margaret Rutherford in build and temperament than was Miss Marple).

If the changes in character and plot are not distressing enough to Christie fans, then the title is surely the most appalling aspect of the entire production. Rather than stay with the original title, *Mrs. McGinty's Dead,* MGM adopted a new title, choosing—apparently by coincidence—a well-known Shakespearean line, "murder, most foul," from *Hamlet.* Unfortunately, Agatha Christie had already expressed a dim view of such a title, calling it "rotten." In "Mr. Eastwood's Adventure" (collected in *The Listerdale Mystery,* 1934), Christie had the main character, the writer Mr. Eastwood, lament that publishers too often changed the titles of his stories, citing such awful examples as "Murder Most Foul."

Despite all of these obvious shortcomings, *Murder Most Foul* is ultimately an enjoyable film, thanks to Rutherford and some amusing scenes. The film opens with the classic discovery of a corpse and a suspect in apparently damning circumstances. There is then a quick cut to a courtroom, where the jury announces that it is hopelessly deadlocked because of the obstinacy of one member. The camera then pans slowly downward, passing the exasperated jury members to focus on the sole juror who refuses to convict—Miss Marple. The old sleuth then sets out to prove the defendant innocent. Her investigation brings her into the world of the theater.

Murder Most Foul boasts several notable cast members. Stringer Davis, Rutherford's real-life husband, plays (once again) Miss Marple's assistant, Mr. Stringer. Also appearing in the role of Sheila Upward is the young Francesca Annis, who went on to play Tuppence Beresford in the London Weekend Television series *Partners in Crime.*

Murder on the Orient Express (1974)

DIRECTOR: Sidney Lumet

CAST: Albert Finney (Hercule Poirot), Lauren Bacall (Mrs. Hubbard), Martin Balsam (Bianchi), Ingrid Bergman (Greta), Jacqueline Bisset (Countess Andrenyi), Jean-Pierre Cassel (Pierre Paul Michel), Sean Connery (Colonel Arbuthnott), John Gielgud (Beddoes), Wendy Hiller (Princess Dragomiroff), Anthony Perkins (Hector McQueen), Vanessa Redgrave (Mary Debenham), Rachel Roberts (Hildegarde Schmidt), Richard Widmark (Ratchett), Michael York (Count Andrenyi), Colin Blakely (Dick Hardman).

Based on the 1934 novel of the same name, *Murder on the Orient Express* is considered by many to be the zenith of the adaptations of Christie works on film. Directed by Sidney Lumet and adapted for the screen by Paul Dehn, the film was released by EMI and produced by Richard Godwin and John Brabourne. Production of the film was made almost impossible because of the initial refusal of Agatha Christie to sell any more book rights. She had been severely disappointed by the MGM Miss Marple movies of the 1960s starring Margaret Rutherford, and she was understandably reluctant to be associated with any further adaptations. EMI, however, was anxious to produce a Christie film, and studio chairman Nat Cohen enlisted help to convince Christie that a faithful, well-produced adaptation was possible. One of the film's advocates was Lord Louis Mountbatten (d. 1979), uncle to Prince Philip, World War II naval hero, and former viceroy of India. Mountbatten also had a hand in bringing to life another Christie masterpiece, *The Murder of Roger Ackroyd,* back in 1926 (for details, please see page 104). After long negotiations, Christie was convinced, especially after being assured by producer John Brabourne that she would not be disappointed.

Under Brabourne, coproducer Richard Goodwin, Lumet, and production designer Tony Walton, *Murder on the Orient Express* was the most lavish Christie production to date. Beyond the superb costumes and cinematography, the produc-

Poirot exposes a masterful murder plot in Murder on the Orient Express *(1974)*. *(Photofest)*

tion also added a grand touch of authenticity by borrowing the real of cars the Orient Express from the Compagnie Internationale des Wagon-lits Museum.

Murder on the Orient Express premiered at the ABC Cinema in London with a star-studded guest list, including Queen Elizabeth II. It was a grand moment for Christie, especially the banquet at Claridge's; it was also the last public event before her death. Critics and audiences loved the movie, and even Dame Agatha confessed her pleasure with the adaptation. She did, however, voice disapproval of Hercule Poirot's mustache. Adding to the prestige of the film was its success in Academy Award nominations: best actor (Finney); best

supporting actress (Bergman); best screenplay adapted from other material (Dehn); best cinematographer (Geoffrey Unsworth); best music (Richard Rodney Bennett); and best costume design (Tony Walton). Ingrid Bergman won her third Oscar for her performance as Greta Ohlsson.

Murder, She Said (1962)

DIRECTOR: George Pollock

CAST: Margaret Rutherford (Miss Marple), Arthur Kennedy (Dr. Quimper), Muriel Pavlow (Emma), James Robertson Justice (Craackenthorpe), Thorley Walters (Cedric), Charles "Bud" Tingwell (Craddock), Conrad Phillips (Harold), Ronald Howard (Eastley), Joan Hickson (Mrs.

Miss Marple (Margaret Rutherford) goes undercover in Murder, She Said *(1962). (Photofest)*

Kidder), Stringer Davis (Mr. Stringer), Ronnie Raymond (Alexander), Gerald Cross (Albert), Michael Golden (Hillman), Barbara Leake (Mrs. Stainton), Gordon Harris (Bacon).

The first MGM film featuring Margaret Rutherford as Miss Marple, *Murder, She Said* was followed by three more productions: *Murder at the Gallop* (1963), *Murder Most Foul* (1964), and *Murder Ahoy!* (1964). None of the films ever met with the approval of Agatha Christie, who complained that the climaxes were weak, and she derived genuine delight from the failure of the films at the box office. She had initially sold the rights to several of her books in the hope that MGM might have more skill in adapting them than other production companies had previously demonstrated. She was disappointed immediately when MGM announced their intention to forego television productions—which Christie had wanted—in favor of feature films. They then decided to adapt the novel *4.50 from Paddington* (1957), and for the role of Miss Marple they cast the well-known ac-

tress Margaret Rutherford. It was a curious choice insofar as she bore little physical resemblance to the literary Miss Marple; Rutherford, however, was ideally suited to the active and rather gregarious Miss Marple created by screenwriters David Pursall and Jack Seddon (who wrote the other MGM Rutherford films). Agatha Christie had great respect for Rutherford, but she thought little of her as Miss Marple (for other details, please see under Rutherford, Margaret).

Murder, She Said announces its departure from the original novel almost immediately by eliminating the character Elspeth McGillicuddy and having Miss Marple witness the murder instead. She then manages to insinuate herself into the Crackenthorpe household, receiving assistance from Mr. Stringer, who appeared in all the MGM Marple films and who was played by Rutherford's real-life husband, Stringer Davis. In an additional interesting casting note, the role of Mrs. Kidder is played by Joan Hickson, who went on to play the definitive Miss Marple some three decades later.

Ordeal by Innocence (1984)

DIRECTOR: Desmond Davis

CAST: Donald Sutherland (Dr. Arthur Calgary), Faye Dunaway (Rachel Argyle), Christopher Plummer (Leo Argyle), Diana Quick (Gwenda Vaughan), Anita Carey (Martha Jessup), Annette Crosbie (Kirsten Lindstrom), Michael Elphick (Inspector Huish), George Innes (Archie Leach), Michael Maloney (Micky Argyle), Ian McShane (Philip Durant), Sarah Miles (Mary Durant), Phoebe Nicholls (Tina Argyle), Ron Pember (Ferryman), Cassie Stuart (Maureen Clegg), Valerie Whittington (Hester Argyle).

A Golan-Globus production of the 1958 novel of the same name, *Ordeal by Innocence* is one of the more forgettable Christie adaptations from the 1980s (see also *The Mirror Crack'd* and *Appointment with Death*). Produced by Jenny Craven and written for the screen by Alexander Stewart, the film is surprisingly dreary, with collectively uninspired performances by the cast. Adding to the lack of atmosphere is a highly inappropriate musical score that includes oddly placed jazz music. Donald Sutherland does his best as the doggedly determined Dr. Calgary, but the script lets him down throughout. The film had a promising premiere in London's West End, with Queen Elizabeth II and the Duke of Edinburgh in attendance for a royal charity screening, but royal attention could not save the film from box-office oblivion.

The Passing of Mr. Quinn (1928)

DIRECTOR: Julius Hagen

CAST: Stewart Rome (Quinn), Trilby Clark (Mrs. Appleby), Ursula Jeans (Maid).

A silent film that is distinguished as the first British-made film version of a Christie story. Adapted from "The Coming of Mr. Quin" (part of the short-story collection *The Mysterious Mr. Quin*, 1930), the film inexplicably spells the title character's name with two *n*'s. The screenplay was penned by Leslie Hiscott, who also wrote the screenplay for *Alibi* (1931) and directed *Black Coffee* (1931).

The director, Julius Hagen, was also the director of *Alibi* and the producer of *Black Coffee*.

The Spider's Web (1960)

DIRECTOR: Godfrey Grayson

CAST: Cicely Courtneidge (Miss Peake), Jack Hulbert (Lord Roland Delahaye), Glynis Johns (Clarissa Hailsham-Brown), John Justin (Henry Hailsham-Brown).

This decidedly low-budget adaptation of Christie's 1954 play by the same name was produced by the Danzigers, a British company. *The Spider's Web* was released and distributed in England by United Artists; owing to its dreadful box-office returns, it was never released in the United States.

Despite its very modest budget, *The Spider's Web* was able to attract the considerable talents of Glynis Johns and the well-known British comedians Cicely Courtneidge and Jack Hulbert. They could not rescue the adaptation from its inherent production and script weaknesses, and the film is all but forgotten today.

Taina chyornykh drozdov (1983)

DIRECTOR: Vadim Derbenyov

CAST: Ita Euer, Vladimir Sedov, Lyubov Polischuk, Natalya Danilova, Elsa Radzinya.

A Russian version of *A Pocket Full of Rye,* this film is all but unknown in the United States or anywhere outside of Europe. The translation of the title is *The Secret of the Blackbirds.*

Ten Little Indians (1965)

DIRECTOR: George Pollock

CAST: Hugh O'Brian (Hugh Lombard), Fabián (Mike Raven), Shirley Eaton (Ann Clyde), Leo Genn (General Mandrake), Stanley Holloway (William Blore), Wilfrid Hyde-White (Judge Cannon), Daliah Lavi (Ilona Bergen), Dennis Price (Dr. Armstrong), Marianne Hoppe (Frau Grohmann), Mario Adorf (Herr Grohmann).

The second film version of the original 1939 Christie novel *And Then There Were None, Ten Little Indians* was released by Seven Arts and produced

A scene from The Spider's Web *(1960). (Collection of the author)*

by Oliver A. Unger, with a screenplay by Peter Welbeck and Peter Yeldham. Director George Pollock was experienced with Christie projects, having directed the popular MGM films starring Margaret Rutherford as Miss Marple.

In creating a new version of *Ten Little Indians,* Welbeck and Yeldham changed the setting for the story from the isolated Indian Island to the higher altitude and greater solitude of the Alps. The change of atmosphere does present a few new wrinkles for the murderer, who has to do away with members of the doomed gathering at a chalet. While the remake does not match the 1945 version, it does have some genuinely inspired moments, especially the beautifully active scenes between Leo Genn and Wilfrid Hyde-White.

Ten Little Indians (1975)

DIRECTOR: Peter Collinson

CAST: Oliver Reed (Hugh Lombard), Richard Attenborough (Arthur Cannon), Elke Sommer (Vera Clyde), Charles Aznavour (Michel Raven), Adolfo Celi (Andre Salve), Gert Fröbe (Wilhelm Blore), Herbert Lom (Edward Armstrong), Alberto de Mendoza (Otto Martino), Maria Röhm (Elsa Martino).

This film is the third cinematic version of the 1939 novel *And There Were None.* It was released by Avco-Embassy and produced by Harry Alan Towers; the adaptation was made by Peter Welbeck, who had worked on the screenplay for the 1965 version. In what perhaps seemed like a good idea at the time, Welbeck and the producers placed the setting not on Indian Island, or even in the Alps, but in a remote hotel in modern Iran. A lifeless and poorly paced fiasco, *Ten Little Indians* is one of those films that should never have been made, especially given the superior versions that had preceded it, the quality of the original material, and the fact that it came out only one year after *Murder on the Orient Express.* It is also a pity that Richard Attenborough, who had been in the original cast of *The Mousetrap,* should have taken part in so worthless a production.

Ten Little Indians (1989)

DIRECTOR: Alan Birkinshaw

CAST: Donald Pleasence (Judge Wargrave), Brenda Vaccaro (Marion Marshall), Frank Stallone

Another adaptation of And Then There Were None, Ten Little Indians *(1965); note the statues of the Indians in the center of the table.* (Photofest)

(Captain Lombard), Herbert Lom (General Romensky), Warren Berlinger (Mr. Blore), Yehuda Efroni (Dr. Werner), Neil McCarthy (Anthony Marston), Moira Lister (Mrs. Rodgers), Paul Smith (Mr. Rodgers).

The fourth version of the 1939 novel *And Then There Were None,* this film was released by Breton Films and was technically the last Agatha Christie work to be brought to the big screen by an American or European production company. This makes for a sad farewell (for the moment, at least) for Christie on film, as it would scarcely be possible for a worse film version to be made of this popular and enjoyable novel; honorable mention for the second-worst adaptation of a Christie work does go to the 1975 movie of the same name. Once again, the producers apparently thought to spice things up by moving the story out of the original Indian Island setting—this time, the film is set in a safari camp. Every possible cliché is thrown into the plot, and audiences are hard-pressed to maintain any interest even before the first of the doomed campers is murdered.

Witness for the Prosecution (1957)

DIRECTOR: Billy Wilder

CAST: Tyrone Power (Leonard Vole), Marlene Dietrich (Christine Vole), Charles Laughton (Sir Wilfrid Robarts), Elsa Lanchester (Miss Plimsoll), John Williams (Brogan-Moore), Henry Daniell (Mayhew), Ian Wolfe (Carter), Torin Thatcher

Sir Wilfrid Robarts (Charles Laughton) in his beloved courtroom, in Witness for the Prosecution *(1957).* (Photofest)

(Mr. Myers), Norma Varden (Mrs. French), Una O'Connor (Janet McKenzie), Francis Compton (Judge), Philip Tonge (Inspector Hearne), Ruta Lee (Diana).

This film adaptation of the 1953 Christie stage play of the same name, based on the original short story (published for the first time in 1931), was the first cinematic version of one of Christie's works since 1947 and was also the first genuinely successful Christie film since 1945. Produced by United Artists, *Witness for the Prosecution* paired one of Hollywood's most prominent directors—Wilder—with a truly inspired cast, which included Charles Laughton, Tyrone Power, and Marlene Dietrich. Laughton, who played the brilliant barrister Sir Wilfrid Robarts, had already portrayed Hercule Poirot in the first Christie-based stage production, *Alibi* (1928).

As is the case with the original stage adaptation of the Christie short story, the film version of "Witness for the Prosecution" does not rely on the short story's rather frustrating ending. Instead, it follows the play's more surprising—and satisfying—denouement. At its heart, of course, the film relies upon the sparkling performances of its impressive cast. Laughton portrays Sir Wilfrid as a towering legal mind who nevertheless suffers from the incessant nagging of Miss Plimsoll, his exasperated nurse, played by Elsa Lanchester. Torin Thatcher also does a fine job in the thankless role of Mr. Myers, the prosecutor who believes he has an airtight case against Leonard Vole. Above all, of course, is the chemistry the actors bring to the peculiar relationship between Leonard and Christine Vole. There is always some new facet to their relationship that is revealed as the trial progresses.

Witness for the Prosecution was one of the most profitable films of the year and was nominated for six Oscars: best picture; best actor (Laughton); best supporting actress (Lanchester); best director (Wilder); best sound; and best film editing. Unfortunately, the film won no Academy Awards. The film was remade for television in 1982 with Sir Ralph Richardson, Beau Bridges, and Diana Rigg.

Zagadka Endhauza (1989)

DIRECTOR: Vadim Derbenyo

CAST: Anatoli Ravikovich (Hercules Poirot), Dmitri Krylov (Hastings), Ilona Ozola, Virginia Kelmelite, Inara Slucka, Andrei Kharitono.

A 1989 Russian film based on the original Christie novel *Peril at End House.* The film is virtually unknown today, although it was one of several Russian films based on Christie writings.

NON-CHRISTIE ADAPTATIONS

Agatha (1979)

DIRECTOR: Michael Apted

CAST: Dustin Hoffman (Wally Stanton), Vanessa Redgrave (Agatha Christie), Timothy Dalton (Colonel Archibald Christie), Helen Morse (Evelyn Crawley), Celia Gregory (Nancy Neele), Paul Brooke (John Foster), Carolyn Pickles (Charlotte Fisher), Timothy West (Kenward), Tony Britton (William Collins), Alan Badel (Lord Brackenbury), Robert Longden (Pettelson), Donald Nithsdale (Uncle Jones), Yvonne Gilan (Mrs. Braithwaite), Sandra Voe (Therapist), Barry Hart (Superintendent MacDonald).

Based on the 1978 novel by Kathleen Tynan and adapted for the screen by the author, *Agatha* offers an imaginative and lushly filmed speculation about the famous ten-day disappearance of Agatha Christie in 1926, following the death of her mother and the collapse of her unhappy marriage to Archie Christie. The topic naturally makes for an intriguing mystery story to rival the best Hercule Poirot or Miss Marple mystery, especially as Christie never spoke about the missing days, not even in her autobiography. *Agatha,* then, seeks to answer the question about the riddle, albeit in a fanciful fashion.

Vanessa Redgrave portrays the long-suffering author, who retreats from her weary existence and signs herself into the Harrogate Hotel under an assumed name to ponder her future. As the days pass and the public begins to wonder where Christie has disappeared to, an American newspaper investigator is able to locate her and becomes involved with Christie; he helps prevent the elaborate suicide she had planned.

Murder Ahoy! (1964)

DIRECTOR: George Pollock

CAST: Margaret Rutherford (Miss Marple), Lionel Jeffries (Captain Rhumstone), William Merwyn (Breeze-Connington), Joan Benham (Matron Alice Fanbraid), Stringer Davis (Mr. Stringer), Nicholas Parsons (Dr. Crump), Miles Malleson (Bishop Faulkner), Henry Oscar (Lord Rudkin), Derek Nimmo (Sub-Lieutenant Humbert), Gerald Cross (Lieutenant Commander L. W. Brewer Dimchurch), Norma Foster (Assistant Matron Shirley Boston), Terence Edmond (Sgt. Bacon), Francis Matthews (Lieutenant Compton), Lucy Griffiths (Millie).

This film heralds the fourth and final MGM outing for Margaret Rutherford as Miss Marple. As produced by Lawrence P. Bachmann and scripted by David Pursall and Jack Seddon, *Murder Ahoy!* is technically a Miss Marple movie, but it is not a Christie adaptation, as the story was an original creation. This is an important point to make, as not only did MGM take severe liberties with Miss Marple, but this final film in the series was so poorly developed that a clear dissociation from Agatha Christie can scarcely be stressed sufficiently.

Murder Ahoy!—as the title indicates—sets Miss Marple adrift with a murderer on board a ship. Rutherford is as enjoyable as ever as Miss Marple, and she labors valiantly to keep the film afloat. She is aided in her task by the always delightful Lionel Jeffries, but neither can do much to salvage the weak plot, poorly executed comedy, and rather claustrophobic sets. *Murder Ahoy!*

was a sad farewell for a memorable Miss Marple; as a curious side note, *Murder Ahoy!* was released in United States before the vastly superior *Murder Most Foul.* As in her other Christie films, Rutherford was joined by her husband, Stringer Davis.

Murder by Death (1976)

DIRECTOR: Robert Moore

CAST: Eileen Brennan (Tess Skeffington), Truman Capote (Lionel Twain), James Coco (Milo Perrier), James Cromwell (Marcel), Peter Falk (Sam Diamond), Alec Guinness (Bensonmum), Elsa Lanchester (Jessica Marbles), David Niven (Dick Charleston), Peter Sellers (Sidney Wang), Maggie Smith (Dora Charleston), Estelle Winwood (Miss Withers), Richard Narita (Willie Wang).

One of the most inventive comedies ever written by Neil Simon, *Murder by Death* affectionately but ruthlessly skewers virtually all of the most beloved detectives from fiction and film. Not surprisingly, Simon does not neglect to include Hercule Poirot and Miss Marple in his gathering of sleuths, although he is careful to give them the new names of Jules Perrier and Miss Jessica Marbles (played by James Coco and Elsa Lanchester). They join spoofs of Sam Spade, the Thin Man, and Charlie Chan. The quirks and foibles of the original detectives are charmingly exploited as the sleuths try to decipher an incomprehensible and insoluble murder mystery. Perrier is obsessed with his appearance, wears a hairpiece because he is so vain, and insists that one should "touch nothing" when examining corpses. While technically unconnected to Christie's body of work, *Murder by Death* demonstrates the obvious possibilities for spoofing her characters.

Television

The A.B.C. Murders (1992)

DIRECTOR: Andrew Grieve

CAST: David Suchet (Hercule Poirot); Hugh Fraser (Captain Arthur Hastings); Pauline Moran (Miss Felicity Lemon); Philip Jackson (Chief Inspector James Japp); Donald Sumpter (A.B. Cust), David McAlister (Insp. Glen), Allan Mitchell (Dr. Kerr), Pippa Guard (Megan Barnard), Donald Douglas (Franklin Clarke), John Breslin (Mr. Barnard), Nicholas Farrell (Donald Fraser).

The London Weekend Television production of the Poirot mystery was the first dramatized version of the novel *The A.B.C. Murders* since *The Alphabet Murders* (1966), starring Tony Randall. Part of the on-going LWT series featuring the cases of Poirot and starring David Suchet, *The A.B.C. Murders* first aired in England and subsequently was shown on the stations of the Public Broadcasting System in the United States. The adaptation takes a few, albeit minor, liberties with the original plot. Nevertheless, the overall structure of the novel is followed faithfully, with the fidelity to period detail that is a hallmark of London Weekend Television productions.

The plot follows the progress of the novel, with moments of genuine menace as the self-proclaimed A.B.C. killer claims the first victims. Poirot displays a mixture of outrage and determination as he is seemingly outmaneuvered by a murderer who uses death as his personal way of humiliating the sleuth and the *A.B.C. Rail Guide* as his calling card.

"The Adventure of the Cheap Flat" (1990)

DIRECTOR: Richard Spence

CAST: David Suchet (Hercule Poirot); Hugh Fraser (Captain Arthur Hastings); Pauline Moran (Miss Felicity Lemon); Philip Jackson (Chief In-spector James Japp); Samantha Bond (Stella Robinson), John Michie (James Robinson), Jennifer Landor (Carla Romero), Nick Maloney (Bernie Cole), Ian Price (Teddy Parker).

Part of the series *Agatha Christie's Poirot,* this television adaptation of the short story "The Adventure of the Cheap Flat" (1924) features several significant, albeit enjoyable, changes to the original plot. Poirot is involved in the curious events surrounding a couple who rents an abnormally inexpensive flat in a swanky part of London. This particular story has several memorable highlights. First, there is Poirot's stint as a house burglar (reminiscent of his work in "The Veiled Lady"), a feat that is neatly concealed by Hastings. Second, Miss Lemon shows off her versatility as Poirot's secretary. Finally, there is Poirot's delight in demonstrating to an FBI agent—sent by J. Edgar Hoover to recover missing navy secrets—that there is such a thing as the Mafia, despite the agent's incessant assurances that there isn't—at least according to J. Edgar Hoover.

"The Adventure of the Clapham Cook" (1989)

DIRECTOR: Edward Bennett

CAST: David Suchet (Hercule Poirot); Hugh Fraser (Captain Arthur Hastings); Pauline Moran (Miss Felicity Lemon); Philip Jackson (Chief Inspector James Japp); Dermot Crowley (Mr. Simpson), Freda Dowie (Eliza Dunn), Katy Murphy (Annie).

This episode of *Agatha Christie's Poirot,* produced in 1989 by London Weekend Television and starring David Suchet, mirrors closely the original 1951 short story "The Adventure of the Clapham Cook" and is distinguished for being the inaugural episode in this series of Poirot mysteries. Premiering in England on January 8, 1989, the episode was the first in a series that has entertained viewers for more than a decade. This first case gives Poirot (wonderfully played by David Suchet) the opportunity to be suitably outraged when his services are no longer required, and he is given an absolutely appalling fee for his services. As ever, of course, he has the last word and solves a far more important crime along the way.

"The Adventure of the Egyptian Tomb" (1993)

DIRECTOR: Peter Fleming

CAST: David Suchet (Hercule Poirot); Hugh Fraser (Captain Arthur Hastings); Peter Reeves (Sir John Willard), Paul Birchard (Rupert Bleibner), Rolf Saxon (Dr. Ames).

This episode of the *Agatha Christie's Poirot,* produced by London Weekend Television, permits Poirot to undergo the "hardships" of a journey to Egypt with Hastings and to investigate a seemingly cursed archaeological dig. The episode exudes exotic atmosphere and a certain dread as members of the dig die from horrible diseases or commit suicide.

"The Adventure of the Italian Nobleman" (1993)

DIRECTOR: Brian Farnham

CAST: David Suchet (Hercule Poirot); Hugh Fraser (Captain Arthur Hastings); Pauline Moran (Miss Felicity Lemon); Philip Jackson (Chief Inspector James Japp); Sidney Kean (Count Foscatini), David Neal (Bruno Vizzini), Vincenzo Ricotta (Mario Asciano).

In this episode of *Agatha Christie's Poirot,* produced by London Weekend Television, the detective must investigate the murder of an Italian nobleman who, it turns out, is also a feared blackmailer. The suspect, an Italian diplomat, must be cleared by Poirot, who is obsessed with the eating habits of the dead nobleman. The episode is notable for demonstrating once again Hastings's interest in fast automobiles—and beautiful women—and for showing a softer side of Miss

Lemon: Poirot's secretary is romantically involved with the butler of the murdered man.

"The Adventure of Johnnie Waverly" (1989)

DIRECTOR: Renny Rye

CAST: David Suchet (Hercule Poirot); Hugh Fraser (Captain Arthur Hastings); Pauline Moran (Miss Felicity Lemon); Philip Jackson (Chief Inspector James Japp); Geoffrey Bateman (Marcus Waverly), Julia Chambers (Ada Waverly), Dominic Rougier (Johnnie Waverly), Patrick Jordan (Tredwell).

In this episode of *Agatha Christie's Poirot,* produced by London Weekend Television and based on the 1950 short story of the same name, the detective is consulted by a concerned family that has received warnings about the impending kidnapping of their son. Poirot is unable to prevent the abduction of young Johnnie, but he does a swift and effective job of retrieving him. This episode shows the rather sedentary habits of the detective, as he is forced to walk a great distance in patent leather shoes. It also develops further the automotive interests of Captain Hastings.

"The Adventure of 'The Western Star' " (1990)

DIRECTOR: Richard Spence

CAST: David Suchet (Hercule Poirot); Hugh Fraser (Captain Arthur Hastings); Pauline Moran (Miss Felicity Lemon); Philip Jackson (Chief Inspector James Japp); Rosalind Bennett (Marie Marvelle), Struan Rodger (Henrik van Braks), Oliver Cotton (Gregorie Rolf), Caroline Goodall (Lady Yardly).

In this episode of *Agatha Christie's Poirot,* produced by London Weekend Television and based on the 1924 short story of the same name, Poirot is consulted by an aristocrat who is worried that her beloved jewel is going to be stolen. Poirot subsequently has to deal with a beautiful screen star and use his connections with the shady underworld in the resolution of the case. In a change from the original story, Japp is obsessed with catching a smooth and unscrupulous gem merchant who spends much of the show frustrating him. Hastings is also at his dim best, running off on an investigatory tangent in pursuit of an imaginary Chinese thief.

"The Affair of the Pink Pearl" (1983)

DIRECTOR: Tony Wharmby

CAST: James Warwick (Tommy Beresford); Francesca Annis (Tuppence Beresford); Reece Dinsdale (Archie).

This is one of ten episodes of the series *Partners in Crime,* produced by London Weekend Television. As with the other episodes in the series, Tommy and Tuppence are a charming couple, and there is a light touch to their adventures. In this episode, the pair are in charge of the International Detective Agency and are consulted in the hopes that they might be able to recover a stolen pink pearl.

"The Affair at the Victory Ball" (1991)

DIRECTOR: Renny Rye

CAST: David Suchet (Hercule Poirot); Hugh Fraser (Captain Arthur Hastings); Pauline Moran (Miss Felicity Lemon); Philip Jackson (Chief Inspector James Japp); David Henry (Eustace Beltaine), Hadyn Gwynne (Coco Courtenay), Nathaniel Parker (Chris Davidson), Natalie Slater (Mrs. Davidson), Kate Harper (Mrs. Mallaby).

This episode of *Agatha Christie's Poirot,* produced by London Weekend Television and one of the best in that series, is based on the 1951 short story "The Affair at the Victory Ball." It offers Poirot solving the brutal murder of Lord Cronshaw at the Victory Ball and the grim death of the actress and cocaine addict Coco Courtenay. Memorable highlights from the episode include Poirot on the radio and the celebration of the harlequinade by Lord Cronshaw and his friends. The costumes are delightful and are used skillfully by the detective to solve the crime. In a nice touch of vanity Poirot refuses to wear a costume to the ball, getting into the spirit by holding up a small mask in front of his face at appropriate moments.

The Agatha Christie Hour (1982)

This limited-run series of ten one-hour dramas was produced by Thames Television and aired in England from 1982 through 1983 (the programs aired in the United States in 1984 and 1985 as part of the PBS series *Mystery*). The ten adapted stories were:

"The Case of the Middle-Aged Wife"
"In a Glass Darkly"
"The Girl in the Train"
"The Fourth Man"
"The Case of the Discontented Soldier"
"Magnolia Blossom"
"The Mystery of the Blue Jar"
"The Red Signal"
"Jane in Search of a Job"
"The Manhood of Edward Robinson"

Agatha Christie's Poirot

CAST: David Suchet (Hercule Poirot); Hugh Fraser (Captain Arthur Hastings); Pauline Moran (Miss Felicity Lemon); Philip Jackson (Chief Inspector James Japp).

This largely successful, consistently enjoyable, and superbly produced London Weekend Television series is arguably the best television series devoted to Agatha Christie's work (fans of the series *Partners in Crime* might disagree). Suchet's Poirot manages to capture the flavor and soul of the original character, while at the same time the production fleshes out the sometimes anemic plot lines or atmosphere of the original material.

The series was launched by London Weekend Television on January 8, 1989, with "The Adventure of the Clapham Cook." The producer was Brian Eastman, and the adaptations were scripted by Clive Exton (who is in charge of a writing team that is responsible for the genuinely excellent adaptations).

The audience does miss the presence of the other police officials who inhabit Poirot's world, but Philip Jackson is consistently excellent as

Japp, and sustains an intriguing interplay with Poirot. While exasperated at times by the success of the inscrutable methods of the Belgian sleuth (especially in "The Cornish Mystery"), Japp is also generous in his admiration of Poirot, even describing him publicly as a brilliant investigator (in "Double Sin").

Hugh Fraser also brings a fully developed sense of character to Hastings, and combines the normally dim thinking of Poirot's faithful sidekick with flashes of vulnerability and insight. The role of Hastings—the equivalent of Dr. Watson in the Sherlock Holmes mysteries—is often a thankless one, but Fraser has managed to keep Hastings fresh and interesting.

As Miss Lemon, Pauline Moran stresses the obsession for efficiency that is a favorite trait of Poirot's secretary. She also makes Miss Lemon more fashionable, diverse in her abilities, and more attractive than the literary model. Her compulsion for efficiency and her impatience with anyone who interferes with or endangers her superb filing system (namely Captain Hastings), is demonstrated delightfully in the episode "How Does Your Garden Grow?" (1991). The success of the ongoing series has sparked a number of made-for-television movies, including *The Mysterious Affair at Styles* (1990); *Peril at End House* (1990); *The A.B.C. Murders* (1991); *Death in the Clouds* (1992); *One, Two, Buckle My Shoe* (1992); *Murder on the Links* (1995); *Dumb Witness* (1995); *Hickory Dickory Dock* (1995); and *Hercule Poirot's Christmas* (1995). Fans of the show who were concerned that the series might have come to an end were delighted by the return of David Suchet as Poirot in the television film *The Murder of Roger Ackroyd* on the Arts & Entertainment channel in early 2000.

"The Ambassador's Boots" (1983)

DIRECTOR: Paul Annett

CAST: James Warwick (Tommy Beresford); Francesca Annis (Tuppence Beresford); Reece Dinsdale (Archie).

Like the other episodes in the London Week-end Television series *Partners in Crime,* this one is set around the efforts of the Beresfords to maintain the International Detective Agency and has a frothy atmosphere.

At Bertram's Hotel (1987)

DIRECTOR: Mary McMurray

CAST: Joan Hickson (Miss Jane Marple), Caroline Blakiston (Bess Sedgwick), Helena Mitchell (Elvira Blake), James Cossins (Colonel Luscombe), Joan Greenwood (Selina Hazy), George Baker (Chief Inspector Fred Davy), Douglas Milvain (Sir Ronald Graves), Philip Bretherton (Detective Inspector Campbell), Preston Lockwood (Canon Pennyfeather), Irne Sutcliffe (Miss Gorringe), Brian McGrath (Michael Gorman), Robert Reynolds (Ladislaus Malinowski).

This enjoyable adaptation of the original 1965 novel stars the brilliant Joan Hickson as the silver-haired Miss Marple. The setting is the venerable Bertram's Hotel, a London institution that has long been a favorite of Miss Marple. Her return visit, however, proves most unpalatable, as the hotel has undergone a grim transformation and exudes a very ominous atmosphere. True to her fears, things are genuinely amiss at the hotel, thanks in large measure to the peculiar guests who have begun to inhabit its once stately rooms. Chief among them is the brash Lady Bess Sedgwick, who is introduced to the aghast Miss Marple when she bites into a doughnut with such force that the jelly explodes all over her face and blouse; to Lady Bess, the disaster is hilariously funny.

Things at the hotel take an even worse turn when murder strikes down the roguish doorman, Michael Gorman. Through the polite and understated investigation by Chief Inspector Davy—a most competent policeman who has the sense to rely on Miss Marple for advice and direction—the inquiry unravels a vast criminal conspiracy.

One of the best of the Miss Marple adaptations featuring Joan Hickson, *At Bertram's Hotel* provides Miss Marple with a genuine puzzle to solve and populates the story with a host of interesting characters. Notable performers include George Baker as Davy, Caroline Blakiston as Lady Bess, and the late Joan Greenwood as Miss Marple's old friend Selina Hazy; Hazy has the best line of the film, when she and Miss Marple are discussing the American tourists at the hotel who have forced Bertram's to serve American-style breakfasts, including cold cereal. With a sigh, Hazy exclaims, "Americans have a lot to answer for."

The Body in the Library (1987)

DIRECTOR: Silvio Narrizzano

CAST: Joan Hickson (Miss Marple), Gwen Watford (Mrs. Dolly Bantry), Moray Watson (Colonel Arthur Bantry), Frederick Jaeger (Chief Constable Colonel Melchett), Raymond Francis (Sir Henry Clithering), David Horovitch (Detective Inspector Slack), Ian Brimble (Detective Constable Lake), Andrew Cruikshank (Conway Jefferson).

Agatha Christie once remarked that the opening of *The Body in the Library* was one of the best starts to any of her books. It remains burned into the memory of any reader of the 1942 novel, and, for the adaptation of the work for television, special care was taken to make the viewer come away with the same sense of ghoulish satisfaction. Using languorous camera movement, the director leads the viewer slowly into the charming country home of the Bantrys. There, in the library, sprawled on a hearth rug, is a corpse. The scene is made complete by the perfectly performed exchange between Dolly Bantry and her still-half-asleep husband, she struggles to make Arthur believe that a corpse truly is in the library and that something ought to be done about it.

Within a short time, Miss Marple has been brought into the case by Dolly Bantry, and she goes to work immediately on investigating the peculiar circumstances of the death. On the scene are two recurring characters, Sir Henry Clithering and Inspector Slack. Clithering is a great admirer of Miss Marple and her methods, while Slack considers her an annoying and intrusive busybody. David Horovitch returns as Slack—he also appeared in *The Murder at the Vicarage* and *They Do It with Mirrors*—and performs the thankless task of crossing intellectual swords with the old sleuth.

A Caribbean Mystery (1983)

DIRECTOR: Robert Michael Lewis

CAST: Helen Hayes (Miss Jane Marple), Barnard Hughes (Mr. Rafiel), Jameson Parker (Tim Kendall), Season Hubley (Molly Kendall), Swoosie Kurtz (Ruth Walter), Cassie Yates (Lucky Dyson), Zakes Mokae (Captain Daventry), Stephen Macht (Greg Dyson), Beth Howland (Evelyn Hillingdon), Maurice Evans (Major Geoffrey Palgrave), Lynne Moody (Victoria Johnson), Brock Peters (Dr. Graham).

The first of two adaptations of Miss Marple novels by CBS Television, *A Caribbean Mystery* marks the first outing of Helen Hayes as Miss Marple. She had appeared the year before in *Murder Is Easy* (1982), with Bill Bixby, in the role of Lavinia Fullerton, but her appearance had been brief, as her character was killed barely ten minutes into the plot. This adaptation for the small screen was undertaken by Steve Humphrey and Sue Grafton, and the plot is faithful to the 1964 novel. It is, however, a distinctly American production with a largely American cast. This results in the unfortunate feeling of a lack of authenticity. All the characters are present, but the spirit of the original is lacking. This becomes even more obvious when the viewer watches the 1989 BBC adaptation of *A Caribbean Mystery* starring Joan Hickson as Miss Marple. As Miss Marple, Helen Hayes is sharp and delightful to watch. Unfortunately, her Miss Marple is a little too friendly and lacks the slightly sinister tinge given to the character by Joan Hickson. Hayes was back as Miss Marple in the 1985 *Murder with Mirrors*, the same year Hickson debuted as Miss Marple in *Moving Finger.*

A Caribbean Mystery (1989)

DIRECTOR: Christopher Petit

CAST: Joan Hickson (Miss Marple), Donald Pleasence (Jason Rafiel), Adrian Lukis (Tim

Kendall), Sophie Ward (Molly Kendall), T. P. McKenna (Dr. Grahame), Michael Feast (Edward Hillingdon), Sheila Ruskin (Evelyn Hillingdon), Frank Middlemass (Major Palgrave), Robert Swan (Greg Dyson), Sue Lloyd (Lucky Dyson), Barbara Barnes (Esther Walters), Joseph Mydell (Inspector Weston), Valerie Buchanan (Victoria), Isabelle Lucas (Aunty Johnson).

In this BBC production, the detective—Joan Hickson in her tenth appearance as Miss Marple—travels to the Caribbean for a holiday. While the notion of Miss Marple actually taking a vacation is perhaps hard to envision, her journey to the sunny shore is not complete without a murder, and she is soon engaged in the enterprise of catching a clever and resourceful killer. The highlight of the adaptation—aside from the always enjoyable Joan Hickson—is the interplay between the old sleuth and Jason Rafiel, a wealthy curmudgeon wonderfully played by the late Donald Pleasence. Rafiel becomes increasingly impressed with Miss Marple's skills as a detective, so much so that he seeks her out years later, in *Nemesis*.

"The Case of the Discontented Soldier" (1982)

DIRECTOR: Michael Simpson

CAST: William Gaunt, Maurice Denham (Parker Pyne), Patricia Garwood, Laaly Bowers (Mrs. Ariadne Oliver).

This fifth episode in the ten-part series *The Agatha Christie Hour*, produced by Thames Television, is based on the short story of the same name that first appeared in the 1934 collection *Parker Pyne Investigates*. Although limited in budget, the episode is fun, featuring an unhappy soldier given a new lease on life by the clever Parker Pyne and the imagination of Ariadne Oliver.

"The Case of the Middle-Aged Wife" (1982)

DIRECTOR: Michael Simpson

CAST: Maurice Denham (Parker Pyne), Gwen Watford (Mrs. Packington), Peter Jones.

This first episode in the ten-part series *The Agatha Christie Hour*, produced by Thames Television, is based on the short story of the same name that first appeared in the 1934 collection *Parker Pyne Investigates*. The primary interest of the episode is actually a bit of trivia. Gwen Watford, who plays Mrs. Packington, also played Dolly Bantry in *The Body in the Library*.

"The Case of the Missing Lady" (1983)

DIRECTOR: Paul Annett

CAST: James Warwick (Tommy Beresford); Francesca Annis (Tuppence Beresford); Reece Dinsdale (Archie).

This is the tenth of the ten episodes in the 1983 London Weekend Television series *Partners in Crime*. As in the other nine episodes, the Beresfords run the International Detective Agency and spend much of their time impersonating detectives from fiction. At one point, with deerstalker in place, Tommy puffs on a pipe; he also plays the violin and cannot resist the temptation to observe that his companion has made an "elementary" deduction.

"The Case of the Missing Will" (1993)

DIRECTOR: John Bruce

CAST: David Suchet (Hercule Poirot); Hugh Fraser (Captain Arthur Hastings); Pauline Moran (Miss Felicity Lemon); Philip Jackson (Chief Inspector James Japp); Rowena Cooper (Sarah Siddaway), Terence Hardiman (John Siddaway), Beth Goddard (Violet Wilson), Mark Kingston (Andrew Marsh).

This episode of *Agatha Christie's Poirot*, produced by London Weekend Television and starring David Suchet, is based on the short story first published in 1924 in *Poirot Investigates*. "The Case of the Missing Will" brings Poirot into the world of the young and intelligent Violet Marsh as she tries to find the will of her late uncle, who had disapproved thoroughly of her hopes for a career. Set in an academic milieu, the episode depicts the struggles of young women in the early twentieth century to attain the same educational rights as young men.

"The Chocolate Box" (1993)

DIRECTOR: Ken Grieve

CAST: David Suchet (Hercule Poirot); Hugh Fraser (Captain Arthur Hastings); Pauline Moran (Miss Felicity Lemon); Philip Jackson (Chief Inspector James Japp); Rosalie Crutchley (Madame Déroulard), Anna Chancellor (Virginie Mesnard), Geoffrey Whitehead (Xavier St. Alard), James Coombes (Paul Déroulard).

This episode of *Agatha Christie's Poirot,* produced by London Weekend Television, offers a glimpse into the relatively unknown past of Hercule Poirot, as does the original 1925 short story. In it, the detective relates the tale of his great failure in crime detection, which occurred during his time as an official in the Belgian police force. This nicely organized story permits Japp's involvement, as he is in Brussels receiving a prestigious police award and has asked Poirot to attend the ceremony. While it is hard to imagine Poirot as a policeman, answerable to superior officers, the remembrances do much to reveal the earlier days of the sleuth. Especially notable is the performance of Rosalie Crutchley in the role of Madame Déroulard.

"The Clergyman's Daughter" (1983)

DIRECTOR: Paul Annett

CAST: James Warwick (Tommy Beresford); Francesca Annis (Tuppence Beresford); Reece Dinsdale (Archie).

The fourth of ten episodes in the London Weekend Television series *Partners in Crime,* "The Clergyman's Daughter" places the detectives in an apparently haunted house and poses them against an all to real villain anxious to acquire the poltergeist-infested domicile.

"The Cornish Mystery" (1990)

DIRECTOR: Edward Bennett

CAST: David Suchet (Hercule Poirot); Hugh Fraser (Captain Arthur Hastings); Pauline Moran (Miss Felicity Lemon); Philip Jackson (Chief Inspector James Japp); Amanda Walker (Mrs. Pengelly), John Bowler (Jacob Radnor), Jerome Willis (Edward Pengelly), Tilly Vasburgh (Jessie).

This episode of *Agatha Christie's Poirot,* produced by London Weekend Television, is based on the original 1951 short story of the same name. Poirot is consulted by Mrs. Pengelley, who is firmly convinced that her husband is poisoning her. She dies before the detective can reach her distant Cornish village, and he sets out to catch her killer. The episode is notable for two vignettes. First, Hastings—as always, easily distracted by good looks—is absolutely overwhelmed by Dr. Pengelley's "stunner" of a dental assistant; he is literally rendered speechless, and Poirot must step in and complete his sentences. Second, poor Chief Inspector Japp, certain at last that he has a nice, simple, airtight case against his suspect, learns to his chagrin that Poirot has not only freed the defendant but has convinced the real killer to sign a full confession.

"The Crackler" (1983)

DIRECTOR: Christopher Hodson

CAST: James Warwick (Tommy Beresford); Francesca Annis (Tuppence Beresford); Reece Dinsdale (Archie).

The last of the ten episodes in the 1983 London Weekend Television series *Partners in Crime,* "The Crackler" features the Beresfords pursuing a couterfeiter. Once again, the Beresfords impersonate a detective from fiction, in this case a sleuth from the works of Edgar Wallace (d. 1875), a popular author of mysteries during the 1920s and 1930s.

Dead Man's Folly (1986)

DIRECTOR: Clive Donner

CAST: Peter Ustinov (Hercule Poirot), Jean Stapleton (Ariadne Oliver), Jonathan Cecil (Hastings), Constance Cummings (Amy Folliot), Ralph Arliss (Michael Wayman), Tim Pigott-Smith (Sir George Stubbs), Kenneth Cranham (Inspector Bland), Susan Wooldridge (Amanda Brewis), Christopher Guard (Alec Legge), Jeff Yagher (Eddie South), Nicolette Sheridan (Hattie Stubbs), Caroline Langrishe (Sally Legge), Joanna Dickens

(Third Woman), Sandra Dickinson (Marilyn Gale), Jimmy Gardner (Old Merdell), Pippa Hinchley (Marlene Tucker), Dorothea Phillips (First Woman), Leslie Schofield (Mr. Tucker), Marjorie Yates (Mrs. Tucker).

To capitalize on the success of its first Poirot film in 1985, *Thirteen at Dinner,* CBS Television chose the 1956 novel *Dead Man's Folly*—the fourth outing for Peter Ustinov as Hercule Poirot and his second appearance as the Belgian detective on television. This meant that a faithful rendering of the murderous events at Nasse House would have to include the presence of Mrs. Ariadne Oliver, who provides great assistance to the Belgian throughout his investigation. For the role, CBS chose Jean Stapleton, best known for playing Edith Bunker in the long-running series *All in the Family.* Adapted for television by Rod Browning, *Dead Man's Folly* features several notable English performers, including Tim Pigott-Smith (famous for his work in the British mini-series *Jewel in the Crown*), Susan Woolridge, and Caroline Langrishe; Langrishe also appeared as Marguerita Clayton in "The Mystery of the Spanish Chest." Despite their presence, the film is handicapped by the American production, which lacks the traditional feel of British mysteries and is tailored toward an American audience.

"Dead Man's Mirror" (1993)

DIRECTOR: Brian Eastman

CAST: David Suchet (Hercule Poirot); Hugh Fraser (Captain Arthur Hastings); Pauline Moran (Miss Felicity Lemon); Philip Jackson (Chief Inspector James Japp); Iain Cuthbertson (Gervase Chevenix), Emma Fielding (Ruth Chevenix), Zena Walker (Vanda Chevenix), Jeremy Northam (Hugo Trent).

In this episode of *Agatha Christie's Poirot,* produced by London Weekend Television, the detective is invited to the home of Gervase Chevenix-Gore, who is found dead in a locked room, the victim of an apparent suicide. Poirot has other ideas, of course, and methodically pieces together the details of murder.

"Death in the Clouds" (1992)

DIRECTOR: Stephen Whittaker

CAST: David Suchet (Hercule Poirot); Hugh Fraser (Captain Arthur Hastings); Pauline Moran (Miss Felicity Lemon); Philip Jackson (Chief Inspector James Japp): Sarah Woodward (Jane Grey), Shawn Scott (Norman Gale), Amanda Royle (Venetia Kerr), Eve Pearce (Madame Giselle), David Firth (Lord Horbury), Cathryn Harrison (Lady Horbury), Guy Manning (Jean Dupont), Roger Heathcott (Daniel Clancy).

This made-for-television production was part of the ongoing series *Agatha Christie's Poirot,* produced by London Weekend Television. A faithful adaptation of the 1935 novel, "Death in the Clouds" gives Poirot quite a puzzle: Madame Giselle, a hideous old French crone, is murdered while flying in a plane from France to England. One of the passengers—among them, Hercule Poirot—is guilty of her death, but the detective must figure out exactly how it was accomplished and why.

"The Disappearance of Mr. Davenheim" (1990)

DIRECTOR: Andrew Grieve

CAST: David Suchet (Hercule Poirot); Hugh Fraser (Captain Arthur Hastings); Pauline Moran (Miss Felicity Lemon); Philip Jackson (Chief Inspector James Japp); Ken Colley (Matthew Davenheim), Mel Martin (Charlotte Davenheim), Tony Mathews (Gerald Logan).

This episode of *Agatha Christie's Poirot,* produced by London Weekend Television and based on the 1924 short story "The Disappearance of Mr. Davenheim," challenges Poirot to discover the whereabouts of the missing (and presumed dead) banker Mr. Davenheim. Adding to the interest in the case is the fact that Poirot has wagered Japp that he can solve the case within a week without ever leaving his house. This leaves poor old Hastings in charge of the footwork, of course, and the redoubtable assistant demonstrates that his "little grey cells" are not the equal of Poirot's. The climax is nicely done, thanks to a fine performance by Kenneth Colley as Davenheim (science-fiction fans will recognize Colley from his work in the films *The Empire Strikes Back,* 1980, and *Return of the Jedi,* 1983).

"The Double Clue" (1991)

DIRECTOR: Andrew Piddington

CAST: David Suchet (Hercule Poirot); Hugh Fraser (Captain Arthur Hastings); Pauline Moran (Miss Felicity Lemon); Philip Jackson (Chief Inspector James Japp); Kika Markham (Countess Vera Rossakoff), David Lyon (Marcus Hardman), David Bamber (Bernard Parker), Charmian May (Lady Runcorn), Michael Packer (Redfern).

This episode of *Agatha Christie's Poirot,* produced by London Weekend Television, is one of the most remarkable because it adapts the 1961 short story that introduced the very memorable character of Countess Vera Rossakoff, the only woman to catch Poirot's heart in all the writings of Agatha Christie. The plot centers around the theft of some valuable jewels during a party and the effort of Poirot to recover them. In the process, he meets the remarkable countess, and the two are soon inseparable companions, at least until the resolution of the case and the safe departure of the countess out of England. Played by Kiki Markham, the countess is both charming and elegant, with a touch of sadness from the tragedies she has suffered and the great loss of her homeland to Communism. There is great chemistry between Poirot and the countess, and the viewer hopefully ponders a reunion, perhaps in a future adaptation of *The Big Four* or "The Capture of Cerberus."

"Double Sin" (1990)

DIRECTOR: Richard Spence

CAST: David Suchet (Hercule Poirot); Hugh Fraser (Captain Arthur Hastings); Pauline Moran (Miss Felicity Lemon); Philip Jackson (Chief Inspector James Japp); Caroline Milmos (Mary Durrant), Elspet Gray (Miss Penn), David Hargreaves (Sgt. Vinney), Michael J. Shannon (Baker Wood).

This episode of *Agatha Christie's Poirot,* produced

by London Weekend Television and based on the 1961 short story of the same name, opens with Poirot and Hastings going on a trip to meet a client. Along the way, they encounter the seemingly charming (at least Captain Hastings thinks so) Mary Durrant, who is traveling on a business trip for her aunt, an antiques dealer. When miniatures in her possession are stolen, Poirot refuses to assist in the investigation and leaves Hastings on his own to conduct the inquiry. Not surprisingly, Hastings makes a mess of things, and Poirot saves the day.

"The Dream" (1989)

DIRECTOR: Edward Bennett

CAST: David Suchet (Hercule Poirot); Hugh Fraser (Captain Arthur Hastings); Pauline Moran (Miss Felicity Lemon); Philip Jackson (Chief Inspector James Japp); Alan Howard (Hugo Cornworthy), Joely Richardson (Joanna Farley), Mary Tamm (Mrs. Louise Farley), Paul Lacoux (Dr. Stillingfleet).

This episode of *Agatha Christie's Poirot,* produced by London Weekend Television and adapted from the 1939 short story of the same name, concerns Poirot's involvement in the investigation into the curious suicide of the eccentric millionaire Benedict Farley. Summoned to Farley's estate, Poirot is interrogated briefly and then sent on his way. Soon afterward, Farley is found dead in his office from an apparently self-inflicted gunshot wound. The viewer has fun with the adaptation's interpretation of Farley's obvious eccentricities and gives Poirot the memorable line concerning Farley's meat pies: "They are terrible, but there are a great many of them." A memorable performance is given by Joely Richardson as Joanna Farley, Benedict's unhappy daughter.

Dumb Witness (1995)

DIRECTOR: Edward Bennett

CAST: David Suchet (Hercule Poirot); Hugh Fraser (Captain Arthur Hastings); Pauline Moran (Miss Felicity Lemon); Philip Jackson (Chief Inspector James Japp), Kate Buffery (Theresa Arundell), Patrick Ryecart (Charles Arundell), Julia St.

John (Bella Tanios), Paul Herzberg (Jacob Tanios), Ann Morish (Emily Arundell), Muriel Paulow (Julia Tripp), Pauline Jameson (Isabel Tripp).

As is the case with several other cinematic adaptations of Christie's novels this one features a number of minor changes in the plot, especially early on, when Emily Arundell changes her will in favor of her companion, Minnie Lawson. In the film, a made-for-television movie based on the 1937 novel, Poirot arrives before Emily is murdered and thus gives her advice as to the disposition of her will in the face of obviously avaricious relatives. Emily is murdered soon afterward, in a very memorable scene in which she dies from phosphorous poisoning; a lurid greenish cloud billows out of her mouth as she staggers along a garden path, a hellish death that is much to the peculiar delight of the Tripp sisters, who believe they are witnessing her spirit passing over into the next world.

Two aspects of *Dumb Witness* are worth mentioning. First, there is the setting for the story, Berkshire, especially the house used for Littlegreen, Market Basing, home of the doomed Emily Arundell. The environment is gorgeous, and Poirot actually does a fair amount of walking, especially after he comes into possession of Bob. The second interesting aspect is Bob himself. An adorable and intelligent wirehaired terrier, Bob becomes the companion of Hercule Poirot throughout much of his investigation and ultimately provides the detective with the much-sought-after solution to the crime. At the end, faithful readers will note a marked change in the dog's ultimate disposition; instead of going off with Captain Hastings (in the novel, Hastings takes Bob because he doubts Poirot's understanding of "dog psychology"), Bob is placed in the care of the Tripp sisters.

"Finessing the King" (1983)

DIRECTOR: Christopher Hodson
CAST: James Warwick (Tommy Beresford); Francesca Annis (Tuppence Beresford); Reece Dinsdale (Archie).

In this episode of the London Weekend Television series *Partners in Crime,* the sleuths find their own mystery to investigate, unraveling a cryptic message in the personals column of the newspaper and setting off for the Ace of Spades, a swanky café that will host a ball at midnight. The title, of course, refers to a murder that will be committed.

"Four and Twenty Blackbirds" (1989)

DIRECTOR: Renny Rye
CAST: David Suchet (Hercule Poirot); Hugh Fraser (Captain Arthur Hastings); Pauline Moran (Miss Felicity Lemon); Philip Jackson (Chief Inspector James Japp); Richard Howard (George Lorrimer), Holly de Jong (Dulcie Lane), Tony Aitken (Tommy Pinner), Denys Hawthorne (Bonnington).

Adapted from the short story first published in 1950 (in *The Adventure of the Christmas Pudding*), this episode of *Agatha Christie's Poirot,* produced by London Weekend Television, follows Poirot's intense interest in the peculiar change in eating habits of a regular customer in a restaurant. The odd event, of course, leads the sleuth to the trail of a murderer, and finds Poirot seemingly obsessed with blackberries.

4.50 from Paddington (1987)

DIRECTOR: Martin Friend
CAST: Joan Hickson (Miss Marple), Jill Meager (Lucy Eylesbarrow), Mona Bruce (Elspeth McGillicuddy), Robert East (Alfred Crackenthorpe), Juliette Mole (Anna Stravinska), Nicholas Blane (Paddington Porter), Katy Jarrett (Mary), Leslie Adams (Desk Sergeant), Rhoda Lewis (Mrs. Brogan), Pamela Pitchford (Mrs. Kidder), Daniel Steel (James Stoddart-West), Alan Penn (Patmore), Will Tacey (Arthur Wimborne), Jean Boht (Madame Joliet).

This film is the ninth BBC production of a Miss Marple mystery featuring Joan Hickson—an actress who, by now, is almost universally acknowledged as the greatest of all the Marples to appear on television or in film. One of the most complicated of the adaptations, *4.50* is delightfully faithful to its original material (contrast this with the 1962 Margaret Rutherford version, *Murder, She Said*). The knowing audience is able to enjoy the labors of Lucy Eylesbarrow, Miss Marple's able agent, in the household of the Crackenthorpes. Portrayed well by Jill Meager, Lucy becomes an essential member of the Crackenthorpe family, and her pursuit by several residents of the house serves as one of the more enjoyable facets of the film. The climax of the story, in which Miss Marple traps the killer by pretending to choke on a fish bone, is one of the best recreations of a Christie denouement.

"The Fourth Man" (1982)

DIRECTOR: Michael Simpson

CAST: Fiona Mathieson, John Nettles, Prune Clarke.

This episode of the Thames television series *The Agatha Christie Hour* (1982–1983) was produced by Pat Sandys, directed by Michael Simpson, and adapted by William Corlett. "The Fourth Man" is based on the short story of the same name originally published in *The Hound of Death* (1933) and concerns the conversation aboard a train among three men. They discuss the mysterious case of Felicie Bault; the young woman died from mental illness at the age of twenty-two, but her multiple personalities are the source of intense fascination.

Ein Fremder klopft an (1967)

DIRECTOR: Kurt Frueh

CAST: Gertrud Kueckelmann (Cecily), Heinz Bennet (Bruce), Edda Seippel (Aunt Loo-Loo), Gudrun Thielemann (Mavis), Rudolf Krieg (Nigel), Karl-Georg Saebisch (Dr. Gribble)

A German television adaptation of "Philomel Cottage." It was adapted by Horst Kloes. The title in German is translated as "A Stranger Knocks."

"The Girl in the Train" (1982)

DIRECTOR: Brian Farnham

CAST: Sarah Berger, Osmond Block.

This episode of the Thames Television series *The Agatha Christie Hour* (1982–1983) was produced by Pat Sandys, adapted by William Corlett, and directed by Brian Farnham. Based on the original short story published in *The Listerdale Mystery* (1934) and *The Golden Ball and Other Stories* (1971), "The Girl in the Train" makes good use of the romantic elements of the source material and plays up the villainy of the pursuing agents hot on the trail of George Rowland and his mysterious traveling companion.

Hercule Poirot's Christmas (1995)

DIRECTOR: Edward Bennett

CAST: David Suchet (Hercule Poirot); Vernon Dobtcheff (Simeon Lee); Philip Jackson (Inspector Japp); Simon Roberts (Alfred Lee); Catherine Rabett (Lydia Lee); Eric Carte (Goerge Lee); Brian Gwaspari (Harry Lee); Mark Tandy (Sugden), Sasha Behar (Pilar Estravados), Andree Bernard (Magdalene Lee), Ayd Khan Din (Horbury), Olga Lowe (Stella).

This made-for-television movie is based on the original 1938 novel of the same name and remains faithful to the original material. *Hercule Poirot's Christmas* can also boast fidelity to the underlying promise of the novel, namely that it will contain a good, old-fashioned, brutal murder. Simeon Lee is not only killed, he is savagely murdered by having his throat cut, and his death is accompanied by total mayhem in his room, for when the body is discovered—apparently only moments after the crime is committed—the furniture has been tossed about violently.

Hercule Poirot (as portrayed by David Suchet) finds himself in his element as his holiday is disrupted by the murder of his host, the monstrously unpleasant Simeon Lee (played with much enthusiasm by veteran actor Vernon Dobtcheff). The suspects are a familiar Christie lot of scheming and avaricious relatives. The solution, however, elevates the film in two ways. First, the viewer is impressed with the murder method; second, the viewer is even more impressed with the method Poirot uses to catch the killer.

Hickory Dickory Dock (1995)

DIRECTOR: Andrew Grieve

CAST: David Suchet (Hercule Poirot); Hugh Fraser (Captain Arthur Hastings); Pauline Moran (Miss Felicity Lemon); Philip Jackson (Chief Inspector James Japp); Jessica Lloyd (Celia Austin), Jonathan Firth (Nigel Chapman), Paris Jefferson (Sally Finch), Damian Lewis (Leonard Bateson), Granville Saxton (Mr. Casteman), Gilbert Martin (Colin McNabb), Elinor Morriston (Valerie Hobhouse), Richard Bell (Mrs. Nicoletis).

This made-for-television movie based on the original 1955 novel of the same name is one of the several cases in which the rather stuffy and archaic Hercule Poirot must deal with crime involving young people. Here, a crime spree takes place at a youth hostel on Hickory Road. The thefts of "odd things" from students' rooms leads ultimately to murder, and Poirot must come to grips with a clever killer and a criminal organization of some ambition. Poirot's interplay with the students—as interpreted by David Suchet—is often fun to watch, especially as the young people begin to realize that this strange Belgian really knows something about crime.

"The House of Lurking Death" (1983)

DIRECTOR: Christopher Hodson

CAST: James Warwick (Tommy Beresford); Francesca Annis (Tuppence Beresford); Reece Dinsdale (Archie).

In this episode of the London Weekend Television series *Partners in Crime,* the sleuths investigate the dangerous events at Thurnly Grange, where someone is the target of a poisoner. As is the case with their other investigations, Tommy and Tuppence adopt the mannerisms, style, and dress of detectives of fiction. For this investigation, Tommy becomes Inspector Gabriel Hanaud, the invention of Alfred Edward Mason (d. 1948), and Tuppence becomes Hanaud's faithful sidekick, Mr. Ricardo.

"How Does Your Garden Grow?" (1991)

DIRECTOR: Brian Farnham

CAST: David Suchet (Hercule Poirot); Hugh Fraser (Captain Arthur Hastings); Pauline Moran (Miss Felicity Lemon); Philip Jackson (Chief Inspector James Japp); Catherine Russell (Katrina Rieger), Anne Stallybrass (Mary Delafontaine), Tim Wylton (Henry Delafontaine), Margery Masson (Amelia Barrowby).

This episode of *Agatha Christie's Poirot,* produced by London Weekend Television, is adapted from the 1964 short story of the same name. It features Poirot investigating the death of a client who is murdered before Poirot can arrive on the scene. Highlights of the episode include the detective's pursuit of oyster shells, a severe Russian young woman who is suspected of murdering her employer, and the efficiency of Miss Lemon. While Miss Lemon is out assisting Mr. Poirot, Captain Hastings searches her files for a bill that is due and then commits the unpardonable crime of paying the bill in cash. He is subjected to the wrath of Miss Lemon for wrecking her files and especially for paying a tradesman in cash. This last sin, however, proves of great importance in the solution of the murder.

"In a Glass Darkly" (1982)

DIRECTOR: Desmond Davis

CAST: Nicholas Clay, Emma Piper.

This episode of the Thames Television series *The Agatha Christie Hour* (1982–1983) was produced by Pat Sandys, adapted by William Corlett, and directed by Desmond Davis. The episode is faithful to the original story, maintaining its brooding sense of dread as a man has a vision of a murder and then hosts both the killer and his victim in his house.

"The Incredible Theft" (1989)

DIRECTOR: Edward Bennett

CAST: David Suchet (Hercule Poirot); Hugh Fraser (Captain Arthur Hastings); Pauline Moran (Miss Felicity Lemon); Philip Jackson (Chief Inspector James Japp); Carmen du Sautoy (Mrs.

Vanderlyn), Ciaran Madden (Lady Mayfield), John Carson (George Carrington), Phyllida Law (Lady Carrington), John Stride (Tommy Mayfield).

This episode of *Agatha Christie's Poirot,* produced by London Weekend Television and adapted from the short story of the same name first published in 1937, brings Poirot into the mysterious disappearance of top secret plans for a British fighter plane. The plans are apparently stolen right from under the nose of high government officials during a pleasant weekend in the country, when there is a suspected German spy in the house. What follows is a delicious game of cat and mouse between Poirot and the suspected spy, Mrs. Vanderlyn (played wonderfully by Carmen du Sautoy). In the end, the detective tracks her to the German embassy—again with Hastings's help and skill with an automobile—but he is seemingly too late to prevent a disaster from befalling England. As usual with Poirot, however, looks can be deceiving.

"Jane in Search of a Job" (1982)

DIRECTOR: Christopher Hodson

CAST: Elizabeth Garvie, Amanda Redman, Andrew Bicknell.

This episode of the Thames Television series *The Agatha Christie Hour* (1982–1983) was produced by Pat Sandys, adapted by Gerald Savory, and directed by Christopher Hodson. The efforts of Jane Cleveland to find a job are brought to melodramatic life in this production, which finds the young English woman caught up in apparent international intrigue and crime. Stylishly presented, this version is nevertheless somewhat overwrought, although it is faithful to the original story, first published in *The Listerdale Mystery* (1934) and *The Golden Ball and Other Stories* (1971).

"The Jewel Robbery at the Grand Metropolitan" (1993)

DIRECTOR: Ken Grieve

CAST: David Suchet (Hercule Poirot); Hugh Fraser (Captain Arthur Hastings); Pauline Moran (Miss Felicity Lemon); Philip Jackson (Chief Inspector James Japp); Trevor Cooper (Ed Opalsen), Sorcha Cusack (Mrs. Opalsen), Elizabeth Rider (Grace), Hermione Norris (Célestine), Simon Shepherd (Andrew Hall).

This episode of *Agatha Christie's Poirot,* produced by London Weekend Television and adapted from the short story of the same name first published in 1924, involves the theft of a pearl necklace from the Opalsens' room at the Grand Metropolitan Hotel. As the Opalsens are friends of Poirot, and as the detective and Hastings are staying at the hotel, the detective undertakes the investigation, despite his supposed need for rest and relaxation. The obvious suspect is the chambermaid Célestine, but Poirot has his doubts.

"The Kidnapped Prime Minister" (1990)

DIRECTOR: Andrew Grieve

CAST: David Suchet (Hercule Poirot); Hugh Fraser (Captain Arthur Hastings); Pauline Moran (Miss Felicity Lemon); Philip Jackson (Chief Inspector James Japp); David Horovitch (Commander Daniels), Timothy Block (Maj. Norman), Jack Elliot (Egan), Lisa Harrow (Mrs. Daniels), Ronald Hines (Sir Bernard Dodge).

This episode of *Agatha Christie's Poirot,* produced by London Weekend Television and adapted from the short story of the same name published in 1924, features Hercule Poirot at his best in a moment of national crisis. The prime minister has been kidnapped, and the detective is the government's last hope of finding him in time for a vitally important conference. The Belgian rises to the occasion with one of his best—and most eccentric—investigations. Instead of running across England and France, the sleuth settles in and, faithful to his methods, prefers to use his "little grey cells." This masterful inactivity is the source of some consternation to the cabinet officials in charge of the investigation, but Poirot does not disappoint them. Fans of the Miss

Marple television adaptations starring Joan Hickson will recognize David Horovitch in the role of Captain Daniels; Horovitch played the recurring role of Inspector Slack in the Hickson-Marple series produced by Thames Television.

"The King of Clubs" (1989)

DIRECTOR: Renny Rye

CAST: David Suchet (Hercule Poirot); Hugh Fraser (Captain Arthur Hastings); Pauline Moran (Miss Felicity Lemon); Philip Jackson (Chief Inspector James Japp); Niamh Cusack (Valerie Saintclair), David Swift (Henry Reedburn), Johnny Coy (Bunny Saunders), Jack Klaff (Prince Paul of Maurania).

This episode of *Agatha Christie's Poirot,* produced by London Weekend Television and adapted from the short story of the same name first published in 1951, brings Poirot into contact with both royalty and the film world. Prince Paul of Maurania asks the detective's help in solving the murder of the odious Henry Reedburn, who was found with his skull crushed in his own home.

The actress fiancée of Prince Paul, Valerie Saintclair, was the only witness to the crime, and the prince is anxious to avoid any breath of scandal.

The primary change in the adaptation for television is that the profession of the lead characters changes from dance to acting. This gives the producers the opportunity to show 1930s soundstages and gives Hastings the chance to enjoy the "scenery." Two notable performances are given here—by Niamh Cusack as Valerie Saintclair and David Swift as Henry Reedburn.

Lord Edgware Dies (1999)

DIRECTOR: Brian Farnham

CAST: David Suchet (Hercule Poirot); Pauline Moran (Miss Felicity Lemon); Philip Jackson (Inspector Japp); Hugh Fraser (Captain Arthur Hastings); John Castle (Lord Edgware), Helen Grace (Jane Wilkinson), Fiona Allen (Carlotta Adams), Dominic Guard (Bryan Martin).

Lord Edgware Dies followed the successful return of David Suchet as Hercule Poirot to television in *The Murder of Roger Ackroyd* (1999). Produced by Brian Eastman, and written by Anthony Horowitz, *Lord Edgware Dies* picks up events immediately after the solution of the case in *The Murder of Roger Ackroyd.* Poirot has returned to London and once more takes up residence in Whitehaven Mansions. Reunited with Chief Inspector Japp, Captain Hastings, and Miss Lemon, Poirot is approached by the beautiful Jane Wilkinson in the hopes that he will help her secure a divorce from Lord Edgware. Twenty-four hours later, Lord Edgware is murdered.

This production is actually a remake of the less interesting 1985 television film *Thirteen at Dinner,* starring Peter Ustinov as Poirot; David Suchet was cast as Inspector Japp, only a few years before he became Poirot himself. Lord Edgware is played by John Castle who appeared in the Joan Hickson-Miss Marple productions, *A Murder Is Announced* (1985) and *The Mirror Crack'd from Side to Side* (1992).

"The Lost Mine" (1990)

DIRECTOR: Edward Bennett

CAST: David Suchet (Hercule Poirot); Hugh Fraser (Captain Arthur Hastings); Pauline Moran (Miss Felicity Lemon); Philip Jackson (Chief Inspector James Japp); Vincent Wong (Chinese Man), Anthony Bate (Lord Pearson), Julian Firth (Bank Teller), Colin Stinton (Charles Lester).

This episode of *Agatha Christie's Poirot,* produced by London Weekend Television and adapted from the short story of the same name published in 1924, brings Poirot into contact with the seedy underworld of London opium and gambling dens. A Chinese businessman, Mr. Wu Ling, is found murdered soon after arriving in London, and there seems to be no shortage of suspects. The episode features Inspector Japp at his officious best.

"Magnolia Blossom" (1982)

DIRECTOR: John Franco

CAST: Ciaran Madden, Ralph Bates, Jeremy Clyde.

This episode of the Thames Television series *The Agatha Christie Hour* (1982–1983) was produced by Pat Sandys, adapted by John Bryden, and directed by John Frankau. Based on the original short story "Magnolia Blossom," published in *The Golden Ball and Other Stories* (1971), the production faithfully depicts the torment of a married woman who must become the emissary of her husband to her own lover; she is forced to confront the question of how far she will go to protect her husband and how deeply she is willing to hurt the man she loves.

The Man in the Brown Suit (1989)

DIRECTOR: Alan Grint

CAST: Stephanie Zimbalist (Anne), Simon Dutton (Harry), Edward Woodward (Sir Eustace Pedler), Rue McClanahan (Suzy Blair), Tony Randall (Reverend Chichester), Ken Howard (Gordon Race), Nickolas Grace (Guy Underhill), María Casal (Anita), Federico Luciano (Leo Carton).

An adaptation of the 1924 novel of the same name, *The Man in the Brown Suit* was produced by CBS Television and Warner Brothers, directed by Alan Grint, produced by Alan Shayne, and adapted by Carla Jean Wagner. While generally faithful to the original story, the TV film updated the setting to the modern era and tinkered with some of the locations. Here, the mystery starts in Egypt, where the smart and inquisitive Anne Beddingfield gets caught up in international intrigue while on vacation. Thanks to delightful performances by Zimbalist and Woodward, and especially the obvious but enjoyable impersonations of assorted characters by Tony Randall (he certainly makes one remember Kirk Douglas in *The List of Adrian Messenger*), the movie provides more fun than it might at first seem to offer. Randall, of course, had already played Hercule Poirot in the film *The Alphabet Murders* (1966).

"The Man in the Mist" (1983)

DIRECTOR: Christopher Hodson

CAST: James Warwick (Tommy Beresford);

Francesca Annis (Tuppence Beresford); Reece Dinsdale (Archie).

In this episode of the London Weekend Television series *Partners in Crime,* Tommy and Tuppence follow the actress Gilda Glen to her house on Morgan's Avenue while the city is blanketed in a deep fog. On the way, the sleuths encounter other people in the mist, including a murderer. The episode continues the custom—of both the original stories and the series—of having Tommy and Tuppence solve their mysteries while impersonating detectives from fiction. In this case, Tommy adopts the persona of Father Brown, the charming priest and detective created by G. K. Chesterton (d. 1936).

"The Manhood of Edward Robinson" (1982)

DIRECTOR: Brian Farnham

CAST: Nicholas Farrell (Edward Robinson), Cherie Lunghi (Noreen).

This episode of the Thames Television series *The Agatha Christie Hour* (1982–1983) was produced by Pat Sandys, adapted by Gerald Savory, and directed by Brian Farnham. Based on the short story of the same name first published in *The Listerdale Mystery* (1934) and *The Golden Ball and Other Stories* (1971), the production features an enjoyable series of car rides as shy Edward Robinson impulsively purchases a sports car and soon is involved with a flashy and adventurous woman of mystery named Noreen.

"The Million-Dollar Bond Robbery" (1991)

DIRECTOR: Andrew Grieve

CAST: David Suchet (Hercule Poirot); Hugh Fraser (Captain Arthur Hastings); Pauline Moran (Miss Felicity Lemon); Philip Jackson (Chief Inspector James Japp); Oliver Parker (Phillip Ridgeway), Natalie Ogle (Esmee Dalgliesh), Ewan Hooper (Mr. Vavasour), David Quilter (Mr. Shaw).

In this episode of *Agatha Christie's Poirot,* produced by London Weekend Television and adapted from the short story of the same name first published in 1924, Hercule Poirot and Arthur Hastings cross the Atlantic to keep an eye on the dubiously reliable Mr. Philip Ridgeway, an official of a bank sending a million dollars in Liberty Bonds from England to New York. Whereas in the original story the ship is called the *Olympia,* in the adaptation it is the *Queen Mary.* The vessel is much to the liking of Hastings, who cannot wait to set sail; Poirot, of course, is deathly afraid of *mal de mer.* In the end, it is poor Hastings who suffers at sea, while Poirot actually enjoys himself and dines on a delicious plate of sautéed calf brains. The voyage takes a nasty turn, however, when Ridgeway apparently has the bonds stolen right out of his compartment while he is playing—and losing badly—at cards.

The Mirror Crack'd from Side to Side (1992)

DIRECTOR: Norman Stone

CAST: Joan Hickson (Miss Marple), Claire Bloom (Marina Gregg), Barry Newman (Jason Rudd), Glynis Johns (Lola Brewster), John Castle (Inspector Craddock), Judy Cornwell (Heather Badcock), Margaret Courtenay (Miss Knight), David Horovitch (Superintendent Slack), Norman Rodway (Dr.

Gilchrist), Gwen Watford (Dolly Bantry), Elizabeth Garvie (Ella Zielinsky), John Cassady (Giuseppe), Ian Brimble (Sergeant Lake), Christopher Hancock (Arthur Badcock), Anna Niland (Cherry Baker), Amanda Elwes (Margot Bence).

It is likely that the BBC waited for a few years before producing this adaptation of the original 1962 novel—the last of the BBC productions of Miss Marple mysteries, starring Joan Hickson as the definitive interpreter of the spinster sleuth—in order to allow additional time to pass after the release in 1980 of the Angela Lansbury vehicle *The Mirror Crack'd.*

For aficionados of Christie in general and Miss Marple in particular, the Hickson version of *The Mirror Crack'd from Side to Side* is vastly superior to the Lansbury outing, in large measure because of the closer fidelity of the script to the novel, the continued brilliance of Hickson's performance as Miss Marple, and the all-British cast, which possesses better chemistry than the more stellar cast assembled for the 1980 production. Notable in the cast are several returning performers. David Horovitch once again plays Inspector Slack, whose dislike of Miss Marple is as strong as ever; John Castle plays Inspector Craddock (he had appeared

Poirot (David Suchet) at sea, in "The Million-Dollar Bond Robbery." (Photofest; London Weekend Television)

previously in *A Murder Is Announced*); Ian Brimble returns as Slack's faithful assistant, Detective Sargeant Lake; and Gwen Watford appears as Dolly Bantry, reprising the role she first played in *The Body in the Library*.

Mord im Pfarrhaus (1970)

DIRECTOR: Hans Quest

CAST: Inge Langen (Miss Marple); Herbert Mensching (Vicar), Ingrid Capelle (Griselda), Heinz Bennet (Lawrence Redding), Willy Semmelrogge (Inspector Slack), Edith Schneider (Anne Hampton), Paula Denk (Mrs. Price-Ridley), Paul Neuhaus (Ronald Hawes).

A German adaptation of *Murder at the Vicarage* undertaken by ZDF and written by Peter Scharff. The director, Hans Quest, was also the director of the German television adaptation of *And Then There Were None, Zehn kleine Negerlein* (1969).

The Moving Finger (1985)

DIRECTOR: Roy Boulting

CAST: Joan Hickson (Miss Marple), Michael Culver (Edward Symmington), Elizabeth Counsell (Angela Symmington), Stuart Mansfield (James Symmington), Andrew Bicknell (Gerry Burton), Sabina Franklyn (Joanna Burton), Rich-ard Pearson (Mr. Pye), Hilary Mason (Emily Barton), Dilys Hamlett (Maud Calthorp), John Amatt (Guy Calthorp), Sandra Payne (Eryl Griffith), Martin Fisk Owen Griffith (Penelope Lee Partridge).

Based on the 1943 novel, *The Moving Finger* marks the second appearance of Joan Hickson as Miss Marple and establishes her firmly as the foremost of all the Miss Marples in film and television. Produced by Guy Slater and adapted by Julia Jones, the film includes virtually all the essential aspects of the original novel, presenting a malicious killer who uses poison-pen letters as a cover for murderous activities. With the chaos being caused in the town by the scurrilous attacks made upon the innocent inhabitants of Little Furze, a murderer is able to move calmly and methodically among them.

Two other plot points are worth mentioning.

First, as in the original, there is much attention paid to romance, especially the relationship between Jerry Burton and Megan Hunter. This is presented quite well in this adaptation, especially when the airman carryies Megan off to London to transform her into a properly dressed and coiffed young woman. Second, and most intriguing, is the characterization of Miss Marple, who stands as a kind of absolute antithesis to the love and merriment of the young people. With her ice-cold stare and bear-trap mind, the old sleuth sits and analyzes the crime, figures out the motive, and devises a means of capturing the brutal killer, ruthlessly using a young woman as a lure in order to complete her plans.

The Murder at the Vicarage (1986)

DIRECTOR: Julian Amyes

CAST: Joan Hickson (Miss Marple), Paul Eddington (Reverend Leonard Clement), Cheryl Campbell (Griselda Clement), Robert Lang (Colonel Lucius Protheroe), Polly Adams (Ann Protheroe), Tara MacGowran (Lettice Protheroe), James Hazeldine (Lawrence Redding), Christopher Good (Christopher Hawes), Norma West (Mrs. Lestrange), Michael Browning (Dr. Haydock), David Horovitch (Detective Inspector Slack), Ian Brimble (Detective Sergeant Lake), Jack Galloway (Bill Archer), Rachel Weaver (Mary Wright), Rosalie Crutchley (Mrs. Price-Ridley).

Based on the 1930 novel of the same name, *The Murder at the Vicarage* was produced by George Gallaccio and marks the fifth appearance by Joan Hickson as Miss Marple. The old sleuth is presented with a suitable puzzle, a brutal and outrageous murder: The much-hated Colonel Lucius Protheroe is shot to death in the supposedly respected precincts of the vicarage of St. Mary Mead and is discovered by Reverend Leonard Clement. All clues point to the bohemian and scandalous painter Lawrence Redding, but Miss Marple is not so sure about the details of the case.

Highlights of the case include Miss Marple's priceless exchanges with Inspector Slack, the over-officious policeman who suffers endless torments as

Miss Marple clearly moves far ahead of him in solving the crime. At one point, the inspector laments that he has run out of suspects; Miss Marple quietly and courteously disagrees, observing that she can think of at least five likely suspects. Another memorable feature is the relationship between Griselda Clement and her husband, Leonard. Paul Eddington (best known for the famous comedy series *Yes, Minister* and *Yes, Prime Minister*) and Cheryl Campbell (who also starred in *The Seven Dials Mystery,* 1981), playing the Clements—longtime favorite characters in Christie's writings—make even throwaway scenes, such as a family meal, delightful. *The Murder at the Vicarage* is one of the best of the Hickson-Marple films and one of the finest Christie adaptations.

Murder by the Book (1986)

DIRECTOR: Lawrence Gordon Clark

CAST: Ian Holm (Hercule Poirot), Peggy Ashcroft (Agatha Christie), Michael Aldridge (Edmond Cork), Dawn Archibald (Sally), John Atkinson (Gardener), Richard Wilson (Sir Max Mallowan).

A charming made-for-television movie about the final days of Hercule Poirot and his creator, Agatha Christie. Planning to release her final Poirot novel, *Curtain*—in which a crippled and decrepit Poirot finally dies—Christie is suddenly confronted by her famous Belgian creation, who demands to know why she plans to be rid of him. Not only is the incarnated sleuth outraged at her ingratitude and her long dislike of him, Poirot is also appalled at the appearance she gave to him. As Poirot complains, she made him look like an overstuffed penguin. Despite his best efforts, the detective cannot convince his creator to spare his life. Ian Holm is wonderful as Poirot, and one wonders why he never had the chance to play the detective in a regular adaptation of a Christie work.

"Murder in the Mews" (1989)

DIRECTOR: Edward Bennett

CAST: David Suchet (Hercule Poirot); Hugh Fraser (Captain Arthur Hastings); Pauline Moran (Miss Felicity Lemon); Philip Jackson (Chief Inspector James Japp); Juliette Mole (Jane Plenderleith), James Faulkner (Maj. Eustace), David Yolland (Leverton West).

This episode of *Agatha Christie's Poirot,* produced by London Weekend Television and adapted from the short story of the same name first published in 1937, pits Poirot against a clever antagonist who seeks to murder a blackmailer. The circumstances of the crime center around the death of Barbara Allen, who is found in her flat with a bullet wound to her head. The investigation determines initially that she committed suicide, but a further inquiry points instead to murder. Poirot uses his "little grey cells" as well as his meticulous attention to detail—an ashtray full of cigarettes, a set of discarded golf clubs, and part of a cuff link—to solve the true crime. A notable performance is given by James Faulkener in the role of Major Eustace.

Murder in Three Acts (1986)

DIRECTOR: Gary Nelson

CAST: Peter Ustinov (Hercule Poirot), Tony Curtis (Charles Cartwright), Emma Samms (Egg), Jonathan Cecil (Hastings), Fernando Allende (Ricardo Montoya), Pedro Armendáriz, Jr. (Colonel Mateo), Lisa Eichhorn (Cynthia Dayton), Dana Elcar (Dr. Strange), Lee McCain (Miss Milray), Marian Mercer (Daisy Eastman), Diana Muldaur (Angela Stafford), Nicholas Pryor (Freddie Dayton), Concetta Tomei (Janet Crisp), Jacqueline Evans (Mrs. Babbington), Ángeles González (Housekeeper).

The fifth performance overall and the third appearance on television of Peter Ustinov as Hercule Poirot, *Murder in Three Acts* was based on the 1935 novel *Three-Act Tragedy* and was produced for CBS Television by Warner Brothers. Adapted by Scott Swanson and produced by Paul Waigner, *Murder in Three Acts* features a number of significant changes to the original work, not the least of which is moving the entire setting for the mystery from England to Mexico. Once one recovers from the shock of seeing Hercule Poirot in Acapulco, there are the usual

Americanisms in the script with which the viewer must contend: the clichés, the overdone performances by American actors uncomfortable with the subtleties of Christie's characters, and the tendency to portray Captain Hastings as an earnest idiot.

A Murder Is Announced (1956)

DIRECTOR: Paul Stanley

CAST: Gracie Fields (Miss Marple), Jessica Tandy (Letitia Blacklock), Roger Moore (Patrick Simmons).

A television adaptation of the original 1950 novel, *A Murder Is Announced* marks the first time that Miss Marple had been brought to life on the screen or the stage and was one of the first ever television adaptations of a Christie work. The program first aired on NBC Television on December 30, 1956, on the *Goodyear Playhouse*. Adapted for the one-hour format by William Templeton, *A Murder Is Announced* offers the well-known actress and singer Gracie Fields in the role of Miss Marple. Aside from its groundbreaking depiction of Miss Marple, the teleplay boasts two significant cast members: Academy Award–winning actress Jessica Tandy as Letitia Blacklock and Roger Moore as Patrick Simmons.

A Murder Is Announced (1985)

DIRECTOR: David Giles

CAST: Joan Hickson (Miss Jane Marple), Ursula Howells (Miss Blacklock), John Castle (Inspector Craddock), Renee Asherson (Miss Dora Bunner), Richard Bebb (Rydesdale), Samantha Bond (Julia Simmons), Joyce Carey (Belle Goedler), Tim Carrington (Rudi Scherz), David Collings (Reverend Harmon), Liz Crowther (Myrne Harris), Paola Dionisotti (Miss Hinchcliffe), Kay Gallie (Sister McClelland), Elaine Ives-Cameron (Hannah), Mary Kerridge (Mrs. Swettenham), Nicola King (Phillipa Haymes), Ralph Michael (Colonel Easterbrook), Simon Shepherd (Patrick Simmons), Joan Sims (Miss Murgatroyd), Matthew Solon (Edmund Swettenham), Sylvia Syms (Mrs. Easterbrook), Kevin Whateley (Fletcher).

The third television adaptation of a Miss Marple novel by the BBC featuring Joan Hickson as the venerable sleuth, this production is based faithfully on the 1950 novel. The adaptation by Alan Plater retains virtually all of the clever and baffling twists and turns of the plot, which commences with the curious announcement of a murder in the local Chipping Cleghorn newspaper. The suspects are one of the most diverse bunches in any Christie murder case, and the assembly of performers ensures an enjoyable time for the viewer. Notable cast members include Elaine Ives Cameron as the self-tortured and suspicious Hannah, Samantha Bond as Julia Simmons (she was also in the David Suchet Poirot series episode "The Cheap Flat"), and John Castle as Inspector Craddock (he also appeared in *The Mirror Crack'd from Side to Side*).

Murder Is Easy (1981)

DIRECTOR: Claude Whatham

CAST: Bill Bixby (Luke Williams), Lesley-Anne Down (Bridget Conway), Olivia de Havilland (Honoria Waynflete), Helen Hayes (Lavinia Fullerton), Patrick Allen (Major Horton), Shane Briant (Dr. Thomas), Freddie Jones (Constable Reed), Leigh Lawson (Jimmy Lorrimer), Jonathan Pryce (Mr. Ellsworthy), Ivor Roberts (Vicar), Anthony Valentine (Abbot), Timothy West (Lord Easterfield).

Luke Williams (Bill Bixby) thinks he has a murderer in Murder Is Easy *(1982). (Photofest)*

A CBS Television movie based on the 1939 novel and adapted by Carmen Culver, *Murder Is Easy* offers one of the most ruthless and industrious murderers in all Christie's works. While overshadowed by the subsequent Christie adaptations that were produced during the 1980s, *Murder Is Easy* remains quite entertaining, thanks to the effort made by the production company to retain as much of the British flavor as possible from the source material. Thus, despite the presence of American stars Bill Bixby, Olivia de Havilland, and Helen Hayes, the movie has the feel of a British-made effort. There is, of course, the primary handicap of being able to figure out fairly quickly who the murderer has to be, but the viewer does not mind because of the enjoyable performances.

One of the biggest surprises comes barely ten minutes into the film. After meeting Lavinia Fullerton on a train, Luke Williams (note the change from the original Fitzwilliam) has the unpleasant experience of discovering Miss Fullerton's mangled corpse just outside a train station. The little old lady who had been on her way to Scotland Yard to report the unusual number of deaths in her village never reached her destination, and Luke decides to carry on in her honor. Unfortunately, Miss Fullerton's death means that Helen Hayes has a very short role indeed; she returned the following year to CBS as Miss Marple in *A Caribbean Mystery*.

Other memorable moments include the chemistry between Williams and Bridget Conway, especially as Williams is not sure about Conway's innocence; the plodding but charming local police constable, played by Freddie Jones; and the use of local color and delightful locations as the backdrop for the multiple brutal homicides being committed.

The Murder of Roger Ackroyd (1999)

DIRECTOR: Andrew Grieve

CAST: David Suchet (Hercule Poirot); Philip Jackson (Chief Inspector Japp); Oliver Ford Davies (Dr. Sheppard), Selina Cadell (Caroline Sheppard), Roger Frost (Parker), Malcolm Terris (Roger Ackroyd), Flora Montgomery (Flora Ackroyd), Jamie Bamber (Ralph Paton), Nigel Cooke (Geoffrey Raymond), Daisy Beaumont (Ursula Bourne), Vivien Heilbron (Mrs. Ackroyd), Gregor Truter (Inspector Davis), Charles Early (Constable Jones), Rosalind Bailey (Mrs. Ferrars), Charles Simon (Hammond), Lizzie Kettle (Mrs. Folliott), Graham Chinn (Landlord), Clive Brunt (Naval Petty Officer).

The Murder of Roger Ackroyd marked the triumphant return of David Suchet as the beloved detective Hercule Poirot to television after an absence of some five years (the last appearance of Suchet as Poirot was in the 1995 TV film *Dumb Witness*). Thanks to the appeals of fans and the sparkling reputation of Suchet as Poirot, not only was Poirot brought back to television but Carnival Films and the Arts and Entertainment Television Channel chose to bring to life one of the all-time favorite Christie mysteries, *The Murder of Roger Ackroyd* (originally published in 1926).

For Christie devotees, the production raised the immediate questions of how producer Brian Eastman, director Andrew Grieve, and writer Clive Exton (all longtime veterans of Poirot mystery adaptations for television) would meet the challenge of the original novel's demanding plot, its boldly innovative narrative style, and especially its shocking conclusion. The plot is presented with considerable care and the usual attention to detail that is a hallmark of the Suchet/Poirot adaptations, including all of the salient clues and devices from the original novel. The narrative—originally written in the first person—is instead here read by Poirot. Finally, the climax, which caused such controversy in the 1920s, is slightly diluted by a gun battle. Overall, however, the retelling is a faithful one. Of note are the interplay between Poirot and Japp, the presence of the inquisitive Caroline Sheppard (played well by Selina Cadell), and the furious combat between Poirot and his vegetable marrows, or zucchinis.

At film's start, Hercule Poirot has decided at last to retire from active detective work and to settle in the country. His objective is to grow vegetable marrows in the lovely little village of Kings

Abbott and to enjoy the pleasant country air and good cheer of country society. His retreat from the world of crime proves a short one, however, for his friend, Roger Ackroyd, is brutally murdered. The list of suspects is a long one, including Ralph Paton, Ackroyd's adopted son, Ackroyd's sister-in-law, and even Ackroyd's own butler.

Unable to resist the intriguing aspects of the case and the chance to work again with his friend, Inspector Japp, Poirot once more puts to use his "little grey cells" and sets out to catch a murderer. The surprising solution to the case leaves Poirot anxious to return to his beloved flat in London and to escape the illusions of a quiet life in the country.

Murder on the Links (1995)

DIRECTOR: Andrew Grieve

CAST: David Suchet (Hercule Poirot); Hugh Fraser (Captain Arthur Hastings); Pauline Moran (Miss Felicity Lemon); Philip Jackson (Chief Inspector James Japp), Bill Moody (Giraud), Damien Thomas (Paul Renauld), Jacinta Mulcahy (Bella Duveen), Ben Pullen (Jack Renauld), Kate Fahy (Bernadette Daubrevil), Bernard Latham (Lucien Bex).

This made-for-television movie, produced by London Weekend Television, was adapted from the novel first published in 1925 and presents Poirot's investigation into the murder of Paul Renauld, who had been taken from his home, stabbed to death, and then thrown facedown into an open grave. Generally faithful to the original material, *Murder on the Links* does downplay the most exciting aspect of the story, namely the first meeting of Captain Arthur Hastings with his future wife, Dulcie Duveen.

Murder with Mirrors (1985)

DIRECTOR: Dick Lowry

CAST: Helen Hayes (Miss Marple), Bette Davis (Carrie Louise Serrocold), John Mills (Lewis Serrocold), Dorothy Tutin (Mildred Strete), Leo McKern (Inspector Curry), Tim Roth (Edgar Lawson), James Coombs (Steven Restarick).

This CBS Television adaptation of the original

Miss Marple (Helen Hayes, left) and her old friend, Carrie Louise Serrocold (Bette Davis), in Murder with Mirrors *(1985). (Photofest)*

1952 novel *They Do It with Mirrors* features Helen Hayes in her second and last outing as Miss Marple (the role was subsequently dominated thoroughly by Joan Hickson). Produced and adapted by George Eckstein, the film boasts a stellar cast and a proper setting in England. Unfortunately, it was soon eclipsed by the Joan Hickson films, especially the 1991 *They Do It with Mirrors.* The two versions provide a suitable basis for comparison between the two Miss Marples. Hayes chose to make her Miss Marple a kinder and more accessible sleuth, while Hickson was more faithful (and hence more sly and ruthless) to the original novels and stories.

The Mysterious Affair at Styles (1990)

DIRECTOR: Ross Devenish

CAST: David Suchet (Hercule Poirot); Hugh

Fraser (Captain Arthur Hastings); Pauline Moran (Miss Felicity Lemon); Philip Jackson (Chief Inspector James Japp); Joanna McCallum (Evie Howard), Eric Stovell (Chemist), Caroline Swift (Nurse), David Rintool (John Covendish), Beatie Edney (Mary Cavendish), Gilliam Barge (Mrs. Inglethorp), Michael Cronin (Alfred Inglethorp).

This made-for-television film, produced by London Weekend Television, offers an exciting opportunity for viewers to witness the first case Hercule Poirot undertook in England and his reunion of sorts with his friend Captain Arthur Hastings, who brings him into the investigation of the death of Emily Inglethorp.

A refugee from Belgium, thanks to World War I, Poirot finds himself and his fellow Belgians dependent upon the charity of the English. He is delighted to meet Hastings—a previous acquaintance—who is himself recovering from shell shock and wounds suffered in the trenches. There is immediate chemistry between the detective and his redoubtable sidekick, and the two fall easily into the give-and-take that has been a hallmark of the Poirot series on television. Hastings is bright and enthusiastic, but he is also utterly out of his depth when dealing with a complicated crime and a subtle murderer, such as the one he faces in the Inglethorp death. Poirot, meanwhile, relies on Hastings as a suitable sounding board, an advisor on things British, and a source of inspiration when Hastings accidentally says something important or insightful.

"The Mystery of the Blue Jar" (1982)

DIRECTOR: Cyril Mark

CAST: Michael Aldridge, Robin Kermode, Isabella Spade.

This episode of the Thames Television series *The Agatha Christie Hour* (1982–1983) was produced by Pat Sandys, adapted by T. R. Bowen, and directed by Cyril Coke. Based on the short story of the same name originally published in *The Hound of Death and Other Stories* (1933), "The Mystery of the Blue Jar" is of greater interest to fans of golf than to fans of mystery, although it does give a generally faithful retelling of Christie's tale of a man who hears a woman's plaintive cries for help.

"The Mystery of Hunter's Lodge" (1991)

DIRECTOR: Renny Rye

CAST: David Suchet (Hercule Poirot); Hugh Fraser (Captain Arthur Hastings); Pauline Moran (Miss Felicity Lemon); Philip Jackson (Chief Inspector James Japp); Bernard Horsfall (Harrington Pace), Roy Boyd (Jack Stoddard), Diana Kent (Zoe Havering), Jim Norton (Roger Havering), Shaughan Seymour (Archie Havering).

This episode of *Agatha Christie's Poirot*, produced by London Weekend Television and adapted from the short story of the same name first published in 1924, gives Hastings a chance to take control of an investigation because Poirot is too ill to attend to an important affair in person. Poirot, of course, knows what he is doing from the start and tries to direct Hastings, but the overly enthusiastic captain has a habit of wandering off into fruitless and tangential aspects of the investigation.

"The Mystery of the Spanish Chest" (1991)

DIRECTOR: Andrew Grieve

CAST: David Suchet (Hercule Poirot); Hugh Fraser (Captain Arthur Hastings); Pauline Moran (Miss Felicity Lemon); Philip Jackson (Chief Inspector James Japp); Caroline Langrishe (Marguerite Clayton), Malcolm Sinclair (Edward Clayton), John McEnery (Colonel Curtiss), Pip Torrens (Major Rich).

This episode of *Agatha Christie's Poirot*, produced by London Weekend Television and adapted from the short story of the same name originally published in 1960, focuses on revenge, jealousy, and a certain brutality not explicitly detailed in the short story. Poirot is asked to assist Major Charles Rich—under arrest for suspicion of murdering Arnold Clayton and dumping his corpse in a chest in Rich's own living room—and the unfortunate widow who is devastated by the crime but who had been troubled for some time by her husband's cool demeanor. The circumstances seem absolutely damning for Rich, who is unable to explain how Clayton ended up in his Spanish chest, let alone how he was stabbed savagely through the eye. Poirot, of course, is able to free Rich and achieve real justice.

The episode is highlighted by the performances of Caroline Langrishe as Margharita Clayton and John McEnery as McLaren. There is also a series of dueling scenes used to frame the story. The duels are nicely staged, and add a complex psychological aspect to the crime that becomes clear only at the end.

Nemesis (1986)

DIRECTOR: David Tucker

CAST: Joan Hickson (Miss Jane Marple), Margaret Tyzack (Clothilde Bradbury-Scott), Bruce Payne (Michael Rafiel), Peter Tilbury (Lionel Peel), Frank Gatliff (Jason Rafiel), Barbara Franceschi (Miss Kurnowitz), Roger Hammond (Mr. Broadribb), Ann Queensberry (Miss Wimpole), Joanna Hole (Madge), Helen Cherry (Miss Temple), John Horsley (Professor Wanstead), Jane Booker (Miss Cooke), Alison Skilbeck (Miss Barrow), Valerie Lush (Lavinia Glynne), Anna Cropper (Anthea Bradbury-Scott).

This fifth BBC adaptation of a Miss Marple novel features Joan Hickson reprising her beloved performance as the venerable sleuth. Based on the 1971 novel—technically the last Marple mystery, as *Sleeping Murder* had been written during World War II—the film was produced by George Gallacio and scripted by T. R. Bowen. *Nemesis* was much anticipated by fans of the BBC adaptations, as it gave Joan Hickson a chance to appear in one of Miss Marple's most memorable cases. Jason Rafiel, who had first met Miss Marple in *A Caribbean Mystery,* leaves a request in his will that the old sleuth should perform the classical role of Nemesis and determine once and for all whether his son was guilty of murdering his fiancée years before. Under the guise of a tourist visiting British homes and gardens, Miss Marple takes on

the task and soon uncovers a dark secret of love, jealousy, and murder.

Nemesis features one of Miss Marple's most memorable endeavors, as she becomes the physical embodiment of the goddess of justice. Her interplay with Rafiel's attorneys is a masterpiece of subtle language and inflection, as the attorneys realize that they have stumbled across a truly frightening intellect who will not shrink at sending someone to the gallows. In confronting the murderer, Miss Marple also meets someone who is as determined as she is, and almost as clever. Bruce Payne does a fine job as Michael Rafiel, a man haunted by his past and brought back into the light of justice.

One, Two, Buckle My Shoe (1992)

DIRECTOR: Ross Deverish

CAST: David Suchet (Hercule Poirot); Hugh Fraser (Captain Arthur Hastings); Pauline Moran (Miss Felicity Lemon); Philip Jackson (Chief Inspector James Japp); Peter Blythe (Blunt), Kevork Malikyan (Amberiotis), Carolyn Colquhoun (Mabelle), Joe Greco (Alfred Biggs), Joanna Phillip-Lane (Gerda), Christopher Eccleston (Frank Carter), Karen Giledhill (Gladys Neville), Sara Steward (Jane Olivera).

This made-for-television film was produced by London Weekend Television and adapted from the novel of the same name first published in 1940. *One, Two Buckle My Shoe* is one of the best of the adaptations by London Weekend Television, thanks in large measure to the nicely constructed screenplay, which very subtly reveals important clues and is supported by strong performances by the principal characters.

Viewers are given the fun of watching the great Belgian detective suffer in a dentist's chair, a moment of human frailty that is galling to one who assures all of his virtual perfection. There is thus an added sense of outrage on the part of the sleuth when the very dentist who had worked on his teeth is found dead soon afterward, the victim of apparent suicide. His death is followed by that of Mr. Amberiotis, another patient, and it is clear swiftly to Poirot that his dentist did not shoot himself but was the victim of murder.

The Pale Horse (1996)

DIRECTOR: Charles Beeson

CAST: Colin Buchanan (Mark Easterbrook), Jayne Ashbourne (Kate Mercer), Hermione Norris (Hermia Redcliffe), Leslie Phillips (Lincoln Bradley), Michael Byrne (Venables), Catherine Holman (Poppy Tuckerton), Louise Jameson (Florence Tuckerton), Martin Kennedy (Tate), Ruth Madoc (Sybil), Jean Marsh (Thyrza Grey), Steve Weston (Ned Thackeray).

An enjoyable adaptation of the original 1961 novel, *The Pale Horse* was produced by Anglia Television Entertainment, scripted by Alma Cullen, and stars Colin Buchanan, who is known to fans of television mystery for his recurring role in the series *Dalziel and Pascoe.* The adaptation is a thorough updating of the novel, meaning that Mark Easterbrook is not a scholar, as he is in the novel, but rather an artist with some prospects and intelligence. He becomes a suspect in the murder of a priest, a death that propels him into a convoluted tangle of murder and conspiracy. There are some excellent red herrings involving the smarmy Mr. Venables, but gradually the focus turns to the eerie inn called The Pale Horse. The chief absence in the film is that of Mrs. Ariadne Oliver, who was in the novel but does not find her way into the screenplay.

Partners in Crime (1982)

DIRECTOR: John A. Davis, Tony Wharmby

CAST: James Warwick (Tommy Beresford); Francesca Annis (Tuppence); Reece Dinsdale (Albert).

This series of ten one-hour mysteries produced in 1982 by London Weekend Television brought to life the popular and often flamboyant couple Tommy and Tuppence Beresford after their successful debut in *The Secret Adversary* that same year. Based on the 1929 collection of short stories, *Partners in Crime* was produced by Jack Williams and features Francesca Annis and James Warwick in the roles of Tommy and Tuppence Beresford. They are assisted by Reece Dinsdale in the role of the ever-faithful Albert.

As in the original stories, the sleuths solve their mysteries while impersonating famous sleuths from fiction, including Hercule Poirot, Father Brown, and Sherlock Holmes. The impersonations, of course, provide them with an excuse to dress up in costumes and lampoon their literary inspirations. More of a comedy and lighthearted mystery than the heavier murder cases investigated by Poirot and Miss Marple, *Partners in Crime* captures wonderfully the original spirit and mood of the short stories. The episodes are:

"The Affair of the Pink Pearl"
"The House of Lurking Death"
"The Sunningdale Mystery"
"The Clergyman's Daughter"
"Finessing the King"
"The Ambassador's Boots"
"The Man in the Mist"
"The Unbreakable Alibi"
"The Case of the Missing Lady"
"The Crackler"

Peril at End House (1990)

DIRECTOR: Renny Rye

CAST: David Suchet (Hercule Poirot); Hugh Fraser (Captain Arthur Hastings); Pauline Moran (Miss Felicity Lemon); Philip Jackson (Chief Inspector James Japp); Polly Walker (Nick Buckley), John Harding (Cmdr. Challenger), Jeremy Young (Bert Croft), Alison Sterling (Freddie Rice), Carol MacReady (Milly Croft).

The plot of this made-for-television film produced by London Weekend Television and adapted from the original novel of the same name, first published in 1932, is concerned with Poirot's efforts to protect a young heiress, Nick Buckley, from death; she has already survived several attempts on her life, and Poirot is determined that none of them succeeds. As with the original novel, the story line is filled with numerous red herrings and blind clues.

"The Plymouth Express" (1991)

DIRECTOR: Andrew Piddington

CAST: David Suchet (Hercule Poirot); Hugh Fraser (Captain Arthur Hastings); Pauline Moran (Miss Felicity Lemon); Philip Jackson (Chief Inspector James Japp); Shelagh McLeod (Florence Carrington), Alfredo Michelson (Comte de la Rochefour), Marion Bailey (Jane Mason), Julian Wadham (Rupert Carrington).

This episode of *Agatha Christie's Poirot,* produced by London Weekend Television and adapted from the short story of the same name originally published in 1951, presents the murder of Flossie Carrington, the wealthy daughter of the even more wealthy Ebenezer Halliday. She boards the Plymouth Express and is later discovered stuffed under a seat on the train, her fabulous jewels stolen. The obvious suspect—certainly in the eyes of her father—is her worthless husband, Rupert Carrington, but attention also focuses on another of Flossie's admirers, the disreputable Count Armand de la Rochefour.

A Pocket Full of Rye (1986)

DIRECTOR: Guy Slater

CAST: Joan Hickson (Miss Marple), Frances Low (Patricia Fortescue), Merelina Kendall (Mrs. Crump), Frank Mills (Mr. Crump), Annette Badland (Gladys Martin), Jon Glover (Detective Sergeant Hay), Louis Mahoney (Dr. French), Charles Pemberton (Sergeant Rose), Susan Gilmore (Miss Grosvenor), Nancie Herrod (Miss Griffith), Peter Davison (Lance Fortescue), Stacy Dorning (Adele Fortescue), Fabia Drake (Miss Henderson), Martyn Stanbridge (Vivian Dubois), Timothy West (Rex Fortescue), Tom Wilkinson (Detective Inspector Neele).

This sixth BBC adaptation of a Miss Marple novel features another memorable outing by Joan Hickson as the venerable sleuth. *A Pocket Full of Rye* was based on the original 1953 novel; it was produced by George Gallacio and adapted by T. R. Bowen (who had also adapted several other Miss Marple mysteries for the BBC). The chief interest of the film is the brilliant performance by Joan Hickson, who relentlessly pursues a cunning murderer, especially after the killer does in a mentally challenged maid who had once worked for Miss Marple.

As does the novel, the teleplay makes good use of the nursery rhyme, and features Miss Marple quoting the well-known line about considering black birds ". . .have you gone into the question of black birds?" The cast is not quite as memorable as in other BBC adaptations (especially *A Murder Is Announced*), but Timothy West is terrific as the much-hated Rex Fortescue (he had already appeared in *Murder Is Easy* in 1982), as is Peter Davison, who plays the perpetually unlucky Lance Fortescue.

"Problem at Sea" (1989)

DIRECTOR: Renny Rye

CAST: David Suchet (Hercule Poirot); Sheila Allen (Mrs. Clapperton), John Normington (John Clapperton), Melissa Greenwood (Kitty Mooney), Roger Hume (Gen. Forbes).

This episode of *Agatha Christie's Poirot,* produced by London Weekend Television and adapted from the original story of the same name first published in 1939, places Poirot once again on board a ship and once again forces him to solve a murder in the difficult environment of a foreign country. The detective investigates the murder of Mrs. Adeline Clapperton, who is stabbed to death in her cabin while the other passengers are off on a port call. While virtually everyone on board had a reason to kill the unpleasant woman, there was seemingly no opportunity for any of them to do so. Poirot, however, dismisses the possibility that some local came on board to kill her, despite the evidence that points to a dealer of trinkets and jewelry. In a delightful scene—enthusiastically brought to life by Suchet—the detective reveals the killer, with the help of a little doll.

"The Red Signal" (1982)

DIRECTOR: John Franco

CAST: Joanna David, Richard Morant, Christopher Casenove.

This episode of the Thames Television series *The Agatha Christie Hour* (1982–1983) was produced by Pat Sandys, adapted by William Corlett, and directed by John Frankau. Based on the original short story published in *The Hound of Death and Other Stories* (1933), "The Red Signal" presents the supernatural experience of Dermot West. He experiences a "red signal" that warns him of impending danger, a feeling that is extremely strong at a certain dinner party. The signal proves most accurate when West receives a dire warning during a séance.

The Secret Adversary (1982)

DIRECTOR: Tony Wharmby

CAST: Francesca Annis (Tuppence Cowley), James Warwick (Thomas Beresford), Reece Dinsdale (Albert), Gavan O'Herlihy (Julius P. Hersheimmer), Alec McCowen (Sir James Peele Edgerton), Honor Blackman (Rita Vandemeyer), Peter Barkworth (Mr. Carter), Toria Fuller (Jane Finn), John Fraser (Kramenin), George Baker (Whittington), Donald Houston (Boris), Joseph Brady (Dr. Hall), Wolf Kahler (The German).

This second adaptation of a Christie work by London Weekend Television marks the first pairing of Francesca Annis and James Warwick in what became the recurring roles of Tommy and Tuppence Beresford. The pair had already starred in *Why Didn't They Ask Evans?* (1981), in the roles of Lady Frances Derwent and Bobby Jones respectively. Based on the 1922 novel of the same name, which introduced the Beresfords, *The Secret Adversary* was adapted by Pat Sandys (who went on to have a major role in other Christie adaptations) and took as its primary objective the recreation of the original material, with all its atmosphere and fun. The Beresfords thus demonstrate the grand flamboyance and the romantic flair that distinguished their first literary appearance. Annis and Warwick were perfectly cast and developed an agreeable chemistry that they never lost in subsequent films or in the ten episodes of their series (1982–1983). One other significant cast member was George Baker as Whittington; he also played Inspector Davy in the BBC adaptation of *At Bertram's Hotel.* (See also *Partners in Crime.*)

The Seven Dials Mystery (1981)

DIRECTOR: Tony Wharmby

CAST: Cheryl Campbell (Lady Eileen Brent), James Warwick (Jimmy Thesinger), Harry Andrews (Superintendent Battle), Henrietta Baynes (Vera), Sarah Crowden (Helen), Norwich Duff (Howard Phelps), Sandor Elès (Count Andras), John Gielgud (Marquis of Caterham), James Griffiths (Rupert Bateman), Lucy Gutteridge (Lorraine Wade), Douglas W. Iles (John Bauer), Noel Johnson (Sir Stanley Digby), Rula Lenska (Countess Radzsky), Robert Longden (Gerry Wade), Charles Morgan (Dr. Cartwright), Terence O'Rourke (Thom Delaney), John Price (Alfred), Joyce Redman (Lady Coote), Lynn Ross (Nancy), Leslie Sands (Sir Oswald Coote), Christopher Scoular (Bill Eversleigh), Roger Sloman (Stevens), John Vine (Ronny Devereux), Brian Wilde (Tredwell), Jacob Witkin (Mr. Mosgorovsky).

The first significant television adaptation of a Christie work since the 1956 NBC production of *A Murder Is Announced, The Seven Dials Mystery* was produced by London Weekend Television (the same company that has enjoyed a long and fine reputation for bringing adaptations of Christie works to the screen) for the *Mobil Showcase.* Adapted by Pat Sandys (who eventually produced *The Agatha Christie Hour,* 1982–1983), this film boasts lavish production values, including the filming at Greenway House, the Christie estate in Devon, by permission of the Christie family.

In terms of Christie television history, perhaps the most notable aspect of *The Seven Dials Mystery* is its casting. British film stars Sir John Gielgud, Harry Andrews, Cheryl Campbell, and Lucy Gutteridge anchor the cast; Andrews's performance is especially significant, as it is the first television appearance of Superintendent Battle. In the role of Jimmy Thesiger, LWT chose James Warwick, who went on to play opposite Francesca Annis in *Why Didn't They Ask Evans?* (1981) and, in the recurring role of Tommy Beresford, in *The Secret Adversary* (1982).

Sleeping Murder (1986)

DIRECTOR: John Davies

CAST: Joan Hickson (Miss Marple), Géraldine Alexander (Gwenda Reed), John Moulder-Brown (Giles Reed), Georgine Anderson (Mrs. Hengrave), Edward Jewesbury (Mr. Sims), Jack Watson (Mr. Foster), Joan Scott (Mrs. Cocker), David McAllister (Raymond West), Amanda Boxer (Joan West), Frederick Treves (Dr. James Kennedy), Esmond Knight (Mr. Galbraith), John Ringham (Dr. Penrose), Eryl Maynard (Lily Kimble), Ken Kitson (Jim Kimble).

An adaptation of the last Christie novel featuring Miss Marple (see also *Nemesis,* above), *Sleeping Murder* marked the seventh BBC Miss Marple movie and another sparkling performance by Joan Hickson, the definitive interpreter of the old sleuth. Once again, the adaptation by T. R. Bowen displays considerable skill in retaining all the nuance and flavor of the novel while at the same time establishing a fine television drama.

One significant casting note is the presence of Géraldine Alexander as Gwenda Reed. Alexander carries much of the burden of the story as a young woman who begins suffering the eruption of long-suppressed memories into her consciousness (she also played Mrs. Maltravers in the London Weekend Television adaptation of "Tragedy at Marsdon Manor").

Sparkling Cyanide (1983)

DIRECTOR: Robert Michael Lewis

CAST: Anthony Andrews (Tony Browne), Deborah Raffin (Iris Murdoch), Pamela Bellwood (Ruth Lessing), Nancy Marchand (Lucilla Drake), Josef Sommer (George Barton), David Huffman (Stephan Farraday), Christina Belford (Rosemary Barton), June Chadwick (Sandra Farraday), Barrie Ingham (Eric Kidderminster), Harry Morgan (Captain Kemp), Michael Woods (Victor Drake).

This CBS Television adaptation of the 1945 novel was produced by the same team that filmed *A Caribbean Mystery,* which starred Helen Hayes and premiered only a few weeks before *Sparkling Cyanide* on American television. *Sparkling Cyanide* makes no real effort to reproduce faithfully the original mystery, and shifts the entire setting of the case from England to Los Angeles. Thus, with the exception of the very English Anthony Andrews, the entire film is distinctly American. Unfortunately, the adaptation possesses little to distinguish it from the assorted Christie adaptations that were appearing regularly on television in America and England during that time. It also lacked the central character of Colonel Race, leaving the detecting to Anthony Browne. While Andrews does well in the role, the absence of Race is felt keenly and deprives *Sparkling Cyanide* of a sense of authenticity.

Spider's Web (1982)

DIRECTOR: Basil Coleman

CAST: Penelope Keith and Robert Flemyng.

A BBC television adaptation of the original Christie play, "Spider's Web" starred one of Britain's foremost comedic actresses.

"The Sunningdale Mystery" (1983)

DIRECTOR: Tony Wharmby

CAST: James Warwick (Tommy Beresford); Francesca Annis (Tuppence Beresford); Reece Dinsdale (Archie).

In this episode of the London Weekend Television series *Partners in Crime,* Captain Sessle is stabbed to death with a hat pin while golfing, and the Beresfords become dissatisfied with the investigation, especially as they are certain that much more is going on than meets the eye. As with their other cases in the series, the fun-loving couple solves the mystery using the personae of detectives from fiction. In this case, Tommy becomes the

Old Man (who solves all crimes from the comfort of a tea shop), and Tuppence becomes Polly Burton, the Old Man's assistant. Both characters were created by Baroness Orczy (d. 1947).

Ten Little Niggers (1949)

As hard as it might be to believe, this title was actually used by the BBC for a television version of the 1943 play (based on the original 1939 Christie novel) *Ten Little Niggers.* Airing on the BBC on August 20, 1949, the horrendously titled teleplay was broadcast live. While virtually forgotten today, the teleplay marked the first ever adaptation of any Christie work for television. It was followed in 1956 by a television version of *A Murder Is Announced.*

"The Theft of the Royal Ruby" (1991)

DIRECTOR: Andrew Grieve

CAST: David Suchet (Hercule Poirot); Hugh Fraser (Captain Arthur Hastings); Pauline Moran (Miss Felicity Lemon); Philip Jackson (Chief Inspector James Japp); Nigel le Vaillant (Desmond Lee-Wortley), Frederick Treves (Col. Horace Lacey), Stephanie Cole (Mrs. Lacey), Helen Mitchell (Sarah Lacey), Tariq Alibali (Prince Farouk).

This episode of *Agatha Christie's Poirot,* produced by London Weekend Television and adapted from the short story of the same name first published in 1960, forces Poirot to do two unpleasant tasks. First, he must—at the behest of the British government—assist the future king of Egypt, Prince Ali (a very thinly disguised King Farouk) in recovering a stolen ruby. Second, he must spend Christmas with the Lacey family, as the thief will almost certainly be in attendance. The detective makes the best of the situation and proves a most amiable guest, even giving a demonstration of how to pit and serve a mango. He also frightens the thief, who panics and hides the ruby in a Christmas pudding. Changes from the original story include a greater role for the reprehensible Prince Ali and a dramatic car chase, in which the participants endeavor to catch a plane being used by the culprits to escape.

They Do It with Mirrors (1991)

DIRECTOR: Norman Stone

CAST: Joan Hickson (Miss Marple), Jean Simmons (Carrie-Louise Serrocold), Joss Ackland (Lewis Serrocold), Neal Swettenham (Edgar Lawson), David Horovitch (Chief Inspector Slack), Ian Brimble (Sergeant Lake), Christopher Villiers (Alex Restarick), Jay Villiers (Stephen Restarick), Holly Aird (Gina Hudd), Todd Boyce (Walter Hudd), Saul Reichlin (Dr. Maseryk), Matthew Cottle (Ernie Gregg).

This eleventh BBC adaptation of a Miss Marple mystery featured the second-to-last appearance of Joan Hickson as the beloved sleuth. Based closely on the 1952 novel of the same name, *They Do It with Mirrors* was adapted for television by T. R. Bowen, who had done an admirable job adapting the often convoluted plots of other novels for television. The original story is of great interest to Miss Marple fans, given the tantalizing tidbits that are provided about the sleuth's younger days; the television movie does not neglect this essential aspect of the story, and assorted references to old home movies are provided, offering a glimpse of Miss Marple when she was a girl, as impossible as it might be to imagine Miss Marple ever being young.

As for the actual murder investigation, the novel is followed in virtually all of its particulars, with careful attention paid to the ongoing relationship between Miss Marple and the easily rankled Inspector Slack (played again splendidly by David Horovitch). His dutiful sergeant, Lake (again played by Ian Brimble), enjoys (not so secretly) every moment of his boss's agonizing dealings with the old sleuth.

"The Third-Floor Flat" (1989)

DIRECTOR: Edward Bennett

CAST: David Suchet (Hercule Poirot); Hugh Fraser (Captain Arthur Hastings); Pauline Moran (Miss Felicity Lemon); Philip Jackson (Chief Inspector James Japp); Suzanne Burden (Patricia Matthews), Amanda Elwes (Mildred), Nicholas

Prichard (Donovan), Robert Hines (Jimmy), Josie Lawrence (Mrs. Grant).

This episode of *Agatha Christie's Poirot,* produced by London Weekend Television and adapted from the original story of the same name first published in 1950, presents a brutal murder in Hercule Poirot's own apartment building. The body of Mrs. Ernestine Grant is found in her third-floor flat by two young men who accidentally find their way into her living room in the mistaken belief that they are on the fourth floor. Poirot is soon involved, and his inquiry leads to the mysterious John Fraser, Grant's estranged husband, and to the murderer. As in several other episodes (such as "The Italian Nobleman," "The Incredible Theft," and "The Kidnapping of Johnnie Waverly"), Captain Hastings displays an ardent fondness for cars, but here the captain also suffers a cruel blow to his beloved automobile. Actress Amanda Elwes also had a role in the television film *The Mirror Crack'd from Side to Side* (1992).

Thirteen at Dinner (1985)

DIRECTOR: Lou Antonio

CAST: Peter Ustinov (Hercule Poirot), Faye Dunaway (Jane Wilkinson), David Suchet (Inspector Japp), Jonathan Cecil (Hastings), Bill Nighy (Ronald Marsh), Diane Keen (Jenny Driver), John Stride (Film Director), Benedict Taylor (Donald Ross), Lee Horsley (Bryan Martin), Allan Cuthbertson (Sir Montague Corner), Glyn Baker (Lord Edgeware's Butler), John Barron (Lord George Edgeware), Peter Clapham (Mr. Wildburn).

This third film featuring Peter Ustinov as Hercule Poirot marks the actor's fist appearance as the Belgian detective on television; he reprised the role three more times, once in film (*Appointment with Death,* 1988) and twice on television (*Dead Man's Folly,* 1986, and *Murder in Three Acts,* 1986). For the transition from motion picture to television, CBS chose one of the more urbane Poirot cases, and the writer Rod Browning created a script that put the talents of Ustinov and the impressive supporting cast, including Faye Dunaway, to good use.

As became the custom in the CBS adaptations that followed—and as had been seen with the earlier CBS Marple adaptations starring Helen Hayes—there was a clear Americanization of the plot and atmosphere. Gone are the many traditional Christie witticisms and phrases in favor of dialogue less disorienting for Americans, although the cast is still sprinkled with recognizable British performers (such as Bill Nighy as Hastings and Allan Cuthbertson as Sir Montague Corner). For any fan of Christie on television, of course, the most memorable part of the movie is the presence of David Suchet as Chief Inspector Japp. Suchet went on only three years later to portray Hercule Poirot for London Weekend Television in its enduring and popular series *Agatha Christie's Poirot.*

"Tragedy at Marsdon Manor" (1991)

DIRECTOR: Renny Rye

CAST: David Suchet (Hercule Poirot); Hugh Fraser (Captain Arthur Hastings); Pauline Moran (Miss Felicity Lemon); Philip Jackson (Chief Inspector James Japp); Géraldine Alexander (Mrs. Maltravers), Neil Duncan (Capt. Black), Ian McCulloch (Jonathan Maltravers), Anita Carey (Miss Rawlinson).

This episode of *Agatha Christie's Poirot,* produced by London Weekend Television and adapted from the original short story entitled first published in 1924, brings Poirot to the estate of a country squire, Mr. Maltravers, who has died under mysterious circumstances. His widow is clearly distraught, and adding to the mystery is the curious behavior of a supposed family friend, Captain Black, who seems to know more that he is revealing.

The television adaptation changes the original story in several significant ways. First, the character of Mrs. Maltravers is much more developed than in the original story. Here, the character is obsessed with her husband's death and evinces a firm belief in the supernatural. Poirot also has an interesting interplay with the local innkeeper, who is an aspiring mystery writer. Finally, Poirot uses an ingenious method for solving the crime—with the help

Poirot (David Suchet) investigates a clue in a murder, in "Tragedy at Marsdon Manor," part of Agatha Christie's Poirot. *(Photofest; London Weekend Television)*

of a local actor. Playing the role of Mrs. Maltravers is Géraldine Alexander, who also played Gwenda Reed in the BBC adaptation of *Sleeping Murder.*

"Triangle at Rhodes" (1989)

DIRECTOR: Renny Rye

CAST: David Suchet (Hercule Poirot); Hugh Fraser (Captain Arthur Hastings); Pauline Moran (Miss Felicity Lemon); Philip Jackson (Chief Inspector James Japp); Frances Low (Pamela Lyall), Jon Cartwright (Chantry), Annie Lambert (Valentine Chantry), Peter Settelen (Douglas Gold), Angela Down (Marjorie Gold).

This episode of *Agatha Christie's Poirot,* produced by London Weekend Television and adapted from the original short story of the same name first published in 1937, is one of the more subtle installments in the series, remaining generally faithful to

the original material and thus developing the plot very slowly and with patience. Viewers must pay close attention to the interplay of the characters to catch the clues leading inexorably toward murder. There is much in this episode (as in the original story) that reminds one of the 1982 film *Evil under the Sun,* mainly because of the similarities in plot and setting; both are set in a lush Mediterranean environment. There is, of course, no confusing the radically different performances of David Suchet and Peter Ustinov in the role of Poirot.

"The Unbreakable Alibi" (1983)

DIRECTOR: Christopher Hodson

CAST: James Warwick (Tommy Beresford); Francesca Annis (Tuppence Beresford); Reece Dinsdale (Archie).

In this episode of the London Weekend Television series *Partners in Crime,* an Australian woman, Una Drake, makes a bet with her fiancé, Montgomery-Jones, that she will be able to create an absolutely perfect alibi by being in two different places at the same time. The challenge is taken very seriously by Montgomery-Jones, who turns to Tommy and Tuppence Beresford for help.

Based on the original short story of the same name, first published in 1933 in *The Hound of Death and Other Stories,* "The Unbreakable Alibi" offers the Beresfords the opportunity to solve a case that has little criminal importance but that is perfectly suited to their romantic inclinations.

"The Under Dog" (1993)

DIRECTOR: John Bruce

CAST: David Suchet (Hercule Poirot); Hugh Fraser (Captain Arthur Hastings); Pauline Moran (Miss Felicity Lemon); Philip Jackson (Chief Inspector James Japp); Denis Lill (Sir Reuben Astwell), Ann Bell (Lady Astwell), Ian Gelder (Victor Astwell), Bill Wallis (Horace Trefusis), Andrew Sear (Humphrey Naylor).

This episode of *Agatha Christie's Poirot,* produced by London Weekend Television and adapted from the original short story of the same name first published in 1951, has Poirot investigating the murder of Sir Reuben Astwell. The plot is similar to that of "The Second Gong."

"The Veiled Lady" (1990)

DIRECTOR: Edward Bennett

CAST: David Suchet (Hercule Poirot); Hugh Fraser (Captain Arthur Hastings); Pauline Moran (Miss Felicity Lemon); Philip Jackson (Chief Inspector James Japp); Francis Barber (Lady Millicent), Terence Harvey (Lavington), Carole Hayman (Mrs. Godber).

This episode of *Agatha Christie's Poirot,* produced by London Weekend Television and adapted from the original short story of the same name first published in 1924, gives Poirot a chance to depart from his usual prim and proper life. Here, he can exercise his "little grey cells" and also play the role

of a house burglar, complete with the requisite black turtleneck. The impetus for his jaunt is the plea from Lady Millicent, the "veiled lady," to help her recover a Chinese puzzle box that contains an embarrassing letter. In burgling the house of a supposed blackmailer, Poirot suffers a mishap and is abandoned by his accomplice, Captain Hastings, and arrested by the police. This dire turn of events is of great amusement to Inspector Japp, and Poirot is so outraged that he pursues the truth of the case with much determination.

"Wasps' Nest" (1991)

DIRECTOR: Brian Farnham

CAST: David Suchet (Hercule Poirot); Hugh Fraser (Captain Arthur Hastings); Pauline Moran (Miss Felicity Lemon); Philip Jackson (Chief Inspector James Japp); Martin Turner (John Harrison), Melanie Jessop (Molly Deane), Peter Capaldi (Claude Langton), John Boswall (Dr. Belvedere).

This episode of *Agatha Christie's Poirot,* produced by London Weekend Television and adapted from the original short story of the same name first published in 1961, is more of a tragic romance than a typical murder mystery. A romantic triangle attracts Poirot's eye—thanks to the photographic interests of Captain Hastings, who captures a revealing scene on film—and he sets out to prevent a tragedy. As in the original story, the detective relies upon the metaphor of wasps to convince a dying man that he should not commit murder. The episode uses the golden sunsets in the English countryside to suggest a man in the sunset of his own young life.

Why Didn't They Ask Evans? (1981)

DIRECTOR: Tony Wharmby and John Davies

CAST: Francesca Annis (Lady Frances Derwent), James Warwick (Bobby Jones), John Gielgud (Reverend Jones), Connie Booth (Sylvia Bassington-ffrench), Leigh Lawson (Roger Bassington-ffrench), Robert Longden (Badger Beadon), Bernard Miles (Dr. Thomas), Eric Porter (Dr. Nicholson), Madeleine Smith (Moira Nicholson), Joan Hickson.

The second 1981 adaptation of a Christie work by London Weekend Television (following *The Seven Dials Mystery*), *Why Didn't They Ask Evans?* was originally intended as a miniseries, but it was edited and subsequently aired as a three-hour television film. Tony Wharmby, who directed and produced *The Seven Dials Mystery,* directed this piece with John Davies (who went on to have a major role in bringing Hercule Poirot to life for London Weekend Television). Pat Sandys, who produced the 1982–1983 series *The Agatha Christie Hour,* adapted the original 1934 novel for the screen.

A fairly routine retelling of Christie's complicated mystery novel of the same name, *Why Didn't They Ask Evans?* is best remembered for the first television pairing of Francesca Annis and James Warwick in the roles of Lady Frances Derwent and Bobby Jones. Two years later, they came together in the recurring roles of Tommy and Tuppence Beresford in the television film *The Secret Adversary,*

followed by the ten-episode series *Partners in Crime.* Sir John Gielgud also makes a report appearance in an LWT production (he had been in *The Seven Dials Mystery*), and of particular interest is the small role for Joan Hickson; three years later, she premiered as the definitive Miss Marple for the BBC.

Witness for the Prosecution (1982)

DIRECTOR: Alan Gibson

CAST: Ralph Richardson (Sir Wilfrid Robarts), Diana Rigg (Christine Vole), Beau Bridges (Leonard Vole), Deborah Kerr (Nurse Plimsoll), Donald Pleasence (Mr. Myers), David Langton (Mayhew), Richard Vernon (Brogan-Moore), Michael Gough (Judge), Wendy Hiller (Janet Mackenzie), Peter Copley (Dr. Harrison), Zulema Dene (Miss Johnson), Jenny Donnison (First Nurse), Wilfred Grove (Photographer), Ceri Kackson (Second Nurse), John Kidd (Court Usher), Patricia Leslie (Mrs. French), Andrew McLachlan (Jury Foreman), Frank Mills (Chief Inspector

The first pairing of James Warwick and Francesca Annis, in Why Didn't They Ask Evans? *(1981). (Photofest; Thames Television)*

Hearne), Barbara New (Miss O'Brien), Michael Nightingale (Clerk of the Court), Peter Salis (Carter), Aubrey Woods (Tailor).

Given the success of the 1957 film version and the even greater success of the 1953 Christie play *Witness for the Prosecution,* it was inevitable that another version of the play should be developed, this time for television. Produced by United Artists and Norman Rosemont, the television film was adapted by John Gay. Gay used both the original play and the screenplay for the 1957 film by Billy Wilder and Harry Kurnitz. This meant that the resulting television script contained virtually all the red herrings and surprising twists and turns in the plot from both works.

There is a perfunctory feel to much of *Witness for the Prosecution,* as anyone who has seen the stage play or the earlier film will know precisely what to expect. There is the monocle test performed by Sir Wilfrid on his prospective client, the shocking arrival of the witness for the prosecution, and the well-deserved rendering of final justice. What ultimately saves the television movie is the gathering of performers. Ralph Richardson, Diana Rigg, and Beau Bridges form an enjoyable triumvirate, although they do not make one forget Charles Laughton, Marlene Dietrich, and Tyrone Power. The story is also ably aided by the supporting cast, including Deborah Kerr, Wendy Hiller, and Donald Pleasence. Rigg starred the same year as Arlena Marshall in *Evil under the Sun.* Wendy Hiller had appeared in 1974 as the Russian countess in *Murder on the Orient Express.* Donald Pleasence appeared in the 1989 version of *Ten Little Indians.*

"Yellow Iris" (1993)

DIRECTOR: Peter Fleming
CAST: David Suchet (Hercule Poirot); Hugh Fraser (Captain Arthur Hastings); Pauline Moran (Miss Felicity Lemon); Philip Jackson (Chief Inspector James Japp); Yolanda Vasquez (Lola), Robin McCaffrey (Iris Russell), David Troughton (Barton Russell), Geraldine Somerville (Pauline Wetherby), Hugh Ross (Stephen Carter), Joseph Long (Luigi).

This episode of *Agatha Christie's Poirot,* produced by London Weekend Television and adapted from the original short story of the same name first published in 1939, is similar to "The Chocolate Box" in that it presents a murder in retrospect. Poirot remembers the grim events of years before, when he was caught, with a group of other tourists, in a revolution in a South American country. In the midst of the political upheaval, a murder is committed at a dinner party. Years later, Poirot is invited to a party that will commemorate the event and recreate the murder exactly.

Zehn kleine Negerlein (1969)

DIRECTOR: Hans Quest
CAST: Alfred Schieske (Sir Lawrence Wargrave), Fritz Haneke (General MacKenzie), Nora Minor (Emily Brent), Ingrid Capelle (Vera Claythorne), Rolf Boysen (Philip Lombard), Alexander Kerst (Dr. Armstrong), Werner Peters (William Blore), Peter Fricke (Anthony Marston), Guenther Neutze (Rogers), Edith Volkmann (Mrs. Rogers), Mathias Hell (Narracot)

A German television adaptation of *And Then There Were None,* the film was adapted by Gerd Krauss and Fritz Peter Buch. The director, Hans Quest, was also the director of the adaptation of *Murder at the Vicarage* the following year, *Mord im Pfarrhaus.*

Stage

Akhnaton (c. 1937)

A play about ancient Egypt, *Akhnaton* was the stage version of Christie's novel *Death Comes As the End* (1945). Like the novel, set in ancient Egypt, it was never staged nor adapted. Christie considered it very unlikely that it ever would be, and the play itself wasn't published until thirty-five years after its creation. As was true with *Death Comes As the End,* Christie was both influenced and assisted in her writing by her husband, Max Mallowan, and the respected archaeologist Stephen Glanville. It is Glanville, for example, who holds the singular distinction of being the only one ever to convince Christie to change the ending of one of her novels, which happened to be *Death Comes As the End.* The result was a play of which Max Mallowan was extremely proud, describing it in his memoirs as "Agatha's most beautiful and profound play . . .The Egyptian court life and the vagaries of Egyptian religion come alive." In the end, Mallowan's enthusiasm was insufficient to secure the play's production, although Christie's longstanding publisher, William Collins, released *Akhnaton* in 1973.

Akhnaton is set in 1350 B.C., in Egypt, during the reign of Pharaoh Akhnaton. It focuses on the efforts of the ruler to establish belief in one god and to build his mighty city of faith, the City of the Horizon. He is challenged by the priestly establishment, his scheming wife, Nefertiti, and his own increasing mental instability. The play ends tragically, with Egypt in ruins from foreign invasion and Akhnaton poisoned by his own wife, who was assisted by the machinations of the chief priests. Horrified at her deed, the queen drinks the poison as well, joining her husband in death.

Alibi (1928)

The first adaptation of a Christie work for the stage, *Alibi* was based on the novel *The Murder of Roger Ackroyd* and was penned by Michael Morton. Produced by Gerald du Maurier, the play debuted on May 15, 1928, at the Prince of Wales Theatre, London, and subsequently ran for 250 performances. It was adapted for the American stage by John Anderson, under the title *The Fatal Alibi,* and opened at the Booth Theatre on February 9, 1932. The American production proved far less successful than its British counterpart, and ran for only twenty-four performances.

From the start, Christie was disappointed in the way that her novel was brought to life. She disagreed with Morton's original plan to make Poirot twenty years younger, but was able to force the playwright to keep the detective the same age he is in the novel. She was unable, however, to change two aspects of the play that she strongly disliked. The first was Morton's decision to alter Caroline Sheppard as she appears in the novel and to make her much younger and hence a romantic interest. The second had to do with casting. In the role of Poirot, du Maurier decided that Charles Laughton was ideal. While Christie liked Laughton's work, she considered him miscast. The critics enjoyed Laughton's Poirot, and the famed actor went on to star in the American adaptation as well. Laughton subsequently appeared in *Witness for the Prosecution* (1957) as the brilliant barrister Sir Wilfrid Robarts.

Appointment with Death (1945)

Based on the 1938 novel of the same name, *Appointment with Death* was adapted for the stage by Christie herself and opened on March 31, 1945, at the Piccadilly Theatre, London. The play did not match the success of *Ten Little Indians,* which had opened two years before. Nevertheless, *Appointment with Death* continued to advance Christie's blossoming career as a playwright and was followed the next year by *Murder on the Nile.* The cast of *Appointment with Death* had a notable member, Joan Hickson, who enjoyed a long career in Christie productions and was arguably the greatest of the Miss Marples. In *Appointment with Death,* she played Miss Pryce.

Black Coffee (1930)

Agatha Christie noted in her autobiography that her play *Black Coffee* was actually completed before Michael Morton finished *Alibi,* his adaptation of *The Murder of Roger Ackroyd* in 1928. Nevertheless, *Alibi* was produced first, but *Black Coffee* holds the distinction of being the first original play written by Christie to be produced for the stage. According to Mathew Prichard, Christie's grandson, writing in the afterword to the 1997 novelization of the play, his grandmother decided to write a play of her own—a new kind of literary undertaking—as a result of her unhappiness with the adaptation of *The Murder of Roger Ackroyd.* Whether the play had been written before Morton finished his adaptation or whether it was written in response to the adaptation became irrelevant when Christie first showed the play to her agent. He suggested that she should not bother to give it to anyone involved in theatrical management, as it was not worth the trouble. Christie chose to ignore the advice and, at the encouragement of a friend, she pressed ahead and found the means to bring her play to the stage.

Black Coffee was first staged at the Embassy Theatre, in Swiss Cottage, London. As it was generally well received, the play was moved to the West End and opened at St. Martin's Theatre. Unfortunately, Christie did not attend the West End opening, as she was in Mesopotamia. The play ran for barely one hundred performances, a pale shadow of the *other* play that ran in the St. Martin's, *The Mousetrap* (1952). *Black Coffee* was also

distinguished by the presence of the well-known stage actor Francis L. Sullivan as Hercule Poirot. Sullivan also played Poirot in the stage play *Peril at End House* (1940).

Constructed around the effort of Hercule Poirot to solve a murder and find a stolen secret formula, *Black Coffee* has three acts. Act 1 sets the scene in the much troubled Amory household. A scientist, Sir Claud Amory, announces to his startled relatives that Hercule Poirot is coming to investigate the theft of a very important secret formula. He then drinks some bitter-tasting coffee and dies soon after. Act 2 follows the investigation of the crimes by Poirot. The detective's inquiry continues throughout act 3, climaxing with a cleverly laid trap in which Poirot pretends to drink poisoned whiskey as Inspector Japp listens to the detective's conversation with the murderer.

A novelization of *Black Coffee* was published in 1997 by St. Martin's Press. It was adapted by Charles Osborne, a veteran actor and writer who played Dr. Carelli in a 1956 staging of the play at Tunbridge Wells.

Cards on the Table (1981)

With the exception of the ongoing and brilliantly successful *The Mousetrap*—the 1952 play was still going strong in 1981—*Cards on the Table* was the last major Christie play to premiere on the London stage. Based on the 1936 novel, *Cards on the Table* was produced by Peter Saunders and adapted for the stage by Leslie Darbon. Saunders was *the* producer of Christie plays, having produced virtually every stage production of Christie's works since *The Hollow* (1951), including *The Mousetrap* and *Witness for the Prosecution* (1953). Darbon had also adapted *A Murder is Announced* (1977).

Cards on the Table premiered at the Vaudeville Theatre, London, on December 9, 1981. It was never produced for the American stage. The primary change in the plot was the peculiar decision to remove Hercule Poirot and Colonel Race. Although

Ariadne Oliver and Superintendent Battle remain, the absence of two detectives wrecks the traditional symmetry of the original novel, which boasts four great detectives and four murder suspects.

Fiddlers Three (1972)

The last original play written by Agatha Christie, *Fiddlers Three* was arguably the least successful of her plays, especially as it never reached the West End. Originally titled *Fiddlers Five,* the play first appeared in the summer of 1971 and had a brief tour outside London. Poorly received in the English equivalent of off-Broadway, the play was rewritten by Christie and subsequently rereleased under the title *Fiddlers Three.* Unfortunately, it still lacked the magic of earlier plays, and Peter Saunders (Christie's long-standing producer) declined to produce it, as it was not up to the Christie gold standard. The play eventually opened anyway, at Guilford in 1972, and never reached the West End. This was Christie's last original play, and it was fifteen years until a new Christie play (really an adaptation of a Christie work) graced the West End, *A Murder Is Announced* (1977).

Go Back for Murder (1960)

Based on the 1943 novel *Five Little Pigs, Go Back for Murder* was adapted for the stage by Agatha Christie. Once again, her long-standing producer, Peter Saunders (who had produced a number of other Christie plays, including *The Mousetrap* and *Witness for the Prosecution*), was chosen to oversee production. The play premiered at the Duchess Theatre, London, on March 23, 1960, and ran for some 250 performances. It was never produced for the American stage.

Hidden Horizon (1946)

See *Murder on the Nile*

The Hollow (1951)

Based on the 1946 novel of the same name, *The Hollow* was adapted for the stage by Agatha Christie. It premiered at the Fortune Theatre on June 7, 1951. The play proved relatively successful, with more than 375 performances. No American adaptation was ever undertaken.

The Hollow's adaptation for the stage gave the author a chance to correct what she had long considered a serious mistake in the original novel. She had felt that Hercule Poirot should not have been included in the plot, and for the stage she removed him entirely. Despite its success, *The Hollow* was soon overshadowed by Christie's next stage work, *The Mousetrap.*

Love from a Stranger (1936)

Love from a Stranger was based on the original short story "Philomel Cottage" (first published in *The Listerdale Mystery,* 1934) and was adapted for the stage by Frank Vosper. The play premiered at the New Theatre, London, on March 31, 1936. It enjoyed a run of 149 performances. The production was then moved across the Atlantic, premiering in New York on September 21, 1936. *Love from a Stranger* proved far less successful in America, closing after barely thirty performances.

The following year, United Artists released a film version of the play in England, starring Basil Rathbone and Ann Harding. A remake of the film

A dramatic scene from the play Love from a Stranger. *(Photofest)*

was released in 1947 by Eagle Lion Studios, Hollywood, starring Sylvia Sidney and John Hodiak.

The Mousetrap (1952)

Perhaps the best way to express the monumental success and longevity of Agatha Christie's foremost play, *The Mousetrap,* is to note the fact that when it premiered at the Ambassador's Theatre, London, on November 25, 1952, Winston Churchill was prime minister of England and Queen Elizabeth II had succeeded her father, King George VI (on February 6, 1952), but she had not yet been crowned (June 2, 1953). *The Mousetrap* went on from its premiere in London to

The longest running play of all time, The Mousetrap. *(Photofest)*

become the longest continuously running stage play in the history of theater and the most successful play ever. At the end of 1999, the play was closing in on its twenty thousandth performance and was headed toward its fiftieth anniversary in 2002, with no sign of slowing down. The colossal success of *The Mousetrap* makes it even harder to believe that it had its start as a half-hour radio play.

In 1947, Agatha Christie was asked to write a radio play by the BBC to celebrate the occasion of Queen Mary's eightieth birthday. The queen was an avid fan of Christie's writings (as were her granddaughters, Elizabeth and Margaret) and when asked by the BBC if she would like to have a special broadcast in her honor, airing whatever she would like to hear, Queen Mary expressed her wish for a radio play by Christie. Honored by the request and aware of the importance and prestige of the opportunity, Christie set to work on a twenty-minute radio play; finished in about a week, the play was given the title *Three Blind Mice.* According to Christie's autobiography, Queen Mary listened to the play at Marlborough House and, apparently, enjoyed it.

It was logical that Christie should put her radio play to further use. The question was the best way to adapt it. Given its length, a short story was appropriate, and Christie soon had "Three Blind Mice" completed. Around the same time, however, she was at work on a stage version of "Three Blind Mice." That she had hopes for the play was revealed by her decision to decline the publication of the short story in Great Britain because it might reveal the end of the play and reduce commercial viability for the stage production. The short story was published in the United States in 1950, as part of the collection *Three Blind Mice and Other Stories,* by Dodd, Mead and Co., New York.

When the play was finished, Christie gave it to Peter Saunders, producer of *The Hollow* (1951), over lunch (it was wrapped in a brown paper bag and Saunders did not know it was a play until he returned to his office and opened the bag). Its original title, *Three Blind Mice,* was changed because an earlier play had the same title. In its place, Anthony Hicks, Christie's son-in-law, suggested *The Mousetrap.* That title was taken from Shakespeare's *Hamlet* (act 3, scene 2) and the "play" that Hamlet stages to discomfort King Claudius. From the start, Saunders recognized the potential for the play, a view not entirely shared by Christie. As she wrote in her autobiography, "[I had] no feeling whatsoever that I had a great success on my hands . . ."

The Mousetrap opened at the Ambassador's Theatre and was given an excellent reception by critics and audiences. Before long, the production departed the confines of the Ambassador's Theatre and moved to the larger, 550-seat St. Martin's Theatre. There it has remained, thanks to new generations of devoted Christie fans and legions of American tourists who have made attending the play part of the required itinerary for their visits to England. It is not possible to see the play anywhere else, as part of the agreement made by Christie with the producers was that there should be no other production of the play on Broadway or as part of a touring company in the United States (the same is true for Australia) until the production closes in England. The prohibition remained in full force after her death, as she had given the copyright to the play as a tenth birthday present to her grandson, Mathew Prichard. Nor has it ever been possible for an audience to see the play in a film version. Victor Saville and Eddie Small acquired the film rights, but the terms were identical to those for a new stage version; no film can be made of the play until the London production ends. Saville and Small are both dead, and their heirs inherited the film rights.

The Mousetrap has been performed essentially unchanged since 1952. Perhaps a little dated today, the play still packs in the audiences, relying more on tradition and genuine love of Christie than its plot or the performances of its actors. Presented in two acts, the plot follows the murderous events at Monkswell Manor, where a group of guests are snowbound and trapped with a killer bent on revenge for some evil inflicted on three children during World War II.

Approaching the end of its forty-seventh year, *The Mousetrap* has been seen by more than ten million visitors and has featured more than 340 actors and actresses, as well as more than 130 understudies. Its two most distinguished performers have been David Raven and Nancy Seabrooke. Raven is honored in the *Guiness Book of World Records* as "the most durable actor," for his record 4,575 performances as Major Metcalf. Seabrooke was the understudy for the role of Mrs. Boyle for 6,240 performances, and appeared only seventy-two times. She retired in 1994 and died in 1997 at Denville Hall, the residential care facility and nursing home for elderly actors and actresses run by the Actor's Charitable Trust.

Denville Hall also benefited from *The Mousetrap*. In June of 1999, after forty-seven years, the set for the play was auctioned off to raise money for the facility. Originally designed by Anthony Holland, the set remained untouched for nearly five decades and included the original wind machine. Following the evening performance on June 19, the set was dismantled and replaced by a new one. The curtain rose on the new set on June 21, 1999, for performance number 19,382, another record in the history-making run of Christie's play.

The Murder at the Vicarage (1949)

Based on the 1930 novel of the same name, *The Murder at the Vicarage* was adapted for the stage by Barbara Toy and Moie Charles and premiered on December 14, 1949, at the Playhouse, London; the play's producer, Reginald Tate, also appeared in the cast as Lawrence Redding. The play marked the first time that Agatha Christie's beloved spinster sleuth, Miss Marple, was brought to the stage. Barbara Mullen portrayed the detective. A considerable success, the play ran for nearly 2,000 performances, although there was never an American adaptation. Its success depended heavily upon the use of virtually all the characters from the original novel, so the audience had the fun of watching characters with whom most of them were already familiar come to life.

A Murder Is Announced (1977)

Based on the 1950 novel of the same name, *A Murder Is Announced* was adapted for the stage by Leslie Darbon and produced by the long-standing Christie producer Peter Saunders (he had produced such Christie hits as *The Mousetrap* and *Witness for the Prosecution*). The play premiered on September 21, 1977, making it the first Christie stage production to debut after the death of the author, the Queen of Mystery, in January of 1976. There was thus a tinge of sadness about the production. The play continued at the Vaudeville Theatre for 429 performances, but there was no American stage production. Dulcie Gray played Miss Marple.

Murder on the Nile (1946)

Based on the 1937 novel *Death on the Nile, Murder on the Nile* was adapted for the stage by Agatha Christie and opened on March 19, 1946, at the Ambassadors Theatre in London. There is very little of the original novel to be found in the play, and the absence of Hercule Poirot is felt keenly. The play was adapted for the American stage and premiered on September 19, 1946, at the Plymouth Theatre under the title *Hidden Horizon*. Despite the presence of the famous actor Halliwell Hobbes, the play was a failure with American audiences.

Peril at End House (1940)

Based on the 1932 novel of the same name, *Peril at End House* was adapted for the stage by Arnold Ridley and opened at the Vaudeville Theatre, London, on May 1, 1940. In an otherwise undistinguished play, the chief highlight was the presence of veteran stage actor Francis L. Sullivan. He had already played Poirot in *Black Coffee* (1930) and was thus a veteran interpreter of the Belgian detective. Even he could not rescue *Peril at End House* from relative obscurity. One other notable casting presence was Ian Fleming in the role of Captain Hastings; Fleming also took part in numerous Sherlock Holmes productions. The play was never adapted for the American stage.

Rule of Three (1962)

Following the production of *Go Back for Murder* in 1960, Agatha Christie next chose to bring to the stage a unique venture—for her: an evening of three one-act plays combined under the title *Rule of Three*. Her long-standing producer, Peter Saunders (who had been producer of *The Mousetrap* and *Witness for the Prosecution*) was again chosen for the task of producing. The play premiered on December 20, 1962 at the Duchess Theatre, London. The three one-act plays were *The Rats, Afternoon at the Seaside,* and *The Patient*. Received poorly by the critics, "Rule of Three" enjoyed only ninety-two performances and was never brought to the American stage.

Spider's Web (1954)

The creation of *Spider's Web* by Agatha Christie marked several significant events in the history of Christie's works. First, it was the first original play written by Christie since *Akhnaton* (1937). Second, it was written especially for one actress, Margaret Lockwood. Third, it was the third Christie play running in the West End at the time of its premiere, along with *The Mousetrap* (1952) and *Witness for the Prosecution* (1953). Finally, *Spider's Web* was the last successful new play for Christie in the world of the theater.

The genesis for *Spider's Web* was the hope expressed by the popular British actress Margaret Lockwood that Christie might write a suitable vehicle for her. She took her hopes to Peter Saunders, the producer of two eminently successful Christie plays, *The Mousetrap* and *Witness for the Prosecution*. Agatha set to work, and the result was a murder mystery and a comedy. Produced and directed by Wallace Douglas, the play premiered on December 13, 1954, at the Savoy Theatre and ran for 774 performances. *The Spider's Web* was adapted for

film in 1960 by United Artists, starring Glynis Johns as Clarissa. In 1953, the BBC adapted the play for television.

As it was written as a showcase for Margaret Lockwood, the play centered around her character, Clarissa Hailsham-Brown, the wife of a Foreign Office diplomat. Act 1 establishes Clarissa as a clever and fun-loving young woman who, for example, fools two of her rather pompous wine connoisseur friends into thinking that they have been tasting different wines when, in fact, she poured wine from the same bottle into three different glasses. She soon discovers a corpse behind her sofa and spends part of act 2 trying to conceal the body with the help of her friends, as it is clear that the killer is her dear twelve-year-old stepdaughter, Pippa. Her hopes are dashed, however, when the police arrive in answer to a call that a murder has occurred. It does not take long for them to find the corpse. As the questioning progresses, things are complicated by the disappearance of the corpse. Events climax in act 3 with Clarissa's realization that Pippa did not really commit the murder. She solves the crime just in time for her husband to arrive home.

An adaptation of this play was produced by the BBC in 1983 for British television.

Ten Little Indians (1940)

Known originally as *Ten Little Niggers* and later given a marginally less unfortunate title, *Ten Little Indians* was the play that first established Christie as a playwright. As she noted in her autobiography, "I suppose it was *Ten Little Niggers* that set me on the path of being a playwright as well as a writer of books." *Ten Little Indians* was Christie's third play, following *Black Coffee* (1930), which was only modestly successful, and *Akhnaton* (1937), which was never produced. Based on the 1939 novel *Ten Little Niggers* (or *And Then There Were None*), *Ten Little Niggers* marks Christie's first adaptation of one of her own books for the stage.

After completing the adaptation, Christie looked for a producer who might bring it to life, eventually winning the backing of the producer Irene Hentschel. The production premiered on November 17, 1943, at the St. James' Theatre, London, and enjoyed a run of more than 250 performances.

The audiences loved the complicated plot, and the ending—different from the ending of the novel—was actually used in the assorted film versions that were produced. In the play, two of the seemingly doomed characters actually survive the gruesome ordeal, a climax that, as Christie noted, was not a betrayal of the original nursery rhyme. One version, the 1868 incarnation by Septimus Winner, concludes with the line: "One little Injun livin' all alone, he got married and then there were none."

Ten Little Indians was brought to the American stage in 1944, opening at the Broadhurst Theatre in New York. It was produced by the Shubert brothers and Albert de Courville. Another, loosely adapted, version was produced in 1976 under the title of *Something's Afoot,* a musical murder-mystery spoof. Although Christie is not credited, the plot is similar enough to *Ten Little Indians* that there can be little doubt as to the original material.

Towards Zero (1956)

Based on the 1944 novel of the same name, *Towards Zero* was adapted for the stage by Agatha Christie in collaboration with Gerald Verner. Produced by Peter Saunders (who had also produced *The Mousetrap,* 1952, and *Witness for the Prosecution,* 1953), *Towards Zero* premiered at the St. James' Theatre, London, on September 4, 1956. No American production was even undertaken, and the play in London was not a major success.

The Unexpected Guest (1958)

Written around the same time as *Verdict* (1958), *Unexpected Guest* is also an original play and, like *Verdict,* was produced by Peter Saunders (who also produced *The Mousetrap,* 1952, *Witness for the Prosecution,* 1953, *Towards Zero,* 1956, and *The Hollow,* 1951). The play premiered at the

Duchess Theatre, London, on August 12, 1958, and was able to enjoy a run of 604 performances. Despite the success, there was no American production. The play, in two acts, centers around the murder of a cruel, wheelchair-confined husband, Richard Warwick, and opens with the discovery of his wife, Laura Warwick, holding the revolver used to shoot him. The person who finds her is Michael Starkwedder, an innocent "unexpected guest" who stops at the Warwick house after driving for hours in fog. [For the novelization of this play, please see *The Unexpected Guest* in Part One.]

Verdict (1958)

An original play by Agatha Christie, *Verdict* was produced by Peter Saunders (who also produced *The Mousetrap,* 1952, *Witness for the Prosecution,* 1953, *Towards Zero,* 1956, and *The Hollow,* 1951) and opened in London in May of 1958. In her autobiography, Christie expressed the opinion that *Verdict* was her best play—after *Witness for the Prosecution.* Unfortunately, few shared her opinion, as the play was savaged by critics and, in an event unique in the history of Christie's work, was actually booed at the premiere because the audience didn't like the ending. Christie also noted in her autobiography that the original title of the play was *No Fields of Amaranth,* after the poem that begins "There are no flowers of amaranth on this side of the grave" by Walter Savage Landor. *Verdict* was written around the same time as *The Unexpected Guest* (1958).

Witness for the Prosecution (1953)

Along with *Ten Little Indians* (1943), *Witness for the Prosecution* is ranked as one of the most successful Christie plays, behind, of course, *The Mousetrap* (1952). Based on the short story of the same name that was first published in 1933 in the collection *The Hound of Death and Other Stories, Witness for the Prosecution* was brought to life the year after *The Mousetrap* began its fabled run. In her search for a producer, Christie was able to call upon Peter Saunders (who also produced *The Mousetrap,* 1952, *Witness for the Prosecution,* 1953,

Towards Zero, 1956, and *The Hollow,* 1951) and Gilbert Miller. The play premiered at the Winter Garden Theatre, London, on October 28, 1953, and went on for a long run of 458 performances. Adapted for the American stage, it opened on December 16, 1954, at the Henry Miller Theatre, New York.

In adapting the original short story for the stage, Christie devoted a great deal of time to researching the details of courtroom life. Of greatest

Sir Wilfrid Robarts (played by the legendary stage actor Francis L. Sullivan) interrogates Romaine Vole (Patricia Jessel), in Witness for the Prosecution. *(Photofest)*

significance, of course, is the stunning climax of the play, a complete change from the climax of the story. Christie was exceedingly pleased with her new ending, so much so that she was adamant in blocking any production of her play that retained the climax in the short story. Indeed, the conclusion was also used in the 1957 film version of the play starring Charles Laughton, Tyrone Power, and Marlene Dietrich (as well as the 1982 television adaptation with Sir Ralph Richardson, Beau Bridges, and Diana Rigg). Christie's confidence in her play was confirmed by its success, which included the winning of the New York Drama Critics Circle Award for best foreign play. While *The Mousetrap* is indisputably Christie's most successful play, critics generally agree that *Witness for the Prosecution* is her finest play.

Actors

The following performers are distinguished for their many or notable interpretations of Christie characters in film and television.

Annis, Francesca (b. 1944) A British actress, Francesca Annis has enjoyed a long career spanning four decades. She has appeared in *Cleopatra* (1963); *Macbeth* (1971), in which she gave a memorable performance as Lady Macbeth; *Lillie* (1977), in which she played Lillie Langtry; and *Dune* (1984), the adaptation of the classic Frank Herbert science fiction novel, in which she played Lady Jessica.

Annis's connection to Agatha Christie's works began in 1964, when she had a role in *Murder Most Foul.* She returned to the Christie oeuvre in 1980 in the role of Frances Derwent in *Why Didn't They Ask Evans?,* costarring James Warwick as Bobby Jones, which was produced for British television. She and Warwick were paired again in the television series *Partners in Crime* (1982–1983) and the television film *The Secret Adversary* (1982), both of which were adaptations of Tommy and Tuppence Beresford cases.

Finney, Albert (b. 1936) The Manchester-born Finney is recognized as one of the foremost actors of his generation and has been nominated four times for the Academy Award. A few of his most memorable roles are in *Tom Jones* (1963), *Scrooge* (1972), *The Dresser* (1983), and *Under the Volcano* (1984). Finney has had only one role in a Christie adaptation. It was, however, one of the most memorable of all film and television versions of any Christie work. In 1974, Finney starred as Hercule Poirot in *Murder on the Orient Express.* His performance earned him an Academy Award nomination for best

actor and a place as one of the great Poirots of stage and film. Interestingly, Agatha Christie liked the movie very much, but she did complain about Poirot's mustache.

Hayes, Helen (1900–1993) Called the First Lady of the American Theater, Helen Hayes was one of the great American actresses of the twentieth century. A few of her most famous performances were in *A Farewell to Arms* (1932), *Stage Door Canteen* (1943), *Anastasia* (1956), and *Airport* (1970).

In 1982, Hayes gave her first performance in a Christie television adaptation, appearing with Bill Bixby in *Murder Is Easy.* Her role, alas, was a brief one, as her character is killed by a homicidal maniac barely ten minutes into the film. The following year, however, she assumed the difficult role of Miss Jane Marple in *A Caribbean Mystery.* This was followed in 1985 by *Murder with Mirrors,* which also starred Bette Davis as Carrie Louise. While enjoyable, Hayes's interpretation of Miss Marple gave viewers a more cheery and sensitive sleuth than they knew from the novels. Unfortunately, her Miss Marple was overshadowed swiftly in the 1980s by the arrival of Joan Hickson, considered the definitive Miss Marple. Perhaps prophetically, Hayes once remarked: "I seem always to have reminded people of someone in their family. Perhaps I am the triumph of Plain Jane."

Hickson, Joan (1906–1998) Arguably the finest interpreter of Miss Marple in history, Joan Hickson had a long career as an actress and a happy association with Christie's works that endured for five decades. Born in Kingsthorpe, Northampton, she began her stage career in 1927 with regional theater and then went on to appear in films, including *The Guinea Pig* (1948), *The Card* (1952), and *The 39 Steps* (1959). In all, she performed in more than eighty movies, all the while continuing her career as a stage actress. In 1977, she won a Tony Award as best supporting actress for her performance as Delia in Alan Ayckbourn's play *Bedroom Farce*.

Hickson's first association with a Christie work was in 1946, when she played Miss Pryce in the play *Appointment with Death* (1946). It is reported that Agatha Christie was so pleased with her performance that she wrote her a note: "I hope you will play my dear Miss Marple." Christie's words proved prophetic as Hickson assumed the demanding mantle of the spinster sleuth starting in 1985 in a series of BBC Television productions, beginning with *The Moving Finger*. She went on to play Miss Marple ten more times, her last appearance being the 1992 adaptation of *The Mirror Crack'd from Side to Side*. From the start, she was hailed as the foremost of all Miss Marples, thanks to her flawless devotion to the character of the novels. She was willing to be cold, calculating, and ruthless, fulfilling completely the title given to Miss Marple by Jason Rafiel—*Nemesis.* It is almost forgotten that Hickson also had a small role in the 1980 production of *Why Didn't They Ask Evans?*

Because Hickson began playing Miss Marple in her seventies, there was a time limitation to her career as the sleuth, and it became ultimately impossible for her to continue in the role. By the time of her final retirement as Marple from the screen, she had received two BAFTA (British Academy of Film and Television Arts) nominations as Best TV actress and was awarded the Order of the British Empire in 1987 by Queen Elizabeth II, a devoted Miss Marple fan. In her final years, Hickson recorded audio books of the Christie mysteries. She died October 18, 1998, at the age of ninety-two, in a hospital at Colchester, Essex. She is survived by a son and a daughter. Her husband, the physician Eric Butler, had died in 1967.

Lansbury, Angela (b. 1925) The London-born Lansbury has had an enduring career on stage and in film in the United States. The daughter of an actress and a political leader in England, Lansbury earned a nomination for an Academy Award for her first film, *Gaslight* (1944). Only two pictures later, she was nominated again, for *The Picture of Dorian Gray* (1945). Perhaps her most famous film role was as Laurence Harvey's truly evil mother in *The Manchurian Candidate* (1962). Her success in film was matched on the stage, where she garnered four Tony Award nominations in sixteen years, and television, where she played the wildly popular character Jessica Fletcher in *Murder, She Wrote.*

Jessica Fletcher was not the first sleuth Lansbury had played. In 1980, she did a memorable turn as Miss Jane Marple in the film *The Mirror Crack'd.* Part of the ongoing adaptations of Christie works by EMI, the film was not as successful as their previous efforts, most notably *Murder on the Orient Express* (1974) and *Death on the Nile* (1978). As for Lansbury, she gave a beautiful performance as Miss Marple, but she was decades younger than the Marple character and thus required extensive makeup to age her for the role. This stretched some of the believability of the film's structure.

Laughton, Charles (1899–1962) This English-born actor, the son of Robert Laughton and Elizabeth Conlon, was one of the most respected performers in both England and the United States. Among his most famous films were *Mutiny on the Bounty* (1935), *The Private Life of Henry VIII* (1933), *The Beachcomber* (1938), and *Spartacus* (1960). Educated at Stonyhurst, Royal Academy of Dramatic Art, Laughton made his first appearance on stage in 1926. Only two years later, he starred in the play *Alibi,* making him the first actor to portray Hercule Poirot. Agatha Christie wrote in her autobiography, "It always seems strange to me that whoever plays

Poirot is always an outsize man. Charles Laughton had plenty of avoirdupois." Laughton became an American citizen in 1950. Seven years later, Laughton returned to Christie's work in the film adaptation of "Witness for the Prosecution," playing the role of defense attorney Sir Wilfrid Robarts. Laughton was nominated for the Academy Award as best actor.

Rutherford, Margaret (1892–1972) A beloved actress of the British stage and screen, Dame Margaret Rutherford is best remembered for two roles: Madame Arcati in *Blithe Spirit* and Miss Jane Marple. She debuted on stage in 1925 and first appeared on film in 1936, in *Dusty Ermine,* at the age of forty-one. Five years later, in the summer of 1941, Noel Coward cast her in his play, *Blithe Spirit,* as Madame Arcati, the fake psychic. Coward was so taken with Rutherford that he developed the role specifically for her, so it was logical that she reprise the role in David Lean's screen adaptation of the play in 1946.

In 1960, MGM acquired the rights to several of Christie's works and announced that Rutherford would be playing the demanding role of Miss Marple. Although she did not look much like Miss Marple (she was actually more reminiscent of Ariadne Oliver), Rutherford went on to star in four Marple movies between 1962 and 1964: *Murder, She Said* (1962), *Murder at the Gallop* (1963), *Murder Most Foul* (1964), and *Murder Ahoy!* (1964). Rutherford accepted the role with reluctance, and Agatha Christie made no effort to hide her intense dislike of the MGM Marple films. Nevertheless, Christie admired Rutherford as an actress in other films and even dedicated her 1963 novel, *The Mirror Crack'd from Side to Side,* to her, "in admiration."

Rutherford was awarded the O.B.E. (Order of the British Empire) in 1961 and was knighted in 1967 by Queen Elizabeth II. Her husband, Stringer Davis, portrayed Mr. Stringer in all of her Miss Marple films and appeared with her in other films as well.

Randall, Tony (b. 1920) This American actor, born Leonard Rosenberg in Tulsa, Oklahoma, has been a perennial performer on stage, film, and television for decades. He is perhaps best remembered for his role as Felix Unger in the television series *The Odd Couple,* in which he starred with Jack Klugman during the 1960s and 1970s. Randall's first performance in a Christie adaptation was in the 1966 film *The Alphabet Murders,* in which he portrayed Hercule Poirot. The film itself was a loose adaptation of *The A.B.C. Murders* and boasted one of the most eccentric interpretations of Poirot ever captured on film. Randall also appeared in the 1989 adaptation of *The Man in the Brown Suit,* starring Stephanie Zimbalist.

Suchet, David (b. 1946) A London-born performer, Suchet has had a remarkable career in film but is today best known for his recurring role as Hercule Poirot in the London Weekend Television series *Agatha Christie's Poirot.* The brother of ITN newscaster John Suchet, his performances are often overlooked because of his ability to disappear into the character he is playing. Thus, many fans will not remember his performances in *Harry and the Hendersons* (1987), *When the Whales Came* (1989), *A Perfect Murder* (1998), and *Hunchback* (1982). He also had a memorable outing in the British television miniseries *Blott on the Landscape.*

Suchet had an early association with Christie's works. He appeared in the 1985 made-for-television film *Thirteen at Dinner,* which starred Peter Ustinov as Hercule Poirot and Suchet as Inspector Japp. Four years later, Suchet made his debut as Poirot in *Agatha Christie's Poirot,* an ongoing television series that has since blossomed into the most popular Christie program in history (with the possible exception of the Miss Marple television films starring Joan Hickson). He has also appeared in numerous television films, including *The A.B.C. Murders* and *Dumb Witness.* Much of the credit for the success of *Agatha Christie's Poirot* rests squarely with Suchet, who has crafted an authentic but approachable Poirot, one that is both plausible as a detective functioning in a real-world setting (even if that setting is England in the 1930s) and likable, despite a host of foibles and eccentricities.

Trevor, Austin (1897–1978) This Irish-born actor had a career that spanned nearly four decades. After a series of romantic roles in the 1930s and 1940s, including appearances in *The Red Shoes* and *Anna Karenina* (both 1948), Trevor became a popular character actor. One of his last appearances was in *The Alphabet Murders* (1965), starring Tony Randall as Hercule Poirot. Thirty years before, Trevor had himself played the great Belgian detective in three films, *Alibi* (1931), *Black Coffee* (1931), and *Lord Edgware Dies* (1934). He is remembered by Christie fans for being the first Poirot on film (the first ever actor to portray Poirot was Charles Laughton, in the play *Alibi,* in 1928) and for being the star of the first Christie film with sound. Trevor was very much a heroic Poirot, adopting a dashing style. While the films are all but forgotten, one lasting detail does linger: Trevor, heretically, played Poirot without his famed mustache.

Ustinov, Peter (b. 1921) A London-born actor of Russian descent, Ustinov is the son of Nadia Benois, a designer and the daughter of Alexandre Benois, the St. Petersburg designer of the Diaghilev ballets. His grandfather was an officer in the czar's army and was exiled from the country after refusing to take an oath to the Eastern Orthodox Church, because he was Protestant. One of the most versatile performers of the last fifty years, Ustinov has worked in film, television, and on the stage, and has both written and produced numerous plays, including *The Unknown Soldier and His Wife,* which opened in 1973 in London. Among his memorable films are *Quo Vadis* (1951), in which he plays Emperor Nero; *Billy Budd* (1962), *Spartacus* (1960), *We're No Angels* (1955), and *Topkapi* (1964), for which he won the Academy Award. For his many achievements, he was awarded the C.B.E. (Companion of the Order of the British Empire) in 1975 and was knighted by Queen Elizabeth II in 1990.

Ustinov's most notable connection with Agatha Christie is his portrayal of Hercule Poirot a total of six times in film and on television: in *Death on the Nile* (1978), *Evil under the Sun* (1982), *Thirteen at Dinner* (1985), *Dead Man's Folly* (1986), *Murder in Three Acts* (1986), and *Appointment with Death* (1988). He also served as the narrator for *The Seven Dials Mystery* (1981). He had two other connections with Christie. First, during World War II, he was batman to Lieutenant David Niven; the two starred together in *Death on the Nile,* with David Niven as Colonel Johnny Race. Second, Ustinov was married to Angela Lansbury's sister; Lansbury played Miss Jane Marple in *The Mirror Crack'd* in 1980.

Appendices

Appendix One

Christie's Detectives

Hercule Poirot

NOVELS

The A.B.C. Murders
After the Funeral
Appointment with Death
The Big Four
Black Coffee
Cards on the Table
Cat among the Pigeons
The Clocks
Curtain
Dead Man's Folly
Death in the Clouds
Death on the Nile
Dumb Witness
Elephants Can Remember
Evil under the Sun
Five Little Pigs
Hallowe'en Party
Hercule Poirot's Christmas
Hickory Dickory Dock
The Hollow
Lord Edgware Dies
Mrs. McGinty's Dead
Murder in Mesopotamia
The Murder of Roger Ackroyd
Murder on the Links
Murder on the Orient Express
The Mysterious Affair at Styles
The Mystery of the Blue Train
One, Two, Buckle My Shoe
Peril at End House
Sad Cypress
Taken at the Flood
Third Girl
Three-Act Tragedy
The Unexpected Guest

SHORT STORIES

"The Adventure of Johnnie Waverly"
"The Adventure of the Cheap Flat"
"The Adventure of the Christmas Pudding"
"The Adventure of the Clapham Cook"
"The Adventure of the Egyptian Tomb"
"The Adventure of the Italian Nobleman"
"The Adventure of 'The Western Star' "
"The Affair at the Victory Ball"
"The Apples of the Hesperides"
"The Arcadian Deer"
"The Augean Stables"
"The Capture of Cerberus"
"The Case of the Missing Will"
"The Chocolate Box"
"The Cornish Mystery"
"The Cretan Bull"
"Dead Man's Mirror"
"The Disappearance of Mr. Davenheim"
"The Double Clue"
"Double Sin"
"The Dream"
"The Erymanthian Boar"
"The Flock of Geryon"
"Four and Twenty Blackbirds"
"The Girdle of Hippolita"
"The Horses of Diomedes"
"How Does Your Garden Grow?"
"The Incredible Theft"
"The Jewel Robbery at the Grand Metropolitan"
"The Kidnapped Prime Minister"
"The King of Clubs"
"The Lemesurier Inheritance"
"The Lernean Hydra"
"The Lost Mine"
"The Market Basing Mystery"
"The Million-Dollar Bond Robbery"

"Murder in the Mews"
"The Mystery of Hunter's Lodge"
"The Mystery of the Baghdad Chest"
"The Mystery of the Spanish Chest"
"The Nemean Lion"
"The Plymouth Express"
"Problem at Sea"
"The Second Gong"
"The Stymphalean Birds"
"The Submarine Plans"
"The Third-Floor Flat"
"The Tragedy of Marsdon Manor"
"Triangle at Rhodes"
"The Under Dog"
"The Veiled Lady"
"Wasps' Nest"
"Yellow Iris"

Miss Jane Marple

NOVELS
At Bertram's Hotel
The Body in the Library
A Caribbean Mystery
4.50 from Paddington
The Mirror Crack'd from Side to Side
The Moving Finger
The Murder at the Vicarage
A Murder Is Announced
Nemesis
A Pocket Full of Rye
Sleeping Murder
They Do It with Mirrors
SHORT STORIES
"The Affair at the Bungalow"
"The Bloodstained Pavement"
"The Blue Geranium"
"The Case of the Caretaker"
"The Case of the Perfect Maid"
"A Christmas Tragedy"
"The Companion"
"Death by Drowning"
"The Four Suspects"
"Greenshaw's Folly"
"The Herb of Death"

"The Idol House of Astarte"
"Ingots of Gold"
"Miss Marple Tells a Story"
"Motive vs. Opportunity"
"Sanctuary"
"Strange Jest"
"The Tape-Measure Murder"
"The Thumb Mark of Saint Peter"
"The Tuesday Night Club"

Tommy and Tuppence Beresford

NOVELS
By the Pricking of My Thumbs
N or M?
Postern of Fate
The Secret Adversary
SHORT STORIES
"The Adventure of the Sinister Stranger"
"The Affair of the Pink Pearl"
"The Ambassador's Boots"
"Blindman's Bluff"
"The Case of the Missing Lady"
"The Clergyman's Daughter"
"The Crackler"
"A Fairy in the Flat"
"Finessing the King"
"The Gentleman Dressed in Newspaper"
"The House of Lurking Death"
"The Man in the Mist"
"The Man Who Was No. 16"
"A Pot of Tea"
"The Red House"
"The Sunningdale Mystery"
"The Unbreakable Alibi"

Mrs. Ariadne Oliver

NOVELS
All of Ariadne Oliver's appearances in novels were with Hercule Poirot, except for her appearance in *The Pale Horse*.
Cards on the Table
Dead Man's Folly
Elephants Can Remember
Hallowe'en Party

Mrs. McGinty's Dead
The Pale Horse
Third Girl
SHORT STORIES
"The Case of the Discontented Soldier" (with Mr. Parker Pyne)
"The Case of the Rich Woman" (with Mr. Parker Pyne)

Superintendent Battle

Cards on the Table (with Hercule Poirot, Ariadne Oliver, and Colonel Race)
Murder Is Easy
The Secret of Chimneys
The Seven Dials Mystery
Towards Zero

Colonel Johnny Race

Cards on the Table (with Hercule Poirot, Ariadne Oliver, and Superintendent Battle)
Death on the Nile (with Hercule Poirot)
The Man in the Brown Suit
Sparkling Cyanide

Mr. Parker Pyne

"The Case of the City Clerk"
"The Case of the Discontented Husband"
"The Case of the Discontented Soldier" (with Mrs. Ariadne Oliver)
"The Case of the Distressed Lady"
"The Case of the Middle-Aged Wife"
"The Case of the Rich Woman" (with Mrs. Ariadne Oliver)
"Death on the Nile"
"The Gate of Baghdad"
"Have You Got Everything You Want?"
"The House at Shiraz"
"The Oracle at Delphi"
"The Pearl of Price"
"Problem at Pollensa Bay"
"The Regatta Mystery"

Mr. Harley Quin

All the stories featuring Mr. Harley Quin also feature Mr. Satterthwaite.
"At the 'Bells and Motley' "
"The Bird with the Broken Wing"
"The Coming of Mr. Quin"
"The Dead Harlequin"
"The Face of Helen"
"Harlequin's Lane"
"The Harlequin Tea Set"
"The Love Detectives"
"The Man from the Sea"
"The Shadow on the Glass"
"The Sign in the Sky"
"The Soul of the Croupier"
"The Voice in the Dark"
"The World's End"

Chief Inspector James Japp

NOVELS
The A.B.C. Murders
The Big Four
Black Coffee
Death in the Clouds
Lord Edgware Dies
The Mysterious Affair at Styles
One, Two, Buckle My Shoe
Peril at End House
SHORT STORIES
"The Adventure of the Cheap Flat"
"The Affair at the Victory Ball"
"The Capture of Cerberus"
"The Disappearance of Mr. Davenheim"
"The Flock of Geryon"
"The Girdle of Hyppolita"
"The Kidnapped Prime Minister"
"The Market Basing Mystery"
"Murder in the Mews"
"The Mystery of Hunter's Lodge"
"The Plymouth Express"
"The Tragedy of Marsdon Manor"
"The Veiled Lady"

Captain Arthur Hastings

All of the appearances of Captain Hastings are with Hercule Poirot.

NOVELS

The A.B.C. Murders

The Big Four

Black Coffee

Curtain

Dumb Witness

Lord Edgware Dies

Murder on the Links

The Mysterious Affair at Styles

Peril at End House

Poirot Investigates

SHORT STORIES

"The Adventure of Johnnie Waverly"

"The Adventure of the Cheap Flat"

"The Adventure of the Egyptian Tomb"

"The Adventure of the Italian Nobleman"

"The Adventure of 'The Western Star'"

"The Affair at the Victory Ball"

"The Case of the Missing Will"

"The Chocolate Box"

"The Cornish Mystery"

"The Disappearance of Mr. Davenheim"

"The Double Clue"

"Double Sin"

"The Jewel Robbery at the Grand Metropolitan"

"The Kidnapped Prime Minister"

"The King of Clubs"

"The Lemesurier Inheritance"

"The Lost Mine"

"The Market Basing Mystery"

"The Million-Dollar Bond Robbery"

"Murder in the Mews"

"The Mystery of Hunter's Lodge"

"The Mystery of the Baghdad Chest"

"The Plymouth Express"

"The Submarine Plans"

"The Third-Floor Flat"

"The Tragedy of Marsdon Manor"

"The Veiled Lady"

Appendix Two

Films and Television Programs

Films

Die Abenteuer G.m.b.H. (The Adventure, Inc.) (1928)

The Passing of Mr. Quinn (1928)

Alibi (1931)

Black Coffee (1931)

Lord Edgware Dies (1934)

Love from a Stranger (1937)

And Then There Were None (Ten Little Niggers) (1945)

Love from a Stranger (A Stranger Passes) (1947)

Witness for the Prosecution (1957)

The Spider's Web (1960)

Murder, She Said (1962)

Murder at the Gallop (1963)

Murder Most Foul (1964)

Murder Ahoy! (1964)

Ten Little Indians (1965)

The Alphabet Murders (1966)

Endless Night (1971)

Murder on the Orient Express (1974)

Ten Little Indians (1975)

Death on the Nile (1978)

Agatha (1979)

The Mirror Crack'd (1980)

Evil under the Sun (1982)

Taina chyornykh drozdov (1983)

Ordeal by Innocence (1984)

Kiken-na Onna-tachi (Dangerous Women) (1985)

Desyat negrityat (1987)

Appointment with Death (1988)

Ten Little Indians (1989)

Zagadka Endhauza (1989)

Television

Ten Little Niggers (1949)

A Murder Is Announced (1956)

"The Disappearance of Mr. Davenheim" (1962; *General Electric Theater*)

Ein Fremder klopft an (1967)

Zehn kleine Negerlein (1969)

Mord im Pfarrhaus (1970)

Why Didn't They Ask Evans? (1981)

Shimofuri-sanso Satsujin-jiken (1980)

The Seven Dials Mystery (1981)

Spider's Web (1982)

The Agatha Christie Hour (1982)

    "Jane in Search of a Job"

    "The Girl in the Train"

    "The Manhood of Edward Robinson"

    "The Red Signal"

    "Magnolia Blossom"

    "The Case of the Middle-Aged Wife"

    "The Case of the Discontented Soldier"

    "The Fourth Man"

    "The Mystery of the Blue Jar"

    "In a Glass Darkly"

Murder Is Easy (1981)

Partners in Crime (1982–1983)

    "The Affair of the Pink Pearl"

    "The House of Lurking Death"

    "The Sunningdale Mystery"

    "The Clergyman's Daughter"

    "Finessing the King"

    "The Ambassador's Boots"

    "The Man in the Mist"

    "The Unbreakable Alibi"

    "The Case of the Missing Lady"

    "The Crackler"

The Secret Adversary (1982)

Witness for the Prosecution (1982)

A Caribbean Mystery (1983)

Sparkling Cyanide (1983)

Spider's Web (1983)

Thirteen at Dinner (1985)
Murder with Mirrors (1985)
The Moving Finger (1985)
A Murder Is Announced (1985)
The Murder at the Vicarage (1986)
Nemesis (1986)
Dead Man's Folly (1986)
Murder in Three Acts (1986)
A Pocket Full of Rye (1986)
Sleeping Murder (1986)
Murder by the Book (1986)
The Body in the Library (1987)
At Bertram's Hotel (1987)
4.50 from Paddington (1987)
A Caribbean Mystery (1989)
The Man in the Brown Suit (1989)
Agatha Christie's Poirot (ongoing TV series; premiered in 1989)

The Life of Agatha Christie (1990)
The Mysterious Affair at Styles (1990)
Peril at End House (1990)
They Do It with Mirrors (1991)
The A.B.C. Murders (1992)
Death in the Clouds (1992)
The Mirror Crack'd from Side to Side (1992)
One, Two, Buckle My Shoe (1992)
Murder on the Links (1995)
Dumb Witness (1995)
Hickory Dickory Dock (1995)
Hercule Poirot's Christmas (1995)
The Pale Horse (1996)
The Murder of Roger Ackroyd (1999)
Lord Edgware Dies (1999)

Plays

Black Coffee (1930)

Akhnaton (c. 1937) (never staged)

Ten Little Niggers (dramatized by Christie) (1940)

Appointment with Death (dramatized by Christie) (1945)

Murder on the Nile (adaptation of *Death on the Nile;* dramatized by Christie) (1946)

The Hollow (dramatized by Christie) (1951)

The Mousetrap (adaptation of the story "Three Blind Mice"; dramatized by Christie) (1952)

Witness for the Prosecution (dramatized by Christie) (1953)

Spider's Web (1954)

Towards Zero (dramatized by Christie and Gerald Verner) (1956)

The Unexpected Guest (1958)

Verdict (1958)

Go Back for Murder (adaptation of *Five Little Pigs;* dramatized by Christie) (1960)

Rule of Three: Afternoon at the Seaside, The Patient, The Rats (1962)

Fiddlers Three (1971)

Adaptations of Christie Works by Other Playwrights

Alibi (adapted by Michael Morton, based on *The Murder of Roger Ackroyd*) (1928)

Love from a Stranger (adapted by Frank Vosper, based on "Philomel Cotage") (1936)

Peril at End House (adapted by Arnold Ridley) (1940)

The Murder at the Vicarage (adapted by Moie Charles and Barbara Toy) (1949)

A Murder Is Announced (adapted by Leslie Darben) (1977)

Suggested Reading List

Aisenberg, Nadya. *A Common Spring: Crime Novel and Classic.* Bowling Green, Ohio: Bowling Green University Popular Press, 1980.

Auden, W. H. "The Guilty Vicarage." In *The Dyer's Hand.* New York: Vintage Books, 1968.

Bargainnier, Earl F. *The Gentle Art of Murder: The Detective Fiction of Agatha Christie.* Bowling Green, Ohio: Bowling Green University Popular Press, 1980.

Barnard, Robert. *A Talent to Deceive: An Appreciation of Agatha Christie.* New York: The Mysterious Press, 1987.

Barzun, Jacques, and W. H. Taylor. *A Catalogue of Crime.* New York: Harper & Row, 1971.

Cade, Jared. *Agatha Christie and the Eleven Missing Days.* London: Peter Owen, 1998.

Cawelti, John G. *Adventure, Mystery, and Romance: Formula Stories As Art and Popular Culture.* Chicago: University of Chicago Press, 1976.

Christie, Agatha. *An Autobiography.* New York: Dodd, Mead and Co., 1977.

Craig, Patricia, and Mary Cadogan. *The Lady Investigates: Women Detectives and Spies in Fiction.* New York: St. Martin's Press, 1981.

East, Andy. *The Agatha Christie Quizbook.* New York: Drake Publishers, 1975.

Feinman, Jeffrey. *The Mysterious World of Agatha Christie.* New York: Grosset & Dunlap, 1975.

Gill, Gillian. *Agatha Christie: The Woman and Her Mysteries.* New York: The Free Press, 1990.

Grossvogel, David I. *Mystery and Its Fictions: From Oedipus to Agatha Christie.* Baltimore: Johns Hopkins University Press, 1979.

Hart, Ann. *The Life and Times of Miss Jane Marple.* New York: Dodd, Mead and Co., 1985.

————. *The Life and Times of Hercule Poirot.* New York: G. P. Putnam's Sons, 1990.

Haycraft, Howard, ed. *The Art of the Mystery Story.* New York: Carroll and Graf, 1983.

————. *Murder for Pleasure: The Life and Times of the Detective Story.* New York: Carroll and Graf, 1984.

Kaska, Kathleen. *What's Your Agatha Christie I.Q.?* New York: Citadel Press, 1996.

Keating, H. R. F., ed. *Agatha Christie: First Lady of Crime.* New York: Holt, Rinehart and Winston, 1977.

Klein, Kathleen Gregory. *The Woman Detective: Gender and Genre.* Urbana, Ill.: University of Illinois Press, 1988.

Lehman, David. *The Perfect Murder: A Study in Detection.* New York: The Free Press, 1989.

Maida, Patricia D., and Nicholas B. Spornick. *Murder, She Wrote: A Study of Agatha Christie's Detective Fiction.* Bowling Green, Ohio: Bowling Green University Popular Press, 1982.

Mallowan, Max. *Mallowan's Memoirs.* New York: Dodd, Mead and Co., 1977.

Mann, Jessica. *Deadlier than the Male: Why Are Respectable Women So Good at Murder?* New York: Macmillan and Co., 1981.

Moers, Ellen. *Literary Women: The Great Writers.* New York: Anchor Press, 1977.

Morgan, Janet. *Agatha Christie: A Biography.* New York: Alfred A. Knopf, 1984.

Murdoch, Derrick. *The Agatha Christie Mystery.* Toronto: Pagurian Press, Ltd., 1976.

Osborne, Charles. *The Life and Crimes of Agatha Christie.* New York: Holt, Rinehart and Winston, 1982.

Poovey, Mary. *The Proper Lady and the Woman Writer.* Chicago: University of Chicago Press, 1984.

Ramsey, G. C. *Agatha Christie: Mistress of Mystery.* New York: Dodd, Mead and Co., 1967.

Reddy, Maureen T. *Sisters in Crime: Feminism and the Crime Novel.* New York: Continuum Press, 1988.

Riley, Dick, and Pam McAllister, eds. *The Bedside, Bathtub & Armchair Companion to Agatha Christie.* New York: Frederick Ungar Publishing, 1979.

Robyns, Gwen. *The Mystery of Agatha Christie.* New York: Doubleday & Co., 1978.

Routley, Erik. *The Puritan Pleasures of the Detective Story: Sherlock Holmes to Van der Valk.* London: Victor Gollancz, Ltd., 1972.

Saunders, Peter. *The Mousetrap Man.* London: William Collins, 1972.

Sova, Dawn. *Agatha Christie A to Z.* New York: Facts on File, 1996.

Symons, Julian. *Bloody Murder: From the Detective Story to the Crime Novel.* New York: Viking Press, 1985.

Toye, Randall. *The Agatha Christie Who's Who.* New York: Holt, Rinheart and Winston, 1980.

Tynan, Kathleen. *Agatha.* New York: Ballantine Books, 1978.

Underwood, Lynn, ed. *Agatha Christie: Official Centenary Celebration, 1890–1990.* London: Belgrave Publishing, Ltd., 1990.

Wagoner, Mary. *Agatha Christie.* Boston: Twayne Publishers, 1986.

Winn, Dilys. *Murderess Ink: The Better Half of the Mystery.* New York: Workman Publishing, 1979.